Call of Elespen

By Missy Sheldrake

Call of Elespen
©2017 Missy Sheldrake
All rights reserved, including the right of reproduction in whole or in part in any form.

First published by Missy Sheldrake November 2017
Printed by Createspace, an Amazon.com Company

Illustrations, Design, and Cover Art ©2017 by Missy Sheldrake
All Rights Reserved.

This book is a work of fiction. Names, characters, places, and incidents are products of the author's imagination. Any resemblance to actual events, locales, or persons, living or dead, is entirely coincidental.

Illustrations for this novel were created using the Procreate iPad App on iPad Pro

Illustrations and other artwork cannot be shared, duplicated, or otherwise used without express permission from the artist.

www.missysheldrake.com
missy@variable.org

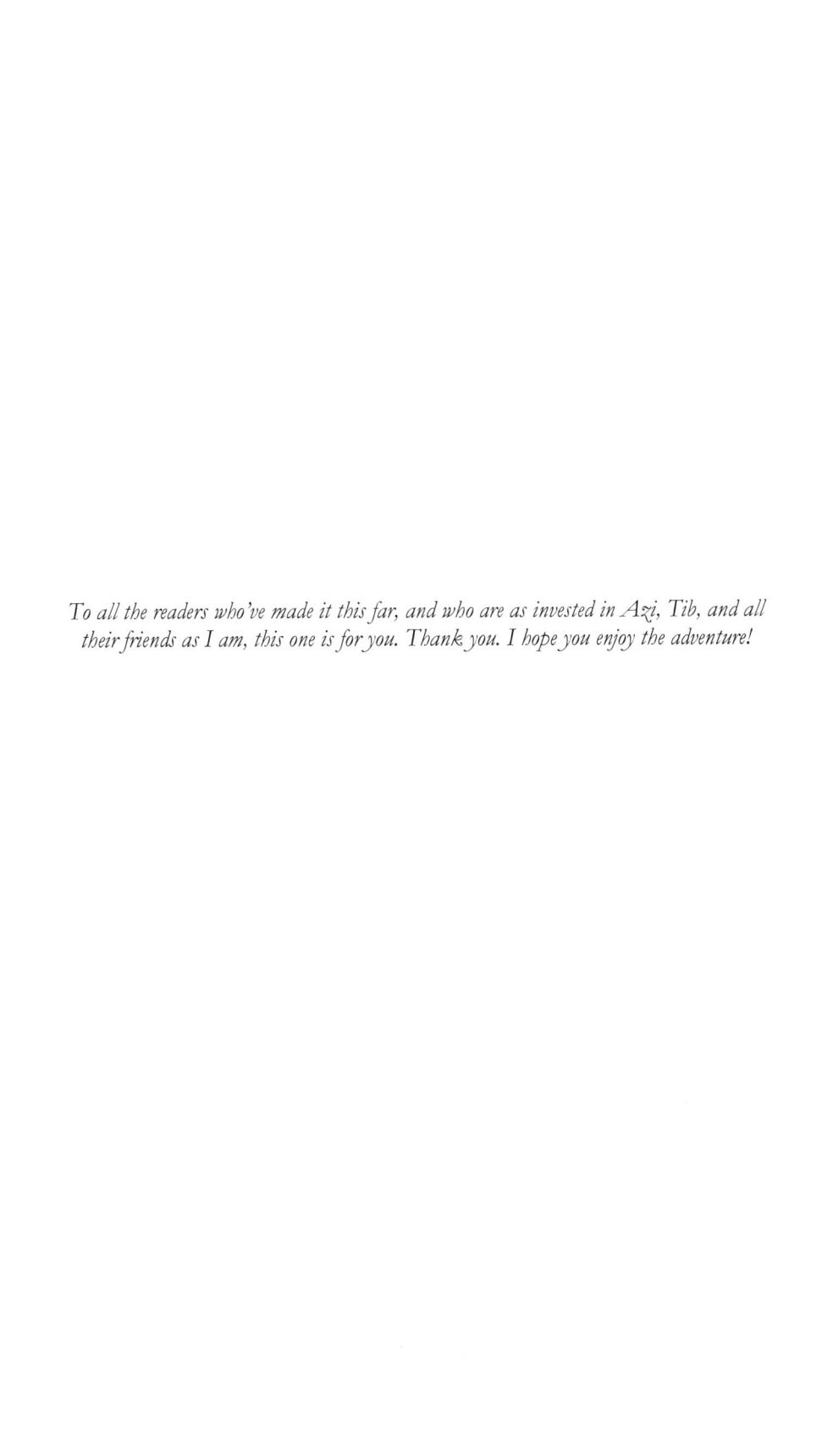

To all the readers who've made it this far, and who are as invested in Azi, Tib, and all their friends as I am, this one is for you. Thank you. I hope you enjoy the adventure!

Table of Contents

Chapter One 1
Chapter Two: 10
Chapter Three 20
Chapter Four 29
Chapter Five 41
Chapter Six 49
Chapter Seven 57
Chapter Eight 65
Chapter Nine 73
Chapter Ten 83
Chapter Eleven 91
Chapter Twelve 97
Chapter Thirteen 105
Chapter Fourteen 112
Chapter Fifteen 121
Chapter Sixteen 132
Chapter Seventeen 137
Chapter Eighteen 145
Chapter Nineteen 154
Chapter Twenty 165
Chapter Twenty-One 176
Chapter Twenty-Two 184
Chapter Twenty-Three 193
Chapter Twenty-Four 201
Chapter Twenty-Five 210
Chapter Twenty-Six 219

Chapter Twenty-Seven 225
Chapter Twenty-Eight 232
Chapter Twenty-Nine 242
Chapter Thirty 253
Chapter Thirty-One 264
Chapter Thirty-Two 275
Chapter Thirty-Four 291
Chapter Thirty-Five 303
Chapter Thirty-Six 314
Chapter Thirty-Seven 324
Chapter Thirty-Eight 334
Chapter Thirty-Nine 342
Chapter Forty 351
Chapter Forty-One 363
Chapter Forty-Two 371
Chapter Forty-Three 383
Chapter Forty-Four 391
Chapter Forty-Five 400
Chapter Forty-Six 412
Chapter Forty-Seven 425
Chapter Forty-Eight 436
Chapter Forty-Nine 445
Chapter Fifty 458
Chapter Fifty-One 468
Chapter Fifty-Two 481

Map of the Known Lands

Chapter One

MENTALIST LESSONS
Azi

Mirrors of my own, my mother's crystal blue eyes have always been a comfort to me. A place of solace and peace. Trust and love, embodied. Home. I gaze into them and allow myself to fall fully, to lose myself into the space behind them. Her mind presents itself in a rush of spectacular threads of light wrapped in sparkling gold. Awed, I watch the perfect, orderly rows as they glide endlessly past. A lifetime of joy unfolds around me. Aside from the Wellspring at Kythshire, it's probably the most beautiful presence I've experienced.

"*There you are, now,*" Kenrick's voice, deep and encouraging, is out of place but not unexpected. "*It is the way of the novice to remain where things are easy, Azaeli. Where there is Light. But to do what you came here for, to heal her, you must turn toward the darkness. Draw your sword.*"

His guidance unlocks an awareness in me. My pulse quickens like it does at the start of a fight. I turn in this remarkable, glittering space and peer into the distance, where the marred and imperfect threads of her memories loom ominous and imperfect. Strands of ink-black tendrils twist around the golden threads, choking them out. Back within my body, far beyond my mother's mind, my hands tingle as the now-familiar elation of magic charges through me. Among the tendrils, I take on a battle stance. With Mercy tight in my grip, I creep into pain and sorrow.

The wicked strands are sharp recollections of recent traumas, memories of Mum's time spent as a prisoner on display in Hywilkin's Menagerie. These are the abuses she suffered, the heartache, the degradation. My first reaction is to strike these awful memories down, to obliterate them, but I remember Kenrick's warning before we began this exercise. I'm not here to erase anything. Memories, good and bad, have value. Destroying them is a forbidden, evil act.

"Good," he whispers. "*Excellent restraint. Now, using great care, unwind it. I cannot tell you how, for we all visualize the mind in different ways. You must seek your own method.*"

I move to the nearest choked strand and observe it. The golden thread is a memory of Da. His face is red from toil at the forge, dotted with sweat. Mum's heart skips a beat as he smiles at her. In an instant, the memory switches to one of Richter's face, the king who held her in a gilded cage. His lip curls in an echo of Da's smile, but this man is nothing like my father. The lewd comment he spews makes my stomach flip with rage. Her helplessness clenches within her, and twined with it is the fear she may never see my father again. This is the black tendril, the darkness choking out the light.

With the tip of the light cast by the point of my sword, I carefully pull the dark coil from the golden one until the two are their own thoughts. Once separated from the memory of Da, the dark tendril clings to my weapon. I drag it away, into a far corner of my mother's mind, and it shrinks to a weak, thin strand. There I leave it to be recalled if needed, but no longer at the forefront where it had been causing so much damage.

It's a simple act, but once it's complete, I feel the energy drain from me. Kenrick is at my side in an instant, cradling me, helping to draw me away, back to myself. My mother's eyes flash before me again just before I leave her mind. We both blink and laugh softly, and a tear trails down her face as she reaches to pat my cheek.

"That was beautiful, Azi," she says, shaking her head. "Truly remarkable. Thank you."

"You see now, why this manner of healing requires the utmost trust between participants," Kenrick explains, going on with the lesson. "So much damage can be done by an untrained practitioner, or by one with sinister intentions."

Mum hugs me and I slump back against the soft cushion of our sofa and adjust to being wholly myself again. The flow of Mentalism has faded to a soft tingle. I close my eyes, like Kenrick instructed, and allow it to leave me.

The silence in the room is broken only by the scratch of a quill across parchment as Uncle takes notes at our cramped desk beneath the window. Beside me, the sofa creaks as Mum changes position. Above us, the ceiling squeaks. Da is awake. His bare feet shuffle across the floor.

"You are a quick study, Azaeli," Kenrick declares with a hint of pride. "Excellent work. Keep focusing on your surroundings. The small noises, the reality of your own presence in this space. Grounding oneself is truly the most important aspect of our work."

"Can you describe in your words, Sister, what took place?" Uncle asks Mum as his quill races across the page.

While he, Mum, and Kenrick discuss her experience, my gaze turns to the details of our small living room. Some of it is familiar, and some is newly replaced following the Dusk's attack on Cerion. I focus on the spindles of the narrow staircase across from me as memories of that battle drift through my mind. I recall my melding with the fairy queen and the Muse of Light, Eljarenae, and how we drove the evil of Sorcery and Dusk out of Cerion together. I remember my moment in the Wellspring, and the warmth of the golden liquid as it caressed my skin.

My eyes drift closed, and when I open them again I find myself looking for old, familiar things. Things which weren't damaged by the fire that ravaged the city, leaving our cozy home half-charred.

"How long ago was it?" The question leaves my lips before I have a chance to think. It's something that has been needling me since we returned from Hywilkin. Our campaign into Kerevorna, I imagine, has jumbled my sense of time. The others pause in their conversation. Uncle turns all the way around on his stool and looks at me, his brow furrowed with concern.

"How long ago was what, Niece?" he asks.

"The battle. The Dusk's attack on Cerion."

I don't miss the worried glance he gives my mother or the slight nod of understanding from Kenrick as Uncle answers me.

"In four days, it will have been a month," he answers matter-of-factly. "Today is the eighth of Autumnsdawn. Do you feel you are confused by time, or have lost your sense of it?"

With his question, he turns back to the desk and flattens a fresh sheet of parchment across its surface. The desk is new. The old one was crushed when the tail of Vorhadeniel, Muse of Darkness, thrashed through our sitting room window. Nearly a month ago, apparently. It doesn't feel like it's been so long.

Uncle hovers his quill over the parchment, waiting for my reply, but the creak of the wooden stairway draws my attention as Da clomps his way down. Most of the stairs are new, but some are still old and familiar. As his head clears the ceiling, Da's expression darkens. He acknowledges Kenrick and Uncle with no more than a half-annoyed grunt. He knew they'd be here. It was discussed between them last night. Still, it's very unusual to have our sitting room occupied by two Mages. Three, I suppose, if you count me—something I'm not quite ready to do yet. Neither is Da, it seems. Before his scowl has a chance to fully form, Mum jumps up from the sofa and rushes to greet him.

"Benen," she whispers, circling her arms around his neck and curling her fingers into his hair. Their kiss has the tender urgency of a first kiss, or a last one. Mum's peace pulses around her, and Da's shoulders relax as he takes her in his arms. Their lingering greeting finally ends, and Da looks again at the strange gathering of Mages in his sitting room. I think he'll say something, but he simply shakes his head and huffs.

"Good morning, Da," I offer, but my cheerful tone sounds forced, even to me. I remember a time not long ago when he would regard me with beaming pride. Now, when he greets me with a stubbled kiss on my cheek, his eyes flick away from mine as if to escape my gaze. I try not to let it bother me. I try to tell myself in time, he'll trust me again, but deep inside I fear he never will. Things have changed between us. I've changed.

"Coming to breakfast, Gaethon?" he asks Uncle over his shoulder as he and Mum walk hand-in-hand to the kitchen door.

"Yes, yes, we have much to discuss," Uncle replies. He turns to Kenrick, offering a hand to shake. "Thank you, Master Kenrick. The lesson was most enlightening. We're quite grateful to have your guidance in the matter of Azaeli's studies."

"I thank you as well, Master Gaethon, for your kind hospitality. I look forward to warm, dry accommodations and the promise of a bustling city to explore after so long in the caves," he pats Uncle's hand warmly.

"I'll be in in a moment," I say to Uncle after they finish their goodbye, and he nods as he brushes past me to join the others in the guild hall.

"Don't be long. And fetch Rian to breakfast, won't you?" he calls over his shoulder.

"I'll try," I reply, aware his irritated tone isn't directed toward me. Rian had the option of joining us at the lesson, but protested too much at my attempts to wake him earlier. I glance up the stairs toward my own room as Kenrick gathers his hat and cloak.

"Fear is a common response to changes in those we love," Kenrick offers quietly, snapping my attention back to him.

At first, I think he's talking about Rian. When I realize it's Da he's referring to, a knot twists in my stomach.

"I wish things could be the way they were between us," I whisper, and Kenrick's smile crinkles the papery skin around his eyes. "He was always so proud of my swordsmanship."

"Life is change, Azaeli," he says gently. "Ask yourself this: could you go back to being merely a swordswoman now? After everything you have become?" He pats my shoulder comfortingly. "Do not fret about your father. In time, he'll come to understand."

"If only I could heal him the way I did Mum just now. If only I could take away that fear and doubt and move it to another place, so he could see I'm still his Azi. I haven't changed. Not that much. Not really."

Kenrick steps closer. His green eyes, framed by his frizz of gray-white hair, search mine. The gold Mark behind his beard catches the pink light of sunrise as it slashes through the shutter slats.

"You can, Azaeli," he explains solemnly. "It is within your power to make him, or anyone for that matter, see anything about you that you wish them to. You have the ability to change his perception of you. The simple fact that you choose not to, that you resist that ability, is a true mark of your purity. You are a valiant beam of light in this world. In time, he will see it on his own. In time, he will trust you as he once did."

"I hope so," I whisper, ignoring the brimming tears that cause his face to swim before me, silhouetted by the light of dawn through the open door as he steps through it. "Thank you, Kenrick."

"Practice," he says firmly. "As much as you can. Do not be afraid to hone your skills. Yes?" When I agree, the Mentalist nods, squeezes my shoulder, and steps away, setting his worn hat upon his head. He looks out over the nearly empty street with the excitement of a child on festival day and declares, "To the market, I think. I haven't been to a proper market in oh…" he chuckles, "you wouldn't believe me if I told you how long."

"The best one is at the harbor," I offer, and he bobs his head without turning to look at me.

"Off to adventure!" he cries. A couple of merchants heading to their stalls pause and give him odd looks, but he pays them no mind as he hops down the stoop. I watch him until he rounds the corner and silently hope he does all right on his own. His tattered clothes and quirky style are at the very least sure to raise a few eyebrows at the market. Still, I'm grateful he could return with us from Hywilkin, and that Uncle was eager to convince the Academy to allow him to tutor me in exchange for lodging there. Apparently, it's been a long time since a Master Mentalist has graced their halls.

With a sigh, I close the door and turn to head to my room. The sudden burst of Flitt's light dazzles me. I yelp and stumble back, and she giggles and tosses a sugar cube into my open mouth.

"Good morning!" she chirps as I gasp and choke on the sweet surprise.

"Good morning, Flitt," I reply between bouts of coughing. Despite the sugary attack, I can't help but smile in her presence. She was only gone overnight, but it feels like we've been separated for ages. Her light is such a comfort to me now. My worries about my father are pushed aside as I make my way upstairs and she chatters in my ear about the latest news from Brindelier, where the Festival of Awakening is still going on in full force.

At the circle hatch in my room, I pause with my hand on the latch and wonder how different things will be when our guild moves to its new quarters on the palace grounds. Will the new housing have secret connections like this one? The thought of change makes me anxious, so I push the thought away. Right now, it's too painful to think about leaving this place. Even though everyone else seems so excited for the move up, this is the only home I've ever known.

While Flitt chatters on and on about Alexerin, the Faedin of Brindelier's princess, I slide the hatch open to peer in at Rian. As usual, all I can see of him is a tuft of auburn curls peeking over the nest of his rumpled bedclothes. *Practice.* I sigh, rest my chin on the edge of the hatch, close my eyes, and focus on Rian.

It's a strange sensation. Something like traveling through the Half-Realm, but only with a small part of my mind. That part splits off, like it's journeying on a different path. It leaves a trail behind it: a tether of golden rope. That rope, Kenrick explained earlier, is vulnerable. If it were to snap, I could lose the wandering part of me. I send it off across Rian's room, into the warmth of his bed. This is allowed. We made an agreement. He knows I'll have to practice, and he's already said I can do so on him whenever I need to. He trusts me.

I wait a heartbeat or two until the scene behind my eyelids shifts to something brighter. A sense of joy and anticipation rushes through me. I can't help but giggle at the pleasant sensation as it floods my insides. I drift away from myself, to another place. Someplace wonderful.

Sweet music and fairy song drift to my ears, pulling me forward. The light dims just enough for me to see Rian standing at the base of a pristine white staircase. He's dressed impeccably, in tailored trousers and a midnight-blue tailed vest, just like the outfit he wore to Princess

Sarabel's birthday ball. His shoes are polished to a gleaming shine. His hair is styled perfectly, the long forelocks cascading over his chest in gleaming slashes of auburn. His hazel eyes dance with excitement and a hint of mischief as fairy orbs dart around him excitedly. Bobbing beside his shoulder, Shush whispers something, and Rian's attention snaps to the end of the long hall.

When I turn to follow his gaze, I realize we're in the grand palace of the Fairy Queen. The arched columns soar into the open sky, and pure white sunlight which glitters across every surface. I squint past the dazzling light to see, at the end of the long hall…myself.

The Azi at the entrance to the Fairy Court steps inside, and the singing and excitement immediately hush. A pair of figures step up to her and bows, and she takes their offered arms. Even with the light washing out most of the scene, I know in my heart it's my parents. My eyes brim with tears at the sight.

The wedding gown is spectacular, seemingly woven of pure light. With each step the dream Azi takes, the gown shifts and sways to reveal what's underneath: the knight Azaeli resplendent in her own midnight blue armor. Mercy, as always, is at her shoulder. In her hands she holds a bouquet, not of real flowers, but a cascade of blooms formed from swirls of golden light. The gown and the bouquet and even the veil adorning her head sparkle brilliantly with every step she takes.

It's so disorienting to see myself as a bride on her wedding day, radiantly marching through the Palace of Dawn on my mother and father's arm, I stare at the scene in awe and disbelief. When the dream Azi finally walks past me, somehow the spell of the dream lifts, and I remember why I'm here.

"*Time to wake up, Love,*" I send to Rian, and my voice echoes loudly through the hushed fairy court.

"Are you even listening, Azi?" Flitt's voice squeaks in my ear, and I wind the golden thread back to myself to find her hovering in front of me, hands on hips, scowling. "Typical! I've been going on and on and it's all been very important, and you weren't even listening!"

She stabs her finger onto the tip of my nose with every word. I dodge half-heartedly, still dazed by Rian's enchanting dream. No wonder he's such a successful Mage. Only someone with an imagination as spectacular as his could be.

"Stop," I whine, covering my nose. Her response is to dive at me, still squeaking in rage.

"Hey," Rian peeks through the hatch, watching with amusement as Flitt chases me around my room, tugging at my hair and hollering.

"What's this?" he chuckles. "Morning exercises?"

"I was telling her about very important business from Brindelier, and she chose to ignore me! Like I'm not important! Like what I say doesn't matter! So typical!"

"Flitt!" I protest, yanking my hair from her grasp as Rian steps through the wall beside the hatch. He's perfectly dressed and looks as though he's been up for hours. Typical Mage, I think to myself, and chuckle at how much I sound like the very irritated fairy who's still poking at my cheek and chastising me.

"I'm very sorry, Flitt" I offer in my gravest tone. With a quick side-step, I dodge her relentless attack and duck my head into a humble bow. "You're absolutely right. I should have been listening. Please, will you tell us both, now that you have our attention, what's so important?"

"That's better," she says with a humph, her fists still digging into her hips. "But now, if you really want to know, you're going to have to play."

Chapter Two:

CATWALKING
Tib

Blue sky. Ship's wheel. Wind in my face. Sunshine flaring yellow in the fan of Ki's black hair. I tip my head to the sky and watch the huge orange bladder of air brush the clouds as we speed through them on our way. I turn the wheel, and we bank east. I turn it the other way, and we bank west. Ki laughs beside me. Her brown eyes sparkle with excitement.

This is how it should always be. From now until forever. As light as a bird. As free as we can be. No obligations, no promises. No offerings. No Sorcerers' threats. No one to protect. Only me, my sister, and the open sky.

"Tib!" Ki grabs my arm like an excited kid. "Are we going lower? Are we nearly there?"

She runs to the bulwark and leans far over to peer out across the sea and sky. She looks back at me again, grinning, and I force a smile.

"Almost," I say, and turn the wheel again. She doesn't realize I've been circling for a while now. I'm not ready to get there yet. Not ready to say goodbye.

"There it is!" she squeals in a very un-Ki-like way. "The gate!"

I don't reply. If I never set foot in Brindelier again, I'd be fine with that. But it's not the place she's excited about. It's who's waiting for her. I imagine the city farther away. I imagine the ship going slower. Just a little longer with my sister. Who knows what happens after this? What the future holds?

"My dear boy," Valenor's voice echoes in the empty space beside me, "the winds seem to be slowing. Shall I help us along?"

"No," I mutter and imagine us going faster. The ship picks up speed. The floating archway in the distance grows larger. "I've got it."

"I imagine you won't be apart for long," he offers. I shrug.

"Who knows?"

"It is for the best," he says gently.

I'm not sure what to say. Valenor was kind enough to offer Ki passage through the Dreaming to Brindelier, even though its gates are still closed to anyone going in or out. Even though the Muses are supposed to stay out of ordinary dealings, he offered to bring her anyway, so she wouldn't have to stay in Cerion and risk being seen by someone who knew her as Viala. She looks a lot different now, but she was still concerned. Afraid. It's the best thing, really, for her. And for me, I guess. Still, I feel like I just got her back. My sister. My only family. We worked well together. I'm not ready to be apart yet.

"Oh, Tib!" Ki bounces on her toes. "I can see the spires! Look!"

I look in the direction she's pointing, toward the towers of Brindelier's castle. The tallest one seems to shine with a light of its own even in the darkness. I know it well. That one holds the Wellspring.

"Ah, it is a splendid sight, is it not?" Valenor asks, lifting his chin to the breeze. His white beard flaps and tangles, and he smiles peacefully.

"How will this work, exactly?" I ask him. "Because Ki and I are back at Nessa's asleep, right?"

"Correct."

"So, how does she get from there to there?" I ask, pointing at the roof of Kanna's Inn.

"It is much the same way as Azaeli and Rian can shift their presence from one place to another with a thought. They have been attuned to the Half-Realm. The place between sleeping and awake. Quite like you have."

"But I can't teleport like they do," I scowl. "I can only hide."

"Yes, well, these things tend to manifest differently depending upon the situation. In this case, I shall help your sister along. Her dream self will arrive first, and her physical self will follow. It is similar to a Mage's teleportation spell, though far less costly because you have my help." He winks at me with amusement.

There's no point in delaying any longer. Ki knows the layout of the city as well as I do. She's aware of the distance between the palace and Kanna's.

"There it is!" she shouts, confirming my thoughts.

I turn the ship's wheel until we're lined up right, and Valenor somehow stretches the height of the inn so we're right against the window of Ki's rented room.

In the streets below, they're still dancing and singing. Fireworks and celebration spells explode all around us, shooting through the hull of the ship and exploding across us like we're not even here. Which we aren't. We're in the dreaming. They can't see us. We don't exist.

"There he is," Ki whispers, draping her arm over my shoulders as I come to her side. She squeezes me and peers through the open shutters of her room with an adoring look, and I follow her gaze.

Efran is there, all right. Sprawled across the bed, his vest half-off like he started to undress and passed out before he finished. The bed is littered with coins, and a tankard of ale lies on its side on the polished floor below his dangling hand.

"He's just as handsome as I remember," she says dreamily as my eyes fixate on the string of drool spilling from his bottom lip onto the coverlet.

"If you say so," I scowl. "He looks passed out drunk to me."

"Well, nobody looks great sound asleep, Tib! And so what if he did a little celebrating?" She slaps my arm playfully and chuckles. Efran's snores drift through the open window.

"I guess," I say with a shrug. Still, with my healed eye, I inspect the room. Look him over closely, for anything sinister. Nothing seems wrong, though. Nothing except for the fact that my sister is so happy to leave me for a witless drunk.

"When you are ready, my dear," Valenor's voice drifts over us, "go and lie on the bed or settle into that chair. You shall drift into your own dream, and when you awake, you shall find yourself there."

"In the chair is better," I say. "No chance of waking him up that way."

"Maybe I want him to wake up." Ki shoves me playfully then pulls me into a hug. Her hand cups my cheek. She tips her forehead to touch mine.

"Be well, little brother." She grins. "I'm so proud of you."

"You too," I mumble, patting her hand. "Hopefully the gate will be open soon, at least for Margy and the higher-ranking folks, and we can visit."

"Oh, I'm sure it won't be long," she says. "Until then, we can meet in the Dreaming. Right, Valenor?"

"Certainly," Valenor replies.

"Be careful," I say, unable to hide my frown as I glance at Efran.

"I will. We'll keep a close watch and send word through Valenor if anything suspicious is going on."

"You still have the white vial I gave you, right?" I ask her. She nods, holding it up.

"I'll be fine, Tib," she says, kissing my forehead. "And so will you."

Her voice goes strange and echoed as she slips away from me. Her form shimmers when she reaches the bed. He wakes up and sees her. Reaches for her. Pulls her close. They kiss. She looks at him like he's all that matters to her.

I turn around. Run back to the helm. Grab the wheel and spin it, hard.

The ship banks sharply away from the window toward darker skies. Night time. Quiet. Peace.

"It's for the best," Valenor's voice echoes like Ki's did, and I realize I'm alone. He's gone, and all that's left are stars and sky. My racing heart slows. My fingers loosen on the wheel. My eyes flutter sleepily.

"Valenor, wait," I call. I had something I wanted to ask him. My voice is too quiet though. I'm drifting back to Cerion. To Nessa's.

My bed beneath me is safe and comfortable. The blankets are heavy and soft. My hand rests on warm fur. As I wake up, I pet it gently. It purrs and nuzzles my palm. It shifts closer to my neck. Its fur tickles my cheek.

Its closeness is such a comfort after leaving my sister that I drift in and out of sleep with my fingers buried deep in its silky fur. The purring grows louder, and the cat stretches itself along the length of my shoulder and burrows its head into my neck.

My dreams shift to Margy in her coronation gown, her crown sparkling on her head as she holds the orb and scepter of state in either hand. Her brown curls dance with the bounce of the carriage over cobbled streets as her kingdom calls her name, throwing petals of sweet-smelling flowers. I was with her through every moment. At her side. Hidden. Nobody knew. Nobody saw.

I stroke the cat tenderly from her head to her tail, still groggy from the memories of my dreams and the excitement of the day before. It's strange to be home again, back in my bed at the Ganvents'. I'm glad to be here. I missed the comfort of Zeze beside me.

"Zeze," I whisper, and my hand stops mid-stroke.

"Mrow," Zeze answers sleepily.

"Zeze!" I whisper harshly and sit up in disbelief, and Zeze digs her claws into my shoulder to keep from slipping to my lap. "What are you doing here?"

She glances at me with big, brown, very un-catlike eyes. Saunters to the blanket at my knees. Stretches her front paws out lazily. Kneads her claws back and forth into my leg.

"Ow," I whisper, and she flops across my legs and shows me her furry belly. "That's not very regal of you."

Her only reply is to lick her paw and rub her whiskers with it.

"You shouldn't be here, Zeze," I hiss, glancing at the door. The wards Lilen set are still in place, but they're not very strong. Not strong enough to protect such an important visitor in the middle of the night. My bandolier is close enough, though. Hanging on my bed post. The glow of the vials tucked in it are the only light in the room right now.

Zeze closes her eyes and turns her face toward the door. The shimmer of a form appears between us. A girl in a nightdress, with brown curls tumbling down her back. She scoots onto the bed, and I tuck my knees under my chin, watching in disbelief.

"Don't," I warn under my breath, but I'm too late. Zeze stands up, stretches again, and steps right into the apparition. When the two forms meet, the girl solidifies.

"Margy," I gasp as the queen shifts on the edge of the bed and turns to me with an excited grin.

"You did it!" A high-pitched voice cries from beside her, and Twig, Queen Margy's Faedin, pops into view beside her.

"I did!" Margy laughs and holds her hand out to him, and he lands softly on her palm. "It was exactly like you said. A little more difficult than just across the room like we usually do, but it wasn't terrible."

"Amazing, Your Majesty! You're getting stronger by the day," Twig says proudly, and Margy giggles.

"What did I say about that, Twig?" She tips her head closer to him with a scolding tone.

"Right, right. Margy. I'm sorry. I'll try to remember."

"My father's closest friends called him by name, and so shall mine," she says with a nod.

"Would someone," I interrupt through clenched teeth, "like to explain what's going on? Am I still dreaming? I hope I am. I hope the freshly crowned Queen of Cerion isn't stupid enough to actually be sneaking around outside the palace past midnight."

"Oh, Tib," Margy laughs and tucks her night dress around her crossed legs. "We were only doing a little experiment."

"Experiment?" I shake my head. "How are you here? What about your room? Your bed? Won't someone notice you missing?"

"Oh, right! I was going to check that," Twig squeaks. Without any more explanation, he blinks away.

"He's set a golem in my bed," Margy giggles. "In case anyone comes to check on me. You should see it. It's an exact copy of me! It's a bit creepy, actually." She scoots a little closer.

"Are you…" I shake my head and stare at her. Somehow, now that I've realized she's here, actually here, I can't think of words. A can't think of anything but the way her curls rest on her shoulders. The way her eyes glitter, even in the dim light. The way the pride of her accomplishment dances in her smile.

"I'm really here. Is that what you meant? Twig has been teaching me. I can walk where I like as Zeze, and then pull my spirit to myself, and when we unite, I can choose whether to be cat or person. It's hard to explain, but it's really useful."

"Useful?" I shake my head in disbelief. "It's a terrible idea. It's dangerous. You need to be in the palace, with guards and wards and—"

"Tib," she interrupts, turning away. "I thought you, of all people, would understand."

"I don't," I say impatiently. "So, explain it to me. Why would you ever in a million years think this is okay?"

"This…" she sighs and looks back at me. Her eyes search mine. Pleading. Warm. I should look away, but I can't. I won't. My heart races. She starts to say something a few times and stops. Like she knows what she wants to say but not how to say it. I can imagine how she feels, actually. I want to tell her it's okay. To comfort her. I can't, though. It's not okay. Not at all.

"I will never be alone again, Tib. There won't ever be a moment when someone isn't with me, watching me, advising me, asking for my counsel or offering theirs. There will never be time during my waking days when I won't be surrounded by attendants, guards…" her eyes tear from mine. "Betrothed."

The word hangs between us like a curtain. The lump in my throat grows. I need to tell her about that. About the Bordas. About Brindelier. About how they don't trust her. Not all of them. Not really.

I can't figure out how to say it, though. Not yet. Not now. If I tried to tell her now, she might think—

"They've invited me to Brindelier, formally," she whispers. "To the festival."

"Will you go?" I ask after clearing my throat.

"My advisors plan to discuss it tomorrow."

"Will he be there?" I ask. I don't have to mention Prince Poe's name. She knows. She shakes her head. Still doesn't meet my gaze.

"Can I go?" I ask. "I found out some things that might help them decide."

Her brown knits. Confused. Surprised. "You want to go to a royal council meeting?"

"Yeah, if I can." Maybe it'll be easier telling them what I found out than telling her. "Will you be there?"

"For some of it." She meets my eyes again.

"So, can I?" I shift a little closer to her. "I learned some things. In Brindelier. Things they'll want to hear. In Ceras'lain, too. And Hywilkin."

The light from the vials in my bandolier dance across her face as it brightens with excitement. This is the Margy I know. The same one who played pretend in the indoor garden with me. The one who read to us from a storybook with hope in her eyes. Hope for her own future and the future of her kingdom. Hope. It mingles with the magic surrounding her, leaping off her skin in swirls. Like leaves in a breeze. I feel the mix of it. The purity.

The magic she carries is different from the spells I usually detect. It's simply there, in its purest, perfect form. White light. Like a Wellspring.

"Oh, Tib! You've been everywhere," she exclaims. "How did you get there? What did you see in Brindelier? What is it like in Hywilkin? In Ceras'lain? Tell me, is the elven homeland as gorgeous as they say?"

"Ceras'lain is warm. Calm," I whisper, taking my bandolier from the bedpost. "Everything is draped with plants. Even the Wall itself is alive. Trees all grown together. They use magic to form it into shapes. To make the rooms and the decorations. All of it is alive. The elves are kind. Peaceful. They gave me a room, and they taught me about things. History. How things were before Brindelier went to sleep."

"Oh, how I wish I could see it," Margy sighs and closes her eyes with a smile. Like she's imagining what it must be like.

"There's a waterfall, the biggest you've ever seen. You can walk behind it. It's so loud, it roars like thunder. But steady. Peaceful," I explain, trying to help her see. I wish I was better at describing things.

"And Hywilkin? What is it like there? I'm told it's cold." She shivers and moves closer. Our shoulders touch. I don't think about it. I put my arm around her. She rests against my side. My heart races. It's wrong. Improper. She's a queen. Betrothed to someone else. But, she's also Margy. My friend.

"It is," I explain. My voice is a little weaker than it should be. I clear my throat. She doesn't move away. Neither do I. I start to think about what would happen if she was discovered here, but I stop myself. Push those thoughts away. Feel her shoulders move with her breath under my arm. I keep going. To keep her here. Close, where I can protect her.

"It's Freezing. Except, I didn't spend much time in the cold part. I was in the mountain. Inside of it is volcano, so it was hot."

"A volcano?" she asks. "How did you keep from getting burned?"

I tell her what I saw. Avyn, Evyn, Stellastera, Sha'Renell. The battle of the Muses. How I opened the Wellspring. How I got the offering.

"We have four now," she whispers. Rests her sleepy head on my chest. "Two to go."

I stay quiet. Think about that. Four offerings claimed. Two left. One, I can easily get. Ceras'lain. The other, Elespen. I don't know much about that place. Only what I saw from the ship while I escaped from Sunteri. A jungle on either side of a wide river. A city, Cresten, which I was forbidden to enter. Forbidden, even though I didn't even realize it at the time. Mevyn had his hold on me then. Kept me on the ship. Mevyn.

Thoughts of him twist my stomach, like always. I miss him. I hate him. I hope I never have a reason to see him again. I wonder how he is. The thoughts pull me southward. Without thinking, I turn my head in that direction. Faedin to a Keeper. *Ili'luvrie. Eftue'luvrie.* Margy's breath goes steady against me. She's sleeping. I let her. While she dozes, I wonder what she'll say when I tell her the truth.

She doesn't know, yet. Has no idea what I can do. That I can simply walk into anyplace, any Wellspring. That it's my right to ask for an offering, and their obligation to give it to me. All thanks to Mevyn. Thanks to his favor. Thanks to his titles. He helped me out of Sunteri, and I helped him restore his people, and now I'm stuck with this responsibility. This power. This choice. It makes me want to get back on my ship. To fly away. To not be left to make these decisions.

I think of Brindelier, where she wants to go. How it's held, still, under heavy spells. How its people are forced to celebrate and they're not even aware. What will happen when all six fonts are filled with offerings? When the Wellspring is open to all the Known Lands again? When the Dawn has won? What, then? Maybe the elves have the right idea. Maybe things are better off as they are right now. No, I'm fooling myself. Brindelier can't stay closed forever. There'd be too much imbalance. The Dusk and its ambitions would always be a threat.

"Azi's coming tomorrow," Margy murmurs sleepily. "She, Bryse, Cort, Rian, and Lisabella are going to tell me of their journeys in Hywilkin after the Reception of Allies. It seems there was an uprising in Belkere. Were you there for that?"

I shake my head no, and she goes on.

"There was a shift in power. I had to order Sir Tanoven, the Ambassador to Hywilkin, to be put to sleep until I could learn of the details. Mother and Master Anod said it was for the best, though I didn't want to. He has always been kind to me."

I look down at the top of her head. So far, she's told me about two important meetings aside from the Reception of Allies, where she'll host ambassadors and visitors from countries across the Known Lands. That's supposed to start at high noon and go through the afternoon.

"You have to go back," I say reluctantly. "To the palace. To your room. You need your rest. There's a lot to talk about, Margy. A lot to do. You have to sleep."

"He's right, Princess," Twig's voice appears before he does. "Err, Queen. The golem is convincing enough, but you do need your rest. You've done a lot of work today, and there's lots more to do tomorrow."

"Margy," she says firmly. "And all right."

"Will you ask them if I can come? Either to the council meeting or to Azi's?"

"Mmm, yes. I'll make sure your name is added to the list." With a stretch and a yawn, she moves away from me. The air shifts between us as she closes her eyes, this time to concentrate.

"That's it. Focus hard. Fur, whiskers," Twig says eagerly.

"Can't you just pop back to the—" I stop mid-sentence as Margy's form shifts from girl to cat right on my bed, and Zeze rubs her temple on my clenched fist. "Palace?" I whisper.

"Excellent!" Twig exclaims, ignoring me. Zeze hops lightly from the bed to my windowsill.

"So, you're just going out the window, then?" I ask, scowling. She answers me with a coy tilt of her head. Before I can warn her against it, she leaps. I scramble across the bed and peer out in time to see her land softly on the cobbles two stories below.

"Wait," I grumble into the darkness, pulling my bandolier over my head. "I'm coming with you."

Chapter Three

THE CLAIM
Celli

Plump red lips whisper above me. A spell, swift and painful, surges through my body. My skin prickles and my stomach clenches, but I force my eyes to stay open wide. The thought of closing them and losing myself again terrifies me.

I don't know how long the darkness held me after Sybel stole me away from the battle. All I know is it's still here, whispering in every corner, watching, waiting. Eyes on me. Breath held. Waiting for any sliver of information.

My throat bubbles. My mouth opens without my permission. I draw a breath. Loudly and clearly, I speak a single word: "Dead."

"There! It's declared. He's dead. Gone!" someone booms from the shadows.

"As we thought, Sybel," someone else hisses.

"Shut up, all of you!" Sybel screams. Her voice is deeper than usual. Choked with emotion. They don't listen to her. The darkness erupts into a chaos of vicious arguments. Sybel grabs my arm and yanks me to my feet. Nobody notices us leave. They're all too caught up in their own enraged arguments. Claims to power I don't understand. I try to make sense of it all, to count them or take stock as she whisks me away, but I can't. My head is swimming. While Sybel shoves me along a passage, my vision follows behind my body in a strange, slow blur.

A door creaks open. We step through, and the thunderous bang of it slamming shut behind us is followed by a series of locks clicking. My head pounds with every small noise. My stomach twists violently again, threatening to empty itself. When Sybel releases my arm, my legs are too weak to support me. I fall to my hands and knees on the plush carpet and gasp as she snaps the curtains closed, shutting out the midday sun which spilled blindingly across the red room.

"Quenson, how could you do this to me?" The Sorceress whispers. "How could you leave me now, when we were almost there?"

His name makes me shudder. I force my thoughts to other things. I know this room. I've been here before. I don't know how long ago. It feels like a lifetime since I woke up on that poster bed with her beside me, inspecting my hand. I stare at it now, my bony fingertips buried in the pile of the red carpet, and remember the red Mark she'd been so interested in. A Mark that faded long ago, replaced by a faint black curl instead. The inky Mage Mark swirls across my wasted hand, dipping into deep crevices and rising over peaks of bones like a mountainous landscape. I remember how proud I was when it first appeared. I don't know what I think about it now.

Osven's bracelet still dangles from my wrist, fully spent. Dead, like Quenson. Truly gone.

The gravity of everything that has happened hits me with such a force I can't even breathe. I want to close my eyes, to let my emotions take over, to sob out all the guilt and hate and wretched feelings, but I can't. Not now. Not with her here.

Sybel, on the other hand, doesn't seem to care about my presence. Her sobs echo like moaning ghosts from the shadows of the ceiling vaults. I don't dare to move. I keep silent and still, watching a sliver of sunlight from the space between the curtains creep across my fingers.

Its slow, steady progress comforts me. The rest of my body is cold and sore, but that sliver warms me. It reminds me of Cerion, of home. Of afternoons running through Redstone, besting all the boys in a footrace. Of the crack in the shutters in our drafty house, spilling morning sun across my mother's sand-blond hair. The golden light brings words with it. Memories of a vagrant, a Mage, walking around me in the driving snow, looking me over. Talking to him, to Quenson. My master. Former master. The Mage's voice rings clearly in my memory: *"What have you done to this girl? What dark magic is this?"*

The sunlight moves from my last finger, leaving my hand in shadow again. Leaving me hopeless. The curl of Mage Mark on my skin taunts me as I remember when it appeared. The baby swathed in a pink cloud of sleep. A woman screaming and throwing bottles in a rage. Lies and deceit. My dagger, plunging into Dub, into Stone, into Muster. The life leaving their eyes. My heart races as the guilt and fury of my past well up inside of me. Sybel sniffles, and I imagine plunging the blade into her, instead. Into all of them. Every single one who's left. Is that what will become of me now? Am I doomed to a life of vengeance and murder, even after he's gone?

Slowly, I slide my hand across the velvety carpet pile, back into the sunbeam. Its warmth is an instant comfort. It reminds me of the guardian on the mountain, terrifying and bold. Its light assures me somehow there are forces out there stronger than Sorcerers and darkness. Can I come back from this?

"*Yes.*"

The voice in my mind is bright and swift, like a flash of sunlight in a raindrop. Unfamiliar. Probably imagined. Still, it makes my heart race with hope. Be strong, the voice seems to hint. Is it someone else, or my own thoughts?

Across the room, Sybel sniffs and clears her throat. Her robes swish closer until she stops just behind me. I keep my head bowed low and my eyes on the sunbeam until her shadow snuffs it out. My fingers tremble in fear and I dig them into the carpet, feeling the rough, scratchy burlap deep at the bottom.

"How?" Sybel demands.

I don't know how to reply. I can't think of what she's asking me. My thoughts are scrambled and confused. I bow my head lower and try with all my will to focus on her question. Somewhere in the back of my mind, memories of my hatred for this woman drift closer.

I despised her when I was his. I didn't like the way his eyes lingered on her, or the way he shut himself away with her and left me to stand in dark places, desperate for his attention. I wanted her dead. I still do, but not for the same reasons. Before, it was jealousy. Now, it's for the horrible things I know she's done. And the things I did for her, for Quenson, for both of them.

She shifts her stance, allowing the sun past again. It spears into the carpet. I focus on the fibers, the light and dark in the red, and imagine a tiny version of myself hiding between its strands, deep at the bottom of the thick pile.

"Answer me," she hisses with an angry, warning tone. I swallow the lump in my throat.

Before I know what's happening, before I have a chance to react, a stinging chill swipes across the back of my head. I imagine bones. Skeletal fingers, gripping me. Sybel stalks into my range of sight. Her clawed hand is aimed at me, her red-rimmed eyes filled with tears and rage. I understand. There's no skeleton. It's a spell, her spell, of terror and pain. She raises her other hand and thrusts it forward, and the chill spikes down my spine, stealing my breath away.

With her graceful upward gesture, my body lifts from the floor. She holds me dangling at her eye level, as though I'm held by ropes from the moaning rafters. My back tingles with pain. I try desperately to gasp for breath, but she's stolen it away.

"Tell me," she growls, her red lips curled back against her white teeth in fury, "what happened to Quenson. How. Did. He. Die?" With every word, she jolts me with that same death-like chill. My breath comes back to me, but only for a moment so she can see if I'll answer. When I don't, she drops me to the floor with a scream of rage.

That same narrow strip of sunlight beams into my eyes, blinding me from her approach as I lie motionless and throbbing with pain. Something is broken. It must be. My skull feels like it's in pieces.

"I swear to Shadow, Celli," Sybel hisses, looming over me. "I will kill you and raise you and kill you again." She kicks me with the pointed heel of her boot, and I curl myself into a defensive ball as she screams again in frustration and crouches to meet my eye. "You do realize you're more useful to me dead at this point, don't you?" Her fingers freeze the carpet beneath them. "Answer me!" she whispers with threatening urgency.

With her face so close to mine, I see something in her eyes that I might not have noticed if she wasn't betrayed by the light dancing in her lashes. Emotions beyond the rage: Desperation. Fear. I realize something in that moment. Something that frees me and gives me hope. She doesn't know I killed him. She has no way of knowing. Sybel is a Necromancer, not a Mentalist. She can't force the truth out of me. If I'm careful, I can lie. I can deceive her. I can go along with them. I might even survive this. What would happen then? I don't know. But at least I'd go on living. Do I want to live, after all of this? *Yes.*

My eyes fill with tears. I let the emotion that's been welling in me spill over. "He fell in," I whisper between sobs. "Into the cracks. He was swallowed by the lava." There is a swirling emptiness and confusion inside of me when I think about Quenson. It's a strange sort of open void. A vacant half of me, waiting to be filled back up, but the broken part of me that remains is still too timid to creep into it.

I watch the realization dawn on her. There will be no remains for her to raise, nothing left to animate. He was swallowed up and burned, body and soul. Defeated, completely. Her hands go into her hair, clenching fistfuls of brown curls. Her eyes snap from side to side hysterically. Her fingers crackle with energy, and I know if she was to unleash it, it'd be the end of me.

"I loved him, too," I whisper, hoping to appeal to her emotions. It's not a lie. I really did. I had no control over it, but I did love him.

"Love?" she scoffs and sneers and pushes herself to her feet, pacing. "You think this is about love? That mess out there," she says, thrusting her finger toward the window, "that utter failure in Hywilkin, that was his fault. His rallying cry, his pathetic folly. If Quenson had survived it, he'd never have seen tomorrow. They know we were partners. After this mortifying defeat, the blame will fall on me." Her eyes widen in terror as she whispers, "You don't know who I'll have to answer to for this. You have no idea."

She whirls in place, searching for something, and I focus on the specks of dust that drift past in the sunbeam she leaves behind, blurred by my tears. Pain, so much pain. It hurts so intensely I can't even pinpoint where it's coming from. Emotional pain, physical pain, it's all the same. The dust, though, the light, comforts me.

"Blood," she utters under her breath. Something thumps loudly on the desk. A tome, probably. Pages rustle. "His blood was in you. I could single it out." The sound of metal sliding against wood rings through the room. She turns, and the golden dagger in her grip flashes threateningly as she stalks toward me.

I know what she's after, just as well as I know I don't have it anymore. The last of Quenson's blood was burned out of me by Evyn, the Guardian of Kerevorna. If she finds that out, she'll know I betrayed my master. She'll know I'm the one who killed him. I shrink away as she crouches beside me and the blade flashes in my thin sunbeam.

Another memory surfaces. Sybel, studying the red Mark on my hand. Writing in a book. Telling me not to forget the gifts she'd given me to help me gain Quenson's favor. She's right. I'm worth more to her dead than I am alive. She'll find that out as soon as she draws my blood. She'll find out the truth.

I know what I need to do to survive. To stay alive, just a little longer. When she presses the blade to my arm, I don't fight. I don't even flinch. I just look into her eyes. "I feel so empty now," I say, letting my voice come out as blankly as I feel. "What will happen to me? Will I be yours?"

My question makes her pause. Her eyes flash with greed at the suggestion of it. She could own me, like he owned me. She looks at me with red-rimmed eyes, like she's thinking about just that. I could be hers now. The Mark on her cheek thickens slightly as she considers it.

"What a delicious prospect," she whispers, moving the dagger away slightly.

A knock on the door causes us both to jump and scream. Enraged by the interruption, Sybel throws the weapon across the room.

"What?" she roars as the handle of the dagger clatters against the door and the weapon thumps to the carpet. "Who's there?"

The locks click again and the door crashes open. I wince as the sound rekindles my brutal headache. I try to look, but something besides the pain holds me still. Even straining my eyes to the side, I can only make out a head of slicked-back blond hair and a blur of crimson robes.

"How dare you, Xantivus," Sybel screams and pushes her hand out to cast something, but a blast from the opposing Sorcerer tempers her spell. The door slams shut, and the locks click securely behind him as he stalks across the room.

"How dare *you*," he snarls and charges her, grabbing her wrists. To my surprise, she cowers from him. "Don't be irrational, Sybel. It didn't go unnoticed that you fled after Quenson's fate was revealed. The blame must fall on someone in his stead. Naturally, that's—"

He stops abruptly, noticing me on the floor. His eyes narrow, white against pure black Mark. He's young, much younger than she is. Handsome, with low-cut robes that show off the prominent Mark on his chest. "What are you going to do with that?" he asks distastefully, pointing at me with his chin.

"Use it," she replies coldly. "His blood mingles with hers, even still. There's a chance—" He stops her with a dismissive wave of his hand.

"Blood memory? Too time consuming, too messy," Xantivus sneers.

"What do you suggest I do, then?" Sybel barks hatefully.

"I can't imagine you'd ask me for help. Even if you did, I wouldn't give it. You had your chance with me and you chose him, didn't you?"

"Even now, I'll never regret it," Sybel spits angrily.

"You say such things as though you think it might wound me," Xantivus laughs. "What happens to her isn't my concern. Nor should it be yours, at this point. You're summoned." He lets go of her with a grunt of disgust.

"What?" Sybel whispers, shaking her head in disbelief. Under the curl of the Mark, her skin goes pale. She sinks to her knees, her breath terrified and shallow beside me.

Xantivus snorts. "If I had known it would only require those simple words to bring you to your knees, I'd have said them long ago."

"Laugh now," Sybel snaps at him, "you know your reaction would be exactly the same."

She stands up, clamps her hand around my arm, and yanks me to my feet. I'm stronger than her. I know I could break away if I chose to. I won't, though. I'm in too much pain to fight. Too curious to know why her hand is shaking so hard despite her grip. I'm also smart enough to know attempting to fight two Sorcerers like these would definitely end in my death. Instead, I stay quiet. Obedient.

The beam of light is narrow, now. Less than a sliver. One word pulses over and over in my mind as I focus on it instead of the pain: "*Survive.*"

Sybel clears her throat and squares her shoulders, all the while glaring at the Sorcerer who has slunk back to her shadowed doorway.

"I had no way of knowing where that battle would lead. Is it my fault they all followed blindly?" She says, failing to mask her shaking voice.

"I don't need to hear it," Xantivus waves his hand dismissively. "Once you're summoned, it's too late for reason. Even if I cared what might happen to you in there, I have no power over the situation. You must think of the cause. Our side. What value do you hold for us now? For the Dusk?" He huffs. "You and your playthings of dead meat and risen bones...what have they really done for us, Sybel? Where is your prince now? Where is your king? Useless, spent energy. Failures of otherwise brilliant, inspired magic, now as worthless as that." I wince as he jabs his finger toward me.

"We've been through this," Sybel glares. "I'm perfectly aware of your feelings about my work. I won't stand here and listen to your abuse."

"Abuse?" Xantivus scoffs. "I'm doing you a favor. A word of advice, woman. If you wish to save your own skin, make your argument now. How have these ventures been worth the time and investment our cause has spent on you? The Void does not show mercy. For your sake, I pray it listens." He doesn't wait for her reply. He simply gestures to the door, unlocks the locks, and disappears into the dark corridor beyond.

"Don't keep it waiting," his voice echoes back toward us.

"Come, Celli," Sybel commands, yanking me along beside her. "If I'm going to face the Void, you'll do as an offering."

My mind races as she weaves us through the dimly lit corridors. I try not to let the carvings on the wall draw me in and confuse me. All of it is too much to make sense of. All I know is this: wherever we're headed is a place even a powerful Sorceress like Sybel is terrified to go to.

"Don't speak," she hisses to me, "don't plead. You will be silent and do as I say. You will answer to Shadow only if they address you directly. You will obey, or you will die."

Her red-painted fingernails dig into the skin of my arm, charged with a spell. Her command is like the cold creep of death. Like a mist in my blood, it travels up to my shoulder and into my eyes, nose, and mouth. It tastes like the smoke from King Tirnon's pyre, ashy and dry. The words she whispers next complete the spell. The ash in my eyes fogs my mind as we step through enormous bronze doors that rend my soul into ribbons of fear. Into darkness. Into the Void.

Chapter Four

RECEPTION OF ALLIES
Azi

The change in the palace since the last time we visited is remarkable. During King Tirnon's vigil, mirrors were turned to face the wall, everything was hauntingly draped, and even the courtiers wore subdued shades of gray, white, and black. Since then, a vibrant transformation has taken place. Somber tones have been replaced by rich, deep autumn colors: rust and gold, magenta, purple and sky blue.

The colors are splashed everywhere: on the upholstered cushions of the thrones, in the tapestries of the walls, and in the drapes that frame the high throne room windows. Laced into it all, dappled across the room, there's a theme of hope and healing. Stunning bouquets of bright pink and pearl decorate every pedestal and alcove, glowing with fairy magic. Queen Margy's throne is draped in airy scarves of the innocent colors, and even Margy herself wears a gown of frothy pink and white, adorned with rows and rows of pearls.

The scepter and orb rest on the arms of her throne as she sits with her hands folded in her lap and her eyes dancing across the assembly. Her seat has been raised on the platform to elevate her higher than her mother, Queen Naelle, the widow of our fallen king, now named Queen Regent. She is dressed much more simply than Margy, in a plain white gown with sleeves that cover her hands, and a high neckline that ends at her chin. It's a mourning gown for His Majesty, a reminder of our beloved King Tirnon, tucked safely in the shadows cast by our bright hope for the future.

"*So, is this all this is going to be? Just standing around?*" Flitt asks as she buzzes impatiently around my head. "*If it is, then I'm going back to Brindelier.*"

"No, it'll get interesting soon," I push to her. "*It's the Reception of Allies. They'll come in one kingdom at a time. They should come in any moment, now.*"

"*All right. Guess I'll stay, then,*" Flitt huffs.

I glance at Queen Margy, who looks much older today than she had yesterday. Perhaps it's her father's crown set neatly on her perfect brown curls that makes her seem more mature, or the fact that she sits rail-straight on her throne, poised and ready for what's to come. I smile to myself at the little balcony at her right shoulder, which Twig has fashioned for himself out of a flowering vine of pink roses. He waves to Flitt, who giggles softly as some of the courtiers follow his gesture and spot her.

It's still so strange, after all the time they spent in hiding, to know our fairies can be seen by everyone, now. Even the most serious and politically-inclined members of court seem to be genuinely intrigued and delighted by their presence.

Beside me, Shush hovers at Rian's shoulder, watching the scene with just as much curiosity. The line of Her Majesty's Champions files from Mya at my left side all the way to Saesa at the other end. Across from us, the Queen's Council stands waiting to receive our allies. Uncle Gaethon and Master Anod are the highest ranking, with the rest of the Council lined up beside them along the plush purple carpet runner which trails all the way to the door at the far end of the throne room.

The only one who hasn't fallen into the proper order is Tib, who leans against the edge of Margy's throne, hidden in the Half-Realm. That's what I assume, anyway, unless he's moved since we arrived to greet the queen earlier this morning. Just before her court began filing in, he moved to pull the shadows around him at Margy's whispered direction.

"You're right! Here comes someone!" Flitt's voice bursting into my mind startles me, but I manage to keep from jumping out of my skin as a trio of elves strides into the throne room. Two of them are elves I know, but the third is unfamiliar. When they reach the steps to the throne and dip into a respectful bow, Margy stands to greet them.

"Representing Ceras'lain, Your Majesty," Master Lowery, Royal High Scholar of National Relations announces. "Zevlain Esen, Knight of the White Line, Julini Ensintia, Deputy Escort of the White Line, and Grandmaster of Histories, Susefen Alvierei."

"My dear allies," the queen's child-like voice is strengthened by its own echoes through the high arches of the ceiling. "It's an honor to receive you in Cerion so soon after your last visit here, when your might in the skies brought us victory against darkness."

The white train of her long cape trails down the steps behind her like sea foam, and she offers her hand to Zevlain and asks the elves to stand.

"The custom, I know, is to accept gifts from those who would call themselves our allies, but today it is I who have a gift for you," she says with an excited smile as Zevlain and the others straighten to tower before her.

"*Look how small they make her seem,*" Flitt giggles into my head. "*Maybe she should grow herself up a little.*"

"*Shh,*" I push, but still I try not to laugh, because she's right. Margy barely comes to Zevlain's elbow when standing in front of him. Even the queen's personal guard, Finn, who stands beside her, barely comes to Julini's chest.

"Your Majesty, a gift is not at all necessary," Zevlain waves his hand dismissively. "The armies lent to us by your father did well to defend our gates against those who would force their entry, especially at a time when they could have been of use to Cerion. We regret that we could not foresee such a circumstance. They would have served you better here."

"In the end, the outcome was favorable for both of us," Margy smiles. "And your diligent care of our soldiers meant that none were lost. For that, and for your continued friendship, Cerion is grateful. So, we present you with this chalice, which has been a treasure of the Plethore family since the time of our great, great grandfather, Asio."

She gestures to a page, who steps forward carrying the chalice on a velvet pillow. To the side of Zevlain, Susefen gasps, drawing the attention of everyone watching, especially the elves.

"Your Majesty," Susefen offers quietly, "this gift is far too generous." With slender white fingers, the elf traces the intricate designs of the silver and gold cup, which is encrusted with jewels of every color. When the other two of her kind exchange glances of curiosity with her, she goes on.

"King Asio's chalice appeared to him on the mountainside of Kythshire's Shadow Crag just before his victory over Diovicus, the Sorcerer King. From it, he drank of the crystal waters of Kythshire. Only then, with the magic bestowed upon him by the cup, was he able to defeat his enemy. It was on that day, when he stood over the fallen Sorcerer King, that he swore his oath. That no monarch or royal of Cerion would ever again wield magic." She glances at Margy, who lowers her head almost apologetically. "It is said that any who drink from this cup will be assured glory in battle, and victory over even their fiercest, most determined enemy."

"That is the tale my father told, as well," Margy says, nodding. "With my grandfather's promise behind us, I can think of no ally more deserving than the elves to hold the chalice. With it, I give you my hope that we shall always stand together in triumph over the darkness."

"Your Majesty, we could ask for no worthier ally than Cerion," Julini says quietly.

"Our gift of a pair of just-weaned cygnets seems to pale in comparison," Zevlain says with a mirthful laugh. He gestures to the door, and the court gasps with delight as a page leads a pair of tethered baby cygnets into the throne room.

"So cute!" Flitt squeals and darts around them, and the dragon-like baby birds follow her light curiously with their eyes. Their coats are soft puffs of lavender, their tails jade-green and pointed.

"Oh!" Margy claps with joy and rushes to the birds, who take to the queen right away. One nuzzles her cheek with the top of its fuzzy head while the other burrows itself into the crook of her arm. Margy giggles and strokes them both, and suddenly she's once again the smallest Plethore, the darling of Cerion. "They're wonderful!" she exclaims, laughing joyfully.

"They should be grown enough to ride by Midwinter," Julini explains. "I've been sent by our council to train them here."

One of the cygnets makes a soft cooing noise and nibbles at the pearls of Margy's gown, and Finn takes a protective step forward.

"I can't even believe it," Margy gasps again with delight, hugging one of the birds around the neck. "Thank you," she giggles, stumbling backward from the birds' overwhelming affections. Finn catches the queen to steady her, and Julini rushes to take the tethers from the page. A quick and gentle whisper in elvish soothes the youngsters, and as the elf leads the pair away, Zevlain offers the queen another bow.

"We have one more gift to offer Your Majesty," he says, gesturing to Susefen, who steps forward.

"Your Majesty, if you are willing, I offer you the gift of knowledge. I was witness to a time long ago, before Brindelier's Age of Sleep, and before the start of your own Age of Peace. I shall entertain your questions of this time when you are at leisure to ask them."

"Your gifts are so very welcome," Margy says reverently, almost whispering. "Of course, our libraries are vast and filled with knowledge, but to have a witness to tell me from her own eyes…Will you be our guest, Lady Susefen? I'm sure I'll have many questions in the days to come."

"I would be honored, *Vieli'sha,*" Susefen bows. When she looks up and sees the confusion on the queen's face, she smiles apologetically. "It means Child of Light," she explains. "It is a reverent title. We have referred to Her Majesty as such since the day of her coming out."

"I see," Margy says with a smile. She nods to the council at her right, and Master Lowery steps forward.

"Her Majesty invites you to her feast table," he says, gesturing to a door at the side of the throne room.

"We gladly accept her invitation," Susefen and Zevlain reply, and both are led off to the feast by a pair of ushers.

There's no time to remark about the elves before the next allies are welcomed to the throne room.

"Prince Vorance and Princess Sarabel of Sunteri, Your Majesty," Master Lowery announces. When the pair reaches the throne, the sisters embrace, and Prince Vorance gently kisses Margy's white-gloved hand.

"My sister," he says with gentle respect, "it is my honor to present to you the auspicious number of six barrels of Sunteri's finest crimson Everlin powder. This is a gesture of gratitude and hope for our strong and continued alliance. May it guide and restore your scholars as their tomes have guided and restored our great city."

A soft growl of a curse drifts from beside Margy's throne confirming Tib's location, but no one else seems to notice as Margy smiles at her sister and brother-in-law.

"That our alliance was forged with love," she says warmly. "That you make my sister so very happy is all the gift I need, Your Highness. Still, I accept your generosity on behalf of my kingdom, and I invite you to join my feast table."

The sisters exchange another hug and the prince and princess leave to join the feast.

"I'll go next!" Twig yelps excitedly as he darts away from Margy's throne. When he reaches the steps before the platform, he pops to human size and bows low to the queen.

"Your Majesty," he says dramatically, and those gathered at court chuckle as they watch the fae with wide-eyed interest.

"Twiggish. That is," Master Lowery clears his throat and announces, "Tufar Woodling Icsanthius Gent Gallant Illustrious Strident Hearken of Kythshire, Your Majesty."

Margy stands on the top step, eye to eye with Twig. The two stare at each other as if sharing some inside joke, both trying their hardest to look serious, but failing. Their bond is obvious to everyone in the room. Beside me, Flitt giggles and darts into my pauldron, patting my jaw with her sticky hand. I can't help but smile. The small gesture makes my skin tingle, reminding me of our own strong bond. I glance at my da down the line, who closes his eyes and shakes his head with impatience.

"Your Majesty, I present to you this ordinary stick," Twig says proudly, grinning with mischief as he places it in Margy's outstretched hand.

"I accept your gift with heartfelt thanks, and invite you to join my feast table," she says, grinning. At my shoulder, Flitt giggles again. All around us, the court whispers in confusion as Margy returns to her throne and Twig is led off to the feasting hall.

"*That was quick, and odd,*" I push to Flitt.

"*Typical. So greedy. She's already got a lot of gifts from us, hasn't she?*" Flitt pushes back a little haughtily. "*A stick will have to do.*"

"*It's brilliant, actually,*" Rian pushes to the two of us. "*He's gone to be her ears in the feasting hall while she continues greeting the others out here.*"

The entry doors swing open again, this time to admit a man I don't recognize. His broad shoulders and heavily muscled chest are covered in armor of burnished bronze scales slashed with orange, like molten metal. The metallic cloak at his shoulders seems to move of its own will, giving the illusion of leathery wings. At closer inspection, I wonder if it's an illusion at all. They could be actual wings. His copper hair is slicked back under a helm fashioned like a dragon's head. The glow of the helm's stylized orange eyes flashes in the man's own eyes like fire. His presence is imposing and commanding all at once, and even the queen seems to watch him with trepidation.

As he approaches the throne, most of our guild stand a little straighter, ready to act if needed. Finn is bolder. He steps to the edge of the platform as if in silent challenge. From her place behind my shoulder, Saesa gasps softly.

"Kerr Skalivar, Royal Consort of the Reformed Kingdom of Hywilkin, Steward of Kerevorna," Master Lowery announces, and the bronze-scaled man dips spryly to one knee.

"Child Queen of Cccerion." When he talks, the tip of a forked tongue flicks between his teeth, giving a strange hiss to his tone. His accent is like Tulya's, though his grasp of our language seems much more fluent. "I ssspeak for my brothers and sssisters, the Faefolk of the North, triumphant over the wicked King Richter, who enssslaved and tortured our kind over decadesss. I, Kerr Sskalivar, am Sssson of Ssscales. Dessscendant of proud dragon kin. On behalf of my brethren of many forms and creedsss, I offer you our allegianccce, and this gift from my ancessstorsss."

He opens his gloved hand to reveal a silvery claw as big as his palm, which catches the light in bursts of every color.

"That is a dragon's claw," Uncle Gaethon declares with awe, and those gathered in the throne room crane their necks to catch a glimpse of it. "Your Majesty, this is a rare gift indeed."

"I can feel its magic even from here," Margy nods, reaching toward it.

"It is more than you know, Majesssty, Magusss," Kerr Skalivar says, puffing out his chest proudly. "Thisss claw of my great-grandfather summonsss a true Guardian. In the north, the sssnow and the moon and the windsss whisssper together of what is to be. The Child Queen of Cccerion, the Light to Come in the Age of Kinship. We offer you thisss protection. I shall show you, when the time comesss, how to call forth thisss Guardian." He turns then and gestures to me and Rian and the others standing beside us. His gaze seems to linger longest behind me, where Saesa stands at strict attention.

"These great warriorsss of yours. Sssome have ssseen Avyn, our Guardian of Kerevorna. They can tell you it isss a worthy protector."

"Yes," the queen says with awe, gazing at the artifact in his hand. "My Champion of Light, Azaeli, has shown me Avyn. She has shown me much of what happened at Belkere. I have seen your victory, and I'm glad. I'm certain if my father had known the truth of King Richter's cruelty, he would not have stood for it."

"As I hoped you would sssay. Sssome of my people believed Cccerion valuesss peaccce over jusssticcce. I am not one of those. I sssaw the actionsss of your Championsss. How they freed usss. How they opened our Ssssource and ssset magic free onccce more, as it should be."

"We're grateful for your faith in us," Queen Margy says meekly. "Be assured that we in Cerion value every life which is good."

"Yesss, Your Majesssty," Kerr Skalivar says with a bow, still holding out the claw.

"I shall ask High Master Anod, my trusted Magical Advisor, to receive your generous gift on my behalf, Kerr Skalivar," Margy says, and gestures to Master Anod, who shuffles toward the man to accept the claw. "Thank you. I have so many questions regarding the state of your kingdom now, but I am afraid this isn't the time. Will you join me at my feasting table, and remain as my guest?"

"I would be honored, Majesssty," Kerr Skalivar bows again, and follows the ushers off to the feast as Margy takes her throne. A hushed murmur drifts across the gathering, and all eyes linger on the warrior until the feasting hall's door closes behind him.

"Princess Amei Plethore, representing Stepstone Isles, Your Majesty," Master Lowery announces as the far doors swing open again.

"She looks lovelier every time I see her," Flitt pushes to my mind. *"It's surprising, considering how much sorrow she's suffered."*

I nod in agreement to Flitt as Eron's former wife approaches, dressed in airy silks of turquoise trimmed with gold. Her outfit is not a gown, but a traditional pair of loose, fluttering pantaloons and a midriff-bearing embroidered top in the style of her island home. When she reaches the steps of the throne, she lowers herself gracefully to her knees and touches her forehead all the way to the floor. Her dark curls tumble to the velvety purple carpet, and the hall goes silent aside from the soft jingle of the princess's bracelets and hoop earrings.

All eyes move from Amei to Margy as the queen stands and descends the steps to the princess's level. When the queen crouches beside her sister-in-law and touches the woman's shoulder, Master Anod gives a disapproving cough.

"Sister," Queen Margy says, and the single word acts as absolution. Amei looks up at the queen and takes her offered hand, and both rise to stand facing one another.

"I would like very much to offer the allegiance of my people, Your Majesty," though Amei's voice is clear, it's filled with regret. "But I am afraid they refuse to acknowledge me, and instead insist upon a formal letter from the throne regarding all…" her voice falters, but she straightens herself and finds her confidence, "all that has happened."

"I'll write them," Margy whispers fervently, taking Amei's other hand and holding them both close to her heart. "Today. Your family's trust is too important to Cerion, and to me. In the meantime, you are welcome at my court, in my house, and at my table, as a sister should be." She smiles, and Amei sniffles as she bows her head again.

Margy embraces her, and the council guides the princess to the feasting hall.

"His Highness Prince Poelkevrin of Brindelier, accompanied by Master Adreen Borda Keyes, Master Councilman of Brindelier," Master Lowery announces.

The prince strides into the room, grinning with confidence as his gaze locks with Margy's. Her own smile is a mirror of his, and she seems to grip the arms of her throne to keep from jumping up to greet him as he reaches the steps before her. When he and his escort bow to her, she steps lightly down the stone stairs to greet him on his level.

"Your Majesty," Poe says with the practiced cadence of a royal, "the Kingdom of Brindelier offers you our heartfelt allegiance."

Beside him, Master Keyes clears his throat disapprovingly, and mutters, "Unless…"

"Unless we are otherwise required, against our wishes, to refute our allegiance, due to the magical bindings enforced upon us, of which we have no control." The prince's caveat is offered with a distasteful curl of his lip. After a glance at his councilman, Poe leans forward conspiratorially. "He made me say it, Your Beautiful Majesty. I know you'll triumph and finish what you've begun, therefore claiming the city and my hand for your own. There is no doubt in my mind that the Dawn will claim Brindelier."

Margy giggles. "That's all right. I understand. And you're right. We will." The air beside her shimmers slightly, and ever so faintly I hear a huff of impatience from the place where Tib must be standing. Margy's glance to the side confirms my suspicion.

"As a gesture of good faith, we offer you this mirror," Poe says, oblivious to the exchange between Margy and Tib. He gestures toward the door, where two pages dressed in Brindelier's livery enter, carrying a full-length silver mirror with an ornate gilded frame. Poe offers the queen his hand as the pages set the object down, and when Margy takes it, he guides her to look at her reflection.

"H-hello?" A female voice echoes from the glass, and Margy steps forward in awe, her hand outstretched as its surface shimmers and swims like the surface of a pool.

A memory jolts me with warning. Mirrors. One at the center of the Sorcerers' lair at the battle of Kythshire, another in Jacek's lair in the darkness of the Dreaming. A flash of a memory of my own reflection luring me in makes me call Mercy to my hands and take a step toward my queen.

Margy startles at my approach and pulls her hand away, looking at me in confusion. "Lady Knight?" she asks.

"Sir Hammerfel," Poe says gently, as if trying to tame a wild beast. My grip on my sword loosens, but only slightly as I glance at the glass.

"I've seen these before," I explain to the two of them as the rest of the court watches with rapt attention. My effort to keep the distrust out of my tone fails. "In the lairs of Sorcerers."

"Aha." Master Keyes chuckles softly. "That is easily explained. These mirrors are rare objects indeed, powerful and difficult to create. It would certainly make sense that their use has fallen solely into the hands of Sorcerers, but I assure you, the magic they convey is quite neutral."

"It is as they say, Majesty, and Niece," Uncle declares, stepping forward to join us at the mirror. "Though this rare magic has fallen out of our hands and into those of darkness, the workings in and of themselves are not of a dark nature. I should very much like to study this artifact."

"H-hello?" the ghostly echo issues once more from the glass, and Poe steps to face the rippling image on its surface.

"Pippa," the prince calls, resting his fingertips on the mirror. "I'm here."

"Brother!" the voice answers excitedly, and the image of Princess Pippa forms crisp and clear before us, as if all she needs to do is step through the glass to join us in the throne room.

"Oh, I see!" Margy says delightfully as she peers through the glass. "Good day, Princess."

"Good day, Your Majesty." Pippa offers a curtsy. "How wonderful to see you. And oh, what a gorgeous gown you're wearing."

"Thank you, and so is yours." Margy giggles.

"Now, even when we're apart, you and I can see each other." Poe beams at the queen and takes her hand to kiss her soft white glove. The air beside Margy makes a faint gagging sound.

"Your gift is most welcome, Your Highness," Margy says with a smitten grin. "I invite you to join my table and feast with us."

"Thank you," Poe whispers, gazing at her as though she's the only person in the room. He looks away only when the councilman begins to lead Master Keyes to the feasting hall, and the prince reluctantly follows.

This time when the queen returns to her throne looking slightly pinker in the cheeks, the doors at the end of the room remain closed. Master Lowery issues no announcement. After a long pause, Margy turns to the Scholar curiously.

"There are no others registered, Majesty," Lowery remarks, checking over his scroll.

"Haigh?" she asks, furrowing her brow.

"Haigh, historically, has been a shaky ally at best, Majesty. Currently, it is dealing with the exodus of Hywilkin. As the new reign overtakes the old and conquerors become leaders, there are always those who would refuse the new government and make efforts to flee their country."

Margy looks as though she'd like to question further, but she checks herself with a glance at the court full of eager ears hanging on the young queen's every word. Instead, she reaches for her scepter and rests it in her lap.

"Elespen?" she asks with measured caution.

This gets an exchange of worried glances among the council, until Hayse, Second Admiral of the Royal Naval Fleet, steps forward.

"Elespen has been uncommunicative since the battle which took place during His Majesty's Rites," he explains quietly. "We have sent scout ships and messengers, and none have returned. There has been no word from any who have been sent there, Your Majesty. It is as though the entire continent has gone utterly silent."

"My champions, my council," she says after a moment of thought, motioning to a set of doors opposite the feasting hall. "I request a quiet word in my side chamber before we proceed to the feast."

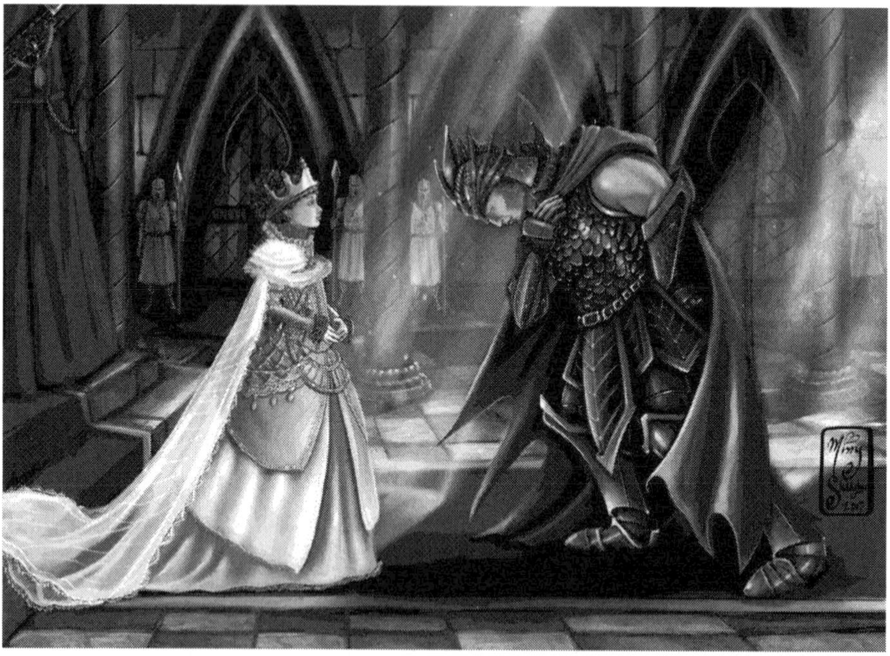

Chapter Five

EYES OF THE VOID
Celli

We step in together, but as soon as we cross the threshold, Sybel vanishes. Everything disappears. I'd say there's darkness, but there's too much chaos and emptiness to describe it that way. My mind goes with it. Disappeared. Stolen away from myself. I'm only aware of my own body. My knees hitting the floor—yes, there's a floor. My elbows, next. My cheek. It feels like nothing, the floor. Like blank space. The pause in speech. The empty pause between breaths.

It's not a peaceful silence. It's fringed with terror. A feeling as though everything is wrong. A threat, hovering, waiting. A suffering. My past drifts to me in pieces, rifled through. Wrinkled and mishandled. Along with it, my emotions trickle back to me. My fear of her. Someone evil and horrible. Someone who would kill me if she knew the truth.

The truth.

What is the truth? I lose track of my hands, my knees, my cheek. Nothing turns into something. A tendril of shadow, licking toward me. I'm not afraid. How can I be, when I'm nothing?

Survive.

The thought is a flash of hope, here and gone. Escaped, leaving me behind. A sliver of light snuffed out by a heavy black drape. Disappeared, like it never was. I'm no one, now. Part of the darkness. Absorbed. I feel the shadows and I don't. It doesn't matter.

What is the truth?

Darkness. It lures me in, placating me, and I sink into it like a comforter. A bed of soft straw. Rainy midnight. My mother's arms around me, and mine around my brother. Baby brother. My family. As soon as I'm aware of them, they're gone again. A page torn out. Forgotten. Again, I'm nothing. No one.

He's here as though he never left. Quenson, my Quenson. His eyes are as dark and terrible as they ever were. No flash of light brightens them or lights my surroundings, but I know he's here. I feel him. His arms and his cloak encircle me. He whispers into my ear and I'm reminded of the charge of importance I felt under his spell. The power of Dusk emanates from him, captivating me, ensnaring me.

The tendrils lift me. Pull me. Everything is still nothing, but I'm drawn deeper into it. Toward the center. Into the thick of emptiness. I have no will to fight, no desire to run. I'm filled with it. It is me, and we're nothing. No one. Endless. My body is gripped tighter, but I don't bother to struggle against it. I lose myself.

"So simple." The whispers come from everywhere, deep and terrifying, high and powerful. Hundreds of voices in unison. "It hardly seems worth it."

I know they're talking about me. How easy it was to take me, to sway me. It doesn't matter. I don't matter. I don't exist.

"Yet, delicious," they hiss from deep within the darkness.

Shadows, feathery-soft, caress my face, pierce my skin, sweep my mind. Ground cracking. Lava. My master, falling. Dying.

"Inconceivable," they mutter, and in the glow of the rocky flames, I find myself again. Celli. *Survive.*

The fear I felt before at being found out is gone, replaced with a sense of accomplishment. Triumph. Power.

"Yes. He was a fool. Impatient. He got what he deserved. Revenge," they whisper. Cackle. Squeal. My ears ring with pain. The noise is horrifying. I feel my body again. My stomach flips. I curl into myself, still held by the tendrils of shadow.

"Vengeance." This voice is set apart from the others. Deep and sure, it stirs me with a desire stronger than I ever felt for Quenson. A need to please. An ache for his favor. "The energy of vengeance is dark. Wicked. Powerful. The essence of Dusk."

As this voice grows stronger, the others around it wane, cowering with unwavering respect. Whoever the voice belongs to is revered by them. Worshiped. My heart races. I am nothing, worthless and unworthy without this force to guide me.

"A quick mind is an asset," he booms. Then, nothing.

The silence stretches on for I don't know how long. The void, the emptiness, fill me to the brim. This time I'm allowed to keep myself. To remember who I am. I'm aware of what a gift it is. What a freedom, to know who I am. I'm grateful. I want to show it. To make some offering, some promise, but there's no one to give it to. Nothing here but me, and darkness. I'm safe in the center of it, a part of it. Cradled by it.

Its power draws me in, like when I used Osven's bracelet. This time, though, it's all around me. A charge in the air. A promise of dark power unlike anything I've ever known.

"You see," the deep voice thunders around me. With each word, the hair on my arms prickles with tangible energy.

I have so many questions. Why? Why am I here? Why me? Why am I not dead? Where is Sybel? Who is this force, this Void, this Dusk? Is he one person? Is he all of them? I don't dare ask. Somehow I know, if I'm quiet, I'll be shown.

"Silence," he rumbles. "Silence and determination."

With his words, I'm flung forward into scenes of dusk and shadow. Battlefields pulsing with arcane power, explosions of magic sending fairies and men tumbling away, defeated. At the center of this power is a man, fierce and terrible. A Sorcerer. A king. The Mark has taken him over so completely that it seems to have formed a shell around him, an armor that no sword or spell can penetrate. Even his face is so melded with dark energy that he doesn't require slits or holes to see out of the inky mask.

I'm pulled closer to him, sucked in until I'm one with his dark form. For an instant, for less than a breath, I become him in this memory of the past.

The charge of power is overwhelming. To go from nothing, from being nothing and feeling nothing to having everything, to pure omnipotence, is a shock of ultimate pleasure. I cry out into the void, gasping as the memory pulls away and I'm once again left in darkness. I want to plead with him not to leave me, not to forsake me this way, but one word warns me otherwise.

"Silence."

I'm rewarded with more information. Further scenes. Keeps, hidden in darkness, filled with battalions of soldiers, readied. Loyal. Waiting for word, for orders from this being, this dark creature, this nothing and everything. Dusk. Waiting for the command to war resting on the tip of his tongue. I've never seen armies so vast and varied. Men and imps, creatures of darkness, giants, rebels and risen dead, all banded together in the name of Dusk.

I soar over them like a bird, the unending formations standing at attention, lined up to strike. To destroy.

"Silence and determination."

Suddenly they're gone, and so is the Void. I find myself in a small unlit room in a soft, comfortable chair. A blanket of shadow drapes my lap, heavy and calming. Across from me sits a man I don't know. It's too dark to see him or make out his features, but my sense is that he's handsome, with a chiseled jaw and a lithe form that lounges casually across his own throne-like chair.

I can feel his eyes on me from the shadows. He watches, waiting. Trying to figure something out. Thoughtful. I can feel the power radiating from him. I know he's the voice in the Void. The king on the mountainside. The Darkness embodied. I'm not afraid. I'm curious. Curious, and even a little grateful.

"Why do you do not speak, even now?" he asks me. "It isn't out of fear. Why are you not afraid?"

I look beyond him, to the walls I can't see in the darkness. To the floor that's black as tar. To him, in his chair, also shrouded in darkness, and look away again.

"Silence," I reply. It seems the only right thing to say.

"And?" He asks with a hint of amusement.

"Determination?" I whisper, overcome with awe that he'd take the time to speak to me so intimately. Just the two of us. Overwhelmed that he hasn't killed me yet, for what I've done. He knows what I've done. He knows everything.

"And what is that? Determination for what?"

My past is behind me. The person I was in Cerion before Quenson, the things I did under his control, and what happened after his hold on me was severed...I'm not her anymore. Something in the shadows emanating from this man pushes it all away. Forgives it, but doesn't erase it. I'm not nothing. I'm allowed to keep my past. Still, what will become of me? Who will I be?

The Sorcerer King rises to his feet and drifts nearer. He seems made of darkness, or darkness is made of him. I can't see him, but I can sense him.

"You look so like her," he whispers, and a thrill charges through me. "Perhaps that is what Quenson saw in you. Perhaps he meant you for a gift, and, in the end, that is what you have become."

"A gift?" I whisper.

"Yes," he replies.

"To you?"

"And why not?"

"With all that you are, and all you command, how can I be anything to you?"

He leans so close I can feel the heat of him. I sense a hand between us and a flash of gold swirls from his palm. The radiance of it in the dark room blinds me at first, and I squeeze the sting from my eyes as the swirls form the figure of a girl.

She's a princess, dressed in a golden gown. Her skin is sun-kissed bronze, and her hair is straight, blond, and cropped short like mine. The image trembles slightly. I feel the shadow's breath catch as he gazes at her. He's right. She could be me, in another age. My sister, maybe.

"Pippa," he whispers tenderly. I look away from her to his face, not covered in the Mark as it was on the crag, but smooth, young, and handsome. His eyes move from the conjured princess and lock onto mine, deep as midnight sky. He sweeps a single finger across my brow and I feel the heat of it enter the sockets of my eyes, claiming them for his.

"*Caviena.*" The word is spoken without explanation. It feels like a title, like a gift to me. My eyes tingle and tear up. When he breaks his gaze, the sensation remains. Right away, I understand. I'm his. His eyes. Whatever I see, he sees.

From one master to the next. I know the wrong of it, I do. Somewhere in the back of my mind, I know. But the might of his armies is unmatched anywhere in the Known Lands. Pretending any other force could ever stand up to them would be foolish. Ridiculous. It might be wrong. Evil, even. But, smart. When he wins, I'll stand among the victors. *Survive.*

"You are not her. Of this I am aware. She was taken from me. Hidden. Enchanted. Blocked, but it is only temporary. Silence. Determination. They have claimed four. Our time is nearing."

He drifts back to his chair to lounge, and my cry of protest catches in my throat as darkness spills once more into the space between us. The raw pain of his defeat hangs heavy over the room, as fresh as if it had happened yesterday. As quickly as he had become a Sorcerer King to me, now he's a teenager, scowling and petulant.

"You are not her," he mutters again, and the anger in his voice swells into rage.

"I can be whatever you make me," I offer, trying hard to keep the desperation out of my voice. I understand. He's the boy and the king. He's both. Everything and nothing. Darkness. The Void. "Just like you can make yourself seem to be whatever you choose."

His reply is laughter, deep and wicked. It ends abruptly, with a single word: "Go."

The chair cradling me falls away, and the shadow blanket in my lap whips around me, flinging me back into the Void.

Nothing, nothing.

Survive, says the candle that flickers nearby.

"Forgiveness granted by one who can mold the very night itself, by one who can fell a giant with a snap of his fingers, who commands armies more vast than anyone can fathom, is a powerful gift."

This voice is different. Not him, so it's unimportant. Still, everything he says is true. The darkness shrinks from me slightly, allowing me to see. The Void is gone. I'm standing in a room, another room. This one is circular, with six alcoves carved into the wall. Each alcove holds an empty pedestal. The man speaking has his back to me. His wine-red robes brush the polished floor as he creeps to one alcove and rests his hand on the empty pedestal. He doesn't turn to face me. Not yet.

I remember this room. Once, two alcoves had bottles in them. Offerings. Until Tib stole one of them. It was important, that vial. I remember the horror that followed. The rage. They failed the Dusk by failing to protect that vial, and now...

"Where is it? The other one? The last one?" I ask.

"Safeguarded by your former master, and so no one knows." He turns around, and my breath catches. Xantivus. "Not yet, anyway."

"That was why she wanted to use me? To find out where he hid it?" I can barely form the words. He's terrifying. Not as much as the other had been, but still intimidating. He steps closer, and a glint of gold Mark flashes under the black that covers his face.

"It would have been a waste. Had you known where it was hidden, the Void surely would have seen it, and so it falls to Sybel to seek its hiding place." He smirks, as if that tidbit of information amuses him. What he said to her earlier was right. The spell she had planned would have been wasteful and useless either way.

He walks around me, eyeing me the way a cat eyes a cornered mouse. Except this mouse is already claimed by another, larger cat. One he won't dare cross. Even knowing that, I lean away from him, repulsed. His gaze bores into me as though it's reading everything about me. As though he can see my thoughts.

"You have seen all of it, then. The glory of our cause. The might," he purrs. It isn't a question, but I nod anyway in reply. "You have chosen wisely."

I try to remember when I made a choice. When I actually said it. I don't think I did, but I know he's right. I'm theirs now. The Sorcerer King's. I belong to the Void. To the Dusk. The idea doesn't scare me. It thrills me that I would be forgiven and accepted after everything I've done. That I would be welcomed.

"Silence and determination. For a century and longer, our High Master has waited patiently, gathering forces and strengthening his followers. He has forged alliances in secret and expanded his reach, drawing followers from every corner of the world. Every discontented heart, every rebellious soul, dead or alive, has flocked to him.

"We have all been given a choice like yours. Those who are wise enough to be open to Shadow, to be drawn in by Dusk, to see firsthand its power and to learn to wield it, are rewarded with his favor, and with even more power. In turn, he has preserved us and strengthened us. He nurtures us, and we feed his power. His allies are Earth and Darkness. They sit at his table, and together, they plot."

While he talks, Xantivus paces around me, circling like a lion closing in on its meal. His eyes go distant and wild. His mouth stretches into a grin. Even his tongue and his gums are trailed with black and gold. Truly, he's a fearsome Sorcerer.

"And now, with the child queen seated on her throne, placated by forces of Light, he knows. The time is nearing. Darkness will cover them first, and when all offerings are in place, Dusk shall strike and claim the All Source for its own."

I picture the armies of Dusk, cloaked in darkness and hidden in some unknown place, waiting for the command of one man. The thought sends a chill through me. The fate of any who would meet against such a force is plain. There could be no victory against the Void.

"These forays and tiny battles have been amusing for our lord. They have determined his truest and most powerful followers. Those who have survived, you see, have gained his utmost favor. In turn, they have provided quite a distraction for the Dawn. Their worthless victories have given them a sense of bravado. They have no way of knowing what comes for them. Our lord has hidden it far too well."

He goes quiet at that, but continues pacing while I think over his words. None of this makes sense. Why, if he's so powerful, would he spare me? Why would Xantivus tell me all of this? I'm just a girl. A former thrall who betrayed her master. Unworthy.

"That is where you are wrong, *Caviena*."

The word sends a rush of heat through my blood and a flash of the Sorcerer king into my mind.

"Yes. You see it now. *Caviena*. Your title. It means eyes. You shall be his eyes, girl. You will go where he sends you, and see what is to be seen. You shall hide yourself and watch."

He moves closer to me and takes my chin with his fingertips as if to kiss me. I don't move away. I don't flinch.

"Pity," he whispers, his rank breath filling my nostrils, "you won't remember any of our little conversation. Or much else, for that matter." Again, he smirks. Tendrils of gold spill from his eyes like serpents, striking the depths of my mind. Vaguely in the distance, I feel lips on mine. His lips. Hands touching me. His hands. Before I can think to push him away, to fight him, everything goes still. Blank. Empty. Dark.

I wake in a strange, bright room, to the sound of singing and distant explosions. My ceiling is draped with silk streamers which flutter in the breeze of the nearby open window. Outside my open window, more streamers and colorful flags wave against the pure blue sky. A shout from the streets below is followed by a chorus of laughter. I turn my head on the pillow and look along my arm at my outstretched hand. It seems disembodied, somehow. Mine, but not mine. A sense of dread fills me when I try to think of what that means. For something to be mine, I need to have a self. But that concept is gone. Far away. Lost.

That dread is quickly pushed out by stronger magic. Joy. Celebration. Happiness. I want to dance, to sing, to cheer. The long wait is over. Now is a time for letting go of old troubles, for throwing cares to the wind. Today is a festival day. I jump out of bed and rush to the window to take in the scene of revelry in the streets below.

My gaze drifts across the crowd and quickly into the horizon, where the colorful spires of Brindelier's palace tower over the rest of the city. It's close. Perhaps just a street over. The sight is so captivating, I can't tear my eyes from it. I take in every carving, every speck of shining glass mosaic, every window. I stare, searching desperately. I'm not sure what for, but whatever it is, I know it's important. More important than anyone here. More important, even, than me.

Chapter Six

COUNSEL
Tib

It's a lot to take in. All of it. As Her Majesty's Champions file into the room behind her, I stay right where I've been since she jumped out my window. At her side. Glued to her arm. Watching. Expecting something bad to happen. Anything.

I don't know why I'm so on edge. She's safer here in the palace than anywhere else. After that Reception of Allies, it's obvious she has more friends than enemies out there. Still, it's too many new people. Too much unknown. It only takes one. A Sorcerer with a spell. An assassin with a blade full of Blackheart, like her father got.

I can't help being suspicious. Now that I'm back in Cerion, now that she's given me titles and positions, I won't let down my guard. *Her Majesty's Eye*. This is my duty. It's why I'm here. To stick with her. To keep her safe. She's too trusting to realize how dangerous things can be. Too innocent.

My thoughts jump around like pebbles in the surf. I keep thinking of the barrels. Six barrels. Prince Vorance was so proud when he told her about their gift. So smug. I wonder if he knows how many slaves suffered for all that powder. I wonder whether anyone appreciates their work, or even knows they exist. I wonder if I'll ever get a chance to talk to him about it, face to face. If I could, would it matter? Would he even listen?

The door closes, and my hand jumps instinctively to my dagger. My healed eye snaps over the six council members who arrange themselves on one side of the round planning table. The Mages stink. I wonder how much Everlin powder they all go through every day. I huff to myself as I look them over. Blow the smell from my nostrils. Gaethon's all right, I guess, but the other two, Anod and Lowery, give me the creeps.

I look down the line at the rest of them. The three non-Mages. The sensible ones. The Second Admiral of the Royal Fleet is here. Hayse. Not Ganvent. The father of my house here in Cerion has been gone for exactly a month now. He and his fleet. They were accompanying a shipment of books to Zhaghen, Sunteri's capital. I remember Osven's threats before Nessa killed him. How he taunted us, implying Sorcerers attacked the fleet.

A pang of guilt stabs at my chest. I could have asked Kaso Viro about him. I should have, but I was too distracted. I promise myself I will, next time I see him. As soon as I leave here today, I'll find out. Sorcerers are liars, anyway, I tell myself. It takes at least a couple of months to get to Sunteri by ship. That's why we haven't heard from him. Maybe it means the Admiral is all right. Probably. Yes, he is. He has to be.

Margy sniffles and I shift closer to comfort her, but her mother swoops in before I can. She takes her daughter in her arms and soothes her. No one else questions or even looks. They bow their heads respectfully and wait. The new queen knows this is her safe place. They won't judge her in here, or think she's weak. All of us, every single one, loves her too much for that.

"Sorry. I needed a moment," Margy says once she's more composed. The queen mother pulls away. Margy dabs her eyes with a square of lace. "Father left me such a legacy. So many friends loyal to the throne. It's overwhelming."

"I beg Your Majesty not to be overly charmed by gifts and promises," Myer warns quietly. He's a good man. I like him. He thinks like I do.

He's loyal. Captain of the Royal Guard. I look him over. No magic on him anywhere, except a necklace warding Mentalism. Most of the guard got those after the battle at the pyre.

"Yeah," I agree with the captain. When I step out of the Half-Realm, there's barely any reaction. Most of them knew I was here. The queen told them. "Like Brindelier and that mirror."

Some of them seem a little annoyed at me for joining in. Like it's not my place. I don't care. This was my main reason for coming to stand around at this boring meeting, anyway. Aside from keeping an eye on Margy. These guys need to know what's happening up there in the clouds. The festival. The Bordas. Azi's eyes meet mine. She nods slightly. Encouragingly. She's on my side.

"What do you know of it, boy?" Elmsworth, the Royal Captain of Arms, asks. His tone isn't disrespectful or dismissive. Still, Margy scowls. She presses her palms to the polished table top and looks sternly down the line at each of her Council.

"Tib is my eyes in the shadows," she says firmly. "He has served me well in my father's time, and proved his loyalty many times over. He may seem only a *boy* to you, Captain, and to the rest of you, but I ask you to address him with respect.

"He lives in the house of our Royal Naval Admiral, Ganvent. I have given him the titles, Her Majesty's Eye and Duskbane. He holds other titles, much more prestigious, from Sunteri, Ceras'lain, and other realms hidden from us. He'll soon be inducted into the house of my Champions. 'My lord' suits him better."

Everyone gives a nod of solemn agreement. Queen Naelle strokes her daughter's shoulder. They seem to look at me differently after her speech. I wasn't expecting her to do that.

Not sure what to do or say, I avoid looking at any of them. Instead, my healed eye flicks toward the wall. In the next room, the outline of a woman walks down the runner leading to the empty throne. She looks timid. Confused. The room is mostly empty now. A page steps up to speak to her.

"My apologies, my lord," the captain clears his throat and I pull my gaze back inside the chamber to focus on him. "What do you know of it?"

"I spent some time in Brindelier recently," I explain. "At first, it's a lot like you'd expect. Lots of celebration and excitement. A great festival. Dancing, singing. But it's not what it seems. All that is a distraction. Something's keeping the people enchanted."

"Enchanted to celebrate?" Master Anod scowls. "Why would they do such a thing? How can you be certain?"

Margy looks at me and nods. She wants them to know what I can do. She wants me to tell them.

"I can tell. I can feel magic. I can see what it does." I don't tell them it doesn't affect me. They don't need to know that. Not yet, anyway. "Like," I point to Anod, "that you're wearing a vest under your robes. One like Prince Eron the Second has. To protect you. And how that cuff on your ear amplifies sound, since your hearing is failing. And your ring—"

"Ahaha," Anod laughs uncomfortably and shoves his hands into his robes. "I see, my lord. I see. No need to reveal all of an old Mage's secrets."

"It would make sense, from what we have learned," Master Gaethon muses, "that such measures would be taken to keep the kingdom of Brindelier calm and controlled, until such a time as the throne is fully secured."

"What does it have to do with the mirror, though?" Azi asks.

"I don't know," I reply. "But I do know there are plots. Some people don't want outsiders coming in. Especially not to rule them. There's a powerful family. The Bordas. They seem to control a lot of what goes on."

I remember my conversation with Lord Borda. How I left him believing I'd try to lure Margy into my arms, just to keep her from joining her kingdom with theirs. I look at her, standing beside me. I take in the shine of her curls. How pretty her upturned nose is when I look at her from the side, like this. I wonder if her cheeks are painted pink, or if that's just her own glow.

She closes her eyes. Takes a calming breath.

"You see, Majesty," Captain Myer says. "And Keyes is one of them."

"Master Adreen *Borda* Keyes," Master Lowery confirms with a solemn nod. "The captain has a fair point, my queen. They are declared allies, it is true. But we must always be vigilant. There is never give without some take. Things are not always as plain as they seem."

"We must act with respect, diligence, and caution," Master Gaethon agrees.

"That's enough for now. It's a lot to take in," Queen Naelle says with a mother's gentle tone. She reaches for Margy, who holds up her hand.

"I'm grateful for your counsel," Margy says. When she speaks, her voice is calm and confident. "The Queen Mother is right. There is much to consider. But I have all of you to guide me, and I have faith in you. I understand the importance of a council, just like my father did before me. Knowing all of this and setting it aside, there are other things which concern me. I worry for Haigh and Elespen. Especially Elespen."

"I agree. The absence of any word from Elespen is troubling," Master Lowery nods.

"We have," she stops herself, glancing at the closed door.

"Silence wards have been set, Your Majesty," Master Anod reassures her, and the queen nods gratefully.

"We have all but two offerings now," she says, her voice barely above a whisper. "Ceras'lain and Elespen."

"That's right," I say. "And we really only need to get Elespen. Ceras'lain will be easy. The elves have already agreed to it."

I don't tell her what else they told me. That as *Eftue'luvrie*, as Faedin to the Keeper of Sunteri's Wellspring, the other Keepers can't refuse me. It's part of the rules. Magic rules. Fairy rules. For some reason, I feel like that information is best kept to myself, still.

"We're so close!" Flitt claps excitedly at Azi's shoulder, and Shush puts a finger to his lips to quiet her as Benen scowls down the line at her outburst. "Well, we are," she whispers, and sticks her tongue out at Shush.

Margy grins at the two fae and steps closer to the Champions' side of the table as if she's drawn to them. Thoughtfully, she looks down the line from Mya all the way to Saesa at the very end.

"Lady Mya," Margy begins hesitantly, wringing her hands.

"Your Majesty," Mya tips her head to Margy respectfully.

"Elespen is your homeland, isn't it? My father told me."

"It is, your Majesty—"

"Margary," the queen interrupts. "Or Margy."

Mya glances across at the queen's council and then at the queen mother before nodding to Margy. It's obvious to everyone how hard the new queen is trying to keep things just like her father had them. Especially here, in the private council room.

"It is where I was born," Mya starts again, "but I haven't been there since I set foot on Cerion's soil. I'm sure much has changed in thirty years."

"Still, you have more experience there than any of the rest of us," Margy smiles.

"That's true. And Cort, Your Maj—Margary. He spent time there as well, in Cresten's port."

"Oh?" Margary asks, peering all the way down the line past Bryse, to where Cort stands between him and Saesa. His braids swing as he leans forward and nods his reply. The queen echoes his nod, gazing thoughtfully across the room.

"I should like to propose a quest," she says to no one in particular.

"That may not be prudent, just yet," Master Gaethon warns. "There are many things we need to research and discuss before we claim the All Source. The elves have promised counsel on the matter."

"And the discussions with Master Keyes are not going as well as we might have hoped," Master Anod adds.

"And, with respect, may I remind all of you this gathering is meant to be a short reprieve for Her Majesty, not a council meeting," says Master Lowery. "Our guests are waiting."

"I know," says the queen. "Even so, I'll feel much better with all of the offerings claimed. The Dusk is out there, and they're not concerned with treaties and agreements. In fact, they probably expect a delay from us because of these many matters. It's the perfect chance for them to gain the upper hand. I dare say that's the reason my father was…" She shakes her head to clear it. "We can't delay. So, the quest."

Beside her, Anod snaps his fingers, and one of the scribes tucked into the corner of the room pulls out a fresh scroll of parchment. Margy's expression twists into a puzzled one while the room goes silent. Finally, she raises a brow and looks at the council. "How do I do it?" she whispers.

"What sort of quest would you like to propose, Majesty?" Master Anod asks gently.

"I should like to send a small group to Elespen, to investigate their silence and the strange disappearance of our scouts," she leans on the table with a twinkle in her eye. "That will be the official reason, of course," she winks. "Mya, Cort, Azi, Rian, and Elliot. Yes, that's a good group, I think. And Tib," she turns to me, "by ship. One of yours."

My heart races. One of my ships. Finally, I can fly. For real, not just in a dream.

Down at the end, Bryse shifts. I can see the scowl in his eyes, but it doesn't reach his face. He's good at hiding emotions. He's annoyed at being left out. Margy's quick. She notices.

"Bryse," she says, this time with a bit more confidence. Bryse squares his shoulders and tips his head toward her. Even that giant is no match for her smile. His granite face cracks into a mirror of it. His brow softens.

"I shall ask you, Donal, Lisabella, and Gaethon to travel to Haigh. I'm concerned about their silence as well."

"Your Majesty," Azi leans slightly toward the queen. "Margy, sorry."

Margy grins and bobs her head at the knight, and Azi goes on.

"Before any official quest is declared, there's another matter you should know about. Something pressing that I think you'll agree needs to be taken care of before Rian and I can go to Elespen. You see, Eron—"

A sharp knock on the door interrupts her.

"Come," Margy calls, and a page steps inside and closes the door behind her with a soft, deliberate click. The silence wards settle back in place.

"Your Majesty," the page curtsies and turns to the council. "Master Lowery, there's another ally outside. In the throne room."

"Another ally?" Lowery scowls. "Not possible. All have been registered and received."

"I think, well," the page scowls, "it's difficult to tell for certain. She doesn't speak."

I look through the door again with my healed eye and find the woman I saw before. She's standing at the edge of the steps to the throne, gazing up at the pillars and arches. She's got an odd crown on her head. Her feet and arms are trimmed with strange wings. It's hard to tell from an outline, but I vaguely remember seeing that strange crown before, in a flash of an image sent to me when I was deep under the sea in Kaso Viro's ship, eye to eye with a merman.

"Where is she from?" Margy asks eagerly.

"The sea," the page whispers. "Definitely the sea."

"Mermaid," I mutter, and Margy gasps.

"Oh! Show her in here!" she says excitedly, but then second guesses herself and looks to her council. "That is, should we? Or should I go out and greet her?"

"By your leave," Master Lowery says, "I'll go."

Obviously disappointed, Margy agrees. Master Lowery is only gone for a moment before he comes back in looking slightly dazed.

"Ah, lady Knight. Sir Hammerfel, that is," he stammers, pointing to Azi. "I believe you'll be much more successful in communicating with her. She seems not to…that is…" he rubs his eyes and shakes his head. Behind him, the door to the chamber creaks, and the woman's pale face peers in at us.

"On'na?" Azi gasps.

"Oh! It *is* a mermaid," Margy whispers in awe. "Oh, dear. Kira, get her a robe please," she orders. I make sure to keep my eyes to the side. Most of the others in the room do, too, until the page comes back with a silky blue robe to cover her with.

On'na doesn't seem to even notice. Her eyes are locked with Azi's. The knight's breath comes in short puffs. The Champions move to protect Azi, but she holds up her hand to reassure them.

"It's all right," she whispers. Flitt's light dances eerily across the room from her shoulder. "She's showing me. Earthquakes. The ground is cracking open. Great chasms split the ocean floor. The rifts shoot like arrows into the cliff sides rending the earth apart. Under cities. Under...Orva." She gasps and tears her gaze away, looking to Rian.

"No," he whispers.

"Orva," Bryse growls. Cort puts a hand on his arm, but the giant doesn't seem to notice. On'na and Azi lock gazes again. The mermaid shows her more. Azi shakes her head. Her eyes widen in terror.

"Aster?" Rian murmurs. He draws the wand from his robes and it pulses softly. "Is it true?"

My thoughts tumble away. Far away. To Hywilkin. Aster. Stellastera, Muse of Magic. Sha'Renell, Muse of Earth. When we left them, they were locked in a furious battle. We didn't stay to see who the victor would be. We didn't try to sway the fight. There were more important things to worry about at the time. Now, it seems like a big mistake. If what On'na is showing Azi is true...

"*Rian*," the wand's eerie voice echoes across us. "*I am lost.*"

"He's out," Azi shudders. "Eron. Released."

"Impossible," Rian shakes his head. "Those wards were above Master level. They were above anything I've ever experienced."

"It's not impossible," Shush whispers from his shoulder. "Not for a Muse. If the earth beneath the Revenant were split open, if Sha'Renell defeated Aster..."

"*Please*," the wand's voice fades weakly.

"On'na, thank you for this warning," says Margy, her voice shaken with fear. "Azi and Rian, do whatever you can. Stop him. Go."

No one argues when Rian and Azi reach for each other. Azi turns to On'na, showing her something between them, and On'na nods and turns to bow to the queen. The mermaid rests a hand on Azi's shoulder.

"Here we go!" Flitt giggles. The air shimmers around them, and in a blink, they're gone. The only evidence they were here at all is On'na's borrowed robe, which flutters to the floor in a pool of blue silk as she vanishes.

Chapter Seven

THE CHASMS OF ORVA
Azi

As we speed through the Half-Realm, I'm overcome by a strange sensation. Along with the usual feeling of ants crawling across my skin, there's a rush of wind that seems to swirl around us. It's puzzling only for a moment, until we come to a sudden stop in cold darkness and a flutter of turquoise fins brushes my face.

"We're in the sea," I whisper to myself, releasing bubbles of my breath toward the surface. I wave my hand in front of my face. To my surprise, it's coated in a thin film of silvery air, the only barrier between me and the endless, dark sea beyond. This uneasy realization is pushed out quickly by a much more urgent one. A nagging feeling I've forgotten something, or someone, nudges at my insides. Immediately my hand flies to my shoulder. *"Flitt?"*

"I'm here!" she calls cheerfully, her voice carrying an odd echo inside our shared cushion of air. When she pushes off from my pauldron, a trail of bubbles follows her as her own air pouch breaks free from mine. It jiggles oddly with the movement of her wings and the flutter of her skirt, and I reach out to her, afraid to lose the tiny creature to the depths of the sea.

The weight of my armor isn't an issue, and turning toward Rian is sort of a strange mix of movement between swimming and walking.

"It worked!" he says with a grin. "I've always wanted to try this one. Depth-Walk. Twelfth Circle. Not bad, eh?" He struts around in midair, or mid-water, with Shush standing on top of his head like the lookout in the crow's nest of a ship.

"It's amazing! Oh! On'na!" I gasp as the mermaid swims between us and her wide eyes lock onto mine.

Visions of a battle jolt me with urgency. A battalion of mermen with spears races through the water, propelled at a dizzying speed by their powerful fins. They disappear into the depths of a gaping chasm. From the suffocating darkness of the ominous space, magical light pulses in erratic patterns like bolts of lightning.

"Where?" I cry, and she grabs my hand and Rian's and pulls us along at the pace of a galloping horse.

"This is amazing!" Flitt giggles as she clings to my collar. "Azi, look how beautiful!" Her sticky hands push my chin toward On'na, whose legs are gone, replaced by a shimmering blue fish tail. Her billowing teal and purple fins ripple with the power of her strokes like fine silks in a breeze, easily the length of her body. Her colorful scales catch Flitt's light like tiny, glittering flecks of iridescent sand.

I find myself mesmerized by the beauty of it, until a sudden realization stabs my gut with a pang of regret.

"*Saesa,*" I push to Rian. "*That's who I forgot. I can't believe it. How could I do that?*" It's not the first time I've accidentally left my squire behind. It's a wonder she hasn't gone looking for another knight.

"*Most likely a good instinct,*" his reassurance takes on an ominous tone. "*It's probably for the best. Look.*"

Onna's fins flick forward, bringing us to an abrupt stop at the gaping mouth of the chasm. Sand churns from the sea floor, clouding our view for just a moment before it settles again. The blue-green tone of our surroundings and the deafening silence add heavy sense of foreboding to the scene. Flitt nuzzles into my neck, trembling as she peers above us.

"*So heavy,*" she pushes, and she's right. The walls on either side of the chasm stretch so high up toward the surface that the edges of them disappear into the murky sea above. It's daytime, I know, but we're so deep, with so much of the ocean above us that it obscures the sunlight completely.

The concept presses in on me, constricting my chest with panic. I shouldn't be so far below. No human should be. No human probably has been. I should be dead. We all should be.

"*Azi,*" Rian's voice is stern in my mind. He takes me by the shoulders, and his amber eyes meet mine. "*Breathe.*"

I gasp, and the magical air surrounding me swirls into my lungs like a cyclone. It stings at first, but comes as such a great relief that I wonder how long I had been holding my breath to begin with.

"*Don't think too much about it,*" he instructs. "*It's maddening if you do. We're here. We're safe. Safe from the sea, at least, as long as my spell goes unbroken.*"

He scowls toward the chasm, and On'na's hand slips from mine as she drifts backward. The terror at what's happening within is plain on her face. Her fearful expression bolsters me. Rian is right. I need to keep my head, to stay strong in the face of danger, just as a Knight is meant to do. I need to protect him and On'na and the others, so we can fight this.

"Mercy," I whisper, and my sword leaps into my hands. Its light beams toward the chasm, sparkling bright white as it dances across the planes of crumbled obsidian, stretching eagerly into the depths, toward the battle. "Stay behind me," I command, and with Flitt tucked safely at my collar, I creep into the narrow crevice.

It's eerie, to say the least, to know a battle is raging ahead and to hear nothing. No clash of weapons rings in my ears, no battle cries warn of the dangers ahead. Occasionally, there is the strange sound of an explosion, but it is so muffled by our air cushions and by the water itself that I can barely hear it.

Behind me, Rian curses and On'na flicks her tail. I'm not sure why until I look up and see the forms of two defeated mermen bobbing motionless above our heads. On'na rushes to one of them and strokes his face. Her wails pierce the silence and ring in my ears. We pause and watch as she draws closer to him, tenderly pressing her lips to his as her webbed fingers sweep across his chest. At first, nothing happens. Then, suddenly, his broad tail jerks. His head snaps forward. Her kiss has brought life back to him. His wounds mend together, his hands ball into fists, and he glares into the depths, toward the battle.

With a quick glance of thanks toward On'na, he bolts away as though his wounds had been nothing but a dream. She does the same for the second one, and for the dozen more we encounter on the way to the battle. Her healing powers impress and encourage me, until we eventually reach the site of the battle and I see what we're up against.

"*It's Orva again,*" Rian pushes. "*Just, under water.*" I nod, tightening my grip on my sword.

Somehow, the coliseum seems to have remained mostly whole on its long journey down the chasm to the sea floor. A number of risen souls swirl like spent magic around the score of brave mermen holding their own against them.

I move to charge into battle, but On'na dives in front of me, blocking my way. Her eyes meet mine and the vision she showed me in the queen's council room flashes between us, this time charged with a sense of urgent warning. As she breaks her gaze, I understand. They can handle the wraiths. I'm here for a more dangerous matter. Eron. He doesn't belong here, and it's up to me, to us, to stop him.

I pause on the fringe of the battle to assess the scene as On'na rushes forward to help her kin. My focus is torn away almost immediately to a jagged hole in the once-dirt floor. Iron, bent and cracked by some unknown force, gapes open like the mouth of a great whale.

I know what it once was without needing to move nearer. The way the darkness clings to the raw edges of rent metal tells me right away. This chasm wasn't the result of a mere act of nature. The sinking of Orva was deliberate, and done for a single purpose: To release the Revenant.

"Rian," I whisper, and the bubble in front of my lips quivers. Past the broken cell, deep within the cover of darkness, something shifts. It's such a subtle movement I almost think it's my imagination, but Flitt's low hiss at my shoulder tells me otherwise.

"*Sorceress*," she pushes. The single word recalls memories, first of the moment I delved into the mind of the assassin who made an attempt on King Tirnon's life. An oath sworn, a spell cast. The second memory is a vision of my time in Eron's mind. His rebirth, with her at his side, orchestrating the entire thing.

"Sybel," I growl. Rian and I exchange a knowing glance.

"*Destroy his maker*," Rian's voice in my mind is a whisper charged with determination. I nod. It doesn't matter how all of this happened, or why. We both know one thing: ending Sybel will destroy Eron once and for all.

"*This way*," he sends, pulling me toward the jagged obsidian rocks that frame the sunken ruins. We cling to the rough stone with ease and propel ourselves upward along the face of the underwater cliff, deeper into the murky shadows until the darkness encloses us like a shroud.

The flashes of battle eventually dim behind us, and Flitt's light does little to push away the insipid gloom of the frigid water. Even Mercy seems dull and weak in this wretched place, and the only small comfort I can find is in Rian's warmth as he bobs beside me. The darkness is so blinding, suffocating, and dense here that it feels like the embodiment of nothing. A void, endless and unforgiving. That same sense of panic creeps in again as I remember how far under we are, and how heavy the water above us must be.

As if to confirm my fears, the last of Mercy's light fails, snuffed out by the impossible weight of the darkness. Flitt drifts to the hilt and perches there. She squeezes her eyes shut and presses her hands to the metal, but the only effect it has is to fade her colorful hair to light pastels.

"*Don't,*" I push to her, and tap my shoulder. Reluctantly, she floats upward and tucks herself deep into my pauldron, but even the warmth of her tiny body is little comfort to me.

"*It's horrible,*" she pushes to me. "*Unthinkable.*"

"*It's pure Dark. Dusk at its essence,*" Shush pushes to all of us. I can feel the hopelessness in his words. He's of no use here under the sea, where there's no wind to command.

"*Maybe we should stop for a moment,*" I push to Rian, and to my surprise, he does.

"*Do you feel anything? See anything?*" he asks, drifting so close to me that our bubbles merge together.

"*No,*" I answer without even attempting to look. What's the point? There's nothing. It's completely empty. I feel myself pulled by the depths, like a current. My fingers slide along the cliff face.

"*This is wrong, Azi,*" Rian pushes. "*We were tricked.*"

I catch a firm grip on the stone and turn to look at Rian, but the darkness is too thick to see him even though I know he's right here.

"*Keep your head,*" he warns, but his voice echoes distant and weak like it's coming from the other end of a long tunnel.

Beside me in the water there's a shift, a spell. It stretches out from Rian, pushing away at the darkness, driving back the shadows.

"*Azi,*" Flitt's voice echoes in my head, and with it comes a sensation of light, warmth, and hope. I cling to that feeling and push it outward, down my arm, into Mercy, which flares to life again now that the shadows are pushed away. The sudden brightness fills me with hope, until I tear my gaze away from Mercy's bright blade into the space beyond.

"Oh no," Flitt's whisper drifts through our bubble into my ear, echoing my thoughts, causing my skin to prickle with chills.

The shadows in front of us shift like the curtains of a stage opening to reveal its players: two figures. Sybel floats in the murky water beside her charge, her dark brown curls drifting around her like extensions of the Mark that swirls over every bit of exposed skin. Beside her, Eron floats with his sword drawn and ready.

I gasp in shock, not because of his presence, but because of his condition. The Revenant seems bigger, somehow. Taller than Eron had been, and broader. It's still him though. His face, pallid and sunken, is unmistakable. His empty eyes narrow as they take me in. The light of my sword seems to drain into them rather than be reflected by them. His presence is terrible, but even more disturbing is the fact that his torso, once a gaping wound delivered by my sword, is healed through. Tendrils of darkness occasionally flick out of the closed-up hole, licking at the creature's armor hungrily even as Eron's gray tongue flicks across his lips.

Beside him, Sybel smirks as she watches me take in my opponent. Her lips move as though she's speaking, but no sound carries to my ears. I can tell it's a taunt, though, by the way the corner of her mouth stretches into a wicked smirk. At her side, his feet dangling without purchase in the depths of the water, Eron takes heaving breaths like a bull preparing to charge.

"*Keep your head,*" Rian pushes to me again, and my grip on Mercy tightens.

Pure light, Uncle had said, can wound the Revenant. I remember that. But he said something else. Killing the creator will end the spell that animates him, once and for all. My target should be Sybel. I don't let on that I know it. I keep my attention locked firmly on Eron.

"*Be ready,*" I push to the others. "*Rian, focus on her. Flitt, stay out of sight.*"

I barely have the command out before Eron charges. He comes straight for me with his sword raised and his teeth bared in a silent battle cry which is made even more ferocious by the shadows that swirl inside his open mouth.

Rian's spell flies over my shoulder, blocking a bolt from Sybel's fingertips. Even through the water the stench of death it emits fills my nostrils, and I gag as I bring my sword up to block a powerful swing from Eron.

Fighting with swords in the depths of the sea is not something I ever trained for. I spend most of the fight ducking away from Eron's blade and parrying his blows as I try my hardest to maneuver myself closer to Sybel. My progress is hindered by the fight; every time our swords meet, I'm propelled backwards through the water. With no ground to plant my feet to, it's impossible to put any power into my own attacks. Rian stays close, mostly blocking any magic the Sorceress sends our way, and sometimes managing to land a spell to break her wards.

I learn quickly that swinging the narrow part of my blade at a certain angle will cause it to slice more easily through the water, but fighting this way is far more exhausting than fighting on land, and it isn't long before my muscles are fatigued from the frigid water and the effort of the fight.

Inside my pauldron, Flitt beams her light at a steady pace, filling me up and warming me, giving me hope and strength, but I know her power is finite. I picture the fae white and withered as Eron drives me back against the wall and smashes my head against the rock with the butt of his sword. My helm does little to protect me from the inhuman force of the blow. My vision closes in on me in tiny points of light. The light grows, replenishing me, pushing the pain away.

From somewhere nearby, Rian unleashes a torrent of bubbles and current that send Eron spinning off into the depths.

"*Flitt*," Shush's voice booms into my head, and I realize it wasn't Rian after all, but Shush who had sent the bubbles. "*You can't.*"

There's no time to react to his warning. Eron is on me again, grinding my shoulders into the stone, cracking my armor. Flitt scrambles back against my neck, whimpering. The bone in my shoulder snaps. A burst of light flashes from the fae, and the pain in my shoulder vanishes. Eron's enraged screams are loud enough to hear, despite the sea between us. He tumbles away in a powerful rush of bubbles. Behind him, Sybel seethes and stretches her claw-like fingers toward us. I steal a glance at Flitt, and her wispy, wasted state makes my stomach flip.

"No!" Flitt cries in protest when a blur as white as she is streaks from Rian to my shoulder. I fling my hand up to protect her, but then I realize what's happening.

"You have to," Shush's whisper brushes my ear as his bubble opens into mine.

"No!" Flitt's repeated cry is cut off as the two vanish.

Her sudden absence is like a punch to my stomach. I steel myself as the darkness seeps closer.

"*It's in your mind, Azi,*" Rian pushes. "*The darkness. Don't let it in. You're stronger than that. Keep fighting.*"

I focus on his voice and push off from the wall with Sybel in my sights. Eron is somewhere further away, carried off by Shush's draining attempt at a gust beneath the sea. This is my only chance.

I know Rian is close behind me. His wards settle over us in layers, bolstering me. His spell propels us through the water, driving me like an arrow toward my target. I lock my arm with Mercy pointed straight at Sybel's chest, and Rian's spells destroy her wards as quickly as she can replenish them.

We're so close. Mercy's tip is just a hand's width from the Sorceress. Her wards are down. This is it. Out of the corner of my eye, I catch a glimpse of Eron. Though he's charging me, I don't change my attack. I imagine my blade driving through Sybel, ending her. Rian propels us forward with his mysterious spell. Mercy's point meets its mark at Sybel's chest. Another ward breaks. Sybel throws her head back, laughing.

I realize my mistake in timing too late. I had thought my strike would have been the killing blow, but I hadn't accounted for more wards, and Eron's progress is much faster than I anticipated. I have no opportunity to dodge his charge. He plows into me from the side, hurtling me away from the Sorceress, shoving Mercy from its target, from Sybel's chest.

A crack so loud I'm sure it'll split my skull pulses over me. Before I know what's happened, Eron is gone. Sybel is gone. I spin in place, grasping for Rian, but find nothing. When I draw a breath to scream his name, I suck in a mouthful of frigid, salty seawater. I try to spit it out, but the weight of the sea presses in on me. A glance at my hand shows me all I need to know. The bubble has disappeared. Rian's spell is broken. He's gone, too.

The dread that strikes me at what that could possibly mean is quickly pushed out by panic. I spin in circles, desperate for some sign that I'm wrong, hoping for some glance of his auburn hair or yellow robes. I fight the urge to scream his name.

The need to breathe overwhelms me and I suck in water instead of air. My lungs burn as they fill up. A flicker of purple fins flashes before me, but too late. I succumb to the dark and silent crush of the unforgiving ocean, and pass out.

Chapter Eight

MERMAID SANCTUARY
Azi

When I finally open my eyes for a blurred peek, everything is dancing. Blue, green, and silver swim in vague forms around me, oddly soothing, until they're washed out with pink and my eyes slip closed once more. Every breath is a painful effort, shallow and slow, even as healing energy cradles my body and fills me up. My thoughts meander slowly, blankly, formless.

Some urgent need nags at the fringe of my mind, but it's too much effort to try and think of what it could be. It feels as though there are holes everywhere. I don't even know how I got here, or where here is. Trying to remember is exhausting, so I set the effort aside and try to focus instead on healing.

Inside and out, I feel saturated, like a barrel that's been filled to the spilling point so that even its wood is soaked to rotting. I remember darkness, cold water, fins.

As the healers move around me silently, charging me through with powerful magic, my body trembles. Despite their efforts, each breath burns like fire. Whoever they are, they're keeping me alive. For that, I'm grateful. I must live. Someone needs me. Someone lost.

My fingers are the first to find themselves again. When I tap them on the surface where I lay, they make tiny splashes in the puddle of water beneath me. Someone takes my hand. Their skin is cold and damp. Another hand presses to my cheek.

Opening my eyes is an impossible effort, but I try again. This time there's more focus, but not enough to really make out anything through the fog of pink light. The forms are people, swaying silently around me. One of them, the one who touches my cheek, leans closer. Her eyes search mine, making a weak connection, and from the exchange I feel a vague sense of apology. My vision is too blurred to see many details, but the flash of gold in her lavender hair is familiar to me.

"On'na," I try to whisper, but my lips are cracked and dry, and my tongue feels over-sized in my mouth.

She answers only with a stroke of a fingertip along my cheek as my eyes drift closed again. I float in the kindness of their healing and allow myself to sleep.

My dreams are slashed with images of a man, a fallen prince, evil and twisted. His body is half-consumed by darkness. As he stalks toward me with his sword raised, he opens his mouth wide. His teeth, once perfectly straight and white, are now decayed and broken. His breath is like death itself. He is my enemy, I know, but I have no recourse. I can't fight, my hands are swallowed by shadows. I can't run, my feet are held to the ankles by the stony earth they stand on. I can't scream, my voice is lost.

In an instant he's upon me, his horrible mouth gaping wider and wider. As he nears, he grows into a dark, wretched, formless nightmare. His mouth, vast and fierce, bears down on me. It will swallow me up, make me part of it. It will force me to become one with Shadow and Dusk.

The reminder of my enemy sparks more memories like a flare in my mind. Memories of allies, especially here.

"*Valenor.*"

I don't say it aloud. I push it out from me the way I push my words to my comrades. To him. My partner. My love. His name comes to me but is yanked away by the wicked mouth gaping to devour me.

It happens immediately. A flash of rainbow scales tinged with gold crashes between me and the nightmare, gnashing its sharp teeth and blasting its breath of pure light at the beast. It guards me with enormous talons, scooping me unharmed from the grip of the earth, and with little effort at all, it drives the beast away until all that remains is peaceful, gentle dawn. The form of my savior shifts from dragon to man.

"They are trying, sweet creatures," Valenor murmurs. "But their limited knowledge of human workings, I'm afraid, may be doing more harm than good." The Muse of Dreaming stands beside me in human form, his cloak of day and night billowing around him urgently.

"Who?" I ask lamely, grateful that at least my voice doesn't fail me anymore.

"The merfolk." He reaches to me and drapes his cloak across my shoulder. Its delicious warmth fills me up, strengthening my spirit. "You see, it seems you drowned, and they were kind enough to restore you as best they could. I do wish they had called upon my brother, though."

"Your brother?" I scowl. My mind is so slow. Was it always this way? I don't think so. If it had been, I'm sure I wouldn't find it so incredibly frustrating.

"Yes, my dear," Valenor strokes my shoulder. "He could indeed help you. I expect they are hesitant to call upon him so soon after all he has done for them recently, but they do not understand how dire the circumstances are. The Dawn cannot lose you."

"What about him?" I ask. I can see his face in my mind, but his name still escapes me. He was it, though. That urgent thing, nagging at me. What happened to him? "My love."

Valenor looks at me curiously. "Rian?" he asks.

"Rian!" I cry, choking back tears. "Yes! Oh, stars, thank you. I forgot his name. How could I have forgotten his name?"

"Oh, my dear girl," Valenor sighs and draws me into a comforting embrace. I'm reminded of someone else when he does. Someone who hasn't held me this way in a very long time. My da. More tears spill down my cheeks. "I do not understand how you could be lured so far away from the Light, so deep into shadow, so easily. Our enemies are clever, Azaeli, and calculating. You must be equally so. You must anticipate their actions. Where is Flitter? Where is your Faedin?"

I try to remember so I can answer him, but my memory fails me yet again.

"As I suspected. They knew how dangerous the sea is for fae. It was no coincidence they'd plot to draw you into its depths. Can you show me what happened?" There's a vague familiarity to the way he searches my eyes, and I know something profound is meant to happen when he does so, but for the life of me, I don't know what.

"Ah," he sighs, doing little to hide the concern in his tone. "There is much to discuss, but this is not the time. Rest, Champion. For now, until I reach my brother, rest, and know that you are safe. I shall guard your dreams until you wake."

He leaves me, I don't know for how long. As he promised, my dreams are peaceful and untroubled. I lay in a field of deep green grass, where golden butterflies chase the sun against a deep blue sky. I watch them for some time, until I feel a gentle pull and hear a deep, familiar voice whisper my name.

"Azaeli," it says, and the meadow fades from beneath me. He calls again, and the golden sunshine shifts to silvery blue-green.

This time when I open my eyes, my vision is much clearer. The room I'm in lies deep beneath the sea, with walls of curved, polished glass. Beyond them, colorful fish swim past in schools. The walls form a seamless dome at the ceiling, and I realize it isn't a room after all, but an enormous air bubble bobbing in the depths of the vast, cold ocean.

"There, now," the same voice soothes. A nearby figure moves closer. His eyes glint with a smile much the same way Valenor's did. His soft white beard grazes my shoulder as he leans over me. "How do you feel?"

It takes me a moment to place the Muse of Water.

I focus on Kaso Viro's question, taking stock of my arms and legs, my head, my body. I wiggle my fingers and test my feet. I take a deep breath and am relieved to find that the burning in my chest has eased almost completely.

"Much better," I reply a little hoarsely. "Stronger. But my thoughts are vague. My head is in a cloud."

"Drink," he says, and raises his hand to offer a conjured mug of hot water. "I know it seems odd to have you drink when you've just drowned, but the saltwater you swallowed is a sort of poison to humans. It is fortunate the merfolk recovered you quickly enough to restore you as they did, but you have a long road of healing ahead, even after their efforts and my own."

When he helps me sit up, I realize we aren't alone. Three women stand to the other side of my bed against the curve of the wall. One of them lowers her hand so her fingertip grazes the glassy surface, and it ripples under her touch. I wonder if they're the same ones who were here the first time I woke. I wonder, too, where On'na went and whether she'll be back.

At Kaso Viro's insistence, I drink a few more mugs, feeling stronger as each one is emptied. My mind, though, is still quite clouded. Kaso Viro doesn't say much. He stands by my side, watching me in silence, alert as if waiting for me to make some sudden move. The others seem to be doing the same thing, expecting me to jump up and run off.

It's a ridiculous thought. Simply sitting up is an exhausting effort right now. Even if I could try to leave, where would I go? Into the sea? Why would I do that?

I huff softly and close my eyes, trying to clear my head and remember. Everything right now is so immediate, but something happened before. Something terrible. A battle into darkness. A fight against some force so powerful and horrendous that I chose to push it out of my memory. A loss—

"Rian!" I gasp and try to leap from the bed, but Kaso Viro catches me and holds me down. The quick movement makes my head pound. My chest burns like that one deep breath tore it to ribbons. I don't care. I try to push the Muse away, but more hands hold me, forcing me down.

"Be still," Kaso Viro says firmly, gripping my shoulders. "The healing you've been given requires it. You must be still, Azaeli. You must rest."

I can't, though. No amount of explanation or logic is enough to calm me.

"Rian," I cry through the burning in my throat. I try to push them off, to get free, but everything hurts. Fighting them takes every bit of my effort. I put my all into it, thrashing, screaming, squirming away from them. It's no use. They're too strong and my body is too broken from its injuries.

If they told me they had him, if they told me he was safe, maybe I could calm myself. But they aren't saying that. No one is reassuring me. No one is explaining that he's off in another bubble somewhere, being tended to like I am here.

"Please," I whisper tearfully, shoving away the hands that hold my shoulders, kicking at those gripping my legs. "Please."

I'm vaguely aware of a splash somewhere in the room, but I don't let it distract me from my attempts to fight free.

"She woke too soon," Kaso Viro utters apologetically.

"So it would seem," says someone else. The same voice. Valenor.

"Take her back," Kaso Viro whispers.

"Mm," Valenor agrees, and once again I find myself in the meadow, the impossible blue sky stretched across me like a blanket. Time passes at its own pace. I watch the clouds drift by. My thoughts are pleasant. Empty.

After a while, I realize I'm not alone. A face in the sky smiles down at me, familiar and kind. I try to remember who she is as I return the smile, taking in her delicate features, her sparkling hair, her enormous, glittering wings. Her gown is spider silk and morning dew; it spills down from the sky like a cascade of clouds. Behind her in the distance, a second sun begins to rise.

"My Champion," she says, and her gentle voice brings tears to my eyes.

"Your Majesty," I whisper. I try to scramble to my feet to show the fairy queen her due respect, but suddenly she's kneeling beside me, her hand on my shoulder, soothing me.

"Be still," she cautions. "You cannot be lost. You have been pulled back from the maw of death. You must remain calm and at peace for the healing to take a firm hold."

A halo of light beams from behind her, so pure and strong that it washes away her wings and her features until she's gone, and all I can see are white, and peace, and love. Time slows. I let the sensation hold me, pushing away that urgent, lingering nagging that stabs at my belly, urging me to get up, to take action.

"Sir Azaeli Hammerfel," another voice echoes from the light, so perfect my breath catches and my skin prickles with chills. "You and I have met only once, yet I know you as though I have always known you," she says. "We were once one. Do you remember?"

As she speaks, something I can't see grazes my forehead, soft as a feather. Memories flood my mind so crisp and clear it seems as though they're happening right now, all over again. I'm one with the fairy queen and the Muse of Light, a centaur, a powerful Knight of Dawn, crashing through Cerion with feathery wings at my back, driving away Vorhadeniel, my enemy: The Muse of Darkness. Her brother.

"Eljarenae," I whisper, and my recognition of her acts like a powerful spell, charging me through with energy and clarity. The light around me beams until I can't even see my hand as I reach for her. It washes me with warmth and strength, filling me up, pushing out any remainder of inky void, salt water, and darkness.

"We are with you," the fairy queen and the Muse of Light whisper together. "The Light is with you, always. Do not falter. We are here."

Eljarenae strokes my hair and presses her lips to my forehead. The act fills me with hope and promise. It's a blessing, I know. A gift of victory. The light fades as slowly as midday turning to sunset, and once more I find myself on my back, gazing into the sky. A breath of sea air tickles my nose. My gaze drifts to my right, where the gentle lapping of glistening teal waves cause the long green grass beside me to sway gently.

"Hello, On'na," I say softly as the mermaid's head and shoulders emerge from the water. She rests on her belly, propped on her elbows, and smiles. Her lavender hair drapes her arms and cascades into the water, where it sways lazily with the motion of the waves. I watch it for some time, soothed by the easy back and forth, until I realize she's staring at me.

The mermaid's eyes sparkle with invitation, and I roll to my side to accept it.

I wish I hadn't. As soon as our gazes lock, I'm bombarded by scenes from the fight against Eron and Sybel and the void. What she shows me is worse than a nightmare. The vision, dark as midnight, jerks me into the battle from her point of view. I watch Flitt and Shush disappear after Eron is hurtled into the depths of the sea by Shush's attack. I see myself charge, with Rian behind me, at Sybel poised at the edge of the Void.

I remember it vividly from my point of view as I watch it from On'na's. How Rian broke the Sybel's wards. How I expected my sword to plunge into her, but didn't account for her one final protection. How I didn't notice Eron charging us from the side until it was too late.

From the outside, I watch in disbelief as Eron crashes into me, thrusting me to the side, leaving Rian open to Sybel's advance. My love's forward momentum in the water is irreversible. Without me between them, he crashes into Sybel, shoving her back, and both are swallowed into the inky cloud. Stolen by the Void.

On'na and I cry out in disbelief at the same time, and I watch myself in her memory as Rian's spell breaks, leaving me at the mercy of the sea. My body convulses and shudders. My sword falls from my grip, sinking into the depths. In the vision, On'na starts to go to me, but hesitates.

Eron is on me. He drives his fist into my chest and readies another blow, but his head snaps toward the void. Something calls him. He sneers, flexing his fingers angrily as he holds me by my chest plate. He looks torn between finishing me and heeding the call of the Void. In the end, it seems impossible for him to resist his orders. He obeys, leaving me floating along the edge of the darkness, lifeless.

Once the revenant is swallowed up by the void, the cloud of black slowly recedes, leaving only the ordinary murky water of the deep ocean floor behind. Only then does On'na emerge from her hiding place to retrieve me. Her lips part with an eerie howl that resonates through the water and forms the bubble where I'm sleeping now.

On'na closes her eyes, breaking the connection between us, and a tear spills down her cheek.

"They took him," I try to whisper, but no sound comes out. My voice is broken. Everything is broken. I made a mistake, a careless one, and now Rian is in the hands of the Dusk. Because of me. What are they doing to him? How will I ever find him? How could this happen?

"Please," I beg her, though I can't seem to form any other words. My mind, once empty, is racing so quickly now I can barely catch a fleeting thought. I have to save him, at any cost. Rian is everything to me. Everything. If I don't have him, I have nothing.

"Please," I repeat desperately, and my surroundings shift abruptly from the soothing cradle of the Dreaming back into my damp, half-broken body lying in On'na's bubble, surrounded by those who would hold me here. Who would keep me from saving him and force me to wait.

Chapter Nine

RUMBLINGS OF THE EARTH
Tib

The page bends to pick up On'na's robe, and her movement breaks the stunned silence in the room like a knife shattering a ward. Margy blinks like she's looked into a light that's too bright. Right away I search for some magic, some spell, but there isn't any. The others around the table shift. Look around. Murmur exclamations of disbelief. Some of them, most of them, I guess, have never really seen those two do that before. Not with their own eyes, even though they knew they could. These are the queen's advisors, after all. They must have known.

At the far end of the table, Bryse shifts his stance. His elbow bumps Saesa's shoulder and she straightens to attention. She tries to hide it, but I know that look. She trains her wet eyes on the table top and forces them to go distant and emotionless.

A twinge of anger jabs my insides. Or pity, maybe, for my friend, left behind by her knight. Margy didn't mention her before, either. When she was talking about the quests. It's assumed, though, that where Azi goes, Saesa goes.

"If I may, Majesty," Lowery's voice seems extra loud when he speaks, and he clears his throat and lowers it. "I must urge you to join the feast and leave this business for tomorrow. Your allies, especially in the light of these events, cannot and should not be neglected."

Margy looks to her mother, who nods in agreement.

"I suppose," says Margy, "there isn't much for us to do until they return." She looks down the table at her champions and her council. "Shall we?" she asks, gesturing to the door.

As it swings open and the others wait for her to leave, I move to step into the shadows. Margy's hand on my arm stops me, though, and she smiles.

"No need for that now, lord Tib," she says warmly. "You don't have to stay in the shadows all the time you're in my presence. In fact, you may sit beside me at the feast. I'm sure you must be hungry."

Some of the council look like they might protest, but Margy doesn't wait for them to. She brushes past all of them out of the council chamber and across the throne room to the great room.

The feast is a good one, with a long table so full of food that there's barely room for plates. With Mya to play for us, it isn't long before the food is forgotten and the guests are all on their feet. The magic of her voice is a spell all its own. I can almost see it as it weaves through everyone here, lifting their spirits. Making them happy. Even Saesa laughs and sings along as Cort twirls her around.

There are things, though. Little things no one else notices. Like how Keyes watches Skalivar once in a while. Cautious, like he can't quite be trusted. Or Gaethon and Anod sitting with their heads tipped together, whispering over the dragon claw in Anod's hand under the table. Or Prince Vorance and Sara slipping out of the room, sneaking away to be alone together. Or how Princess Amei spends the whole feast staring past everyone, out the window toward the ocean. Or the way Prince Poe and Princess Pippa steal longing glances at each other through the mirror when they think no one is watching. Even while he's dancing with Margy. Which he does all day and past sunset, not even giving anyone else a chance. No one else seems to mind. Not even Twig, who spends the entire time darting around the queen's head, silently filling her in on everything she missed while she was in the council chamber.

He's in the middle of recounting a quick disagreement between the elves and Master Keyes when Gaethon gets up from the table and approaches the queen.

"Your Majesty," he says just as Mya's song ends.

"Master Gaethon," Margy nods breathlessly. She steps away from Prince Poe and tucks a loose curl under her crown. She seems a little grateful to be finished dancing. Maybe that's just my wishful thinking.

"After a short conference, Master Anod and I agree it would be wise, sooner rather than later, to activate Kerr Skalivar's generous gift." He holds his hand out, revealing the silvery claw. Again, Margy steps close to it like she wants to touch it, but restrains herself. I can see why. Its power is immense. Intimidating. I guess to a Mage, it would be really appealing.

"Massster Gaethon, Massster Anod, you are mossst wissse," the dragon-man replies. Off to the side, the elves whisper together.

"If I might make a suggestion," Susefen speaks up, stepping toward the group. "Such magic is most potent, in this case especially, at the start of the day."

"At dawn, then," Margy nods.

"Of courssse, it would have to be." Skalivar bows low.

"Wouldn't it be best," Princess Pippa interrupts from inside of the mirror, "to wait until our kingdoms are united? Then, the Guardian would be loyal to Brindelier as well."

"Princccesss," Skalivar bows to the mirror, "I'm sssure you meant no offenccce, but thisss gift is intended sssolely as protection for the kingdom of Cccerion."

"Of course. I only meant—"

"How dare you take such an accusatory tone?" Master Keyes interrupts the princess in a fury, stepping between the mirror and Skalivar. "She is our princess. Show some respect! After all, if it hadn't been for your people, if not for Hywilkin—"

"Enough!" Prince Poe interrupts, throwing his arm across Master Keyes. "That's enough. This is neither the time nor place—"

"How can you accusssse my people, when it was *your* king," he jabs a clawed glove toward Poe, "*their* father'sss own lack of—"

"Please." Margy moves to the center of the group. Twig hovers beside her, his arms crossed.

Their presence seems to bring everyone to their senses. Skalivar is the first to back down. He turns abruptly away, his cloak swirling behind him. I can feel the ring of magic around Margy, pushing out like rose petals. Soft. Strong. Tempering them. Lisabella moves closer, but she doesn't need her pulse. Even without magic, Margy commands enough respect. To the side, the elves watch with quiet reverence. Nobody interferes. No one has to. They all know it. Right now, an alliance with Cerion and the favor of its queen is too important to all of them.

"Your Majesssssty, I humbly beg your pardon," Skalivar whispers sincerely. "I shall bite my tongue and hold my opinionsss."

"Quite so," Keyes grumbles. When Poe nudges him, he bows, too, and murmurs an apology. At the edge of the gathering, the surface of the mirror goes blank. Poe glares at Keyes, shaking his head slightly in disappointment.

"In the morning, Kerr Skalivar," Margy says with a quiet, firm tone, "we shall be grateful to employ your gift at whichever site my Mage Advisors see fit."

"As you wish, Majesssty," Skaliver bows again.

"The hour grows late," the queen mother announces, coming to stand beside Margy. "We are all, I'm sure, exhausted. If it pleases the queen, we invite you to retire to your rooms."

"Yes," Margy nods. "Please. If there's anything you require, our attendants will assist you. Thank you all for your company and friendship. Cerion is grateful to each and every one of you for joining us this day, and for your pledges of allegiance to our humble kingdom."

The allies bow to her one by one before they file out. When the last one is finally gone, Margy sinks wearily into her throne at the head of the table. The queen mother whispers something to her, but she shakes her head and holds up her hand.

"There are bound to be squabbles, Majesty," Master Lowery says. "I thought it went rather well, considering."

"I agree," Mya says, sidling up to lean against Elliot's chair while she talks to Margy. She plays with his hair. He snores. "There is so much history between them all, Majesty. Songs that have since been lost to time."

Behind the group, Master Anod casts silence wards across the room, concentrating them on the mirror and the door.

"I cannot imagine how difficult a task Keyes has before him," Lowery goes on, "having to form new relationships when his kingdom has lost touch with the world for so long. They are certain to require much guidance."

I scoff to myself and move off toward the edge of the room. If Lowery knew more about the Bordas, I'm sure he wouldn't be so sympathetic. While the others talk, I watch through the door.

Skalivar is there. Right outside, lingering. Waiting. A page approaches him, but he waves him off gently. I glance behind me at the others, who stay bent over the table, deep in conversation. Gaethon's eyes are dark with concern. I'm too curious about the Hywilkin ally outside to care about what they're discussing. They're all so involved, they wouldn't miss me. I turn to step into the shadows and nearly crash into Saesa.

"Gah!" I whisper. "How long have you been standing there?"

"About as long as you've been creeping toward the door," she whispers. "What's going on?"

"Skalivar's outside," I reply. "I was going to go have a chat. I'm trying to figure him out."

"Hm," Saesa glances past me at the others gathered around the feast table. "They could be at it for hours. You hide. I'll talk."

Before I can agree or disagree, Saesa slips out of the room. I duck into the shadows, step into the Half-Realm, and squeeze behind her just as the door clicks shut.

"Oh, Kerr Skalivar," she exclaims with surprise, offering a curtsy to the huge man when he turns in her direction. "I thought everyone had already gone to their rooms."

His eyes narrow to slits, and he takes two broad steps to close the space between them. His leathery cloak swings forward, almost closing Saesa in. "The queen, she isss sssstill within?" he asks. Saesa nods. "She isss guarded well?" Again, Saesa nods.

"They'll be talking for some time, I imagine," she explains. "I don't expect you'll be able to get an audience with her tonight, if that's what you're waiting for."

"You are?" he tilts his head to the side, looking her over. I can't help it. I step closer. Grip my dagger hilt. There's nothing threatening about him, though, other than his size. His demeanor is gentle. Kind, even.

"My name is Saesa Coltori. Squire to Sir Azaeli Hammerfel."

"Ah, Champion of Light. Yesss," he nods. "In truth, it was not Her Majesssty I wasss waiting for, but the Lady Knight. She wasss not at the feassst, though. Nor was the Mage, Rian. I hoped to sssspeak to them. To thank them. I was waiting to asssk their guild how I might make a meeting with her."

"Oh, I see," Saesa smiles. "Well, My Lady Knight was called away on an urgent matter, along with Mentor Rian. I could pass them a message if you'd like, when they return."

"What matter?" Skalivar hisses. His armor and eyes flare orange. His cloak-like wings stiffen and spread like a gut reaction. I draw my dagger. Ready it. He catches himself when Saesa takes a step back from him, though. Goes calm.

"Forgive me, Sssquire. It isss in my nature to react quickly. Boldly. You sssee, I have conccccern for the well-being of your kingdom. Your queen." He glances over his shoulder. Watches every shadow.

"Thossse of Brindelier would poissson her againssst usss. All of usss. The All-Sssource must remain firmly in the Plethore's grasssp. It isss my undersssstanding that the Championsss of Light are fassst approaching that end. They mussst not be disssstracted or ssstopped.

They mussst sssuccceed. There mussst be no opportunity for Dusssk to claim the cccity. It mussst go to the Dawn. Only then will the Dusssk be vanquished. Only then will Sssorcery meet itsss final end."

"Y-yes," Saesa leans away slightly as Skalivar's armor sends sparks skittering across the floor. "We're all working toward that goal."

"Not all," he shakes his head, pointing to the door of the great hall. "Sssome wish for a different end. Sssome pray in sssecret that the Championsss of Light will fail. You mussst tell your Lady Knight. Wassste no time. Ssseek the final offeringsss. Do not be lured into plotsss of darknesss. Dissstractions. Rumblingsss of earth."

"I'll…I'll tell her, sir. Th-thank you," Saesa stutters, doing little to hide her shock. I don't have to wonder why. What Skalivar is saying, rumblings of earth. That's exactly what happened. That's exactly why Azi and Rian are gone now. Plots of darkness. Distractions.

"Take thisss," he says, pressing something into her palm. It pulses with magic. Friendship. Companionship. Trust. "When your lady knight returnsss, use it to sssummon me. I shall go to my chambersss now. I do not wish to inssspire dissstrussst."

Saesa nods her agreement, and Skalivar strides off toward the guest wing. Once he's out of site, Saesa turns in place, searching for me.

"Tib?" she whispers, still holding her closed hand out in front of her.

"Yeah," I reply, stepping out of the shadows. Saesa moves closer, nearly bumping me with her closed fist. The object in her hand, oddly, makes my boots tingle.

"What is it?" she asks, opening her hand to reveal a sleek orange opal the size of a peach stone. It reminds me of things I've seen. Azi's diamond. Margy's bracelet.

"It's…I think it's a tether," I murmur.

Saesa's eyes widen. "But, why? That's not something you just…give away to someone. Just like that."

"Unless it was someone you really wanted to make an impression on. Really wanted them to know you trust them."

Together we gaze after Skalivar, even though he's long gone now.

"How could he know about that? Rumblings of the earth? It's exactly what hap—"

"Tib! Saesa!" Margy gasps as we jump away from the path of the great room door. "There you are. I thought you might have gone home."

"Oh, no, Majesty. We were just talking," Saesa bobs a curtsy.

"Well," Margy says with a deep yawn and a stretch. "The day has gotten far too long for me. It's time we all went to our rest." She turns her face toward me and gives me a tiny wink.

"Indeed, Majesty," Lowery agrees. "And tomorrow promises to be just as long. Good night." He bows to those gathered, and everyone else says their good-nights and farewells.

"No break for you, Saesa," Bryse winks at her as he and the rest of the Champions file past. "Midmorning tomorrow, guild hall."

"Yes, sir. Thank you," Saesa shoves her fist into her pocket and steps aside as Cort playfully punches her shoulder.

"It happened so fast," I say to her later, about Azi leaving her behind, as we walk home together. "I'm sure she would have brought you if she'd had another second to think about it."

Saesa shrugs. "You're probably right," she says, clearing her throat. "Anyway, Bryse is showing me the shield tomorrow."

"That's good," I mutter. Not sure what else to say. The more I think about what Skalivar said, the more my stomach twists to knots. What if it was a plot? Shouldn't we have heard something from them by now? How long does it take to investigate an undead prince? What if something went wrong?

My mind races over those questions all the way up the stoop and into the house. Saesa's silent, too. I bet she's wondering the same things. When she stops abruptly inside the doorway, I think that must be why, until Nessa's yelp breaks me out of my daze.

"Praise the stars, you're back!" She swoops in on us, gathering us into her arms. I blink over her shoulders to see a crate, a packing crate, right in the middle of the foyer. The lid stands open, with stuffed sacks spilling out. "I was so worried I wasn't going to be able to leave you word," Nessa whispers.

"What's happening?" Saesa asks, staring at the crate.

"It arrived this morning," Nessa explains, pulling us with her into the sitting room. With a shaking hand, she reaches for a note on the desk. Its cracked seal bears the Ganvent crest. Saesa smooths it out and reads it in a whisper.

"Perhaps it's time we settled down. I grow weary of the sea life. -Tristan."

Nessa chokes back a sob and squeezes both of our shoulders. "Go and pack your things. Only the important things. The carriage will be here shortly. If you must stay, I understand, but I can't leave word of our new address."

"What?" Saesa steps back and looks at Nessa in disbelief. "You're leaving?"

"But," I whisper, not able to finish. I can't fathom it. The Ganvent manse, empty. Cerion without Nessa.

Nessa takes the letter in her shaking hand and sinks to the carpet. "This," she whispers so low that Saesa and I have to touch our foreheads to hers to hear. "It's Tristan's warning phrase. I never thought I'd see it. I prayed I never would. It means…" she chokes on her tears and buries her face in her fists, sobbing.

"I remember," Saesa whispers in disbelief. "It means something's happened to the Admiral, and we aren't safe here now. It's his code. Nessa told us all when we first came here. She said if he ever sent these words, we were to leave the manse immediately and not come back."

"Why are you still here, then?" I hiss, lifting Nessa to her feet by her elbows. "Where's everyone else?"

"I sent them on while Raefe and I saw to that last crate," Nessa sniffles. "I couldn't bear to leave until I could see at least one of you. Please, we have to go. There's no way to know what will happen, or when."

She gazes up at the ceiling, as though the danger the Admiral warned about could be hovering overhead as we speak.

"Nessa, I have the last of Lil's spell books. I think we'd better close it up," Raefe calls from the foyer.

"Raefe!" Saesa cries, and rushes out to greet him.

"Oh, Tristan!" Nessa sobs. I pull her to me. Pat her back. My pulse pounds in my ears. The Admiral. It can't be. My thoughts race to the conversation in the council chamber. Elespen. How it's gone so quiet. How there's been no word from anyone sent there.

"It's not true," I whisper to her. "The Admiral. He's got to be safe. He's got to be."

Nessa doesn't answer, except to burrow her face deeper into my shoulder.

"I'll figure it out," I vow. "I'll find him. I'll bring him back."

A soft, sweet purring fills the silence between Nessa's sobs, and Zeze appears out of nowhere, weaving between my ankles.

"Zeze, no! Go home!" I growl, nudging her away with my toe. "I mean it. Not tonight. Get out of here. It's not safe!"

Zeze yowls with obvious annoyance, raises her paw, and slashes the back of my knee with razor-sharp claws. When I scream in pain, Saesa runs into the room to investigate.

"Get them out of here," I shout, and push Nessa gently toward her. I chase after Zeze, who takes off in a blur up the stairs toward my room.

"Zeze!" I shout as I skid to a stop in my bedroom, where I find Margy sitting cross-legged on my bed in her sleeping gown. "Are you out of your mind?" I yell, slamming the door shut behind me.

"Tib," Margy laughs, "when are you going to realize that no amount of lecturing is going to keep me from—"

A low rumble from deep inside the ground interrupts her. The floorboards of my bedroom shudder and creak strangely. A dagger rattles along the surface of my nightstand and clatters to the floor.

Margy grips the coverlet, peering up at the ceiling as another rumble causes a small crack to splinter the plaster overhead.

"What is that?" she whispers, wide-eyed.

"Rumblings of the earth," I mutter, diving to shield her as chunks of plaster rain down with another quake.

The door flings open at the same time Twig appears at Margy's wrist.

"Tib!" Saesa shouts.

"Margy!" Twig cries.

"Your Majesty?" Saesa gasps and goes to curtsy, but the shaking floor makes her stumble forward right into Margy's lap. "What are you doing here? You have to get out!"

The floor shakes again and Margy reaches for me. "Get us all out, Twig. Hurry!"

"Nessa and Raefe are downstairs!" I shout over the now thundering quake.

"I saw them out," Saesa coughs as another crumble of ceiling crashes down on us. "They're safe."

"Go then, Twig! Hurry up!" I yell.

"Everyone hold tight!" Twig squeaks. Margy's arms close around me. Saesa grips my hands. Twig dives into the group of us, and together we lurch forward through the Half-Realm, narrowly escaping the ceiling of the Ganvent manse as it collapses onto my bed.

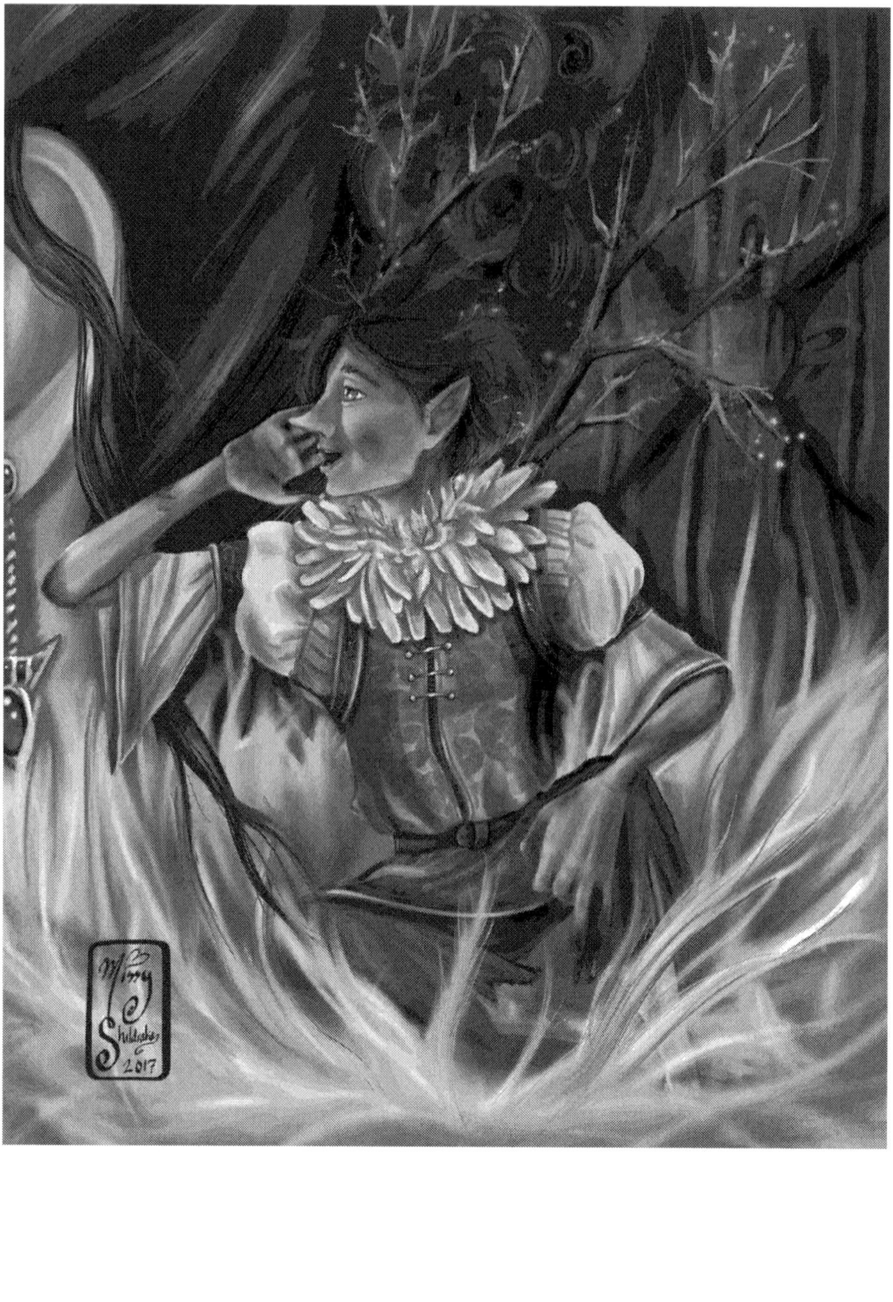

Chapter Ten

OPAL AND ORBS
Tib

Flowers. Singing. Perfume. Magic. So much magic, everywhere. Everything around me is coated with it. Made from it. Enhanced by it.

The branches of the dome over us breathe with it. It's so thick, so rich, the hairs on my arms stand straight up. Moonlight seeps from outside, dances across my knees and my hands on the mossy floor.

Saesa appears beside me. Her green eyes lock on mine, alarmed, and then flick to her pocket. Inside, the stone Skalivar gave her buzzes softly with magic of its own. Different magic. Hywilkin magic.

"Twig," Margy whispers from somewhere behind me. "Why are we here?"

"It's safe here," Twig replies, darting to the wall of the dome. The vines untangle and open to the night sky, and he floats out to peer around. "We can be sure of that."

"If it isn't safe in Cerion, I need to be with my people. I can't be here," Margy argues. She jumps up from the cot and runs to Twig's side, peering out with him. "What's happening?"

"I'm not sure," Twig whispers. "It's quiet here."

"Rumblings of the earth," Saesa says, but neither of them reply to her. They're already locked in silent conversation together.

"*Muse of Earth?*" Margy pushes to Twig. He nods.

"*They know. They know how close you are. How close the Dawn is, to victory. The attacks will come quicker now. Stronger.*"

"*How can we stop them?*" Margy asks. "*How do I protect my kingdom?*"

Twig pops to human size and hugs her.

"*I can only think of one way,*" he explains.

"*Claim Brindelier,*" Margy shakes her head slowly.

"*Persevere,*" Twig pushes back with a nod. "*And fast.*"

Beside me, Saesa growls in frustration. She gets up, turns on her heel, and shoves her way out of the vines at the back of Twig's dome.

The other two don't notice. They're too caught up in their silent conversation.

"Saesa," I whisper, following her out.

"Huh," she scowls at me as the vines close behind us. "I guess I'm not invisible after all."

"What are you talking about?" I bat at an annoyingly close trumpet flower as it sniffs at me, and duck away when it doesn't let up.

"Forget it. It's not important," she says, crossing her arms and rolling her eyes. Another flower is fixated on her pocket. The one with the opal. A few of the trumpet's vine-mates gather with it to investigate. Saesa doesn't react to them. Instead, she glares at the dome. "You could hear them, right? Talking in their heads, like Azi does with Rian and Flitt?"

"Yeah," I shrug.

"Don't shrug like that, Tib. You act like it's no big deal. Everyone does. Maybe to you it isn't. But to people who are left wondering, it's..." she rolls her eyes again. Huffs. "Just, never mind. I'm letting things get to me when they shouldn't. It's not about me. It shouldn't be about me. So, what's happening? What's the plan?"

"Saesa, nobody's trying to—" I start, but she puts her hand up to stop me.

"I said forget it," she scowls. "All of this, it's bigger than I am. I have to remember that. Remember my place."

"Your place? What's that supposed to mean? You're just as important as—"

"Don't."

For a while we stand, just staring at each other. She doesn't say anything, and I don't know what I can really say. She's hurt. Mad at everything. Even me, and I don't know why. I know Kythshire can make people irrational. It's the magic here. That's probably it. Once we leave, she'll be fine. Back to herself.

After a while, she turns away. Looks up at the stars. Hugs herself. The vines curl out, following her pocket. "Azi's out there," she says. "Something's happened. Something's wrong."

"Something, like what?" I ask.

"I don't know. I can just feel it. Like a warning. Like what Skalivar said. Distractions." She reaches into her pocket and pulls out the opal. It doesn't do much. Just sits there in her palm, glowing. Tether magic is strange. Constant. Like a beacon, but so quiet. "She would have been back by now if it was nothing."

"Aha!" A flare of red-orange flames bursts into the space between us, hovering over Saesa's hand. White-hot sparks rain down over the opal, and the fae creating them flashes to our size. "What do you mean, bringing outsider magic here?" She screeches, stalking closer to Saesa. Her red dress swirls around her like fire. Her charcoal skin crackles with heat.

"Back off," I warn, stepping between the two of them as Saesa holds the opal to her chest. The trumpet flowers rustle and whine.

"All right, all right," Twig chuckles from inside the dome. "I'm coming."

The vines part and a flurry of orbs darts through them, swirling around the three of us. They glow in pulses of every color. Orbs from the trees and the sky and the brush.

"Ah, Ember. What brings you out this far?" Twig asks. If he's annoyed, he's hiding it well. Behind him, Margy peers with awe at the orbs and the fire fae.

It's a lot of magic all in one place, but I can see through it. Fairies. Tiny ones, all fragile and naked and curious. They're not like Twig or Flitt or Shush. These are less real than they are, but more real in other ways. It's hard to grasp. Hard to understand. They hold so much power. So much knowledge. And they're all connected, their minds, their hearts. Like they're one, but different.

Some of them float to Saesa's arm, sliding around her hand, investigating the opal. Others dart around Ember, who stands with her hands on her hips and a smoldering look of annoyance on her face.

"That." Ember jabs her finger at the opal. "Exactly that. As you know, my kind is charged with keeping our borders safe. Keeping such things out."

"Yes, I know," Twig mutters.

"Don't you take that annoyed tone with me. Show some respect." Ember huffs and tosses her head. Sparks tumble to the grass at her feet.

The orbs cling to Saesa's hand until it's so covered that half her arm is hidden. Saesa doesn't seem to mind them, though. Actually, she seems tickled by their attention. Their multi-colored lights twinkle in her eyes and flash brightly across her red hair.

"Hywilkin," an orb whispers, and word echoes through the rest of them.

"Just as I said. Outsider magic," Ember sneers.

"It's starting," they all sing together.

"Age of Kinship."

"Friendship."

"Dawn."

"How has she done this?"

"Is it not too soon?"

"It's forbidden," Ember growls. She lunges to snatch the opal from Saesa's hand, but Twig and I jump to block her. "It isn't welcome here!" she screeches.

"Don't be such a wildfire, Ember," Twig says gently. He cups his hand around Saesa's, gently brushing the orbs away. He starts to touch it, but holds back. "It's Dawn magic, you can see that plain as day. Where did you get it, Saesa?"

"It's..." Saesa looks to me, and back to Twig. "Skalivar gave it to me. Tib says it's a tether."

"A tether?" Twig steps closer and pokes it with his fingertip. "Well, so it is. But, how? It shouldn't have been able to cross into Kythshire. It's from Hywilkin."

"Maybe since the Hywilkin offering is claimed by the Dawn now?" I suggest, but Twig shakes his head.

"It hasn't been given to the All Source yet, though. This is curious. Very curious."

"Dangerous," Ember says, darting upward in a flash of flame. "I'm telling the Ring."

"They're asleep," Twig calls up to her in a sing-song voice.

"This is worth waking them," Ember spits sparks and vanishes.

"Good luck with that," Twig chuckles. Some of the orbs dance around his head. Rest in his hair.

"Should we go, too?" Margy asks.

"They won't wake up for Ember," Twig shakes his head. "She's too much of an alarmist. Always in a spark about something."

"I didn't mean to cause trouble," Saesa says quietly, tucking the opal away.

"You didn't. If it wasn't supposed to be here, it couldn't have come in." Twig smiles and pats her shoulder. "Don't worry."

"Anyway, it won't be here long," Margy steps closer. Looks from Saesa to me.

"Are we going back to Cerion?" Saesa asks.

"We can't," Margy's brow knits together with concern.

"Not yet," Twig explains. "See, my tether is here." He points to Margy's bracelet. "I wasn't thinking ahead about getting back. I was just trying to get us all out safely."

"So, what then? What if someone discovers the queen's missing?" I ask, throwing Margy an I-told-you-so glare.

"They won't. Twig did some enchantments before I left the room…" Margy's voice trails off. She looks away from me. She knows the mistake she made. Good. I hope it's the last time she goes sneaking around at night.

"We'll handle all of that," Twig says. "Don't worry. At Dawn, we'll appeal to Crocus for a special case, and Margy will be back home before anyone is the wiser."

"Unless the earthquakes reached the palace, too," I argue.

"They didn't," Twig explains. "My trees in the forest park would have let me know."

"Great," I mutter. I wonder if Cerion knows the fae have literally planted spies right outside the palace.

"In the meantime," Margy turns to me, "Twig and I were discussing it. You said you have a way of claiming Elespen's offering quickly, right?"

"I think so, once I get there," I reply.

"I was going to send you with the others and make a quest of it, but I'm not sure that's the best thing to do now," Margy whispers, moving closer. She takes my hands in hers, looking grave. "I think it would be better to keep it quiet, instead. I don't want the risk the Dusk knowing our moves, and if I declare a quest, word is bound to reach them. Do you think you'd be able to do it on your own? Could you be safe?"

Beside me, Saesa presses her lips together. Her nostrils flare out. I can tell she's annoyed. Margy notices it, too.

"Saesa, I'm not confident you'd be safe if you went, too. Tib has ways of going unnoticed."

"I know that," Saesa says a little shortly, then catches herself. "Sorry, Your Majesty," she says more softly. "I know what Tib can do."

"I want her to come," I say it without thinking. I'm not sure why. I guess because I don't want Saesa to feel bad anymore. I want her to feel needed. She and Margy both look surprised. "I do. Saesa helps me keep my head. It would be better to have her there."

The look Saesa gives me is worth it. This time, the tears in her eyes are happy ones. That makes me grin. Until her face falls.

"But, what about Azi?" she whispers.

"Our next step is to go see Flitt," Twig explains. "She's here. I can tell. Weak, but here. Don't worry about Azi. We can sort that out. If Tib needs you, you should go with him."

He flicks his wrist and hands Saesa a tiny green bud. "Take this. It'll bring you both back here, just once. Keep it safe, and only use it if you really need it, all right?"

Saesa nods, grinning. "Thanks."

"Tib…" Margy's hand on my arm sends a tingle of warmth all the way to my shoulder. "If it's too dangerous, if it takes longer than a few days, come home. Promise."

Her eyes, deep and sparkling, meet mine. When they do, I can't think. What she said to me is lost. It's not magic. It's just Margy. I have to close my eyes and look away to focus.

"Promise." I agree, once I can get my thoughts together. "It shouldn't be a problem, though."

"How will we get there?" Saesa asks. Above her, the stars in the sky seem to shine brighter, fighting for my attention. Glittering against the black like jewels, they remind me of the last time I was in Kythshire. On the seashore, with Ki. The memory makes me smile, and the idea it gives me charges me with excitement.

"He knows a way," Margy says proudly. She steps closer to me. Kisses my cheek. My whole body tingles. "Be safe," she whispers in my ear.

I reach for Saesa. Grip her elbows. Look into her eyes. Green. Jungle green. Ships and rivers. Burning towers.

"We're going to go to the coast and call for Kaso Viro. Ready?" I ask.

"Ready," she nods, grinning. Echoing that same excitement. That promise of adventure. I close my eyes. Think of the shore at the border of Kythshire. The sea. Our feet leave the grass and land in soft sand. A beacon of light beams across us. The ground beneath rumbles and shudders. Saesa clings to me to keep from falling.

"Another earthquake?" she shouts over the rumbling.

"Nah, it's only—"

"We are Aren," a pair of deep voices interrupt me. Salty wind rushes from the mouths of the two giant heads emerging from the sand in front of us. Each face holds a single eye in the center of its brow. "The Golden Coast embodied—"

"Hi Aren, it's just me," I call up to them. The heads tower over us, their light beaming across us, pondering. "Tib. And Saesa. You met her before, through Oren. Go ahead and ask."

Saesa presses closer as the white eyes flash in unison.

"Yes, it is so. Squire to Azaeli Hammerfel, The Temperate, Pure of Heart, Reviver of Iren, The Great Protector—"

"Yeah. That's the one," I call over my shoulder, already halfway to the water with Saesa in tow. They keep on going with Azi's titles while Saesa gazes behind her, looking both awed and a little guilty as I pull her by the hand into the waves.

"Kaso Viro!" I shout as soon as my feet are wet. A water spout swirls up from the surf, sweeping us up, and I grab Saesa to hold on to her.

"Good evening, Tib." The voice that greets us isn't Kaso's, but Loren's. The apprentice's figure, a blur of yellow and brown, swirls inside the wall of the rushing cyclone. "My master is indisposed, I'm afraid. I can deliver a message to him, if you'd like."

"Indisposed?" I scowl. "Doing what?"

"I couldn't say," Loren replies.

"Couldn't, or won't?" I ask, annoyed.

"Couldn't. You know the way of things." Loren's blur shrugs. "Is there something I can help with?"

Secrets. Kaso's sworn Loren to secrecy about something, but what? Why? I glance at Saesa, who's gazing at the swirling water around us with a mix of fear and wonder. I put the questions out of my head. Focus on the quest. The offering.

"Not unless you can get us to Elespen," I answer.

"Actually, I just completed my studies in inter-aquatic movement and mass-portation. It's a complicated series of elemental shifts, made even more difficult by the fluid nature of water, and my method is rudimentary compared to my master's, but—"

"Is that a yes?" I interrupt.

"Yes," Loren splashes.

"Great, we'd really appreciate it, then. Whenever you're ready."

"What part of Elespen?" Loren asks.

I think back to my journey along the Jairun river on Cap's ship, when I fled from Sunteri to Cerion. "Cresten," I say. "The capital."

"Very well. Please hold on to each other. And you should probably close your eyes. I'll try not to get you wet, but the spinning is unavoidable."

Saesa moves closer to me. Puts her arms around my shoulders. Stares into my eyes. I hold her around the waist.

"Ready?" Loren asks.

"Ready," we reply together.

The cyclone picks up speed. Lurches forward. The sound of rushing water drowns out everything else. When we start spinning, Saesa's the first to close her eyes. She tucks her head against my shoulder. Holds me tighter. So close I can feel her heart racing.

We speed off across the surface of the sea, and my thoughts rush to Elespen and its Wellspring. I think of the task ahead. Think of Margy's reaction when I finally place the fifth offering in her hand. Her victory. Her eyes. Her smile.

Chapter Eleven

CAVIENA
Celli

It's odd to feel two opposite emotions at once, but here in this strange place, I'm both confused and excited. The festival below is in full swing. The streets are crowded with merchants, entertainers, and all sorts of people. So many people. A twinge from deep inside me makes my heart race. They're so packed in, well dressed, and wealthy. It could be a good day of pilfering. I could make a small fortune.

From my high window, I can see deep into the center of the main marketplace. There, the crowd thickens around a stage where someone is performing. I can't quite make out what's happening, but it looks like it's a dancer. The spires of the castle catch my eye again. I spend a good portion of the afternoon staring at it from top to bottom, but it's no use. Whatever I'm looking for is hidden deep inside. Whoever I must see wouldn't be standing in plain view of a window or balcony.

Reluctantly, I tear my eyes from the scene and turn to the door. The skirts of my gown swish around me, surprising me. Something is odd about wearing a gown. I don't know why, but it's unexpected. I smooth the fine green satin with my hands and shake out the thick petticoat.

My hands. I stare at them, trying to place why they seem so strange. Something is missing. I graze each wrist with my fingertips, looking at the bare skin curiously. Something is gone. Lost, but I'm not sure what. I find pockets in my skirt and reach into them, pulling out an elegant lady's dagger, a jeweled purse filled with gold, and a pearl-encrusted mirror which opens and closes with a satisfying click.

I look at each item for a long time, trying to connect with them somehow, but the only thing I have any stirring about is the dagger. When I hold it, I think of blood and snow. Unsheathing it fills me with a strong sense of betrayal and violence. It scares me, so I tuck it back into my pocket and try to forget I have it.

I look to the door curiously, trying to remember where I am. An inn? A home? I'm not sure. What will I find when I open the door? A part of me wants to stay here, where things are becoming familiar, but something compels me to leave. The strong desire feels like a lingering order. Go to the palace. Find her. See her.

I open the door and peer out. In the hallway, a man has a woman pressed against the wall. They're kissing. She's got a quiver and bow, and long black hair. He's more of a brute type, with a thick short sword at his hip. I size up their gear. They're smart. Their purses are well hidden. So are the variety of daggers and knives on each of them. They've been out. Some of her arrows have a strange sort of white glow on them, and his sword hilt is splashed with a few drops of blood.

It makes me think again about snow and betrayal as I walk past the two of them, puzzling over why I know to look for things like purses and hidden weapons.

"Stairs are the other way," the black-haired woman calls after me.

I nod my thanks and turn around while they get back to kissing.

"You going to tell me your secret? That was incredible," the man murmurs.

"Just a little trick my brother taught me," the woman replies. A key clicks in the lock. They open the door, duck inside, and close it behind them.

Her arrows stay on my mind while I go down the stairs. How they glowed was notable, I'm not sure why. My interest fades as the aromas of supper strike me full-on. I pay for a plate and eat, all the while thinking about the palace.

"Shall we try our luck at the soiree?" A woman at the table beside me asks. "It would be a thrill to get to see the princess."

"Sure, sure. It couldn't hurt to at least get in line. Perhaps we'll make the list."

The princess. The sun is already setting when I leave the noisy tavern, and the streets are just as crowded as they had been when I woke up, which apparently was mid-afternoon. I find it a little strange that I was so sound asleep in the middle of the day, and fully dressed, too. Thinking about it brings up those same feelings of betrayal, that memory of snow and darkness. I ignore them and make my way along the short route to the palace, thinking about the conversation back at the tavern. If I could get in, I could look at her.

At the outer gate, a man holding a scroll and quill stands at the head of a long line of richly dressed people. He calls to them to make order and straighten the line, but there isn't any need for that. They're all quiet and polite as they wait. The couple in front of me is dressed alike, in maroon silk draped with chains of gold. They're so involved with each other they don't notice me exploring his pockets. I come away with the reward of a small purse of gems and a sense of mild disappointment. Too easy.

Something darts around my head and I stash the purse behind my back. When my hand flies up to swat it away, a high-pitched voice yelps in protest.

"Hey, watch it! What do you think, just randomly waving your arms around like that? You should be more careful!" The fae scolding me gets close to my nose and wiggles a finger at my eye. "That isn't how you get on the list!"

She's cute. Dainty and bright, with pale pink skin and shining yellow eyes. She's dressed in what looks like a uniform, with a light blue tunic and dark blue pants.

I duck my head in apology and reveal the stolen purse, emptying the jewels into my hand. The fae looks from it to me, and squeals happily.

"Oh, is that a gift for me? How kind of you! I'll have you added to the list for sure!" She swoops down, waves a hand at the jewels, and they disappear, replaced by a silver token. "The princess will be excited to meet you. You look very much like her. Did you know that? Come back at dusk, and show your token. See you then!"

Dusk. The word sends chills through me. Excites me. Something about it empowers me. Makes me feel part of something bigger.

I lose the time between. I'm not sure how. It doesn't matter. At dusk, I'm where I should be in the courtyard of the palace. My gown is blue, now. Royal blue. It glitters with jewels and silver-white threads. This one has no pockets, except a tiny one at my bodice which holds the silver token.

It's like a dream, how they show me in with the others bearing tokens of their own. How my heart beats so fast I feel I might take off flying. We stand in a foyer, waiting. They cast spells and search us, then we're guided through the palace, up a spiral stairway, into a small dining room. I'm seated at a table with a few others. They try to talk to me, but I don't speak. I can't be bothered with them. I only stare at the door, knowing at any moment she'll walk through.

When she does, the room stands. They bow and curtsy, so I do, too. I look at her, unable to tear my eyes away. Unable to blink. I watch her receive each of her guests with grace and kindness. Listen to her speak to them and accept their gifts of song and their tales. She invites us to dine with her, and we do. When it's finally my turn to meet her, we stand face to face.

I have nothing to say, but I don't need to speak. She looks at me curiously as I stare at her hair, her nose, her lips, her chin.

"How curious," she says with a soft laugh. "I feel I might be looking into a mirror! You and I could be each other's reflection! Isn't it droll?" she asks, turning to the other guests. I don't see their reaction. I see only her. Her profile, her eyelashes, the paleness of her cheek. The way her earlobe pulls under the weight of the earring decorating it. How her gold-white hair makes a perfect frame for her pretty face.

"What is your name?" she asks, turning her attention back to me.

My mouth opens, but my mind goes blank. I can't think of any name at all, let alone my own. I can only think of looking at her, gazing into the pools of her eyes, following the line of her shoulder.

"Won't you answer me?" She tilts her head to the side. Her short-cropped hair slides over the gold collar of her gown. Slowly, I shake my head. "Can't you speak?"

"She hasn't said a word to us, Your Highness, the whole time she's been sitting here," a man from my table says, standing respectfully.

"Not even when we tried to get her to," says his wife. They're the couple from the line. The ones with the jewels.

"Have you lost your voice?" the princess asks. I nod. "How dreadful," she whispers. "When did it happen? Was it recent?"

I nod again.

"Were you ill?"

I shake my head, no. I don't think I've been ill. I watch the soft dip of her collarbone as she speaks. How it rises and falls. How the shadow of her chin spills across her milky throat.

"Oh!" she gasps, startling me. "It was the sleep, wasn't it? Could you speak before? Before we all slept?"

Everyone else gasps at the thought of it. I don't deny it. I honestly don't know.

"If that's so, then oh!" she presses a dainty hand to her brow. I watch her eyes fill with tears. "We must seek a healer for you. Certainly, someone could reverse this terrible ailment?" She looks over her shoulder to a man standing by the door. He's the one from earlier. The one with the scroll.

"Princess, I know what you're thinking, but you are not responsible for—"

"Nonsense," the princess waves her hand at him and steps closer to me. She rests a hand on my shoulder. "We'll see what can be done. In the meantime, I'd be very amused if you'd help me."

Her eyes dance with a hint of mischief. She leans closer to whisper in my ear. I watch the candlelight flicker in the white-blond streaks of her hair. "I should like to play a trick on my brother. What do you say?"

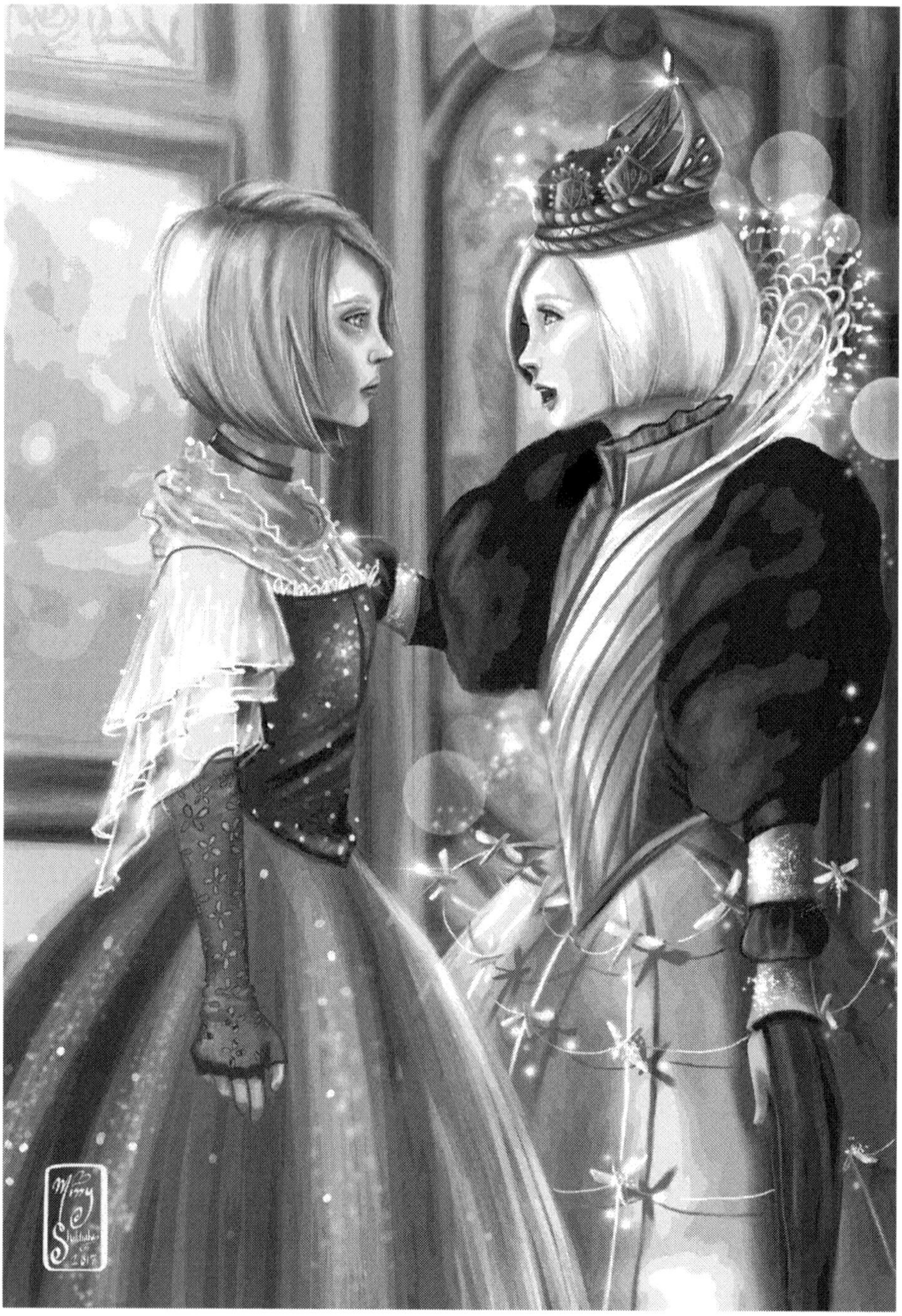

Chapter Twelve

SEE WHAT I SEE
Azi

I drift in and out of consciousness, vaguely aware of a conversation between two voices which match each other in tone. Valenor and Kaso Viro, together in one place. The thought of it is strange and dream-like, but I imagine that's because of who's talking.

"It is as it was, Brother. Though our sister is free, she has been battered, mind and body. It is her shame which keeps her hidden from us now."

"Her shame? Or her pride, Valenor?"

"Indeed. Either way, it would be pointless to chase after Stellastera now."

"It is impossible to know what abuses she suffered at the hands of Sha'Renell."

"Hands, and tongue. I cannot imagine being pent up with that woman for as long as she was. Still, I fear it unwise to leave her alone in such a time. She could easily be swayed. In the interest of neutrality, we cannot ignore her absence."

"In the interest of neutrality..."

It's obvious they think I'm still asleep. They don't know I can hear. I lie still, even though I know I should move or signal somehow that I'm listening. I remember Aster's call at the council meeting, from Rian's wand: *I am lost.*

"Perhaps it is for the best. If she hides, it might mean she is wary of meddling on either side."

"Quite so. And that makes her much wiser than any of the rest of us at this point."

"They make it so appealing..." One of them rests a hand on the side of my head. It's warm, gentle, and loving. Almost fatherly. Valenor. "Why must they be so confoundedly endearing?"

"That may be, but men cannot be blamed for our missteps. We know their ways. We always have."

"Balance is key."

"If that is so, then why this constant push to victory? There is no balance in victory, Kaso. We both know this."

"There is, when one side makes relentless efforts to overcome the other, and must be snuffed and put in its place. It is the downfall of mortal societies, Brother. The memory of Man only reaches so far. Peace, sadly, is unsustainable in the long term."

"You say that, but have you forgotten our own family? Our history stretches further than any other, and still we have Vorhadeniel, who insists upon tipping that balance every chance he gets, and now he has Sha'Renell under his thumb, and we both know how stubborn she can be."

"The push between light and dark will never cease."

"And always, it seems the dark is the one doing the pushing."

"There is more to it than a simple thirst for power. Corruption…"

The more philosophical they become, the further I drift from their conversation and the more I grow aware of the strength of my body as I lie here. My chest is clear. I test it with slow, deep breaths and my lungs fill with warm, salty air. My body is no longer broken. I feel the charge in the muscles of my arms, legs and stomach. My fingers flex and close, and to my surprise I find the grip of Mercy in my right hand. The presence of my sword brings me even more strength.

My mind, too, seems healed. I remember everything: the battle, my injuries, how they kept me safe, so I could heal, how hard I fought to leave, the Void swallowing Rian. I still want to jump up and charge to his rescue. My heart aches at the thought of him in the hands of darkness, at the mercy of Sorcerers. I'm more rational now, though, than I was when I was healing. I'm calm. Centered. Instead of jumping to action, I continue to lie still, working out the puzzle. Why, this time, with my own heart, my reason for living captured and surely suffering, am I so calm?

A moment in the Dreaming comes to me. Eljarenae, Muse of Light, hovering close, kissing my forehead. I remember the flare of light as she did so, and the peace it brought me. Without thinking, I raise my hand and press my fingertips to the spot.

"Ah, she wakes," Valenor sighs with relief.

Trust. That's what it is. As Valenor and Kaso Viro help me to my feet and I look around the strange observatory that's exactly as Rian had described it to me some time ago, I know. I trust Rian. I know his mind and its strength. I have faith in him. If anyone can endure the darkness, the wickedness of Sorcerers, he can. The notion keeps me calm and centered, until something catches my eye as it flutters from my mattress to the floor.

A blue hawk feather.

"Shush's tether," I whisper, crouching to retrieve it.

"Ah, yes, it was recovered by the merfolk after the Void had retreated," Kaso Viro explains.

"I owe them my thanks, and an apology," I wince, remembering how hard I fought them in my frantic attempts to leave.

"I would say they understand," Kaso Viro shakes his head, "but I believe they were quite relieved when I decided to bring you away to my tower. The merfolk bear little trust for men. As far as owing them, I think not. If not for you, many more of their kind would have surely perished in Richter's menagerie."

I nod, not fully convinced. My thoughts drift to Flitt. She was so white, so drained during that battle, and even then, she was reluctant to leave me.

I loop my thumb around the cord at my neck and pull it free from my armor. The light of her diamond spills across the room, coloring every dark corner with rainbows. The sight of it fills me with both relief and dread. Thank the stars I still have it, but if I do, then where is she? It hasn't taken more than the span of one night for her to heal at home in the past.

"How long was I out?" I ask them.

"Not long. A night and half of the morning," says Kaso Viro.

"And they haven't returned? Is there some magical reason they'd be unable to come here, Kaso Viro?" I hold up the feather and the diamond.

Both men shake their heads apologetically.

"No reason, except that they are not yet strong enough to travel, I'm afraid," Kaso Viro replies.

I sink back to the mattress and close my hand around Mercy's hilt. With my other hand, I press that same spot on my forehead. Should I check on the fae, or go after Rian? Or go home to Cerion to report what's happened and gather help? Eron escaped, after all. He went with the Void. They need to know that in Cerion. He's free, and his purpose is to end Margy. They need to be on guard. But how can I turn my back on my love and the unknown tortures he's sure to be suffering? And how could I face the Dusk alone? It would be so foolish. If Rian was here, he would know what to do. Then again, if he was here, I wouldn't have such a difficult decision to make.

"I am certain once she is well enough, Flitt will return to you," Valenor says. "Wherever you choose to go from here."

"I have to go to Rian," I say, shaking my head. "There's really no other option. Knowing he's there with them, knowing what they're capable of…"

"We expected as much, Lady Knight," Kaso Viro sighs. "To be perfectly honest, I find it a wonder you're still here at all."

"I don't suppose we could warn you against it?" Valenor asks. "Try to talk you out of it?"

I shake my head slowly and look from one of them to the other. "No, I don't suppose you could."

"Well then, I imagine we'll have to do what we can to assist you." Valenor says with a twinkle in his eye.

"After all that talk about meddling?" I offer them a guilty smile.

"Oho, you were listening, hm?" Kaso Viro chuckles.

I reply with a shrug. "I was waking a little, but still not completely awake. It's strange to feel so calm in the face of all of this. I feel I could simply walk right into Sixledge and take him out of there untouched."

"What's that you said? Sixledge?" Kaso Viro straightens and takes a slight step back, scowling.

"Yes, that's what Sybel said just before she vanished from the mountain in Hywilkin. I assume that was her destination," I explain. "I'm actually surprised I remembered it."

"Well," Kaso Viro mutters, stroking his beard and pacing. "Well."

"Azaeli, if you would be agreeable, I suggest you give Rian's tether to Kaso Viro for safekeeping, and bring the diamond with you, on the chance that Flitt recovers while you are there. It would be unwise to bring both tethers with you."

"Sixledge," Kaso Viro whispers under his breath. He takes the feather from me absently and tucks it into the pocket of his vest. "You know Sha' had something to do with that, brother. You know she must have."

"I don't understand," I say. "What's the significance of Sixledge?"

"Never mind," Kaso Viro waves his hand dismissively and casts a warning look at Valenor, who seems just as rattled as his brother.

"Sixledge is—" Valenor starts after a long moment spent in what seems to be an internal struggle.

"Ahem!" Kaso Viro coughs. "Really, it is no matter. If you're going to go, then you ought to go while the sun is shining. Going at night is walking into the very maw of death itself. And I do not mean that lightly!" He says, jabbing his finger toward me with every word.

"Come, Azi," Valenor beckons, opening his cloak so the sunlit sky beams out from it.

With a quick word of thanks to Kaso Viro, and not missing the warning look he gives to his brother, I step into Valenor's cloak and allow myself to be swept off into the Dreaming.

This time, it isn't only my mind he carries with him, but all of me. We glide together over rich green meadows filled with golden roses, and soar past the towers of a glittering white castle. Every moment reminds me of Rian and the time we spent here when the Dreaming was under Jacek's control.

"He never gave up on me then," I whisper to Valenor as we sweep over a dense forest, causing colorful birds to scatter from its canopy. "I swear I won't give up on him, either."

"You have the Light on your side, Azaeli," Valenor says. "Keep your wits about you, and you cannot fail."

The meadow gives way to decimated, red-trunked trees and hillsides of glowing ash, and then to darkness.

"I'm here," Valenor whispers. "You have the mark of my sister on your brow, Azaeli. You are protected. Trust in that."

Arcs of powerful lightning crash to the ground all around us, charging the air with electricity. The black sky above thunders so loudly my ears ring. Valenor is quiet for a long while as we dart through this terrifying place. Finally, he settles us on the edge of a craggy peak and holds tight to my arms to keep me safe.

"My brother would warn me against telling you this, especially knowing Sixledge is the very place you mean to venture, but my conscience could never be clear if I delivered you to such a place without telling you the truth of it first."

I turn to face him, and his cloak envelopes us while flapping in the wind like a writhing cocoon. His milky white eyes, crinkled at the edges with kindness, reflect the lightning that strikes around us eerily.

"A place too dangerous to mention, even in myths, Azaeli. When Diovicus, the Sorcerer King, was struck down by Asio Plethore, the blow was said to be so powerful it drove what was left of Asio's foe into dust. The Sorcerer King's remains were gathered together, and Asio's most trusted men journeyed to the edges of this world to find a place to cast it away. That place was named Sixledge, for the series of cliffs descending deep into the earth. It was said the king's men gathered the most powerful Mages known, and those Mages cast spells to close the rift, encasing Diovicus's remains in the deepest grave known to man.

Valenor gazes out over the crags of the Dreaming, far into the distance.

"I visited the Sorcerers' keep in Tib's dreams, only twice. Never was I given an indication that it had been erected in such a sinister place. It sat upon an island, surrounded by the sea. "

"I don't understand," I say, following his gaze. "If the sea surrounds it, wouldn't Kaso Viro be aware of what had happened there?" For a moment I panic, wondering if maybe, somehow, Kaso Viro did know. Maybe he was aware of this from the beginning.

"We are not so omnipotent," Valenor explains. "Yes, my brother is of the water, and may go where the water goes, and must remain where it is. He is able to command it and search within it with ease, but the water does not reveal all its secrets. Not unless he seeks them out specifically. And my brother, as you have heard, wisely prefers to keep his distance from the conflicts of men."

"He didn't, though, when he gave Cort that letter for me. When he told us about Eron and the sons of the prince. Why is that?"

"Sometimes, as much as we wish to, as hard as we try to, it is impossible to sit by and watch imbalance and corruption take hold. You may think us above this world, but in the end, it is a world we all share. Though we are meant to be neutral, my brother and I much prefer it when the balance is tipped to Light. It is not always easy to turn a blind eye, especially knowing our brothers and sisters had a hand in the tipping. This time, Darkness has quite a heavy hand."

The Void in the ocean billows in my memory, with Sybel standing before it. Flashes of her face appear again and again, first in the memory of the assassin who made the attempt on King Tirnon, and later in Eron's memory. The darkness swirls around her to reveal something else. Something I had somehow forgotten. The face of

Diovicus himself, his pointed teeth bared as he swipes furiously in my direction.

I scream, and Valenor grips me tightly.

"Azaeli," he says with a commanding tone, "what is it?"

Without a thought, I gaze into the Muse's blank eyes, showing him that same vision, that awful moment in Eron's mind which was somehow erased from my memory until now.

"As I feared," Valenor whispers. "As we all feared, and in so many ways, suspected."

"Eron, Sybel, and now Diovicus himself," I shake my head, holding Mercy with a white-knuckled grip. "And Rian is in there with them. How can I possibly reach him and get us both out safely?"

"Can you think of nothing you might try before storming the keep in person?" Valenor asks, his eyes twinkling with possibilities. "Perhaps a change of scenery might help."

His cloak flutters and we swirl away like leaves on the wind before settling to a gentle stop in a familiar field of small hillocks and wildflowers. As soon as my feet find purchase, the hillock in front of me rustles and shimmies, and a wide-eyed creature peeks up from the dirt, grinning at me.

"She has come back to see Stubs! Oh, I did miss her," he exclaims. "Will she tell me all of her adventures since she left? It has been a very long time, it has. And it is peaceful here now, thanks to her."

"Hello, Stubs," I say, trying for his sake to keep the confusion out of my voice.

"She remembers, doesn't she! How Stubs taught her about the threads. And what else? See what I see! Yes, she remembers."

"See what I see?" I whisper. Without much effort at all, I fall into his huge amber eyes and see myself from his perspective. With a shake of my head, I'm back to my own viewpoint again. My heart races. If I could do that, if I could look through Rian's eyes, I could see that he's safe. I could scout out what's happening to him, and I could make a plan. A part of me would much rather storm into the keep and put my sword through everyone who stands in my way, but I know it would be foolish to even think about attempting such a thing by myself. This is the best first step. Reconnaissance.

"It's brilliant!" I yelp, hugging Stubs around his muddy neck. "Of course! Oh, but could I do it if he's not nearby? Is it possible?"

"She could, if she concentrated hard enough. If she knew her target well. Yes, I'm sure she could."

"Try it," Valenor urges. "You are safe here, and I agree it is the best approach. I shall be by your side, watching over you. Try."

He's right, I know. I settle on the grass and lean against Valenor to get comfortable. When I close my eyes, Stubs's scratchy voice instructs me.

"She should focus on him, like she can see him in front of her. She can imagine him someplace familiar if it helps. It doesn't matter if it isn't where he really is."

I do as he says, imagining Rian in his bed, and myself peeking through the circle hatch. I summon little details of the experience, as many as I can. How the edge of the hatch is worn smooth from my fingers, how the blankets on his bed crumple and spill over the edge of his mattress.

"Move closer," Stubbs guides me, his voice further away than before.

In my mind, I drift through the wall, focusing on Rian's auburn hair and his steady, peaceful breathing as he sleeps.

"Closer," Stubbs's voice is so distant I can barely hear it. I press my cheek to Rian's. My body tingles with a charge of magic. I'm in the Dreaming, and I'm here, too. With Rian. Within him. Part of his mind and body, occupying it beside him. He's standing. The fact that he's standing fills me with relief. If he's on his feet, he can't be badly injured. Both within him and back in the Dreaming, I take a deep breath.

"Now, she should open her eyes."

Slowly, cautiously, I do as Stubs instructs. I open my eyes and peer out into Rian's surroundings.

Chapter Thirteen

SIXLEDGE
Azi

"Worthless, half-elf scum," a man's voice, echoed and cruel, resonates from somewhere to Rian's left.

Rian doesn't make any sound or motion at all. He stands with well-practiced quiet, staring at the shelving on the opposite wall. His hands are folded in the sleeves of his robes. His breathing is measured and calm.

"What does she see?" Stubs asks, pulling me slightly back to the Dreaming, interrupting the vision.

"He's in a room," I whisper, "some sort of study. He seems unharmed."

"Concentrate. Feel what he feels. She can. She can be him," Stubs urges. In the field with the sun warming my face, Valenor's cloak stretches across my shoulder. I feel its power seep into me and I know Stubs is right. With the Dreamwalker beside me, the possibilities are endless. Rian is alive. He's safe. That fact alone gives me confidence.

"Shh," I whisper to Stubs in the field as the voice in the room creeps closer.

"We have given you concessions," Rian's heckler says as I draw myself back to my love. *"Still, you refuse to acknowledge us. Perhaps a bit of encouragement?"*

Rian's attention remains locked on the shelves in front of him as if he knows what's to come. A hand, cruel and firm, clamps his shoulder, bursting with magic. I don't know how he doesn't cry out at the pain that follows, how he doesn't turn and lash his own powerful spell at the Sorcerer who delivers it, but he doesn't. He doesn't react at all. Not even a gasp. The sickening odor of sulfur and burnt skin fills the air, swirling around us.

The pain trails across Rian's back to his other shoulder as the man delivering it circles to face him, and still Rian remains strong, his gaze fixed forward.

His attacker isn't anyone I've seen before, but he's most definitely a Sorcerer. He's middle aged, with a sand-blond beard flecked with silver. The Mark on his face is a single line, a curl of black brambles stretching from his jawline under his beard to his temple. The scarceness of the Mark frightens me more than it would have if there was a full-fledged Sorcerer in his place. This man is new to the practice. Obviously, he's looking to prove himself, and he means to use this time with Rian as his chance to do just that. When he presses his palm to Rian's chest and the sizzle and smoke bursts between them, his Mark pulses broader.

Still, Rian doesn't move. His refusal to acknowledge the man only serves to infuriate the Sorcerer further. His nostrils flare in rage, his eyes narrow as he leans close, boring into Rian's. He raises his hand and strikes Rian hard across the cheek, hissing, "Fight back! Fight back, you weak, worthless—"

"You used 'worthless' once already. Surely you're clever enough to come up with a new insult rather than offering the same, tired ones again and again?" Rian smirks, his gaze still fixed on the shelves, his back still straight, his bruised, throbbing chin raised in defiance.

His chiding only serves to infuriate the Sorcerer to a level that could only be described as utter insanity. He lashes out against Rian with a series of powerful spells: acid, fire, dark energy. Still, Rian shows no reaction. The only evidence that the Sorcerer's spells are doing anything at all is the force of them causing Rian's feet to slide backwards along the smooth wood floor. The pain he would have felt from such a barrage is surprisingly muted. At first I wonder whether it's just because I'm not really him, and therefore can't feel it fully, but when Rian takes a deep, centering breath I understand. Somehow, he's diminishing it. The injuries are still there, of course, but the sensation of them is pushed away, shoved back from his focus.

The more enraged his opponent becomes, the more Rian seems to draw peace into himself. His entire body buzzes with that familiar magical elation, strong and controlled. I follow his focus and notice something I hadn't before. On the shelf beyond this raging Sorcerer is a single burning candle. Its flame is so etched in Rian's eyes that whenever it flickers it leaves a blue shadow of itself burned into his vision. His connection to it is almost tangible, as though I could reach out and scoop its energy into my hand.

Now that I'm aware of it, I realize what he's been doing all this time. With that single flame as his focus, he's been allowing the energy of Light inside him to build. It seeps into his eyes, filling up his skull, his shoulders, his torso...all the way to his feet. His skin seems to pulse with it. His heart starts to race. He knows it's time. His patience and focus are about to pay off.

When his opponent draws a hand back in preparation to thrust another wicked spell forth, Rian remains still. The Sorcerer's hand comes forward, and in a simple, quiet gesture, Rian raises his own hand to meet it. Their palms touch.

The burst of light comes so suddenly and so powerfully I can't keep my hold on him. I'm scattered away by the force of it as it charges through Rian's body and explodes outward.

"What happened?" Valenor shakes my shoulders gently. "Azaeli?"

"Why was she shut out?" Stubs asks.

"I cannot tell. I have no way of entering that place," Valenor replies.

I blink rapidly, trying to clear the light from my eyes, trying to find myself back in the Dreaming, in the meadow, but a tentative voice calls me back to him.

"*Azi?*" he whispers aloud, and I'm pulled into his mind once more.

He's on his hands and knees on the well-worn stone floor. All around him, the light he'd harbored clings to the walls, the ceiling, and the furniture. It drips from the closed drapes, glittering to the carpet. It shines from the crumpled heap before him, the lifeless form of his defeated enemy. It sizzles softly as it eats away at the man's dark form, pulverizing it into glittering ash. Rian watches in silence, as if trying to wrap his head around what he's just accomplished. He sits back on his heels and stares in disbelief at his hands, then up to the shelf where the candle still flickers, innocent and unassuming.

"*Azi?*" *he whispers again.*

"*I'm here,*" *I reply into his mind, and he cries out in relief.*

"*I thought I lost you. I thought you were dead,*" *he pushes to me. He might have whispered it if the lump in his throat hadn't gotten in the way.*

"*I thought you were, too,*" *I reply. I wish, more than anything, I could feel his arms around me.*

"She's going," Stubs's voice is so foreign and surprising that it makes me pause, but my desire to be with Rian, to feel his warmth, pushes out any distraction. I feel a shift, a rush through the Half-Realm, a sickening lurch.

A warning sensation comes over Rian. His stomach flips and he jumps to his feet. His fingertips crackle defensively, but his spell is quickly extinguished. I look out from his view to see, to my shock, myself kneeling on the carpet across from him. My eyes are open and blank, and the gold Mark on my skin pulses softly with light as the tangible magic shifts around me like a breeze, rustling my hair.

I drop away from his mind into my own. The switch is a sudden, uncomfortable convulsion that causes my body to quake with chills. My breath comes fast as I'm barraged with wicked sensations of fear and hopelessness.

Rian closes the space between us in an instant and takes me in his arms, and as much as I want to relish the moment, all I can do is make a strong and concerted effort not to vomit.

The room spins around me. Horror-filled screams ring in my ears, searing into my aching head. I feel I'm at the precipice of a cliff about to fall. I see my family lying dead at my feet. All my most horrifying fears have come to pass. I feel cowardly, useless, abandoned. Despite my efforts, I can't keep myself from getting sick. The darkness of this place is miserable and oppressive. It's a creature all its own, lingering in shadows, pummeling me with the most wicked, disturbing thoughts imaginable.

Rian leaves my side, whisperings words in Mage tongue, leaving me to fend for myself in the cruel, endless darkness until my thoughts go blank and hollow. I know he's setting wards, but all I can think of is that he left me, and now I'm alone. He must know I'm a coward. He must hate me.

"Azi."

His hands rest on my shoulders. His soft auburn hair brushes my forehead. His lips are rough and chapped, but still they charge me through with the power of his love as they press to mine, soft and cautious. When I lean closer to him, our kiss deepens until I feel whole again, until we are as close as I was when I entered his mind and saw through his eyes.

When we finally pull away from each other, I'm immediately disgusted. It stinks in here, like decay and rotten flesh. I have to get out. My heart races. My stomach churns. I can't breathe. I have to escape this place, to run away and never come back, but his grip on my shoulders keeps me still, and his stern whisper snaps me out of it.

"Wards, Azi. Those are wards. The smell, the feeling, all of it. They're meant to terrify and incapacitate any intruders," he explains. Swiftly, he runs his hands down my arms, murmuring in Mage's tongue as he traces strange runes over me. The relief comes gradually. Instead of death and decay, the fragrance of fresh flowers tickles my nose pleasantly. Instead of panic and fear, my mood shifts to hopeful determination.

The better I feel, the more aware I become of our surroundings. The room's high ceilings disappear into the shadowy rafters where the darkness seems to hang over us, listening. The walls are covered in carvings of some ancient language which pulses with power and sinister energy.

Rian moves closer, giving me time to take it all in while we stand in each other's arms. I cling to him and close my eyes, relishing his closeness, grateful we're both safe despite where we are.

"*What happened?*" I push to him, and the familiar dull headache that comes with Mentalism throbs vaguely at my temples. After everything I just accomplished, I'm actually surprised it's not more pronounced.

"*Not here*," Rian replies, hugging me closer. I feel a shift and know he's pulled us into the Half-Realm.

"We won't be hidden here for long," he says aloud as he scans the room suspiciously. On the shelf, the candle flickers in silence. "When the next one arrives, they're bound to use Reveal if they find the room empty," he scowls at the large iron door beside it.

"The next one? How many have there been?" I ask in horror.

"Three or four," he shrugs. "That's not important. What's important is what they're hiding here. We've got to put a stop to it."

"Three or four?" I stare in disbelief at the pile of dust on the carpet which was once Rian's tormentor. That reminds me of his injuries, and I hold him at arm's length to look them over. His robes are scorched in a diagonal line from his shoulder to his belt, and the skin beneath is angry and raw. When I start to turn him around, he shakes his head and brushes his hand over himself, restoring the robes to pristine condition with a simple spell.

"You can't fool me, Rian," I frown. "You can fix the robes, but the wounds—"

"It's fine," he says dismissively.

"It's not—"

"Azi, I'm beyond it," he explains.

"Beyond it? What does that mean?"

"It's hard to explain. I don't feel it. I haven't for a while. For at least a half day now. It didn't matter what they did to me. I could withstand it."

I think of the candle flame and the sensation of Light filling him up, and on some level I understand.

"I even found a way, somehow, to allow healing in that state," he chuckles softly. "That really infuriated them."

"Healing?" I whisper in disbelief. Healing magic, as far as I know, has always been completely separated from Arcane magic. One is a Mage or a Healer. One can't be both.

"It's not unheard of for a Mage to be able to do it," Rian explains. "It's rare, but there have been records of Mages who possess the ability to heal themselves at certain Circles."

The way he scuffles his feet and looks away with a hint of guilt makes me suspicious. It's been a long time since I've seen Rian push at the boundaries of his studies and sheepishly try to cover it up. It reminds me of a time long ago, before all of this happened, when were still children. I used to be terrified of the wrath he'd face from Uncle. Now what scares me is the effect it might have on him. In this dark place, it's easy to see how quickly a Mage could succumb to the temptations of Sorcery.

"What Circles, Rian?"

"Well," he swallows nervously, "the records I read were vague…"

"Rian." I say softly, tilting my head and drawing him to face me.

"I think it was probably…forty-third or so," he mumbles. "Forty-Third Circle."

His hazel eyes meet mine, and in them I see a mix of wonder and a hint of fear. Forty-third Circle magic is more than twice the power he should be able to wield.

"Was it Aster? The wand must have helped," I offer weakly. To my dismay, Rian shakes his head mournfully.

"They took the wand. I think they're holding her here, too. Stellastera," he says.

I think of Kaso Viro's earlier conversation with Valenor. How they had discussed the strange disappearance of their sister. Rian's expression softens to relief for a moment, until I realize he thinks he's distracted me and I turn the conversation back to his sudden ability to wield magic more than double his Circle.

"How?" I whisper. "Uncle is only Forty. Master Anod, the highest in Cerion, is Forty-First…"

"Shh," he warns, looking around us as if the shadows are listening. The specific Circles of Cerion's Mages is highly guarded information. While he's distracted, I pull his robes open at his chest, expecting to see the Mark curling there. Instead, there's soft pink line of nearly-healed flesh. The blistering red scorch mark is gone.

"How?" I whisper again, tracing my fingers across his skin. Rian shivers and gently takes my hand away.

"All I can think of," he murmurs as he closes the buttons again, "is that the ways of Magic are changing. The rules, the way we learn, are evolving. It's not unheard of for a Mage to gain Circles and skills through practical usage rather than—" he stops abruptly as footsteps approach from outside of the iron door.

Reflexively, I turn. Mercy leaps to my waiting hands as we take a defensive stance.

"*We got off on a tangent,*" Rian pushes. "*There's a lot you need catching up on. I'm stepping out. You stay hidden. We'll see if whoever it is can detect you. If so, be ready to fight. If not, when this is done, we'll have free reign of the place.*"

"*Rian, wait,*" my thought to him is pleading, but he kisses me softly, winks, and steps out of the Half-Realm just as the locks click.

"*Trust me, Azi,*" he sends, and I cling to Mercy beside him as he fixates on the flame and the door creaks open.

Chapter Fourteen

MISTY GREEN
Tib

    The inside of Loren's cyclone is soothing. The sound of rushing water reminds me of Ceras'lain's waterfall. His spell keeps us dry and comfortable. It's not long before Saesa and I are leaning against each other, drifting to sleep.

    When Loren wakes us, it's early morning. Just before dawn. The sea on the horizon is a sharp black line against the gray sky. Instead of a cyclone, we're in a boat. A rowboat, bobbing at the far end of a long pier. Beside me, Saesa stretches and turns to look around us.

    "Ships," she gasps. "Look, Tib! Cerion's ships!"

    "Shh!" Loren warns as I turn in the direction Saesa points.

    "We're here," I whisper. "Cresten."

    I scan the long pier with my healed eye. There are three ships docked here. Their masts poke out of a thick mist. Like Saesa said, two of them bear Cerion's flag. The third one flies a banner I haven't seen before: a pale blue leaf over a green circle. Probably a merchant ship.

    "Something's off," I mutter.

    "I'll say," Loren shakes his head. "I've never seen a ship stand so still in the water before. And this mist. Look how it just stops like a wall." He reaches toward it, then pulls his hand away before his fingertips touch the fog.

    "You're right," Saesa observes, reaching out, too. She stops short, just like he did. "I've never seen a mist like this. It's so dark."

    "It's not just that," I say, peering through the fog that chokes the length of the pier, into the insides of each vessel. "Where is everyone? It's not normal for a ship to be left with nobody on it. That's one the first things I learned, sailing. There's always someone to guard the plank. Especially on a merchant ship like that one."

    I raise my hand to point out of the boat toward the docks, and my finger slices into a field of magic like a wall in front of me. Right where the fog starts. It reminds me of the borders outside of

Kythshire. Magic meant to make people leave. To turn them away. This magic comes from a darker place, though.

"I can't see it," Saesa says. "The mist is too thick. I can only see the flags on the highest masts."

"Nor can I," Loren says. "And I'm afraid this is as close as I can bring you. Master will be wanting his braziers lit and his morning brew set out." He peers away from the docks toward the west. Away from the wards and the mist. Beside me, Saesa shifts on the bench. Her hand grips her sword hilt like she's ready to draw it at the slightest threat. The mist looms over us, heavy. They both feel it.

"Thank you, Loren," Saesa says while I turn my attention back to the city. I only look away when she nudges me in the side.

"What?" I ask, and she gives me a look and tilts her head toward Loren.

"Oh, yeah. Thanks, Loren," I offer him my hand to shake, and when he takes it I feel the wards around him. Good wards. Not as strong as Rian's or Gaethon's, but powerful enough to keep him mostly safe.

"It was an interesting experiment," he grins. "I'd never tried a inter-aquatic movement with someone other than myself. And a Dreamstalker, at that. Master will be pleased to hear about my progress. Keep the boat, by the way."

I don't know what to say to that, so I just shrug. It would have been good to know it was going to be an experiment beforehand. Mages.

"You did a great job," Saesa offers, smiling. "It was a very soothing journey."

"Yeah," I agree lamely.

Loren drops my hand and looks toward the mist with the kind of fearful awe of an apprentice opening a forbidden tome. "Are you sure about going in there?"

"We're sure," I answer, following his gaze with my healed eye. Back through the mist.

The docks being empty is eerie enough, but something even stranger bothers me. There are no guards posted at the gates or on the low city walls, no people wandering the streets inside. I look as far as I can from here as our boat bobs silently against the ward barrier. Into buildings and stables. Empty. Torches are lit, lanterns glow, but who for? The city is completely deserted.

A sharp elbow from Saesa makes me gasp.

"What?" I grumble, rubbing my ribs.

"You could have said goodbye to him," she says, pointing to the rippling water beside the boat.

"I didn't mean to," I say, still distracted. "Or not to, I mean."

"Tib," she says sternly, and only then do I tear my attention away enough to see the determination in her eyes. Jungle green.

"It's just, where is everyone, Saesa?"

"Sleeping, probably," she replies, taking the oars. "It's still early." She starts to row, but only moves along the invisible wall which runs parallel to the ships.

"They're not. There's no one anywhere. I can see," I say.

I reach out and graze my fingers along the wards. Nothing happens. I didn't expect it to. I feel what would have, though: a shock of deathly fear. A sharp instruction to leave and never come back. Pain. Some sort of alarm. Once we cross, whoever is trying to keep everyone out will know we're here. I think about it, watching Saesa row. I shouldn't have brought her. I could go straight through that with no trouble at all. She can't, though. She's just going to slow me down. Right away, I feel awful for thinking it. We used to do everything together, before I became Dreamstalker. Things are so different now.

"Riptide?" Saesa growls. "I don't know what it is, I can't seem to get us closer."

"It's not a riptide," I say. I tell her about the wall. The wards.

"So, it's like Kythshire's border, only more sinister," she says, and pulls the oars into the boat.

"Not as powerful, but yeah."

"No one is inside, and everyone else is shut out," she stares at the docks, so close but unreachable. "We can imagine who would have done it."

"Dusk," I agree.

"But, why?"

"To stop us. Distract us. They know what we need. Elespen is the last one, since I can get Ceras'lain easily. They expected us to come, and now whoever they left in charge of this place will know we're here if we're brave enough to cross through that," I explain, pointing at the air in front of us. Some other reason crosses my mind. They know what I can do. That I can cross through borders like that with no consequences. They know others won't. Whoever set these wards wants me inside, alone.

I look away from the city toward the horizon. The sun hasn't moved. Even though it should have risen by now, it's stuck just below the black slash of the horizon, covered in churning storm clouds. The stars are blocked out. It seems like the sky will open up over us, like the rain will start to pour down any time now. It doesn't, though. There isn't even a breeze. Everything is too still.

"You mean, if I am." Saesa whispers. "You could go through with no issue. They couldn't detect you at all, if I wasn't here."

I don't say anything. I don't know what to say except she's right, but I don't want to admit it to her. There must be a way. The whole thing makes me angry. Furious. My fists clench around my knives. I want to run them through someone. Destroy them. Sorcerers. My hatred toward them, toward the Dusk, runs as deep as ever. I want to make them see they aren't as clever as they think. Show them they have no power over me or my friends.

My feet tingle inside of my boots. Mevyn. The last time I was here, was with him. Because of him. I push aside my anger at the reminder of that time. Try not to be so on edge. Distract myself to thoughts of the elves, instead. Of my time in Ceras'lain.

I bow my head. Close my eyes. Try to push past my anger. All I can focus on, though, is how much I want to draw my knives. Cut through something. Slash. Through my eyelid, with my healed eye, I see the glow of my vials slung across my chest. Aids to help me fight. Gifts from the elves. Some I haven't used yet. The clear one. That's not for right now. The misty one is. Green. Elespen.

I draw my elven dagger, a gift from Rian all the way back when we first met. The green vial from my bandolier smells sharp and cool.

Bright sunshine. Fresh mint. Cut grass. Clarity.

Saesa watches me coat my blade. My heart races. This will work. I know it will. There's a magic all its own created from this blend. Gifts. Allies. Light. Friendship.

"I'm sure this will do something," I explain to Saesa, gesturing her closer as I raise the dagger. "I'm just not sure what. Stay close. Be ready to cross through."

She moves closer. The boat doesn't tip. The repelling wards it leans against keeps it steady. The hairs on my arms stand up. I raise the dagger and push the point of it into the wall of mist.

The fog sizzles at the touch of my blade, which drips with the water that collects on it. I motion straight downward, and the slice opens a hole in the mist large enough for us to climb through.

I take Saesa's hand and step through first, onto the damp boards of the low dock. It's not just the mist that was cut away. I feel it when I pass across the space where the wards had been. The spell has parted, too. Just enough to let us cross. I pay close attention as Saesa's hand passes through. No alarm. No reaction.

When she looks at me through the opening in the mist, I nod and tug her hand, and she steps through. Here on the other side, it's clear. The mist itself is a wall, just a few paces thick.

"Alright?" I ask Saesa once both her feet are planted on the pier. She nods and grips her sword, still sheathed. I let out a breath of relief. The mist had no effect on her.

"Should we close it back up?" she asks, pointing at the hole in the mist. It just stays there, like a weird cloud formation. A sliced-through opening between us and the boat.

"Maybe, to cover our tracks," I consider. I try to push the edges of the mist wall back together with the flat side of my dripping dagger, but it doesn't move. "Or maybe we should leave it open. A breach in the Dusk's borders couldn't be a bad thing, right?"

Saesa chuckles half-heartedly and shrugs. Her attention is already on the nearest ship. One of the ones bearing Cerion's banner. She keeps my hand tight in hers and guides me toward it.

"What if it's his, Tib? The Admiral's ship?"

I know we're both thinking of Nessa and the strange note he sent her. All these missing people, this empty city, isn't something we can ignore. Nessa is desperate to hear news of her husband. Margy wants an explanation about Elespen's silence. This is where the answers are. It couldn't hurt to take a quick look and try to figure out what's going on here.

I start to warn her to be careful as she creeps up the gangplank with her sword in one hand and my hand in her other, but there's no point. There's nothing ahead. No people, no spells. It's completely deserted.

We explore the main deck and find the galley empty, with bread and other food just sitting out, half-eaten. The ship doesn't rock under our feet. No flies or rodents pick at crumbs. Out on deck, no sea birds circle overhead.

"It's completely lifeless," Saesa whispers. She's right. Everything within the misty wall is gray. Even her fiery red curls and the flash of her bright green eyes seems snuffed out. Covered in a colorless shroud. She turns in place, squinting thoughtfully.

"The Captain's quarters," she mutters, pulling me along. "They keep records. A diary of days. Maybe there's something…" her voice trails off as we duck under the low awning that leads back into the officers' area.

My stomach sinks slightly when Saesa reaches the door to the Captain's quarters. It's a gut reaction, leftover from my time on Cap's ship. Officers only. If I'd been caught going in there, I'd probably have been beaten and thrown overboard.

"Whoa," I whisper when Saesa pushes open the door and we step inside.

The oil lamps are still lit, but their flames are low and eerily still. Every polished, dark wood surface is covered in a scattering of maps and parchment. Saesa lets go of my hand and rushes to a long desk against the crisscrossed windows at the end of the room. I stick close, watching everywhere while she rifles through the piles.

"Tib," she gasps, holding one letter up to the lantern light. The handwriting on it is Nessa's. "It *is* the Admiral's ship," she says in disbelief as I start to read it.

"My sweet love," I mutter, and quickly skip to the bottom, where Nessa's neat signature is scrawled.

"Oh, the ship's log!" Saesa exclaims, and I drop the letter to look over the neat, even lines of the Admiral's script in a worn-looking book. "But everything's normal," Saesa whispers with a scowl. "How can there be nothing here?"

The rest of the cabin is just as disappointing. Nothing is disturbed. It's like the captain and crew just vanished, and no one has been here since. Even things thieves would have taken are left lying out on the polished table tops: silverware, bronze goblets, gold-trimmed quills and a good set of calipers, spyglasses, shelves of detailed maps which would fetch at least a gold apiece, daggers and swords.

Below deck, it's the same. No life. No one here, and everyone's belongings are left untouched. It isn't until we reach the third deck that we find what they must have come for. Crates of books, all tipped over and spilled out. Rifled through.

"This is the shipment for Sunteri," Saesa breathes, stepping cautiously over the piles of hand-copied tomes. "The last one they were on their way to deliver." She crouches at the other side of the pile, in between two huge crates, and picks up a tome. "But they left over a month ago, before His Majesty…" she shakes her head as her voice trails off, and starts going through the books, stacking them in neat piles.

With my healed eye I scan the hold, searching for any sign of magic or movement. Just as before, there's nothing at all. Not even a rat. "They've been here a while," I agree. "But look, no cobwebs. And upstairs, the lamps were still lit. And that food in the galley looked like it was fresh today."

"So someone waited for them to dock, made everyone disappear somehow, and then came down here and took just some of the tomes? How? And why?"

"I don't know," I sigh. "But I'm sure it was Sorcerers. All the wards that would have been set down here are broken, and there's nothing magic on this ship at all. Come on. Let's check out the other ones and see if we can figure it out."

As we go through the next ship, a different worry starts to nag at me. What if I can't detect anything because, somehow, my abilities as Dreamstalker are fading? What if there really is some clue here, some sign of life, and I'm missing it? The thought puts me on edge. Halfway through the second of Cerion's ships, I draw my knives. Saesa glances at me curiously. She doesn't argue, though. The silence is unnerving. Taunting, almost.

We find this ship in the same state as the first one. The third, the merchant ship, is just as untouched except for its cargo, which has been ransacked like the book crates. Jewels, silks, and gold have been left behind, though. Valuable things anyone motivated by riches and greed would have snatched up without a second thought.

"If they left all this, what do you suppose they took?" Saesa asks.

"Enchanted things," I reply. "Just like this ship, nothing here is magical. Not even a coin."

"That, and the people," Saesa says, stroking her fingers across a roll of velvet.

"There have got to be answers inside the city," I say with a sudden urgent need to see something, anything, with my healed eye. I offer my hand to her. "Come on."

We run up the stairs, down the gangplank, and jump onto the dock at a sprint. Saesa giggles, and the sound along with the freedom of sudden speed goes to my head. I pull her along until she lets go and starts a foot race along the pier. She edges me out, and I pump my legs harder until we reach the ramp to the stone walkway. A white sand beach stretches along the shore on either side of the walk, grayed out by the black clouds overhead. I beat her to it and leap to the walkway with both feet. Saesa follows, laughing, and lands beside me at a crouch.

As soon as her bare hand touches the stone, the ground rumbles. The sand on either side of us roars like a tidal wave. Great mounds of it rush skyward and plummet toward us, threatening to crush us. Saesa dives into me and shoves me to the side, and we narrowly dodge the attack.

We jump to our feet and keep trying to run, but the sand is relentless. I have no time to search for the source of the magic, or try to figure out what exactly is happening. The sand takes the form of dozens of fists smashing toward us.

"Get back to the dock," I yell.

Saesa and I try to stay close to one another, but it's no use. The force of the sand as the fists barrage us is like slivers of glass driving into my skin. Something cracks along my chest, and I try not to panic when I see spatters of glowing yellow, green, and pink fly off with the sand-fist that smashed my vials. Another fist drives into my back, knocking the breath out of me. I fall to my knees, and another upper-cuts me to the chin, sending me flying as stars burst across my vision.

Somewhere among the fists, Saesa screams.

"Saesa!" I shout, and my mouth fills with sand. I sputter and cough as the grit hits the back of my throat, and I fight through the fists toward the sound of her voice.

With my eyes closed against the rush of sand, I search through my eyelid for her. At first I think I see her standing at the edge of the city gates, gesturing toward me.

"Help me!" Saesa screams, but her voice is behind me. The figure at the gates is someone else. Her laughter rushes in the sand, carried by it. I recognize the voice. Remember how she tried to claim me under the mountain. Under Kerevorna. How she tried to sway me.

Another barrage of fists flies at me from the side. They smash my shoulder. Pummel my knees. My legs buckle. The pain is too much to bear. At the gates, Sha'Renell laughs. It all makes sense now. She couldn't touch us on the pier. She was waiting for us to reach solid ground. As soon as Saesa touched the stone, she knew, and flew into action. We dropped our guard. We should have been ready.

The sand collects around me, shoving me along the stone, pushing me toward the Muse of Earth. Something strikes me hard from behind. More fists, I think, but no. Something different. Claws. They clamp around me, scooping me up. Flying me away. Up into the sky, out of the reach of the sand fists. Into the churning clouds.

"Saesa!" I scream toward the city far below, but the only reply I hear are Sha'Renell's wails of disbelief. I try to squirm free from whatever's holding me, but its grip is too strong, and even that small movement is agony. Something's broken, I'm sure. My knees. My back. It's hard to tell.

"I'm here, Tib! Can you believe this?" Saesa squeals from somewhere above me. "This is incredible!"

My head dips with relief, knowing she's with me. She's safe. My fingers graze the scales of whatever's holding me. They're warm and smooth, like hammered copper. The edges are laced with bright orange, like molten metal. I try to look up, but moving hurts too much. I can only make out the tip of a long, bronze wing as it flaps down and up again, and the flash of a flame-orange eye as the creature's head snakes down to wink at me.

Dragon.

Valenor? No. Too different. Too unfamiliar.

Saesa's laughter catches on the wind above me as our rescuer soars away from Cresten. It isn't long before the dark clouds break. My head aches, but I force myself to stay awake. Focus on the jungle below, where the sun shines brightly across deep green treetops. Watch them blur and tilt as we near.

Bright. Rich. Alive. Elespen.

Chapter Fifteen

SAVARIKTA
Tib

We fly along the line where the dark fog meets the jungle for a while. It's disturbing. The wall of gloom. It stretches from as high into the sky as I can see, all the way to the ground. Like the wall of a violent storm that looms, but never arrives. Except we've been in there. There's no storm. No rain. Just mist, dark and thick.

Far above me, Saesa talks on and on. She sounds worried. I wonder who she's talking to. I can't hear what she's saying, though.

The dragon's talons cradle me. I don't dare to move. It would hurt too much. I could fall. I could break. I wish I knew where it we were going, though. I wish I could tell who it is. I rest my forehead on the scaly foot holding me. It seems more metal than creature. My legs throb. Pain pulses in my head. I can't focus. I rest my cheek on smooth scale. Look out at our surroundings.

We circle lower and lower until the broad wings fold around us and we plunge through the canopy of the jungle. Birds cry out as we pass. A chorus of creatures shrieks at our arrival. Trunks of massive trees and vines streak beside us. There's something else. A shift of energy. Protections. Barriers. Not like the fog one. This one is bright. Light. Safe. Joyful.

A powerful relief washes over me. I can feel it. Sense it. I didn't lose it. My healed eye flicks around the jungle. Magic is in everything, raw and rich. Inside the trees, in every leaf. In the colorful birds that watch us from their perches. In the strange, furry creatures who hang in groups by long tails, chattering to each other. In the tree cats who doze way up at the top of the canopy. Everything is magic. Like Kythshire. It pulses and flows around us with an emerald glow. Elespen.

Our rescuer slides me onto a huge fern leaf. Saesa is at my side in an instant. The glow of excitement fades from her eyes as soon as she sees me.

"The pink," I croak. My throat is raw from the sand. Even my jaw hurts when I try to talk. I have to clench my teeth. "Pink vial."

Saesa traces her fingers along my bandolier. Scowls. Looks at me apologetically. I remember the sand fist hitting my chest. The sound of glass breaking. The splattering of pink, green, and yellow with the force of the blow.

"It's gone," she whispers.

I growl with frustration and tip my head back, then groan from the pain in my neck. Saesa tries to soothe me. Holds my head in her lap. Strokes my hair out of my eyes. I try to focus on her. On anything but the pain. Her face and neck are slashed with tiny cuts. The corners of her eyes and mouth are crusted with sand. Her leather vest is shredded and caked with it, too. One of her sleeves is completely torn off. A huge bruise blooms across her bare shoulder. She tries to hide the wince when she moves that arm, but I notice.

Fury surges through me. Sha'Renell. How long had she been there, waiting for us? Did she know when we were on the ships, looking around? I imagine how she must have lurked. How she watched us run down that pier like fools. Completely oblivious. Her cruel laughter rings in my ears, taunting me. Calling me stupid. Telling me I should have known. I should have seen. I shouldn't have let my guard down.

"Tib," Saesa calls softly. Her thumb sweeps the corner of my eye, wiping away a streak of tears. "Try to stay awake."

I force my eyes open without realizing I had closed them. Her face hovers over mine. She smiles, but the smile doesn't reach her eyes. Green, like the jungle above her. Worried. Scared.

"How many vials are left? Which ones?" I ask, trying to distract myself.

She reaches down. Picks some broken glass out of my vest and tosses it aside. "Only three got smashed. Pink, yellow, and green. Everything else looks whole."

"White?" I ask.

"It's safe," she nods, patting a vial to the side.

"But the pink is gone," I moan and squeeze my eyes shut, wincing at the pain.

"Just...we'll figure this out," she whispers. "Try to stay still. Look here. Look at me."

I try to clear my head. Focus on her and not the pain. Her curls are all messy. They float around her face. Something dark pokes through her cloud of red hair. Saesa seems to be aware of it. She raises her good shoulder slightly as the small, coppery creature emerges to peer at me. Its eyes glow with orange flames. Its leathery wings are folded neatly across its back. Its tail flicks lazily as it follows her gaze into the jungle.

"Saesa," I say hoarsely. My teeth crunch with grit, making me wince. "I'm either seeing things, or you have a baby dragon on your shoulder."

"She's not a baby," Saesa says softly. "She's the one who saved us." She offers a hand to the creature and it slides into her palm, so she can hold it closer to me. The dragon flicks its head from side to side like a snake. "She just made herself smaller to keep from causing damage to anything here."

"She?" I ask. The creature hops from Saesa's hand to my chest. Sniffs at my bandolier. My broken vials. It feels like nothing's there. Light as a feather. I sense the magic in it. Tether magic. Fire. Metal. Lava. Raw power. Hywilkin.

"I think it's a she, anyway," Saesa coos and the dragon hops back into her hand. "When I hit the ground at the end of the pier, the opal fell out of my pouch. It started to glow before I snatched it up. I called for someone to help us, and the next thing I knew, we were being carried off."

"She's really pretty," I say, fixing my attention on the white scales along the dragon's body that shine with pure white light. Dawn light. "That opal was meant to summon Skalivar, though, remember? That's what he said. To use it to call on him when your lady knight returned."

"She must belong to him," Saesa reasons. "He must have sent her through the opal to save us. That's what I'll call her, I think. Opal."

"Yeah," I agree. Even though it seems off to me. Tether magic doesn't work that way. I can't focus, though. The last time I was in pain like this was when the Sorcerer Osven dropped me off a cliff. I push the dark memory away. Let my eyes close, just for a bit.

"Tib," Saesa's voice drifts to me from far away. "Stay with me."

I try hard. I do. Try to force my eyes open. I can't, though. The pain is winning.

"Someone's here," Saesa whispers, shaking my shoulder. The leaf trembles under us. Pain jolts through me. I bite my lip to keep from crying out. I try to push through the grogginess. Look with my eye to see what's happening. Opal's form grows slightly. Figures creep onto the edges of the enormous leaf. I fight my body's need for rest. Fight hard. It's too difficult, though. Too much of a struggle. I can't help it. I lose the battle and black out.

It's hot when I wake up. Hot and bright. The thin, silky blanket covering me sticks to my skin. The hammock holding me does, too. Every once in a while a burst of breeze drifts over me, but it isn't enough to keep me cool for very long. The air is so thick it's like breathing water. Inhaling mist. I'm careful not to open my eyes. Not to let anyone who might be watching know I'm awake.

The first thing I notice aside from the heat is the music. It's distant, but it comes from every direction. Drums. Flutes. Cheerful singing, all in time. It's quick and primal. A celebration, a heartbeat. It mixes with the humid air like magic. Like Mya's songs, it holds power. I let it touch me. Just a little. Enough to see what it does. My heart soars. I feel a part of it. Welcome, like family.

I push it away again. Disallow it. I need my feelings to be my own right now, and this reminds me too much of Brindelier's forced celebration. It's not as sinister, though. It has a purity to it. An innocence. A light.

I pretend to stay asleep. Peek through my eyelid with my healed eye, looking for Saesa. Searching the room.

It's more a shelter than a room. Broad leaves stretched over strong branches. Long, colorful strips of silk sway lazily from the ceiling. On my right side, a young boy fans a huge leaf over me. I can't see too many details of him without turning my head. He's the only one here, and he's no threat.

They must have Saesa somewhere else. I have to get to her. As still as I can manage, I check myself. My arms and legs. My back and neck. Everything's healed. Completely painless. Even the gritty scratchy feeling in my throat is gone. My mind is clear. Not just soothed, charged up. I feel I could leap from this hammock and take on the Dusk itself.

My sudden burst of energy is crushed quickly under the memory of my shattered vials. Without thinking, I slide my hand to my chest. My hip. My bandolier is gone. My dagger, too. My feet tingle in my boots. I find it odd they left them on but took off everything else except my small shorts.

"Akkoti!" The boy calls out as soon as I move. His voice is high and perfect. Like it belongs outside singing with the others instead of in here. It gives me chills. The leaf fan stops. His bare feet slap on the floor as he runs across the shelter. "Akkoti!" he shouts again. This time he says more, but I don't understand his language.

Whoever he's calling comes quickly. They chatter excitedly and rush inside together.

"Tibreseli Nullen Ganvent. *Evtu*," the second voice greets me beside the hammock. This one is deeper than the boy's, and even more melodic. "You are awake now?"

No reason to hide it anymore, I guess. I turn my head and open my eyes. The woman greeting me is short and plump. Her rich, dark skin peeks out through the cracks of red, green, blue, and white designs painted all over her curves. Her eyes are deep brown. The beads in her long hair slide off her shoulders, clicking together as she leans over me.

"How do you feel, *Evtu*?" she asks, smiling wide and bright.

I shift in the hammock, making it sway gently. On the opposite side of me, the boy starts fanning again. The silks draping me start to slide free, and I tug them up to make sure I'm covered.

"Undressed," I mutter, looking around for my things.

The woman throws her head back and laughs with so much joy that I can't help but smile, too. She takes my hand and pats it kindly. Grins at me like I'm some wonder or mystery. The way a mother looks at her baby.

I look her over carefully. The gemstone beads in her hair hold magic. Knowledge. The lines painted across her rolling skin do, too. Each one was put there with a purpose. Embedded with some thread of wisdom. She feels like a Mage to me. A powerful one. Someone who has studied the craft and knows how to mold it.

She seems young to know so much. Not at all like the stuffy old men of Cerion's Academy. I look past the painting and the gold plates and green silks decorating her chest. Really look at her skin. No Mark shows at all. Not a hint of Sorcery.

"Many of your things were damaged and are being repaired," she explains. "Do not worry. Our craftsmen are skilled. Your items will be returned to you much improved. I am Akkoti, a Dona of the Savarikta. The Great Riders. I shall be your guide as you remain our guest in Mokti Jungle, *Evtu*."

"A Dona?" I ask.

"In your language, it is Mage. A wise person, one who has studied and can mold the Lifesap," she explains. Keeps my hand in hers. Mine's sweaty from the sticky air, but hers is cool and dry. It's a spell on her, I realize after I search for it. One that keeps her comfortable in the heat.

"And *Evtu?*" I ask.

"*Evtu.*" She smiles and shakes her head with that same look of wonder. "*Evtu Luvari* is a title most cherished by our people. You are welcome here, my friend. You and your companions."

"*Evtu Luvari*," I repeat under my breath. It's so close to what the elves call me, *Eftue'luvrie*, I feel a shiver. "You mentioned my companions. Where is my friend?"

"She is our honored guest. You arrived just in time. Come. Pelu will help you dress, and I will take you to her. Come. They are waiting to see you." She gestures toward the opening in the shelter, toward the music and voices. She nods to the boy with the fan and bows to me, then slips outside to wait.

The boy, Pelu, helps me out of the hammock. He works in silence, winding fresh orange silks around my legs for trousers, and tying a sash of blue-green across my chest. He fastens it all together with a belt of gold links. When he's finished, he crosses to a row of baskets tucked to the side of the shelter and brings one to me. It holds my dagger, belt, and all my vials neatly wrapped in gold silks.

"Where's my bandolier?" I ask, making a motion over my chest and pointing to the vials.

Pelu shakes his head, then gestures across his own chest like he's breaking something open.

"Broken," I scowl, remembering the sand fists that smashed the vials and shredded my clothes. I'm lucky it didn't fall off while the dragon was carrying us away. Lucky most of the vials were saved.

Pelu taps my arm and points to the basket he holds, then to his own eyes. He holds the basket close, guarding it, and I understand. It's his job to watch my things. My vials. It's his duty, and I trust he's serious about it. Still, I sift through the neatly bundled vials until I find the most important one. The white, stripping one. I buckle my dagger belt under the gold one and tuck the vial into it. When I'm done, Pelu bows to me and gestures to the opening where Akkoti is waiting.

A curtain of beads and ferns separates us from the music beyond. The sunlight streaks through it, making reflections of it dance around us like orbs. Akkoti turns to me, her eyes dancing with excitement.

"Be warned, *Evtu*. They will greet you with much enthusiasm." She holds her hand out to me and a long sash of tattered silks appears. "Best to wear this."

Puzzled, I pull the sash over my head and run my hand over it. Some of the scraps are wound with gold, others have beads of precious stones sewn in. I'm about to ask what the meaning of it is when she pulls the curtain aside to reveal the village beyond.

It's hard to take it all in, but the first thing I notice is how huge it is. Dozens of huts like the one I came from dot the jungle floor, with at least a hundred people at the center of the village. They dance in time with one another, singing with the beat of the drums. The crowd shimmers with color, glittering from the sunlight that splashes off the gold and jeweled decorations on their clothes. Some of them wear elaborate headdresses that sway dramatically with the movements of the dance. Others are dressed like the animals of the forest: monkeys, birds, forest cats.

Everyone is gathered, from babies to elderly, and all of them take part in the dance. When they see me, they rush forward in a swarm. Akkoti holds my arm, shouting to them in their language, guiding me forward through them.

They reach for me, calling out "*Evti!*" and "*Tib!*" They stretch out long arms and strong hands, trying to touch me. Some of them pull at my sash and manage to grab a silk scrap with cries of triumph. Others just stroke my skin or my hair and step away to let the next person through. Through it all, they keep singing on the outskirts. Singing, drumming, and dancing.

Beside me, Akkoti sometimes sings along as we creep through the mass of people. Other times, she barks out in a scolding tone, "*Ogun tadi!* Be gentle! *Se terna!* Step away, move aside! Nearly there, now, *Evtu*. Thank you, thank you for your kindness, my friend." She pats my shoulder with encouragement.

The whole thing is confusing. Irritating. I try not to frown. I try to just push through it. Get through it. For some reason, they love me. They need to see me, to know I'm real. The power of their song lifts them up. Even though I don't allow its magic to touch me, I can't help but be charged by the rhythm of it. Their closeness and brotherhood are as contagious as their joy. By the time we reach the other side of the village, I'm grinning and laughing.

We stop at the steps of a huge platform, and everything goes quiet. A huge stone structure towers over the outskirts of the village, its steps and walls overgrown with vines. Where the sunlight hits it, its surface sparkles with flecks of gold and silver.

The building is a backdrop to two thrones of live trees growing right up from the platform. One of them is empty. The other one is draped with silks of orange and blue-green like the ones I'm wearing. They trail from it down a row of root steps, which have been piled with offerings of flowers, fruits, and burning candles. Perched on top of them, dressed in shimmering gold jewelry and light, gauzy silks, is Saesa. A delicate band of gold sparkles on her forehead like a princess's circlet. Opal lies draped across her shoulders like a strange, elaborate epaulet. When she sees me emerge from the crowd, her eyes light up and she jumps from her seat.

"You're awake!" she shouts happily, and her voice sends birds crying and flapping from the canopy high above.

She starts to move toward me, but the piles of silks slow her, and a man standing beside her puts a hand up and whispers to her. Saesa pauses and nods to him.

"Come up," she says, grinning, and Akkoti takes my elbow to guide me up the winding roots. The drumming and singing start again, pushing out the hushed silence as the crowd surges forward. They stop at the steps, though, respectful of the boundary.

We hug, and even with her shouting right into my ear it's almost impossible to hear her over the voices of the Savarikta.

"Are you healed?" she asks. "They gave you potions. They asked me first."

I nod, holding her close. Opal slips to her opposite shoulder, shrinking a little to make room for herself.

"Are you all right?" I shout into her ear. She nods, too. "What's going on? This can't all be for us."

"It's not. Their riders are coming back. It's a huge holiday. They've been gone for weeks, and we happened to show up right when they're returning. Dona Kruti explained it all to me." She tips her head toward the man at her side. He's painted up just like Akkoti, with a huge headdress of feathers and reeds and golden beads. "We're to be their honored guests for the welcome home ceremony."

"We can't stay here," I say, and Saesa pulls me to the tree thrones.

"We owe them at least a night," she explains. "Dona Kruti said they know who we are and why we've come. They want to help us, and they need our help. They've had some of their own tribe vanish, too.

They said they'll discuss it with us after the riders return. They were out scouting."

"How do you know they can be trusted?" I ask just as the drumming and song suddenly stop. My shouted question hangs in the air around us. I look around awkwardly, thankful that most of them probably didn't understand.

Akkoti and Kruti step forward together, to the edge of the root steps. They say something in their language, and the crowd cheers and parts to form two lines with an aisle in the center. They bow their heads.

Akkoti turns and smiles at me, her eyes flashing with excitement, and says quietly, "They come."

Saesa reaches across the trunk-like arms of our two thrones and grips my hand. The jingle of her gold bracelets is the only sound in the vast jungle. Even the wildlife seems hushed as we squint past the aisle in front of us into the dense jungle to try and see the riders.

With my healed eye, I scan through thick trees and underbrush, but nothing is out there. In the lines below, no one is looking toward the jungle. The ground starts to rumble and quake, and many of those lined up drop to one knee to steady themselves.

Saesa squeezes my hand as the quaking grows stronger. Her eyes meet mine fearfully. I know she's thinking the same thing I am: Sha'Renell. She knows I'm here. She tracked me, and now all these people are in danger because of me.

I draw my dagger, even though I know it'll be useless against anything the Muse of Earth could throw at us. Over the thundering quake, I yell at them to run. Some of them look up and laugh. Others stay bowed and reverent. None of them does what I say, though. Akkoti hushes me and urges me to sheath my weapon and sit.

"Tib," Saesa whispers, pointing at a crack in the muddy jungle floor. It shakes and rumbles and moves like something's under it, burrowing. Coming up from inside. I peer into the earth and see a strange beast beneath it, pushing its way closer. Behind it, five more of them follow.

The first one sprouts through the mud like a seedling. Its head is covered with a rough, muddy shell. It emerges, flapping its broad ears from side to side, spraying the onlookers around it with dirt. It stretches a long trunk toward a few of them, and they reach to touch it like they reached for me before.

The creature is gray, wrinkled and enormous. Its wide, flat feet are like stumps of trees as it lumbers forward out of the ground. On its back is a second shell, like a tortoise shell, which drips with dirt. Once it has cleared the earth and all four feet are above ground, the villagers cheer and start to sing and drum again.

As the huge creature nears, a man emerges from beneath the creature's back shell, near its neck. He's lean. Muscled. Painted in the same style as the Donas. He stands on the highest point of the shell, lifts his spear to the sky, and raises his voice to match the others in song.

Behind him, one by one, the others climb free of the earth, too. Their riders take the same stance as their leader. Their mounts stomp forward along the line. Saesa and I are directed by Akkoti and Kruti to stay seated in our tree thrones and wait to be greeted by the riders of Savarikta.

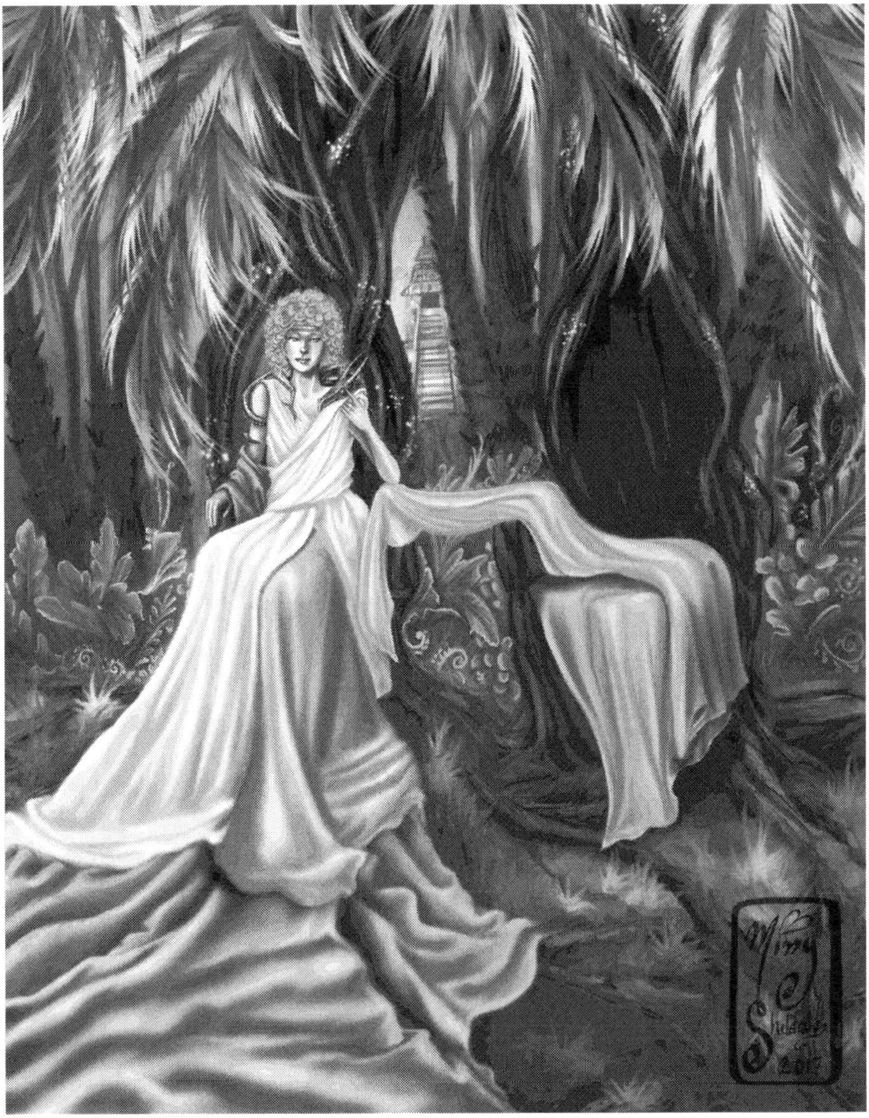

Chapter Sixteen

THE RUSE
Celli

"She amuses me, and I shall have her as my guest. And you are forbidden to say another word about it." Pippa's tone is final. She doesn't even look at the attendant who lost the argument. He's the one from before, with the list.

"Have them prepare Salvia's old room for her." Pippa waves her hand and the man bows, looks at me hesitantly, and rushes off.

"Make her cheeks pinker, Lia. And see what you can do about that gray under her eyes. I want there to be no mistaking," Pippa directs the lady-in-waiting who works in front of me, sweeping powders and paints over my face.

She keeps telling me to look forward, but I keep turning to the side to watch the princess. I can't help it. Everything about her is intriguing. I can't take my eyes off her.

The maid catches on eventually. She has the princess stand behind me so she can compare, and so I can look into the looking glass and see her standing with me. My eyes meet hers in the mirror, and neither of us looks away.

She seems like she knows something about me. Something I don't even know. She seems like she wants to ask me things, more things, but she's biting her tongue. Instead, she rests her hands on my shoulders and watches her attendant work.

"That will do," she says some time later, when the girl sweeps a brush across my lips. "Look at that. Two reflections of myself!" The princess squeals with delight and takes my hand. "Come, I hope he's still awake. The moon is nearly risen, and as I'm sure you know, my brother sleeps by night and I by day."

She doesn't acknowledge the group of ladies and guards who file behind us through the corridors of the palace. It seems normal for her. For some reason, I take in an interest in them and crane my neck behind me to get a good look. There are two guards, a frazzled-looking older woman, and two lady's maids. All of them seem very awake for this time of the night. I imagine they stay up all night, like she does.

Something compels me to focus on each of their faces, to linger on them even while the princess pulls me through the maze of her private rooms. It's important to see them, really see them, and then her, again. How the fringe of her hair grazes the back of her neck. The way the silk of the gown clings to the curve of her waist. The grace of her steps, even at this speed, as she navigates the corridor.

"Wait here," she orders the group, taking my hand. "We'll just be inside for a moment."

The room she pulls me into is dark and cozy, with walls draped in deep purple velvet and trimmed in gold. There are no doors other than the one we entered through, and no windows that I can see. A beautiful tufted chair and carved desk sit to one side, and in the center stands a single, ornate mirror. When the door closes and we're alone, she turns to face me and look me over.

I watch how her chest rises with her quickened breath. How the high collar of her gown grazes her jaw. She walks around me, and I don't take my eyes off her until I can't turn my head any further.

"This is my private study," she explains, stepping to where I can see her again. I watch her lips move as she speaks. "I come here for meditations and solitude. It's difficult work, presiding over Brindelier at night. The effort to keep light in my heart as I should is...overwhelming."

Her eyes meet mine and linger again, like they did when she watched me getting made up in the mirror. She steps closer. Her breath catches. She reaches toward my face, but pulls her hand away and turns her back.

With a whisper and a gesture, she thrusts her fingers toward the door and it crackles with a spell. Another flick of her wrist lights a candle on the desk, and she crosses to it to stare into its flame.

"I know why you're here," she whispers. "I see it in your eyes. Deep within them. The question is, do I allow it? I shouldn't."

I don't answer. Even if I could, I wouldn't know what to say. She knows why I'm here, but I have no idea. It's not important. I'm doing what I'm meant to do. Watching her. Looking. That's my purpose. It doesn't matter why. All that matters is her. The way her hand rests elegantly on the table. The flicker of the candlelight casting delicious, deep shadows beneath her nose and in the corners of her eyes.

She seems to gather herself, and looks at me again.

"Your gown," she says, and wiggles her finger. I feel it change around me, but I'm too drawn to the motion of her hand and the softness of her wrist to care what she's done to my dress. When she's satisfied with how I look, she stands me in front of the tall looking glass. Side by side, we do look almost the same. Dressed in the same gown, I can't tell the difference between us at all. It's disorienting until she steps away and leaves me to look at my reflection.

"Brother," she calls, and the surface of the mirror shifts. My image disappears, and the glass becomes a window into another place. A palace, from the looks of it. A dining hall. A boy steps into view. A prince, dressed in white and gold, with blond hair like mine and eyes like Pippa's. She stands away, far to the side where he can't see her. An uneasy feeling hits me in the stomach when we look at each other, and his mouth curves into a smirk.

"What trick is this?" he asks with amusement. "Pippa? Who is this girl?"

"Oh, Poe," Pippa groans with disappointment. "We worked so hard, and still you couldn't be fooled!" She laughs and steps to my side, and Poe looks us both over.

"She's very close," he chuckles, "but I know my sister too well."

He presses his fingertips to the glass and Pippa does the same, lining them up perfectly to his, closing her eyes like she can feel his energy.

"Who is she, Pippa?" he asks, this time a little suspiciously.

"Just a girl. She was on the list today," she explains, and waves at me to step aside. I do as I'm told, and she centers herself in the mirror and presses her forehead to the glass. "I miss you."

"I know," Poe says apologetically. "I miss you, too. But they're close, now. Very close. Soon it will be as it should be. We'll be together again in Brindelier. Until then, you must be strong for our kingdom."

Pippa steps back. Nods, but doesn't answer otherwise.

"Where is Alex?" he asks.

"Entertaining," she replies quietly. "I only meant to amuse myself. Things have been dull here, and you seem to be having such fun."

"It isn't all fun, Pippa," Poe says with a scolding tone. "I'm doing my duty, as you should be doing yours. We are all working, Sister."

"Except your work involves wooing a beautiful princess, dancing, and feasting. My own task is much more lonesome."

Inside the mirror, Poe presses his lips together. He looks up at the ceiling. I can't tell what he feels. Concern, maybe. A little annoyance. Guilt.

"It isn't all dancing and feasting. There were quakes tonight," he whispers.

"Bad quakes?" Pippa asks fearfully, peering past him into the room.

"Not terribly bad. Frightening and damaging, but no lives were lost. Still, it sent a message."

"The Dusk is getting more brazen," Pippa says quietly.

"I fear they may attack soon. Have you been to speak with Mother?" Poe asks.

"She doesn't answer me anymore," Pippa sighs. "Not for days and days."

"We're on our own, then, for now."

"As always," Pippa scowls.

"Sister, be strong. Meditate on the light, as you've been taught to. Gather your ladies around you. Surround yourself with love as much as you can. Don't ever forget how loved you are by them. By all of us. By me."

They press their hands together again and look at each other for a long stretch of silence before the prince finally breaks it.

"It won't be long, I promise. Don't be consumed. And you ought not keep her," he says, pointing to me. "You don't know who she might be."

Inside the mirror, in the other palace, the ground rumbles and the mirror shakes. Poe grasps the frame of it, steading himself and the looking glass. Behind him, a pair of tall candlesticks clatter to the ground.

"Poe!" Pippa cries, pressing closer to the glass.

"It's all right, Sister," he says as the rumbling fades. "Just...be strong for me. Have faith. I have to go. They'll be wondering where I'm off to."

Before she can say anything, Poe sweeps his fingers across the surface, leaving Pippa staring at her own reflection. I watch her eyes fill with tears. Watch her hair swing to cover her face as her head tips forward and her own hand drags along the surface. Watch her cry in the flickering light of the candle on the desk. Watch the shadows dance around her. Feel them taunting her. Calling her.

She turns to face me. Her wet eyes bore into mine, deep and searching. The shadows swirl around us. My ears ring, and strange sensation comes over me. I lose control of myself as something else takes hold. Something dark and sinister.

My hand drifts to the princess's face without my telling it to. I trace something across her cheek. Some unfamiliar letter or rune. She gasps, her eyes wide, and pushes my hand away.

"My brother is wrong," she whispers. "I know exactly who she is. As soon as I saw her, the way she stares, I knew it was you."

"What about it?" I whisper in reply. My dark, unfamiliar voice startles me.

Pippa takes a shaky breath. She looks at me with a mix of horror and desire. She knows how wrong it is, but she still wants this company. Aches for it.

"There is still a way for us, my love," the whisper seeps from my lips.

She tears her gaze away, shaking her head. Her lips move, but no sound leaves them. She wrings her hands and paces, glancing toward the door where she knows her attendants wait.

After a moment, she spins to face me. With a gesture in the air between us, she whispers a phrase, a spell. My eyelids grow heavy. My knees buckle beneath me. I sink to the floor as pink dust settles around me, lulling me to sleep.

Chapter Seventeen

CIRCLE OF SPIRES
Azi

  Two more of them come in and toy with Rian, and twice more, he bests them with this new light magic he's achieved. With each new pile of ash, my heart races faster. What is the point of these torturous sessions, and when will they stop? When will they reach their limit of tolerance for his victories, and start to truly punish him for what he's done? My hatred for the evil in this place swells inside me, ready to burst out. I want to hurt them the way they've hurt him. With every cruel taunt and senseless injury, I want to make them pay.

  Rian's light surges, and another Sorcerer crumbles to glittering ash. I sheathe Mercy and draw him close to me, and he slumps into my arms. His hair is singed, his face scarred with some wicked spell which caused his flesh to dry and crumble.

  "How much longer will you take this, Rian? They're only going to keep coming until you have nothing left to fight with."

  "That's exactly what they're doing. Testing my limits. Breaking me down." He swipes his foot to the side, through the ashes of defeated Sorcerers. I can feel his remorse for their deaths weighing heavily on him. Rian has never been a killer. Even in the face of the most wicked foe, he has always tries to figure out a way to win the fight without ending lives.

  I don't know what's worse, knowing that these people are so evil they would discard their own allies for such a pointless exercise, or having to watch Rian go through this. I imagine what it must be doing to his spirit, and the thought is too much to bear.

  "And when your magic is spent?" I ask him as he droops further. *"When you can't fight back any longer? You're giving them exactly what they want, and they're not going to let up until you're destroyed. We have to get out of here."*

  His only answer is a long, deep breath. His gaze is still fixed on the candle. I can feel the light strengthening him.

  "Aster's here," he pushes. *"We have to find her. And this may be our only chance inside their lair, to find out how to put a stop to them and end this for*

good, Azi. They're hiding something horrible. Something unthinkable. You got in, but there are wards here. There's no way out. Not through the Half-Realm. I tried already, more than once."

His argument is interrupted by more footsteps outside the room. My heart jumps to my throat. Blood pounds in my ears.

"*I won't stand by and watch another round of this, Rian,*" I push to him, tightening my grip on his arms.

"*Azi, don't,*" Rian warns, but I don't listen. I hold him closer, concentrating, and pull him with me into the Half-Realm.

The next Sorcerer steps inside, his face hidden by a dark hood. I know I've succeeded when the Sorcerer's hood sweeps from side to side, searching the small room for Rian. At his shoulder, an imp emerges from the darkness, his dark eyes narrowed, his pointed teeth bared in a cruel grimace.

"A little game," the imp jeers in a high-pitched voice. "Where is he hiding, hmm?" He drifts into the room as the Sorcerer flings his hand backwards and the door slams shut with a series of clicking locks.

With another swift movement, the man gestures quickly over his head and his hood vanishes. With his face revealed, I gasp in shock and my skin prickles in warning.

"*Xantivus,*" I push to Rian, who tries his best to straighten even though he still needs me to support him. "*I told you about him. Do you remember? He was at the pyre. He's the Mentalist who challenged me. The one who took control of the Elite and made them fight against us.*"

Rian doesn't answer. The silence between us makes me cringe. Xantivus creeps into the room, leering into the shadows. Rian focuses on the candle flame, gathering it to him, letting it fill him up. He doesn't heal himself this time, though. The scars on his face seem to spread slowly rather than fade.

"We were wondering how long it would be until you used that little trick," he says with a smirk. "Hiding away is useless, Eldinae. We know your secrets. All of them." The swish of his black robes kicks up one of several piles of dust. It's the most recent, the second Sorcerer who Rian faced while I watched in hiding. Xantivus pauses and looks down at his fallen ally with a cold stare.

"Do something about that, won't you?" he says to the imp, who dives to the floor while Xantivus closes his eyes. A strange sensation comes over me as I watch a thin stream of shadow, like smoke, push away from him. The Mentalist in me recognizes it as a part of his mind, searching in silence. The smoke breaks into tiny particles, dissolving into the air, drifting out to find us.

Rian doesn't protest when I guide him backwards, away from the particles. He keeps his gaze locked on that same candle as the motes of dust float over us. Some of them are the Sorcerer, I know. They settle on Rian's robes, even here in the Half-Realm. They speckle the stone surface of my armor. The candle's flame gutters and dies, leaving us in darkness.

"*He knows you're here*," Rian pushes. He clings to me with one arm, able to stand mostly on his own, but stays close in the sudden pitch darkness.

Xantivus hisses a spell. Rian replies with his own, canceling out Xantivus's Revealer before it can take effect.

"Silence," Xantivus declares, and this time when he casts the Revealer, Rian is mute. His ward fails, and the Mentalist's spell meets its mark, pulling us from our hiding place in the Half-Realm. I wish Mercy to my hands and stalk toward our foe with Rian still leaning heavily on my arm for support.

The Sorcerer's satisfied smirk disappears behind the crook of his arm as he shields his face from Mercy's sudden blinding light. Beside him, the mounds of ash swirl rapidly under the imp's direction, molding into ghostly forms. The defeated Sorcerers solidify, coming back to life as strange golems of their former selves, made of ash and dust. They barrage us with spells, aiming mostly for Rian, who is helpless to cast a ward without his voice. He grasps his throat and then thrusts his hand forward, trying to use the collected light he'd gathered to stop the missiles of stone and acid which spear toward us, but it isn't enough to block them all.

I shove him behind me to shield him from the attacks, and their stone missiles and orbs of acid crack against Mercy's blade and my bracers, bursting into clouds of mist and dust that sting my eyes and burn my throat. I duck my head, coughing, and when I look up again, Xantivus is standing right in front of me. His eyes lock onto mine, wild and maddened and black with Mark. I try to look away, but the veins of tendrils which stretch across the whites of his eyes into his pupils hold my stare locked to his.

In an effort to fight his grip, I step back, stumbling into Rian. My hands fly up, gripping my sword, and Mercy's light flashes between us as I swing it hard at the Mentalist, breaking his gaze and slicing through his wards.

"*Rian*," I push, and he circles his arm around my waist to let me know he's all right.

Xantivus advances again and I turn my face from him and swing, but his eyes are everywhere I look, taunting me, pulling me in.

"I have you," he says with deep satisfaction. Furiously, I slash upward with Mercy into the space where I think he is. My sword meets another with a clang. Mercy's light floods the space around me so brightly, it burns my eyes. I duck away, shielding my face, gasping for breath.

My attacker is relentless. Despite my efforts, it drives me further away until I fall. When I catch myself, my hand meets soft grass and mud. The sound of a crowd rushes to my ears, disorienting me. Someone calls my name, cheering. I squint away from the sun into the crowded stands of the arena. Somewhere close by, two horses thud the ground in a dance of battle. My mother's sword clashes against Dar's battle axe.

I tear my attention from the fray and scramble to my hands and knees, where a dozen rings lay scattered across the grass. I stare at them in disbelief and squeeze my eyes shut. I try to convince myself this is wrong, that it isn't happening, but the roar of the crowd and the grass underneath me are too real to deny. I stare at the sword in my grip in disbelief.

Mercy is gone. In its place is my first real sword, the one Da gave me on my sixteenth birthday. My hands are gloved in leather and my arms are covered in chain mail, not the beautiful fairy armor gifted to me by Iren. The gold and blue surcoat of His Majesty's Elite pools on the ground at my knees. Dazed, I snatch up a handful of rings from the grass and push myself to my feet.

As I stand up I'm aware of Dacva charging me. His sword is raised, his teeth are bared ferociously, his battle cry lost among the roaring crowd. I'm so disoriented, I barely have time to shove the rings into my surcoat and raise my sword before he's upon me, slashing furiously.

I remember this battle. I know how it ended. Dacva and I fought each other while Mum and Dar battled on horseback. In the end, I was wounded but Margy's ring was the only one in the count. I won and was named a squire, while Dacva lost and suffered Dar's punishment.

This time, it plays out differently. A horse screams in the distance as Dacva's sword pierces my shoulder. I watch in disbelief as

Mum's mount buckles underneath her and falls to the side, pinning her beneath it.

"Mum!" I scream. My doubts about the reality of the scene disappear, pushed out by my need to save her as Dar looms over her with his axe raised. I shove Dacva aside with a slash to his leg and race across the pitch toward my mother, but Dar's axe falls before I can get there, and Mum's scream for mercy is cut short. The crowd goes silent as Dar holds his bloodied axe aloft in victory.

Dacva catches up to me. He grabs my braid and yanks me back. Margy calls my name in the distance. King Tirnon shouts for the match to stop. Redemption ignores his commands. Dar charges toward me, tossing aside his axe in favor of a lance. I let my sword drop to the grass in surrender, but he doesn't stop.

I reach into my surcoat and pull out a single ring. Oddly, it's the ring Margy gave me at the end of the battle, the one which won me the match. Its purple ribbon is frayed and stained with blood from my shoulder wound. I wonder at it as the hoof beats of Dar's horse thunder closer.

When I look up into Dar's helm, the face that leers back at me isn't his, but Diovicus's. He lowers his lance to aim for my heart and I know there's nothing I can do. I will never be a squire, never become a knight. My past is changed. The unthinkable has happened. My mother is dead. I close my eyes, defeated, and wait for the strike.

It hits me hard, driving through the amateurish chain mail armor, boring into my chest, straight into my heart. The pain sears through me and I feel myself lifted from the pitch, dangling.

"*AZAELI HAMMERFEL YOU SNAP OUT OF IT RIGHT NOW!*" Flitt's high-pitched squeak screams into my head and the burning in my chest eases slightly as I somehow manage to catch my breath. Dar's lance is gone, the cheering of the crowd has faded. Shadow spills over me, pushed out by Flitt's constant effort as she smacks my face repeatedly with tiny, sticky hands. Her diamond vibrates so intensely that its power burns my chest, right at the spot where I thought Dar's spear had struck me.

"Rian," Shush cries, and a torrent of wind rushes ahead of me. I blink my eyes rapidly to adjust to the shift in my reality. The gust breaks apart the resurrected piles of dust, sweeping them up into the shadows of the rafters. Sticky hands continue slapping my face as Flitt endlessly barrages my mind with my own name.

"*I'm here,*" I push to her, jumping to my feet with Mercy in hand.

"*Took you long enough,*" she pushes back. "*Hurry, before they finish!*"

My vision finally clears enough to see Rian across the room, lying on the floor. Xantivus and the imp hover over him, and a strange glow of light blue energy streams between Rian's motionless body and something in the imp's hand.

"She's free," the imp warns Xantivus.

"A moment too late," the Mentalist chuckles. He sweeps his hand over Rian, and the stone floor beneath him starts to rumble. Shush bolts toward the Sorcerer, screaming a torrent of wind as Rian sinks into the stone. The imp tumbles away, the object in his hand glowing as it absorbs the rest of the strange blue light. Shush blows a gust toward it and it tumbles free to skitter across the floor toward me. I gasp and snatch it up, then dive at the floor where Rian disappeared.

"Rian!" I scream, slamming my fists into the stone as Shush and Flitt face Xantivus.

"*Azi,*" the object in my hand replies with Rian's voice. Shocked, I look down and open my fist to find Margy's ring resting there, the bloodied ribbon swaying gently in Shush's breeze.

"Rian?" I whisper in disbelief. The ring buzzes and glows softly with that same blue light.

"*Where am I?*" he asks.

"Trapped!" the imp cackles, snatching the ring from my hand before I even know he's there. I growl, flinging myself to tackle him, and the wretched creature vanishes the moment I would have reached him. I swipe at the air around me, desperate to grab the filthy thing, but he's gone, disappeared into darkness. Across the room, Flitt and Shush yelp in surprise. Everything goes quiet, and I don't have to look in their direction to know that Xantivus is gone, too.

"Rian," I whisper, pressing my hands to the stone that sucked him in. Its surface is solid and unchanged, like nothing ever happened. Flitt drifts to the space between my thumbs and kneels, and Shush settles beside her.

"He's in there," Flitt whispers. "Trapped in the stone."

"Not all of him, though," Shush says mournfully. "They have his mind in that ring."

"Why?" I whisper, watching my tears splash on the worn stone. "Why would they do this? I don't understand."

I sit back on my heels, pressing my palms into my eyes, trying to make sense of what just happened. What was real, and what wasn't? My thoughts and memories swirl around me like cards scattered by the wind. My reality feels cracked and unreliable. I try to collect myself, but all I can think of is Rian. Rian, trapped in the stone beneath us, smothered and suffocating in the dark. I can't help the panic that rises in my chest at the thought of it.

"Rian," I cry, raising Mercy above my head. I drive the point of my sword into the stone, ignoring Flitt and Shush's warnings not to. Its tip glances off, jarring my arms and shoulders.

"You can't get him out of there like that," Flitt explains. "We need to get that ring back."

"That's the only way," Shush whispers.

"But why?" I ask again, unable to stop the flood of tears that slip down my cheeks into my collar. "How could I let this happen?" I choke.

"They know the Dawn is close," Flitt explains, smearing away the tears from my neck and settling into my pauldron. "They know our victory is nearing. They know who we are. Champions of Light. They'd rather keep us here, distracted from our quest to restore Brindelier and claim the Wellsprings."

"Determined," Shush whispers.

"They know you and Rian are inseparable," Flitt explains. "So, they made a game to keep you occupied."

"A game?" I shout in disbelief.

"We should have seen it coming," Shush whispers.

"We should have known it when they lured you into the sea," Flitt mutters apologetically. "They scolded us at home. After we were healed up, we really got an earful."

"It was our job to be mindful of that sort of thing," Shush whispers. "To keep track of you and keep you safe."

"I'm really sorry, Azi," Flitt flies up and pats my cheek again.

"They'll pay," I growl, my hands curling into tight fists around Mercy's hilt. On one knee, I lay the sword on the stone between myself and Rian. I squeeze my eyes shut and tears of rage spill down my cheeks as I imagine the might of the fairy queen and the Muse of Light, Eljarenae behind me. How foolish these Sorcerers were, to draw me into the heart of their lair and taunt me by taking away the one person who matters to me more than anything.

"This is no game." I hiss my threats into the shadows. "When I'm through with this place, they're going to regret every move they ever made against us. When I find them, they'll know the Dawn is no force to toy with. Their cruelty, their evil, wretched existence will be smothered by the Light. The shadow of Sorcery will be reduced to a distant memory. They'll wish they never thought to challenge us."

Chapter Eighteen

SORCERER HUNTING
Azi

My oath to Rian and his torturers settles on my shoulders like a mantle. I push myself to my feet and stalk toward the iron door, prepared to rain my fury over this keep and everyone in it.

"*Whoa, whoa, whoa,*" Flitt and Shush push to me in unison. Both fairies swoop into my path, holding their hands up to stop me.

"*You can't just stalk out after them,*" Flitt pushes.

"*We need to make a plan,*" Shush agrees.

"I'm tired of planning," I growl aloud. "I'm tired of being sensible and methodical while they attack us with chaos and cruelty."

"Shhh!" they both hiss frantically, their gazes flicking into the shadows above.

"*Shadows have ears,*" Shush pushes. "*They're listening.*"

"*You can't think that way, Azi,*" Flitt warns. "*The more you act out of revenge and hate, the easier it'll be for them to get you.*"

"Get me?" I glare. "They have me already, Flitt. Or haven't you noticed?"

I grab the slender handle of the door, wrought in the shape of a striking serpent, and Flitt lands on my gloved hand.

"*Argh! Here we go. Dunderhead Azi again!*" she pushes in frustration. "*Just, listen to us before you go charging off to kill people!*"

"*Think about it,*" Shush pushes. "*They had you. They could have killed you, both of you, but they didn't. They know you'll go searching for that ring. They're expecting it.*"

"I don't care," I push back. "*Every breath we spend standing here arguing is one breath Rian is forced to take trapped—*" I stop, gasping.

"No," I whisper. "How can he breathe in there? He'll die!"

"Shh!" Flitt hisses again, and Shush darts to my face and presses his long, cool hands over my lips.

"Don't think about that," he pushes. "*What they did, it's like a sleep spell. His body will stay alive, and he won't even feel like he's trapped. The rest of* him, *the part that can feel, is in that ring. That's why I said we have to get it back. Remember?"*

"*Yes, but how can you be sure he's alive? That he's not suffocating?"*

While he and I fall into the question game, Flitt slowly pries my fingers free of the door handle, one by one.

"*The same way you're sure,"* Shush replies. "*I can feel it. Now, can you think of a way to locate that ring other than by fighting aimlessly through the Dusk's main stronghold?"*

The solution comes to me as Flitt guides me by the hand, away from the door, back to the stone encasing my love. She pulls me down to it again and presses my fingertips to it.

"*Close your eyes,"* she pushes. "*Try to find him."*

I fight my instinct to jump up and rush out swinging, and instead try to follow the fairies' guidance. At first, despite Shush's reassurances, all I can imagine is Rian lying beneath me in the stone, unable to see or move. Panic grips me at the thought of it. My breath comes in rapid bursts and then stops altogether until my lips tingle and the rest of me goes numb. I feel myself falling, slipping away from here, into darkness and emptiness.

"*She can be him,"* Stubs's voice echoes into my mind from a distant time and place.

I suddenly wish for Valenor and remember what he said when I was straddling his world and this one, that he's shut out of this place. Whatever I'm doing, now that I'm fully here, I have to do it without his help.

"*Try to find him, Azi,"* Shush pushes to me.

I practice again like I did in the Dreaming and before that at the Circle hatch between our rooms, sending out a thread of myself, searching for Rian's thoughts. The feeling of panic leaves me, set free the moment the part of my mind leaves my body. It swirls in threads of golden light, spearing into the darkness, winding through the mouth of the serpent door handle and into the corridor beyond.

Flitt's warmth at the crook of my neck grounds me. Her hand on my jaw centers me. It's an odd feeling to be in two places at once. I think of Rian being cruelly forced from his own body this way, and imagine how much worse it must be for him.

"*Shift your thinking,"* Flitt pushes. "*Don't fall into darkness and anger. Look what you can do now, Azi! It's amazing!"*

"*Focus,"* Shush pushes.

I listen to the fae as the golden thread weaves through dark corridors, reaching out for Rian. The memory of his dream that morning when I tried to wake him guides me. I imagine the light of the Fairy Queen's palace surrounding me. The reality of our surroundings is the complete opposite. There are no torches lining the walls. There's no life anywhere. The black stone and metal doors that enclose these narrow passages are dark, forbidding, and endless.

The shadows seem to press on the thread of my mind in an effort to snuff it out. I remember Kenrick's warning, that if I wasn't careful, this wandering part of my mind could be lost. I wonder whether the Dusk knows what I'm doing. Are they watching me? Will they attack?

"*Azi,*" Flitt pushes. Her light bursts into my thoughts, pushing away my fear. My forehead tingles where the light of Eljarenae touched me. Both give me courage.

I press further, trusting in myself and my friends. I know he's somewhere close, just out of reach, right at the end of the path my thread is taking. I can feel his presence like a beacon, calling to me from the center of hopelessness.

My thread pauses at a metal door decorated with intricate designs. At eye level, a circle of six skulls surrounds the same design on the spindle coin from Brindelier: A spire in the clouds with an outspread hand at the top of it.

Through the door, I sense Rian's watchful presence tinged with fear. I can feel his calculating quiet so strongly that it comes to me like a vision of him: his hazel eyes distant, his mind focused, his hands balled into fists, tucked inside the long sleeves of his robes.

I guide my thread through the keyhole, careful not to go in so far that my golden light might be seen. It's dark within, and even with the aid of Flitt and Eljarenae's light to strengthen me, my head begins to throb. The shadows obscure what's inside like it's behind a thick veil, and I have to concentrate hard to see anything beyond it.

"*What's there?*" Flitt pushes. Her voice in my mind is a reminder of the split I'm experiencing. It makes me dizzy until I remember her advice and push away the negative. What I'm doing is powerful and unique. I'm doing it for love, for light. The thought bolsters me as I send myself back through the thread to watch through the keyhole.

"*A room paneled in black,*" I push to Flitt and Shush, making every effort to see through the darkness. Describing it to them helps me stay in my body and remember I'm not there, but here. That disconnect keeps me calm, somehow, and for that I'm grateful. A part of me knows if not for that, I'd be thrown into a sheer panic over what I'm seeing at the end of my thread.

"*It's a round room, a tower room. An enormous hearth stands right in the center of it, but there's no fire. Instead, there's a churning darkness that seems to swallow up everything around it. A Void.*" I shiver. "*There are two Sorcerers. Xantivus is watching Sybel do something. There are three pillars in between the hearth and a large slab. One of them has a sealed bottle on it, filled with something green and glowing. The second holds the wand, Aster. On the third is the ring. Rian. Sybel is hovering over him, whispering in Mage tongue. She's flanked by six skeletons dressed in plate armor. The slab has a man lying on it. It's Richter, the king we defeated in Hywilkin. He isn't alone. Eron is laid out next to him. They're both stripped of clothing and neither of them is moving.*"

"*Find Stellastera,*" Rian's voice booms as clearly in my mind as if he was standing right beside me.

Xantivus's eyes snap to the door. Before he sees me, I pull my thread away. It reels back like a snapped fisherman's line, jolting into me with a stinging force that sends me stumbling backward. Shush blows a breeze that catches me, helping me regain my footing. The vision of Sorcerer, Necromancer, and Void looming over Rian burn into my mind like a branding iron. Flitt drifts to look at my face, and she and Shush exchange frightened glances.

"*The wand is Aster, the ring is Rian, the bottle…*" Shush trails off thoughtfully.

"*I've felt energy like that before,*" I push. "*It was an offering from a Wellspring.*"

"*Oh, no,*" Flitt pushes. "*That's bad.*"

"*We have to stop them,*" Shush agrees, "*before they finish that ritual.*"

"*We have to find Stellastera first,*" I push to them both with Rian's voice still echoing through me.

I reach for the serpentine latch expecting them to protest, but neither of them does. Flitt plunges into my hauberk and Shush perches on the edge of my shoulder guard beside her. I yank the door open and feel the shift as one of them pulls us into hiding in the Half-Realm.

A thousand thoughts enter my mind as I creep into the darkness of the hallway. They must be aware of us, they must know we're coming. What if this was all a trap? Some elaborate set-up to get me alone in these halls? What if they can see me right now, what if they're watching? Where is everyone? How can I win against a keep full of the worst evil the Known Lands have ever seen? What if I was wrong in hearing Rian, and that was a trick to distract me from rescuing him? What if I find Stellastera too late, and Rian is lost?

"*Filling your head with what-ifs is a dangerous slope to slip down,*" Flitt pushes with a burst of colored light into my mind, and I scold myself internally for letting the shadows affect me.

"*Stop that, too,*" Shush pushes, chuckling, and I growl in frustration.

"*We've got to be vigilant,*" Flitt's gentle tone lifts my spirits. "*I believe in you!*"

Flitt's glow blends with Mercy's as we venture into the depths of the lair, but neither does much to guide our way. The shadows here are entities all their own which fight to prevent any light from traveling farther than a few paces ahead.

I'm not confident enough in my abilities to try to search for the Muse with my mind and leave myself less aware of my surroundings out here in the open, so instead I try my best to push away feelings of doubt and search for some shift or change in the energy around me.

"*Can you feel her at all?*" I ask the fae.

"*Stellastera?*" Flitt asks. I nod. "*We can try, but I imagine anywhere she is must be shielded from magic.*"

"*Flitt's right,*" Shush pushes. "*The only way to imprison a Muse is to keep them from their element.*"

"*Yep! Being kept from magic will weaken her, and make her easier to control.*"

I think of the iron room where Bryse imprisoned Eron in Orva. "*But Aster could pass right through that iron door where Eron was being held, remember? How could she do that in Hywilkin, where magic was so sparse?*"

"*She pulled magic from the Wellspring where she had been trapped. She channeled it into the wand, so Rian could use it.*"

"*She probably could have escaped that, if she really wanted to,*" Shush pushes.

"*But Muses are still human in a way,*" Flitt explains. "*And she must have been in and out of hope in her prison.*"

"*And now she's prisoner again.*" I scowl.

"*I don't think the Dusk will give up on her so easily,*" Shush pushes. "*Imagine having someone who can bend all the might of magic to her will on your side.*"

"*The trick,*" Flitt agrees, "*is getting her on your side.*"

The conversation reminds me of a deep chasm in an icy mountain, where we freed Valenor from his cruel prison. His friendship has been invaluable to us since then. Kaso Viro, too.

"*I see now why Rian wants us to find her first,*" I think, and Flitt and Shush both nod their agreement.

"*We have to find a place where—*" Shush's suggestion is interrupted by a chill shriek which pierces my skull like an arrow. My knees weaken and wobble, and I stumble sideways and cling to the wall to steady myself.

"Banshee," Flitt squeaks, and as though she had been waiting for the introduction, the ghostly figure of a woman appears a few paces in front of us. She shrieks again, and bile rises in my throat. The sound is like death itself. It makes my blood curdle and my mouth go dry. I want to turn and flee, convinced her next attack will be the last sound I hear.

Shush responds to her screech with one of his own, and she tumbles backward into the darkness. Flitt's attack is a concentrated beam of light which spears into the darkness and bursts into a spray of color. The banshee shrieks again, but this time it's a wail of pain rather than rage.

My companions' quick thinking and powerful attacks snap me out of my terror. I charge her with Mercy raised high, and slash the ghostly form in two. She disappears in wisps of bleak, gray energy which hang around us eerily and slowly fade away.

"Yes!" Flitt cheers. "*Did you see that? Did you see what I did?*"

"*I saw it,*" I push. "*You learned a new trick.*"

"*That's not the only one! Wait and see!*" She giggles and settles in my pauldron again.

We creep in silence for a while, our hackles raised, ready to take on whatever lurks beyond the reach of our light. Often, I catch myself sinking into dark thoughts, fearing for Rian, wondering why it's so quiet, feeling hopeless that we have no idea what we're looking for in our search for Stellastera. When the fairies notice, they start chattering in my head, filling me with purpose and strength, encouraging me to keep going deeper into Sixledge.

The place is a maze of doors and hallways, some so narrow one would have to turn sideways to allow someone else to pass. It's these that make me the most uneasy, knowing any foe we'd face in such a small space would be nearly impossible for me to fight with my sword. Still, we go deeper into the winding passages, listening at door after door, searching for some sign that Stellastera might be behind one of them.

It's in the narrowest of these that our enemies begin to appear. The first one is a young woman, probably my age, whose perfect light brown skin is defiled with the Mark up to her earlobe.

At first she's unaware of our presence, and I take a step backward to avoid her. The passage is quiet, and she's so absorbed in her book she's almost dazed. I jog further back, my plate boots ringing on the stone in the otherwise silent space. In her dreamy state, she hears. Her head snaps up. She closes her book and narrows her eyes. When she raises her hand to cast the spell I can only imagine will be a Revealer, I think fast.

With golden threads, I reach to her hand and lower it. I back her up against the wall and keep her flattened there, and I slip past. As I do, I look into her eyes and pull quickly at the threads of her memories. My thought is to take one away, just this quick moment of our meeting. I almost manage it, but Flitt's warning bursts through my head.

"*You can't! Remember?*"

I know she's right. Kenrick warned about it. Destroying a memory is an evil, forbidden act. I let it go and rush past, hoping the girl will think it some fluke of a ward or some mystery best left alone, but she doesn't. As soon as we're past, she whispers the Revealer.

When we're exposed, she calls out in a language that sounds native to Elespen. I rush forward, binding her hands and mouth with threads, and meet her eyes with mine. I thrust Mercy against her throat, holding her in both mind and body.

"Stellastera," I demand, keeping her gaze, pushing the sense of the Muse of Magic into her. "Where is she?"

"*She wouldn't know, Azi,*" Flitt pushes. "*She's just a baby Sorceress.*"

I don't listen to Flitt. I push deeper into the girl's thoughts, slipping past the threads of her memories, looking into each one for some small clue that would lead us to our goal. The threads grow dimmer the deeper I go, past family and loved ones into moments of terror and abuse.

The darkest times take place here, within the walls of Sixledge. She was a witness to such evil and cruelty. I watch as she was abducted from her home with so many others, and how the Sorcerers who stole her broke her down to build her up again. I see her life since she's been here, her empowerment, her nurtured talent.

Her lust for power started when she thought she might use their teachings to break free of this place, but since then she has faced so much cruelty and despair that her hopes are only shriveled, blackened remains of memories long forgotten. As her power grew and she became more and more consumed with the elation of it, her hopes dwindled to nothing. I wonder how many more like her are here.

The part of me inside her mind pokes at the threads with the tip of Mercy, and like I did in my mother's mind, I carefully free the light from the shadows and fling these dark thoughts of hopelessness and defeat far into the distance of her mind. I fight my way through several more, freeing them, allowing them to shine and brighten.

When I finally drift back into myself, the Sorceress blinks at me in disbelief. Tears of gratitude spill down her cheeks. She whispers her thanks in that same strange language while the tendril of Mage Mark that had curled up to her ear fades. Her book falls to the floor and she takes my hand, pulling me urgently along.

"Where are we going?" I whisper, and she turns and presses her finger to her lips to quiet me. Our eyes meet for a quick flash, and I see our goal inside them. Stellastera, sealed behind a door of iron. Its face is carved with runes of warning. The center of it bears a horrific, snarling ghoul bearing fangs which drip with real poison.

A thunder of footsteps approaches from the darkness, and our new ally skids to a stop at the edge of the shadows. I don't see what it is that strikes her. It comes too fast. She falls instantly and they're on me, swarming like bats.

The black, wing-like forms batter my face and scratch at my head, screeching with eerie battle cries that make my head spin and disorient me. I try to fight them off, but the passageway is still too narrow for Mercy to be of any use. Beside me Shush screams, calling up a squall that sends the creatures scattering back into the shadows. At the same time, Flitt beams her light, allowing me to see where the passage opens up just a few paces ahead.

At the edge of Flitt's glow, a pair of Sorcerers stand waiting for us. One of them raises his arms to cast. His partner places his hands on them as if channeling their energy together. The resulting spell is slow-acting. A purple, oozing slime creeps across the floor toward us. The stone it touches hisses and sizzles as the slime corrodes it. It reaches our new ally, now motionless, and devours her arm. Shush screams another squall, but nothing happens. The slime stretches from wall to wall in the corridor, and as long as I am tall. Behind it, it leaves a hole of rotten, crumbling stone.

"*I learned a new trick or two, too,*" Shush pushes to me as I back away from the ooze. "*Don't be alarmed.*"

He dives behind me and a gust of wind billows my cloak. My feet lift from the floor as I fly, carried by the wind, across the devouring ooze and am set down gently on the other side.

The pair of Sorcerers move to cast another spell, but Flitt throws out a ball of light from my shoulder which bursts in front of them in an explosion of tiny, colorful lights. They drift in strange patterns which seem to enthrall the Sorcerers, mesmerizing them into a stupor.

"That's new, too!" Flitt giggles. I blink away the effects easily and charge both Sorcerers at once. Neither of them flinches when I thrust Mercy, piercing through their wards first, and then their robes. Both crumple to the ground with barely a sound aside from a final, shuddering breath.

"It's disturbing how easy that was," I mutter.

"That was easy?" Shush whispers, pointing at the path of destruction behind us. I turn to follow his gaze past the fallen Sorcerers and dancing lights, beyond the sizzling hole in the stone, past the acidic lump of goo that was the Sorceress I tried to save, and shiver.

"Maybe not," I whisper, horrified by the goo, regretful that I couldn't save her from her fate. I stand in silence for a moment, thankful for the aid she gave us.

"At least now I know what to look for." I say quietly. "We must be going in the right direction if they were here to try and stop us."

I look at each of them in turn, showing them the same poisoned door the Sorceress showed me. They nod in understanding, and together we slip back into the Half-Realm to venture further into the shadows of Sixledge.

Chapter Nineteen

VELU'S TEMPLE
Tib

One at a time, the Savariktas' huge mounts clomp to the root platform. The creatures bow. Their riders dismount, gracefully sliding down the beasts' massive front legs. Each one gets a cheer from the crowd, and each one joins in song as the drums beat faster. They line up side by side, facing us, their mounts behind them.

While Akkoti introduces them to us, I stare at the huge creatures. They're called *sava*, Akkoti says. They tower over their riders at least twice their height. Massive. Quietly powerful. Each one rests its long trunk on its rider's shoulder. There's a magic between them. A connection, like Faedin. As a group, they bow to us. Akkoti says we should bow, too, so we do. Some of the riders eye Opal with curiosity or hesitation. None of them asks about her though. They trust and respect the Donas. There's an understanding between them.

With the greeting done, the riders and their *sava* join the celebration. They mingle with the crowd which swarms them the same way they swarmed me. It isn't long before they're swallowed up by groups of their family and friends, and the only sign of them is the enormous shell backs of the *sava* bobbing through the sea of villagers like boats on the ocean.

The song goes on and on. They dance and sing through the afternoon. The noise thunders into the canopy above, and even the birds seem to sing along. Saesa sits on the edge of her throne, tapping her feet. She seems like she wants to join in, but I imagine we're not supposed to.

We don't bother trying to talk. We'd have to scream our throats raw and still we probably wouldn't be able to hear each other. After a while, it's a little irritating. I'm tired of sitting. I want to get up. Take action.

The whole thing reminds me of the Ring at Kythshire, where the fae would celebrate wildly around the circle for hours on end. It's the same sort of energy.

That gets me thinking. I scan through the crowd with my healed eye, searching for magic. As I figured, it's everywhere. It's strongest around the huge *sava*. Their riders glow with battle magic and wards, too. The villagers hold their own power.

Their songs swirl around them like veils. The louder and faster they sing, the stronger the magic. Their voices meld and glow, pushing protections to the tops of the trees and out past the borders of the village. For as far as they can be heard, the magic flows out in rivers.

I gaze as far as my healed eye will reach, through tree trunks and huge ferns and green underbrush. At the edge of their spell, the edge of the song, that heavy wall of mist looms. It pushes now and then, testing the villagers' power, searching for some small opening. The setting sun seems to encourage it. Its shadow seeps closer.

"And now, it is time for the closing ceremony," Akkoti shouts into my ear. "When it is through and night falls, we shall go with the riders to the temple, to greet mighty Velu."

She gestures behind us to the vine-covered temple. It's a lot more imposing at this time of day. The orange glow of sunset reflects like fire from the spaces between shadowy overgrown leaves. Even greater power lies there. Its magic surges from every crack in the stone, strong and forbidding.

I try to sense what's inside, but something blocks me from looking too deep. It makes me uneasy. I should be able to see, to know, what's there. The only sense I get is of something mighty. Bright. Green. Life.

Beside me, Kruti talks to Saesa. Opal lifts her head. Looks toward the temple. Blinks with heavy eyelids. Saesa strokes the small dragon's neck absently as she meets my gaze. I give her a slight nod of reassurance.

It may be powerful and forbidding, but I don't think there's any threat in life and light. We probably don't have anything to be afraid of. I hope. They can help us, and they need our help. That's what Akkoti said.

The Dona offers me her hand. Guides me to the edge of the root platform. Saesa and Kruti step forward, too. When the Donas start to chant in the villagers' language, I expect the singing to stop so they can listen. They don't, though. They raise their voices higher. Even the *sava* point their trunks to the sky and trumpet loudly.

A rush of energy flows from the temple behind us. It mixes with the voices. Strengthens them. Bolsters the protective power of their song. Pushes its borders further.

As the last sliver of sunlight disappears, the Donas' spell rushes over the village. Their magic hardens over the people's song like a bubble. It stretches to the far edges of the protections they've spent all day weaving with their voices. It freezes their magic in time, strengthening it. Wards. Invisibility. Confusion. Like a border spell. Like the protections Kythshire uses.

The temple's magic is a beam of glowing green light as it drifts from behind us into the crowd. At first they cheer, but as the magic settles, their voices slowly quiet. The celebration is over. The village is safe. Mothers carry children on their backs. Fathers clap each other's shoulders and say goodnight. They go to their huts. Peace settles over the tribe. My ears ring in the sudden quiet.

"And now," Akkoti says with reverence, "we join our riders to meet Velu."

As if summoned, the *sava* trudge to the village center. Their riders straddle their broad necks. Their spears are tucked away, into side harnesses. Kruti beckons to Saesa as the first *sava* bows to the platform's level, offering a leg to climb up on.

"You will ride the *sava* into Velu's temple," he explains. "You will be safe with Resai."

Resai offers his hand to Saesa from high atop the *sava*'s neck. Saesa hesitates, glancing at me. When I nod, she gathers her long orange silks around her and climbs up the creature's leg to sit behind the rider, tucked between his back and the creature's thick shell.

"*Evtu*, you will go with Meheli," Akkoti explains as the first *sava* stands and the one behind it comes to bow.

I scramble up its offered leg. Its skin is thick and gray. Stony, dry, wrinkled. Dry earth and mud crumble under my fingers as I pull myself up. Sit wedged behind Meheli, whose shoulders are so broad I can barely see around him.

He says something in their language and flashes a wide grin over his shoulder.

"Meheli insists you hold onto him, *Evtu*," Akkoti calls from the back of the third *sava*.

Almost too late, I wind my fingers into the loops of Meheli's straw belt. The sava lurches to its feet and I slip to the side, nearly falling off. Meheli reaches behind him and shoves me back to center, laughing.

Even Saesa seems to have a better handle on riding than I do. Her back is straight. Her arms are tight around her rider's waist. Her head is tipped to peer ahead at the temple. Opal stays still, like an ornament. Her eyes are closed. I guess she's sleeping.

Side-by side with Saesa's, my *sava's* steps are lumbering and heavy beneath me. As we ride two by two to the temple, his back pitches and rolls like a ship on heavy seas. I keep my grip with my legs. Try not to slide off.

"I've never even ridden a horse!" I shout to Saesa. She laughs.

The temple is bigger than it seemed from our thrones on the root platform. When we finally get to it, I realize why we had to ride the *sava*. The steps to the top of the overgrown pyramid are the height of a man. I'm a fair climber, but I doubt I would have been able to make it to the top. Especially not in this heat.

Even now that the sun has gone down, I'm dripping with sweat. I'm no stranger to heat, either. I grew up in Sunteri's desert, after all. But this heat is different. Thick with moisture. So heavy, it makes me feel as lumbering and slow as the *sava*.

They climb the steps effortlessly. The higher we go, the stronger I can feel the energy inside of this place. It's not a specific type of magic. It's every kind, mixed together. Familiar. Wild, like the vines that grow across the stone. Actually, the vines seem to glow with the same energy. It fills everything: riders, *sava*, Dona, leaves, trees. Even the air around us is thick with it.

We climb higher than the tops of the trees until all that's above us are the stars. The sky touching the horizon in the distance is red and angry. The land is dark. From this high, I can see the edge of the mist blanketing everything up to the bubble of magic set by the tribe and the Donas.

The final tier of the temple jabs the sky like a spear. Lower down, the temple was crumbled and overrun by vines. Up here, the stone looks like it was just carved today.

Pictures of dancing men and women, and animals baring pointed teeth decorate every bit of it. Sava, too, on hind legs, with their trunks curled over their heads. The open entrance to the inside is a huge, gaping mouth. A single eye is carved above it. It glows yellow, orange, and pink. I recognize the magic right away. It's like Iren and Aren in Kythshire. Like Avyn in Hywilkin. Guardian magic. Watcher.

It finally dawns on me. Why they sing all day to conceal it, to protect it. The Savarikta. Inside this temple is their source. The Wellspring of Elespen.

Saesa's *sava* approaches the eye. Its light beams over her rider first, then her and Opal. It looks at her for a long time, reading her mind, searching for her motivations. I watch images flash between them. Elespen, empty. Sha'Renell's sand fists flying. Us, all of us, sitting at Nessa's table. The Admiral's face. Nessa, fleeing the manse. Saesa saying farewell to her brother. Azi smiling at her. Azi disappearing with Rian from the Queen's court. My face. Margy in Kythshire. Skalivar giving her the opal. Saesa, flying on a dragon. Me, nearly dead on that giant leaf.

"Enter," a voice booms over us, and the eye closes.

Something strange happens as soon as the eye looks away. Opal swishes her tail, just once. I watch the spell creep over Saesa from the tip of it. A ward, a strong one. Meant to push out whatever influence we're about to face. A wall around her, to protect her. It's especially thick around her eyes and the top of her head.

Their *sava* disappears into the giant mouth, and mine steps up next. The eye opens again and reads my rider first. The images that flash between them are different. Dark, with only threads of greenish-yellow light. Like roots in the earth. They blur past in streaks, mixed with black. It feels forbidding to me. Closed off. Frustrated.

The eye's light moves from the rider to me. Its power is rich and complicated. Same as Aren and Iren and Avyn, it only takes a glance at me and knows right away who I am. Good thing, too, because I wasn't about to let it see into my head.

"Enter," the voice booms. The eye closes. We clomp into the darkness of the temple mouth.

Except, inside it's not dark at all. Once we're through the door, it's bright as midday. The huge, circular room is filled with pillars and columns carved like the inside of the Sorcerers' keep. Intricate patterns cover every surface, even the floor. At the center of the room, weaving in between the pillars, life-sized statues of sava on hind legs, standing in a line, raise their trunks over their heads just like in the carvings outside.

Strange music echoes around us. Chanting. Fast. High-pitched. Quiet, though. Distant. We lumber past the *sava* statues and Saesa and I crane our necks to look up at the towering creatures as they point their trunks up into the night sky way at the top of the dome.

In here, no one speaks. It's understood this isn't a place for talking. The magic is so thick. Almost overwhelming. It seeps from the walls and hangs heavy in the air around us.

The pillars and statues open to an alcove draped with all different shades of blue silks. Gold drips from the space: coins, chains, platters. Candles flicker in the puddles of silk. Offerings of fruit and teas pile up all around it on the floor. The *sava* bow to the alcove and our riders dismount and help us climb down.

It's not until my feet are on solid ground that I notice the child sitting cross-legged in the alcove high above, weighed down with all kinds of gold and jewels, adorned with the same silks that are draped down to the floor.

Her head is turned slightly to the side, but her wide eyes are locked on us. I can't help but stare at her. She's young. Probably six or seven. Her eyes are lined with thick black paint. Her slightly smiling lips are painted bright pink. I can't think of any way to describe her other than perfect.

She reminds me of Margy. A gift. Deep understanding. Peace. She raises her hands, palms facing us. They glow with soft blue light. The riders and *sava* step closer. The light that touches them cleans their skin and clothes. It washes away the dirt and grime. I allow it to touch me, and the cool breeze that grazes my skin wipes away the sweat and dirt of the jungle.

The riders leave their sandals here and Saesa's Dona instructs her to take off hers, too. Mine doesn't. I think she knows about my boots. Mevyn's tether. Good thing. I wouldn't have taken them off, anyway.

The next room is the same as this one, except the statues inside aren't *sava*. These are tall, spindly animals with necks longer than their bodies, like dragons. Except they're covered in spots and fur, not scales, and they don't have wings or horns. Their feet have two-toed hooves, like camels. A set of arms sprouts from their shoulders above their long front legs, and their tails are long like a monkey's.

One of them has been carved all the way at the top of one column, to look like it had climbed up to the ceiling with its strange set of arms and its long, gripping tail. Its head pokes out of the top of the dome, like it's peering up out of the jungle canopy.

It's impossible to walk past the statues and carved pillars without being a little awed. I wonder if these creatures are real, like the *sava*. They seem too strange to be, but in this place, I feel like anything is possible. I never imagined, those years ago crossing through this jungle on Cap's ship, that this is what was hidden by the thick green leaves and trees I watched as we sailed past.

We walk up to the second alcove, this one draped in pink, and I feel a shift in myself. It's not a spell or the result of any magic. It's a thought. A feeling. A peace, like Margy's. A trust. Hope for the Light. I wonder how many more places like this are out in the world, hidden away. Untouched. Pure. Amazing.

The child in this alcove holds the same pose as the first one. She's painted the same way, and just as thickly adorned with jewels, gold, and candles. This one offers healing, though, to the riders and the *sava*. Once that's done, we're guided by the Dona through another huge archway and down a wide set of stone stairs until we reach another room.

Just as bright as the first two had been, this room is completely undecorated. The walls are smooth, untouched stone. The ceiling opens completely to the sky, which is strange because I'm sure those circle rooms with the alcoves are above us.

In the center of the huge room is a hole in the floor big enough to fit a *sava*. Greenish light floods from it, spilling over the smooth walls and floor.

Saesa inches closer to me. Her hair and skin are washed grayish in the strange green light. Opal is still draped across her shoulders, sound asleep. Without a word, Saesa takes my hand. With the other, she points to the far end of the room, where a pointed golden arch frames a doorway of pure white, sparkling light. Something appears in front of it. A silhouette. A figure, tall and slender like an elf, with broad wings and some sort of bushy headdress.

"There is Velu," Akkoti explains. She sinks to her knees. Kruti does, too, and tugs at Saesa's silks until she does the same. Even the *sava* and their riders kneel. Nobody tells me to, so I don't. I don't know this Velu, and as great as this place seems to be, I'm not about to bow to someone I've never met.

"Velu is our sage, our connection to the Lifesap, our protector and our guardian. Velu is neither 'he' nor 'she'. Velu rises above mortal understanding of such things. Velu is a sacred presence. A mystic. Velu has touched the earth and sky, and commands the growth of trees, ferns, and vines. Velu guides our people with vast knowledge, love, and understanding. Velu protects us, past, present, and future."

Akkoti and Kruti tell us these things in unison. This is a practiced speech. A recitation. It's meant to inspire awe and respect. It's not really needed. Velu drifts forward, wings barely moving, feet hardly skimming the floor.

They're a fae, I think, but the magic in them is mixed with something even more mystical and powerful. As tall as two people at least, Velu looks down on us with a raised chin as they approach. The crown headdress Velu wears is gold, with an eye of pink and orange at the center. It's stuffed with real leaves, fronds, and vines that shimmer and drip with Lifesap like dew.

"Tib," Saesa hisses, tugging at my silk garb. It doesn't take much convincing. As the crown's eye gazes at us both, and Velu looks down their perfect nose, I sink slowly to my knees. I can't help but stare at the fae's gold-green skin, at the interesting spots of midnight blue that dot their face and neck, not like Mage Mark. More like the spots on a frog or a butterfly.

There's so much about Velu that's intriguing. A sense of caring and concern for their people. They aren't like the unpredictable fae who lord over their magic in Kythshire and Sunteri. They're not like the Mages and Sorcerers who selfishly suck up every bit of knowledge they can muster for their own gain.

Just kneeling in their presence, I understand. Respect. Velu respects the Source, which gives the Savarikta everything they need. It keeps them healthy and joyful. That joy comes out in song, and that song is a protection for the temple and Velu.

It's not like in Cerion, where magic is borrowed from Kythshire with so many rules and restrictions. It's not like in Sunteri, where the fae are forced to guard their source from the ever-thirsty Sorcerers of Zhaghen. It's not even like Ceras'lain, where the elves have had to build enormous walls to keep out invaders to guard their Wellspring. This place is too well hidden and too respected, and Velu is the reason for that.

The sage whispers over the *sava* and the Savarikta in their language, and an orb of green light floats up from the well. It drifts to our group and touches each of them. I can feel the magic: blessings of peace, power, strength, and wisdom.

While the orb distracts them, the eye of Velu's crown flicks over each of them. It pulls visions from the riders, learning about their discoveries. I get a sense of what it's doing, but I can't see exactly what it's seeing. The magic in here is too overwhelming. Picking out details is hard.

My boots tingle at this realization. That tingle creeps up from my toes through my legs into the rest of me. It charges me with clarity. Pushes away Velu's tricky enchantments.

This place is just like any other Wellspring. Velu is just like any other fae. These people are just like everyone else. My mouth goes dry. I push myself to my feet with the crown of my head still tingling. Velu turns to me wearing an expression between curiosity and offense.

"My name is Tibreseli Nullen-Ganvent," I announce.

"Tib!" Saesa hisses, tugging at my boot strap. I pull away from her. Take a step closer to Velu, whose chin goes even higher. The mystic's eyes are strange. Orange, pink, and yellow. No pupils, like Flitt's. Light fae.

Wings bearing huge eyes on the top section glare down at me, trying to intimidate. It doesn't work. The others are too enthralled by the green orb and the eye of the crown to notice me take a bold step forward. Only Saesa watches, slightly mortified.

"Steward of the Last," I declare. "Knifethrower, Dreamstalker, Bearer of the Guardian, Slayer of Shadows, Liberator of Valenor, The Dreamstalker, The Untouched, Key to the Skies."

Velu's expression is blank as those strange eyes look past their yellow-white nose tip and raised, perfect chin. Haughty. Arrogant. There's a long stretch of silence before the sage's attention switches from me to the others.

"My children," Velu says. The guardian's voice is perfect. Not too deep or too high. I watch the others shiver with pleasure at the sound of it. Even the *sava*. Even Saesa. While the sage's attention is on the Savarikta, I grasp Saesa's hand and pull her to her feet. Pull her a few paces away, while Velu speaks to the others in their language.

After what just happened, the adoration I felt, the warning from my boots, I'm not taking any chances around this Velu. I understand now, what I was admiring so much. Power. Beauty. The awe inspired by this place and its guardian.

Some of it is magical, but most of it is in its design. The majesty of the temple. The artistry of the pillars and statues. The beauty of the children in the alcoves. Even without a magical influence, it was easy to get drawn in by all of that.

I wonder what would happen to someone without my abilities. Without the protections Opal gave to Saesa. How captivated they'd be. How enraptured. And why? To keep people obedient? To force respect? I look at Akkoti, still kneeling, her forehead pressed to the floor. That's what would happen, exactly.

"Dreamstalker," Velu interrupts my thoughts. "Come."

Without waiting to see what we'll do, the mystic turns, drifts across the room to the golden archway, and disappears into the light.

"It is a great honor to be invited into the depths of Velu's temple," Akkoti whispers, looking up from her bow. "Go quickly, *Evtu*, and bask in the honor you've been given this day. Even we Dona are forbidden to venture further than this. Go," she urges me, smiling with pride. "Go, and when you return to the village, you will tell us all of the wonders you have experienced within."

With Saesa's hand gripped tightly in mine, I cross the huge room and step through the archway. The light inside is so bright my eyes water. Beside me, Saesa gasps. To her, it's blinding. Overwhelming.

I've seen this magic before, though. Flitt does it, too. It's just light. Nothing special. I squint into the glare, searching for Velu. With my healed eye, I finally spot the fae a few paces ahead. The sage is much smaller, though, in here. Not the imposing figure it was outside with the others.

In the wash of light, all I can make out are the eyes: two on the wings, one on the crown. They drift closer to me, emerging from the glare of light, and narrow to scowling slits.

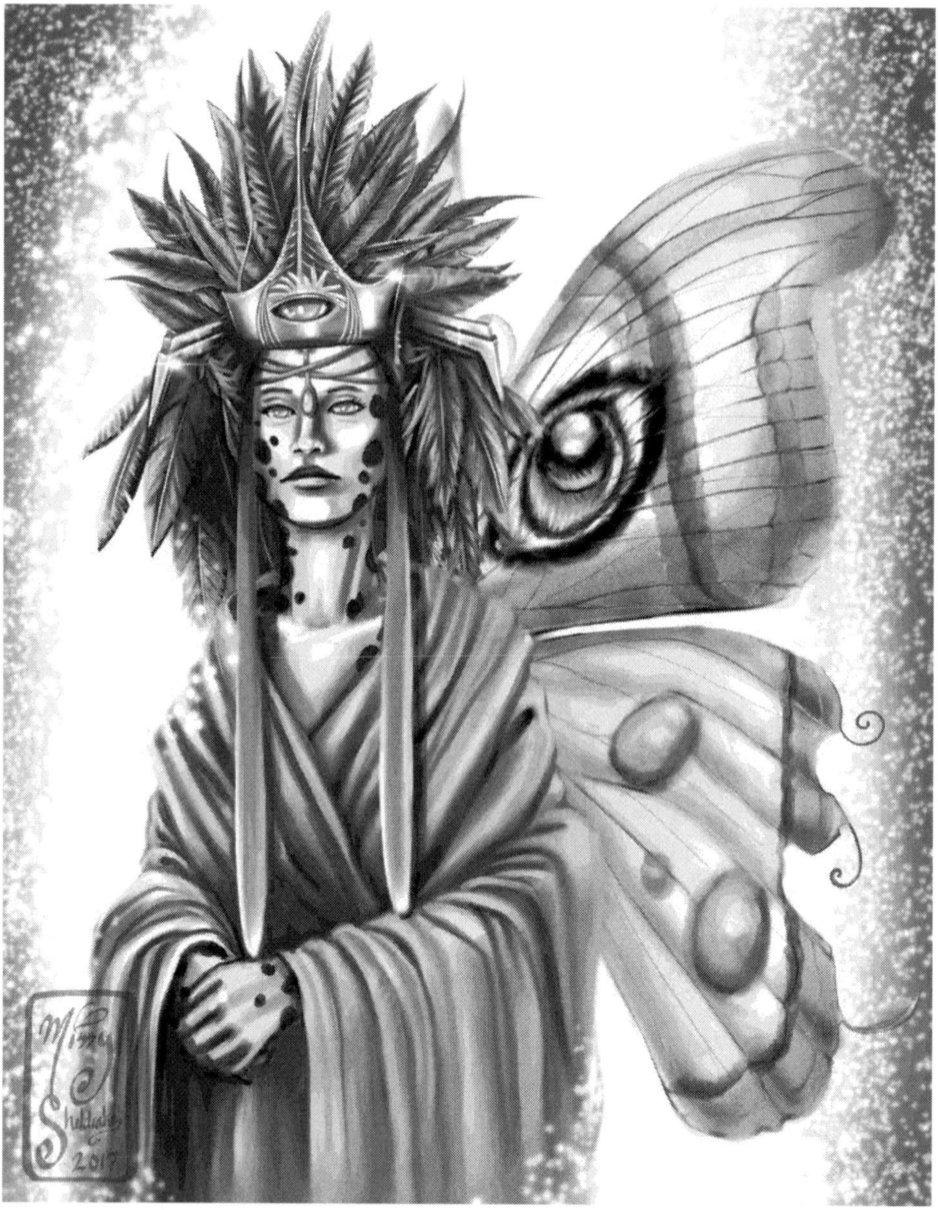

Chapter Twenty

MUSES' REACH
Tib

With Velu standing so close, I have stop myself from chuckling. The sage has changed their size again. They're just a bit taller than me now. Tall enough they can still look down their nose at me as they raise their chin.

They expect me to be intimidated. To be enthralled, like I should be. Like the strong powers in here command me to be. I'm not, though, and that just seems to irritate them more. I tuck Saesa behind me slightly, just in case that ward on her fails somehow.

"We know why you have come," Velu scoffs. "And you know of our obligations. Go, then, Dreamstalker. Take what is yours to claim. Do not expect me to simply hand it to you."

The tone of wry amusement in their voice prickles me with warning. Part of me wants to do exactly that. Get the offering. Get back to Cerion. I wonder quickly how much damage those quakes caused. Whether Margy got back to the palace without anyone realizing she was gone. Whether Nessa and the others really did flee the city.

"Why do you pause?" Velu chides. "If you can't be bothered to worship us, to wonder at our beauty, then what is the point of remaining in our presence?"

The mystic drifts across the room until they're surrounded by light. Hidden.

I can't help it. I laugh aloud. The mighty Velu is actually pouting. Saesa grabs my arm and whispers my name in warning.

"Ignoring us is a slight we can overlook," Velu says.

"Yeah, right," I mutter.

"Tib! Stop it!" Saesa whines, tugging me backwards.

"But mocking us? That is unforgivable."

The flash is like a bolt of lightning, quick and instant. It shouldn't affect me, but it does, somehow, throwing us both back with a furious force. I land on Saesa, who pushes me off.

"I told you not to," she hisses in annoyance.

"What is your problem?" I growl at Velu, drawing my dagger as I spring to my feet. Saesa grabs my hand and shoves the weapon back into its sheath. Her eyes meet mine. Fearful. Warning. Jungle green. They center me. Calm me.

"You. Outsiders," Velu spits. "The Lifesap belongs to the jungle. Despite what you might think, the Source is not infinite. We have given you a vial already, haven't we? Against our better judgment, we gifted it, based upon your silky words and broken promises. Yes, we gave in when we shouldn't have. Yet you steal it from beneath us. As if that were not insult enough, you return, sending a boy we cannot refuse to our temple to mock us."

"What?" I scowl. "I've never been here before, and I never stole anything from you."

"You deny, then, the poisoned blackening of the earth surrounding my village? The sapping of our outlying plants and trees? The disappearance of innocent creatures, including my own people, in the path of dark fogs? Fogs, mind you, which only appeared after your last agent left this place with our offering. We should not be surprised. We expected you would show no compassion for our tribe, the last of the Savarikta. We are aware of the greed of Sorcerers."

That last word makes it all fall into line in my head. Sorcerers. My thoughts race into the past, to the moment I ran with Vae in my arms through the circular room in the Sorcerers' keep. To the alcoves in the curved wall, where two of them held vials.

A gray one, Haigh. A green one. The same green as that orb and the light in the well. Elespen. That's what Velu is talking about. Sorcerers must have come here, somehow gotten through all of that outside, and talked their way into getting an offering.

"Of course. They have Elespen. Argh!" I groan and start to pace. "Why did we even come here? We could have gone there instead and stolen it from them. It would have been so much easier than dealing with all of this!"

"You see?" Velu scoffs. "You *are* a thief."

"You don't know anything about me," I shout. I take a few steps forward. Reach for my dagger again, and again Saesa shoves my hand back.

"Stop!" she yells. "Both of you, please, just stop. The answer is here if you'd just listen to each other."

"Insolent cur." Velu sneers at Saesa.

"Hey!" I warn. "Don't call her a cur!"

Saesa sighs and rolls her eyes.

"Tib. Listen. Velu obviously doesn't trust anyone from the outside, and can you blame them? It sounds like the last run-in they had was with a Sorcerer. That's all they know." She turns to Velu and gives a slight bow.

"Velu, Tib and I are just as against Sorcerers and their workings as you are. We, too, are concerned by the dark fog and the disappearances. To the north of here, there is an entire city cloaked with it, and everyone has vanished."

"They are not our concern," Velu huffs.

"Maybe not, but your own villages and creatures are, right? It's all connected," Saesa explains.

"What would you have me do?" Velu looks away, into the light. "Our *sava* exhaust themselves searching for any resolution, and find nothing. The fog encroaches daily, creeping ever closer, threatening our village and our temple. Our Dona receive no visions to fight against it. Our *kipta* have vanished within it, as have their riders.

"When we make efforts to reach their essence through the roots and the flow of the Lifesap, we find nothing. We have tried on our own to drive the chaos back. We have even left the temple, a forbidden act, only to find our own light cannot touch it. It surrounds us above and below the ground, and there is no recourse. We are preparing for the inevitable."

"What? You're giving up? Some mighty leader you are," I growl.

"Tib. Shut. Up!" Saesa cries, shoving me back. She turns to Velu. "We know about the Dusk, and we're willing to help. Your Dona saw something in us, didn't they? If they didn't, they wouldn't have allowed us to meet with you. They knew we could help."

"Don't go too far, Saesa," I warn under my breath. The last thing we need are more promises and pacts with the fae. Things are complicated enough as it is.

"How precious. You think you are special, do you? That you could possibly understand the plight we face? That you have capabilities beyond my own and those of my people?" Velu snorts in a very undistinguished way. "Get out of my sight, both of you."

Saesa takes a step toward the fae, and I grip her arm tightly to keep her from getting drawn in. She calls out to the light where Velu hides, "Please, if you would just—"

"Get what you came for, and leave!" Velu's shout causes the walls around us to rumble with the power of their voice.

I don't waste any time. I pull Saesa across the room, toward the draw of the Wellspring. The light blinds me, but my healed eye sees a path of glowing green and I follow it with Saesa in tow. She clings to my shoulder as we inch past Velu, whose rage I can feel rolling off them like steam from a boiling pot.

"Just hold on to me," I mutter to Saesa, "and keep moving."

"You shouldn't have provoked them," Saesa whispers.

"Quiet," I reply, pulling her through the alcove on the opposite side of the room from where we entered. Velu's light dims right away. We turn together to look back the way we came, and are greeted with the same blinding light inside the arch.

"Look at that," Saesa whispers. "The light doesn't spill out into this room. How strange."

"Yeah," I agree, waving my hand across the surface of the light. "Wards, probably." I try to make sense of what is magic and what isn't, and it makes my head spin. Everything here is soaked in it. Drenched with magic. We turn to look into this new space and gasp.

"What is this?" Saesa asks, wide-eyed.

"Stepwell," I reply. "We had them in Sunteri, in the desert. It's so dry there, they'd have to build these deep steps into the earth to reach water."

We shuffle to the edge of the walkway and peer down to the sparkling green Wellspring shimmering at least a dozen stories below. A maze of zig-zagging steps leads the way from top to bottom in an upside-down pyramid that mirrors the shape of the outer temple.

"How do we get down there?" Saesa asks. "None of the steps match up."

With my healed eye, I peer along the many paths we can take, searching to see if any of them are magically disguised or changed in any way. Saesa follows my gaze, while on her shoulder Opal snores quietly.

"Something feels wrong in here," Saesa whispers. I don't answer, even though I agree.

I trace countless paths of steps, bridges, arches, and doorways leading to the Wellspring at the bottom, but each one seems to end in a dead-end. The silence in the vast, dark space is deafening, and after a while the sound of blood pounding in my ears mixed with Opal's snoring and Saesa's breathing are enough to make me crazy.

"Does she have to snore so annoyingly loud?" I snap.

"She's tired," Saesa replies, patting Opal apologetically. "She worked hard saving our lives, in case you've forgotten."

I press my lips together, biting my lower one. I know she's right. The dragon blinks sleepily, raising her head. She nuzzles Saesa's cheek with her nose. Then, in a burst of orange glitter, she vanishes.

"Opal!" Saesa cries, her hand flying to her neck. "See what you did? You scared her away!"

"I didn't mean to," I mutter.

"You need to think about holding your tongue sometimes," Saesa snaps. "People—and dragons and mystics—have feelings."

"Sorry," I say. "Really, I am."

She doesn't answer. Glaring, she pulls a pouch from the folds of her silks and empties two objects into her hand: Skalivar's orange opal, and Twig's bud. The bud pulses with the essence of Kythshire. The opal glows softly. She tucks the bud away and whispers to the opal, "Tib's sorry. Please come back."

We stand in silence, waiting. Nothing happens. Saesa purses her lips. Her nostrils flare out angrily. She drops the opal back into the pouch and shoves it into her sash.

"Come on," I sigh. "The sooner we figure this out, the sooner we can get out of here."

Saesa doesn't say anything.

"It was supposed to be so easy," I mumble, hoping to get her to talk to me. "Go to Elespen, get the offering, get back to Cerion. Instead, we find an empty city, we're almost killed, and then rescued by a tribe full of people whose leader hates us just because we're outsiders like the Sorcerers are."

"Can you blame them, really?" Saesa asks with an edge of accusation in her voice.

We stop abruptly at a dead-end ledge.

"I can blame that Velu for thinking we're with Sorcerers," I scowl, gazing back up the stairs for another route. "I mean, how thick can you be? I thought Guardians were supposed to be wise. That one was so conceited and self-serving it makes me sick. Did you see how those Dona and Savarikta groveled? They practically worshiped them. It was disturbing."

"It's all they know, Tib," Saesa says defensively.

"It doesn't make it right, Saesa. A fae isn't a god."

She doesn't answer with anything but an exasperated sigh, and the last words I spoke hang in the awkward silence that follows. It's something that bothers me. That's always bothered me. Ever since Mevyn. Ever since I got hung up in all this mess with fairy-kind. I see it in Brindelier, sure. It's really strong there. But I see it in Cerion, too. The way Twig and Margy are so close. The way she listens to his advice over the advice of her own people. The warning of the elves when I stayed with them in Ceras'lain.

All of it nags at me. Is it really a good idea, I wonder, to go on with this? To get this offering and the others and unite the Wellsprings? That's a lot of power in one place. A lot of responsibility to make sure it's controlled. How can we be sure the fae won't grow even more powerful when everything is linked? How can we trust them not to take over everything? How can we keep places like Cerion from becoming like the village outside, singing all day to protect their Source? Or like Brindelier, where everyone is still dancing, enchanted by fairy magic?

I reach the top step and keep walking, this time across a skinny stone footbridge to the opposite side of the stepwell. Far below us, the eerie green glow of the Wellspring splashes against shadowed, twisted staircases. Inky swirls churn beneath the glow, flicking at the surface ominously.

I stare thoughtfully at it as I jog down a staircase which zigs one way and zags another. Behind me, Saesa's bare feet pad on the stone. That bleed of black can't mean anything good. The thought of it charges me with warning, and I shiver, remembering my bandolier and armor left behind in the village.

For the first time, it dawns on me that Saesa is unarmed, too, and dressed only in soft silks. I groan in frustration. How did we let that happen? How could we leave there without even the clothes on our backs?

"What?" Saesa questions warily.

"Where's your armor? Where's Feat?" I ask.

"I gave them to Kruti," she replies. "He said they had artisans who could repair them."

I stop and turn to face her, trying hard not to glare. "You gave him Feat?"

"Well, yes," she says, at first sure of herself but then going paler. "It needed some honing..." Her face reddens. Her eyes widen. "You don't think..." she trails off.

"I think it's pretty clever of them to take all our things and lead us in here unarmed."

"But Tib, they healed you. They were kind to us," she murmurs. Even as she talks and we stop at another dead end, I can hear the doubt flooding in. "How could we let that happen?" she whispers.

I decide to take her earlier advice. I don't reply. I know if I did, I might say something I couldn't take back. I just jog down another staircase in silence.

"Kind is different than good," I say finally.

"That doesn't make any sense," Saesa insists, catching up to me. "Why would they take the time to heal you just to throw you into danger?"

"I don't know," I grumble. "Maybe the insane fae guardian they worship ordered them to."

"Now you just sound paranoid," Saesa snaps as we reach another dead end and turn around. "That was a Light fae."

"Paranoid? There's good and bad in everything. Maybe even in light." I retort, and stop myself short of yelling at her about how I'm the only one with half a brain to figure this stuff out.

This annoying maze of stairs makes me want to scream. I spin on my heel and take yet another staircase. We've been at this for what feels like hours already, and we're still only one flight down.

"Take what's yours to claim," I whine in a mocking tone. "Generous of them, when we can't even get to it!" I shout down at the Wellspring, and my voice echoes back at me. As it fades, it's replaced by whispers and the slow rise of giggles.

Orbs of green and yellow light drift from the Wellspring far below. Some of them go past us into the ceiling. A few others bob in front of us, drifting like dandelion wisps around our heads. Watching us. Shadows follow them, but they dart away, keeping their distance.

"You're letting this place get to you, Tib," Saesa warns, reaching out to one of the orbs. It calls to her, enticing her. Her toes hang over the ledge.

"Come," the orb whispers. She starts to take another step and I push her back.

"That fall will kill you," I hiss, swatting at a group of green orbs swirled with black. "Cut it out!" When they scatter, I turn to Saesa again. "This place can't affect me, Saesa. I'm immune to magic, remember?"

"It's not just magic," she says, her eyes squeezed shut, her back pressed against the wall. "It's trickery. Mind games. These stairs, our goal, all of it. You're letting it get into your head. We both are."

The orbs keep bobbing around us, whispering and giggling annoyingly. I swat them away again and lean on the wall next to Saesa, closing my eyes, too.

Her hand closes over mine, warm and reassuring. She forgives me. The gesture makes my stomach twist with feelings I don't want to be having. Especially not now, in this place, where it's hard enough to make sense of anything. I push them away. We have to get out of this together.

"You're right," I say.

"Just think," she whispers, squeezing my hand. "Think hard."

I try to push away the sounds of pixie giggles and whispering shadows for long enough to form a thought that doesn't consist of how much I hate this place.

"Saesa," one of the orbs calls, "come with me! You said you would help us!"

"Help us!" the other orbs whisper.

I feel her hesitate, but then she steps forward. I fling my arm out to stop her.

"Argh," I groan as a thought I wish I'd had hours ago springs into my head.

"Sorry," Saesa whispers sincerely.

"No, it's not you," I explain. "Opal. If she was here, she could have flown down to the Wellspring to get it. Now I really feel bad."

"Are you trying to get down to the Wellspring?" One of the orbs giggles. A shadow flickers across it, snuffing it out momentarily, and it darts away. "We can show you!"

"Oh yes, follow us!" a group of them calls, hovering at the center of the well in a cluster. "Just step out!"

"This place is corrupted," I growl, slashing at the orbs with my dagger.

"Go into shadow and we shall be saved," the orbs whisper.

"Save us!"

Saesa fights the urge to do as they say, watching the scene in confusion. Her hand slides instinctively to her waist, to the sword hilt that isn't there. I sigh and rub my forehead, squeezing my eyes shut. There must be a way out of this. The pixie giggles are louder now.

They flood the entire space with their annoying little voices until I can barely get a thought in.

"Shut up, all of you!" I yell, and our surroundings instantly go silent. Saesa and I look at each other, shocked.

My boots tingle. My heart races. My ears ring with a sudden realization. They listened. They did what I said. I raise my finger. Point at the nearest green orb.

"You," I order. "Go back to the Wellspring."

Without hesitating, the orb plunges into the glowing pool below. My mouth goes dry. My feet go numb. I turn to Saesa and shake my head in disbelief.

"You can control them," she whispers. All around us, the orbs freeze. "Is it me, or do they look nervous?"

We stare in disbelief at the glowing balls of light, frozen in place in front of us, waiting for me to make my next move.

"You," I point to a small yellow orb. "Bring us an offering from the Wellspring."

The orb shoots away. We watch in disbelief as it returns almost instantly. It nudges my hand, and I open the fist that's been balled at my side. Gently, carefully, it sets a leaf-shaped vial of sparkling green liquid into my hand. Shadows swirl around it, licking it with darkness. I stare at the vial, stunned, and swipe at the shadows angrily with my other hand.

"Tib," Saesa whispers, horrified, pointing to the Wellspring below. I flick my healed eye in the direction of the pool and spy the figure of a golden fae rising from it. Tendrils of inky shadow cling to the Keeper, weighing him down, slowing his progress.

"You have the offering. You are no longer safe here," the Keeper warns. His voice is tortured. Twisted.

"Come with us, Dreamstalker," the shadows whisper, "and we shall leave this place untainted."

"Surrender," the darkness echoes, "and the mist will recede."

"Get ready with that bud," I whisper to Saesa, closing my fist around the offering.

"What about the Savarikta? And the empty city? We can't just leave them," she whispers, staring at the blackening Wellspring below. "They need us."

"Just have it ready," I say.

"You have the power to stop the darkness. Just come with us. Agree," the shadows swirl together, taking the form of a man. I reach to Saesa. Grip her arm.

"Don't let them get to you," I warn under my breath. "We're here for the Dawn. We investigated Elespen, we got the offering. We did what we came to do."

"But, Tib..." Saesa whispers, trying to pull from my grip.

Suddenly it dawns on me. The reason why Velu was so angry, so resigned. They're already here. Dusk. They've been here all this time. We trusted them, the Dona, the Savarikta. We let ourselves be stripped of our defenses. We walked right into it. I wonder how many of them knew. Kruti? Akkoti? No. I can't believe that. They were just doing what Velu commanded. And Velu was just doing what they thought they had to in order to preserve what little they have left. The Wellspring here is so low. Drained by roots. Sha'Renell's roots. Tainted by darkness. The whole situation enrages me. I turn toward the shadowed figure, floating at our eye level. I reach for my white vial and my dagger.

"When are you people going to get it through your thick skulls?" I shout. "I DON'T BARGAIN WITH SORCERERS!"

"Sorcerers?" The shadow's deep laugh echoes around us ominously. Saesa steps back from the ledge, shivering with fear. Below us, the Keeper wails pitifully.

"I am no Sorcerer," the shadowed man grins. "You know who I am. Darkness embodied. Partner to Earth. Consort of the Void."

My stomach twists in anger and fear. I know exactly who he is, even without him spelling it out. The way he was able to simply appear, ignoring the magical borders protecting this place. The way he blocked out the light as soon as we entered... I should have realized it then. The shadows all over this place. The darkness, being pushed out by the weakening light of the Wellspring. Vorhadeniel. Muse of Darkness.

As soon as I think it, the stepwell around us rumbles and quakes. She's here, too. Skulking. Prepared. Sha'Renell. Both of them have been lying in wait. Like vipers on their bellies, waiting to strike. Beside us, a crack snakes across the wall. Darkness seeps from it, ambling closer like enormous bony fingers as stone crumbles and splashes into the pool below. The green light of the Wellspring beams up, pushing both forces back, fighting to keep control.

"You are a fool to think you can refuse us," Vorhadeniel whispers. "To think you have any choice at all."

"If that was true," I yell back at him, "then why are we still here? If you're so powerful, why don't you just take us? Kill us? You can't, and you know it!"

"Tib," Saesa groans, clinging to me.

"It is too late for us. Do not forget us when the All Source is opened," the Keeper wails as another quake threatens to knock us off the ledge. The temple around us creaks and crumbles. "Flee!"

"Don't have to tell me twice," I shout, throwing my arms around Saesa to shield her from the collapsing stepwell. A statue of a woman in a stony gown emerges from the rubble, bearing down on us. Vorhadeniel joins with her, swirling around her in a black cyclone.

"Hurry, Saesa! The bud!" I scream, allowing its circling magic to affect me.

The Muses cackle and raise their hands together. Dark energy gathers around their outspread fingers, swirling like a miniature cyclone. It pulls its power from the Wellspring below, growing more and more terrible. Magic surges around us like armor. The earth splits open. The Wellspring drains. The Keeper charges the Muses, spraying them with green light that makes them scream in pain. The light beams brightly, washing us in its glow, drowning out the battle until it's nothing but sounds, and those sounds fade, and we're floating in clouds.

Spinning. Falling.

Moss. Chimes. Fairy magic.

Peace.

Chapter Twenty-One

SLIVER OF LIGHT
Celli

The streets of Redstone Row are cleaner than I remember. Old houses that were crumbling before I left Cerion have been repaired with fresh red bricks. Sunlight splashes across the front of my house. A new lintel decorates the front door, coated in bright, cheerful blue paint. My father's signature scroll-work is carved masterfully into the wood. I'd recognize it anywhere.

I pause on the doorstep with my hand on the latch, listening. My mother's voice drifts into the street along with the fragrance of cut flowers, yeast, and flour. This is home, like it used to be. Before Quenson, before Sixledge, even before my baby brother, Hew.

A beam of sunlight spears across the shutters and over my hand, and I look down at the latch. It's not the same. It's new. I understand, this isn't before. It's Cerion today. Right now. The sunbeam warms my hand, and I stare at it in wonder and confusion.

"*Survive.*"

My heart races. I squeeze the lever on the latch. I push the door open. My mother looks up from the kitchen table and drops the dough she'd been kneading. Her mouth opens in disbelief when she sees me. Her eyes brim with tears.

"Celli!" she cries, running to throw her arms around me. I step in and close the door, shutting out the sunbeam. The scene spirals into shadow. The house is gone, the kitchen gone, my mother…gone.

I float in the Void, wrapped in darkness. Eventually, the single word offered by my mysterious advisor fades. My name is lost to me again. My past is stolen.

I wake to the sound of fluttering wings, a soft rush of air, a flash of gold. A fae hovers over my face, peering into my eyes. Threads of gold light wind between us, curling like tendrils of Mage Mark in the otherwise dark room. When he realizes I'm awake, the tendrils vanish. I scramble away from him, sliding on satin sheets, buried in thick pillows against the ornate headboard.

He laughs softly and drifts closer, watching. I don't say anything. I'm entranced by this fae, his handsome chiseled features, the gold that pulses over his skin in strange patterns, the sturdiness of his build even though he's small enough to fit into my palm.

He seems okay with the silence. He just hovers, watching. Thinking. Looking impossibly gorgeous.

"I should not have woken you," he says to me finally. His voice comes in puffs of gold dust that glitter in the candlelight between us. The flecks bring me comfort.

"Survive."

I bite my lip and try to look away. I don't know what he wants from me, or what I'm supposed to do. I try to think back, to grasp one of those golden threads, but no memory comes to me. I feel emptied out. An unimportant vessel. It frustrates me. I know I'm more than this empty girl nestled in rich, soft pillows. I'm deeper than a blank mind and a hint of hope. I know this, but as hard as I try to push beyond it, nothing comes to me.

This fairy, is he friend or foe? I don't know. Something tells me it doesn't matter. I'm compelled to obey him. Just look, watch, go where I'm led.

"I'd introduce myself, but there's really no point. You don't care who I am, and the one who does care already knows," he chuckles to himself. I want to argue that I do care. That I have a thousand questions about who he is, and who I am. Every one of them rests on the tip of my tongue, but can't be set free. I have no voice, no ability to speak.

"Come on, then," the fae orders. He glances to a far door of the room, ornate beside a window draped in long, partly closed curtains. Outside, it's still dark. "Get up. She's gone to bed early, which will make this much easier. I honestly didn't expect you to manage it."

I know he's not talking to me. Not really. He's talking to someone else through me. The realization makes me uneasy. I push against the shadows in my mind, the strange darkness obscuring who I am. The action fills me with warning. I do as instructed and slip out of bed, watching the fae carefully. I wonder if he's the one who has blocked me from myself.

Something deep inside tells me he isn't. He's here to help me do what I'm meant to do. To look. To see. I slide my feet into slippers waiting on the plush carpet, and when I turn to face the fae, he flicks his fingers and dresses me in an elaborate gown fit for a princess. A crown rests on my head. Earrings dangle from my ears. I look down at my hands to find a ring on every finger and golden bracelets peeking out of cuffs of pure white lace.

"Most of the kingdom is oblivious, of course. They've been kept busy," he chuckles again and guides me out of the room, into a quiet corridor. "Shoulders back, now," he instructs. "Chin up." He settles into the crown on my head and guides me up a spiral staircase.

The guards along the stairs don't suspect anything. They seem used to the idea of their princess passing this way alone with her Faedin perched in her crown. Beautiful lanterns cast shimmering light across the polished stone and wood lining the walls.

I gaze into the light and a flash of a memory comes to me. My fingers on a latch. My mother's shocked face as I open the door. The sunlight beaming brightly between us. I pause on the steps. My vision floods with light. A soft, warm breeze rustles my hair. Gauzy, glittering white fabric flutters before me. Its welcome brightness covers everything with a golden-white haze.

"*Draw yourself into the light, child,*" a woman's voice, pure as sunshine, enters my mind like a dream. "*I am with you. I will guide you. Close your eyes. Do not let him see.*"

"Come on, now," the fae says with a hint of annoyance, and I realize I've stopped in the middle of the staircase. "Do you want to look, or don't you? There's little time left before dawn."

The strange film of light remains as the woman's voice fades and I feel her presence leave me. With it comes tiny starbursts of color whenever I look at a lantern or light source. It stings my eyes, and I squeeze them shut as I reach the top of the staircase. My heart races with my thoughts, trying to make sense of what just happened.

Panic catches my breath and holds it. I need to see. I'm desperate to look. I blink rapidly, trying to clear my vision. I rub my eyes. I push the light away and take in what the fae has brought me to see. The light remains, but dimmer now, and only the brightest spots of my vision are flooded with strange, prism-like sparkles.

We pass through a set of golden gates into a lush garden. The sound of trickling water lures me deeper. The air is thick with magic. We arrive at a perfectly round pool, where three basins spill liquid from strangely-shaped glass bottles into the swirling well below.

"There is your proof," the fae whispers. "With one more on the way, if Keyes is able to negotiate it. I imagine it'll be just a few days."

I stare into the pool, losing myself in the endless, glittering swirl. The starbursts return, and this time I allow them, letting them fill up my vision and flood everything out. A dark warning inside me threatens death itself, but I can't bring myself to push the beauty of it away. The elation of magic fills me up, charging me with its power, entrancing me. I breathe in the spray of it, let it enter my body, feel the tingle of it in my nose, mouth, and lungs.

I have wielded magic before, the light tells me. I have memories of it. They swim just below the surface of my mind, drumming against a sheet of black ice, trying desperately to crack it, to return to me through some weak fissure. The power of this pool and the magic surrounding it emboldens me.

I raise my fist, as if the sheet of black is right in front of me. I throw a punch as powerful as I can muster, and meet nothing but air. The punch is a reminder in itself. Part of who I was. A blocked memory on the fringe. I draw in a deep breath. I want to scream from frustration, but when I open my mouth, no sound is allowed to escape.

"She can't stay here long, my lord," the fae says, "She was a good find, and the princess is fond of her. We can't have her going mad."

The ice turns to thick shadow, taking me over. I feel myself nod, and my gaze is torn away from the pool, away from the beautiful light that would help me become myself again. I turn against my will. My feet carry me away, my vision dims. My will leaves me with every step as I go further from the pool and the darkness in my mind shadows my hope until there's no memory of it but a dull glint of light when I look at the glowing lanterns. Even then, my eyes are forced to cast themselves down. To focus on the shadows at my feet.

The fae flies in front of me this time, guiding me back through the pristine corridors of the palace. The battle inside me has receded, leaving me exhausted and sluggish. By the time we return to my room, all I can think about is my bed. The door closes behind me and the fairy gown transforms on its own, back to my plain night shift.

"Alexerin," a voice whispers from across the room, "what have you done?"

"Sleep," the fairy whispers to me, but the spell that sweeps over me as I lay back against the pillows only closes my eyes. The rest of me remains awake. Pinpoints of light dot my eyelids, calling to me. I pull myself toward them, desperate for more of the hints I was shown at the pool, but there isn't enough light behind my eyes to guide me. It's too dark.

"Princess," Alex coos. The fae's voice drifts away, moving toward Pippa. I struggle to open my eyes, to look at her as I'm supposed to do, but I can't. I can only listen.

"How could you, Alex?" Pippa asks in a hushed and desperate tone. "After everything we've done to stop this, after how hard I've fought to keep him out…how could you let him back in?"

"Each side deserves an equal chance, Princess," Alex explains. "Sometimes night is longer than day, and sometimes day is longer than night. But there is never a time when one reigns completely. We have had some very long days, and the nights are growing shorter."

"It isn't about that. Not for me," Pippa says quietly.

"Isn't it?" Alex whispers. "What happened to you, dear girl? What happened to your plans, your dreams? We three would have been—"

"I was a child," Pippa interrupts sternly. "I didn't realize what he had become. I didn't know what any of it meant. How grave it could be. I was alone, and the thought thrilled me. I shouldn't have encouraged him."

I wonder, as I listen, who they're talking about. Whoever it was, he sounds like someone powerful, someone the princess regrets associating with. The shadows press close. My eyes burn with the effort to open them, but the spell holds them tightly closed.

Suddenly I know exactly who they're talking about. The shadow of a man lounged across a chair lurks in the darkness of my mind. A young man, handsome and alluring. A prince. A Sorcerer. A king. He sweeps his fingertip across my brow. I'm his. His eyes. I'm failing him. I need to look.

"You were not alone," Alex says firmly. "You had me, and him. You had your brother and Ali. You were never alone. That's not an excuse. You were in love."

"Stop it," Pippa says.

"You're still in love."

My heart races. I know this feeling. The longing, the need, the awareness of how wrong it is, but the inability to stop it. The lure, the draw, to darkness and to power. The sensation of belonging, of being owned and valued and wanting to fight it, or knowing we should want to fight it, but being unable or unwilling. I understand the princess. Her struggle. I know who she is. Who he is. The man on the throne in the darkness. Her suitor. The Sorcerer King.

"I said stop! Don't. You know who he was, how horrible," she sniffles. "Or have you forgotten the wretched things he did in my name, after all this time? I haven't. I was sleeping. For me it seems like yesterday. For you, it's been ages."

"I haven't forgotten," Alex replies. "It's as fresh in my mind as it is in yours. Princess, I am only asking you what is in your heart. You know I'm the last one you can deny it to. I feel your ache. My concern is for your happiness."

"You're supposed to be the closest to me, Alex. You're supposed to understand me and protect me, as I am to do the same for you."

"Perhaps that's exactly what I'm doing, Pippa. A heart's true desires aren't to be ignored. I know your heart better than you do. If he should win—"

"I won't hear another word. And I won't have the girl used that way again, do you understand me?"

"Orders from the human," Alex snorts. "Is this what we've come to?"

"She's listening," Pippa replies. "But you probably knew that."

A rush of peace flows through me, soothing me to sleep. I'm not sure how much time passes. This time, my rest is dreamless and quiet. When I wake again, it's midday and I'm not alone. The princess sits on the edge of my bed, staring at me. Her hand is posed as if she's just finished casting a spell. Her expression is instantly regretful.

"What is your name?" she asks me with a hint of fear. "How did you get into the city?"

I want to tell her I understand her. I want to confide in her and help her. I want her to know who I've been and who I am, but how can I tell her when I don't even know, myself? Again, I push against the darkness in my mind, and again my stomach twists with warning.

I look past her into the light that streams between the drapes and follow it to the richly embroidered coverlet that drapes my knees. My fingers slide into it and I gaze at them thoughtfully. A single starburst glistens and spins in my vision, as if I'm looking through a teardrop. Across the room, the drapes slide open further. The light spreads across my arm, warming me, calling to me. White gauze flutters and I gaze into it, searching. Warmth spreads through me and the flash of a memory bursts into my mind. A woman, shocked to see me, dropping her work, rushing to greet me. The light gives me a gift, pure and beautiful. The gift of myself. My own name.

"Celli," I whisper hoarsely.

The princess gasps. A glint of silver by the window darts to her side.

"She couldn't even speak yesterday," Pippa explains. "Not until after the mirror…"

"What did Alex say about it?" the silver fairy asks, bobbing at her shoulder.

"Nothing useful," Pippa sighs.

"Typical," the silver fairy snorts in reply. "Boys."

Pippa doesn't reply. She just stares at me. I stare at her, too. At the brightness in her tired eyes. The way her long lashes brush her round, pink cheek. A strange feeling comes over me. Dark mist. Shadow. Even with the sunbeam still warming my hand, he pushes the light out of my mind. I feel far from myself, edged aside by his presence.

"You swore," I utter in a strange, deep voice, reaching for her.

"I never swore," Pippa whispers, glancing uneasily at the silver fae. "Never."

"You forget," I reply. "Or you lie."

The silver fairy swoops close, calling out a spell. The pink clouds of a sleep spell drift around me, lulling me into a drowsy state.

"Please, no," I whisper, clinging to the warmth of the sunbeam. I don't want to sleep. Not now, when I might finally have an ally to pull me away from darkness, to show me who I am and how to get home again.

"I need my brother, Aliandra," Pippa pleads as I drift off. "I can't do this alone anymore. He needs to know. He needs to come home."

"I'll tell him," the silver fae promises. "I'll go right now."

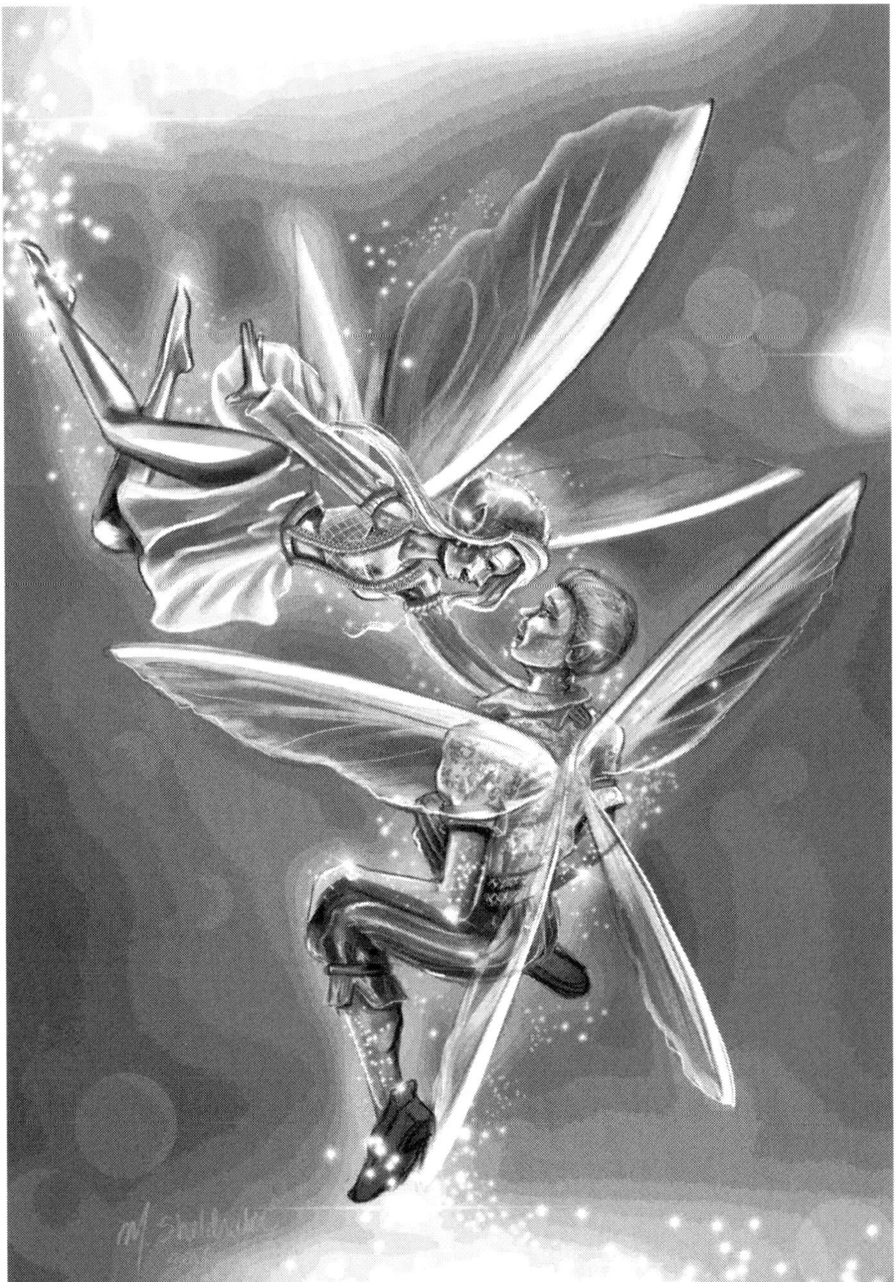

Chapter Twenty-Two

NEUTRALITY
Azi

The walls of the inner keep, carved with intricate patterns of runes, pulse with what seems to be flowing black ink. The etched stone channels the energy of the Void, dark and foreboding, like lifeblood through the narrow, imposing corridors. They call out constant warnings of our passing, even as hidden as we are in the Half-Realm, and summon creatures of darkness in droves to stop us. It's like Orva and Kerevorna all over again, except this time I'm alone, with only the fairies to fight beside me. We battle swarms of skeletons, shadow cyclones, giant spiders, wraiths, banshees, and of course, imps and Sorcerers as we press deeper and deeper into the shadows of Sixledge.

Each foe has a different edge, and there are times I fear we might fail, but the fairies bolster me, pressing me on. My body aches with exhaustion, bruises, wrenched muscles and wounds, but I fight through it for Rian. I know we're his only hope and my love for him and my belief that we'll triumph gives me strength.

Even though it's just the three of us, we're unstoppable. We face poisoned gasses which Shush blows away with his breath, and cackling hags who lie down to my will, surrendering. We combat swirling shadows with Flitt's prisms of light, and droves of walking dead with Mercy's might. Despite the narrow passages, my sword is nimble. With each victory, I feel my confidence rising.

Whenever I reach the end of my stamina and start to fall back, Flitt comes to my rescue, healing and charging me with light. Each time she does, Eljarenae's blessing pulses on my forehead, multiplying the effects of Flitt's healing, pushing me forward. I feel better than alive, the further I push into the depths. I feel like I did as the giant centaur, one with Light and the Fairy Queen. I'm in my element, here to prove a point. Light pushing against darkness, fighting for love, for life, for victory over chaos and evil.

A handful of ruthless Sorcerers is the last group to face us. They try their best to intimidate me, but I see them only as obstacles waiting to be struck down. The battle is fierce, and it leaves us breathless but victorious. When the last of them falls, we find ourselves faced with a dead end: a wall of obsidian which seems to absorb the surrounding light, snuffing it out.

I reach to touch it and it hisses at me in warning. Tendrils of black malice flick out at my fingers, testing me. Flitt drifts close to my hand and they lash out at her light, sucking it into the wall, devouring it.

"We can't go any further," I push to Flitt. I think back along the route we took, trying to remember a place where we might have taken a wrong turn to end up at this dead end. The wall seems to beckon me, and I'm so weary from the endless battles I want nothing more than to lean against it and rest, just for a moment.

Flitt notices right away and flings a fairy-sized handful of sparkling purple dust at me from one of her belt pouches. I breathe it in, closing my eyes, and my thoughts travel to home. My bed is soft and warm, bathed in sunlight from the open window. Outside in the forge, Da's hammer rings on the anvil. My door squeaks open, and Mouli bustles in bearing a tray piled high with hot sweet rolls and steaming tea. She sets it on my lap and I breathe in the aroma of the sweet spices. The welcome feelings of home rejuvenate me, filling me with the strength and energy I need to keep going.

"Oh! What I wouldn't give for some yummy icing! Time to come back, though," Flitt pushes.

Reluctantly, I open my eyes and find myself back in the dank, stinking dead end.

"Better?" she asks.

"Much," I reply. With a sigh of disappointment that Mouli's sweet rolls were just my imagination, I turn and look back the way we came.

"I'm sure this is the way," Shush pushes, keeping a safe distance from the glistening, inky liquid that flows along the carvings in the wall.

"Shush is right," Flitt pushes. *"I can feel it on the other side. An empty space."*

The blood-like stream in the wall whispers a constant, maddening chant. It reminds me of the tendrils in Mum's mind, strangling out the golden ones, twisting them into something sinister and hopeless. I trust the fairies and raise my sword, and the glow from Mercy's blade sizzles and crackles against the darkness.

A memory comes to me from a long time ago, when Rian and I had just learned about our place in the Half-Realm. Despite the darkness and foreboding of this mysterious obstacle, I find myself chuckling.

"Do you remember," I ask the fae, "the night we stripped Viala? We went to the palace after that to see Eron. He was in his chambers, and we were hidden in the Half-Realm. Twig showed me something that night. Something I'd forgotten about."

I show them the memory in flashes of golden light.

"You don't need all that," Twig says to Rian as he starts to cast a spell to breach the polished wooden wall. "You're in the Half-Realm. You can just go through. Like this." He dives at the wall and disappears through it. A moment later, he's back again. "See?" Just like everything else, it's a matter of belief. The wall is there, and it isn't, too. Believe it isn't, and you go right through. You try it."

I show them a little further into the memory, when Twig slid back and forth along the wall with only his head showing and a silly grin on his face.

Flitt giggles. "How about that? She does listen to us after all! Even if it did take years for it to sink into that thick skull."

"I'm fine with my thick skull, Flitt. Thick means it can take a blow or two," I wink at her, and we all laugh again. The moment of levity makes my forehead tingle and gives me confidence to do what I'm about to do. I try not to think about strange flow of inky black, like the lifeblood of Sixledge rushing along in sickening streams. "Besides, they're throwing everything they can at us to stop us. I need to embrace what I can do. Everything I can do..."

"It's there and it isn't..." I whisper, and give Mercy a slight push. The wall gives way to my sword hand. It swallows my blade and the light it gives off. There's no pain or sensation at all. It's just like I thought. There is no wall.

"It isn't," Flitt whispers, and dives straight at it, disappearing. Shush does the same. I hold my breath and step forward. As I pass through the wall, the black streams flow over my face, through my hair, into my eyes and nose. I pause halfway through, tangled up in it, twisted and held, just for a moment. My ears are filled with tortured screams, my eyes see horrors I can barely fathom. Shadowed tendrils grab me, pulling, trying to lure me into their darkness. I feel the fae take hold of my arm and yank me through, and I stumble sideways out of the wall and land breathlessly in the darkness beyond.

"*What is this place?*" I push to the others. It's so dark no light can penetrate, and the acrid stench of decay hangs heavy in the air around us.

Flitt tucks into my pauldron and Shush clings to my braid, and even though I feel them right here with me, their voices are distant in my mind.

"*Void,*" Flitt pushes. "*It's nothing.*"

"*No,*" Shush pushes. "*There's something. Azi, take a few steps in. Just a few. Hold your hand out. Keep Mercy ready.*"

I follow his instruction, trusting in his direction, and take a tentative step forward. Whispers of warning flick out at my mind, taunting me. I shouldn't be here. I don't belong. If I remain, I'll be lost forever. What will happen then? How will Rian ever be saved, if I don't survive this? How could I be so careless? How disappointed the Dawn must be in their Champion of Light.

"*Keep going, Azi. It's close!*" Flitt pushes. "*I feel it now, too!*"

Warily, I take another step. What if they're wrong? What are we trying to do, anyway? I should go back. I should run. How could I be so foolish to come here? How could I be so naive to think I could save Rian? I'm weak, powerless. Mercy is so heavy in my hand. Too heavy to bear. The fae are gone. I'm alone. I've failed.

Rian will die in this awful place, encased in stone, and it'll be my fault for being so weak and powerless. I'm lost, I'll be lost forever in shadow, drifting, fading from reality. And what does it matter? Love is weak and fleeting. It abandons us, it brings us pain. If I never loved him, I'd be free from the paralyzing fear of losing him.

I could let go of it, just let go of Mercy and my quest and float here in the never-ending silence of the Void. Others are here, too. Hundreds. Thousands. I feel them drifting, just like me, their cares faded, their presence calm and peaceful. They're part of something greater, some building force. It's quiet, too. Patient. Silence and determination.

My fingertips graze a smooth, cool surface. The sensation brings me back, grounding me.

"*There,*" Flitt and Shush say together, and I'm jolted back to my senses. The Void and its empty suggestions slink away, pushed out by my own recognition of its existence.

My heart races as I sheathe my sword and slide both hands along the iron wall. The lure of the Void is still strong, but I know I've overcome it. Awareness itself is enough to keep it at bay, even though it's a constant effort. I wonder as I pace along the metal wall, how the fairies were unaffected.

"*Do you feel it?*" I push to them. "*The emptiness? It's a void, like a blank space.*"

"*Oh, Azi!*" Flitt gasps. "*We should have realized. Push the light away from you, just a little. It will make a cushion. Like when we were under the sea with Rian's bubble.*"

I try it, focusing on my forehead where Eljarenae's light is most concentrated. A ripple of bright energy spills down from the crown of my head, shimmering with prisms like Flitt's. In the soft glow of it, I can see the metal wall beneath my fingers. It's dull and covered with flakes of rust and cobwebs.

I walk alongside it, and in a few steps, I find a corner.

"*It's a box,*" I push. "*A metal box surrounded by nothing.*"

I round the corner and stop in my tracks.

"*It's that door,*" Flitt gasps. "*Be careful.*"

"*Remember what the baby Sorceress showed you,*" Shush whispers. "*Poison.*"

I could die. Memories of King Tirnon bubble to the surface of my mind, lying on a plush carpet, his veins filled with Blackheart, his wife the queen sprawled over him, weeping. I stare blankly at the door, watching the poison drip slowly from the ghoul's pointed teeth. What good would I be to anyone, dead? It's probably not Blackheart, but how could I possibly triumph if my flesh were to be eaten away by painful, disintegrating poison? What would the point be of rescuing Rian when the sight of me would make him ill?

"Rian," I whisper, pushing away the doubts and wicked thoughts. The shadows hover over us, imposing dread and cowardice.

I close my eyes and let the golden strand loose again, guiding it toward the door the young Sorceress showed me in her mind. The maw of the ghoul molded in the metal door smacks its glistening lips, watching that part of my mind with a greedy hunger that makes my stomach sink.

That strand, Kenrick explained earlier, is vulnerable. If it were to snap, I could lose the wandering part of me. Could I really, I wonder, or is it just the Void taunting me again?

I pull the strand back and blink rapidly, staring at the door. The runes of warning circling the ghoul's head make my stomach twist in fear. The ghoul smirks fiendishly and runs its metal tongue along its pointed teeth.

"What's wrong?" Flitt asks.

"Why did you stop?" Shush pushes.

"She knows she will fail," the goblin sneers. "Turn back now, feeble warrior, before the choice is lost to you. Dawn is no match for the Dusk."

"That's what you think! Eat light!" Flitt cries. Before I can react, she dives from my shoulder. A ray of light spears from her fingertips, shooting into the mouth of the goblin, cleansing the poison. Shush calls my name, but it's too late. The goblin's tongue latches onto the light, reeling it into his mouth, slurping up Flitt and Shush together.

"No!" I scream and Mercy leaps to my hands. I raise the blade and, with all my weight behind the strike, I drive it between the goblin's eyes.

A blinding burst of light flashes the moment Mercy meets its mark, and I feel myself tumbling away, plummeting down a chute that seems to have no end.

"Flitt!" I scream, both in my mind and aloud. "Shush!"

"Azi!" Flitt cries. "You did it!"

"Hang on!" Shush shouts, and a weak puff of wind rushes up from below, trying to cushion my fall. It fails miserably, and I hit the bottom hard with an ear-ringing clang of stone on metal. The force of my impact with the iron floor knocks the breath out of me. I feel both saved by my stone armor and crushed under the weight of it. Flat on my back, I lie gasping for breath with Flitt perched on my chest.

"Glad I figured that one out," she beams. "You'd have probably just stood there talking to him all day."

"It was risky," Shush agrees. "But it worked."

With a groan, I roll onto my side and push myself up to sitting.

"Just once, I'd appreciate it if you let me know ahead of time before you do something like..." my voice trails off when I realize we aren't alone.

The figure huddled in the corner of the cramped space doesn't move or acknowledge us at all. Her hair, both black and white, hangs in long, stringy locks over her face and tumbles down the front of her tattered gray gown. Her large wings droop from her shoulders, torn and limp like heavy canvas. Her bony knees are tucked to her chest and her sunken cheek rests on her shoulder. She stares blankly ahead, and I can't tell whether she's watching us or whether we just happen to be in the line of her disinterested gaze. I can tell just by looking at her how beautiful she must have been once, before her eyes grew sunken and her body withered to skin and bones.

"Stellastera?" I whisper. The fairies scramble along my armor and sit on my shoulders in silence, waiting, but the Muse says nothing in return. "Can you hear me?" I ask. I crawl closer and she watches, but refuses to answer. When I reach out to her, she flinches and ducks her head, hiding behind her hair.

"Don't be afraid," I whisper. "I'm Azi. These are the fairies, Flitt and Shush."

Flitt climbs down my arm and perches on my wrist. Her light is dim, and her wings can't carry her in the iron confines of this place. My heart races with the sudden realization that we're all trapped in here without magic to get us out. I push the panic away quickly and focus on one thing at a time. Stellastera's gaze drifts to the fairy, but her expression remains blank. There's no hint she has any idea who we are.

"We've met, remember? Your wand helped us in Orva. In Kerevorna, it was our ally, Tib, who opened the Wellspring and released you."

"Yes, I remember you," she replies with a haunting, emotionless tone.

She speaks like someone who has been broken and discarded. Someone who has lost all sense of self-worth. It brings to mind Valenor and Kaso-Viro's conversation about their sister: *"She has been battered, mind and body. It is her shame which keeps her hidden from us now."*

"We weren't aware of what happened since, but we're here now. Your brothers are worried for you. We came to rescue you."

"Rescue?" she whispers.

For a long stretch of silence, she looks me over. Her halfhearted gaze slowly drifts into the vast space above us. I follow, looking up into the chute as far as I can before the walls are swallowed into shadow. She doesn't have to say a word. The hopelessness she feels hangs heavy in the dismal space.

"Even if you could," she whispers. "To what end?"

The question makes me pause. I thought she'd be thrilled to have rescuers ready to do whatever we could to see her released. Having to explain it to her doesn't make any sense to me.

"To get you out of here," I say. "Away from the Dusk and the Void. To free you."

"I have been free," she replies quietly. "My freedom brought nothing but misery and heartache. The world outside is better off if I remain apart from all of that, shut away from those who would suffer the consequences of my choices."

"You can't truly believe that," I take her frail hand in mine. "We need you. Rian has been captured by Dusk. They're doing something to him, performing some awful ritual. We fought through unthinkable terrors to get to you, when we could have stopped them first. We don't have much time. We have to get back to him. Please, Stellastera. Help us."

The Muse of Magic pulls her hand from mine and slides as far as she can into the corner. With her face turned to the wall and her hand pressed to her eyes, she slowly shakes her head.

"I am sorry you wasted your time," she whispers. "Your journey was for nothing. I cannot help you. I must remain neutral."

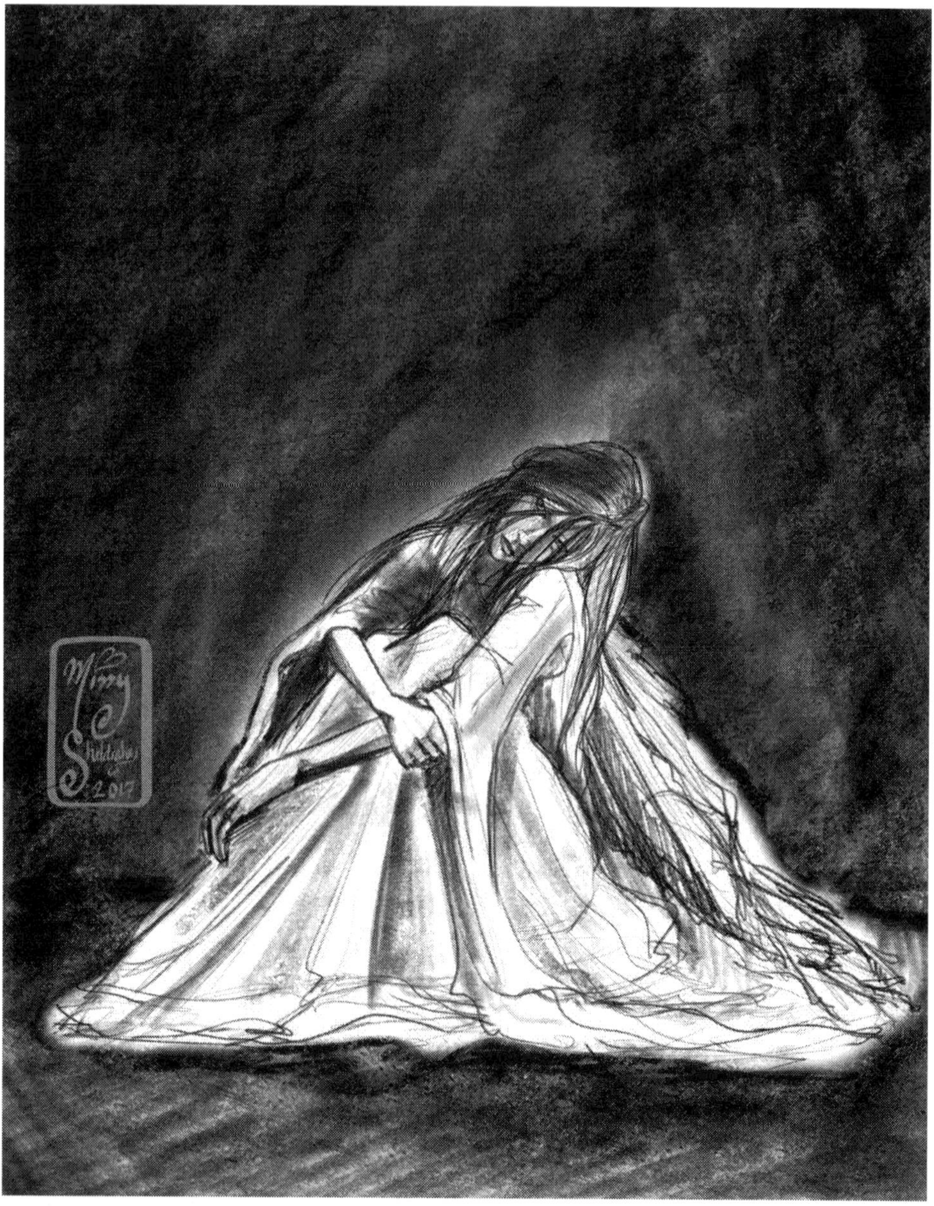

Chapter Twenty-Three

BREAKING SHADOW
Azi

"Neutral?" I ask in disbelief. "Why? How? Do you have any idea what's happening out there?"

Stellastera's response is to do nothing more than shrink deeper into her corner and bury her head in her arms.

"Flitt," I whisper, my heart racing. I can't stop thinking about Rian. This is urgent. I need to sway the Muse, and we need to figure out a way out of here so we can put a stop to whatever they're doing before it goes too far. "Do you have any more of that purple dust?"

"No," Stellastera utters. "No more magic. No more. You're a warrior, brave and strong. You must be, to have made it this far. You don't need me. Go and do what you will. Leave me here."

"We're not leaving you here," I say sternly.

"I will not go with you."

"Argh!" I groan in frustration, and Stellastera cringes like an abused child.

"*Be patient, Azi,*" Shush pushes. "*You have to convince her.*"

"*Gently,*" Flitt urges. Her dim light grazes Stellastera's arm, and as weak as it is, it seems to push away the shadow just enough to give the Muse's skin a soft, peachy glow.

I creep forward on my knees and rest a hand on Stellastera's shoulder. Even in the confines of the iron, Eljarenae's touch buzzes on my forehead the closer I get to her sister. The Muse of Light is with me. I feel her faint presence spread from my forehead and down my nose to my lips. I welcome her words, speaking them on her behalf.

"Sister," I whisper, and a puff of light glitters forth, mingled with my breath. "I come to you carried by the hope of this Champion of Light, whose heart has guided her to you."

The fairies and I watch the glittering breath drift to the Muse. It clings to her stringy hair and dingy gown like dewdrops, casting a light of its own. Her dark eyes catch the light, reflecting it dully until she closes them.

"I cannot be swayed, Elja. What's done is done," she mumbles.

The Muse of Light's glow stretches into my fingers, guiding me closer to her sister, urging me to take her in my arms. Her love fills me with comfort and hope as I draw Stellastera to me, willing that energy to grace the broken Muse.

"That is our brother talking, and our sister," Eljarenae whispers through me, stroking the long tangles of her sister's hair. "We are aware of their harsh words and harsher treatment. They will come to understand what they have done is inexcusable. Valenor and Kaso Viro search for you, even now. They love you, as they always have. Your children, as well. They—"

"Don't," she interrupts with a strangled cry. "Don't speak to me of my children. Can't you see where love has brought me, and by my folly, all of the rest of you?"

"Tell me," I whisper in glittering puffs, "how you've been forsaken by love. Help me to understand."

"You were there," Stellastera says softly. "Why bother retelling what we both lived?"

Eljarenae's influence slips away slightly, lingering only on my forehead. Despite her reluctance to speak, Stellastera rests against me, clinging to my arm like she's afraid I'll let go. Flitt and Shush remain quiet, but both of them slide from my shoulders to perch in the folds of Stellastera's gown. Silently, Flitt digs into her pouch and produces a sugar cube, which Stellastera takes hesitantly. Instead of eating it, she rolls it between her fingers, watching the light from the glittering beads in her hair catch on the granules of white sugar.

"You don't play with it, you eat it!" Flitt giggles. She snatches the cube from the Muse's fingers and pushes it into her mouth. "See? Yum."

The specks of light from Eljarenae's whisperings don't change over time. They twinkle in bright little pinpoints, like stars in the night sky. Stellastera takes a long, deep breath and swallows the sugar.

"He was so handsome," she says, and for the first time her voice holds a hint of warmth and softness. "A king. Though I tell myself that would not have mattered to me, perhaps I would never have noticed him, had he been an ordinary mortal."

"She means Emhryck, the King of Brindelier," Flitt chirps.

"Shhh!" Shush waves his hands at her. "Let her tell it herself." He points to the beads of light, which have slowly begun to creep along the folds of her gown, leaving streaks of white behind, collecting over her heart. Flitt's eyes light up with excitement, and she takes a giant bite out of her sugar cube, crunching it loudly.

"Emhryck," Stellastera sighs. "How could I have forgotten his name?' Her lips curve into the hint of a smile. "Paulin."

A tear slips down her cheek, glistening and rich with magic. It splashes onto the droplets of Eljarenae's light, and they pool together and spread. In a fist-sized space just over her heart, the dull gray fabric whitens and sparkles as if coated in diamond dust.

I know how she could have forgotten his name. Shadow. Darkness. It's happened to me more than once. I don't tell her, though. She's already far in the past, I can tell, and I don't want to interrupt the magic taking place within her as she remembers.

"My sisters and brothers warned against it. I knew it would be disastrous to fall in love with a mortal, but my heart could not be reasoned with. I loved him desperately, and nothing I tried could change my feelings. I forsook my blood-right and turned my back on who I was. I tried to pretend I could live among mortals as one of them. I wed him and sat beside him on the throne of Brindelier, and as they rightly should, the Muses turned their backs on me."

Strange tears spill down her cheeks as she speaks. From her right eye, the tears sparkle with bright, joyful magic. From her left, they drip like the black liquid that flows through the walls of Sixledge. Each splashes and pools on whichever surface it lands on, spreading like ink on wet parchment in spidery swatches of black or white.

"I longed for the company of my siblings, but soon that longing was edged out. I was with child, and the feeling of life growing within me brought me more joy than I ever imagined possible. When my twins were born, the celebration and outpouring of love from the kingdom was like nothing I ever knew before. My darling babes..."

She whispers those last words and her tears spill in steady streams, splashing her chest and arms, streaking her gown with oily black shadow and glistening white diamonds. Some of the white spreads to Flitt, and her light beams a little brighter. Her wings flutter, and she pushes off and flies to rest on my shoulder. Shush catches a tear and darts up to join her.

'It's working,' Flitt pushes to me.

"Pippaveletti and Poelkevrin," I whisper, gifting the Muse the names of her children.

"Yes," her voice cracks, and she nestles deeper into the comfort of my arms, weeping, spilling tears of dark and light magic.

Both drip onto my arm, mixing together, streaking the deep blue stone of my armor with silvery light.

"The celebrations went on, but I slowly began to see the truth. No one else recognized the warnings, but I knew. Though I loved my children, a twin birth was a portent. A split of power, a fissure between light and dark. Vorhadeniel came to see his nephew and niece. He held my daughter and whispered his dark suspicions to her: that her birth was a wicked ploy, designed to bring her mother great power and favor. His words were a spear to my heart, and once they were uttered I knew I could do nothing to remove the cruel seed he planted within my child.

"Eljarenae heard tell of my brother's whisperings and came to me soon after. She gifted my son with light to balance his sister's darkness, and she urged me to do everything I could to ensure that he, and not my daughter, would take the throne when the time came."

She pauses here and says no more. Her eyes, still spilling tears of black and white, are distant as she relives those moments in her past. They flash in surges of love, fear, hatred, and hope. They stream thickly with magic, drenching her from head to toe, spilling over her, changing her. Her gaze drifts along my arm and rests on Flitt at my shoulder. Recognition slowly dawns on her as the fairy's light reflects on her wet skin.

"You are the Paladin. The Mentalist," she whispers. When I nod in reply, her eyes slide to mine and lock there. My forehead tingles with light, and the silvery magic on my shoulder seeps into me, giving me strength and guidance. Stellastera leans closer, searching my eyes, pleading silently for help. Golden tendrils swirl between us, locking us together, and I fall past the shimmering black and white pools into the mind of the Muse.

Unlike my mother's mind, Stellastera's greets me with just three strands of gold: one for her husband, one for Pippa, and one for Poe. All three are twisted with shredded shadows, and I know right away that small healing is a result of our conversation. I call Mercy to my hands and aim the light at the remainder of the shadow on each thread, unraveling the darkness and flinging it into the depths.

Aside from those three threads, her mind is infested with black. It sticks to my boots, slowing my pace, it stretches from endless rows of shriveled black threads, calling out to me with maddening, tortured screams, overwhelming me.

I aim Mercy at the nearest thread and pull away at the sticky darkness. The golden thread beneath reveals a memory of a fairy to me. Its beauty is unmatched, and its power reminds me of Sapience, the Keeper of the Wellspring at Kythshire. The memory is shrouded with guilt and regret, and as I pull away the shadow I watch the scene unfold before me.

"We shall do what you ask of us, my queen," the fae says with a slightly mournful tone. *"But you must realize it has not been done before. We do not know what will happen."*

"I understand," Stellastera replies. *"If there can be one for each of them, they shall easily achieve balance together. I won't have them quarreling like I do with my siblings. This way, you can be Faedin to both, and neither of them will feel left out or slighted."*

"You must be the one to do it, Your Majesty, if it is what you truly wish."

"It is."

"Take us, then. Rend us apart," the golden fairy says.

Stellastera holds the creature in her shaking hands. With the Wellspring of Brindelier as a sparkling backdrop, she takes its hands between her fingers and pulls, forcing her will, whispering her apologies. She closes her eyes as it happens, so I can't see the fairy as it splits. When she opens them again, she holds a gold fae in one hand and a silver in the other.

"You will be Alexerin," she says to the gold, *"and you, Aliandra,"* she tells the silver.

I stumble backwards from the memory and nearly drop my sword in shock. My breath catches, and I scramble back to my own mind, pulling the threads of myself with me.

"Azi!" Flitt cries as I return to myself.

"I'm all right," I whisper, my open eyes filled with tears as Stellastera squeezes hers shut and turns away. The movement causes the black tears to spill to the white side of her, shifting the balance.

"It was my attempt to achieve true neutrality," she whispers. "To protect my children, to ensure the health of Brindelier's treasured Wellspring. I never could have foreseen what a terrible mistake it would be. I didn't realize my actions would introduce darkness to the kingdom. I was shortsighted. Things became complicated and confused. Dusk fell early, and its followers were bolstered by the prospect of ownership over the All Source. They laid in wait, knowing that when Pippa came of age, they would have their chance. They began to groom a suitor of their own.

"Warnings came from all across the Known Lands. In Hywilkin, they threatened to close off their Wellspring. Paulin saw how it affected me. I fell into fits of panic and despair over what I had done. I meant to go to Hywilkin, to plead with Juvask not to disrupt the balance any further than I already had. I swore to make it right. My husband agreed, and we traveled together through the Wellspring.

"Hywilkin's king was wiser than Paulin. Wiser than I, even. He saw the future and knew his kingdom would be safest if it had nothing at all to do with me. With Magic. He was stubborn, but so was my husband. They spent years trying to come to an agreement, but their talks were heated and proud. When Juvask finally decided to exile his Mages and close off his Source, I fell into hysterics. I knew what it would mean for my husband's kingdom, and I knew it was my fault. Paulin was enraged by the effect it had on me, and he challenged Juvask. Juvask came out the victor of that challenge.

"You know much of the rest of the story. I was unable to stop the sealing, and so overcome with grief was I over what I had done, I followed the Mages of Hywilkin into Kerevorna, and I hid like a coward away from the rest of the world. I turned my back on my children and lost myself to darkness under the strict confines of my sister, Sha'Renell.

"It is fair for you to hate me, knowing what you do now, but I assure you I hate myself enough for the both of us."

She wipes her right eye with her left hand, smudging the diamond tears with darkness. I take her hand and dry it with my cloak.

"I can't even begin to imagine," I whisper. "I don't hate you, Stellastera. As much as you believe what you did caused so much pain, I see it differently. All of your actions came from love."

"No," she shakes her head. "I was selfish, I was greedy."

"There's no crime in allowing yourself to love," I offer gently. "You loved your husband and your children. You tried to do what you could to ensure their happiness. You reached out even in your darkest hours and offered us help. I'll never forget that. We never could have gotten through Orva without you. I can't believe you're lost to darkness."

"I couldn't be satisfied with what I had. I had to push for more, always more. Even shut away, I couldn't keep from meddling."

"That's Sha talking," Eljarenae's voice whispers through mine. "And Deniel. Azaeli is right. You loved, and found light. You saw hope, and you acted upon it. There is honor in that, Sister."

"Honor?" Stellastera asks as though it's a concept long lost to her. She gazes up at me, diamond tears spilling over the black, pleading silently for me to help her see. Without a second thought, I slide into her mind effortlessly.

This time, the golden ropes are thickened. Even those twisted with black seem ready to burst free of their confines. I hesitate at first, but a rush of light streaks past, melding with Mercy's glow, guiding me. I feel Eljarenae here, and with the love of a sister to guide me, we sweep through the Muse's mind. I'm careful not to look. I learned my lesson before. These memories are private, and I don't care to know their secrets. I concentrate only on pulling at the dark cobwebs and tendrils, clearing the sticky darkness, and flinging it into the infinite reaches.

Our work is rewarded with pure magic. It swells around us, seeping from every freed rope, swirling like cyclones of pure white energy, filling the space with tingling power. I feel elated, carried by it, floating as I did the time I stepped into Kythshire's Wellspring. I see from inside of the Muse that she is magic, and it is her. She had been so skewed by darkness, so consumed by all of it trapped inside of her, wrangled down, suppressed. I work until the glow of her mind blinds me with its brilliance, and there's not a single shadow left for me to unravel.

When my work is finally done, I drift peacefully from the Muse's mind and settle back into my buzzing, charged up body. I gaze down at my hand, and the golden light that pulses from the swirling Mentalist Mark on my face reflects brilliantly in the polished surface of my glove.

Shush and Flitt dart excitedly around me, giggling and whooping in celebration. The air is as thick with magic as it is in Kythshire. It drifts around us in orbs of silver, gold, white, and black. Through it, a figure emerges. Her gown swirls around her legs like churning clouds, glittering with sunlight. Her long black hair shines brilliantly as it tumbles in silky waves over her smooth, perfect skin. Wings of white with deep black spots spring from her back, bursting with glitter. More remarkable than any of that, though, is her wide, joyful smile.

"Come, Azaeli," she says.

She holds her arms outstretched, offering a hug, and I push myself to my feet and rush into her embrace. As soon as we meet, my feet leave the ground. Flitt and Shush cling to my shoulders as the

Muse of Magic shoots upwards with impossible speed. I watch the trail of magic she leaves behind, and squeeze my eyes shut as I realize how high we've gone in such a short time.

My heart races and tears fly from my eyes as I feel us breech the confines of the iron.

"Rian," I push into the suffocating darkness of Sixledge. *"We did it. We have Stellastera. Please hold on. We're coming."*

Chapter Twenty-Four

RED
Tib

Lying flat on my back on the mossy floor of Twig's dome, I try to get my bearings. My heart still races from the battle we just escaped. I try not to think of Elespen's Keeper, or the attack. I try to believe the scene we just left wasn't as bad as it seemed. That maybe the Wellspring and its Keeper are still safe. That maybe it was okay to leave them in the middle of the worst of it.

The shift between Elespen's magic and Kythshire's is abrupt, and slightly confusing. Elespen's magic is more green, earthy, and filled with life. Like the jungle, it's mysterious and powerful. Kythshire's energy is lighter. It's a mix, bright and cheerful, like a rainbow. Through the vine canopy, orbs of light mingle with the sunlight, drifting past, giggling.

"Ugh," I groan, covering my eyes with my arm. Whatever they feel like, both places are equally annoying. "More fairies."

Without a word, Saesa gets up. Stomps away. Leaves rustle, trumpet flowers sniff.

"Great," I utter under my breath. "She's still mad."

When I go out to join her, her head snaps up to look at me. She shoves the opal away, back into her sash, and scowls.

"No reply from Opal, still?" I ask.

"What do you think?" she huffs.

"I said I was sorry."

"That didn't make her come back, did it?" She crosses her arms over her chest and looks away from me.

Fairy magic glitters in her orange hair. Her silk scarves drift around her like she's under water. Her eyes narrow. Her jaw clenches. She doesn't say anything, but I can tell she wants to. Something's boiling up under the surface. She's furious, and it's not about Opal.

Not really sure how to deal with it, I try changing the subject. "Guess Margy left. Hope she got back to Cerion before they figured out she was gone."

"Too bad you came running back here for nothing," Saesa shakes her head slightly, fuming. Without even telling me she's going to, she closes her eyes, whispers, "The Ring," and vanishes.

"Hey!" I shout into thin air. "What's your problem?" I mutter under my breath. Reluctantly, I close my eyes, too. I let the magic here touch me, just a little. I know where she went, and I really don't want to have to follow, but it's really the best course at this point, especially with Twig and Margy already gone. With a deep, reluctant breath, I think of the Ring and whisper it.

Like Saesa, I vanish from Twig's dome and reappear in the middle of the dancing. Fairies of every shape and size trample over me, skipping and singing and cheering and laughing. I try to dodge their path, but I get swept up into it instead. They carry me around and around until the forest is nothing but a blur. One of them links her arm through mine and beams a smile at me. Her eyes glitter like sun on fresh snow. Her hair is long, blue, and tangled. She calls out to me, but her words get buried in the music.

I squint around, trying to spot Saesa, and a blur of orange hair streaks past.

"Saesa!" I yell, but the singing is too loud and the dancing's too wild.

The blue-haired fairy takes both my hands in hers and spins us around like a whirlpool as we're carried around the mushroom ring by the rest of the dancers. She throws her head back, laughing, and I yank my hands free, annoyed.

This is exactly what I didn't want to get caught up in. We have the offering. We need to get to Margy and tell her what we saw in Elespen. Then get Ceras'lain. Then get to Brindelier, fast, and claim it before the Dusk can act.

The blue-haired fairy scoops me into her arms. Pulls me close. Laughing, she tips her head to the side. Gazes into my eyes. Kisses me. Her lips are soft and warm. My stomach flips. My body tingles. For some weird reason, I think of Margy.

"Cut it out!" I yell, shoving her away. "Leave me alone! Stop this dancing! STOP!"

The circling slows, the music dies off, the fairies pause. Across the circle, Saesa's eyes meet mine. Her nostrils flare, her green eyes roll in annoyance. She shakes her head.

"We recognize Tibreseli Nullen-Ganvent, Steward of the Last, Knifethrower, Dreamstalker, Bearer of the Guardian, Slayer of

Shadows, Liberator of Valenor, The Untouched, Key to the Skies, Duskbane, Her Majesty's Eye," a sweet voice drifts out over the circle.

I tear my gaze from Saesa to Crocus, who smooths the pink petals of her skirt dreamily and stretches her arms up over her head like she's just waking up.

"Tibreseli, please join us," she sweeps one hand toward the grass in front of her, and I slip away from the dancers to stand in the center of the Ring. "I would ask you why you stopped our dancing, but I can see with a quick glance that your business is urgent."

"Yeah," I agree, surprised to see efficiency from a fairy. "I need to get back to Cerion. Well, me and Saesa do."

"Saesa?" Crocus asks curiously. "Saesa Coltori, squire to Azaeli Hammerfel, The Temperate, Pure of Heart, Reviver of Iren, The Great Protector, Cerion's Ambassador to Kythshire, Knight of His Majesty's Elite, The Mentalist, The Paladin, Champion of Light?"

"I'm here," Saesa calls, and the crowd parts to let her join me.

All around us, the fairies whisper curiously. Some of them sound concerned. Others confused.

"How is it you are here, Squire of Azaeli? We thought her to be lost among Sorcerers," Crocus asks just above a whisper. "If she has returned, if you have any news, we should very much like to hear it."

"Lost among Sorcerers..." Saesa murmurs with concern. "She left me—that is, I stayed behind. I didn't go with her. I went with Tib, instead, to Elespen. What's happened? How is she lost?"

"Ah," Crocus bows her head. "You've forgotten how to play, so I shall answer the first question. Please be mindful of the game."

"Big of you," I scoff, and Saesa smacks my arm hard and shushes me fiercely.

"We know only this," Crocus offers with the soft sigh of a breeze ignoring our exchange. "Our own Flitter and Shushing left some time ago to aid her, and are obscured by shadow. You see, when our kind travel too far, they are hidden to us. We hope desperately to have them safely returned."

"They're too brazen!" Ember shouts from a mushroom top. "They never should have been allowed to go! If they are discovered, they leave Kythshire open to attack! Their love for that human will be the end of us, I swear!"

The red fairy's hair bursts into sparks, and the others around her dip away cautiously.

"The Ring does not recognize Ember at this time," Crocus waves dismissively.

"How long ago did they leave?" I ask.

"Pity," Crocus sighs and smooths the puff of yellow-green hair piled on top of her head. "We've only just begun, and the game is already lost. It was our turn for a question, after all," she says, offering a mirthful smile.

"Oh, my—" I start to curse, and Saesa punches me.

"Shut. Up," she growls. "Just," she turns to me, shaking her head, "stop talking. Hold your tongue. Please."

Crocus smiles sweetly and says, "You know nothing of our lost charges, and have failed to provide us any useful information. We grow bored of this conversation, and wish to return to dancing."

"Seabee Ophie Racing Wishful Adventurer." Crocus's voice mixes with Scree's and the ground rumbles under us. The fairies around the ring whisper excitedly to each other, and in a pop of color like a firework, a fairy appears between us.

"I'm here!" she shouts, reaching up to pat the sparks out of her still-smoking purple hair. "Oops," she laughs sheepishly. "Overdid it a little on the poppers." She digs around in several pouches tied all over her body until she pulls a flower petal from one of them. "A little less popping on the purple pepper peepers," she whispers to it. The flower squeaks, and she shoves it hurriedly into a different pouch.

"Sorwa," Crocus giggles.

"Your Grace," Sorwa curtsies, and a few trinkets spill out of her pockets and pouches. "Get back here," she whispers urgently to them, and they scramble back to where they belong.

"Sorwa, would you like to go on an adventure?" Crocus asks.

"Does a frilly beetle have twenty-eight legs?" Sorwa whispers out of the corner of her mouth to Saesa, who offers a bewildered laugh. "The answer of course, is yes!" the fairy replies loudly. "Yes, they do! I mean, I do!"

She turns to look at me, her eyes magnified by a pair of huge goggles, and adjusts them. I knit my brow at her, and she turns back to Saesa.

"What's with cranky?" she whispers.

"These are Tibreseli Nullen, Dreamstalker, and Saesa Coltori, Squire to Azaeli Hammerfel," Crocus explains.

"Oh! Flitt's Azi?" Sorwa gasps, clinging to Saesa. "Do you think I could meet her?"

"Sorwa," Scree's voice booms from beneath the grass where Crocus stands.

"Yes!" Sorwa squeaks, fumbling to catch what looks like a glowing pin that jumps out of her pouch as the ground shakes.

"We ask you, traveler," Scree rumbles, "to return these two to Cerion."

"Oh?" Sorwa looks around, slightly frantic, and starts patting at her pouches. "Oh, yes, of course, I just need to, I have to find…uh, oh! That's right. I left it there. Ha! Of course! What good would it be to have my tether here, if I'm going to it there?" She giggles, and the rest of the fairies laugh, and the singing starts up, and with it, the dancing.

"Safe travels," Crocus says before the voices rise too loudly. "Please have our kin send word, if you see them. And best wishes for the victory of Dawn."

"Thank you, Crocus!" Saesa shouts.

Sorwa bobs her head in time with the music, clapping. She drifts slightly toward the whirling blur of dancers, and Saesa taps her arm.

"Yes?" Sorwa shouts, slightly annoyed at the distraction.

"We're ready," Saesa says.

"Oh! Right!" Sorwa offers each of us a hand, then closes her eyes behind the watery lenses of her huge goggles. "Cerion, Cerion," she whispers. "Concentrate."

I sigh and close my eyes. Part of me would rather walk to Cerion than trust this bumbling fae, but we don't have much choice if we want to get back quickly. The fae pulls at my hand, and I allow her magic to swirl around us, transporting us away from Kythshire.

The journey is quick, but bumpy and strange. Saesa at some point finds me and grabs my arm, and we emerge in a dark, cramped space that stinks like horse manure.

"Oops!" Sorwa giggles. "Not that one! Hold on!"

We pop away and end up in an overly-perfumed tangle of thread, fabric, and feathers.

"Wrong again!" Sorwa sputters, sneezing as she pulls us back into the Half-realm.

"Here we are! Perfect!" she says in a sing-song voice, and we emerge inside of a treetop and start to fall. "Oh sisslefigs! You can't fly!" she yelps as a branch smacks the back of my head.

I see another one coming and grab it, and thankfully Saesa catches her own fall just a few branches below me.

"Sorry," Sorwa says, bobbing in front of me. "I forgot!"

I glower at her and she yelps and dives down to Saesa's level.

"Seriously," she whispers, "is he always like that? It's kind of scary."

"Most of the time," Saesa shrugs, glancing up at me. "It's best to ignore it. You get used to it eventually."

While she untangles her silks from the nearby branches and carefully climbs down to the ground, I sniff at the air around us. It's full of magic, bright and colorful. Cheerful. Kythshire magic.

"Great," I call to the fae below. "You brought us back to Kythshire!"

"Did not, dummy!" Sorwa replies as I pick my way down out of the tree. "This is Cerion. See? There's the Elite hall, and the palace, and the new Guardian…oooh it's very intimidating!"

"The new what?" I ask, dropping into the grass beside Saesa.

"Guardian," Saesa whispers, pointing to the towers of the palace. She grabs my elbow and we run out of the forest park to get a better look at it.

When we reach the street, I realize there's no real shift in the amount of magic between the forest park and the rest of the city. Cerion is brimming with it, now. Protections. Wards. Safety. Look-aways. Powerful enchantments meant to bolster every single building. I gasp at the might of it. Concentrated, intricate spells cast by dozens of Mages seep into every stone and sink deep into the ground below us.

"Wow," I whisper, wondering how much effort and skill must have gone into so much magic. I've never felt this amount in Cerion before. That's when I notice it, kicked up under our feet as we make our way toward the palace. Trailing in clouds behind passers-by as they rush off to market. Everlin powder, rich and red, sprinkled over the cobbles of the street. Dusting the walls surrounding the palace. Swirling in the breeze that dances from the sea. Everywhere.

I shield my nose and mouth from it with the tatters of my sash, but the floral perfume still taunts me. My heart races with fear and anger as memories of my past flood through me. The crack of the whip. The sting of fine thorns. Its presence makes me gag.

Saesa doesn't notice. She gasps and points up at the tallest tower of the palace, where an enormous stone dragon sits perched, watching.

"Pretty amazing, huh!" Sorwa crows. "Wait 'til it wakes up! Come on, you'll see."

She darts toward the palace gates and Saesa runs after her.

With my eyes on the dragon and my mouth still covered, I race past them. All I can think about is getting away from the powder. Red, everywhere. Flowers. Petals. Baskets. Sorcerers. Little sister, staring at me across the dark carriage, terrified. Nan. Roots. Darkness.

I thought I'd moved past this, but the strong smell of the fields is inescapable. I tear past Saesa and through the palace gates, and the stone of the tower cracks and rumbles with a thunderous sound.

I skid to a stop and watch the enormous dragon stretch its webbed wings, blotting out the sun behind it. It cranes its neck and peers toward us, narrowing its glowing purple eyes as Saesa slides to a stop beside me.

"I am Valor," the dragon booms, leaping from its perch on the tower and crashing to the sweeping lawn in front of the palace. Its enormous head is the size of a fisherman's boat, its eyes as wide as I am tall. "The White Coast embodied. Guardian of the South. Keeper of the Palace of Cerion. Spirit of the Arcane. Gift of Hywilkin. Protector of the Queen. Scourge of Sorcerers."

"Whoa," I whisper. Saesa steps closer to me and Sorwa ducks behind us as the dragon lowers its head to peer at us at eye level. I glance down at its feet, where a glint of silver flashes in the afternoon sunlight. There, melded to the middle toe of its right foot, is the silver dragon claw Kerr Skalivar gave to Margy during the Reception of Allies. I remember how the elves had suggested they use it at dawn, and again I find myself wondering how long we've been gone.

"That's incredible," Saesa breathes, reaching toward the creature. The guardian's stony nostril snorts at us, blowing Everlin powder off us with a single puff of breath.

Specks of glowing blue dance in the deep purple of its eyes, and its black irises widen and narrow as it gazes down its long, scaly nose at us.

"Friends of Queen Margary Plethore of Cerion," the dragon rumbles, "you may pass. Fairy, your entry is not required at this time."

It pushes off from the grassy lawn with a sweep of its enormous wings and lifts into the sky to its perch on the tower.

"Well, goodbye, then!" Sorwa says, and with a cheerful wave, she blinks away.

"Thank you, Sorwa," Saesa offers, just a moment too late.

"Whoa," I say again, shielding my eyes to watch the dragon as it takes a regal pose and freezes, transforming back to smooth statue-like stone, like it's been carved into the palace spires.

"Yeah," Saesa whispers, following my gaze. "Amazing you managed to hold your tongue instead of mouthing off as usual."

With her fists clenched at her sides, she storms away from me in a flutter of dirty, tattered silks.

"Saesa!" I call after her and catch up once she's in the alcove of the palace doors. When she doesn't stop, I grab a fistful of her sash. "What's your problem?" I shout.

"What's my problem?" she growls, yanking the silk out of my hand and waving it at me furiously. "You think you're above everything! You just run around, making decisions without asking anyone, you do whatever YOU think is best without considering anyone else!"

"What are you talking about?" I mumble, stepping back. I can feel the color drain from my face. My lips go numb. I've never seen Saesa like this. I wonder if it's the Everlin powder affecting her. She purses her lips. Her eyes brim with tears.

"How could you just leave like that?" she cries. "You heard what they said, you knew what would happen, and you didn't care. You got what you came for, for her," she jabs her finger toward the palace doors. "Did you think about what would happen to the Savarikta? To the Wellspring? And what about our gear? Feat! Your bandolier! You just…you just left." She looks away, shaking her head.

"What was I supposed to do, Saesa?" I ask in disbelief. "Give up? Go with the Dusk? Let them stop us?"

"We could have figured it out," she whispers. "You and me, together. Instead, you just decided for us. For them. All those people, gone. The *sava*, the Dona." She shakes her head again and looks away, sniffling.

Before I can answer, the door of the palace swings open and Master Gaethon peers down his nose at us.

"Ah, it *was* you, after all. Come, Her Majesty is eager to see you," he says, ushering us inside.

Saesa sniffles again and glances over her shoulder at me as she turns to follow the Mage. My pulse pounds in my ears and I shove my hands into the folds of my makeshift trousers where my pockets would be, thinking longingly of the elven clothes I left behind in that village. And my bandolier, and Pelu, who guarded my vials. And Akkoti.

With a pang of guilt, I follow Saesa, watching her red curls bounce in the light that beams through the windows. Maybe she's right, I think, as we rush through the throne room and into the council annex to the side of Margy's empty throne. Maybe I should work on my temper.

The notion is short-lived, though, when the first face I see gathered around the planning table is Vorance's. The prince of Sunteri's presence floods me with the perfume of Everlin powder. As much as I try not to, when the door closes behind us, all I see is red.

Chapter Twenty-Five

SLAVE'S RAGE
Tib

"You," I hiss, stalking toward the prince with my fists clenched at my sides. His personal guard steps forward defensively, flanking him. The prince looks at me with such a shocked expression that I'd laugh if I wasn't so furious. His red cloak pools around him. He wears it. He stinks of it. Everlin. I can still feel it clinging to my skin. Dusting my legs. My fingertips tingle with the sting of the needles. Hours of my life. Years of it.

"Do you have any idea?" I roar. Lunge at him. Throw a punch. His guard catches my fist. Pulls me back. Someone shouts my name. I don't know who. I'm too furious. Everything is a blur.

"We suffer, we hurt, we die!" I bellow. "And you throw it in the street! Like dirt! Like it's nothing!"

I squirm in the iron grip of the prince's guard, fighting to free myself, reminded of the roots that held me. The dirt. The desert.

"You slaver! You vile, selfish, wicked, worthless cur!" The words spill out of my mouth like venom. I don't even know what I'm saying. Someone shouts my name in horror. I don't care. I kick frantically. I want to hurt him. To make him feel the whip, the fear.

My vision is blurred with tears of fury. All I can see is a smear of red as he moves back, behind his guard. Safe, like we never were. Protected. I don't give up. I want him to see, to know. My boots tingle a warning. I ignore them and lunge again, scrabbling for my dagger. Someone grabs my hand. Wrenches it back painfully. My weapon clatters to the floor.

"Have you ever been there?" I wail, struggling to break free. "Have you ever even seen it? Do you even know the cost? The real cost?"

Someone comes to help the guard. They force me to the floor. Pin me down. Lisabella. I feel her peace pulse. It doesn't touch me. I don't let it. I kick. I scream. Years of pain spill out of me in a torrent of curse words and violence. All the loss, all my sorrow. Everything I've kept walled up. Everything I thought I put behind me. My throat is raw, but I carry on screaming. I want him to know the pain I've suffered. Want him to feel it like it's his own.

"Tib," Saesa hisses in my ear. "Calm down."

She holds my shoulder. Someone else has my legs. They press me to the floor. Panting, I try to fight free. Lisabella's pulse gets stronger. Heavy. Thick magic. It works on them, not on me. Their hold loosens a little.

A glint of pearls catches my eye. Purple satin. Gold crown. When she comes into view my rage fades a little. I quiet down. Watch the fabric of her gown shimmer in the glow from the table above.

"Majesty, I wouldn't," someone warns. Finn, I think.

The queen waves him off and kneels beside me. At my side, opposite Saesa. Her white-gloved hand touches my shoulder. Her face swims before mine. Her eyes, deep, brown, and warm, bring me to my senses. She looks different. A little older. Distinguished. She's concerned, but still smiling. Always smiling. I can't help but smile back at her, only a little.

Her warmth soothes me. I want to reach for her, to hold her, but my arms are still pinned. I try to pull away, but they're too strong, and I don't want to fight them anymore. Don't want to scare her. Tears spill from the corners of my eyes into my ears. The air burns my throat as I try to catch my breath.

"Tib," Margy says gently. "It's all right. Be calm."

Her peace, her trust in me soothes me. The realization of what I just did hits my stomach in a wave of nausea. I swallow and squeeze my eyes shut. I can't look at her. Not now. Not after that.

I concentrate on the warmth of her hand through her glove until I'm as settled as I can be. When I open my eyes, she looks away from my sash to my face again. At first I'm confused, but then I remember the offering. She must know I have it. It must be obvious to her. At her shoulder, Twig whispers something too quietly for me to hear. Margy nods slightly.

"I'm sure what you've been through was difficult," she says gently. "Just try to be calm, and we can talk about it."

"Talk about it?" Vorance scoffs from somewhere behind her. "Surely you're joking. He just attacked me, Your Majesty."

"Tib is my trusted friend," Margy says, squeezing my shoulder. "I'm certain he's not himself right now. Please, give him a moment."

Her eyes meet mine. They try to reassure me, but every word the prince speaks grates on my resolve to stay calm.

"I'm sure I have no idea what reason that boy would have to rant at me in such a way," the prince sniffs. He creeps closer, looking down at me like I'm beneath him. Small. "He's mad, certainly. Dangerous." His guard, still holding my legs, glares at me in warning.

"You're going to pretend you don't know?" I sneer through clenched teeth. My fists ball tightly at my sides. Saesa squeezes my arm. "That you have no idea how many slaves it takes to get six barrels of that powder you threw all over the streets? That most of them are kids who could never even dream of the sort of comfort you live in every day, because all they've known is filth, and sun, and red, red, red." I say hoarsely. My throat tightens. My eyes ache with the tears that spill down my neck, stinging my skin, soaking my hair.

I watch his haughty expression go slack. He turns away, shaking his head. I close my eyes again and let myself sob. I can feel them all watching me. Awkward. Pitying. I want to disappear. To run away and never come back. To go someplace where none of this matters. Where I can just be myself. Just Tib, without this pain. Without this past.

"Just breathe," Margy whispers. She rubs my shoulder. Dries my tears. Waits patiently for me to be calm. Quiet. Saesa pats my arm, then gets up. She walks across the room. Whispers something to someone. I can't hear all of it. Just one word: volatile. My heart flips with anger. Shame.

"Come now, Tib," Margy says kindly after a long stretch of silence. "Let's get up off the floor, hm?"

I nod after a while. One by one, they let go of me. My legs are the last to be freed. Someone props me up. Lisabella. She helps me to my feet. Keeps an arm around me. Margy strokes my arm, gazing up at me. She leans forward like she'll hug me, but someone at the far end of the table clears his throat and she catches herself and steps back, folding her hands in front of her.

I swipe my arm across my eyes. Sniffle to clear my nose and swallow my tears. A hug from Margy would be nice, right now. I feel like it's the one thing I really need. She keeps herself distant, though. Stands apart. Plays her role. The queen. Everyone stares at me, waiting. Like they expect me to do it again. To attack. To rage. I try my best not to. I work to distract myself.

My attention is drawn to the table, where a magical model of the city glows across the surface. Dots of light flow through the streets and in houses throughout it. People. My eyes travel from the palace to the Ganvent Manse. My stomach sinks to find it empty. It sinks even more when I realize we left Elespen without figuring out what happened to the Admiral. Without stopping it. I glance up at Saesa, who's staring at the same spot. Her eyes meet mine, jungle green. Tearful. She looks away.

Back at the table, a floating ship lifts off. One of mine. My idea, taken for Cerion. Beneath the ship, my healed eye spies an official looking paper. A few words catch my eye. Brindelier. Marriage. My gaze flick past it. At the far end of the table, in the direction of the earlier throat-clearing, sits Keyes, Poe's Master Councilman. He looks at me with interest. Like I'm something to be studied. Like silently, in his head, he's making a case against me. He'll tell Poe about this, I'm sure.

My gut churns with embarrassment. My heart races. I try to think of the elves, to remember what they taught me. To calm myself. It's impossible, though. Too long ago. Too far away. Too much has happened. Too much is at stake.

"I'm sure if you offered an apology," Lowery, the national relations scholar urges, interrupting my thoughts, "we could move past this and on to the matters at hand."

The prince and I exchange an expectant look, but he says nothing. I glance around the room to find everyone's looking at me.

"Me?" I ask in disbelief. "You want *me* to apologize to *him*?"

"Never mind, Lowery," Margy says. "We can address it later. I'm sure Tib has a great deal to share about his travels." Margy turns to me. Her eyes drift to my sash again. To the offering. "I'm eager to hear what you've learned."

My boots tingle again. I scrunch my toes. I want to pace. To help myself feel better. I can't, though. Lisabella's hand twitches on my shoulder. I glare at Margy angrily.

"Do *you* want me to apologize?" I ask Margy.

She glances over her shoulder at Lowery. At Keyes, standing next to him. He nods to her, and Twig whispers something else, and Margy looks sorry for what she's saying, but resigned.

"It's complicated," she sighs. "You must understand why it would be asked of you." When I don't reply, she goes on. "Perhaps you should go and rest, and we can discuss all of this later. I'm sure you're weary from your travels."

The lump rises in my throat again. I shake my head slowly. Does she even care? How could she ask this of me? She should be making him apologize instead. Making him admit to it. Making him put a stop to it. Instead, she's protecting him. Putting it off. Trying to appease me, temper me. I know exactly why, too.

My hand slips to my sash. Closes around the offering from Elespen. My eyes flick to the table again. To that contract. Brindelier. Marriage. Everything I've done was for her, and why? For this? So she could turn her back on me?

"You've changed," I say through quivering lips. "I thought we were friends."

"Tib," she whispers tearfully, "we are."

"I'm not apologizing," I say firmly. "Not now, not later. Never. If you knew, if you really cared, you wouldn't ask me to."

"Tibreseli," Gaethon interjects, "if you wish to attend such gatherings, you must understand the nuances of compromise."

"I don't need your Mage lessons," I seethe. "And I'm not a child. I've done more than any of you put together!" I pull the bottle from my sash and hold it up. Its green light glints across the gathering, washing everything in eerie green. Gaethon's eyes light up. Twig drifts toward me.

Margy gasps and steps closer. She reaches for it. Across the table, Saesa shakes her head frantically in warning. It's like she knows what I'll do before I do it. Before I even know. Her green eyes try to catch mine, but I look away, glaring. Back at the queen who won't stand with me after everything I've done for her. Back at the rest of them, who apparently think I'm insane. A liar. A child.

"I'm done. You can take your offerings and your Wellsprings and your Everlin powder. Take your prince and your fairies and your stupid magic!" Furious, I raise the offering over my head.

"No!" Saesa cries. She dives toward me, sliding across the table, but it's too late. Before I know what I'm doing, before I can stop myself, I fling the bottle across the room. It smashes against the wall, spraying glowing green liquid all over everything.

Everyone screams. Twig dives to the mess, working magic over it. Gaethon and Margy rush to help.

"I'm done," I mutter. I don't wait for the consequences. I pull the cobwebs around me. Slip backwards into hiding. Fling the door open. Run.

Someone chases after me. I don't know who. I don't look back. I just keep going. Through the palace, into the courtyard, past the gates, toward the sea. My feet pound on the cobbles, kicking up puffs of red dust. It clings to me, filling my nostrils, making me cough. I feel it inside me, in my lungs, trying to work. Trying to amplify the magic in me, but there's none. I don't wield it. I can't. I never will. I'll never want to.

I run past ships that blot out the sun, through the market, into the richer quarter. I don't know where my feet are carrying me until I arrive. Home. Nessa's. I know she isn't here, that's what the model said. Still, when I reach through the locking wards and push the door open, I'm disappointed when she doesn't greet me. The house is still. Quiet. Clean.

I go back outside. Shake the powder off me. Kick it from my boots. Pull off the filthy makeshift trousers wound around my legs. My heart pounds with anger. With regret for my things left behind. With fury at myself for letting them trick me into giving everything up. And for what? I feel sick thinking about it. For Margy. For the offering just smashed. For nothing.

I growl, toss the Everlin-caked silks into the street, and run upstairs. My room is exactly as it was. Like the earthquake never happened. I press my hand to the wall and close my eyes. Imagine what must have happened. Cerion was attacked. Things were destroyed. I feel the remnants of magic lingering in the walls. Repaired by Mages.

I think it over while I do my best to clean myself off and get dressed in fresh clothes. Using a trick the elves taught me, I try to see things from their perspective. That's why they sprinkled that powder everywhere. Why everything looks untouched. It helped them work. Boosted the magic. The reparation spells. Again, I wonder how long we were gone. How long Sha'Renell attacked the city for. What happened. How they triumphed against her. Whether anyone discovered Margy missing before she made it back.

I feel better in my own clean clothes, with my face and hair splashed with cool, clean water. At home. In my room. Quiet. I turn in place, considering my bed, but I'm too wound up and this place is too obvious. Anyone looking for me would come straight here, so I leave. Up the steps, through the hatch, up the ladder into the widow's walk. I perch on the railing, leaning back against the sloped roof. From up here, I can see the entire city. Watch the sun dipping lower in the sky.

See the ships floating out on the sea and on the air. Watch the Everlin powder drift in swirling clouds, blown by the ocean winds.

My thoughts turn to the first time I ever came up here. With Saesa. How she spent hours huddled next to me, showing me everything she knew about Cerion. She's been with me, by my side, through so much. She knows me. She'd never ask me to apologize to that prince. She was the first to comfort me in there. She knew I'd throw that bottle. She tried to keep me from my mistake. To warn me of my own actions. I close my eyes, and her green ones linger in my mind. My boots tingle.

"Alright, what?" I grumble, slightly relieved for the interruption of my thoughts. "What do you want, Mevyn?"

"I sense a great deal of turmoil in you, my friend," Mevyn replies. A flash of gold appears in front of me. Gold wings. Gold spear, gold armor. He's brilliant in the late afternoon sunlight. Hearty. Muscled. A warrior. A true Keeper. I think of the ruined one in Elespen, tangled with black shadow, wasting away. I swallow the lump in my throat. I shove the thought away angrily. No more. I meant what I said. What's done is done.

"I'm fine," I say, but my hoarse voice cracks, betraying me. "I just want to be alone."

"I can help you, you know," he says with concern. "Take away that which brings you pain."

I close my eyes. Shake my head. Memories shuffle through my mind like cards in a deck.

"There wouldn't be much left," I laugh mirthfully.

"Wouldn't there?" he asks.

I think about it. Really think. The cards shuffle. Show me things. Triumphs. Friendships. Victories. All the things I've done, everything I've overcome. Battles with Sorcerers. Sipping nectar with Margy in the palace garden. Being welcomed by the fae of Kythshire. Being a guest in the sacred home of the elves, inventing a flying ship. Laughing with Nessa's other kids around the Ganvent's dining table. Running through the streets with Saesa. Racing. Winning. Riding a *Sava* up the steps of Velu's temple. Convincing Iren to free my sister. Sister.

I'm not sure when I drift off, but when I wake up, Mevyn is gone, and so is the sun. I stretch and hop down from the railing, and a glimpse of red hair catches my eye in the street below. It's Saesa, and she's not alone. Walking with her, his bronze armor flashing in the orange glow of the setting sun, is Kerr Skalivar. He towers beside her, his cloak flicking in the sea breeze, his smile wide. Saesa's hands whip around her as she talks, animating her words in a flurry. Skalivar throws his head back. Laughs. Shakes his head. They pause at the bottom of the steps of the manse, and I crane over the railing to watch.

"Here we are," Saesa says, her voice carried on the breeze up to me.

"I'm glad I ran into you," Skalivar bows. He takes her hand. Kisses it. Reaches to touch her face, but stops himself. I feel my own cheeks go hot. My hands grip the railing tightly. My insides churn.

"Me too," Saesa replies with a nervous laugh.

"I do hope you find Tib, and your lady knight asssss well," he says, still holding her hand. Even though there's no reason for it now. He could let go at any time, really.

"I have a feeling he's here," she says, glancing up. Straight up here. To the widow's walk. Her eyes drift back to him. She steps a little closer. Doesn't take her hand from his. "Will you remain in Cerion much longer?" she asks. He smiles.

"For sssssome time, I imagine," he replies.

"Well, thank you again," she says, pulling her hand away. Even from way up here, I see her reluctance. The way her cheeks go red. The way neither of them wants to look away. To go away. I think of Margy and Poe. Wonder whether they're like that, too.

Saesa and Skalivar manage it, somehow. To separate. Saesa jogs up the stairs. The door closes. He stands there a while. Waits. Looks around. Starts to walk away. His cloak ruffles in the wind. Flaps, like wings. Something shifts. Magic around him. Like he's stepped away. Into the Half-Realm. Hidden, or so he thinks, he transforms.

His coppery wings glint in the sunlight. His pointed tail flicks as he lifts into the sky. As he flies away, the white scales along his sides shift in rainbow colors, like opals.

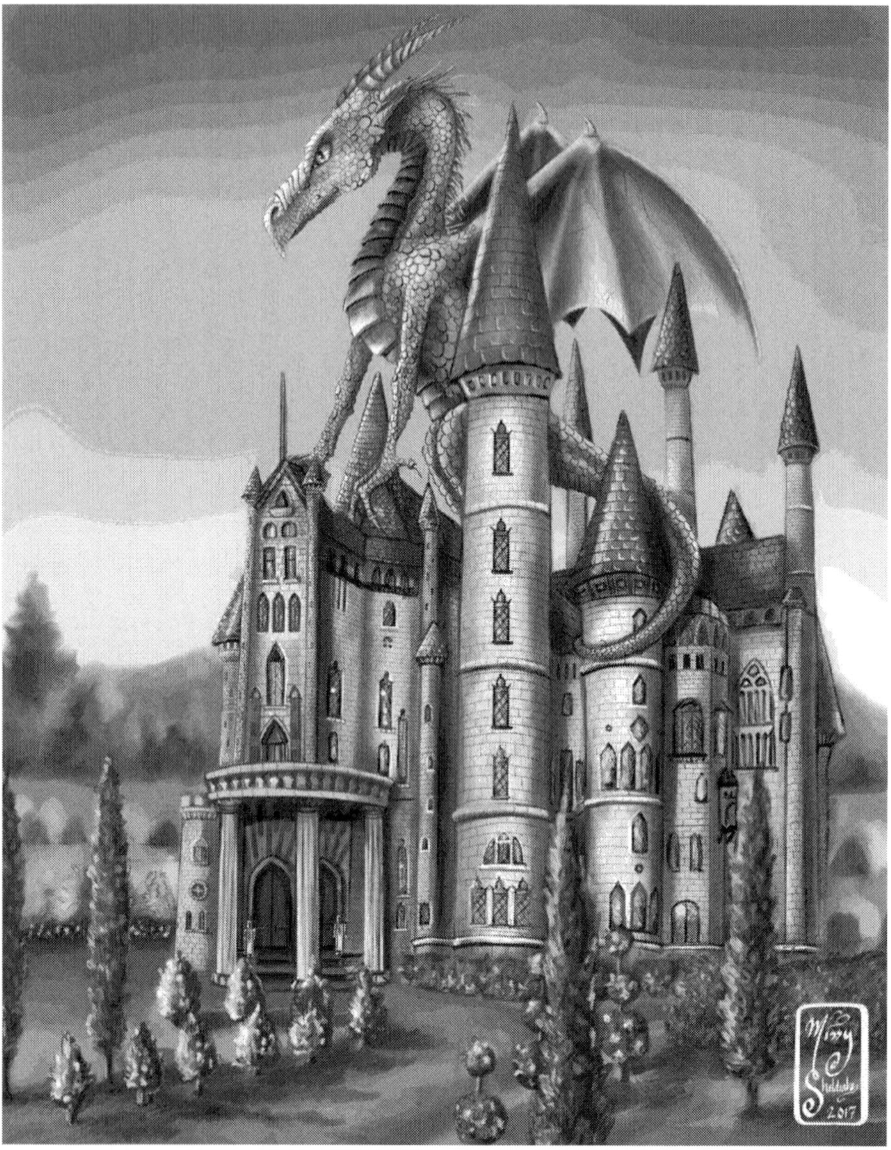

Chapter Twenty-Six

SISTER
Tib

"Opal," I mutter, shaking my head. "Opal's not a she, he's Skalivar."

I hop down from the railing, ready to sneak away. I don't want to see Saesa right now, and I know if I stay here, Zeze's likely to show up, too. With my arms crossed over my chest, I huff into the wind, scanning the red-dusted streets below. I don't want to go down there, either.

"Tib?" Saesa calls from somewhere inside. I step back against the railing. Look around. Think of what Mevyn showed me. Think of the one person I want to see right now more than anything else. We promised we would, too. In the Dreaming. My sister.

"Valenor?" I call into the Half-Realm.

The swish of his sky cloak tells me he's heard me. He drapes it around me like a cocoon of pure clouds. I feel its soothing magic hovering, waiting for me to allow it. I do, and am blanketed in the joyful feelings of an impossibly good dream.

"You have seen and done much since we last spoke," Valenor says. "You have suffered."

I can't answer. My throat is too closed up with my emotions. I just nod.

"I know why you have called me. Your sister is eager to see you. Come," he says gently. I nod again. Let his magic take me away. As Nessa's widow's walk fades from view, the trapdoor snaps open. Saesa peers out. My heart thuds in my chest. I almost call out to her, ask her to come, but I stop myself with a pang of guilt. She'll be fine. She's got Skalivar, after all. I won't be gone for long, anyway.

I drift off, carried in the comfort of Valenor's cloak. My sleep is dreamless and restful. I wake up refreshed, tucked in the comfort of a huge, soft library chair. Ki sits in a cozy nook across from me, nestled into a chair of her own with her feet curled up under her. Books are piled everywhere around her. The air is thick with the scent of old paper. Light spills into the room from huge windows and a skylight way up in a dome. Valenor slips away quietly, leaving me alone with my sister. She turns her head to the side and her black hair slips down her shoulder like satin. When she tears her eyes away from the book in her lap and looks at me, her face lights up.

"Brother!" she shouts, leaping from the chair, closing the space between us in two strides. She throws her arms around me. Hugs me tight. I do the same, squeezing her until she gasps for breath, burying my face into her shoulder, letting her hair tickle my nose.

I can't stop the tears. They come in ugly torrents. My whole body shakes with them. Ki holds me through the whole thing, stroking my back, whispering comfort. Her patience gives me permission to take as long as I need. When I'm finally calm enough to talk, I tell her about everything. Margy. Zeze. Cresten. Sha'Renell. The fists of sand, the dark fog. The Dona and the Savarikta. Velu. The Wellspring, swallowed up. Cerion and the Everlin powder. My confrontation with Vorance.

"You didn't," she gasps, pushing me away a little to look into my face. When she sees I'm telling the truth, instead of scolding me, her eyes brighten. She laughs with admiration. "Do you have any idea how many hours of my life I've spent dreaming of doing exactly what you did? Oh, I wish I could have been there to tell him off with you!"

"It was awful," I sniffle. "They thought I was a madman."

"Even the queen?" Ki asks. I nod. Look away. Think about her. Think about Saesa.

"I smashed it," I tell my sister. "The offering from Elespen. The one we worked so hard to get."

"You were angry," she says. "And rightfully angry. I can't believe they did that. All that powder. I can see why, though. Word in Brindelier was that Cerion was nearly completely devastated by earthquakes. Most of the homes there were flattened. Many people were hurt or died…"

I stiffen a little, and she squeezes my shoulder.

"I'm not making excuses," she hurriedly assures me. "It's unthinkable what they did. But I could see how the Everlin would have helped. It amplifies magic. It speeds it and purifies it. It would have allowed the city to recover in just a day or two, with only a few Mages. It even helps with healing magic as well. I learned all about it when I studied in Cerion. They used to be very strict about its use. I imagine it's because of the new queen that regulations on magic are changing there."

When I don't say anything, she goes on. "Do you want to talk about them? Margy? Saesa?"

"I don't know," I reply. "Every time I think about them, either of them, my thoughts get all twisted up. My heart races. My stomach gets sick. I want to punch something."

Ki laughs softly through her nose.

"What?" I ask.

"You don't do anything halfway, do you?" she says, squeezing me.

"I don't know what you're talking about," I mumble.

"You're not a boy anymore, little brother," she says, resting her cheek on top of my head. "You're bound to start having these feelings. And two at once, too. So, what are you going to do about it?"

"What do you mean?"

"Come on, Tib," she groans in disbelief, "I know you're not that dense. Who do you like more, Margy or Saesa?"

"What?" I shove her away. Start pacing. Shake my head. "What kind of a question is that? What difference does it make who I like more?"

Ki covers her mouth, but her eyes are smiling. Laughing. My heart thuds in my ears. Her question rings over and over in my mind. I think of Saesa. How she fought beside me. Saved my life, even. How she tried to keep me from getting in trouble. How she knew, before I did, even, that I was going to rage and throw that vial.

I think of Margy. How she took to me when we first met. Helped me and Mevyn, when I didn't even know about him. When he took my memories of him away. She believed in us before I even did. She knew, and she did everything she could to help us. I think about how my stomach flips every time I see her. About the light in her eyes. Her hope for the Dawn. How I want to keep her safe. Happy. Protected. Victorious.

"It's a stupid question," I grumble.

"Is it?" Ki laughs.

"Margy's queen. She's got to marry Poe," I say bluntly. "And Saesa's like my sister."

"But she's not your sister, is she?" Ki asks.

"She's got someone else, anyway," I reply. I tell her about Skalivar. The warrior who walked her home and kissed her hand. The copper dragon who saved us in Cresten. That leads to more questions about the things that happened in Elespen. I'm happy to change the subject and answer them. I tell everything I can remember about the Dona, and the Savarikta, and Velu and the temple. What it was like in the Stepwell, how I made the choice not to go with the Dusk. How I chose to let the temple fall, to let the Wellspring be taken.

She tries to convince me I did the right thing. I want to believe her, but I keep thinking about how angry Saesa was, and how kind the Dona had been to us. The song of the Savarikta echoes through my mind. The drums, like a heartbeat. The pulse of Elespen.

"Come here," Ki says. "I want to show you something."

She puts her arm around me. We walk away. Out of the library. Into the streets. Sea air and sand greet us. It's sunny. Hot. Sticky. Crowded. Merchant tents packed with wares line the streets. We pass a stall where a huge line waits to buy a roasting spit of sizzling, spiced meat from a singing cook behind it. The spices drift to my nose, fueling memories. I'm on Cap's ship, staring into Cresten. I pause. Look around.

"Where are we?" I ask.

"The Dreaming," Ki replies. "We can go anywhere in the Dreaming. Remember?"

"But this is exactly like Cresten," I say. The capital city, the way it should be.

"I know," Ki says. "When I left Sunteri, we traveled by ship through Elespen along the Jairun river. We stopped here," she explains, taking two spits from the cook. She hands me one. "I remember thinking how beautiful it was. So colorful and joyous and filled with life."

I take the spit and bite into the flavorful, juicy meat as we meander through the stalls. People greet us as we walk past, smiling warmly. I think of the cloud that hung over the city when Saesa and I arrived.

"It's not like this now," I tell Ki. "It's empty. Everyone is gone. Shadow has taken over."

"There are rumors of it in Brindelier," Ki says, wiping hot grease from her chin with the heel of her hand. "A darkness spreading. It's said to swallow up any life it touches. It's reached distant places: Haigh, Stepstone, Elespen. Barely anyone is aware of it, because no one remains to tell of its presence. I even heard someone say it had breached the borders of Cerion, in the north."

I stop walking. Swallow a lump of meat. Look at her.

"Who'd you hear it from?" I ask. "The gates of Brindelier are still closed, aren't they? They're still enchanted. Still celebrating."

"Sorcerers," Ki says under her breath. "Efran and I have been spending our days hunting them down, putting an end to them. There aren't many left in the city anymore, but they do tend to talk a lot. Especially with a coated dagger pointed at their throat." She grins at me. "That vial was the best gift you ever gave me."

I don't answer. I just think about my vials. My bandolier.

"We've been skulking around, destroying sigils. That's how they get in, you know. They use those coins set into the carvings they make," she explains. I pause.

"You mean the spindle coins?" I ask, remembering the first time I found one in an empty alley in Cerion.

She nods, her mouth too full to answer. I think about her and Efran running around Brindelier, Sorcerer hunting. It makes me kind of proud. Maybe that guy's not so bad, after all.

"It's so strange there," she goes on once she's done chewing. "There's no semblance of leadership, other than the Bordas keeping a loose order on things. Just rumors about the prince's comings and goings, and the princess's melancholy moods. Even those are talked about in whispers and dismissed. The people are too busy dancing, singing, eating, and drinking. It makes me wonder what it'll be like, eventually," she ponders. "Once all the offerings are in place and things go back to normal."

"Me too," I agree. My earlier vow to keep out of it seems foolish, now. The gray clouds, the Dusk gaining ground, the city hanging in the balance. It seems like the world is hanging on the precipice, ready to tip into oblivion. I imagine it swallowed up into darkness. Everything. Ruled by shadow and Sorcery, with Vorhadeniel and Sha'Renell on the throne.

What's to stop everyone from being slaves then? Good people, like these? People who deserve to live their lives free of the influence of magic, if they want to? It'd be like Sunteri, before I burned the towers. Sorcerers would rule. No one would stand a chance. I stop in the middle of the crowd and close my eyes. Take a deep breath. Listen to the chatter and the laughter. Feel the sunshine on my face. I can help them. All of them. I'm one of the only people who can.

"All right," I say after a while. "Where am I going, then?"

"Hmm?" Ki asks.

"Well, I smashed Elespen's, and who knows if there's any hope of getting another one. I think that temple collapsed and Sha'Renell drained the Wellspring. There's another offering in the Sorcerers' keep. We could try to get that one."

"I don't know," Ki says quietly, looking around as we walk through the crowd. "Maybe we should ask..." she trails off. Laughs softly. Points.

Sitting at the flaps of a colorful turquoise tent, a boy in bright yellow silks calls out a greeting to us in the language of the islands.

"Tib!" he shouts as we get closer, "and Ki! We've been expecting you! Come in, they're waiting." Loren pushes the tent flap aside, and a billow of bluish vapor puffs out of it into the sky. When we duck into the tent, the sounds of the market are shut away, replaced by the rush of ocean waves.

I gaze around in disbelief. We're inside Kaso Viro's tower. A pool of water in the center of the room sparkles. More blue vapor hangs in the air. Across the room, Valenor stands among pillows scattered over the floor.

"Welcome," he says, opening his arms in greeting. "Brother, they've arrived."

Chapter Twenty-Seven

SHIFTING LIGHT
Celli

Light, everywhere. It beams through my mind, pushing out every current thought, every memory of the past, every emotion. It washes over me, cleansing me, clearing me, absolving me. I feel peace, pure and beautiful. Love, acceptance, and beauty fill me up into the tips of my fingers and the corners of my mind.

In this moment there is no sense of self, good or bad. There is only light. It nurtures and guides me. It comforts and reassures me. I stay this way for countless hours, cradled and soothed by it, drifting in soft, sunlit clouds.

"Can you hear me?" A familiar voice calls. It's deep and gentle. A boy. A twin. A prince. Poe, the soon-to-be-heir of Brindelier's throne. Betrothed to Margary Plethore, Queen of Cerion.

A smudge of black streaks across the light, like a spot on my eye from looking too long at the sun. Tendrils of shadow seep through it, feeling around, searching. The light beams brighter and snuffs it out.

"Celli?" Poe calls.

I try to reply, but my body is far away. It doesn't exist here. All that does is pleasant, vast white. I'm not sure my answer is heard. All goes silent again for a while, and I drift on, neither here nor there, content in the purity of this state.

"*Celli,*" another voice calls. This one is a woman's. It's the same voice which spoke to me in sunbeams and dreams, giving me hope, encouraging me to survive. I know this presence, though it had been blocked from me. She's a friend, a caring entity. From her, I get a sense of nurturing kindness, a motherly sort of love. Her voice is accompanied by an even brighter light, and for the first time I'm aware of my own self in this strange and beautiful space.

I realize I can move through it, and I do, gliding closer to the light, flying as if I have wings. As I near her, I'm overwhelmed by her beauty. Her hair is long, pure strands of white light, dusted with flecks of prisms. Her eyes are just as white, framed with white lashes. Her gown is threads of sunbeams woven into gauze that drifts around her with impossible grace and beauty.

She opens her arms to me, and an echo of a memory mirrors the moment.

I remember a dream like this one, when darkness held me fast, and a smudge of gray called to me. That time, it was him. The Sorcerer, Quenson. He was all I needed then. He was my life blood, my breath, my sole reason for existing. He called to me this same way. He opened his arms to me. He held me and kissed me, and my life was complete. I was his, held fast. Owned, body and soul.

The Lady of Light sweeps her hand before me, and the shadow of a vision is obscured. I step into her arms as I did his, and she bends to embrace me. Her silky hair drapes my shoulders, sending tingles of perfection through me, forgiving the darkness, filling me with love. Real love, not spell-crafted. Not trickery. Not a selfish, controlling, cruel mockery of it. This is the love of my mother and father, and their hopes and dreams for me. It's my love for my lost brother, the way his smile lit me up with adoration. I find this love and hold it, keeping it close to me like the most precious gift. It gives me back my self. My voice.

"Who are you?" I whisper into the glistening beam of her shoulder.

"*I am Eljarenae, Muse of Light,*" she replies. "*I am with you. Whatever darkness befalls you, I offer you light to combat it tenfold.*"

Her voice echoes through the vastness like music, soft and sweet. It fills my heart to bursting with joy.

"Why me?" I ask her. Somehow, I recognize how special it is for her to show herself despite my tainted past.

"You have been drawn to the depths of my opponent, and you have survived. You hold within you a unique perspective. A doorway which until now has been closed to me, and to my allies, the Dawn."

"I do?" I ask, dazed by the tingle of the light that touches me.

"You do, dear one," she replies. "But I do not work in the same fashion as they. Though I covet the qualities you hold, I shan't take advantage of them unwillingly. I shall offer you two choices, and honor your decision, whatever you choose."

"What are they?" I whisper, leaning against her. Her warmth and caring are sensations I haven't felt in so long, I'd forgotten what it was like to simply be held.

"One, I shall return all of your memories, your knowledge of yourself and your past to you. I shall offer you healing from the cruelty you have suffered, and absolution of your dark deeds. You shall walk away to live however you choose, as long as you remain in the light. Two, I shall return all of your memories, your knowledge of yourself and your past to you. I shall offer you the same healing and absolution, and you shall work beside myself and those who stand with me against the darkness. This choice is far more dangerous, for you shall sometimes be asked to face your dark past head-on."

I sink deeper into her light, letting it surround me and wash over me. Far away, past the beams of sunlight, starlight, and moonlight, I can feel the darkness hovering. I have a detached understanding of it here in her presence. I know its terror, its evil, its hopelessness, but I'm protected from it. This close to the Lady of Light, I feel I can overcome it. I can be free of it. I can drive it back and diminish it.

I look up into her perfect face. Just as I'm about to give her my reply, I feel a shift. My body returns to me, or I return to it. I feel my hands, my feet, my shoulders and legs. My head is heavy against soft pillows. Warm sunshine bathes me from head to toe. Someone touches my arm.

"She wakes, Highness," someone says. A man. His voice is vaguely familiar.

"Ah," Poe says. I hear his footsteps approach, swishing through grass.

It's too bright for me to make out the prince's features as he comes to my side. Even when I blink rapidly, my eyes can't seem to get used to the glare of the sun. It washes everything in dancing prisms, blotting my surroundings with strange, shimmering colors. He rubs my arm.

"Did it work?" he asks the other man.

"I did my best to draw her as far into the light as I was able," he replies. "I could see nothing but the presence of Eljarenae, in the end."

I try to place his voice. It reminds me of snow and frigid cold, of a night filled with betrayal and lies. A distant, unimportant moment, now that all has been forgiven.

"You met her?" Poe asks me excitedly. His hand tightens on my arm slightly. I sit up a little and rest my opposite hand on his. Slowly, I nod.

"She's beautiful, isn't she?" he sighs. "I've met her only once, a very long time ago. She tries to stay away from the affairs of our people, but things are different now."

I nod again, still buzzing from the charge of beauty I just experienced. I squeeze my eyes shut and keep blinking, trying to clear my vision. It doesn't help.

"Come," Poe says. "Stand up. Stroll around some. It will ground you."

He takes my hand and pulls me to standing, and I feel soft grass beneath my feet. I cling to his arm and let him guide me in silence with the sun beaming overhead. My arm brushes delicate leaves. The fragrance of roses drifts to my nose. The further we walk, the sharper my mind becomes. My memories, long lost to me, begin to seep back.

They come slowly, gently, day by day, week by week, year by year. They file into place in my mind, neatly arranged, perfectly set. The darkest times seem distant. I can recall them fully, but they're brighter and emotionless. I see them as if they belong to a stranger, unattached and calm. Quenson is among them, shelved beside Sybel and her plots and spells. The layout of the Keep at Sixledge, the incantations whispered within its walls, the plans and schemes of the Dusk revealed to me in the Void…all are available if I choose to recall them.

Poe pauses at a flowering rosebush and breathes in the scent of the flowers.

"This was my mother's garden," he explains. "She made it for me and Pippa. She wanted to share her love for simple things. Things that grow."

We walk on, letting the sunshine warm us, until eventually we reach a wall. I feel its rough stone under my fingers, and I turn my face to the breeze. Far below us, I hear the sounds of revelry, the celebration festival still coursing through the kingdom. I squint my eyes, to really look, but the sunbursts still blind me. For some reason, being unable to see doesn't disturb me. I remember a moment in the darkness when my eyes were taken from me. Possessed by another. *Caviena*. I understand why, for now, my sight is blocked.

I wonder whether he can still see through me. Whether his grip still holds me in some way. The thought doesn't frighten me. It's more of a curiosity. The answer to my question, when I think about it, comes quietly: "*Only if you allow it. It is up to you, now.*"

My thoughts drift to other things. I wonder about the woman who would choose to make such an enchanted place for her children to spend their time, and the thought reminds me of my own mother back in Cerion.

Poe and I lean against the wall and I turn my face to the sun, letting it warm me. The autumn air is crisp. A soft breeze blows, carrying with it the perfume of flowers and the soothing cool of the season. I try to remember the last time I found myself completely free of influence and simply enjoyed being me. The thought makes me uneasy and puts me on edge.

"I imagine it's overwhelming," Poe says quietly. "What you've been through. What you're still going through, even now."

"Do you know?" I ask, not defensively, but genuinely curious. I'm at peace, but confused. I understand what's happened, but not fully. "How? And how much?"

"See there, you've found your voice," he says, and I can hear the smile in his tone. "When Pippa showed you to me through the mirror, I knew who'd sent you. I could see its influence around you, like a halo of shadow. It had consumed you a long time ago. Pippa didn't see it. She wouldn't have. She has—" he stops himself. "Sorry. I'd better not say too much. Not until you choose, anyway."

"Choose?" I ask, vaguely remembering the lady and her proposal.

"She gave you choices, didn't she?" Poe urges. "Eljarenae?"

I close my eyes and think, letting my past play out over and over in my mind. I long for the days before I swiped that coin from Quenson, cloaked in black and lurking in the shadows of the Academy. I long to be that girl again, the one who bested nearly every boy on the block in foot races, spent her days casually pilfering, and came home to supper on the table and the affections of her parents. I know I can't, though. I can never go back to a mundane life. That girl has changed too much. She's seen things and done things that could never allow her to return to the way things had been. She knows too much now. I know too much.

"Your Highness," I admit shakily, "I am no hero. Even before all of this, I was a thief. A brawler. It doesn't make sense why your lady would offer any kindness to me."

"Everyone has their dark places," the man beside Poe says thoughtfully. I imagine a glint of gold. Windblown, wiry hair. The orange glow of the Firestone. Quenson's screams of anguish as I failed to stop that Mage from taking it. I think back at the things I did that night. At the blood on my hands. I shiver.

"You remember me," the man says quietly, "though we were never properly introduced. Your plight troubled me that night, Celli. I hoped one day I might meet you again." He chuckles softly. "And here you are. My name is Kenrick. I am a Mentalist, and I hold no ill will against you for your actions. You were, after all, a thrall.

"The Lady of Light sees beyond the darkness. She whispered to me and told me of your plight. She finds the hope in a person, you see, as small as it might be, and she draws it out of them. Just as darkness can be fostered, so can light. It is all in the mind, after all. You have been offered a chance to turn things around. To right past wrongs. I hope you'll find redemption a welcome offer."

I think on it long and hard, relishing the moment. My life is my own. I have a choice. I can do what I want, whatever I choose, with no one controlling me. Though the emotions that go with my memories have been healed and detached, a new flame lights inside of me. I understand the wickedness of the Dusk, and I know of its vast reach. I'm aware of things even the Lady of Light has no knowledge of. I can be a deciding force in the battle to come. I can help the right side win. Before I tell him, though, before I decide, there's something I need to know.

"What would she have me do?" I ask warily. "What task?"

"You shall tell us all you know of the Dusk. Their reach, their plots, their holdings and movements. You shall tell us all that you have seen, and all that you know is to come. When you've told us all you know, we might delve into your mind to search for things you may not know the value of. In time, if necessary, you might be allowed returned to the hold of Dusk, as an agent of Dawn, to face those who kept you and to bring justice to them, if you choose it.

My heart races when I realize what it means, when it fully strikes me. I'm free of them. All of them. I'm free to choose. I can do nothing, or I can fight. I can stand up against those who held me captive and manipulated me. I can put an end to their wickedness, to keep others safe from it.

I have a choice. I'm not powerless or hopeless. I can be forgiven. I can fight.

"I choose to stand beside you," I say to both of them. "I choose Dawn."

My words hold power. A burst of energy explodes from my center, filling me with light, banishing the last of the darkness. My eyes tingle, my vision returns. I feel the last of his hold on me leave, the last of the influence of the Dusk erased.

Poe grips my hands, watching with an expression of awe and amazement. His long white-blond hair rustles in the breeze of the rush of light, and he takes a deep breath as if inhaling the power of it.

"What a relief," he says once everything goes quiet.

"Indeed," Kenrick says. I look him over. His face is metallic, brushed in gold Mark. It pulses and sparkles with glittering light. He's not so threadbare and weather-worn as he was that night. His hair is better kept, and his traveling clothes and hat are of the same style, but newer. His eyes are crinkled and his mouth upturned in a constant smile. He winks at me, and a shiver of laughter bubbles from my chest.

"How did you come to be in Brindelier?" I ask him. "All the way from Hywilkin?"

"I arrived with the prince," he replies, "who rushed home from Cerion with an urgent concern for his sister. Imagine my delight when I found the mystery thrall was behind all the turmoil. Quite curious indeed. Your mind is a delightfully complex place, my dear."

I shift a little, unsure whether to be flattered or insulted by his assessment.

"Come," Poe says, breaking the awkward silence. "There is much work to do, and little time."

"Indeed," Kenrick agrees. I accept the arm the Mentalist offers me, and with his guards flanking us, I follow Poe along the parapet to the inner annex of the castle eagerly toward my future, on the path I've chosen myself. My freedom. The light. The Dawn.

Chapter Twenty-Eight

RITUAL'S DREGS
Azi

Deep in my heart, I listen for a reply from Rian. When he doesn't answer me, I try hard not to worry. If something serious had happened, if Sybel had succeeded, then I'm sure I would have felt something. She didn't, I tell myself over and over. She couldn't have. Shush would know. The fairies would tell me.

The battle that follows our escape from the chute is a blur. The Void is nothing to Stellastera, and her magic ensures we're invisible to it as well. We dart through the Void-filled room beyond the iron door as if it's any other space, and the shadow doesn't even think to touch us.

With her spirit rekindled, Stellastera is a force to be reckoned with in the dark corridors beyond. The inky liquid magic that courses through the walls seeps toward her, drawn like a magnet. It winds around her arms and weaves into her gown. With Flitt and Mercy's light to kindle her spirit, she commands the arcane to her will, casting it out again to plow over those who stand against us.

Sorcerers crumple at her feet without a word spoken between them, and she draws their magic to her in powerful streams. I barely have to raise my sword against our enemies. She breezes past them, invoking fear, devastating their resolve, leaving them stripped witless in our path. Risen skeletons crumple at the sight of her, and ghostly wraiths are sucked in by her breath and released in wisps of pure, silvery magic.

"*This way,*" Shush pushes, and he streaks ahead of us in a blur of iridescent green. We weave through the winding hallways, leaving bright, pure stone and the remains of our defeated enemies in our wake.

We're met with fewer and fewer opponents the further we go, until eventually the passages are deserted and silent.

"They know," Stellastera warns. "They know I escaped. The energy has shifted. They have fallen back into the Void. It pulses with the energy of them, it siphons away into darkness, to their furthest retreat." She slows her pace, looking back over her shoulder.

"What do you mean?" I ask. "I thought this was their stronghold."

"No," she whispers in reply. She drifts slightly away from me as if drawn toward it. "I feel it. A great, wicked gathering to the north, in a city unknown to maps and lost to the memories of humans. A rival to all the cities of the Known Lands."

I follow her distant gaze until Shush grabs my braid.

"Hurry," he cries, "Rian!"

His voice gusts over me in a torrent, snapping me back into action. We race through the keep until we finally arrive at the door with the serpent handle, where my golden threads wove through the keyhole. I pause. A lump rises in my throat. My hand rests on the latch. Fear pulses through me. I don't know what I'll find on the other side. All I do know is I can't feel his presence at all.

"Wait," Flitt pushes. "Try to look through like you did before."

"There is no need," Stellastera says, closing her eyes. "The wand and the ring are within, but the Sorcerers have fled. All were called back into the darkness by their master, Diovicus."

His name makes my heart sink into the pit of my stomach. Even Flitt and Shush spin to stare at her, wide-eyed.

"It's true, then," Flitt squeaks.

"We didn't want to believe it," Shush whispers.

The flash of rage in Stellastera's eyes is fleeting. She turns her attention to the door with confidence, and with a wave of her hand, the wards are broken and the door swings open.

"Remain here. Allow me to see what I might glean from the essence within before you enter," she says.

Reluctantly, I nod. My feet shuffle as close to the threshold as I can get without entering. My gaze locks on the pedestal holding my ring, my love. Nothing else in the room matters to me. At my shoulder, Flitt clings to my neck, her eyes wide, her breath held in suspense. On my other side, Shush wrings his wiry hands. I reach up to offer him comfort, and he settles in my palm to cling to my thumb hopefully.

Stellastera glides through the room, her chin raised as her toes graze the floor. Her wings barely flutter. She seems to float on magic itself as she moves.

"The residue of magic here is foreign to me," she explains, sniffing the air. She drifts to the pedestal holding Aster, the wand, and hovers her hand over it. "Its devising was brilliantly crafted," she sighs with a shudder of appreciation. "Mortal Sorcery with immortal flavors. The Necromancer's spells were intricately woven, complex and obscure. She melded shadow and death into her workings to hide its intentions from us. I have never felt anything so dark, so forbidden."

She sweeps her hand over the first platform, where the bottle that once held glowing green liquid lies on its side, emptied of its contents.

"Their only remaining offering," she whispers. "A great sacrifice." She holds her hands before her, as though catching some imaginary flow of magic. Her wings flutter softly, propelling her to the platform. Her eyes are half-closed, entranced by the memory of the ritual that lingers behind in the room like the thin smoke that streams from an extinguished candle. Her musings guide her to the two platforms which held Eron and King Richter.

"A fallen prince, blood of the sworn enemy," she shakes her head slowly, stretching her hand across the stone where Eron had lain. She pauses for a moment, then turns to the other slab. "A fallen King, blood of the victor," she whispers. When she faces me, wide-eyed, my stomach sinks all the way to my toes.

"Such remarkable, intelligent magic," she says shakily. "Such wise, thoughtful manipulations. Eron Plethore, descendant of he who struck Diovicus down. His sworn enemy. The one who destroyed his lofty ambitions. And Richter, King of Hywilkin, descendant of he who triumphed over the King of Brindelier."

"Oh," Flitt whispers in my ear, trembling.

"I don't understand," I croak, even though a small part of me does. I just don't want to believe it.

"In Hywilkin, as I'm sure you saw, Azaeli," Stellastera explains, "the victor over the king claims the throne. By drawing from the bloodline of the victor over my husband," Stellastera explains, "the Necromancer strove to infuse some entity with the right to claim his throne."

"Some entity," Shush whispers. No one needs to say aloud what we all know. Who else could that entity be but their master? Diovicus, the defeated Sorcerer King.

"What about Rian?" I ask, my vision blurred with tears as my eyes rest again on the ring. "What did he have to do with it? Is he still…" I can't bring myself to finish my question. It takes all of my restraint to keep from charging into the room and scooping up all that's left of him. Instead, I watch Stellastera, wishing with all my heart that I could be her, close enough to reach out and touch him. My heart aches with fear as she drifts to the ring on the pedestal and hovers her hands over it.

"Blood of the Protector," she nods to me, indicating the blood on the ribbon of the ring. My blood. "Essence of the Champion," she whispers, closing her eyes.

"Rian," I push, focusing hard on the ring. *"Please answer me. Please."*

"Do not fret, Azaeli," Stellastera says after an agonizingly long pause. "His essence has diminished, but he is not lost to us. He has retreated into himself. Tucked far from their reach is he, guarded by all the wards he could muster, cloaked in the shadows of his mind, but surrounded within that by the light of my sister, Eljarenae." She looks away from the ring, into the hearth that churned with the energy of the void in my earlier vision. Now, it's empty. She gazes at it for a thoughtful moment, taking deep, centering breaths.

"Come," she says finally, motioning to me. I step over the threshold and creep closer to her. My fingertips tingle with a charge of magic. They're drawn to the ring, compelled to take it from the pedestal. My vision closes in slightly, but Flitt's grip on my earlobe and Stellastera's voice keep me grounded and alert.

"Once you take it," she whispers, "there will be little time. They will know. They will come. I shall remain to face them."

She drifts to me and lifts my chin with the tips of two fingers, guiding me to look into her face.

"Azaeli," she says with a grave tone, "when I tell you to do so, take the ring and the wand. Run as fast as you can. Bring it to the room where Rian lies encased in the stone. In that moment, the Muse of Earth will be occupied with me. She will not realize straight away what is being undone there. The wand will free him, but you must act quickly. Do not go to Kythshire, though you might be tempted. Take Rian, the ring, and the wand to my brothers. Valenor will know what to do. Show them what you have seen here. Tell them I stand with Dawn. Plead on my behalf for their aid. If they do not come, I shall indeed fail. I have learned I cannot stand against the earth and the darkness alone."

"You're willing to stay and face them again, even after what they did to you, just to make sure we get out safely?" I ask her in disbelief.

Her smile is soft and warm. Her fingers trail from my chin to my forehead. The touch of her sister lingers there, buzzing with soft light.

"Do not allow the same faith you have enlightened *me* with to fail *you*," she says. "The Dawn will triumph. It must. But it cannot do so without its champions."

I don't know what to say. I hug her tightly and she hugs me, too, and I feel the power and essence of magic swirling around her like a storm. She's different now, it seems to tell me. She has the power and determination, this time, to fight against them.

She drifts away and looks to the fairies at my shoulders, offering them the same warm smile.

"Ready?" she asks. I nod.

"*Stay on me,*" I push to Flitt and Shush. Flitt tucks herself deeper into my pauldron. Shush clings to my collar.

"Now," Stellastera says calmly.

I snatch Rian's ring first. In the two steps it takes me to reach the wand, the floor starts to rumble. The walls ripple like fishermen's nets airing in the sea wind. The ceiling cracks. I grab the wand and take off through the door without looking back. I try to push back my panic as the floor rolls beneath me and everything around us goes dark as pitch.

"*I can't see!*" I push to the fairies, and Flitt peeks out from my pauldron and beams her light through the blindness. From his perch on my other shoulder, Shush directs me through the rumbling, thundering passages. Several times, I stumble and crash against a wall and come away covered in the dark, sticky substance that flows through it.

"Here, here, in here!" Shush shouts, and the door that barred our way smashes open with the force of the wind that rushes from his voice.

Another quake throws me to my knees, and I grip Rian's ring tightly in one hand and Aster in the other as I crawl to the spot where I know he's lying trapped in the stone.

I realize in this moment as the darkness billows around us and the floor rises and falls like a stormy ocean wave, that I have no idea what to do. Stellastera gave me no directions. I take the wand and point it at the floor, and I do the first thing that comes to me, I scream Stellastera's name.

With a shuddering quake, the floor splits open between my knees. I start to fall into the chasm and scramble frantically to grab the side of the wall, but I refuse to let go of the ring or the wand, and the rumbling floor makes it impossible for me to find purchase. Shush darts away from my shoulder and bellows something I can't hear over the thundering of the quakes. The wind he creates holds me steady, keeping me from falling.

Flitt leaps from my shoulder and dives into the deep crack. Her light casts sharp shadows across the broken stone until she disappears into the depths below.

"He's here!" she pushes. *"Come down!"*

Shush takes my hand. He creates a wind around us to ease me gently downward, deeper into the cracking earth, until I'm sure we'll all end up buried alive. When we reach the very bottom, Flitt's light grazes across Rian's prone form. He lies on his back with his eyes closed, surrounded by rubble. His hands rest peacefully on his chest, which rises and falls with his breath.

"Rian!" I choke. Shush sets me gently beside him and I scoop him up into my arms. His body is limp, unresponsive, and so cold it gives me chills. The chasm roars above us. Flitt's light is snuffed out.

"They're coming," she whispers.

"Got it!" Shush calls. I feel his hand on my cheek. Flitt clings to my shoulder. The air around us shifts. My body tingles from head to toe. I grip the ring and the wand and Rian tightly as we're pulled into the Half-Realm. An instant later, we arrive in a spray of warm sand. The sun beams down from overhead, but the usually soothing sound of ocean waves crashing on the seashore brings me little comfort.

On my knees in the sand, I hold Rian close and feel little more than bones buried within the thick layers of his robes. His eyelids don't flutter when I tip his face toward the beaming morning sun. His freckles are deep spatters of red-brown against the pale white translucence of his skin. I swallow back tears at the sight of his gaunt cheeks. He's almost skeletal in my arms.

Sniffling, I draw his face to mine and kiss his rough, parched lips. With the ring looped around them, I slide my fingers into his hair. My own heart races being so close to him, but his pulse remains steady and slow.

"Kaso Viro!" Shush calls toward the sea. I hear some splashing at the shore, but I'm too concerned with Rian to care what's happening there.

"Rian," I push to him tearfully. *"My love. Please, if you're there, please say something. We found you. It's over."*

She can be him, I think to myself, remembering Stubs' guidance. I squeeze my eyes shut with my lips still pressed to his.

"Azi, that's not a good idea. You'd better wait for the Muses," Flitt warns. Her voice is far away, obscured by the golden threads that curl between me and Rian, licking at my closed eyes, calling me away from myself.

"Greetings, friends!" Loren calls. His voice is even further than Flitt's.

I don't open my eyes. My need to speak to Rian, to know he's all right, keeps me focused. I feel myself slipping deeper, carried by golden threads toward my love. I feel the shift and know that I've entered his mind, but there are no thoughts, images, or memories to greet me. I'm surrounded by a still gray fog which muffles the sound of my boots and the light in my heart. It's neither sad nor happy, it just is. I remember what Stellastera said, that Rian has tucked himself beyond reach and is guarded by countless wards within his mind.

"Rian!" I shout into the gray. My voice echoes endlessly through the fog, repeating until my ears ring and I have to cover them to keep from going mad with the sound. I take a deep breath and try, like I did in my mother's mind, to go deeper and find the darkness Stellastera told me about. I wander in wide circles, searching desperately for some shift or difference in the gray matter, but I find nothing at all.

"So, what am I supposed to do?" A voice echoes from deep within the gray. It takes me a moment to figure out who it is, mostly because it's entirely out of place.

"Tib?" I call out.

"Search for a source of magic. Most likely wards," Valenor replies.

"I don't know," Tib mumbles. "I'm no Mentalist."

"Well," Valenor chuckles, "you might have noticed our reliable Mentalist has gotten herself into a tangle, so you'll have to do, Dreamstalker."

"Valenor!" I shout.

"Sh-sh-sh! Did you hear something?" Valenor asks.

I turn in place, trying to face the direction of their voices, but there is no direction. They're coming from all around me.

"No," Tib answers. "But I found some black stuff over here. And some white stuff behind it. It's all jumbled up with gold thread."

"Excellent!" Valenor says. "Now, just take this dagger and—"

My breath is knocked out of me as I'm flung violently off my feet. I careen through the space and fly out of Rian's mind with the speed of a cannonball. My body jolts with the force of my expulsion. Pins and needles prickle my skin from head to toe. I gasp for breath and squint, blinded by pinpoints of colorful light.

"You stupid dunderhead!" Flitt squeaks at me. Her tiny hands batter my face with little stinging slaps that amplify the pins and needles and ripple out like rings around water drops. "I told you not to! When are you ever going to listen to me?"

I try to bat her away, but my hand is too heavy. My heart thuds in my chest. My ears drum painfully with every word she chirps. My eyes fly open. I search frantically until I see him lying beside me. Turning my head is a colossal effort, but I manage it. His eyes are open. He's staring up at the ceiling, where the reflection of water dances above us. Shush sits on his chest, his head bowed, his eyes closed.

"What happened?" I try to push, but Flitt doesn't reply. I don't think she got it.

When I'm finally able to tear my gaze from Rian, I realize others are kneeling on cushions beside him. Valenor, Kaso Viro, and as I heard in his mind, Tib. It's strange to see him there, flanked by the two larger men, his eyes closed, his hands resting on Rian's chest. He's holding the ring. I can see the stained purple ribbon dangling from it.

"What are they doing?" I whisper to Flitt when I finally find my voice. Her reply is a yelp of relief followed by a great, big, sticky kiss on my cheek.

"Rian did a good job of hiding himself away from the Sorcerers," she explains. "So good, even Valenor couldn't find him. Thankfully, Tib was here. He went into the Dreaming with Valenor and figured out what was going on. You were all tangled around him. Now that you're out of there, they're getting him back."

"I feel so strange," I groan. The pins and needles prickle through me still, not subsiding.

"Well, what did you expect, going into someone's head when their head isn't all in one place?" she huffs. "Honestly."

"I want to help," I whisper.

"Nope!" She chirps. "You need to rest. Let them work. Go to sleep, and maybe they'll catch up to you in the Dreaming when they're done."

"I can't sleep now," I cry, gazing over at Rian.

"Sure you can. Here," she says, reaching into her belt pouch. "I'll help."

Before I can protest, she flings a handful of sparkling pink powder into my face. My eyes flutter closed, and I drift to sleep.

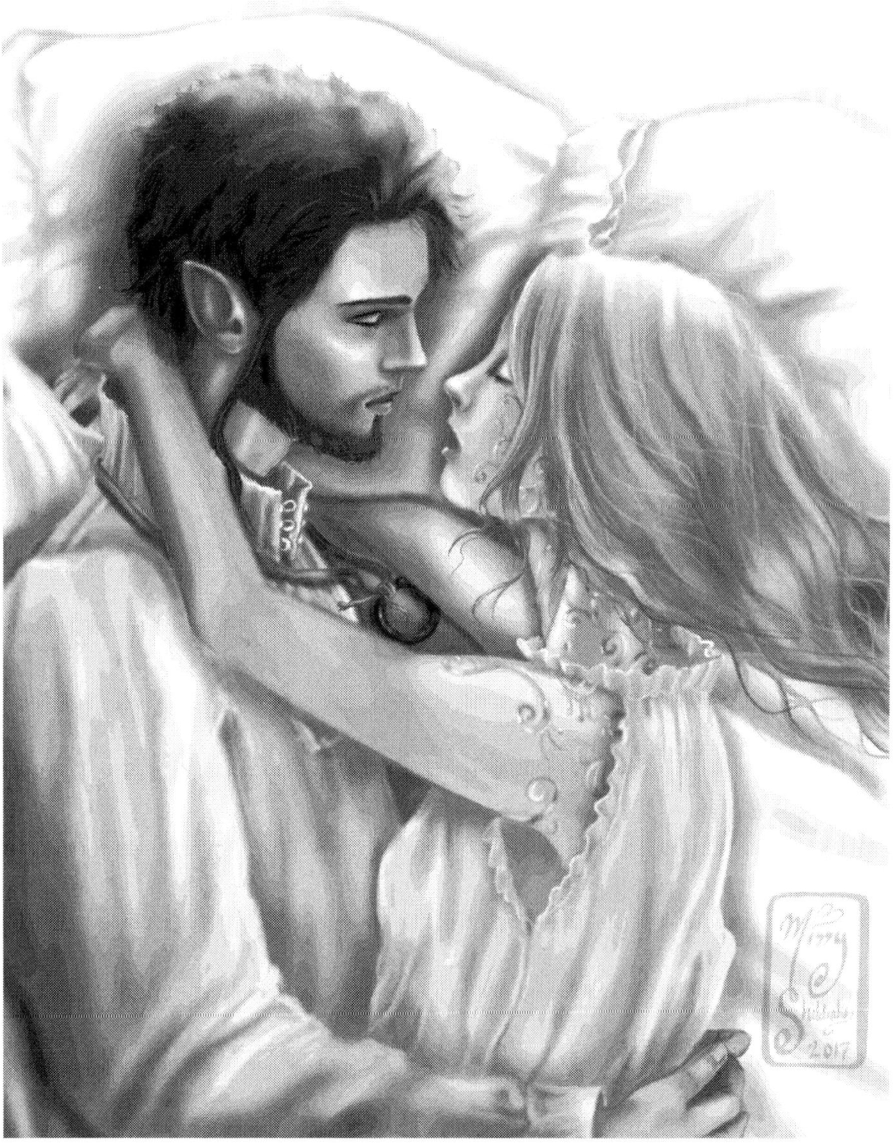

Chapter Twenty-Nine

MEETING OF MUSES
Azi

Cocooned in the soft warmth of Rian's arms, I wake slowly to the sound of wind chimes and singing birds. Rather than open my eyes right away, I burrow deeper into the comfort of his embrace, breathing in the smoky scent of his robes, listening to his heartbeat as my head rests on his chest. He tucks me closer to him, stroking my back. The scruff of his beard catches in my hair. His breath warms my forehead as his lips graze my brow.

"Azi," he whispers, and I tip my head back so his lips can find mine.

Relief cascades over me in delicious waves, filling me with the warmth of his love as our kiss deepens. Fleeting thoughts travel through my mind as he caresses me: Where are we? What happened? Where are the others?

Each thought, each worry is pushed away as quickly as it comes. Right now, it doesn't matter. Rian is back, and we're together. Everything else can wait. It doesn't take long for us to lose ourselves in the moment, to allow ourselves to be together, just us two. Despite what we've been through, despite what's happening elsewhere, nothing has changed between us. He's mine and I'm his, and our world is here, safe and complete in each other's embrace.

"Azi, you have a stinky Mage stuck to your face," Flitt squeaks, giggling.

Without breaking our kiss, I groan and throw a pillow in her general direction. She yelps and sends it flying back at me.

"Hey! Don't be rude!" she cries.

I respond by deepening my kiss. To my surprise, it works. Flitt goes silent. Her light behind my eyes fades.

"They're still at it," I hear her say to someone nearby.

"Let them be," Shush whispers. "Give them some privacy."

"Just thought you might want to watch the battle," Flitt pushes to me. *"It's been going for a while now, and you're missing all the good parts shut away in here with a Mage sucked onto your face."*

I throw another pillow, and Rian laughs through his nose. To our relief, the fairies go, leaving us content in the privacy of each other's company.

***

"Battle?" I gasp sometime later, bolting from my dreamy state.

The bed where we sit is draped with a canopy of gauzy pink billowing fabric. Flowering vines drip thickly from it, filling the air with a sweet, light perfume. It's a lavish, wide bed in an incredibly spacious room. The walls are the soft color of dawn, matching perfectly with the open sky above us. In the far corner, my suit of armor stands polished on a form, with all the underpinnings freshly laundered and laid out beside it. On a nearby rack, Mercy glints in the soft glow of morning, waiting patiently to be called into action.

"Where are we?" I ask sleepily. "The Dreaming?" Rian takes my hand. He sits up much more slowly, blinking into our softly lit surroundings with a confused look on his face.

His other hand drifts to his chest and closes over something I noticed there earlier, but was too distracted to give much thought to. The ring, Margy's ring, the one that held Rian's self apart from his body, hangs from his neck on a sturdy leather cord. He glances at me and tucks it into the collar of his linen shift.

"Mm-mm," he replies between kisses to my knuckles and wrist. "The Palace of Dawn, I think."

"Why do you still have that?" I ask, resting my hand on the ring through his shirt.

"For now, I need it," he replies vaguely.

He pulls me to him and we kiss again, but before it goes too far I lean back and look him over. It's all so perfect, so wonderful, it's hard to believe it's real.

His eyes are the same as always: hazel, warm, smiling. He looks much better than he had on the beach. His face is fuller now, his skin still pale, but healthier. I stroke my hand down the length of his arm as he leans in to kiss me again and am relieved that he's not as wasted to bone as he had been when we recovered him, but he's still quite thin.

"How long has it been?" I push, not wanting to interrupt our kiss.

"I don't know," he replies.

"How do you feel?" I ask.

"I love you."

"Azi! Ugh! Don't you two ever come up for air? Honestly!" Flitt darts between us, shoving my face away from Rian's, beaming her light so brightly that we're forced to turn away from each other.

I reach behind me for another pillow, but before I can throw it, it disappears in a burst of sparkling sunbeams.

"No more of that! Really!" she squeaks indignantly. "They said you'd need time to recover, they said let you be together, but this is ridiculous! Get up, get up! You're missing all of it, and it's really impressive, and you're going to be sorry if you don't! Get! Up!" she emphasizes each word with a sharp tug to my braid.

Beside me, Shush is giving Rian a similar speech. My love glances over his shoulder at me and rolls his eyes.

"All right, all right…" I agree, batting Flitt away. "Just let me talk to Rian for a moment."

I shuffle closer to him, sliding my arms around him, and he leans back against me and closes his eyes, savoring our closeness.

"I love you, too, Rian," I say, "but you're avoiding answering me. How do you feel? What happened, exactly? And why do you still have that ring?"

To my surprise, the fairies don't interrupt. Instead, they float close to each other and quietly wait for Rian's reply. He draws a long, deep breath and lets it out slowly. Wherever we touch pulses with bright energy.

"I watched for a long while," he explains, his voice just above a whisper. "I analyzed every movement Sybel and Xantivus made. I couldn't see well from where I was. It was like looking through a dark veil. I had to use my Arcane training to tune into it and really feel their magic. It was so complex, so dark and wicked, I had trouble setting my emotions aside. Fear welled in me. I knew what they were doing was beyond the realm of forbidden. It made me angry. I wanted to lash out at them, to destroy them and their makings, but I knew that without my body I was powerless."

He shudders, and I hold him tighter. He goes on to tell us things we already know, things Stellastera gleaned from the residue of magic in the chamber. Rian's account is far more difficult to hear, though. When he tells us of the moment he retreated to deepest reaches of his mind, his voice breaks several times.

"Show me," I whisper, but he shakes his head.

"Not so soon," he replies softly and turns to me. His eyes graze my nose, my lips, but never meet mine. "I need my thoughts to be untouched, just for a little while." He takes my hands in his, turning the rest of his body to face me. Seeing me seems to bolster him enough to go on.

"The Mentalist entered my mind. He chased me. I only knew what he was doing because I'm aware of what you can do. I tried to fight back, but he was ruthless. He tore into me, stealing every thread of myself that he could reach. That's when I gathered myself and retreated as far as I could from him. Eljarenae, the Muse of Light, was with me. She helped me build a wall of light to barricade myself from his attacks. After that, I couldn't see any more. The next thing I remember is feeling your warmth, and falling, and being brought to the sea."

He closes his eyes, skipping ahead.

"Stellastera infused the wand with enough power to start the restoration from here," he grazes our fingers over the hidden ring in his shirt, "to here." He raises our hands to his temple. "The restorative magic is still working. It'll take some time for me to be wholly myself again. Until then, and even after that, I need you. The love between us is a power unlike any other. It will work to nurture their magic, to strengthen and speed it. As unthinkable as things were in there, I learned so much. The purity of light, the importance of love."

He pulls me close, pressing me to him. His lips brush mine and I slide into his lap and fall more deeply into his kiss.

"Ugh," Flitt gags in my ear dramatically. "Come on!" She tugs on my bangs, separating us.

"When the Muses return," Rian says quietly, "Stellastera will be able to speed the process. She has the ability to completely unravel and restructure even the most complex spells. It's remarkable, truly."

"Stellastera," I gasp. "She's still there! Oh, Rian. I was supposed to tell them, and I didn't! I couldn't because—" I whirl in place, pointing at Flitt with a glare. "You!"

"Don't blame me!" Flitt squeaks. "You were being Azi again! Always rushing into things, trying to fix stuff you don't know anything about!"

I lunge at her, swiping the air she leaves behind. I want to shake her, I'm so irritated with the little fae. She thinks it's a game. She giggles and ducks, leaving rainbow trails of glitter behind her.

"Oh, settle down," she laughs. "We told them about her."

"Right," Shush whispers. "They made sure Rian was recovering well, and they had us bring you here and then went to help her."

"Yeah," Flitt agrees. "And you're missing it!"

Her excitement is lost to me. Rian's skilled hand playing with my hair is too distracting. He trails his knuckles softly along the nape of my neck. I fall back into his arms, and we kiss again.

"Really?" Flitt chirps, enraged.

"They're right, you know," Rian murmurs between kisses. "We can't stay here forever. All good things must come to an end."

His words crash over us like the severing of a spell. The urgency of what's happening at Sixledge hits me in torrents. We separate and look at each other, wide-eyed, and I know he's having the same revelation. This was a spell to keep us soothed and happy together. A necessary spell for his recovery. He must have known, deep down, the words he'd need to speak to break it.

"Finally!" Flitt yelps. "Hurry!"

We jump up from the bed and race to dress ourselves. The fresh, soft chausses and gambeson laid out for me are easy enough to dress myself in, but my armor is another story. For the first time in a long while, I think of Saesa as I heave my newly-polished chestplate from the mannequin. I feel that same pang of guilt for leaving her behind, and I wonder what's happened to her since we left Cerion.

Rian notices my plight with the armor. He waves his hand effortlessly, and the pieces fit themselves to me. Mercy settles on my back. My braid combs and re-plaits itself.

"What's happening?" I ask Flitt as Rian offers me his arm. "Was she fighting alone for very long?" I groan. "I was supposed to tell them about her as soon as we returned!"

"Don't worry," Flitt huffs as she leads us through to the main annex of the palace. "No thanks to you, she's winning. Even Eljarenae went to help her."

"Don't feel bad," Shush whispers, throwing Flitt a look that seems to order her to behave. "No one blames you. You two needed to recover, after all."

"Well, they wouldn't have needed to *recover* so intensely if Azi hadn't gone and barged into his head when she shouldn't have!" she argues.

"I was only trying to help," I say.

"You did," Rian whispers, kissing my temple. "I felt you with me. It kept me from panicking."

I look up at him, but he keeps his eyes ahead. My gaze trails to the ring hidden beneath his shirt, and I ask, "Are you well enough to do this? Is it safe?"

"I'm with you," he pushes to me, nodding. *"As long as we're together, I'll be fine."*

The throne room of the fairy queen is a place I've visited before: once in person and once in Rian's dreams, where I walked down the aisle in my wedding gown. Both of those times, Rian and I were the center of attention. This time, no one notices us as we enter through a side door. As always, hundreds of fairies are gathered between the rows of elegant columns, hovering in crowds all the way up to the vaulted open ceiling.

Their breath seems to be collectively held, their attention fixed on the long aisle that runs through the center of the throne room. There, a stretch of space is open before them like a vast portal. Upon its watery surface, an unbelievable scene unfolds. The images overlap each other, like several memories observed all at once.

Rian and I edge closer, hand in hand, our eyes fixed on the scenes that play out there. Once we set our attention on the sights, sounds emerge, too, bursting in our ears, rumbling through our bodies.

One view is the scene outside of Sixledge. The black keep towers upon its island, a dark sky broiling over it, churning in angry shades of green and purple. The sea pulls back from the land, exposing the ocean floor for as far as we can see. At the foreground, Kaso Viro rears up in the form of a sea dragon. His scaly lip curls in a fearsome snarl. He screeches a powerful, eerie cry, and the sea rushes in in torrents, charging up the mountain, crashing into the walls of the keep in tidal waves, crumbling its outer walls as though it were merely a sandcastle. The waves spill back and crash in again and again, relentlessly pounding the stone, washing it to pebbles and sand.

A figure, the finely carved statue of a woman, appears on the parapet. She raises her arms and the crumbled stone rolls toward her. It arranges itself perfectly into place, repairing the walls with barely a word uttered from her lips. She sinks into the stone and the earth rumbles violently. Another ocean wave pulses out from the keep, driving toward Kaso Viro.

"She's under the sea," Rian whispers, his lips brushing my ear.

Sure enough, a moment later the black water swirls into a whirlpool. Kaso Viro dives into it and the surface of the sea shudders and crashes with the power of the battle going on beneath it.

The ocean's storm creates turmoil in the clouds above. Lightning pulses within them, growing moment by moment in power. With each crackle of it, the sky lights up like daytime. Its electric energy sizzles in the clouds, pushing them back, exposing the stars in the night sky.

The images shift and fade, and we watch from a new perspective: the sky high above Sixledge. As the sea rumbles far below, the lightning strikes once more, revealing a breathtaking, pure white draft horse. Lightning arcs across the night sky, charging it with power. The horse's hooves pound at the black clouds that churn beneath it. It rears up and kicks again and I gasp and cling to Rian in awe. It's not a horse at all. It's a unicorn.

The glorious creature races along the edge of the clouds, churning them up, leaving a trail of open sky. Above it, Valenor hovers, his cloak of night sparkling bright pinpoints of stars over the scene. One of the stars strikes out again. A bolt of lightning spears into the churning storm, and I understand. The unicorn is Eljarenae. The storm is Vorhadeniel.

The clouds release a deafening peal of thunder, and the spiked tips of horned wings emerge from them. The creature rising from the black is too terrifying for description. It emanates hate, fury, hopelessness, and despair. Even the sight of it makes me sick to my stomach. Its horns drip with black like the ink that ran through the walls of the keep. Its tongue lashes out, spewing poison and disease. Eljarenae dodges the spray and it falls to the sea, sizzling as it splashes in. She lowers her head, her horn sharp and bright, and prepares to charge.

Far below, the sea crashes and rumbles. The keep shakes violently. A spout of water swirls up from the center of it, and the walls of the wretched place explode outward, crumbling. The spout stretches up to the sky, catching the clouds, whirling them into a mass of razor-sharp water droplets which slice the dark creature into ribbons. Vorhadeniel lets out a horrifying, agonized screech and the creature swirls itself together again, though this time it seems slightly weakened.

As Kaso Viro summons the might of water to join the battle in the sky, the crumbling keep erupts with a pillar of sparkling light. Finally freed from the confines of the Sorcerous keep, the Muse of Magic flutters up through the beam like a playful butterfly.

For the first time since we arrive, the gallery of fairies erupts into cheers. They call her name and dart toward the screen, reaching out as though they might be able to touch her. The perspective shifts again, this time centered on the Muse of Magic.

It's difficult to focus on her exactly. Her form shifts and changes, much like Vorhadeniel's churning in the clouds. Except with her, the only way I can think to describe it is magical. Arcane energy swirls around her in lighthearted curls of colorful filigree. Its shape reminds me of Mage Mark or Mentalist Mark, painting itself around her like wards. Glittering tendrils of blue, orange, purple, yellow, red, and green merge into a layered globe that obscures her from view. The globe draws magic to it, building and growing and floats up into the sky.

The dark creature pauses to watch. The unicorn lies down in the shifting clouds. Valenor's cloak goes still. Kaso Viro sinks back to the cradle of the peaceful waters below. The fae go silent. Everything stills as all eyes remain on the globe.

"My brothers and sisters," Stellastera's voice drifts over the scene like perfect fairy song. With each word, the globe encasing her pulses softly. "We have overstepped. We have breached the boundaries of this world, and our actions held grave consequences for its people. I beseech you all: Leave these dear ones to their conflicts. Step away. Do not meddle further. We must act as we are bound to, and keep each other in balance. Sister Eljarenae, Brother Vorhadeniel, light shall always cast shadow, and shadow shall always obscure the light. Be at peace with one another. Sister Sha'Renell, brother Kaso Viro, the sea must always touch the shore. Do not quarrel."

The globe rises higher until the light it casts shimmers across the night sky of Valenor's robe. It beams so brightly it catches in his beard and flashes in his crinkled eyes.

"Brother Valenor," she says softly, her voice heavy with apology.

"I never blamed you, sister," Valenor answers gravely. "In fact, I tried to reach you until I was outsmarted and held fast in stone and shadow."

I shudder at the memory of Valenor the dragon, deep in the crevices of Hywilkin's mountain peaks, strapped down by wraiths of shadow, wasted nearly to nothing.

"The Dusk will triumph," Vorhadeniel's thunder rumbles.

"You know it cannot," Eljarenae replies with a pleading tone.

"We will not stand down," Sha'Renell cries from the rubble of the island keep.

The earth roars and shifts and the stone of the keep piles upon itself until it takes her form once more, except this time she's so immense her head nearly touches the clouds. She swipes at the globe and it darts forward. The unicorn leaps to her feet and charges toward the magical light. Above them, Valenor's cloak ripples and swirls. He dives into the globe and it swoops down to the sea. When it splashes into the water, the spray left behind shimmers with magic. We watch a swirl of yellow and turquoise fins meet with it, and as soon as the two forms join, the enormous orb vanishes.

The vision before us ripples and fades, leaving nothing behind but lazily drifting orbs. I blink in confusion as the gathering erupts into murmurs of astonishment. It's disorienting being here in the throne room when it seemed as though we had just been standing in the middle of the clouds watching the battle unfold. Everyone turns their attention to the far end of the bright walkway, where the fairy queen has remained silent on her throne, watching with just as much interest as the rest of the fae.

With impossible grace, she stands to address her people. The train of her gown glitters with light and drifts out behind her as she moves, held in place by a team of hovering pixies all dressed in white.

"We have all borne witness to the Muses' attempt to reconcile," she explains with a soft, gentle voice that echoes through the hall. "Many of you have come to these halls to seek asylum from the goings-on of men. Some of you more recently than others."

She sweeps her elegant hand in a gesture toward a gathering of strange creatures to the side. Riders with painted skin, adorned in feathers and leaves, sit astride enormous gray beasts with long noses and hard shell backs. Others of their gathering stand at the creatures' stump-like feet, watching the fairy queen in awe. One of them is taller than the rest, with enormous green wings decorated with eyes that seem to stare imposingly at everything around them.

"That's the tribe of the Savarikta," Rian whispers to me. "They're from Elespen."

"A scourge of darkness encroaches upon your homes," the queen gestures to the other side, where a group of stone giants and charcoal-skinned imps with dragon-like wings crowd together. "You have been patient in our solace, and we have welcomed all fairy-kind to our halls during these trying times. But I say to you now, friends, the time is nearing. You have seen firsthand the opposition of the Dusk. You have heard the corrupt Muses refuse peace and resolution. A great turning point awaits, poised on the horizon. Should the Dawn fail, your homelands shall be lost forever in shadow. Night will reign, and balance will be forsaken."

"It is true, as some of you believe, that men are at the root of this imbalance," the queen says, her voice deepening with command. "And I have seen the distrust seeded in this belief. But men are not the enemy. Dusk is the enemy. Azaeli Hammerfel, Rian Eldinae, step forward."

I glance back at Flitt, who gives me a sheepish grin and prods me forward. Hand in hand, Rian and I approach the steps. Flitt and Shush remain behind, having not been called forward by their queen.

"As I said, a good number of you have only recently arrived," she says to the crowd. "Many of you have not had the great privilege to be in the presence of these, our greatest allies among humankind. Azaeli Hammerfel, The Temperate, Pure of Heart, Reviver of Iren, The Great Protector, Cerion's Ambassador to Kythshire, Knight of His Majesty's Elite, The Mentalist, The Paladin, Champion of Light."

I bow to the queen, and she goes on.

"Rian Eldinae, Oathkeeper, Windsaver, Arcane Guardian, Steward of the Wellspring, Champion of Light."

Rian bows as well, and the Queen beckons to Flitt and Shush.

"Felicity Lumine Instacia Tenacity Teeming Elite Reformer, and Soren Hasten Udi Swiftish Haven Illustrious Noble General, Champions of Light."

The two fairies dart to our sides and pop to match our heights, both standing alert and proud in the presence of their queen.

"These Champions have claimed each other as Illi'luvrie, as Faedin. They were among the first to do so, to begin the journey of the true merging of our worlds. They have shared in each other's triumphs and heartaches, supporting one another. Thus doing, they have defeated evils they never could have on their own, and they have brought our worlds closer together.

"We are aware that some of you believe this joining fed into the turmoil our world is facing, but I assure you that is not true. Working together is the only way we will ensure the victory of the light. Our worlds have ever been linked, and to divide them is to bring division to the greater balance. The time for hiding is over. I ask you all, please, go forth. Find those who call to you. Seek them, and join with them. Now is the time to unite. If Dawn is to be victorious, we must stand together as one against the darkness."

A cheer erupts from the crowd, bursting into the sky above, filling the hall with colorful light. Several of the fae dart forward to shake our hands or pat our backs, and others whisper excitedly among themselves before shooting up into the sky.

In wide-eyed disbelief, Flitt turns to me, her mouth hanging open.

"There it is," Shush whispers from Rian's side. "She's started it, just like that. The Age of Kinship."

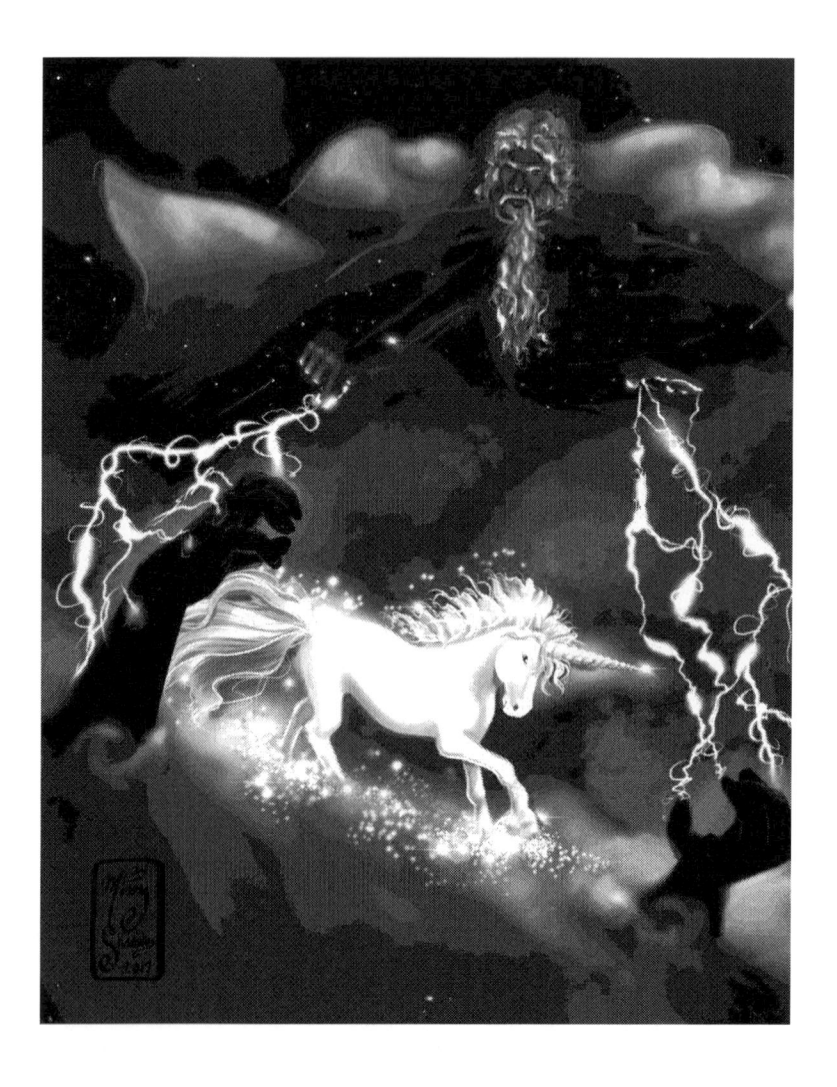

Chapter Thirty

HIDING IN DREAMING
Tib

The wind rustles my hair as my ship cuts through it, speeding over treetops, bobbing and gliding through the bright blue sky. I lean against the bulwark with Ki beside me, and we watch the leaves blur past, shivering in our wake. I don't really see them, though. My thoughts are a world away. Out beyond the Dreaming, a battle is taking place. A war is brewing.

I wish I hadn't promised Valenor I'd stay here after he brought Azi and Rian somewhere else. Where else would I go, though? My hand slides to my sash absently, to rest on my dagger. The dagger that's not there. I groan, and Ki tears her gaze from the trees below to look at me.

"I left my dagger in the palace," I grumble. "And my bandolier's in Elespen."

I shove away from the railing and start to pace. Ki turns to watch me, leaning on her elbows against the bulwark.

"You'll get them back," she says with a certainty I don't feel.

"What difference does it make?" I grumble. "What would I do with them, anyway? I hate this, just waiting around. Hiding. I want to do something."

"Try to be patient," she says.

I answer with a scoff, a shake of my head, and more pacing.

"You know you can talk to me, little brother," she offers. "In confidence."

My thoughts race. My feet pause. I stare at the horizon. Out there, a kingdom lies in shadow. A Wellspring has crumbled. Sorcery is on the rise. Out there, Saesa wonders where I am.

Out there, Margy…

My hands ball into tight fists at my sides. My stomach twists. Margy what? What is the Queen of Cerion doing right now? Preparing to travel to Brindelier? Making her wedding plans?

"She's just a kid," I growl under my breath. "Younger than me, even."

"Hm?"

"Nothing," I mutter.

"Thinking of Queen Margary again?" she asks with a smile that suggests she knows more than I do about my own feelings. She probably does.

"A lot depends on her victory," I shrug, trying to change the subject. The truth is, I'm always thinking about her. I wish I could stop. Then again, I don't want to. Even though it hurts. Even though it feels like everything would be so much easier if I could just put her out of my head.

"Come on," Ki laughs. "Be honest with yourself. You deserve that, at least."

"So what if I am honest?" I ask her. "Then what?"

The ship lists to the side. I stumble, then start pacing again. Every time I think about Margy, I remember that conversation I had with Lord Borda. How he wanted me to pursue her. How he and his Faedin believed they convinced me to veer her off the path of a suitor. Why would they want that? Even if I could tell her how I felt, I wouldn't. She needs to do what she's supposed to, as Queen. Just like she did in that council room when I lost control. My heart pangs with anger and guilt. What kind of selfish person would I be if I told her the truth?

"I know it's complicated," Ki says. She sighs. Looks away toward the bow of the ship. Her hair blows back from her face, trailing behind her. She squints against the wind.

"She doesn't feel the same way," I mutter.

As soon as the words leave my lips, I hope she didn't hear them. It's too close to an admission of how I feel. I wish I could take it back. I force myself to shift my thoughts, but they linger on the council room. How Lowery was going to make me apologize. How Margy didn't take a side. Didn't stand up for me. That helps me to keep from admitting how I really feel about her. I stick to that. It makes me want to run my dagger through something. It's a good change from those other feelings.

"Maybe she does," Ki offers. "Try to think of things from her perspective. She's a queen, a new one. She's trying hard to do the right thing and to show she's capable of leading. She needs to think of her kingdom first. Her choices need to ensure the safety and happiness of so many people. She has expectations and responsibilities no one else can fathom. There's really not a lot of room for her true feelings, Tib. Plus, she's still so young. It's easy to forget that. I remember thinking what a wise child she was when I spent my time in the palace. It was as if she'd lived a lifetime already. But she's only, what? Thirteen? Fourteen? She's probably just as confused as you are. Even more, really."

I let Ki's words sink in. I think about them. Scenes of my last meeting with her flash through my head, and I see them from a new perspective. It makes sense, thinking of it that way, why Margy didn't jump to my defense. It doesn't make the hurt go away, though. Just lessens it a little.

"I don't know," I mumble. "I don't even know what I feel, really." My heart pounds so hard it booms in my ears. I feel my face go hot. "I care about her. I want to keep her safe. I know she's young. I guess that's part of it. I want to protect her from all the things she's got to face now. I want her to be happy."

"That's love, brother," Ki says gently. I don't want to hear that. Don't want to name it. I wish I'd never started this conversation. I scramble to change the subject.

"But I smashed the offering," I tell Ki. "I swore I was done with all of this. I stormed out. I don't know how to fix that."

"You were hurt," Ki says. "You were angry. It's all right to change your mind after you've had some time to think about it."

"I don't know if I want to," I scowl.

"Tib," Ki sighs. She pushes away from the bulwark and links her arm through mine. "I understand your confusion. You've been thinking for a while now that your actions were for one person, for someone you care about deeply. But I imagine if you truly think hard about it, you'll see that with or without her, barring oaths and forgiveness, even, there's still a fight to be fought."

She stops my pacing, taking me by the shoulders. She looks into my eyes, hers filled with stern determination.

"Don't lose who you are for the love of one person. The Dawn needs you, Brother. If you have to, for now, set aside your feelings. Think about what you said you saw in Rian's mind. If even the Champions of Light aren't safe, who is? Do what you know in your heart is right. Everything else will sort itself when the time comes.

"But imagine if you hid away sulking and missed your chance to stop the Dusk. Imagine what our world would be like ruled by

Sorcerers. What we suffered in the fields would be a reality everywhere. The cruelty our family faced would be faced by thousands more innocents. You must agree we have to do everything in our power to keep that from happening. You have been given gifts unlike anyone else. They can't be wasted while you dwell on how you might or might not feel. Stand up. Don't do it for her, Tib. Do it for yourself, because you know it's what you must do."

"Rise above it," I huff. My hand goes to my absent dagger hilt again. I drop it to my side and look up at my sister with her hair fanning out behind her and her bow slung across her chest. I remember the girl she used to be, avoiding the whip, hiding in the fields with a book on her knee. I remember the Sorcerer who came, whispering promises, and lured her away. "How'd you get to be so smart, anyway?" I roll my eyes, shaking my head.

She doesn't answer, except with a hug. I hug her, too. Breathe in the scent of her. Leather. Old books. Some strange, sweet spice. Together, we watch the sun sink low over the landscape of the Dreaming. Thoughtful. Quiet.

"Does it feel like it's been too long?" I ask Ki after a while.

"I don't know," she replies. "How long does it usually take a pair of Muses to break their sister out of the evil keep of wicked Sorcerers allied with Muses of their own?"

"I don't know," I smirk. "Half a day, maybe?"

"Right," she snorts. "Then I guess they might be a little behind."

"I think I need to go back to Elespen," I say. "I want to see what really happened to that temple, and try to get another offering to replace the one I broke. I want to figure out what happened to everyone in Cresten, too. What really happened."

"You saw what happened to some of them," Ki says. "They're here in the Dreaming."

"What?" I ask, leaning away from her. I look up into her eyes to see if she's joking with me. She's not.

"Tib, you saw them. You were there. Don't you remember?"

"I thought I was dreaming them. Isn't that what that was? It was a dream," I search my memory, trying to make sense of what she's saying.

"Well, it was. But those people were just as real as we were. Couldn't you tell?" she asks.

"I don't...I didn't even think about it." I shake my head, confused. "But, how?"

"I imagine Valenor had something to do with it," she says. "We can ask about it when he returns."

"I wonder why he didn't tell me."

"Things did get a little hectic when Azi and Rian arrived," she says reassuringly. She's right, I guess.

"I don't want to wait," I say, racing to the helm of the ship. I can only think of one thing: The Admiral. I have to know if he's there. If he is, then she's right. The people of Cresten, of Elespen are safe. Just hiding.

The same way Brindelier did the first time I had Ki aboard with me in the Dreaming, Elespen appears on the distant horizon once I think of it. The trees beneath us give way to sea, and the sails fill out as wind carries us forward.

I turn the wheel to steer us on course. It isn't long before we reach the city. Here in the Dreaming, it's obvious the streets are still full. As we soar over it, the sounds and aromas of the market are as real as ever.

There is a sheen to it, though. A strange sort of veil that settles in every corner. I reach out to sense them. Protections. Dreams. Constructs. It's obvious this isn't the real Cresten. It's only a place in this realm meant to seem like the city. We cross into it through the veil, and I feel the shift into someplace new.

The same three ships Saesa and I explored are still tied to the pier. I lower ours to the end of it and unlike before, dock hands rush to greet us and help us put in.

In the back of my mind as Ki and I walk down the gangplank, I can't help but think about that moment that seems so long ago, when Margy declared we'd be going to Elespen. This is how it was supposed to happen, except with Azi and Rian, and Mya and Elliot. And me. On my ship.

We reach the end of the dock, and I pause right where the wood stops and the cobbles start. I squint along the sand-covered walkway, past the guarded gate, into the bustling city. My healed eye scans beneath the sand, along the beach that stretches between the walls of the city and the sea on either side.

Ki rests a hand on my arm. Gives me a questioning look. "Tib?"

"This is where she attacked us," I explain. "Sha—"

"Shh! Don't say it. If you say her name, you might allow her in. This is the Dreaming, after all. You have to be careful what you imagine." She looks around warily. "When I spent time here before, before the previous Dreamwalker was dismantled, I learned that quickly."

"I wonder if it's different," I ponder, "when we're here, mind and body rather than just in our dreams."

"I don't know," Ki whispers. "But it's probably better to be safe than sorry. And it might be best not to mention it to anyone within the city. I don't know whether they're aware of what's really happening."

"We're not even aware of what's really happening," I murmur, my healed eye taking in the crowd beyond the city gates.

"Best be careful, then," she says.

I nod. Hold my breath. Take a step onto the cobbles. Nothing happens. We stay close together and walk through the city gates under the stern, watchful gaze of the guards.

Inside, it's just like it should be. Just like I remembered seeing it from Cap's ship. It makes me pause. I turn around. Gaze back at the Admiral's ship. Two watchers are set at the gangplank. With my healed eye, I look past them. Through them. A few crew are in the galley, eating. The Captain's lodge is empty. I turn back. Look into the city. Pull Ki to the side, against a wall, away from the crowd.

"Where would he be?" I wonder aloud.

"Who?" Ki asks.

"Admiral Ganvent. His ship is docked here, but nobody has heard from him or his crew since they left with the shipment for Zhaghen's new libraries. He disappeared, but not before he sent a note of warning to Nessa to get out of Cerion," I explain.

"The best way to find out is to ask around," Ki says, pointing to the tavern across the way. "Come on."

She adjusts her leather vest, pulling it down a little in front, and flicks her hair to tumble down her back. As we walk across to the tavern, the crowd seems to part for her. I don't miss how the men pause. How their eyes are glued to her. I make sure they see me too, though. I give them all a good glare. Eyes off my sister, I want to say, but I don't. I couldn't do anything about it, anyway. I sigh. Hook my thumb through my belt loop where my dagger should be.

The inside of the tavern is strange. Perfect. There's no scraps on the floor, no spilled ale. No stench of sweat. Every table is piled with food. Everyone's singing, laughing, and making merry. No shadowy figures lurk in corners with their backs to the wall. No hulking men throw insults and threats at one another across the room.

A few look up from their meals as we enter, mostly focused on Ki. When they see my narrowed gaze, though, they go back to their suppers. My sister sidles up to the bar, orders a mug, and asks for the innkeeper. I stand beside her, on edge. Drum my fingers on the bar. Scan the tavern over and over. Keep an ear on Ki's conversation with the innkeeper.

"Just a mo'," I hear the innkeeper say. He ducks out. Into a back room.

"We're in luck," Ki says with a grin. "I think he's here."

As if to answer her question, the innkeeper pokes his head out of the door he just left through. He nods and beckons to us.

"Go on," says my sister. "I don't think I'd better."

I start to protest, but then remember her wariness about being seen by anyone in Cerion who might remember who she used to be. I wonder vaguely how the Admiral would recognize her, but the thought disappears when I walk through the door.

Ganvent's eyes light up the moment he sees me. He gets up from his chair with a clap of delight and bellows, "Tib, my boy! What a surprise!"

Behind me, the innkeeper shuffles out and closes the door. The Admiral's officers watch me with interest. Some of them whisper to one another. One of them reaches out and pokes me with a finger, like he's testing whether or not I'm real. When I reach the Admiral, he claps me on the back. His face, as always, is red and scrunched from the sun. His beard is neat and trimmed. His uniform is impeccable. Perfect. He even still smells like the sea when I hug him.

"We've been hoping to find you," I say.

"We?" His eyes flick toward the door hopefully.

"Saesa and I came to Cresten," I explain. "We saw your ship."

His eyes cloud over darkly. He looks to his men.

"Dismissed," he tells them. "Back to your duties. Steklin, make certain those charts are checked over. Greshel, the inventory."

The two salute him. A third gets up and says, "I'll check around, Admiral, for some brawn."

The Admiral nods. Salutes him. Waits for them all to leave. When the door shuts behind them, he sits heavily. Taps out the ash from his pipe. Fills it back up again.

"Some of them don't know," he says quietly, glancing up at the door. He gestures to the chair closest to him, and I sit there.

"Sir?" I ask.

"They don't know this isn't really Cresten. They think we're about ready to push off," he grunts. "Maybe I should've told them, but no one else in this place seems to realize it, either. I thought it'd just cause trouble. Hate keeping things from them, though. Nothing admirable in that."

"Sir?" I ask again, confused. I watch him light the pipe. He draws in the smoke and puffs it out thoughtfully. "What happened?"

He glances at the door. Leans forward. Draws another puff of smoke. His thoughts are far away, until his narrowed eyes snap to mine.

"Did she get it?" he asks. "Nessa? Is she safe? Are the kids?"

"Yeah," I scowl, thinking back. "She had everyone leave when she got your note. It was right on time. There were earthquakes that night."

"What did it say?" he asks me, his voice filled with suspicion.

"The note?" I ask. He nods, one eye almost shut as he looks me over.

"It said, 'I grow weary of—'"

"Good enough!" he interrupts, holding up a hand to stop me. "Good enough. Bah, I hate having to be so cautious. I miss the sea, where things are so much more straightforward. The stars don't lie. The sun is a constant."

"How are you here, sir?" I ask him as his gaze grows distant again. It's strange to see him outside of the Manse, without the chaos of the other kids climbing on him and making him laugh. He's much more serious. Almost a different person, really. Or maybe that's the Dreaming. I don't know.

"Night we docked," he says with that same distant gaze. Like he's looking into the past. "We followed procedure. Half stayed aboard with the cargo, other half went ashore. The night passed without any incident, or so we thought. During morning checks, it was discovered that our hold was breached. Stuff everywhere. Crates opened. Wards broken. Our Mage was nowhere to be seen. Disappeared."

The hand holding his pipe shakes. He rests it on the table to stop it.

"Never saw anything like it," he shakes his head. Closes his eyes. "Tanis was a Master. Thirty-seventh circle. The best the Academy had to offer us, aside from Gaethon or Anod, of course. He knew procedure. There were alarms that should have sounded. From the looks of the crates, it seemed like there were at least half a dozen attackers. No one heard them. They came in and left without a trace. The only thing strange we found was a sigil carved into the low deck."

"Was it round?" I ask. "Like a coin with prongs around it?"

"Aye," he narrows his eyes at me again.

"Sorcerers," I spit.

"Seems so. How did you know about that? The sigil?" he asks.

"I've seen it before, when some of my friends disappeared in an alley. It's how they can get from one place to another. They must have carved it there another time. Maybe before you left."

He frowns. Nods thoughtfully. Goes on with his story. "We took an inventory of what was missing and determined that the stolen books were the most powerful of the cargo. They had been wrapped up, and were only cataloged by number, as Tanis warned us to not even attempt to read the titles.

Now it's my turn to frown. What business did Cerion have, sending books like that to Sunteri? If they were so powerful, why would they allow them to be copied and shared? Another thought nags at me. What information did the Sorcerers hope to learn from those books? And would they ever have been able to get their hands on them if I didn't burn their libraries to begin with?

I shift uncomfortably in my chair. The thought makes me want to pace, but I force myself not to.

"What happened after that? After you found the books missing? How did you know to send that warning to Nessa right before the earthquakes? How did you get here?" I ask.

"Well, we spent that day trying to find out whatever we could about the intruders. I had my men ask around. I reported the attack to the captain of the city guard. Wouldn't you know it? They did some searching and came up with three Sorcerers sheltered in place in some merchant's house. Their Mages put them to sleep and threw them in the dungeons. No one could find our missing tomes, though.

"That night I was here at the tavern, meeting with the Captain of the High Guard. The ground started shaking. I never saw anything like it before. The floor of this place rumbled. The walls cracked and broke apart. We ran outside and found chaos. The streets rolled like the sea in a storm. The stars were blotted out. Torches guttered. All over the city, people screamed and cried for mercy.

"'Join us', a voice rose above the chaos. A female. I could see her through the dust, moving along the ground like she was part of it. Riding the rolling wave of the street like a ship. 'Join the Dusk and know true power. Deny us, and know death.'

"That was when the visions came in a cloud of shadows and darkness. I saw things that terrified me. Cerion, crumbling. My home destroyed. The might and power of the forces who wished to lure me. I took it as a warning. I turned my back on the threat.

"Long ago, I had nightmares of things like this happening. Of being away and knowing Nessa was threatened at home, and being unable to warn her. I took the note from my pocket. I carried it everywhere, you see. I wrote it years ago, and had it enchanted for just such an event. I whispered to it what the Mage had instructed me to say, and I let it go, to drift into the sky."

"I tried to keep my crew together, but there was so much chaos I could barely see them through the mist. It choked us out, mind and body. Some of us kept our heads. Others did not. I fell into a daze. I felt a shift around me. It felt like I was being pulled forward into a different space. Like I'd stepped through a veil of cobwebs that tickled my face and skin.

"I heard a voice whisper, then, secretly. 'Come with me, and I will give you sanctuary,' it said. 'Turn your back on shadow and destruction.' It was a woman's voice, beautiful and clear. It carried light and peace with it. I had no other choice. I trusted it. I followed it. It brought me here, to this place which is Cresten but isn't. To this alternate Elespen, where we make empty plans to continue our journey. Where it's like those quakes never happened."

He sighs and takes a pull of his pipe, not realizing the smoke went out a long time ago.

"Several of my crew were lost to that mist," he says. "I have to hope they were taken by force. I cannot face the alternative, the possibility that they went willingly to the Dusk."

"I don't know," I say quietly. "What I do know for sure is that there's definitely no one left in Cresten. Most of the north of Elespen is covered by that mist you mentioned."

The Admiral taps his pipe to empty it. Packs it again. Gazes off thoughtfully.

Something soft grazes my shoulder. I get the sense of stars. Of sunlit sky. A cloak, flapping in the breeze. A familiar mantle.

"Tib," Valenor whispers in my ear. "It's time to say farewell to the Admiral, for now."

I feel a sense of peace drift past me. It flicks at Ganvent's beard. Strokes his cheek. The Admiral's eyelids go heavy. His head tips back against his chair. He snores softly.

"Come," Valenor says. "There are urgent matters at hand."

Chapter Thirty-One

STELLASTERA'S AID
Tib

Ki is with Valenor. I feel her before I see her. I feel something else, too. Another shift, like the one I felt when we arrived here. Except, this time it's more pronounced. A crossing of borders.

"What was that?" I ask him.

"Felt it, did you?" he chuckles softly. "We have just returned fully to the Dreaming."

"I thought we were in the Dreaming already," I say.

"No, indeed, my friend. The asylum city of Cresten only brushes the edge of my realm. It is seated mostly within the Realm of Magic. A construct of my sister, Stellastera, in one of her more lucid moments, I imagine."

"Magic has its own realm?" I ask, looking back over my shoulder. The city grows smaller and smaller as Valenor carries us through the sky, over the ocean, toward those same rustling trees. Back the way we came. Beside me, Ki spreads her arms out to the sides and lifts her face to the wind like a bird. She grins, listening to the two of us talk.

"Indeed. I am pleased you found the Admiral," he says, changing the subject. "His absence has been troubling the dreams of quite a few of those close to you for some time now."

"Yeah, me too," I say. "But how did I do it, if that wasn't the Dreaming?

"As you know," Valenor explains, "each Muse is bound to our domain. Mine is the Dreaming, as Kaso Viro's is the water. In turn, each domain encroaches in some places upon the other. The Dreaming shares a border with every other Realm. Mine is much like a central space to the others. The other domains overlap each other in places as well, much the same way the sea meets the shore, and light and shadow exist together."

"Oh," I say thoughtfully. "So, is that Elespen whole, then? All of it? Or just Cresten?"

"I believe it is a creation modeled after the areas Dusk has claimed," Valenor replies.

"All of the areas?" I ask. "Even the Wellspring?"

"I am afraid not. A Wellspring cannot be duplicated in any fashion," he says.

I don't reply. I know what it means. There isn't any other option. Elespen's Wellspring was destroyed. I smashed our offering. There's only one bit of it left, and they have it. I'm going to have to go to the Sorcerers' keep.

"What happened at the battle?" I ask, realizing that's where he just came from. "Did you get Aster out?"

"There was much contention, but we recovered our sister. Lines were drawn. That came as no surprise. We knew Vorhadeniel and Sha'Renell would stand together. He convinced her long ago that Dusk would triumph. I am grateful, at least, that our sister Stellastera could see reason. She awaits us now, in the place where the realms of Magic, Dreaming, and Light converge."

"Forgive me," Ki asks, pushing her billowing hair from her face as she turns her head toward Valenor, "couldn't you just bring us straight there? As much as I'm enjoying the journey," she breathes in a deep breath, smiling, "you did say it was an urgent matter."

"Indeed I could, but, you see, I am expecting someone to join us. And ah! There he is now."

A red-orange blur streaks toward us. Black paws. White chest.

"It's Elliot!" I shout.

The fox runs on the wind, his paws striking thin air. He catches up to us and Valenor's cloak swirls close to him. As soon as it brushes his fur, we spring forward as a group and lurch to a stop at our destination. My skin prickles with static. Ki and I cling to each other's hand, gaping around at our surroundings.

It's impossible to know where we are. It feels like a tower, but all I can see are pillars of light that twist like ribbons from the ground to the sky, and we are somewhere in between. The ribbons swirl and shift in every color, and when I step closer to the nearest one, I peer into what seems like another world. The magic that flows from it is thick, rich, and flawless. It drifts to my hand when I reach toward it, coating my fingers. Joy emanates from it. Excitement. Simplicity. I can't help but allow it to affect me. It's too overpowering to deny it.

I step a little closer. Within the pillar, the ribbon of light, the image of a forest emerges. The floor is dotted with lush ferns and bright red mushrooms. I watch with amusement, intrigued as tiny men climb up onto the spotted caps. One by one, they crouch, then stand, raising tiny spears. The mushrooms pop out of the ground. They drift upwards and speed off into the depths of the forest. I don't tear my eyes away until the last one disappears, and the surface of the twisting pillar shifts, and a new scene shimmers.

This one is a perfect glen dotted with sunlight. A woman in a beautiful yellow gown steps into it. Her song seems to carry all the beauty of the world with it. She sinks into the grass and sweeps her hand across it, leaving a trail of glistening dew droplets. Each droplet echoes her song as they cling together and grow, becoming a globe of crystal nearly the woman's size. It swirls into the spiral of a perfect glass snail shell. A purple eye stalk pokes up from beneath it, and she speaks to it in a soothing voice.

"Tib," someone nudges my shoulder and I gasp and whirl to face them. Him. Valenor. He squeezes my shoulder. Gestures to the side, away from the swirling ribbons of light. Toward the others gathered around. They don't notice me. They're too absorbed in something else. Confused, I shake my head, rub my eyes, and fight the urge to glance back at the scene.

"Ah, that was something I had not anticipated," Valenor chuckles. He rests his arm across my shoulders. Walks me further away from the pillars. "It would make sense for you to be drawn to the portals," he explains. "The others are not quite so enticed, as there are protections upon this place to keep them from looking. It might be best if you allow the magic, friend. If for no other reason but to permit you to focus on the matters at hand. For someone so attuned to magic as you are, this place is certain to be overwhelming."

I take a breath. Close my eyes. Do as he says. Allow the magic. The pillars of light fade some. Their images go blurry until they're only smudges of color. It helps me to see our true surroundings: the top of a pure white tower at the edge of a mountain peak. The sky is crisp, perfect blue. The gentle trickle of a waterfall bubbles beside us, carried along in grooves in the stone to the edge of the tower wall, where it spills over into the vast mountain peak below. It reminds me of Ceras'lain, but it's purer. More peaceful. More impressive, which is saying something. The place feels ancient. Powerful. Sacred.

I turn back to the twisting pillars and feel the block between myself and the magic there.

"They're portals?" I ask Valenor. "To where?"

"Anywhere magic can be found. Across the way," he points to the opposite side of the tower, "there are portals to any location where there is Light. And there," he motions to another area, "points of Dreaming. I have not ventured to this place in some time, for it is impossible to do so without the consent of all those whose realms converge here. It is a rare occurrence for the Muses to come together this way."

"Da," Rian's voice echoes around us.

"Rian!" Elliot cries.

I turn my attention to the gathering. Watch Rian and Elliot—the man, not the fox—embrace. Azi stands beside them, wiping tears from her face. On Rian's other side, Stellastera bobs with her feet barely touching the ground. An object dangles from her fingertips. The ring. The one they had me hold when I went into the Dreaming to try and help Rian. It's empty now. I can feel it. She did what was needed to restore him. He's whole again. That's a relief. He had been in pretty bad shape, before.

I look Stellastera over. She's different than she was when I left her back in Kerevorna. Much different.

There, it was obvious how she tried to keep balanced. Her hair was black as night, her skin was bright white. Her gown was gray. Her wings were white with black spots. Now, she's completely changed. Her gown is a swirl of colors that shift depending on how she moves. Her hair is kind of like Flitt's, who seems to be missing from the gathering. It's rainbow colored, but not tied up in ponytails. It drifts around her like she's under water. It glitters with flashes of light as it moves. Her wings are clear like crystal. Iridescent.

I feel the energy surging off of her in waves. It's fascinating. Overwhelming. I can't pin any of it down. It's like wind through the treetops. Like pouring sand. Impossible to focus on any one thing. It reminds me of the ocean or the sky. Deep. Unending. Vast.

"Thank you," Rian says to Stellastera earnestly. "Truly. I've never been so afraid. The magic they performed was unthinkable. I honestly didn't know whether it could be undone."

"All magic has two sides," Stellastera says with a smile, "and, with effort, can be reversed. You stood your ground impressively. It was a joy to discover your patience and restraint."

While she's talking to him, another presence moves forward. A figure of white, taller than anyone else in the group. Light beams from her so brightly that I can only see her basic form, even with my healed eye. I know who she is without any introduction. I can feel it about her. Eljarenae. Muse of Light. She starts talking to Azi and Rian, and Stellastera's eyes flick to the side. Away from them.

"Dreamstalker," the Muse of Magic calls.

"Stellastera. You look good," I say, moving closer to her.

She smiles at me. Nods slowly. I know we're both thinking of the same thing. A time that seems like forever ago. When I met her beneath the mountain, when I released the power of the Wellspring with a swift stab of my dagger. A dagger lost to me now. I think of how she helped me escape. How she broke the stone encasing my feet and lured her sister's wrath from me, distracting her so I could escape. I remember Sha'Renell scooping her hand across the rubble and flinging it at Stellastera. I wince.

"I'm glad," I say quietly. A little apologetically. It's not like me to run from a fight, but at the time I knew it was what I had to do. For Cerion. For the Dawn.

"Do not fret," she offers gently. "Though at times I wondered whether I would ever be the same, as you see now, I am restored. Had you not freed me from Kerevorna, I would not be here today. I am indebted to you, Dreamstalker."

"No, you're not," I say quickly. I feel my face go red. Beside me, Ki squeezes my arm. I don't need or want to be owed anything by her. "I did what I had to do, and then I left you there." I think of Elespen. How I did the same thing there. How mad it made Saesa. It wasn't heroic. It's not something to be proud of or appreciated for.

"You did what you needed to do. If you had remained, my sister surely would have killed you," she insists. "Tibreseli, allow me to offer you a gift of gratitude. I have already done so for the Champions of Light. It would ease my heart to offer you something as well. A wish."

She twirls her hand gracefully in front of her. Conjures something small and bright. Offers it to me, palm up. A tiny ball of light, like a marble.

My stomach clenches and twists into knots. I lean closer to the Muse. Feel the promise in that little globe. The endless possibilities. A wish. I could have anything I want. Ki steps forward, too. She reaches toward it like she can't help it. Can't resist. I take her hand gently. Guide it to her side. She looks at me, blinking like I broke some spell. She smiles and shrugs her shoulders apologetically.

"Anything?" I ask the Muse. Across the way, the gathering quiets. Everyone's eyes are on us. I could take the wish. Use it to help fix things. To help us win.

"Nearly anything," Stellastera replies.

My thoughts race with what I could ask for. I glance to the side. Knowing they're watching makes me uneasy. I reach to accept it and ask, "Do I have to decide now? Can I take it with me?"

"Once you leave my presence," she explains, tipping the glowing marble into my hand, "its magic shall be lost."

I close my hand around it. Start to pace. Think hard. There are a lot of things I want. My bandolier, my dagger. The offering from Elespen. But then I start to think bigger. I want the slaves of Sunteri to be freed. I want my little sister, Zhilee, back. I want the end of Sorcerers everywhere. I want the Wellspring of Brindelier in Margy's hands, and victory for the Dawn. I look down at the glowing object. It's heavy in my hand. Heavier than something so small should be. It buzzes with magic. Its power weighs on me. My hand starts to shake. Ki puts her arm around me. Stills my pacing. Whispers something. I don't hear her. My thoughts are humming too loudly through my head. What can I ask for? What should I wish for? I don't want this responsibility. I want it to be over. I want peace.

"Peace," I announce as soon as the thought comes to me. "I wish for peace for the Known Lands and victory for the Dawn."

I look up at Stellastera, who offers me a warm smile with a hint of regret. She shakes her head slightly and explains, "I'm sorry I was unclear. The wish can only be for an object. An item."

"All right, then. I wish for the Wellspring's offering from Elespen."

I look down at the vibrating marble expectantly. When nothing happens, Stellastera sighs. "I am afraid an offering is not something that can be wished for. It must be bestowed willingly."

"Well," I growl, getting angry, "what's the point of offering a wish when I can't actually ask for anything useful?"

"Tib," Ki hisses a warning.

"Why do you wish for the offering from Elespen?" Stellastera asks.

The others, Azi, Rian, Valenor, Elliot, and Eljarenae move closer, watching. Listening.

"We only need that one," I say. "That and Ceras'lain. To claim the Wellspring in Brindelier for the Dawn. I had it. The Elespen offering. But I—" I look from Valenor to Azi and Rian, whose eyes go wide at the mention of it. "It got smashed," I say, embarrassed to admit the whole truth. "It got smashed, and the Wellspring of Elespen is destroyed, and the only other offering I know of is at the Sorcerers' keep. I was going to go there—"

"It's not," Azi interrupts quietly. "We found the container it was in. They used it for something already."

"Sister?" The Muse of Light asks, addressing Stellastera. She nods and sighs.

"It was a construct magic unlike anything I've seen before. Devious and complex," Stellastera explains. She takes Eljarenae's hand. Guides her and Valenor away, out of earshot, leaving me with the other non-Muses.

"Used it?" I ask Azi. "What would they possibly use it for other than claiming the Wellspring?"

She tells me rather than showing me with her mind. About their underwater battle with Eron and Sybel. About the keep and Xantivus and the ritual. About her fight through it to find Stellastera.

Rian listens while she explains. Sometimes, he goes pale. Sometimes, he reaches up and strokes her cheek as she talks, where the Mark of Mentalism curls and sparkles on her skin. Sometimes, he takes her hand and watches her with awe. With a sort of appreciation that makes me envy the both of them. More than once, my thoughts flick to Margy and I yank them back again.

"So Diovicus has a body now, and it's Eron?" I growl. My pulse thumps in my eardrums. I feel my face go hot with anger. Beside me, Ki goes rigid. Her jaw is clenched She shifts her weight closer to me. Her eyes narrow. Her nostrils flare. I can tell this news is just as disturbing to her as it is to me. Maybe even more. I know what she went through with Eron. I'm sure she was relieved when she knew she'd never see him again. I take her hand. Squeeze it.

Rian nods. "The ritual performed by Sybel was an attempt to restore him to this plane. Well, the human plane, that is. Not this one."

"It was Stellastera who determined that," Azi explains. "She seemed quite convinced of it."

"So what do we do now? How do we stop him?" I ask. "How do we stop all of them?"

"Keep fighting," Azi says. "Stay on our path."

I shake my head. "The Void, Sha'Renell, Vorhadeniel, Diovicus, the Dusk. The sacrifice of their only offering…oh." I whisper the last. My face drains of heat. My fingertips go cold. "It wasn't a sacrifice at all," I hiss. "They've got the entire thing. It was swallowed up by the earth. By Sha'Renell."

I look into Azi's eyes. Allow her magic to curl into my head. Show her everything that happened in Elespen from the moment we arrived until we left. I keep going, too. Show her everything afterward. Even my outburst at the prince. How I smashed the vial. It feels good to share it. To know she can see it from my perspective.

When she breaks the connection, her eyes glint with tears. She pulls me into a hug.

"I can help you with your pain," she whispers for my ears only. "Say the word and I will. At the very least, I'll help you fight for them once we have our victory. I'll help him see the wrong of it."

"Thank you," I whisper. Tears sting my eyes again. I clear my throat. Step back. Not yet, I think to myself. Not now. I'm not ready to be fixed yet. Not ready to let go of the pain that drives me to do what's right. She understands. Smiles. Nods.

"Those creatures," she says, quickly changing the subject. "We saw them at the Palace of Dawn." She looks at Rian. Shows him.

"*Sava*," he says. "After you came to aid me—thank you, for that, by the way— Valenor brought us to recover at the Palace of Dawn. They were there. The Sava and their riders."

"They were?" I gasp. "What did they look like? Show me!"

She looks into my eyes again. Draws me in. Shows me the image of them. The same riders that brought us up the steps of the temple, and next to them, unmistakably, is Velu.

"Yes!" I whoop and punch the air. "They're safe!"

"We were able to watch the Muses' battle from there," he says. "When it was through, the Fairy Queen declared the Age of Kinship."

"What's that?" I ask, still partly distracted. If they're safe, then the tribe must be, too. They have to be either in Stellastera's Elespen, or the Palace with the Sava. I hadn't realized how guilty I'd felt over all of that until now, now that I know they're okay.

"From what Flitt explained," Azi says, "it means fae from all the reaches of Dawn are free to leave their domains, to seek out their own Faedins. She was actually kind of surprised when I told her we didn't realize that that was the reason they were always gathered around the Ring and the Queen's throne room."

I scowl thoughtfully. "Yeah, I kind of thought they were just nosy and liked dancing and singing."

Azi laughs and shakes her head. She leans into Rian. Gazes up at him, still smiling.

"Apparently," Rian says, "they've been waiting for that declaration ever since the first time Azi and I set foot in the Ring at Kythshire."

"So where are they now?" I ask them. "Flitt and Shush?"

"Back home at Kythshire," Azi says. "They wanted to give them the news."

"Oh," I say, bumping closer to Ki. I don't know how I feel about it. The Age of Kinship. Fairies everywhere. Magic. I guess it's a good idea. If we're going to fight the Dusk, we can use all the help we can get. It makes sense. It's going to be annoying, though.

"Speaking of home," Elliot says with a stretch and a yawn that makes me echo him. "A lot has happened there in the days you've been gone, Azi and Rian. I've been looking everywhere for you both. Mya's frantic. So is Lisabella, of course." He yawns again. Smacks his lips. Ruffles his shaggy red hair. "It would probably be a good idea for you to head back there."

"What happened?" Azi, Rian, and I ask all at the same time.

"The night you left, there were quakes. Terrible ones." He rubs his eyes sleepily. "Woke me up out of a dead sleep. Half the city was destroyed. The ground under the catacombs cracked open. A lot of the cells were swallowed up into the earth. Most of them held the Sorcerers who attacked Cerion during the rites. Remember?"

"Yes," Azi whispers. Her eyes are wide with concern. Her arms wrap tighter around Rian's waist. "Half the city was destroyed? Were there many injured?"

"Not as many as you would imagine," Elliot says. "There was a strange kind of glow about the street lamps when it happened. Anywhere the light touched was saved. The conclave came out in full force. Donal and Dacva have been working ever since, tending to the injured. The Academy used the dragon claw Kerr Skalivar gifted to Her Majesty. That was incredible to see, I have to tell you. Cerion has a dragon guardian, now. Gaethon and Anod decided to use the Everlin powder gifted by Prince Vorance to speed rebuilding. The Mages have been working tirelessly ever since to restore the damage that was done."

I stiffen slightly at the mention of Everlin, and Ki rubs my back to soothe me and whispers, "What's done is done. It's in the past. Don't let it anger you anymore."

"Cerion's restored," I tell them. "I just came from there. It looks like new again."

"Even so," Elliot says, "a visit home would be appreciated, if you can spare the time. Both of your mothers are sick with worry. And your master, too, Rian."

"All those Sorcerers, freed," Rian whispers, shaking his head.

"With everything I just mentioned," Elliot scoffs, "that's the thing that troubles you? The deaths of Sorcerous war criminals awaiting trials and executions?"

The look in Rian's eyes says it all. He knows the truth. I do, too. Those earthquakes were Sha'Renell, for sure. And it's no coincidence that all the Sorcerers in the dungeons were swallowed up into the earth. Just like Elespen's Wellspring.

"They're not just causing destruction," I mutter, "they're building their forces. Preparing."

"We have to get home," Rian says to Azi. "To warn them."

"The sooner the better," she agrees. We look to the Muses, tucked to the side, caught up in their own conversation.

"Fitting," says Eljarenae, "a Plethore. It is almost lyrical, is it not?"

"It has come full circle," Stellastera agrees.

"I see no choice but to allow it to play out," Valenor says, shaking his head. "This quarrel has been simmering for far too long. Decades of hate and rivalry have brought them to this point."

"Valenor is right," Eljarenae agrees. "We may offer aid to our own side, as I am sure our brother and sister have to theirs. But no finality can truly be accomplished until one is victorious over the other."

"It's true," Stellastera says. "Victory holds an energy. A power all its own. I only hope…" she trails off. Valenor pats her back reassuringly. Stellastera turns away from them, shaking her head. "Had I not been so weak…"

"Weak? There is power in love, Sister," Valenor says, draping her with his cloak, hugging her.

"You did what you thought was best, Stella. For your children, and for their kingdom. You did not foresee the reach of Dusk. Had you, I'm certain you would have put a stop to it."

"I wanted them to be happy," Stellastera sighs. "I wished for balance, for equality."

"What's done is done," Valenor says. "There is no way to change the past. We must look to the present. To the victory of Dawn."

"We shall rally behind the Champions," Eljarenae says. "And your fears shall be unfounded, Sister."

"Yes," Stellastera says, sniffling. "I'll watch from the pool of Brindelier. My daughter aches for my company, and I will not allow her to falter now."

"Well, enough standing around talking," I say. I squeeze the marble in my fist. "I wish for the stuff Saesa and I left in Elespen," I say. The marble crackles and pops, and my bandolier, clothes, and vials lie at my feet, along with Saesa's armor, and Feat.

"Yes!" I whoop, scooping the items into my arms. "Let's go, Ki."

"Where are you going?" Stellastera asks.

"I guess to Elespen," I say. "There's got to be something I can do to recover that offering."

"Rian," Azi asks, "if an offering was smashed, as Tib said earlier, is it possible to restore it? In the memory he showed me, it seemed as though Twig and Uncle were attempting to do just that."

"I'm not sure," he says, scratching his head. "Even if it were simply a potion in a bottle, there are issues of clarity and pollution that come from a restoration spell. I fear if the offering was spilled, it would have lost a great deal of its potency.

"An offering must be treated with the utmost care and respect," Stellastera interjects. "I am afraid if it was tainted, it cannot be recovered."

"That settles it," I sigh. "Back to Elespen."

"I know a few who will be eager to aid you on your quest," Eljarenae offers. "I shall gather them, and meet you at the borders of Shadow."

"Quickly, Tib," Valenor beckons me close. "The Dusk is growing stronger by the hour. We haven't a moment to waste."

Chapter Thirty-Two

SIPHON
Celli

The streets of Redstone Row are cleaner than I remember. Old houses that were crumbling before I left Cerion have been repaired with fresh red bricks. Sunlight splashes across the face of my house. A new lintel decorates the front door, coated in bright, cheerful blue paint. I stroke my fingers along the grooves of my father's carving work and imagine him at his bench, sunlight catching in the wood dust that drifts through his workshop.

My hand falls to the latch silently, and just like in my vision, I listen. My mother's voice drifts through the slats in the window shutters, raised in song. Home. The sun warms my hand and I stare at it and smile. I've experienced this once before, recently. This time, I know what it means. Eljarenae, the Lady of light, here with me.

My whole body trembles with anticipation as Kenrick's words rush back to me: *"Before you are to be of any aid to anyone, you must find yourself. You must go home and reconnect with who you truly are, Celli. Seek out who you were before you were seduced by Sorcery. The Light, as always, will be with you, but we shall not. You must go on your own, and be free to act as you choose."*

The prince smiled at me then. He was so proud of me for the choice I made, and so kind. It was a true kindness, too. Not a ruse. It hadn't been guided by any selfish ambitions or hidden motives. Trust, Kenrick explained, is an element of goodness, as are freedom, nurturing, love, and loyalty. They put their trust in me, and I should trust myself as well.

The notion of it, of actual freedom, is both exhilarating and terrifying. If I let myself, I could fall just as easily into the grips of Sorcery again. I won't, though. I have seen the darkness. I've been a part of it. I've lost myself to it. Never again.

I close my eyes and breathe in the scents of home: Baking bread, flowers in the window box, sawdust. How long has it been? How long ago did I disappear? The air is cooler today than it had been that day I stole the satchel from that rich boy. My stomach twists with guilt. I remember how I'd pinned him against the wall. How I beat him. I shudder. Had I been under Quenson's influence even then? I'd like to believe that's the case. That I'm not capable, on my own, of an act like that. I don't know, though. There's no way to be sure. I'd gotten into plenty of brawls before that. Still, there's only moving forward, now. Doing the right thing.

I push down the latch with my thumb. My heart races like I just ran two laps around the city. My parents are inside. I hear Da's voice, too. Will they be angry with me for leaving them without a trace? Can they forgive me for the pain I caused them? How could I have allowed myself to do it, to just disappear and never say why? The questions nag at me, fueling my fear. I could turn around right now. I could run, and they'd never know the difference.

Sorcery. I tell it to myself over and over. A dark enemy, enticing and sneaky. It seeps into your heart and holds it. It's alluring, captivating. It makes you want more. It makes you stop caring about anything else but the power and reach of darkness. Standing here, it feels like an excuse to me. Even after the Muse of Light's assurances, I find it hard to believe forgiveness and absolution can be so easy to come by.

Will my parents understand, if I tell them? Will they be forgiving, too? Do I even have to do this? No, I don't. Kenrick said so. This is the good path to take, the righteous path, but I can choose not to. My life is my own now. If I walk away, what then?

I rest my head against the door and close my eyes to listen to their voices blended with my own blood pumping through my ears. The sun beams so brightly it burns the side of my face. I squint toward it and draw on the strength of Light, of good, to guide me.

My fingers flex on the latch. I push the door open. Just like in my hopeful dream, my mother looks up from the kitchen table and drops the dough she'd been kneading. She gapes in disbelief when she sees me. Her eyes brim with tears.

"Celli!" she cries, running to throw her arms around me. I step in, not bothering to close the door. My father, who had been sitting with his back to me, jumps up from his chair. He closes the space between us before Mum does and buries me in his embrace. She crashes into us a moment later and we stand in the doorway holding each other, tearfully shaking, laughing, and crying.

"My darling girl," Mum whispers into my hair. "I thought you were lost forever."

"Where have you been?" Da cries, his voice cracking as he squeezes me. "What happened to you?"

He's different, I can tell. He's strong again. His arms are like rocks around me. He doesn't carry the odor of cheap, stale mead on his breath or his clothes. He smells like he used to before everything went bad, like fresh cut wood and faintly of sweat. He feels different, too. More confident. Brighter. Light. I follow that feeling. Mum has it, too. It's a hopeful feeling, like a seed of grace planted in them. It reminds me of Cerion, of peace. It seeps toward me and touches me with the same cheerful sensation.

"What is that?" I whisper, ignoring Da's question. "You both have it." I step back and place my hand on Da's chest. My fingertips tingle with the soft, sweet magic that's drawn into them. I close my eyes again and visions come to me, memories that aren't my own, of a lively parade to celebrate Princess Margary. She holds the gift of a magical dewdrop in her hand. With the care of a true leader, she shares the fairies' gift, spreading it through the kingdom with any who wish to accept it.

I smile at first, until more thoughts come to me. My own actions after that time were the opposite of hers; wicked and malicious. I remember standing at the king's pyre, scooping up his ashes. I remember skulking through the dungeons, freeing prisoners with Dub beside me. Dub. Stone. Muster. My hand goes cold and starts to tremble. I can almost feel the dagger in my grip as it plunged into the three of them in the driving snow. I clench my fist and turn away. I can feel the blood drain from my face. My lips go numb. My ears ring.

"Celli, Nugget, what is it?" Da asks. He strokes my back to soothe me. Nugget. He hasn't called me that since I was a little one. My eyes brim with tears. I wonder for a moment if this is real. How can they be so well? How is it possible? Mum's cheeks are rosy and plump like they used to be. Da's arms are thick as an ax-man's. Mum pulls me to the table, and I sink onto the bench.

The light, I tell myself. *Hope. Focus on that.*

"You two look amazing," I whisper. "You have no idea how relieved I am to see you."

Da smiles. His eyes twinkle with that same light they used to when he looks across at Mum. Her hand drifts absently to her stomach, which seems a little rounder than it had before I left. She sees me notice and turns abruptly to the washboard to pour a mug of milk. Da sinks to the bench beside me. He leans close, taking my hand.

"The new queen is generous," he says with a smile. "She's given us hope for the future."

"With you gone," Mum whispers, "we thought we'd drown in our sorrow. We searched for you day and night. We appealed to the palace, and as soon as Queen Margary took her throne, men were hired to find you and the others. There was nothing for us to do but comfort each other and pray, then. Your da started working again. We knew, we truly believed, you would return to us. The change in the kingdom gave us hope that anything was possible."

She sets the mug in front of me and comes around the table to rest a hand on my shoulder and Da's.

"The others?" I whisper, staring at the milk in the mug, white as snow. "Who?"

"Mikken and Griff disappeared around the same time you did," Da explains. "Some suspected Sorcery."

At the word, I press the rim to my lips and gulp the milk, creamy and sweet, until the mug is drained. I remember the last time I had a mug of milk. It was in the shelter given to me by an imp in Hywilkin. She had warmed it, and sweetened with honey. I was cruel to that imp. I was cruel to so many. I focus on the white liquid as Mum pours more from the jug. I took things like the kindness of strangers and the rich, simple creaminess of milk for granted. I even refused them most of the time. Now, when I set the mug down and Mum fills it up a third time, I take a sip and let it sit on my tongue so I can relish its flavor. In my mind, I apologize to the imp who saved me from freezing and starving to death.

Sorcery. Unable to admit it aloud, I simply nod at my Da's suspicion.

"It was, then," Da whispers. "Sorcerers." He glances at Mum, who shakes her head slightly. The jug rattles on the table as she sets it down with a trembling hand. I swallow the last of the milk.

"I've done things," I tell them both. "Under their thumb, I did terrible things I hope you never find out about. Things I wish I could take back." Again I think of my fallen comrades, and the prisoners broken free, and all the other terrible acts Quenson forced me to perform. I have a vague memory of my old friends from Redstone Row, Mikken and Griff, staring pleadingly at me through the bars of a cell. I shake my head slowly and start to get up.

"I don't think I should have returned to Cerion," I whisper.

"No!" Mum wails. Da grasps my hand tighter. His eyes search mine.

"Whatever you did, it doesn't matter now," he says. "You're home."

"We can be a family again," Mum sniffles. She wipes her eyes with the corner of her apron and comes to hug me again.

I sink into the warmth of her arms. Breathe in the flour and the soft lavender fragrance of laundering that I'd forgotten.

"I want that," I whisper. "I do. But a threat is looming out there. I used to be on the wrong side of it. I know where Griff and Mikken are. I know things that no one else on our side knows. Things that can keep us safe."

"What threat?" Da asks. "What's happening?"

"An evil is coming, Da," I tell him, just above a whisper. "A war unlike anything Cerion has seen in years. Dusk. It started here with that battle at the king's pyre, and it continued with the earthquakes that just shook the city."

"We recovered well from those, though," Mum says. "The kingdom rallied together. It brought us all closer."

"I understand," I say. I kiss my mother on both cheeks. Da's beard scratches my face when I give him the same affection. "But I know what I must do now. I have to stay in the Light. I have to redeem myself for what was done. I love you."

With each kiss, my heart fills up, pushing out the sorrow of my past. When Da nods and lets go of me, telling me he's proud of me and he'll be waiting for my safe return, I'm brimming with hope and purpose. I hug them both again say my farewells and, without looking back, I pull up my hood and leave my parents and my home behind.

At a brisk pace, I keep to the edge of the street until I reach the market where I can easily hide in the crowd. My eyes flick over the wares of merchants who stand at their stalls, calling out to passersby. My hand twitches as a pair of well-dressed nobles pauses at the table of a metalworker. Not long ago, I would have been unable to resist the challenge of reaching into one of their pockets and seeing what I'd come away with. Thinking of it now is almost laughable. What could they possibly have that would hold any value to me? What would I gain that would be worth the risk of getting caught, found out, and thrown in the dungeon?

I smile to myself and shake my head. Is this really me? I can't believe how quickly things have changed. I can't think of anything other than getting back to Brindelier and getting to work. I need to see Kenrick again to tell him I'm ready. Poe, too. As I cross out of the market toward the docks, I start to daydream about the prince. Lost in my thoughts about how kind he was to me, and how much faith he placed in me to allow me to take this journey knowing who I had been just days before, I wander past the docks all the way to the forest park that borders the palace. Only when I reach it do I realize how it was drawing me in.

The magic that flows from it is sweet and bright. I can feel its charge, warm and inviting, all the way to my bones. Fairy voices call from its depths. Their giggling and singing entices me to step from the cobblestones into the soft grass.

"Celli," someone calls. Her sweet, merry voice is tinged with laughter.

"Celli," calls another, with a deep, funny kind tone.

"Who's there?" I ask quietly, creeping deeper into the enchanted woods. "Hello?"

"What have you seen?" a third fairy asks me, darting around my head, encased in a glowing orb of light.

"She has ventured deep into darkness," yet another whispers.

From everywhere, they move forward slowly. The bravest ones graze my sleeves and my fingers, clinging to me.

"From darkness into the light," some sing.

"Is this a dream?" I ask, raising my arm to get a closer look at the giggling orbs.

"Who will she choose?" they ask in unison, ignoring my question.

Their presence is overwhelming. I feel their draw like water to a sponge. I want to be one of them, to accept them and have them accept me. The enchantments in this place fill me like a pitcher. The light bubbles within me, charging my skin with the thrill of its bright energy. I feel uneasy, as though I've lost control of my choices and my freedom. These are light fae. Good fae, I tell myself. Still, I don't like it. I back out of the forest and stumble into the street again. The orbs drift from me, returning to the green canopy of the trees, and I stand staring until the last of them disappears.

"Celli," someone says firmly beside me, and I get the sense that it isn't the first time he's called my name.

"Kenrick," I murmur, shaking my head. "How long have you been standing there?"

"Long enough to see what happened," he mutters, looking me over. "Are you all right?"

I nod, though I'm not sure I really am, and he narrows his eyes to inspect me more cautiously.

"Are you certain?" he scowls.

"I..." I trail off. "They..." I gaze back into the forest. Part of me wants to run after the orbs so I can feel that same elation again. Part of me wants to run the other way and never look back.

"I understand," he says gently, and I honestly believe him.

"I saw my parents," I tell him, turning so my back faces the forest. It helps to have it out of view. "Before that."

"And?" he asks.

"I'm ready to return and do what I can to aid the Dawn," I say.

"Good girl," he replies, offering me his arm.

Our return journey to Brindelier is both a blur and a thrill. We board the *Tibreseli*, bobbing in the air, tethered to the newly-built docks that jut from the tops of the cliffs near the sea market, and drift through the sky to the island in the distant clouds.

"Is this a dream, Kenrick?" I ask him more than once.

Each time he replies he gives me the same answer: "It is reality, my dear. Give your mind time to adjust. I realize it is a lot to take in."

We disembark and show our coins to the gatekeeper, and Kenrick walks beside me through the Festival of Awakening, where the blur of colors, dancing, and singing are overwhelming. More than once I get lost in the crowd and Kenrick is forced to search it, only to find me whirling in the arms of a stranger or clapping to the beat of some minstrel's song. I let the magic that drifts around us fill me up and lift my spirits. I welcome it, feeling the joy and promise the festival brings.

"I can't help it," I say breathlessly after the third time he recovers me. "It's so alluring. I can feel so much pleasure all around me. It's like..." I can't find the words. I raise my arms and scoop at the air, letting the magic of the kingdom's enchantments soak into me. Kenrick doesn't try to stop it. He simply smiles and guides me ahead with his hand firmly on my back.

It's better in the palace. Quieter. We're lead by pages past by guards and attendants without being stopped. They all know him, the trusted Mentalist who is friend to the Champions of Light, who was there at the opening of the Wellspring of Hywilkin, who hails temporarily from Cerion. Mentalist. I look at him from the corner of my eye. My parents, happy and healthy. An enchanted forest. A flying ship. He said they were all real, but can I trust him, truly? Why would he trick me? What would he gain from it?

I shrug away his hand, suddenly very aware of his presence. He doesn't seem to notice. The page shows us to a parlor where velvety purple drapes are elegantly tied back to allow the polished wood and plush carpeting to flood with light. I walk away from Kenrick quickly and go to the window to let the sun warm my face. My heart races.

"Might I step away to peruse the library?" Kenrick asks the page. "There is something I want to be sure of before we meet with His Highness."

The page must answer agreeably, because Kenrick calls across the room to me, "I won't be long, Celli."

I nod, not turning from the light of the window. I touch the smooth glass with my fingertips. It feels real. The view is remarkable from here. The spires of the palace spear toward the sky above and below this window. Each one is carved with figures of animals and people and magical creatures, and painted with bright, cheerful colors. I feel I could look at them for hours and never see everything there is to see.

See. *Caviena.* Eyes. His eyes. I shiver and swallow the sick feeling that makes my stomach flip. Kenrick explained to me exactly what he'd done before we left for Cerion. He said he'd built a sort of partition in my mind, a ward that stands between me and Diovicus. When he tries to see through me like he had before, he'll see only darkness. He'll think I'm held by a sleeping spell. He'll only be let in when and if I allow it.

I stare into the sunshine, soaking in the light, gazing at the smallest details of dragons and mermaids.

Knowing that I have control, that one slip could let him back in, is terrifying. I don't understand the magic. I don't like that Kenrick has meddled with my mind, even with good intentions. Even though I gave him permission to. I suppose it's because I don't know how far his reach goes. How much of my thoughts are mine, and how many are tainted by his intentions, as good as they are? And does it really matter in the end, if we're both on the same side?

"His Highness, Prince Poelkevrin Emhryck," someone announces distantly.

"You're back," Poe says. His voice jolts me from my thoughts. I tear my gaze from the window as the prince crosses the room to greet me. My vision is obscured with blue haze and shadows of the towers as my eyes adjust from the sunlight to the indoors, but I can see he isn't alone. His attendants file in behind him: a page and two personal guards. He doesn't seem to pay them any mind. He's used to their presence.

I curtsy, and his fingers graze my arm, guiding me to stand up.

"How were your parents?" he asks. "What happened?"

He leads me to a sofa bathed in sunlight and sits beside me while I tell him about my visit. He listens attentively, offering thoughtful comments through the conversation, leading me to tell him more and more. When I'm finished talking about my parents, I describe the forest, and the flying ship, and even my journey through the city back to the palace. He seems genuinely fascinated to hear my perspective of the festival. In his eyes I see a longing to be out there among the commoners. His slightly sad smile doesn't seem to fit right on his perfect lips.

My eyes rest on them as he talks, and my thoughts drift far away, to the moment Quenson first kissed me. At the time, it was all I wanted. Now, looking back, I almost shudder. His lips were rough with the scab of the Mark, but I didn't notice that. All I knew was that he chose me, that I was important to him.

"Celli?" Poe asks gently, and I blink my eyes rapidly, clearing away the memory.

"Sorry," I whisper breathlessly, flicking my gaze away from the prince's lips. How long was I staring at them? I'm sure he noticed. He's moved closer, I realize, on the sofa. His arm is on the back of it, around me, but not really. He leans slightly toward me. I lean toward him, too. He's the first to break our locked gazes to glance at his attendants.

We both stand up at the same time and walk away from each other. He goes to a bookshelf, I return to the window. My heart races as I turn my face to the light. What was that? Am I insane? How can I feel this right now? He's a prince. Betrothed to my queen. I steal a glance at him and find him watching me, too. He looks away quickly, to the open book in his hand. I stare out the window, and we ignore each other until Kenrick returns.

"It's as I thought," the Mentalist announces after a quick bow to the prince. "Celli, your experience has led you to uncover a unique gift." He strides across the room to me, pulling out a book that was tucked under his arm. The prince comes to stand with us in the window.

"Siphon," Poe reads over Kenrick's shoulder as the Mentalist points to a passage in the tome. The prince keeps reading aloud, "A siphon is a rare talent which allows its savant to attract and channel the flow of the arcane. With practice, this talent can hone the ability to store magic within his body, and at even rarer high Circles, can shift the manner of magic from one type to another. Thus, dark magic can be drawn in, and light magic expelled. Early signs of this ability include extreme susceptibility to arcane workings, and unusually intense attraction both on the part of the siphon and any nearby presence of the Arcane. Recognizing the early signs: An untrained siphon might be quick to anger, violence, and frustration, and easily compelled by stronger outside forces of Light or Darkness. He or she is prone to fall easily into patterns of self-destructive behavior."

I grip the sill of the window and lean back onto it, letting the prince's words sink in. The passage is word for word a description of me. I shake my head, unable to fully grasp it. Poe's thoughts move quicker than mine.

"She can siphon magic from dark to light?" he asks.

"It's a rather rare talent," Kenrick says. "And will take a great deal of work to refine it, I imagine. I knew a siphon some time ago. What he could accomplish was remarkable. Sadly, he perished within Kerevorna."

"I want to learn it now," I say quickly. "If it's true, and what you told me before is also true…" I trail off, thinking of the possibilities. He could guide me, Kenrick had said, through my own mind, into the reaches of the Void, since I had been there. I could explore it. Gather information. Shift it from the inside, into something better.

"Proper training in such things takes time, my dear. Years. Decades, even," Kenrick says gently. "And that is with a master to guide you. I know of no other Savants in this age."

Poe looks at me, recognizing the disappointment I'm sure is plain on my face. He glances at Kenrick, then back over his shoulder at his attendants.

"Do not be discouraged, Celli," Kenrick says, chuckling softly. "Just because I am unaware of any, does not mean none exist."

"I think I know a way," Poe says. "Wait here. I won't be long."

Celli

We wait in silence for Poe to return. Kenrick becomes absorbed in the pages of the tome and I in the details of the towers outside again. The setting sun casts a warm, pink glow across the beautiful faces of rabbits and deer. As it creeps lower, I watch the long, dark shadows crawl slowly across the carved surfaces, contorting them. It makes me long for the afternoon sun again, with all its beautiful colors and soft warmth. I imagine being out there, with all of those enchanted creatures. I think of what it would be like to make a new home, here in Brindelier. Something about it makes me feel like I belong here. Like I'm meant to be here.

"The prince will receive you now," someone in the doorway announces. I tear my gaze from the window to blink at the waiting page.

Kenrick offers me his elbow, and I slip my hand into the crook of it. The page shakes his head and says, "Not you, sir. I'm sorry. His Highness has only summoned milady Celli."

"Oh," I whisper, looking up at Kenrick apologetically.

"I expect I know why," he says graciously. "No matter. We'll have much to talk about when we see each other again."

His eyes crinkle with that same warm smile they always hold, and he pats my hand reassuringly and nods toward the page.

"I'll see you soon, then," I say. "Thank you, Kenrick."

The page guides me through a series of corridors until we reach a spiral staircase I'm familiar with. The gold fairy, Alex, led me through here, dressed as Pippa. I remember how the light from the lamps along the walls called to me, and how it filled my vision with prisms, obscuring my sight. At the time, my confusion had been suppressed by the power of the spell that held me. *Caviena*. Now, I understand. The Muse of Light was with me even then, inching her way into my heart, trying her best to guide me.

I wonder whether Diovocus realized it then. Surely, he could see how the light obscured my vision. Did he know I was slipping from his grip? Does he know it now? My thoughts drift back to Alex again. Pippa knew what he'd been up to. Her battle with the darkness reminds me of my own. She feels the lure of it, just like I do.

I could tell that although she denied it, she does still have feelings for him. Diovicus. I could tell how hard she fought against them, desperate to convince everyone, even herself, that she didn't feel the way she did. I wonder how it came to be. He loves her, too. I felt his desperation when he met me in the Void. I knew his longing and his pain.

My heart skips into my throat and I stop on the stairway, right under a gilded lamp. I stare up at it, letting the light burn into my eyes, welcoming Eljarenae, letting her good chase the wicked thoughts away.

"Just a bit further," the page says. He probably thinks I'm tired from so many stairs. I'm certainly breathless. With each step upward, my pulse quickens. Why would Poe summon me to the Wellspring, I wonder? Is it safe for me to be in the presence of all that magic? The last time I stood before the pool, my entire body buzzed with energy. I felt like a plucked harp string. It was pleasant and unpleasant all at once, but maybe the discomfort was caused by the enemy's dark presence. I don't think his name. I don't want to be pulled off balance again.

To my relief, when we reach the top of the stairs, Poe is waiting for me on the landing. He offers me his hand and I slip mine into it gratefully.

"Thank you, Davi," he says to the page, who bows and jogs away from us, back down the steps. I stare at my hand in his, relishing the warmth in our contact as the sound of the page's footsteps fade.

Once we're alone, I expect him to guide me through the gates, but he doesn't. We remain in the quiet of the alcove, in a place just out of sight of any guard or attendant. He steps closer, and I feel the lingering magic of the Wellspring drift with him like perfume. He keeps my hand in his, and with his other, he strokes my cheek.

My heart races, my cheeks blush hot, but I keep my eyes trained on his hand. I know if I look up into his face, I might end up falling into something I don't dare hope for.

How has this happened? I keep wondering. How has everything come to this? I don't deserve the attentions of a prince. If he knew the things I've done, he'd be disgusted with me. The dark thoughts edge their way in, and I step closer to him without thinking, drawn to his bright energy to help push out the doubt in my mind.

"You said you had an idea?" I whisper. I can feel his eyes on me.

"I did," he says, pulling me closer. His breath grazes my forehead. This close, I know all I have to do is tip my head back...

"Po-key!" A singsong voice calls. "Is she here yet?"

I step away quickly, just as the silvery fairy flies around the corner. My foot misses the edge of the top step, and I slip backward. Poe tightens his grip on my hand and pulls me, and I stumble forward into his arms.

"What are you two up to?" the silver fairy giggles, darting around us. I recognize her. She's the one who pulled the curtain back when I was alone with Pippa. She promised the princess she'd fetch her brother. Her brother, Poe, who had been in Cerion, wooing the queen. My queen. I extract myself from his arms and take a step away again, careful this time to be mindful of the stairwell.

"Never mind," she says, waving her hand dismissively. "They're waiting, you know."

She hovers between us with her hands on her hips, looking from me to him with a hint of mischief in her strange, silvery eyes. Almost like she knows what we were up to.

"Of course," Poe says. He glances at me and gives a little nod, motioning toward the gateway that leads to the Wellspring.

"Are you sure?" I ask. Even from this distance, my skin is tingling. It's the magic, I tell myself, and not the perfect crystal blue of his smiling eyes. His playful wink clinches it. It's not the magic after all.

"I have faith in you," he says. "I think you'll like my idea. Wait 'til you see. Come on."

"I like her," Aliandra whispers to Poe as she floats along beside him through the gate.

"Stop," he swats at her playfully, disappearing into the glow of magic within.

The guards flanking the gates eye me through the slits in their gleaming helms. They each hold huge, gleaming spears that look so sharp they could slice me in two with hardly any effort. At first, I'm disappointed Poe left me behind instead of escorting me through, but when I step to the threshold and they don't budge, and I feel the rush of magic from within, I understand. This is a test. I must enter on my own.

I take a deep breath and peer inside. This time, I notice the lush garden that grows on either side of a gleaming walkway which disappears eventually behind broad ferns and colorful flowers. I smell the soil and feel the warmth and moisture in the air. I feel the intense magic that flows from center of the space, hidden at the end of the path.

Why does Poe want me to go in there, I wonder? How is this going to help me? I close my eyes and test the wall Kenrick built against Diovicus. The thought of his name weakens it a little until I push against it to make sure it stays firmly in place. Again, I wish I knew what Poe had in mind for me. I don't like going into situations like this blind.

Trust, they'd said. Trust, hope, faith, love. I understand now. These are things I have to fight to always keep my focus on. Doubt, despair, Distrust…these will tip me into darkness.

I take a deep breath, step through the gates, and walk along the path until the greenery on either side parts to reveal a breathtaking scene.

The pool hasn't changed since the last time I was here. Three basins spill their contents into the sparkling liquid below. Light beams up from it like the reflection of sunbeams from rippling water. I stroll to the edge of the pool, entranced by the beauty of it, drawn by the sheer power and purity of the magic it holds. It is neither light nor dark. It's magic in its untainted form, perfectly neutral.

I start to sink to my knees in front of it, to reach out to it, when some movement across the pool draws my attention. There, across an ornate footbridge, are two golden thrones. Neither is occupied. Instead, the princess, wearing a gown so opulent I can only imagine it was created from the magic of the pool itself, clings to the waist of a woman, or a fae. I'm not sure. She has wings like one, which sparkle with the light of the pool and shift through the colors of a rainbow. She curls her left arm around Pippa, and with her right, she welcomes Poe, who has just reached her side.

At first, none of them acknowledge me. The woman bends to kiss Poe on the cheek. The gesture reminds me of my mother, and I understand in that moment that she must be theirs.

"Celli," Poe beckons to me.

As I cross the bridge, I can't help but get caught up in the magical details of the scene before me. The twins look so alike, dressed in silver and gold, clinging to their mother. I can feel the magic surrounding them, light and loving. Aliandra, Poe's fairy companion, has found her seat in the cushion of Poe's crown, just as Alex perches in Pippa's. Pippa's eyes glisten with tears as she gazes up at her mother. Her smile beams with joy, and she seems as if she might never look away from the beautiful woman. I don't miss, as I approach, how the fairies' eyes move in unison, alert to my every movement.

"I see," the woman says without any introduction. She closes her eyes and breathes in, and glowing motes of light swirl to her nostrils from the Wellspring. This close, I can see how each strand of her long, tumbling hair shifts with color and glamour, and how the shimmer of her gown seems to be made of pure, endless magic.

She steps forward, taking her hands from her children, and offering them to me. Pippa moves with her, still clinging to her waist, and Poe puts a hand on his mother's shoulder. I hesitate and look to Poe, who offers me a reassuring nod. My hands are sweaty and shaking with nervous energy. The magic in this place pulls at me, confusing my thoughts. I feel the power swirling from the pool, calling to me. I want to fall into it, to let it spill over me and fill me and use me. I fight that urge and take a step closer. With the prince's reassurance, I place my hands into his mother's. She bows her head and closes her eyes, and I do the same.

Strange whisperings cascade around me too quickly to grasp anything being said. I get the sense that they're voices from everywhere, all across the Known Lands, casting spells, creating enchantments, and wielding the Arcane. They come and go like the rustle of wheat fronds in the breeze, until only one of them remains.

"I know the struggle of balance," she says. As she speaks, her whisper grows stronger until her voice rings clear and perfect. "I have suffered much the same as you have, forsaken by darkness, lured into hopelessness. I have reached into the depths of despair, and I was drawn back into the light by a sliver of hope, a promise of love, a forging of trust."

Her words crash over me, each one carrying with it the full impact of the emotion behind it. I feel each of the things she lists off; the dark ones like a punch to my insides, the light ones like a passionate kiss. I cling to her hands, feeling the charge of those emotions rushing through them.

"You have been touched by my brother, Vorhadeniel, and held by my sister, Eljarenae," she says. "Your experiences and choices have brought you to me. I am Stellastera, Muse of Magic. If you so choose, I shall guide you in the ways of the Siphon, Celli Deshtal of Cerion, and welcome you to my side as a Champion of Balance."

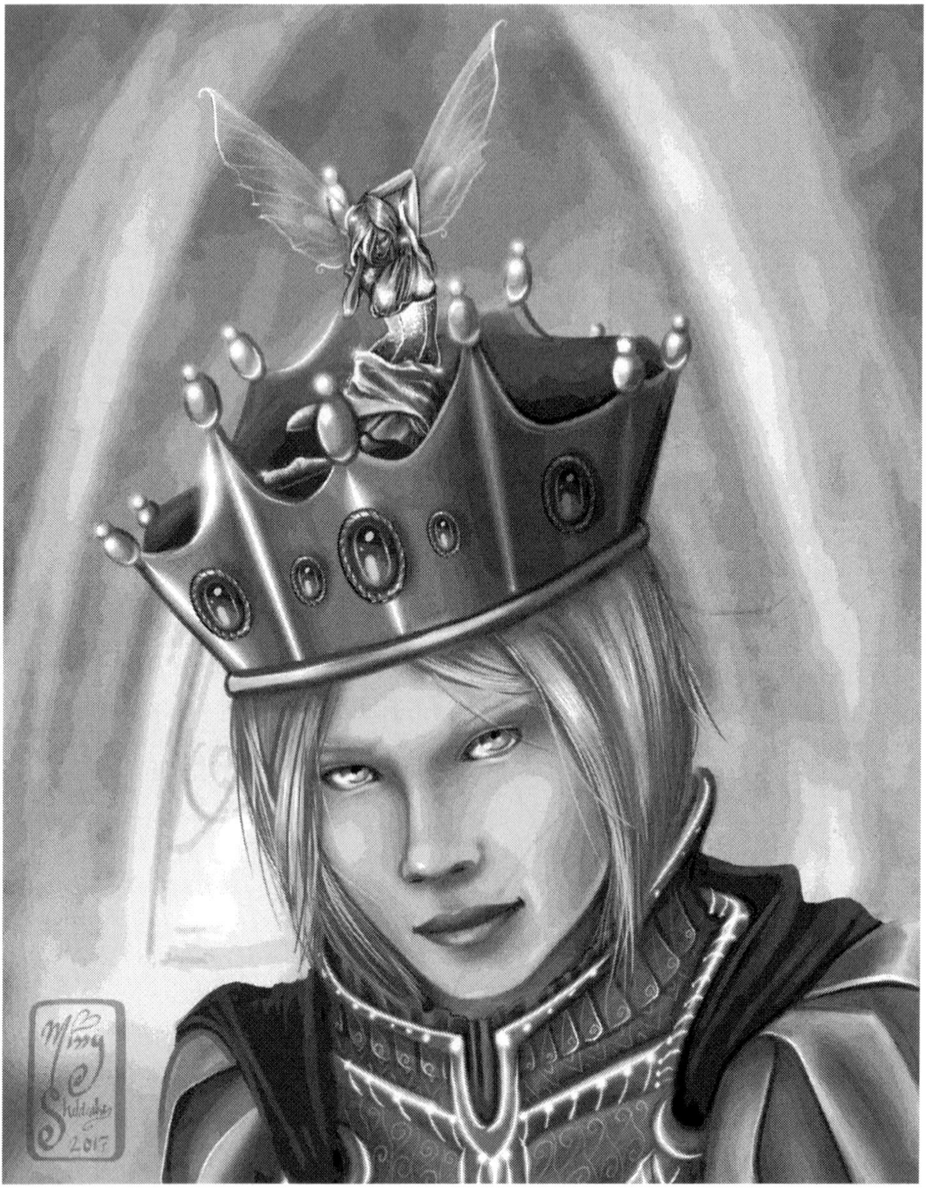

Chapter Thirty-Four

VALOR AND SUGAR CUBES
Azi

"Saesa, you're dripping all over the lists," Mya's voice echoes through the guild hall as we emerge into it from our journey through the Half-Realm.

"Sorry," comes Saesa's breathless reply. "Bryse didn't hold back today. I thought he was going to cleave me in two."

"Luca!" Mouli shouts from a short distance away. "Did you forget the sugar again?"

"I didn't forget it the first time," Luca grumbles under his breath. "No, dear!" he shouts louder.

"Well, where is it?"

"On the washboard!"

"It isn't!" Mouli's voice grows closer. "Why can't you just admit you forgot it again? Second day in a row, too."

"I didn't, woman!"

"Go and find it, then."

"Better things to do," Luca mumbles.

Things come into focus around us, and before Rian whispers the Revealer, we watch Luca's lanky, hunched form stomp off through the serving door that leads to Mouli's kitchen, brushing past her as he goes.

Mouli sighs and wipes her hands with her apron. She steps closer to Mya, who's busy shuffling through a dozen pages scattered across the hall table.

"I'm starting to think," Mouli confides in Mya under her breath, "maybe retirement isn't such a bad idea, if the man can't even remember something so simple as sugar. That'll be two days in a row with no sweet rolls. What if they come home today?"

"No sweet rolls again?" Bryse booms as he clomps in from the training square. "What gives, Mouli?"

Mya's eyes flick from Mouli to Bryse and back to her pages. She presses her lips together, hiding her amusement at the exchange.

Beside her, Saesa gulps water from a mug, mopping sweat from her neck and face with a towel.

"Dadgumit," Luca shouts from the kitchen. "What'd you do with it, woman? I got a double sack of it just yesterday!"

"Watch," Mouli says with a huff. "This'll be the day they finally come back, too."

"Serve 'em right," Bryse grumbles. "Those two gotta learn to send a bird once in a while."

"We're in trouble," Rian whispers in my ear. I shuffle closer to him and giggle softly, pressing a finger to his lips.

"Maybe we should come back bearing gifts of sugar," I push to him. *"To the market?"*

"I can think of a better use of our time," he replies, bending to kiss me. While our lips are pressed together, I feel him fidget a little. When I pull away and open my eyes, he holds up a bag of sugar cubes. *"Conjure confectionery. Third circle."* He grins, wiggling his eyebrows at me.

"That sounds like a made-up spell," I push, swatting his shoulder playfully.

"Ow," he whispers, feigning a wounded scowl.

"Come on, Luca," Mya calls. "We only have until mid-afternoon to get through these. Do you think we should start packing Benen's forge before Midwinter, or after?"

"Guess I'm going to market," Mouli sighs. "Wish me luck."

"No need for that," Rian says, and with a flourish, he casts the Revealer. Everyone yelps and jumps. Bryse lets out a string of curses that burn my ears. Mouli screams and collapses dramatically against Luca, who just happened to reappear in the doorway beside her at the right moment. Mya jumps to her feet. Saesa's hand darts to her sword.

"I heard you needed this," Rian says with a bow, presenting the sugar to Mouli.

"You're back! How wonderful!" Mouli cries. She hugs me and Rian tightly, accepts the sugar with a quick thank you, and turns to Luca.

"I told you. Now they're here, and I don't have Azi's favorite," she whispers, smacking him on the chest.

"And somehow, it's my fault." Luca glowers and rubs the spot.

"Of course it is! You forgot the sugar!" Mouli hisses, over her shoulder as she rushes back to the kitchen.

"Did not," Luca mumbles.

"Never mind they're my favorite too," Bryse grunts, scooping me into a damp hug. "Bout time you two got back," he says as Rian goes to hug his mum. I laugh and pat Bryse's broad sides, doing my best to ignore the unpleasant odor of half-Stone-Giant sweat.

At the long end of the table, Saesa's eyes lock with mine. She gives a respectful nod as she sets her mug on the sideboard. She turns to leave, and my laughter falls flat as guilt seeps in over leaving her behind again.

"Saesa," I say. All around us, the room goes quiet.

"Lady knight," she replies, curtsying graciously.

"May I have a word?" I ask, pulling free of Bryse, who steps awkwardly aside.

"Certainly," she nods with a smile that's obviously forced. "Forgive me, though. It must be quick. I've been asked to report to the queen the moment you returned."

"I'll walk with you," I say.

"Best not, Azi," Mya interjects. "Stay inside until the queen sends an invitation for you."

I look from her to Rian and then Bryse questioningly.

"Aye," Bryse agrees. "It's near impossible for any of us to go out there without causing a scene anymore. Everyone wants to see the Queen's Champions. Good thing we've got Saesa to pass our messages, eh? She's excellent at moving around unnoticed." He grins at her, punching her arm. She shrugs. I recognize the look in her eyes. It's the same one I'm sure I had when Mum and Da were on the quest to Kythshire, and I was left behind with Bryse and Cort at the guild hall. He did the same thing then, trying to keep me busy and distracted.

"I have ways of going unseen," I remind them.

"Her Majesty is concerned about you and Mentor Rian appearing on palace grounds before you're introduced to Valor," Saesa explains.

"Valor?" I ask.

"Remember that dragon claw from Hywilkin?" Bryse says in between gulps from his mug. "Valor." He winks.

"Oh," I reply, still slightly confused. Rian and I exchange a curious glance, and his gaze drifts toward the east wall of the guild hall, in the direction of the palace.

"Pardon us," I say to the others, beckoning Saesa to follow me out. We walk in silence through the passage that connects the guild hall to our townhouses, and I push open my family's door and step into the kitchen. Saesa trails me without a word and stops just inside the door with her hands clasped behind her back.

"Mum?" I call as soon as the door clicks shut. "Da?"

"Sir Hammerfel, that is, your mum," Saesa says quietly, "is at the palace, milady. Sir Hammerfel, your da, went to oversee a shipment of arms to Kordelya Keep after rumors reached the queen of a threat encroaching from the north."

"Oh, I see," I say, shifting from one foot to another. I tap my fingers on the insides of my gauntlets nervously and turn to face her. "I owe you an apology," I say. "Things happened so quickly, but that's no excuse. I should have thought to grab you as we left. I'm so sorry I left you behind."

"My Lady Knight," Saesa says, bowing her head, "you don't have to apologize to me. These things happen. I'm actually glad I was here, so I could be your eyes in Cerion, or elsewhere, while you were gone."

"You still call me that," I ask with a smile, "even though I left you behind?"

"Of course," she smiles, too. "I swore to serve as your squire, didn't I?"

The question hangs between us uncomfortably. She did swear it, just as I swore an oath to her.

"Really, My Lady," she says, stepping closer, "there are far more important things happening right now. I'm sure you agree. What happened with the mermaid?"

Her question brings me back to the moment in the queen's council room with On'na. It feels like it was ages ago. I reach for her and she moves even closer.

"Look," I whisper, holding my hands out before me. She tips her head forward and I play the scenes for her, from the moment we arrived at the crevice, through to Rian disappearing into darkness, and then on to the mermaids' healing, and to Stepstone and even the Palace of Dawn and the Muses' meeting.

She reacts in hushed whispers, taking in everything I show her with earnest concern. When I'm through, her green eyes meet mine.

"Now, you should look, My Lady Knight," she says, and the gold tendrils swirl between us into her dark pupils. I fall into her memories of Cresten, and the opal dragon, and the jungles of Elespen, and the temple of Velu, and the Wellspring, and her and Tib's return to Margy, all through that meeting until the vial smashed.

"They tried to repair it," she explains, "but I don't think it worked. I told the queen of what happened in Elespen. She's not worried. She believes if we're meant to claim Brindelier, we'll find a way to retrieve another offering." At that she pauses and looks over her shoulder. "I think," she whispers, hesitating.

"What?" I ask, resting a hand on her arm.

"My Lady, I wonder whether the queen intends to wed the prince of Brindelier, as everyone expects her to. As far as I can tell, she's been delaying talks with Master Keyes. After the quakes, rumor says she all but turned her back on the negotiations for marriage. Since then, she has been spending long hours with Lady Susefen, the elves' scholar, shut away in her study. I've been paying close attention, and it really does seem like she has other intentions. Since Prince Poelkevrin returned to Brindelier, it's starting to seem more and more like she might refuse their throne, after all."

"But why would she…" I trail off as images from Saesa's memory come to mind. She saw the pain in the queen's eyes as plainly as I did while Tib was on his tirade. Anyone could have seen it. Anyone but that boy, apparently. I sigh and look at Saesa, shaking my head.

She looks away tearfully, clears her throat, and changes the subject slightly, "I'm so relieved the Savarikta are safe. I wonder how many of them will go with him to Elespen?"

"I'm not sure," I say. "But I have faith that this time he won't fail. His sister seems to have calmed him and set him back on the path he needs to follow."

She doesn't say anything to that. I can tell what she must be thinking. I saw what happened from her perspective, with her own emotions tinting her memories. "The heart wants what it wants," I offer to her quietly. "He can't help it."

She nods. "Perhaps I should go to Her Majesty now."

She doesn't mention anything about Kerr Skalivar, and I'm not sure I ought to have seen the flashes of memories which peeked in as she showed me other things, so I don't bring him up. I wonder about his intentions with her, though. Knowing what little I do know makes me feel rather protective of my squire. I vow to myself to arrange a meeting with him to find out, as soon as everything else quiets down.

A knock on the kitchen door makes both of us jump, and I open it to find Rian on the other side of it.

"Sorry to interrupt," he says. "I filled Mum in, and now I have to find Master Gaethon."

"Come in first," I whisper, pulling him in and closing the door. "Saesa, tell Rian what you just told me about the queen."

Saesa repeats herself, and Rian paces as he listens, scratching his beard and nodding his head thoughtfully.

"Well," he says after she's finished, "in Brindelier, the prince did say Margy was under no obligation to marry him. Remember?"

I think back to that moment when the twins woke on their throne. "He did, didn't he? He said she'd be free to choose, without any pressure or obligation. But what will happen once all the offerings are in place?" I wonder. "The passage Margy read to us, the one that started all this, said, 'their kingdoms shall unite, and none shall divide them.'"

"That can be taken a lot of different ways," Rian muses. "It doesn't necessarily mean marriage... As for what will happen if they aren't married, I'm not sure. If anyone knows, it's probably Susefen. I'll bet that's why they've been meeting. Do you know if Master Gaethon is at the palace, Saesa?"

"The last I knew, he was at the Academy," she says.

"Thanks," he says. He gives me a quick kiss and sets off, stepping into the Half-Realm to hide himself before he slips out the back door.

"I'll be quick," Saesa says with a curtsy. I walk her to the outer door and then return to the guild hall, where Elliot stands looking over Mya's shoulder, scratching his scruffy head.

"Hey, Azi," he says around a deep yawn.

"Elliot," I reply, smiling. "Where did everyone else go?"

"Luca's outside checking a crate delivery, Bryse is in the bath, Mouli's baking," Mya offers distractedly.

"Cort's at the Conclave," Elliot finishes for her as she checks two pages against each other.

"What happened?" I ask. "Is he all right?"

"Saesa caught his elbow with her long sword in practice," Mya explains absently. "Clean break, but more than I could heal with a song."

Elliot winces and wiggles his elbow, then goes to slump in one of the armchairs by the hearth.

"Going to check out past Kordelya," he says, yawning. Mya nods, her brow furrowed in concentration, and Elliot closes his eyes.

"No one has gone to Haigh yet?" I ask, thinking of what Stellastera said about forces gathering in the north.

"That quest was postponed after reports from Stenneler that Kordelya Keep was threatened," Mya explains. "Her Majesty sent armies to reinforce the offensive efforts there."

"Saesa mentioned that," I say, thinking of Da.

When Mya doesn't reply, I go to her side and slide onto the bench to look at the papers she's shuffling around: packing lists, orders for crates, schedules. It's strange to imagine after everything we've been through and everything we know is coming, that she's been here, doing something as ordinary as this. I wonder whether she enjoys it, or simply does it because it's her duty as guild leader. My pulse quickens at that thought as I remember Margy's declaration just before her coronation, the one that named me deputy leader of the guild. I feel like I should take more of an interest in this work, but it seems so mundane in the face of what's happening that it's practically comical.

"Don't you want to know what happened?" I ask her.

"Rian told us most of it," she says. "I'm sorry, Azi. I know it seems ridiculous, but I've been putting all of this paperwork off for too long. I really just need to get through it."

"Can I help?" I ask, pulling a parchment toward me.

"I appreciate the offer, but not right now," she replies, sliding the parchment back into place. "I have everything the way I need it to get it finished quickly." Just like that, I feel like a child poking my nose in important work I have no business being around.

"All right," I say quietly, and she barely acknowledges me when I get up to wander off to the kitchen.

Just inside the service door, I'm greeted with the fragrance of sweet spices and a scene that makes me clap my hand over my mouth to keep from laughing. The top part of the kitchen's half-door is agape, and Mouli is just outside talking to Luca. Unaware of my presence, a group of a dozen or so fae hover whispering over the sack of sugar cubes, deftly shoving one after the other into the pouches of their belts. They giggle and crunch and pilfer until half the bag is gone, and just as they're about to make their getaway, I clear my throat.

"Eek!" three of the fairies yelp and dart off in a blur of color. The remaining creatures freeze in place, staring at me, wide-eyed.

"It's her," one of them squeaks. "Flitt's Azi!"

"It really is!" chirps another.

"What do you think you're doing, all of you?" I ask. I cross my arms over my chest and tilt my head to the side, trying hard to take a scolding tone, but the scene is just too funny for me to keep a straight face. "Poor Luca, taking the blame for forgotten sugar."

"We can't help it," a fairy with bright pink hair shoots toward me and darts around my head. "It's so yummy, we couldn't resist."

"Why don't you just conjure your own?" I ask, thinking of Rian's spell.

"They never come out the same," one of the fairies explains. "Her cubes always taste so much sweeter. So filled with joy."

I can't really argue with that. It's true that everything seems to taste better once Mouli's had a hand in it.

Another fairy dressed all in bright red rose petals with a shock of green hair spins in the air in front of me, shouting, "Mouli is the best! She always has the most delicious treats for us!"

"She's going to be my Faedin," a third, very round fairy mumbles around a mouthful of sugar.

"No, I already flashed ideas to her!" a fourth one yelps. "I made her daydream and smile and make more autumn apple biscuits!" She is even rounder than the third, with broad blue wings and a dew-kissed smile. Or perhaps not. Perhaps it's just glistening with stolen sugar.

"Where did you all come from?" I ask with an exasperated whisper.

"The forest park!" They reply.

"She's coming!" a lanky fairy bobbing in the doorway warns, and before I can say another word, the fairies vanish. A moment later, Mouli pulls open the door.

"Azi, dear," she greets me with a smile and goes to wash her hands in the basin. "Are you hungry? I'll fix you a tray. Just let me get the sweet rolls fin—" she gasps as she turns to see the pilfered sack of sugar on the table and the messy footprints left behind in the spices and the rolled-out dough.

"Flitt!" she cries in exasperation, shaking her head at the mess.

"It wasn't her," I say, covering my bemused smile. "You have admirers, Mouli," I chuckle, pointing toward the door where the bravest of the fae hover, peering inside.

Slowly, Mouli turns her head, hands on her hips. "Now, now," she says, clicking her tongue. "Is that so?"

The two round fairies drift inside a little, the one with the blue wings pushing the other one backwards.

"Well then," she laughs softly. "Come in out of that breeze before your wings get all rumpled. Help me clean up, and I'll fix you a treat. Apple biscuits perhaps? First, though, I think you owe poor Luca an apology."

***

There's not much to be done while I wait for Saesa to return, so I eat the tray of goodies Mouli fixes for me in the kitchen and spend time visiting with her and the fairies and gossiping about all the things I missed while we were away. Eventually, Mouli masterfully steers the conversation in a direction I should have anticipated, but wasn't prepared for.

"You realize it's less than a year from Summerswan," she says with a slightly impatient tone, looking up from the dough she's rolling from a sheet into a spiral. My mouth waters when I think of the sweet rolls, and my stomach growls loudly.

"It's eleven months," I say, biting into a deliciously ripe plum.

"Barely ten, and I don't think you realize how much there is to do!" Mouli exclaims. "With the move in Midspring, it'll be here before you know it! Best not to let these things sneak up on you, Azi."

She expertly slices the rolls into perfectly shaped portions as she talks, and I wonder at her skill. Her hands move expertly, almost without a thought to what they're doing.

"I'd very much like your help," I say honestly. "I don't think I could even begin to do any of it without you."

Her deft hands stop abruptly. She turns to me, her eyes brimming with tears.

"Oh, Azi, my dear! Of course!" she cries. She rushes close, nearly tipping my tray, and flings her arms around me. "It'll be a wedding like no one has seen in the history of Cerion. It'll rival even that of Amei and Er..." her voice trails off as she realizes what she's said. No one, I imagine, looks back on the marriage of Eron and Amei as something to aspire to after what's happened.

"It'll be amazing," I say, squeezing her around the shoulders. "I believe if anyone could make it perfect, you could, and I can't imagine asking anyone else, Mouli."

She sniffles and wipes her eyes, then steps back and pats my cheek affectionately. "All grown up," she whispers, and goes back to her dough.

While she rambles about all the wonderful plans for my marriage to Rian, my thoughts wander back to the last big wedding

Cerion had seen, the one that was doomed to fail. Those thoughts lead me to Eron, and the Revenant he's become. I shiver as I think of his fate now, how he was created to destroy our queen, and how she most likely hasn't seen the last of her brother, yet. I wish more than anything I could have ended Sybel at the chasm, or in Sixledge. Destroying the creator would have destroyed the creature, that's what Rian and I had discovered before. I wonder if that's still true, now that the magic Eron has been imbued with is so much more complicated.

These are the things Rian must have gone to talk to Uncle about. That and the newfound abilities he wielded when faced with those Sorcerers. I shift on the stool and pluck an apple biscuit from the tray to nibble on it thoughtfully.

"...and of course, cornflowers, and your favorite, yellow roses..." Mouli goes on, and I nod absently in agreement. It seems utterly ridiculous to even think about a wedding, knowing how much more is at stake right now.

The blue-winged fairy, who told us her name is Kit, pops into view right in front of Mouli's face, startling her.

"We apologized, but he sure is a grump!" she says.

"I apologized first," says her rival, a plump little boy fae with bright orange hair who introduced himself as Leif, "and I don't think he's that bad."

"Well now, that's a gleaming appraisal, isn't it?" Mouli chuckles.

"Now can we have a biscuit?" Kit asks.

"Pleeease?" Leif grins adorably.

"Yes, yes, but keep your footprints out of the spice blend this time," Mouli sighs, gesturing to the platter behind her.

Just outside the door, Luca calls to someone out of view, "What've you got there?"

"Hi Luca! Just a few things," comes Saesa's breathless reply.

I watch Luca's head go bobbing past the half door, and I get up to peek out. When I pass the fairies, they fade from view. Too many people around, I imagine, for their comfort.

Just beyond the door, Saesa stands with her arms laden with trinkets and baubles. She laughs apologetically, explaining, "I usually bring a sack with me, but I forgot this time. Thanks, Luca."

He only grunts in reply, collecting as many things as he can to help her out. "Every day, more and more of this," he grumbles. "And who's going to pack it all?" he asks me, wiggling what looks like a pretty lace handkerchief in my direction.

"Hush, you!" Mouli hisses, brushing past me to push the door open for them. "Come inside. I won't have anyone thinking we're ungrateful."

"What are they?" I ask Saesa, who stumbles up the steps with her arms still laden and ducks into the kitchen. Mouli closes the door, both top and bottom halves, behind her. Before she does, I catch a glimpse of the crowd that apparently followed my squire from the palace. Bryse wasn't kidding.

This close, I can pick out all sorts of things in the pile Saesa's carrying: necklaces made from polished, gleaming seashells, little carvings out of wood in the shapes of fairies, horses, and dragons, delicately embroidered kerchiefs, and even a banner of gold and blue that spills across her arm and down to her knees.

"Gifts," she says, tipping them toward me. "All for you."

"What?" I whisper. "Why?"

"Why, she asks!" Mouli snorts. "Come now, Azi!"

"I imagine she's not been to her room yet, has she?" Luca grunts.

"I'll go put them with the rest, and then we have to hurry back. Her Majesty wants to show you something," Saesa says. Before I can ask any more questions, she jogs off through the kitchen into the hall.

"What's in my room?" I ask, scowling with confusion.

"More things to pack!" Luca grumbles. "I better go tell Mya to order a few more crates."

"You have well-wishers," Mouli smiles as Luca disappears into the hall. "Admirers. They've been sending you things for a while now. Some for you, some for Rian…some for both of you." She winks.

Part of me wants to go investigate my room and see just how much the two of them are exaggerating, but the other part shifts uncomfortably at the thought of strangers I barely know feeling the need to send me gifts. I stand conflicted, stuck to the spot, watching Mouli work until Saesa rushes back in, snapping me out of my awkward silence.

"Has Cort gotten back yet?" she asks Mouli.

"Not yet. Did the queen want him, too?" Mouli asks.

"No, milady," Saesa replies. "I just wondered whether it was as bad as it looked."

"Well, I don't see why you couldn't practice with wooden swords, if you're going to be so rough with each other," Mouli scolds.

"Honestly, what's the point of working yourselves so hard that you're injured for the real fight?"

Behind Mouli's back, Saesa meets my eyes, her brows raised as if to ask how she should respond to that. I roll my eyes and shake my head slightly.

"Don't roll your eyes at me, Azi," Mouli tsks. "I've been saying it for years, haven't I?"

"Yes, Mouli," I say, kissing her cheek. "Thank you for the tray."

"Go on, don't keep the queen waiting," Mouli says, swatting me away with her flour-dusted hand as she takes my empty snack tray to clean it.

Chapter Thirty-Five

MAGE QUEEN
Azi

The short journey to the palace gates is not as bad as everyone made it out to be. A crowd is waiting to greet me when we leave the guild hall, but they're all very warm and kind, and they understand my rush to the palace and don't keep me long.

Our arrival at the palace gates is another story altogether. The crowd here is much larger, but they're not waiting for me. Instead, they crane their necks to gaze at the tallest tower, shielding their eyes from the sun, waiting for something to happen.

As I approach the gates, the subject of their attention is obvious. Valor, the dragon, is a sight to behold. Its scales are the same color as the whitish gray stone that makes up the castle, and it looks as though the dragon is nothing more than an impressive, decorative statue perched upon the highest peak of it.

The guards at the gatehouse wave us in, and a whisper of anticipation rushes through the crowd. High above, the dragon's eyes flash a bright warning. With the grinding sound of stone on stone like a miller's wheel, its wings stretch out.

Behind us in the street, the people gasp and cheer. Valor lifts off from the tower and lands lightly before me, its huge, shining talons barely making a mark in the sprawling lawn.

"I am Valor," the creature booms, lowering its enormous head to peer at me with sparkling purple eyes. "The White Coast embodied. Guardian of the South. Keeper of the Palace of Cerion. Spirit of the Arcane. Gift of Hywilkin. Protector of the Queen. Scourge of Sorcerers."

"You are stunning," I whisper to the dragon, stepping closer with my hand outstretched. To my surprise, it snakes closer until the scales of its right nostril graze my outstretched fingers. A charge of magic sparks between us, golden and purple and bright. The dragon's eyelids flutter with pleasure, and it huffs its warm, glittering breath into my hair as it takes in my scent.

"Azaeli Hammerfel," it says. "The Temperate, Pure of Heart, Reviver of Iren, The Great Protector, Cerion's Ambassador to Kythshire, Knight of Her Majesty's Champions, The Mentalist, The Paladin, Champion of Light, Agent of Light, Duskbane," it says with reverence. "You are welcome here. Enter. Her Majesty awaits your company."

It bows its head to me, then looks toward the palace doors.

"Thank you, Valor," I say, still awed by its majestic presence. If this is our Guardian, our version of Iren at the palace of Cerion, I know we have little to fear from those who would threaten us.

"Remind me," I tell Saesa as we step inside, "to be sure to give Kerr Skalivar my sincere thanks for such a thoughtful and powerful gift."

I glance over my shoulder at her and don't fail to notice the blush that covers her cheeks.

"I will, my Lady Knight," she says.

"Ah! Sir Hammerfel!" To my surprise, the attendant who greets us isn't a page, but a Mage, and familiar one, at that. His slightly-too-long orange robes seem hitched up over his ankles by some strange, unseen force. His floppy hat is skewed on his head, and part of his hair is singed from some event that seems like it must have been recent, since it's still trailing a thin stream of smoke.

"Ah, Dumfrey, wasn't it?" I ask the Mage, whose eyes bulge wide in shock.

"You remember me?" he gasps and stutters and looks behind me at Saesa, whispering, "She remembers me!"

For an awkward moment he stands blinking and grinning and shifting in place. Once or twice he starts to offer me a hand to shake and then pulls it away quickly, as if he's unsure what the protocol is.

"Sorry, sorry, Lady Sir. I mean Sir Knight. I mean, ah, they're waiting. We're supposed to hurry."

"Your hair," Saesa warns as the smoldering strand goes alight again.

"Right, it was just a small accident," he says, waving his hand dismissively, fanning the fire to burn brighter.

"No, I mean, it's—" Saesa starts, and I step forward quickly and blot the flame out.

"Oh, was it still..." he sniffs the air nervously and pats the side of his head. "Well, thank you, lady. I mean, sir. Sir."

"You can just call me Azi," I say, which I realize immediately was a mistake, because his eyes go wide again and his mouth goes agape and he looks from Saesa to me, speechless.

"Can you show us to the queen, please?" I ask, and he nods, still silent, and trips over his robes as he turns to lead us off through the palace.

"Poor Dumfrey," Saesa whispers once there's enough space between us to keep him from hearing. "Rumor has it, he was assigned to the dungeons when the earthquakes hit. He managed to create a barrier for himself and the guards posted with him to keep them alive until rescue came, but apparently, he hasn't been quite the same since then. Queen Margy gave him a post above ground after that, something easy to help him keep his head."

"She's at her lessons, of course," he bumbles over his shoulder. "She's coming along nicely. It's a pleasure to watch, of course. Despite some hiccups." He reaches up and pats his head again, but the fire has since died out completely.

Just as I'm about to ask him exactly what lessons he's talking about, he pushes open a set of double doors and ushers us into an enormous courtyard surrounded on all sides by the palace, but open to the sky above. When we step in, the doors close behind us on their own. Dumfrey holds up his hand, signaling for us to wait.

At the center of the plain courtyard, Queen Margy emerges from thin air. Her form wavers slightly, then strengthens until it's as solid and real as she should be. She's facing away from us, looking toward the distant archway, where Master Anod stands watching. She's dressed in the plain robes of an apprentice, but dyed to signify her status as royalty. Such a simple thing seems like it wouldn't be remarkable, but I'm struck by the meaning of the color. I doubt anyone in Cerion has worn purple Mage robes since before the time Asio Plethore claimed the throne from Diovicus.

She looks terribly small in the center of the room, standing alone, facing the old master in his red robes. Anod raises a single hand, and Dumfrey waves behind himself at us, his eyes glued to the scene. Saesa backs up against the door and pulls me to stand beside her, pressing as far away from the queen as we can be without leaving the courtyard.

"One!" Anod shouts, and Margy's form blurs so rapidly that my eyes tear up in my effort to focus on her. The faster her form shifts and vibrates, the further apart the images break away from each other, until there are two Margys, then four, then eight, and sixteen.

"Two!" Anod shouts, raising his left hand. He spreads the fingers of both hands, and they crackle with sharp energy.

All the Margys thrust their arms to the sides. Her voice echoes from the line of them, speaking in Mage's tongue. A bubble of light pushes out from them all, creating a ward to protect her from Anod's threat.

"Three!" The master shouts, and swoops his hands up and over his head. A strange sort of bluish purple magic crawls across his face, morphing his features into a completely different person. On instinct, I take a battle stance as Master Anod disappears, robes and all, and Eron takes his place. Mercy leaps to my hands as the Revenant stalks down the few steps to Margy's level, his own sword raised, his charcoal armor absorbing the afternoon sunlight, so it glows like embers in a fire. He sneers at the line of queens, taking each of them in, trying to discern which one is really her.

I stride forward, my own sword raised to attack, but Dumfrey jumps to me and grabs my arm.

"It's not really him," he whispers. "Keep watching. Don't break her concentration."

I know he's right, but it's still difficult to watch the former prince sneering and shouting obscene threats at the line of queens who stand composed and calm in the face of his abuses.

One of the queens breaks form. She reaches to brush a curl from her face. Eron doesn't miss it. His eyes snap to her. He speeds across the courtyard at an unnatural pace and slashes his sword at Margy. I take a couple of steps before Saesa grabs my arm and pulls me back. The Margy under Eron's attack vanishes, and so do the others along the line, one by one, until the queen stands alone about thirty paces from him.

"Four," Eron growls, and Margy plants her feet and turns toward him. With a scream of rage and power, she thrusts her hands forward. The ball of light that suddenly appears between them is bigger than her head. It crackles with bright, searing energy like a miniature sun. She pulls it to her chest and shoves it outward, and it shoots toward the prince faster than an arrow. It strikes him with a deafening crackle, throwing him backwards through the air.

He lands hard at the edge of the courtyard, but the spell doesn't stop there. The globe of light grows and spreads, coating the prince's chest, arms and legs. He convulses and screams as his skin crackles with the power of it, until he's completely consumed by the light.

"Five," Margy whispers. She pulls a hand through the air in a line parallel to the ground, summoning a spear of that same pure, crackling light. She raises the weapon in her steady hand, readying herself for the attack she assumes will come, but Eron's prone form lies still, glowing and shimmering.

Immediately, I'm concerned for Master Anod. Surely, he couldn't have taken an attack so powerful as that and still survived. Saesa clings to my arm, holding her breath. I glance at Dumfrey, who looks from Margy to the Master, also concerned.

"Should we—?" I whisper.

"Shh!" he replies, his hand flying up.

Sure enough, a moment later, the prince flips over and spins on his hands and knees with unnatural speed to face her. His shoulders heave as he sneers at Margy, baring his teeth like a wild animal.

"Six," Margy mouths to herself. She pulls the spear back, pointing directly at Eron's head with her free hand. With a strange sort of grace and a measured power, she throws it forward. The spear doesn't fly like a normal one would. It's much faster, and it doesn't curve in the air with the weight of its tip. It takes a straight, driving path, striking Eron directly between the eyes. He releases a horrible screech before his image disintegrates, leaving the master kneeling in his place.

"That was," Anod pants, "better, Majesty."

She rushes to his side, allowing him to lean on her to stand up. I let out a long held-breath and sheathe my sword. Beside me, Saesa lets out her own breath as well.

"That was excellent, your Majesty! Truly brilliant!" Dumfrey cheers loudly, clapping as though he's a spectator at the joust.

"You hold back," Anod says hoarsely, tugging his robes straight in front.

"I don't want to hurt you," Margy says quietly. "You're not him."

"In that case, I am. If you don't work to your full potential, you will not ever reach it," he chastises.

"We'll do it again, then," she says with determination.

Anod looks her over as any concerned friend would. I see his eyes linger on her pale cheeks and drooping eyes, and I wonder how long they've been at this.

"I require rest, your Majesty. Forgive me," he says quietly. Saesa and I exchange a glance. He doesn't look half as drained as the queen does. He's making excuses to give her a break.

"Very well," Margy sighs. "I suppose I could use a break as well."

"And you have guests," he smiles, gesturing toward me and Saesa. We curtsy as the queen turns in our direction.

"Azi!" she shouts, hiking up her robes to run to me.

"Did you see?" she asks, her eyes bright with excitement despite their obvious exhaustion.

"I don't even know what to say, Your Majesty," I tell her earnestly. "It was very impressive magic."

I look to Anod, who stands behind her with his hands tucked into his long sleeves.

"Her Majesty is preparing for any eventuality," he explains.

"You heard of our failure, then," I sigh, bowing my head apologetically.

"In my dreams," Margy nods. "Which I have come to trust as much as my waking."

She steps forward and throws her arms around me, and I sink to my knee and hug her tightly.

"I'm so relieved you came through it," she whispers so only I can hear. "When you didn't return straight away, I feared the worst."

"I'll always return home, Majesty, to serve you," I swear it as firmly as an oath, and she pulls me to standing.

"Come with me," she says, her voice thick with emotion, patting my back.

"Center yourself," Anod murmurs his instruction, leaning forward to address her. "You are the queen, our regal and respected sovereign."

Margy nods and closes her eyes. She takes several deep calming breaths, and when she's through, she sweeps her hands from the top of her head to her feet. Her purple robes shimmer with magic, spilling out wide into a sparkling violet gown that glitters with pure white pearls and tiny jewels. Her hair binds itself up in perfect curls, and her crown sits neatly on top of them.

"Oh, and here," she says to Dumfrey. With a soft giggle and a swish of her finger, she restores his singed hair. "I do apologize for that," she says, and Dumfrey gives her a low bow of thanks in return.

The doors swing open on the queen's command, and a group of attendants just outside stand waiting for her orders.

"Tea in the garden please," Margy says sweetly. She folds her gloved hands in front of her and nods to them gracefully, and they all rush off to do her bidding.

The change in her as she leaves the courtyard is remarkable. In there, she was a practiced, fearsome Mage, quickly honing her craft to overcome her most threatening enemy. Out here, she's the darling young queen: sweet, dainty and bright-eyed. Both somehow, are Margy in her element. I shake my head admiringly as I follow her and her attendants through the shining corridors with Saesa trailing behind me.

We pass the alcove of tapestries where Eron made advances on me, and I can still hear her small feet sprinting across the polished floor and her high-pitched voice calling my name. I remember playing at swords with her in the sunshine of the same garden where she leads us to join her for an elegant afternoon tea. The silver pot which the head server expertly tips to fill my cup shines with the reflection of the blue sky above. It reminds me of the fairy house given to me by the same girl who sits beside me now, commander of her power, a rising force to be reckoned with.

Who would have thought then, I wonder to myself, that she'd settle so easily into the role she plays now: Margary Plethore, Mage-Queen of Cerion? Her father would be so proud.

"This is where it all started," she says quietly, seemingly following the same train of thought. Her footman steps away and she sips her tea, gazing out at the well-manicured hedge where she once knelt calling for Twig. Her smile brightens, and I can almost see the memories playing in the twinkle of sunlight reflecting from her deep brown eyes. "Do you still have that old pitcher?" She laughs.

"I do." I smile back at her, thinking of the first moment I saw the rainbow of Flitt's light dancing from it.

"I never thought, then..." she says, her voice trailing off. I let her sit in silence, waiting for her to continue. She takes a few more sips of tea and her cheeks grow slightly pinker while she gazes distantly toward the city.

"I always imagined Eron would be king, as most everyone did. And Sarabel and I were to marry off, to strengthen our alliances. I dreamed maybe of marrying to Ceras'lain, to the elves. The other options weren't very appealing to me at all," she sighs. "Honestly, no option was appealing to me. My heart yearned to stay here in Cerion, my beloved kingdom. Still, I never imagined things would go the way they have. That it would be me on the throne. That I would have to rule, and make decisions for so many who depend on me."

At the last, her voice goes quieter. She glances to Finn, who stands with the rest of the guards at the entrance to the garden. Even her footman and maid servants are stationed far enough away that the queen and I can talk in complete privacy. Only Saesa, seated opposite us at the small round table, is close enough to hear. Even so, Margy leans forward and drops her voice to a whisper. "I have a secret I must share with you."

"You can tell me anything in confidence, Your Majesty," I whisper.

"I wish to show you," she whispers. At that, she nods and beckons me close, gesturing to her eyes.

My heart races as I'm immediately aware of what she wants me to do. With Tirnon, I never would have dreamed it. I feared it, actually. The prospect of looking too deeply into his eyes and unintentionally seeing secrets that could have been dangerous if they fell into the wrong hands terrified me.

This is different, though. She's inviting me. She knows what I can do, and she's asking me in. I shift closer in my chair, locking my gaze onto hers, drawn to the golden orange flecks in the brown. Blood thumps in my ears. The elation of magic fills me up, prickling me with its energy, drawing me deep into the mind of the queen. She has the memory prepared for me, it seems. I see it through the Queen's eyes:

The setting is the same library where Margy read me the story of the Protector of Kythshire, the lady knight with blond hair who seemed so much like me. Where I met Twig, and fairy tales started to become something much more real than I ever dreamed they could be.

The room has changed, but only slightly. The floor is no longer strewn with toy models of the kingdom and its people. Eron's things have of course been cleared away, and the desk that was once Tirnon's now holds the queen's trinkets, papers and studies. On the sofa across from it, Margy sits beside Susefen, the Grandmaster of Histories sent by the elves. She sits close enough to Margy that they're almost touching, as unassuming as a student and teacher would, with a large tome resting balanced between them on their knees.

Margy looks down at the elf's slender finger on the page, following it as the woman reads aloud in Elvish. Something nags at the queen while the conversation goes on. There is a draw to the elf which hasn't been there before. It's something alluring and compelling, tucked away in secret. It makes the queen both curious and uneasy, so much so that she has difficulty concentrating on the lesson.

"The Age of Sleep was set in place to avoid a war like no other. You see, with no king to rule it, and only children as his heirs, victory against the Dusk was uncertain. Especially so, since the princess's heart had been drawn toward darkness from an early age. It was agreed that this advantage could not be allowed, and so of course the enchantments of sleep were set," Susefen explains. "As were the conditions of the Age of Awakening and the Claiming of the All Source."

"In the book I read," Margy ventures, "it said, 'Prince and Princess, brother and sister, hand in hand they abide, wrapped in enchanted sleep until woken by one worthy to rule beside them. Of royal blood the suitor must be. Their kingdoms shall unite, and none shall divide them. They will be a beacon of power, where magic flows freely and all manner of creatures are welcome as equals.'"

"Yes," Susefen agrees. "Can you imagine ruling over such a place as that?"

"I think it would be difficult," Margy says. Her gaze drifts across the room. "For many reasons."

"What reasons, Majesty?" Susefen asks quietly.

Margy swallows the lump that rises in her throat. A flash of Tib's face surfaces in her mind, and she pushes it away. "'All manner of creatures are welcome as equals'," she says, quoting her book again. "I imagine that means there would be some darkness allowed, to balance the light. Such a balance would be difficult to achieve, while also ensuring the safety of the innocents who might fall victim to those who are drawn to shadow."

"That is so," Susefen agrees. "And at such a time when the Dusk has been building its forces over decades, I'm certain you can imagine the sort of conflict that would be invited by the restoration of the Wellspring. Our council has foreseen it. War is inevitable."

"My kingdom hasn't seen war for generations," Margy whispers.

"And yet, your father and his before him maintained a hearty force of strong, capable, loyal armies to serve Cerion," Susefen says. "They have been prepared, and in so doing, have left you prepared. Even a people as wise as my own see value in cultivating strong warriors who will defend their innocents from the threat of those less inclined to peace." Susefen closes the book and pats Margy's arm gently. "No matter how we look at it, Majesty, through no fault of your own, Cerion's Age of Peace is ending."

Margy goes quiet, thinking over the elf's words. Scenarios shuffle through her thoughts.

"It ended already," she says after a while. "The attack at my father's Rites, the ruse of earthquakes which acted as cover for them to steal back their own kind from my holdings," she looks at Susefen, her heart racing with determination. "The Age of Peace is over."

"Through no fault of your own, Majesty," Susefen repeats. "And please do not mistake my intentions. I have not come to teach you in order to incite you. I mean only to prepare you. The elves are resigned to it now. The council has agreed, war is to come. You have seen the might of your allies, and have been well-informed and wise to gather them close. As we have read together here in the knowledge of the ages, the time is ripe for you to walk the path upon which you have been placed."

"To open the Wellspring," Margy whispers. Her gaze goes distant. She wrings her hands in her lap.

"Why do you hesitate?" Susefen asks, tilting her head to the side with concern. "Something troubles you. Something which has nothing to do with kingdoms joining, and Wellsprings uniting, and war on the fringes. Something more personal. Forgive me for being forward, Majesty, but I am here to offer my wisdom to you on all matters. If you intend to take on this role, your heart must be free from doubts and misgivings."

"Their kingdoms shall unite," Margy says, choosing her words carefully. She looks to the door, where she knows wards have been placed. Only Susefen can hear her now, and over the past few days of her teachings, Margy has come to trust her. She musters her courage to confide in the elf the greatest misgiving that has been digging at her from the moment she woke the heirs.

"I know," the queen says, her voice just above a whisper, "throughout the history of our world, marriages have been made as tactical agreements. Rarely is a princess or a queen fortunate enough to wed the one her heart longs for. Perhaps I'm no different than any of those in the past have been. Perhaps it's best for me to set aside my feelings, or lack thereof, for Brindelier's prince."

She looks up, searching Susefen's eyes. The elf smiles softly and takes the queen's hands in hers.

"You are so young, to be troubled by such matters of the heart," Susefen sighs, shaking her head. "I cannot tell you how to feel, Majesty, nor should anyone else presume to do so. But I will ask you this: Do you think it wise to begin your reign over the Age of Kinship with a lie in your heart?"

"What choice do I have?" Margy asks. "It said, 'the suitor'."

"Suitor, in Elvish, is a word which can hold many meanings. Do not let semantics trouble you, Majesty. Even His Highness Poelkevrin himself assured you a marriage is not necessary, did he not?" When Margy nods, Susefen goes on, "Do not be mistaken. Once the final offering is in place and the Wellspring is open, the Void and all it hosts shall be called to its gates. Its power will be a lure unlike anything anyone of this age has seen. But such a lure can be used to our advantage."

"If we know they're coming," Margy muses, *"we can be prepared for them."*

"Quite so," Susefen agrees. *"And so it shall begin. With your allies and champions prepared, our council firmly believes victory will go to the Dawn. When it does, Cerion and Brindelier shall be joined as they once were, and the two kingdoms will reign over the All Source. The risk of your defeat grows deeper, though, if you cannot trust in your own heart."*

Margy closes her eyes, thinking over Susefen's words. Susefen takes her hands from Margy's. As she does, that same strange lure pulls at the queen. This time, it's much stronger. It's a familiar magic, and she focuses on it, trying to recognize why she knows it, trying to discern what it could be. When she pinpoints it, her heart starts racing.

Strange light dances behind her eyelids. She opens her eyes, and Susefen holds her cupped hands toward Margy. The vial she presents is clear crystal, shaped in the form of an elegant bird. Its insides swim with sparkling liquid, so pure and white that the queen's breath catches as she looks at it.

"Ceras'lain puts its faith in you, Majesty," Susefen says firmly. *"By our grace, we give you this offering as our promise to stand beside you in the name of the Dawn."*

Margy's hands tingle as Susefen gently tips the crystal bird into her hands. My vision floods with gold, and slowly I return to the garden.

The tendrils between us dwindle into dust, and Margy and I blink to return to ourselves.

"Oh," I whisper, unable to say more. My hands still seem to vibrate with the energy Margy felt when she held the Offering. I understand the importance of the secret Margy has entrusted me with. The Dawn has five, now. All we need is one more.

Chapter Thirty-Six

The Edge of Shadow
Tib

The border between light and dark is about what I expected it to be. Eljarenae's realm feels like Kythshire, except it's about a thousand times more irritating. It presses on me with light, happy and carefree. Peaceful and joyful. It tries to needle its way into me, to fill me up. It calls me, promising me love and pleasant things. My eyes shift around, trying to focus on something in our pure white surroundings, but there isn't anything to see. It's like staring straight into the sun.

"Glad you talked Ki into staying behind," I mumble as Valenor's cloak flicks around me. "This would have been too much for her."

"As would that have, I imagine," he says. I feel his hands on my shoulder. He turns me around, facing me toward the convergence. Darkness. Blacker than I can describe. It swallows everything around it, calling to me wickedly, trying to draw me close, whispering unthinkable evils.

"Remind me why we came here, again?" I ask, stepping closer to him. His hand on my shoulder gives me confidence. It helps me push out the constant pull between dark and light happening all around me.

"Eljarenae has gone to the Palace of Dawn, to appeal to the Savarikta," he explains. "They will be able to bring you into the depths of the earth where their temple once stood. If anyone is able to find the Wellspring of Elespen, or the remnants thereof, it will be them, and you."

"Great." Into the depths of the earth. All that gets me thinking of is Sha'Renell.

"Are you coming, too?" I ask, suddenly feeling slightly unsure of this quest I got myself into.

"I shall be nearby to offer as much guidance as I can," he replies, "but departing my own realm completely would leave us vulnerable in a way that would be quite dangerous to our cause at this time."

"Oh, right," I say, trying hard not to shudder.

"Sha'Renell will remain distracted by Kaso Viro. At least that is our hope," Valenor explains.

"They're still fighting?" I ask.

"He is drawing out the duel for the benefit of this quest," he says. "I cannot speak for the other, Vorhadeniel. He has not been heard from since we left Sixledge. We expect he has retreated to the Void. It would be prudent to assume you will meet with his agents or him personally once you enter his reaches in the depths."

"Perfect," I say, my hand gripping my dagger's hilt. I'm ready for a fight. A good one.

The Savarikta arrive before Valenor can reply. They lumber out of the glow of the light with their heavy, clomping, trunk-like feet. I'm disappointed at first that there are only two *sava* and two riders. I was sort of hoping to see Akkoti and Kruti again. Still, I guess I'm glad one of them isn't Velu.

"*Evtu*," one of the riders says as they lurch to a stop in front of us. He slips down from the *sava* with little effort and bows to me, thumping his chest.

"Meheli," I say, relieved I remember the rider's name from our short time together at the temple. "And Resai, right?"

The second rider slides down and thumps his chest and bows the same way.

"*Evtu*," he says.

The respect they show me makes me uncomfortable. They must not realize it was my fault they're where they are now. My fault their temple collapsed, and they're stuck in this weird, other realm. I don't deserve to be honored by them.

"These most respected, fiercest warriors of the Savarikta have volunteered to join you on your quest, Tibreseli." Eljarenae's voice echoes all around us. "Take with you this token of my Light, and know that I am always nearby."

Three little globes break free from the white light in the direction of Eljarenae's voice and drift to each of us.

I feel the magic of my globe as soon as it settles into my palm. It's something like a cross between the wish Stellastera gave me at the convergence of the realms, and the gift of light Margy shared with the people of Cerion.

The Savarikta tuck their globes into their belts and climb back onto their *sava*. I put mine in a pocket of my bandolier, relieved to have it back again. My knives across my chest and my dagger at my belt give me confidence. I stand up a little straighter and look way up to Meheli. Without a word, he offers his hand to me.

I climb up onto the swaying back of the *sava*, and he tucks me deep into the safety of the creature's enormous shell.

"How does this work, exactly?" I ask him. He turns to look at me, his brow furrowed with warning, and presses a finger to his lips. His head disappears behind the shell as he stands on the *sava's* thick neck. With one arm draped on the top of the shell, he looks over to Resai and shouts something in their language.

"All right, no talking for me, I guess," I mutter under my breath.

"Just sit back and enjoy the ride," Valenor whispers beside me. "It is a great privilege to be taken aboard a *sava*. Isn't it remarkable?"

Remarkable? Sure, I guess, I think silently. Inside the shell is strange. Looking at the creature on the outside, it's definitely huge, but its shell sits pretty snugly on its back. It doesn't seem like there'd be any room between its body and its shell. I never would have guessed what it's like inside. In here, there's a rug for me to kneel on and plenty of space for Meheli to join me. There's a small stash of food, too, and a few extra weapons strapped to the ceiling of the shell.

It's magic, I can tell. Magic woven between creature and rider, to expand the area making it more comfortable for both of them. If I reach out, I can feel the subtleties of it. Love. Familiarity. Home. There's another sort of magic, too. A stronger bonding. A kinship between the rider and his mount. It's not forced. It feels more like a split. Like they're both the same thing, even though they're not. Like Faedin, or Ili'luvrie.

I wonder, as Meheli slips into the shell beside me, how a rider gets a *sava*. Or how a *sava* gets a rider. I don't ask, though. He wouldn't understand me if I did, and he told me to be quiet, so I am.

"Aleetah," Meheli says to me. He takes my hand and places it on the rough, warm skin of the sava beneath us. Wiry, sparse hairs poke up from the skin under my touch, like gooseflesh. "Aleetah," he says again, and I understand. He's introducing us formally. That's her name. I pat her gently, nodding.

"Aleetah," I whisper, "I'm Tib."

"I am with you, Tib," Valenor's voice drifts in through the shell. "Do not be alarmed. Allow them to take you where they will."

Aleetah trumpets and rakes her foot beneath us. I can feel the excitement pulsing from the two of them, Meheli and his *sava*. He turns to me and points forward, and I understand. Time to go. As soon as I let their magic in, the Savarikta lurch forward.

My skin crawls as we slip from one realm to the next. It's not the same brush of cobwebs as stepping into the Half-Realm is. This is rougher. It feels like stone scraping my skin. My ears rumble with a strange sound. My stomach sinks. Meheli turns to me. Pats my shoulder. Gives me a reassuring nod.

Above our heads, Aleetah's shell sounds like it's going to crack. Something loud and heavy scrapes along it. The seams of light peeking in around the edges of it are snuffed out. I feel the air grow heavy.

I remember being in the village, surrounded by the tribe, with Saesa and the Donas standing beside me. How the ground rumbled and arched at our feet. I remember the *sava* poking up through the soil. Too late, I realize what's happening. This is how they plan to bring me to the fallen temple. I guess I knew it on some level. I had to. I'm not stupid. I just didn't want to fully grasp it. Didn't want to think about it. We're boring into the earth. We're tunneling.

Aleetah picks up speed. Her shoulders and hips rock underneath us, jostling us with every pounding step. Under the earth, she's forceful. Agile, even. It's like the rock and dirt propels her forward.

How did I get myself into this? I wonder, swallowing the sick feeling in my stomach. We're underground. In the earth. With the roots. With the darkness. This is her territory. Sha'Renell's. She'll know we're here. She'll leave the fight with Kaso Viro. She'll crush us. She'll pin us, the way the savage, broken fae bound me at the drained Wellspring of Sunteri. She'll constrict us, and we'll never escape. Zhilee's eyes float before me, terrified. Pleading. Sister. Little sister.

Panic grips me. My breath comes in short bursts. My knuckles go white as I cling to the rug. My ears ring. My lips go numb. How could I let this happen? I trust Valenor. I trust Eljarenae. They're my allies. They'll keep me safe. I tell myself that over and over, but my fear lingers. We're plunging deeper. Into the depths of earth and shadow, my two greatest enemies.

"Breathe, Tib," Valenor commands, and I suck in a breath that brings me back to life. The *sava* race through the underground, thundering into the soil, trumpeting to each other.

With my breath comes clarity. I can feel the wards around us, hiding us, protecting us. These creatures are of the earth. They belong here. They thrive here. I understand how, like the roots of innocent trees, this is their home. They know where they are. They're friends. They're allies. They've agreed to help me, to fight beside me. We have the same goal. Find the Wellspring. Recover their village.

The deeper we burrow, the harder I work to remind myself that the earth itself isn't my enemy. Just like the Dreaming, the Realm of Earth holds good and evil. Just like in the Dreaming, its steward, its Muse, can be corrupted and changed. It doesn't make everything here wicked.

I'm comforted by that. Inspired by it, too. I remember what Valenor said. How he'd be vulnerable if he completely left his realm. It makes me wonder, would Sha'Renell be just as vulnerable? Could she be lured away from her earth and stone? How could it be done? What would it mean, for her to be isolated from her domain? She could be tricked into water, or sky. Anyplace that doesn't touch the ground.

I bet Kaso Viro knows that. Imagining he does helps me forget how far below the ground we are. How trapped I'd be if something happened to the *sava*. He's probably winning right now. He's probably doing something to bind her. To keep her held.

My mind goes over and over the different ways the Muse of Water could hold the Muse of Earth as the *sava* charge further into the underground. It isn't until they start to slow and the arcane energy around us changes, that I finally set the thoughts aside. The slower they go, the more urgency I feel. The magic in this place, wherever we are, is strong. It's like the fog in Elespen, fearsome and forbidding. It screams for us to leave, to go back and never return. I push it away, close myself to it.

When I do, I become more aware of the mood inside the *sava*. It's a heightened alertness. A warning to prepare. I push myself to crouching. My hand goes to my dagger. Meheli swipes his spear from the clasp on the ceiling. He turns to look at me, sees my dagger, and nods silently. The *sava* huffs and stomps beneath us. It's disturbed. Something else is out there. Something other than the fog. I search beyond the shell with my healed eye, looking all around until I'm facing backward into the tunnel we just burrowed through. What I see makes my heart race. Something's coming. Chasing us.

Meheli knows. He turns Aleetah to face it, ready to charge. I pull out a blue vial. Fairy fire. I coat my blade. Peer out.

Bugs. They're like the tiny ones that used to crawl around my workshop under the shack in Cerion. The kind that curl up into a perfect ball when they're poked. I used to take a handful back to Ruben. He thought they were great. He'd flick them around with his fingertips, playing with them like marbles.

These, though, are a lot more intimidating. Bigger than me. Half as long as a *sava*. They're armored on the outside with the same hard carapace. Their underside is all legs and fangs. Four of them charge through the tunnel at us. I risk a glance to the side. Resai's *sava* is beside us, head low in a defensive stance, tusks ready to strike.

Both *sava* stomp warnings, but that only serves to provoke the beetles. They charge faster. Start screeching. Earsplitting. Bone wrenching. The sound cracks the earth above us, threatening a cave-in. Meheli moves deftly to the front of the shell, places a hand on the edge of it. Crouches to ready himself. I move up alongside him. Again, he nods at me. His eyes are narrowed. Focused. His jaw is clenched. The muscles of his arm bulge and flex as he adjusts his grip on his spear.

I think of the spear and the enemy outside, wondering what good it'll do against them. I don't have to wonder too long. The *sava* start to charge. The shell opens up. Meheli leaps out, landing right in front of one of the beetles. He thrusts his spear upward just as the vermin opens its mouth to strike, and drives the point of it straight through its mouth.

Black liquid spills from the wound, and the creature writhes and gurgles, then slumps lifeless.

Meheli shouts something to Resai, who's already taken down the second of the bugs, and Resai shouts something back. They laugh and advance with the *sava* beside them. In the short time it takes me to jump from mine and run to help, the third and fourth bugs are dead.

I skid to a stop at the edge of a pool of the black liquid. Meheli turns to me and smirks, like he's asking what took me so long. I shrug an apology and start to say how easy that was, but he hisses through his teeth and claps his hand over his mouth in warning.

Got it. Still no talking. I shift slightly, wondering why we don't get back on the *sava*, when both Meheli and Resai bend down. They each swipe what looks like a small water skin through the black goo, collecting a good amount of it carefully. I crouch close to the nearest puddle of it and stretch my hand toward it. The magic it holds feels sinister. Dark. Death. Instant and irreversible.

"Do not touch it, Tib," Valenor's whispered warning sends a shiver through me. "That is Blackheart poison."

I take a couple steps back. Blackheart. The poison that killed king Tirnon with a single arrow strike. That's not the sort of stuff that should be left around. I take out my blue vial and drip a couple drops of the liquid onto it. The black goo sizzles and catches flame. The flames eat across it in a line, leaving dust behind.

Meheli nods, clapping my shoulder gratefully. I look at the two warriors with a new kind of respect. They've been down here before. They must have known what that was when they were fighting. They knew one scrape from the fang of one of those bugs would mean an immediate, painful death, and they fought anyway.

There's no time to think about it longer than that. The *sava* start to get all agitated again. The tunnel rumbles in the distance. I peer into it, expecting more of the same, but the bugs that charge us this time are different. These are long and thin, with huge, serrated pincers that snap threateningly as they charge. They skitter closer and the Savarikta brace themselves for the battle. These are about the size of a horse, but there are lots more of them. Dozens.

I don't wait for them to get close. I shove my dagger back into its sheath and grab two knives from my bandolier. When I reach for my blue vial to coat them, I realize the blades are already tinged with blue. Fairy fire. I fling one knife and the next, each at a different target. Two of the bugs squeal in pain and writhe on to their backs. The flames catch, spreading across them in a quick line, leaving a pile of ash.

The ash doesn't last long. Five more charge through it, spreading it around. Resai shouts a battle cry. Charges them with his spear raised. Aleetah follows, spearing two at once with her tusks. The tunnel shudders with the echo of their shrieks. I dive into the ash. Retrieve my knives from it. Duck under Aleetah's belly for cover to coat them again, but, curiously, they still shine with blue.

One of the impaled bugs snaps its pincer at Aleetah's trunk desperately. Its serrated tip slices into her thick gray skin. She rears up on her hind legs, roaring in pain. I roll out from under her. Fling my knives, one at each of the impaled bugs. They meet their mark, plunging straight into the thick carapace. The creatures fall to dust.

Aleetah barely has time to react before three more are on her. I pull two more knives, two I'm sure I haven't used since Stellastera granted my wish, and am shocked to find those already glowing blue, too. For just a moment, I stare at the blades in disbelief. Aleetah shuffles sideways, thrashing her head to avoid another pincer, and I stab at the bug she flings past me.

Ash rains down over me as the fairy fire catches.

"Tib, move!" Valenor shouts.

At the same time, something strikes me hard from the side, shoving me away from the fight. I spin to stab at it, but strong hands stop my swing. Meheli grabs me, pulling me back just in time to avoid the swarm. We separate from Aleetah, who charges fearlessly toward the scourge of bugs, stomping and roaring and spearing.

"*Evtu*," Meheli says, his voice tinged with relief.

"Thanks," I reply sincerely. We both turn to watch her charge. It happens so fast. The *sava* drives into the swarm of creatures with her head low. Her tusks plow into them, tossing them into the tunnel walls which still shudder with every echo of their awful screams.

It's not long, though, before she's overcome by the insects. They spill over her even as she stomps and tosses her head. Meheli shouts a stern command as they break the *sava's* defense and skitter toward us. It feels like an order to the *sava*: Fall back. She doesn't listen. Nearby, Resai and his *sava* are overwhelmed, too.

I fling my daggers, two, three, four, five. Every bug that falls is replaced by another. They come in an endless swarm. Beside me, Meheli spears them again and again. There's no time to risk a glance at Aleetah, but there's been no trumpeting or thudding footsteps from her direction for way too long.

Meheli's choked battle cry confirms my fears. His fighting style changes. His movements are filled with rage and mourning. Revenge. I feel it rolling off of him in waves. Even so, I can't believe it. It can't be true. Aleetah brought me here. She risked her life for me.

I fall into the rhythm of the fight. Fling another knife and another. Something occurs to me after the tenth one or so. I don't carry this many knives. I don't have this many sheaths in my bandolier.

Resai's call echoes through the tunnel. Meheli answers him, then starts pushing me back. Away from the fight. I pull another knife, but his hand closes over mine and he shakes his head. His eyes are red and wet with tears. His lips curled back in anger. With a firm, insistent motion, he jabs his finger into a split in the wall at my shoulder. It's just big enough for me to squirm through, but too small for the bugs or for the two large warriors.

"You want me to run away?" I shout. "No way!"

"You must, Tib," Valenor says sternly, "or this will all have been for naught."

Meheli's back is to the fight. He doesn't see the bug charging toward him. I wrestle my hand from his and fling the knife. A puff of ash spreads over us. He glances back, shakes his head slightly, and points again into the crevice.

"*Evtu*," he growls.

Valenor whispers something to him in his own language. Meheli reaches into his belt and pulls out the small globe that was given to us by Eljarenae. He points to himself, to the unmoving mound of his *sava* beneath the steady stream of insects, and then to Resai and his *sava*. He thumps his chest once, and points upward.

I understand. This is as far as they can take me. They'll fight to the fallen *sava*. They'll call Eljarenae. She'll get them back to safety. I'm on my own from here. I've got to leave them behind and keep going. I glance behind him again, to where Resai and his *sava* are still fighting. I look past to the unmoving lump beneath a steady stream of the insects and clench my jaw. My nostrils flare. My eyes sting with tears.

"Here," I say, pulling two vials of blue from my bandolier. "Use these. Get out as fast as you can." I clasp his forearm with both hands and look up at him. "She'll be okay. I'm sure someone can heal her."

Meheli swallows hard and nods urgently, then shoves me into the crevice. I have to hold my breath to wedge myself between the stone, which rumbles and quivers with every screech from the bugs. I try not to panic, thinking of how far below we are. Of how much rock is pressing in on me. Of how, with one good quake, I could be crushed into pulp. I try to ignore my racing heart. To slow it.

As I wriggle myself away from the fight, I can't help but keep my eyes glued to it. Even when the wall blocks me and I can't see anymore, I watch with my healed eye through the stone. Here I go again, I think to myself. Running away. Leaving others to their probable death. I watch Meheli toss one of my vials to Resai. They coat their blades. Meheli dives below the swarm, toward his *sava*. A few of the bugs catch with fairy fire and spill to ashes. A bright light flashes right where the *sava* had fallen. In the blink of an eye, the mound disappears. Good. Meheli and Aleetah made it out.

Resai lets loose another battle cry and leaps up onto his *sava*. The bugs crawl up the side of it, threatening to overtake it. The warrior pulls out his own globe of light and calls into it. It flashes once and they, too, vanish.

Their disappearance causes a flurry of screeching and skittering as the bugs search for them. Some of them scatter back down the tunnel. Others crash against the crevice, snapping their pincers, somehow sensing me. They're too big, though, to fit. I wait, holding my breath, listening. After a while, the clicking of their feet clatters away.

Their screeches die off. Everything goes silent. Empty. Dark

Chapter Thirty-Seven

SOLITUDE
Tib

"This way, Tibreseli," Valenor whispers from the other side of the crack.

My heart thumps against the jagged wall. It's so narrow I can't even turn my head in his direction. I press my hands on either side of the rock behind me and push myself along. My vials and knives catch and pull, slowing my pace. I start to panic again. The fear of being trapped, of being suffocated, is overwhelming. There's no room for my chest to take in any more than quick, shallow breaths.

I try to think of something else. Anything else. The previous battle. Aleetah. I hope Meheli got her out in time. I hope Eljarenae can save her. Those thoughts don't calm me. They only make my heart thump faster and my breath quicken as I wedge myself along the crack. My mind races to something else. Anything else. Another of my knives snags on the rock, and as I wriggle to free myself, I remember how the blades already glowed blue. How could that happen? Stellastera's gift. The result of a wish. It's like they already held the power I wanted to use. Like they knew. I realize something else, too. I threw a lot more knives than I know I own, and my bandolier is still well-stocked with them. I think I got more than I wished for.

I concentrate on that as I keep a steady pace. Focus on my bandolier. On the knives and the vials. Now that I'm paying attention, I do notice it. Magic. Quiet. Subtle. Powerful. My awareness that it exists opens my mind to it. I remember a time in the icy shadows of a mountain chasm, when I sliced through the shadows that held Valenor prisoner in dragon form. Mevyn had told me at the time that the vials didn't mean anything. Somehow, I had forgotten since then. I kept depending on the serums.

It's confusing, though. The elves gave me those other vials. The stripping one, the one that could slice into the wards outside Cresten and let Saesa through. Was that me, too? Or the vials?

"Almost there," Valenor's voice comes so quietly it might just be a thought.

The crevice widens enough that I can turn my head. My neck aches stiffly with the movement. I roll my shoulders as much as I can. Tip my head from side to side to stretch. Take a deeper breath than I've been able to. My thoughts swirl around that one memory of Valenor, tied down by shadows, trapped outside of his realm.

"It was him," I whisper in the direction of Valenor's voice. "Vorhadeniel. He's been a part of it since way back then. Since Mevyn."

"Tibreseli," Valenor replies so quietly I have to stop moving in order to hear him over the sound of my shuffling boots and my clothes scraping against the wall. "…courage…here."

"What?" I whisper.

"…cannot…courage."

"Valenor," I hiss through my teeth. My healed eye flicks along the jagged opening. If I couldn't see him before, I don't know why I hoped to now. I close my eyes. Take as deep a breath as I can. Try to feel his presence. The flick of his cloak. The sense of someone else nearby. I'm met with nothing. With emptiness. Shadow. Void.

"Valenor?" I whisper again, and my only reply is a thought that could be him, or could be my own: *Courage*.

The rough surface of the stone is washed in complete darkness. Even with my healed eye, I can't make out my surroundings. If it wasn't for my fingers on the stone, I'd think I was plunged into nothing at all.

Courage. I slide my arm out to the side, up to shoulder height. I feel my way along the stone, edging further, until it takes a sharp angle to the side. When I reach it, I take one more cautious step and slip out of the crevice into a much more open space.

My vision is still blotted by the utter darkness. I step to the side with my back against the wall and pull the cobwebs around me. Just because I can't see doesn't mean I can't be seen. Once I'm hidden, I try to think. He's gone. Valenor. Something happened. I don't know what, but it must have been something he couldn't foresee. Something that kept him out of this place. Some force he wasn't aware of.

I close my eyes. Take several deep breaths. Let the air fill my lungs as deep as it'll go. Feel the magic around me.

Darkness, yes. There's that. There's also that same forbidding magic we were met with in Cresten, except it has a spent feeling to it.

An expiration. It's still strong enough to keep people out, but it's not active anymore. It's lingering. Left over. Finished, but not cleared away.

Why, though? This magic is meant to repel people. To protect something. To keep enemies out. The only thing it could mean, really, is there's nothing left here to protect. The purpose of the magic, the reason it was here to begin with, is gone. Still, this is the strongest I've ever felt wards like this, and I'm sure they're the same as the fog outside Cresten.

Even when I breathe, I can feel the dampness in the air filling my nose. I squeeze my eyes shut and open them again, straining to see something. Anything. I will my healed eye to bore through the darkness, to pick up even the slightest shift in the black. I scan the space in front of me with all of my might, and just as I'm about to slump back in defeat, a blur of glowing green flashes, just once, several paces ahead of me.

My heart leaps to my throat in a quick flash of excitement. I creep carefully in the direction of the blur, alert to my surroundings. There's nothing here, though. No one. I inch along, aware of my feet on the stone, cloaked in my solitude. The magic of the wards brushes across me like leaves on trees. I think of the jungle, far above. How filled with life it has been.

Down here, it's the opposite. Emptiness. Silence. Just a sense of abandonment. Of hopelessness. Of ancient magic. I pause. No, that wasn't here before. The magic has shifted. My healed eye flicks forward. The pulse of green comes again. I feel its sorrow. Its defeat. Its desolation. I'm filled with regret, almost instantly. Deep inside, I know exactly where I am, even though I don't want to believe it.

My foot slips off the edge of something and comes down hard. Steps. A step. I crouch to my knees and reach out with my hands. A staircase, covered in crumbled stone and cracks. I feel along the length of the first step. There are no walls on either side. I crawl down backwards on my hands and knees, just to be safe, and find another staircase going down at a strange, sharp angle at the bottom of it.

I pick my way down silently, through the thick shadows of magic, into the fringes of this spell. The further I go, the more aware I become of the magic and its workings. This wasn't originally an evil spell. The edges of it are tainted. Corrupted by evil. On the outsides, it feels like death and terror. As I get closer to the heart of it, though, the source, it becomes purer. It lightens. It changes.

Green. Jungle green. Gold. An eye. A lost protector. I think of Velu. I think of the Keeper, bound by strands of inky black. I blink rapidly, trying to see. I hold my hand up right in front of my face. Nothing. The darkness has taken a firm hold, even here. I keep going. A fallen pillar blocks my path. I climb over it. Trace my fingers along the carvings. Feel a series of cracks, like wrinkles in folds of skin. An eye. A long trunk. *Sava.*

My heart races. It can't be. It can't be this easy. I crawl down another set of steps and turn and find another, and realize yes, yes, it can. I'm here, at the stepwell. At the Wellspring. With that realization, I pause. Crouch low. Breathe deep. Focus. I'm here. I made it. Aleetah's sacrifice wasn't wasted. Resai and Meheli did what they set out to do. I hope they know how close they got me to my goal. I hope, some day, I can tell them. Thank them. But I'm getting ahead of myself. Focus.

The last time I was here, I could feel the pull of it. The pool of green life in conflict with the darkness that threatened it. This is what it's become, now. I remember Sunteri. How its Wellspring was nothing but an empty basin when Mevyn and I got back to it. A memory of something else edges its way into my mind. A title I was given, then. One I had forgotten about.

Lifebringer.

For some reason, that title grips me. Calls to my heart. Compels me. I feel an overwhelming need to push on. To investigate deeper. Something is there. Something that needs me.

The last time I was here, this place was facing ruin. The walls were crumbling. The earth was quaking. The Wellspring was fated to be swallowed up. Sha'Renell. Vorhadeniel. The Keeper, wrapped in inky tendrils.

Everything that's happened until now is in the past. What I do from this point on, this is what matters. It's not about offerings and victories. It's about saving something on the brink of being lost forever.

I crawl deeper, pulling myself up over rubble and around broken stairways. My boots seem to guide me, to urge me further, to steady me. The closer I get to the empty pool, the stronger I feel the presence of something unusual.

It's not empty. It's filled. Filled with Void. Shifted and replaced. The Wellspring's magic was never drained. It was corrupted and stained with Dusk, with evil. I creep onto a fallen pillar which had plunged into the liquid. I can't see it, but I have a sense of where it is.

What it is. The pool. The former Wellspring. The pulse of green comes again. Fainter. Dying.

Lifebringer. My title. My calling.

Tendrils of darkness writhe around me, flicking at the air near my face, taunting me to fight them. They know I'm close. They know what I'll do. They don't scare me. They're no threat. They can't touch me. I'm the Dreamstalker. The Lifebringer.

It's there. At the bottom of the black pool. A presence. Something that was once powerful and glorious. Something that held the knowledge of Elespen's ages. Something that never could have, never should have been defeated. Something ravaged, and left for dead. Something that ought to be dead. Someone.

For the first time, I'm relieved to be alone. If someone else had been here with me, I might have missed it. If Valenor or Ki were here, or even Saesa, they might have stopped me. I know what I have to do. I know how crazy it is. But that light pulses again, and I know it's almost spent. It's the last pulse. The last chance.

I fix my healed eye on the spot. I take a deep breath and hold it. I don't think too hard about it. I dive headfirst into the corrupted pool.

If I wasn't the Dreamstalker, I'd be dead. That's my first impression. It's thick, like tar, the magic. Vicious. Suffocating. Merciless. I feel what it would have done to me. How it would have torn at my skin, eating it like acid. It's a pool of Blackheart, it feels like. Thicker than nothing. I squeeze my eyes shut and pull myself into the deep part of it. Follow my gut. My instinct. It's nearby. I know it is. I sense it. It needs me. It's lost.

My fingertips graze something tiny and sharp. A pin. A spear. I push my legs. It's like trying to swim through mud. My muscles ache with the effort. My lungs burn from holding my breath. I stretch out my hand, grasping, aiming for that feeling. That energy. The green. This time, I find it. A motionless, tiny body. Smaller than my palm. Smaller than a pixie in an orb. I scoop it up, along with a handful of the corrupted Wellspring. My knees hit the bottom. I pull my feet underneath me and push hard back to the surface, tucking the fairy close to my chest with one hand.

The black pool swirls and churns furiously. It senses what it's lost. It knows.

I scramble out of it, climbing back up that fallen pillar, careful to keep a gentle hold on the fairy. The Keeper. Crawl away from the pool awkwardly, still blinded by darkness. Up rubble and debris, I feel my way back. Tuck myself into a safe corner.

I feel like I can breathe again when the liquid from the pool slides off of me. It can't stick. It has no power over me. I feel released. Victorious, even though there was barely a fight. I feel strong. Protective. Unbeatable. Right.

Gently, I tip my hand away from my chest and open my palm. I still can't see, but I can feel it. It's a little stronger now, like it's been fueled by the hope of my arrival.

Not sure what to do, I take a vial from my bandolier. I think it's a pink one, but it's difficult to tell. I hold it right up to my healed eye and check. A tinge of pink peeks through the shadows at me. I pull the cork out with my teeth. Douse the fairy with it. I feel it working, washing away the black. It sizzles and bubbles in my palm. The creature moves weakly. Coughs. Starts crawling up my arm.

"What are you doing?" I whisper, but it doesn't answer me. It clings to my sleeve, to my bandolier. To the pouch where I tucked Eljarenae's globe of light. It pulls open the flap. The glow of it spills into the darkness, splashing across the blackened fae, bathing my arm in pure white.

Right away I feel stupid for forgetting I had it. Then again, I guess it's not a bad thing, after all. The fae reaches his hands toward it. Presses its palms to the light. It stretches across his black skin, restoring it to greenish gold, bringing back its life. I watch the change travel up his tiny, fragile arms, across its chest, into its heart.

The strength of the magic there takes my breath away. I know what it is without even having to ask. A drop of the Wellspring. The last uncorrupted drop, there inside of him. Eljarenae's light drains into him, but it isn't enough to restore him completely. It's only enough to give him strength to speak to me.

"I swallowed it," the fae whispers. "The last of the Lifesap. It was my last resort. I shall bestow it to you, *Evtu*. The final drop of our Wellspring, which I have saved, hoping for this moment. Take it. Restore the All Source, and my polluted Source will thrive once more. Protect it with your life, for once it is gone, all the hopes of Elespen shall go with it."

As he speaks, I tuck myself deeper away from the churning pool. It feels more sinister by the moment. Ready to attack. To take back what was stolen. From the dimming light of Eljarenae's globe, I see spears of it writhe up like tentacles, slapping at the stone sides of the basin.

I know what it means. What he means. Once I take that drop, he's dead. He's held on this long just to keep it safe. He's prepared to sacrifice his own life, just to give me what I'm entitled to as *Evtu*. To put all his faith in me. To uphold some promise I don't even know about. It's touching, but it makes me angry, too. That someone so powerful could be reduced to this. That some force, somewhere, says I'm more important just because of a title I was given for a task I didn't even choose. That this fae would think, even for a moment, that I'd take that drop from him and just let him die. What kind of Lifebringer would that make me?

"Hold on," I say firmly. "We're getting out of here, together."

He doesn't reply. Doesn't have the strength for it, I guess. I slip him safely into the pocket of my bandolier. The same one that holds Eljarenae's globe. He's already drained it enough that I'm sure it won't be able to take us anywhere. He needs that energy more than I do, anyway. If I could get out of here, I could hopefully reach Valenor again. He's probably waiting just outside of this block. Waiting for a glimpse of me. Trusting I'm right, I start the climb out of this awful place.

The shadows cling to me, pulling my arms, whispering things. Doubts. Warnings. Threats. The darkness tries to take its hold, but it can't reach me. I'm too protected. Too determined. Too far from its grasp.

The muscles in my legs pump hard, pushing me up stairways, carrying me further from the pool. The more distance I put between us and the ruined Wellspring, the quieter it gets. The silence makes my ears ring. It's dizzying. Confusing.

I focus on the feel of the rough rubble under my fingers. I hone in on the fae in my pocket, checking on the strength of the magic it holds. I think of everything I can to keep from letting shadow drive me mad.

Valenor. I keep my mind on him. My hope. I try not to imagine he met with the darkness, too. Was Vorhadeniel close? Did he intercept him to keep him from me? Why was the Wellspring unguarded? I expected to meet with Sorcerers, with imps, with something to keep me from collecting the offering, but there's nothing. No resistance at all. Why?

I climb in silence, thinking it over. If I was the Dusk, I'd have assumed I'd come back for the offering. Maybe they don't know it was smashed. Maybe they figured there was no reason to guard a polluted, drained site with an almost-dead Keeper in it.

Or, maybe they know everything. Maybe they're watching me right now. Maybe they want me to get this last drop. Maybe they're waiting for me to bring it to Brindelier. To open the All Source. Maybe this is what they want.

I reach the top of the collapsed stepwell. Ground level. I can tell, because when I look toward the rubble with my healed eye, I can see the forms of trees on the other side. I can feel the energy of the jungle, cloaked and suppressed by the dark fog of the Void.

Paranoid, I set the intention of stepping into the Half-Realm, even though I know I'm already there. The cobwebs brush my skin. In the pouch at my bandolier, the fae shivers.

"We're leaving the stepwell," I mutter to him under my breath, cupping my hand over the pouch. "Brace yourself. I'm not sure what to expect."

As soon as the words leave my lips, before I can even take a step, the rubble under my feet shifts. An energy, swift and wicked, surges around me. It churns and pulses, drawing power from the blackened Wellspring, pulling the corrupted magic through it. My hair rustles softly as it surrounds me, closing in on me. Shadows of faces jeer at me from inside of it, their eyes open sockets of darkness, their mouths stretched in silent screams.

I know this is magic. I know it can't touch me. I know, as it closes in, that it's not going to hurt me. Courage, Valenor had said. Courage. I screw my eyes shut. I step through the wall of the cyclone.

The pressure in my ears is agonizing. The darkness fills my nose, my mouth. I try to look through my eyelid with my healed eye, but all I see is streaking, swirling black. I try to scream for help, but no sound comes out. My throat is raw. My skin prickles from the arcane power surrounding me.

I don't understand how it can be. How darkness has become something tangible. Something non-magical, that can cause me harm. Like Sha'Renell's sand-fist. Something that can hurt. It scrapes through my leathers, clawing at my skin, scrabbling into my brain. I drop to my knees, both hands clamped over the pouch where the fae curls up. I can feel him trembling. Feel the light of Eljarenae dwindling to nothing.

"Help me," I whisper as the darkness bears down on me. "Help us both."

"Your knives," comes the answer, clear as a bell. I think of what I need to cut through this cyclone. Green. Misty green. I draw a knife and slash it hard through the shadow. The pain fades slightly. I push myself to my feet. Keep one hand over the fae. Slash again. The shadow breaks apart. Spirals away. More come, and more. I fight them until my arm feels like it'll fall off, then I switch to the other and keep going.

In the distance, a shift of energy ebbs. I feel it before I see it. A change. A transformation. Dark into light. It's so subtle, so soft, I'm not even sure it's real. There's no time to try and figure out what it is. No break in the fight. I keep slashing, keep pushing back, ignoring the ache in my arms and legs, denying my body any small break.

I fight harder, gaining ground one foot at a time, pushing through the rubble, breaking through the shadows until the border is breached and we're free of the stepwell. The dim light of dusk greets us, and I have no time to dwell on the village left in ruins on the outskirts of the collapsed temple. Even here, beyond its borders, the cyclones press in on me. The darkness is relentless, but so am I.

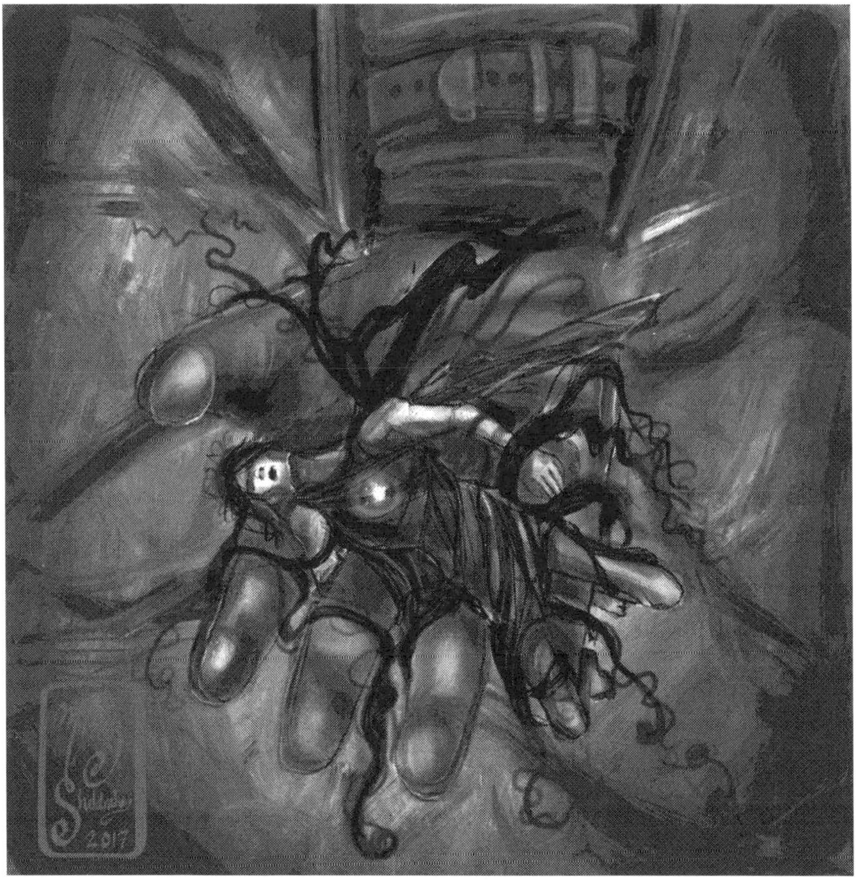

Chapter Thirty-Eight

THE DOORWAY
Celli

Stellastera, Lady of Magic, is the teacher I always dreamed of. She guides me with patience and compassion, showing me the depths of the talent I've been given. Her teachings come from her heart, and my triumphs and failures are hers, too.

When I was much younger, I imagined myself as a Mage studying in Cerion's Academy, but there was no way my parents could pay the steep fees of a serious apprentice. I realized that from a young age, and I kept my hopes to myself. I see what a mistake that was, now. If my parents had known, I'm sure they would have found a way for me to get the guidance I yearned for. If I had told them, perhaps I wouldn't have been so quick to fall into the grip of Sorcerers, so compelled by their wicked power.

My Lady has warned me more than once against allowing myself to think negatively. Balance, she says, is key for a student of my talents, so I let my thoughts drift to other places, to other people…like the prince.

I know I shouldn't. I know my teacher can probably sense it, but I can't help it. His hold on me isn't something I can deny. How I feel isn't something I can control. She tells me while I'm practicing to think of what pleases me, what makes my heart soar. Right now, that's him. The way he smiles at me. The way he watches me at my lessons and gives bits of advice to help me stay positive. The admiration he shows for my abilities. The way my skin tingles when he grazes my arm with his fingertips. Most thrilling of all is I'm sure he feels the same way I do. It's no trick or spell. It's love, pure and simple.

"Celli, focus on your lesson," Stellastera instructs. I nod and raise my hands, and she presses her palms to mine. The long sleeves of my robes swish forward elegantly, brushing the sides of my acolyte's vest. When I close my eyes and concentrate, I can feel the tendril of dark energy she creates. It charges through my left hand, filling me with a sense of Sorcery. I imagine Mage Mark curling across my skin, even though I know it's not there. I know the darkness. I've been consumed by it before. It's familiar, and so I'm not afraid.

Like we've practiced a hundred times already in this impossibly short period of time, I draw the shadow into me. It swirls into my spirit, tingling through my bones. "It isn't a fight," she says quietly. "It should not be thought of as a battle. It is simply a change. A shift. Feel it filter through you."

My right hand prickles softly as she links her fingers through mine, and I make myself aware of the darkness. Just like I did with my thoughts, I shift the energy. Through my right hand, I release it. When I open my eyes, a swirl of golden-white light curls around her wrist like a trail of glittering light.

"Well done," the Lady says quietly, smiling. "Pippa," she calls, and the princess comes to join us.

My eyes flick between them, and I feel myself blush with embarrassment.

"I'm not ready, My Lady," I protest. It's one thing to practice on the Muse, but the princess is another story. What if I make a mistake? What if I hurt her? Poe will hate me.

"Nonsense," the Lady of Magic says gently. "Your mind is far quicker than I expected, and we have little time to waste. Remember what you are working toward, my Champion. Have faith in yourself."

Champion. The word seems empty to me. I haven't done anything to prove myself a champion, yet. I feel unworthy of the title and the status she's given me. If the Lady of Magic senses my doubt in myself, she doesn't show it. She offers me a warm smile and slips her hands from mine, placing them into Pippa's. The princess interlaces our fingers together. Her hands are soft and warm, and the smile she offers is genuine, much less forced than my own.

"Help my daughter," My Lady whispers as she moves to stand beside me. She tucks a lock of hair behind my ear soothingly. "I believe in you."

My eyes meet Pippa's like I'm looking in a mirror, and the princess nods encouragingly.

"I trust you, Celli."

The darkness within her takes me a short time to find. When I do locate it, it seeps toward me with very little effort. I can feel her letting go of it, releasing it to me. Trusting me with it. It's different with her than it is with the Lady. With her, the flow is much weaker and easier to siphon. I take the doubt, weakness, and darkness from her and replace it through my right hand with hope, strength, and light.

Even though I barely feel like I've done anything, Pippa sighs and steps back. My eyelids flutter open and I watch as tears run down the princess's cheeks. Her mother swoops to catch her, holding her up.

"That was incredible," Pippa whispers. "What a gift. It felt almost the same as when you do it, Mother."

Once she gets her bearings, the princess steps forward and hugs me tightly.

"Thank you, Celli," she whispers, "you have no idea what a comfort that was."

"It was nothing," I say, hugging her back. I mean it. I barely felt any effort on my part. It doesn't feel like I did much at all.

"One last exercise," the Muse says gently. "I know you must be exhausted, my dear, but sometimes we must push through our fatigue in order to continue our work."

"I'm not tired," I insist truthfully, glancing at Poe, who's been watching from the sofa. He gives me a smile and my heart flutters. I haven't felt him look away since we began, though he has stayed silent and respectful through the lesson. Pippa sinks dreamily onto the sofa, and he puts his arm around her to let her rest against him.

I'm glad it's early evening, a time when we can all be together. It must be strange, I think, my eyes still stuck to the two of them, to have to live opposite each other the way they do. It hasn't taken me long to learn the workings of the palace, where Poe and Ali rule by day, and Pippa and Alex rule by night.

It isn't just the prince and princess who I find curious and interesting. I'm also fascinated by the fae and how they interact with the subjects of Brindelier's palace. Poe says it's like that throughout the kingdom, fairies and humans paired together. Watching their close relationships makes me long for a fairy of my own. I understand how wary one might be to choose me, though. I am, after all, a former thrall of Sorcerers. I have a dark past, I know. Even though I can't ever erase it, at least I have hope now that I can rise above it.

"Reach out to me, my Champion," the Lady of Magic instructs, interrupting my wandering thoughts. Each time she uses my title it seems to lend the word more weight. I offer her my hand, but this time she refuses it. Instead of touching me, she simply turns her hands at her sides with her palms facing me.

"For one such as myself," she explains, "the flow of magic is constant. It is present all around me. It enters my being. I am one with it, I am the arcane. Thus, I must always be vigilant and aware of the Balance. Mirror my pose. Close your eyes and reach out to this energy. Try to become attuned to the power surrounding you, as abundant as the air we breathe."

Again, I do as she instructs. I take the same pose she does with my hands by my sides and my palms facing forward. My eagerness to learn drives me quickly through the lesson. Like she taught me before, I plant my feet. I breathe up through them, centering myself, making myself aware of my own energy first. Once I'm ready, I reach out and feel the arcane energy that swirls around us.

I've learned in this short time how magic flows. It seeps from the Wellspring, dissolving into the air. It's always there, drifting. The closer we are to the Source, the more concentrated it is, and the easier it is to manipulate and to cast spells. The further away we are, the less concentrated, and the more difficult and complex spell casting becomes.

My Lady is like a channel of the arcane. She collects it around her far more powerfully than any ordinary Mage or Sorcerer would. She's almost like a walking Wellspring on her own. I feel the pull of her magic and allow myself to be drawn to it. It's as compelling as my desire for Quenson had been, as dark and delicious. On the other side, it's also bright, peaceful, and alluring.

Even now, no matter how aware I try to be, it's the darkness which calls to me more strongly than the light. It draws me closer, enticing me. I imagine the beautiful swirls of Mage Mark, how they attracted me, how I longed to display them on my own skin, how utterly thrilled I had been to see them peek beneath the cuff of my sleeve. I allow my awareness to be pulled further toward it.

"*Sister, I need you,*" a man's voice calls, distant and strange. I steer myself toward it, letting it draw me in. It conjures images of beautiful things. Dreams, precious and perfect. Nightmares, fearsome and terrible. The figure of a man swims in the space between us, but only in glimpses. I see a cloak of both day and night, dark skin, a white, curling beard.

"*Valenor.*" My Lady's stance changes. She turns her hands toward her sides, closing herself off to me. I'm aware of the change and I know it's a signal that I should cut myself off, too, but I can still hear their silent conversation as though they're speaking aloud.

"The Darkness is too present. The Dreamstalker is lost to me," he cries. His tone is panicked. Thick with fear. *"Vorhadeniel is stronger than we feared."*

"My token is too faint," a woman's voice whispers. Eljarenae. *"I cannot find the boy's precise location."*

"I beg you, help," Valenor replies. *"He is like a son to me, and I have failed him. He has slipped from my reach, blocked by darkness. By our brother. Please, Sister. I cannot lose him."*

"Of course," My Lady answers urgently. *"I know how dear he is to you."* With her reply comes a rush of desire to ease her brother's suffering. I follow it to her like I'm walking down a trail. Her attentions turn away from me, too distracted by the urgency of her brother's request to realize I'm following her along the path of Darkness. I stay quiet, cautious, and close.

"Celli," Poe cries. His concern creates an energy similar to the arcane. Like the magic surrounding us, it takes a path of its own. A similar path swirls from the voice, the one who is so afraid for the boy he says is like a son to him. So many paths to follow. Though I'm drawn to Poe's the most, I feel this is some sort of test. His hand closes around mine and I yearn to stay with him, where it's safe, where I'm loved. But I know I should choose the way that gives me the best opportunity to help. Redemption comes from action. I don't know where I heard that. Maybe I've just thought it up on my own.

My hand slips from Poe's and I feel myself fading from the practice room. I'm not afraid. I choose the path of urgency, left behind by Valenor.

Closely, I follow My Lady along a trail of darkness, pressing deeper into the depths. Jungle leaves rustle around us. Strange animals call out, their voices echoing over thick fog. The air grows heavy with heat and moisture. Sweat beads my brow.

"Turn back, Celli," My Lady commands. "The darkness in this place is certain to consume you. You are not ready for this, yet."

I try to obey My Lady, but I can't. The lure into the fog is too strong, too compelling. The need is too great. It leads me along a strange and winding trail, ending with a face. I know this boy, this near-son of the voice who fears for him. At least, I knew him once.

"Tib," I whisper.

Vague memories come to mind. Tricks and commands of Sorcery which led to his capture. Tib lying broken on a slab. A cat in a cage. My former Master's greedy gaze lingering on them. I've wronged him. I owe him.

This is my chance to prove myself, to show I'm truly changed. I choose to break free of my Lady's link. Hopefully, she'll think I followed her direction. Hopefully, when this is over, she'll be proud of the choice I made.

I delve into the depths of the fog. It tries to drive me out, to terrify me, but I've known this darkness and I'm not afraid. I pull it into me, swirling it around my insides, releasing pure white light in its wake.

The action propels me forward, shifting and changing as I draw it into me in and push it out again. I focus on him. On Tib. My former rival, even before the Dusk gripped me. I focus on the pain of my Lady's brother. It isn't long before I feel them with me, the Lady of Magic and the Lord of Dreaming. They know I've found him. They chase me deeper into the jungle, calling my name. I soar into the fog, siphoning it, leaving a trail of Light in my wake.

The power I sift through charges me with energy, driving me ahead through the jungle faster and stronger than I ever could have imagined possible. The negative magic is an endless, undeniable source. Ahead, I feel a concentration of it like no other. It feeds on something, taunting, heckling.

I push through the fog toward the beacon of darkness, cutting into it, ignoring its forbidding pulses. I trust My Lady to protect me. I know I'll be safe. I arrive at the source: a fearsome cyclone of ink-black energy, whipping and swirling violently.

"Hold on," Tib's weak voice echoes from inside of it. "Just hold on."

"He's here!" I shout, reaching toward the cyclone. My Lady calls my name again, but she's far away this time. I wonder as I draw the darkness through me, how she could have been so easily lost. "My lady!" I scream so she's sure to hear me, and I feel her drawing nearer.

The jungle air is hot and sticky. Sweat rolls between my shoulder blades and makes my cotton robes cling to me. The force of the cyclone, though, is frigid cold. It whips my hair around my face and stings my skin with frost, and I'm reminded once again of that snowy night. The night I took three lives. How could I think I'd be anything more than a thrall, a murderer?

"Poe," I whisper, steeling myself against those wicked thoughts. I force out the darker images in favor of his smile, his touch. My heart swells, pulling in shadow and flinging away light. In between blurs of black, I see him. Tib. His face is slashed with cuts, his hair tangled and matted. One hand is pressed to his chest. With the other, he drives back the shadows from the inside with his dagger.

Oddly, I feel nothing where he's standing. The energy is blank and empty in the space he takes up. The cyclone tries to touch him, to taunt him and change him with its cruel thoughts, but its relentless attacks never meet their mark. Still, I can see Tib is exhausted. More than once, he stumbles to one knee and fights to stand again.

My attempts to siphon the energy of the cyclone are not enough. I can feel the endlessness of the storm as it draws power from the fog around it. I don't break my concentration, but I know that my attempts are futile.

"My Lady!" I scream again. "My Lord! He's here! Please! We're here!"

I fling a trail of light away from me, thrusting my palm toward the sky, imagining a beacon of golden light like the swirls that danced up My Lady's wrist. My left hand gives against the side of the cyclone. Inside, Tib falls to his knees. He tries to get up, but he's not strong enough. I feel Stellastera nearing, but I fear there won't be time to save him. Tib is spent, but the energy I mold has invigorated me. I know what I must do. It's only thing I can do.

I take a deep breath to prepare myself. I know I only have one chance. With all my strength, I dive into the center of the cyclone, shoving Tib free of its hold. He rolls away across the jungle floor, tucked into a tight ball.

The cyclone unravels slightly, as if trying to decide which one of us is a better target. I pull more strands of it in through my left hand, releasing the light with my right as cold, sharp shards slice into my skin with the force of the swirling energy. The tendrils of shadow seem to regroup. They pulse around me, strengthening.

Outside, blurs of My Lady and My Lord peek through the darkness. A cloak of stars sweeps over Tib, and he vanishes behind its folds. I can't hear them speaking, but I can sense their relief in finding him.

That sense, though, is short-lived. The Dusk has lost Tib as a target, so its energy focuses on me. I feel the force of Shadow pulled from the surrounding fog, fueling the cyclone. There's nothing left for it to protect. This place is worthless to them now. I'm all that remains. Me and My Lady.

The cyclone rages around me and I continue to pull the darkness and push the light. Outside, I feel My Lady doing the same. I know, working together, we can siphon all of it. Change it to good. I have faith. I believe.

This darkness is thicker than the forces I practiced with. It has a firmer feel to it, a substance and a history I'm not used to. As it churns inside of me, readying to change, I get a sense of its origins. I'm reminded of my moments in the Void, face-to-face with Diovicus. I remember what he showed me, how his armies are gathered in distant cities, waiting. I see them now as clearly as if I were standing among them. They aren't waiting anymore. They're on the move. They march through mountains at an impossible pace, charging southward.

"What new trifle is this?" the Sorcerer King's voice echoes through the cyclone. "Deniel, look. Have you seen such magic wielded by a mortal before? She had been mine. They stole her from me."

"Then claim her again," comes Darkness's reply.

"Celli!" My Lady screams. Her voice is shredded by the storm. My hands shake with fear, but I keep them firmly posed, maintaining my stance. "Elja, help us!"

The trail of pure white light from my right hand wraps around my wrist firmly. "Celli, it is I, Eljarenae," she whispers. "Come with me."

The darkness flowing into my left hand sweeps up my arm, clawing at me, pulling me to it. "You are mine," it growls. "You are nothing without me."

They tug on me, swirling around my insides, churning and melding within me. The words she spoke when I first met her come back to me: *"I am with you. Whatever darkness befalls you, I offer you light to combat it tenfold."* Then, *"You have been drawn to the depths of my opponent, and you have survived. You hold within you a unique perspective. A doorway which until now has been closed to me, and to my allies, the Dawn."*

A doorway, I think to myself with The Muse of Light pulling my right hand and the Muse of Darkness pulling my left.

"The doorway is open," I cry, pulling Eljarenae's energy through me into the darkness, allowing her passage, channeling light forward like the shots of a hundred archers. "Use it!"

Chapter Thirty-Nine

THE BEGINNING
Azi

After a long day of meetings, planning, and preparing for the Dawn's next steps, I fall into my bed and bury my face in my pillow. The sweet, familiar lavender and rose fragrance of Mouli's laundering soap soothes me to sleep almost instantly. I dream of pleasant, fleeting things as I burrow deep into my soft, downy bed.

"Azi," tiny hands pat the side of my nose and Flitt's light dances behind my eyelids as she raps on my brow. "Azi," she whispers again, this time a little more insistently.

I groan and burrow deeper into my bed in protest, and she tugs at the unraveling strands of my braid.

"Azi, wake up!" she squeaks just above a whisper. "It's urgent!"

My eyes fly open. I bolt upright in my bed. My heart races. Across the room, Mercy jumps in its stand. "What is it?" I gasp, flinging my warm, downy blanket away. "Is it the Dusk? Are they attacking?"

One bare foot touches the cold floor as my sword lands in my outstretched hand. I'm halfway to my armor stand before Flitt darts into my face.

"Shh, shh, shh!" she hisses, pressing her surprisingly non-sticky hands to my lips. "It isn't anything like that! You're out of sugar cubes again! It's like Mouli's forgotten all about me!"

I stare in disbelief at the bright fairy, blinking the sleep from my eyes. Mercy slides from my loosening grasp and floats to set itself in place on its stand. With a groan, I fall back into bed and pull the blankets up over my head.

"You said it was urgent," I say thickly through a yawn.

"Well, it is. I'm hungry!" Her squeaky voice, muffled by the comforter, drifts closer. I feel her feet on the side of my head and pull the blankets tighter around myself. "I can't help it if I've been up dancing all night while you were being lazy. A fairy has things to do, you know. Important things."

"Sure, important things," I yawn again.

"You don't believe me," Flitt huffs. I feel her land by my arm. There's the sound of a scuffle and a tug on the blanket. She manages to get an edge pulled out of my grasp, and she peeks inside. Light bursts from her face, blinding me with sudden, twinkling rainbows. I screw my eyes shut in protest.

"Of course I believe you," I say, poking my head out into the cold in surrender. "Could you tone it down a little, maybe?"

"Sorry," she whispers, giggling, and dims her glow. "But you're awake now! Hurrah!"

"Hurrah," I mumble, scooting back to prop myself against my pillow. I glance to my shuttered window as I reach for the cup on my bedside table to take a sip of water. The light of the waning moon spills through the slats, competing with Flitt's colors as it stretches across the floorboards.

I set the mug back on the table and open the drawer, revealing the stash of sugar cubes I'd grabbed earlier on the way back to my room.

"There," I say, utterly annoyed.

"Yes!" Flitt squeaks. "You're the best, Azi. Really." She dives into the drawer and shoves several cubes into her belt pouch. To my surprise, as hungry as she claimed to be, she doesn't eat any.

"Do you want to know who I was dancing with?" she asks, now that she's sure I'm fully awake. She keeps her voice much quieter than usual and glances over her shoulder toward the circle hatch. The ribbons of her skirt rise and fall as she sighs dreamily, twirling in place. "Bet you can't guess."

My mood shifts. Maybe it's because I was just dreaming, or maybe it's because I'm overly anxious over the looming battle, but something about her here in my room, dancing and glowing in the moonlight, makes my heart swell with love for the little fae. My irritation over being woken up in the middle of the night is easily pushed aside by my affection for her. Just a few short years ago, I never would have imagined a scene like this could be real. If I'd told someone there was a fairy in my bedroom, Uncle most definitely would have had my head examined.

"Hey, Dreamy," Flitt whispers, diving toward my face. She stops short of my nose and taps it with her finger. "You're supposed to guess!"

"Oh," I say. "Um, Twig?"

She shushes me again, clinging to my cheek, and glances toward Rian's room.

"Not Twig," she whispers. "And can you keep your voice down?"

"Why?" I ask.

"You can't answer a question with a question!" she whispers.

"I didn't know we were play—"

"Shh!"

"For the ever-loving—" I start to growl, and Flitt squeaks and darts to my ear.

"I don't want to wake up Stinky," she whispers. "When was the last time we had a talk, just you and me, huh? If he comes in here, he'll stick himself to your face all the way 'til morning, and I just want to talk to you without him around because you're mine and I'm yours and just this once I don't want to share!"

Slowly, I turn my head to face her. She hovers in the air, even with my eyes, her fists clenched at her sides, her cheeks red, her eyes narrowed.

"Flitt," I whisper, trying hard to keep the bemusement out of my voice, "are you jealous of Rian?"

"Don't be ridiculous," she huffs, crossing her arms. She purses her lips. Her nostrils flare out. This close, I can see the beautiful shift of color in her eyes: fuchsia, orange, violet.

"You are," I say, biting my lip to keep myself from smiling.

"That's not the point!" she squeaks, then claps her hands over her own mouth. "This isn't working," she whispers. "Maybe you should just look instead."

She comes to perch on the pillow beside my head and pats it with her hand until I lean back enough to look at her. Her eyes swirl from the warm, energetic shades of orange and yellow to the cooler, more soothing greens and blues. Arcane energy tingles through me, spilling from my heart and warming me all the way to my toes and fingertips. Our eyes lock together, and the golden tendrils swirl between them as I fall into the memory she's prepared to show me.

Shimmering clouds of color drift past me, sparkling like dew or like dust in a sunbeam. The beauty of Flitt's mind is something I've experienced only a few times, and every time, I forget how breathtakingly beautiful it is. The colors shift like leaves in the wind, filled with stunning disorder, flashing with life and promise.

"This way," her sweet voice calls to me like fairy song.

I float toward it, eager to see what she's invited me here for. The sounds of a festival fill my ears, and the glittering clouds begin to part to reveal first the bright spires of Brindelier's palace, and slowly the rest of the city sprawling out from it.

It hasn't changed much since the last time I was here. The streets of the lively kingdom are filled with revelers, dancing, singing, and cheering. I soar through crowded streets on fairy's wings, Flitt's wings, past flapping banners and through bursting, bright fireworks. From her perspective, everything is magnified. The sounds of the festival boom in her ears, the smell of cook smoke and fry bread hang heavy in the air around her.

As she makes her way through the city, the sun hangs low in the sky, casting a radiant shade of red-orange over the faces of the buildings she passes. In the distance, a voice rises above the crowd in song. It's a man's voice, clear as crystal, with a pitch so pleasing that even back on the bed, in my own body, I gasp.

Within the memory, Flitt's heart starts to race. She's almost there. She can almost see him. She reaches the end of the long street which opens up to reveal the main square, where the same stage we saw on the day we arrived with Margy is nearly engulfed by a crowd of onlookers.

There, Prince Poe's Faedin, Aliandra, floats high above the crowd on silver wings. To the sound of Alexerin's voice, she performs a graceful dance that flows perfectly to the song. She has grown to twice the height of a human, and though Alex's voice fills the square with an upbeat melody that has everyone dancing, he stays to the side of the stage, unseen.

Excitement fills the audience, charging the air with tangible energy that both fae seem to thrive in. When the song ends, Flitt darts to his side at the edge of the stage, and he turns to her and beams a smile.

Aliandra raises her hands to quiet the crowd, and the cheering quickly fades. Her silver skin flashes like flames in the light of sunset, and she smiles at the crowd as though she knows what they're waiting for and is drawing out the wait just to tease them.

Hidden from the audience, Alex drifts closer to Flitt. Her heart races faster, and he flicks his eyes to the stage. Flitt follows his gaze to find Aliandra peering offstage at them.

"One more song?" she pushes to both Flitt and Alex, and Alex nods and offers his hand to Flitt. Beautiful music swells across the square, and this time, Alex doesn't sing. He draws Flitt closer, and hand in hand they spin in midair, like two leaves carried in the breeze.

Their eyes lock together, and everything around them seems to disappear.

"You were gone for so long," he says to her, "I was afraid you'd never return." The quiet tone of his voice which she knows is meant only for her sends a shiver of pleasure all the way to the tips of her wings.

"I was on an adventure," she replies. "We're getting closer to the end, you know. And the beginning."

"The princess has passed her test," he whispers, leaning closer as they float and spin. "I'll tell you the whole of it, but not here."

"They made it in? The Dusk?" Flitt gasps. "How?"

"They sent a girl," he murmurs, tipping his head closer to her. "One to spy, to watch. It was a clever spell, one that was easily detected, but I led our enemy to believe there could be a chance for him, for Pippa's benefit. She withstood his lure, though. She was strong in the face of it. I'm proud of her."

"You're right," Flitt whispers. "You shouldn't say any more here, with all these people around." Her eyes close slowly, and she tips her face toward him as his breath grazes her brow.

"What people?" Alex whispers. "I only see you."

His lips brush hers, soft and warm, and they keep spinning and spinning as their kiss deepens.

"Flitt!" I gasp, pulling away from the memory, spilling out of her mind and tumbling back to my bed.

"What?" she asks innocently.

"You kissed Alex!" I hiss.

"So, what?" she shrugs, wide eyed.

"You hate kissing!" I whisper.

"I do not! Only when you do it. Ugh. I mean, Mage kisses," she falls back on the pillow, her hands clamped around her throat, her tongue stuck out in an exaggerated mime of choking.

I stare at her in disbelief, and she pops up to a sitting position, her legs stretched out in front of her.

"Fairies kiss, Azi," she says with a roll of her eyes. "You saw him. You heard him sing. Can you blame me?" She looks off into the distance dreamily. "Anyway," she whispers, snapping her eyes back to mine and scooting closer on the pillow, "that's not what I was trying to show you. Come on." She beckons to me with a flick of her finger and points to her eyes.

"All right," I whisper, "but do you think we can skip the kissing part?"

"Who's jealous now?" she asks, winking. I roll my eyes and shake my head, and she huffs and nods. "All right. Watch."

"And so, another day has passed. Can you believe it went so fast?" Ali's voice echoes across the crowd, and they cheer in response. She gestures offstage, and the cheering grows louder. Alex gives Flitt one more quick kiss—

"Sorry," Flitt whispers to me in my bedroom. "I forgot about that one."

—*before drifting onto the stage, growing in size as he reaches the center, to match Aliandra's size.*

"The cycle of day to night and night to day is a comfort to all of us," they say in unison to the instantly hushed crowd. "The sun shall always rise, and the night shall always fall upon our sweet kingdom."

"Brindelier, Brindelier," the crowd replies together, their voices raised in song. They continue to sing the anthem of their kingdom as Alexerin and Aliandra come together on the stage to dance in perfect unison, as though they're two bodies with one mind. After what Stellastera showed me in Sixledge, it makes perfect sense how in sync they are. Their dance holds absolute magic, melding with the song of their people, a ballad of deep history, of loyalty and pride of country, of hope for the future.

The words are lost to me even as they're sung, but the emotion lingers long after the song is through. When the final notes fade, Aliandra takes her bow and floats from the stage, shrinking down to fairy size.

"Hello," she greets Flitt with a smile. Though she looks exhausted from a long day of entertaining the crowd, she offers Flitt a warm hug. "Coming?" she whispers.

As soon as Flitt nods, they blink away from the square and appear in the garden tower of the palace, where the Wellspring bubbles softly with the constant flow of the three offerings. Ali excuses herself to plunge into the pool and emerges looking quite refreshed.

"I'm glad you're back," she says with no evidence of the exhaustion she'd shown just moments before. "Alex was getting worried. A lot happened while you were gone."

They dive expertly into the question game, excitedly sharing information between them as they dart through the corridors of the palace. Ali recounts the events of the palace to Flitt, filling her in on the mysterious girl who looked so much like the princess; how she had been an agent of Dusk sent to attempt to lure the princess, and how Kenrick pulled her into the Light to discover a rare talent no one could have foreseen. She recounts the return of Stellastera, and describes how delighted the prince and princess had been to have their mother return. By the time the game is through, Ali is fully filled-in with Flitt's latest adventures in Sixledge, and Flitt has found out everything the fae knows about the recent goings-on with the prince and princess.

I pull away from the memory again, shifting my focus to Flitt's eyes, blinking as the connection fades between us. "You two told each other everything," I whisper.

"Of course," she whispers, shrugging. "We're on the same side, after all, and you should know fairies are terrible gossips. Honestly, it's like you don't know anything about me! Now, stop interrupting. We're getting to the good part."

She pulls me back in again, this time to Prince Poe and Princess Pippa, who stand clinging to each other in the middle of the room. Neither seems to notice when the fairies enter. Only the personal guard posted just inside seem to acknowledge the arrival of the fae, both offering a respectful nod.

"It was uncle," *Poe sniffles softly.* "Uncle Valenor, I'm sure of it. She wasn't supposed to go with them."

"She'll be safe," *Pippa whispers reassuringly.* "Mother is with her."

"I don't know," *Poe replies, his face drained of color.* "I don't think she realized Celli was with her."

"My prince!" *Aliandra cries, darting toward him. He looks up from his sister's shoulder and smiles.*

"Ali," *he says with relief, reaching toward her. The fairy lands in his hand and he brings her to his cheek, where she wipes away the tear that trails down it.*

"What's happened?" *she asks him, and while he tells her about the lesson, the three of them shuffle to the sofa to sit, still clinging together for comfort, staring at the empty space on the carpet.*

"What if something happens," *Pippa ventures,* "and Mother doesn't return? What if it's Uncle Vor—"

"Tsst!" *Ali interrupts her briskly.* "Don't even think about that, Princess! Don't allow those dark thoughts to seep in!"

"Ali's right," *Poe agrees, though doubt hangs heavy in his tone.* "We have to be positive and have hope."

"Flitt," *Ali says, gesturing to her to come closer.* "Tell their Highnesses what you told me, about how Azi drew their mother out of the darkness."

Flitt recounts the tale, and she's almost finished when a crackle of energy booms like a thunderclap through the palace. The prince and princess gasp, and Ali cries out, "The Wellspring! Hurry!"

In a blur of silver and gold, the prince and princess leap to their feet and charge along the corridor. Their guards keep pace, weapons drawn, cloaks of purple billowing out behind them. Flitt chases after the group, her wings buzzing loudly behind her as she flies up the spiral staircase beside them.

They don't stop until they reach the pool, where, upon the long stone bridge that stretches across the Wellspring, a figure crouches on hands and knees. He looks as though he's been to the depths and back. His clothes and cloak hang from him in shreds. Though his face is hidden by a fringe of matted black hair, I still recognize him by his slender form and by the bandolier that crosses his chest.

Aliandra shoots toward him like a silver arrow, but he doesn't pay her any attention. He leans far over the bridge, dangling his arm toward the sparkling liquid below.

"How dare you trespass at the Sacred Source?" *Aliandra shouts, raising her hands to cast a spell.*

"Guards!" *Poe bellows, giving the two who had raced up the stairs with them permission to enter the gates.*

"Don't!" *Flitt cries, racing to meet the fae.* "That's Tib!"

"Brother," *Pippa says quietly,* "what's in his hand?"

Poe throws up his hand to halt the charging guards. At the edge of the pool, the group stands watching as Tib drops to lie flat on his belly, reaching as far as he can toward the Wellspring. He opens his hand to reveal a pathetically drained, emaciated fairy who seems to have been doused in black ink. Dim green light pulses within the fae's chest, barely bright enough to be seen through the black.

"Go on," *Tib whispers. His focus is on the fae in his hand. Nothing else seems to exist to him.*

The fae takes a rattling breath, too weak to even turn his head to look at Tib.

"He's dying," *Flitt whispers. She starts toward the fae, but Tib tips his hand before she can reach him, and the blackened fae drops into the pool with a sparkling splash.*

A collective gasp echoes through the garden, and the prince and princess inch closer to the edge of the basin, peering at the space where the fae disappeared. Bubbles of green and black rise to the surface and burst. On the bridge, Valenor's cloak drapes Tib's shoulders as the Dreamwalker crouches to rest a hand on the boy's back. Tib lets his head drop onto his forearm in exhaustion.

"Just wait," *Valenor whispers.* "Watch."

Flitt is the only one brave enough to get close to the surface of the Wellspring. I feel in her memory the sensation of its power causing every hair on her head to stand up. She peers into the glittering surface, and something green and bright moves beneath it.

"He's all right!" *she yelps and darts away just in time to avoid the jet of jungle green magic that shoots from the pool. It spikes all the way up through the open ceiling and dives down again, spiraling around Tib, who jumps to his feet in shock.*

"He's a Keeper," *Flitt gasps in wonder at the spectacular golden green fae who swirls around Tib, washing him in curtains of glittering light.*

"Allow it," *Valenor's laughing voice booms across the garden.*

Tib seems to do as the Dreamwalker suggests, and the fairy's magic bursts over him, healing his wounds, shining his hair, repairing his cloak and clothes. Tib reaches out to him, and the fae touches his hand in a flash, leaving a green orb glowing there. Before anyone can react, the fae shoots up again through the ceiling in a jet of brilliant color. The trail he leaves behind echoes with the sounds of the jungle: cawing birds, chattering monkeys, and the drums of its tribal people which pulse like a heartbeat.

Flitt drifts up from the pool to hover beside the orb held in Tib's outstretched hand. He follows her gaze to it, and the light around it fades to reveal a vessel in the shape of a pure crystal leaf, filled with shimmering green liquid. His eyes travel slowly to each empty basin until they rest on the one that holds the same shape.

In disbelief, he blinks at Flitt, then Poe and Pippa, and shrugs.

"I guess," he says hoarsely, clears his throat, and tries again, "guess we just need Ceras'lain, now."

I pull away from Flitt's mind, my heart pounding in my chest like those tribal drums. "He got it," I whisper through numb lips as the energy of Mentalism drains away. Flitt giggles, nodding excitedly.

"Rian!" I shout around the sugar cubes she shoves into my mouth. I stumble out of bed and race to the hatch. "Rian," I shout again, coughing as I inhale granules of sugar.

"There's no reason to wake up Stinky," she says with a pouting tone. "We still need Ceras'lain, anyway."

"You couldn't have just told me right away?" I ask, exasperated.

"Well, I told you it was urgent, didn't I?" she argues as the wall quivers behind her and Rian steps through.

"I thought you were talking about sugar cubes!" I cough again, and Rian conjures a cup of water and offers it to me, looking between me and Flitt as he blinks the sleep from his eyes.

"Come on, Azi," Flitt says, rolling her eyes. She turns to Rian, shaking her head. "Typical. It's like she doesn't know me at all."

Chapter Forty

A FALSE PEACE
Azi

The looking glass gifted by Prince Poe still makes me uneasy when I see it standing alone in the center of the palace sitting room we've been summoned to. Lavender light from the rising sun spills through the curtains of the towering windows and dances on the mirror's ornate gilt frame in a way I'd find beautiful if it didn't bring back such awful memories.

The mirror reminds me too much of my first true battle at the keep at Kythshire's border, where a similar glass acted as a tool for the Sorcerers gathered to breach its borders. The memory of my first real fight, my first kill, lingers on the outskirts of that thought. Until that battle, all of my fights were spars against others in training squares.

Try as I might to forget that moment, I can still see my ice sword slicing through Gorgen's robes, and the life leaving his eyes. I remember Flitt's eyes meeting mine, and I remember wondering whether she'd feel different about me from then on. The thoughts hang in my mind like the strings in Mum's. I wonder whether I'd be able to heal them the way I healed hers, to unwind the dark feelings of fear and regret at taking a life, no matter how evil. I wonder if I truly want to. If I didn't have that moment to weigh on me, I might lose my compassion, my temperance. I might lose who I am.

As though he senses my unease, Rian slips his hand into mine and squeezes it. Flitt lounges on my shoulder. Saesa stands just behind me. Her Majesty's Champions are gathered around us: Uncle in his red robes, his gaze solemn and distant, Cort nursing his freshly healed elbow with Bryse beside him, Mya and Elliot, and even Brother Donal. Mum stands on my other side, looking determined and focused although I'm sure she's concerned for Da, who is still hard at work overseeing armament for the battle to come.

Among us, Her Majesty's most trusted allies are gathered: her mother Queen Naelle, Princess Sarabel and Prince Vorance of Sunteri, Kerr Skalivar of Hywilkin, Master Keyes of Brindelier, Susefen and

Zevlain of Ceras'lain, and her Council: Master Anod, Admiral Hayse, High Scholar Lowery, Captain Myer, and Captain Elmsworth.

Her Majesty enters the room at a brisk pace with her personal guard, Finn, by her side. She wears a full-skirted gown of royal purple satin which fades to the floor in shades of earthy brown. Her bodice is plates of moss-covered tree bark which sparkle with green and white gems like dewdrops. A nest of vines sweeps up her shoulder, creating a perch for Twig, who sits by her right ear. Her hair, usually done in perfect curls, is bound into a bun on top of her head and dressed with her father's plain, gold crown.

A certain sort of awe fills the room in her presence, and everyone gathered sinks to a knee to greet the queen. She weaves among us, touching each of us on the shoulder, offering us a warm smile and words of gratitude. Her eyes flash with barely-controlled excitement, her lips are curved into a smile which seems eager to spill its secrets.

"Twig!" Flitt squeals, darting to greet him.

"Flitt!" he shouts, and dives at her. They link arms and feet and spin into a blur of green, brown, and rainbow colors all the way up to the ceiling. Far above us, they whisper in secret as the group cranes their necks to watch, most with smiles of amusement on their faces. The fairies finish whispering, and drift back down to our level.

"To think, just hours ago, you had an Alex stuck to your face," I tease Flitt secretly as she returns to her spot in my pauldron.

"Typical. You're so uptight," she pushes back, winking at Twig with a sparkling smile.

As the queen moves toward the center of the room, Uncle Gaethon and Master Anod set wards of Silence over the doors and windows. Margy waits until they're finished before she addresses the group.

"Thank you all for coming so quickly," she says as she steps into place beside the mirror. "I realize it's quite early, but this could not wait. What I have to share with you must remain a guarded secret among us all. Each of you is here because I trust you deeply, so I beg you, please, do not share what I'm about to say with anyone outside of this room until I ask you to do so."

She takes a deep breath and glances at the mirror beside her, explaining, "I have called this meeting in order to create a plan to move forward. You see, a remarkable triumph in the name of the Dawn has been brought to our attention."

Her hand drifts toward Twig, indicating he's the one who reported the news, and she goes on.

"An agent of Light has successfully recovered the Offering from Elespen. With that, we now possess the remaining three required to claim Brindelier's Wellspring and unite our kingdoms."

A collective gasp issues through the room, followed by a round of eager applause that doesn't fade until Queen Margy raises her hand to quiet it. Beside her, the surface of the mirror ripples, revealing two figures: Princess Pippa and, surprisingly, Tib.

"Margy," he calls anxiously, stepping closer to the glass.

"Tib," Margy and Sacsa gasp in unison. The queen whirls to face the mirror, her brow knit with concern.

"How I hoped you'd join us." Margy's gloved hand moves to touch the surface, her eyes on Tib alone. Queen Mother Naelle clears her throat softly, and Margy guards herself and lowers her hand. Tib drops his own hand with a slightly annoyed glance at the Queen Mother. His once eager expression shifts to brooding as he peers deeper into the room at the rest of us. Pippa looks from Margy to Tib in thoughtful silence. As if to mask any reaction to the two of them, she reaches gracefully to tuck a lock of hair behind her ear.

Master Keyes is the first to break the awkward silence that follows. He scowls, muttering under his breath, "What is *he* doing there?"

His question seems to permit a flurry of whispers on our side of the mirror. Mum shuffles closer to me. Her worried glance around the room and the reaction of the others reminds me that many who are here now were also present during Tib's tirade. Margy raises a hand to quiet us. She glances at Prince Vorance, and he nods to her and pats a scroll case that hangs at his side. Beside him, Princess Sarabel links her arm through the prince's and smiles at him proudly. Margy looks away from them both, her own secret smile disappearing as she faces the mirror once more.

"Your Majesty," Pippa says, bowing. Alex, who had been perched in her crown, pushes off to hover beside her tipped head.

"Look, Pippa," Alex whispers, wide-eyed. "They've got a stone half-giant, and a dragon kin." Pippa looks up from her bow, her eyes trailing across the group on our side with wonder and appreciation. Next to her, Tib bows, too. He pats a pouch on his bandolier and grins at Margy, ignoring everyone else.

"I got it," he says. "Sorry about the first one." His silvery eye flicks to Vorance and away again. His hands ball into fists at his sides and then relax.

Margy laughs softly and presses her fingers to the glass, ignoring the queen's throat-clearing this time. "It's all right," she whispers, the crowd behind her forgotten for a moment. "I'm sorry, too."

"I hoped to give it to you in person," Tib says, "but, well, it's complicated. I was stuck coming here, instead, and it seemed kind of reckless to bring it back to Cerion if this is where it had to end up, anyway. We only need one, now, for the Dawn."

"No," Margy whispers, smiling only for him. "The elves gifted me with theirs already. We have all of them!"

"We do?" Tib asks in disbelief. His eyes flick around the room through the mirror. I can almost see his mind at work as he realizes what it means. They run through a series of emotions: Excitement, relief, resolve. He looks at Margy and away quickly, hiding his sadness expertly. He doesn't know yet, about her conversation with Susefen. Pippa watches the interaction between them with curiosity plain on her face. She seems relieved in a way that makes me wonder exactly what's going through her mind. A part of me is curious whether I could peek in and try to figure it out, but I know how wrong that would be.

Instead, I tear my attention from the pair in the mirror and glance at those in the room with me, worried that the feelings between Margy and Tib are as obvious to everyone else as they are to me and the princess. They don't seem to notice, though. Even Master Keyes seems distracted, glaring through his bushy eyebrows into the room beyond Pippa and Tib.

"Forgive me, Your Majesty, Your Highness," Master Keyes says. "Where is the prince? I must say it's quite inappropriate for him to be absent from such a critical meeting."

Pippa looks over her shoulder with concern, then looks to Tib, then back through the mirror at Keyes.

"I'm not sure how much I should say," Pippa says, peering through at our crowd. "I'm sorry, Your Majesty. There are quite a few unfamiliar faces there."

"This room holds Cerion's most trusted council, allies, and champions," Margy explains. "If you would trust your own advisor to know it," she gestures to Master Keyes, "then you can trust any of these equally."

"Very well," Pippa says, looking past the queen to her council member. "He's at the Source, Master Keyes. A battle continues at the site where the offering was recovered by Lord Tibreseli. Poe awaits word from our mother, who has joined that fray."

"Your mother?" Keyes's jaw drops. He sputters in disbelief, looking from Pippa to the empty room beyond her shoulder as if trying to catch a glimpse of Stellastera herself. "How can that be?"

"That's right," Alex says excitedly, "she's returned."

"Isn't it wonderful?" Pippa asks, beaming.

"Well, this…" Keyes shakes his head and starts to pace. "This changes everything, doesn't it? We thought her lost in Hywilkin. We presumed the twins orphaned. If she is alive…" he trails off, his thoughts obviously racing faster than he can convey.

"The Muse of Magic has revealed herself after all," Anod mutters to Uncle. "What a remarkable turn."

"Indeed," Uncle replies, stroking his beard with a twinkle in his eye.

Beside me, Rian squeezes my hand. When I look up at him, he winks at me proudly. The two of them, Rian and Uncle, had been in meetings since the moment we returned from the Dreaming. I wonder how much Rian told about what happened in Sixledge. One glance across the room at Uncle is all the answer I need. His eyes are fixed on me, his smile filled with pride. My cheeks go hot. When I duck my head, Rian bumps my shoulder with his playfully.

"If it is so," Susefen speaks up. "If Queen Emhryck is truly returned, then the reasoning behind the enchantments over Brindelier no longer applies."

"Quite," Keyes agrees. "Everything Brindelier's council has done has been based on the premise that the twin heirs must be honored and guarded until balance and security can be restored to our world. If Our Lady, the Queen, has truly returned, then it is as the elf says. The Age of Awakening is truly upon us, with or without a proper suitor to claim our kingdom."

"You are forgetting, Master Keyes," Susefen interjects, "that which had been written and declared by your own Master Mages at the time of enchantment. Once the offerings are set in place by the suitor, the kingdoms would be joined, and our world would be restored to its former glory. So, in order to restore the Wellspring and set Brindelier firmly in the hands of the Dawn, the suitor is quite necessary."

"Yes, yes," Keyes agrees, glancing from Margy to the mirror as he strokes his chin thoughtfully. "So, Your Majesty, marriage or not, if you intend to follow through, you must be prepared for the consequences of your action."

"What's that supposed to mean?" Tib scowls, leaning closer to the glass.

"It means that even should she choose not to wed our prince," Keyes explains, "Her Majesty will still be responsible, in her part, for anything which might happen once the offerings are in place and the Wellspring is restored."

"Anything like what?" Tib asks impatiently. "That sounds like a threat, to me."

Behind me, Saesa lets out a tiny, almost imperceptible sigh.

"I'll try to explain it as Susefen has explained it to me," Margy says, wringing her hands before her and glancing at the elf. "But please, correct me if my understanding is flawed."

"Of course, Majesty," Susefen bows, smiling, and Margy goes on.

"Brindelier was not always a city apart from our world," Queen Margy says. "At one time, at the peak of its glory, it was as Cerion has been, a kingdom of peace at the edge of the ocean. It had a port like ours, a popular one where people would come from all reaches of the Known Lands to trade. It was of course known for its magical commodities, but also offered a vast variety of wares and exports. It was a normal kingdom, just like ours, or Ceras'lain, or Hywilkin, or Elespen, except for the Wellspring at its center, which offered a link to every other one throughout our world."

"When that peace and balance became threatened, the Mages of Brindelier tried to hide the kingdom away in order to protect the hub of magic. They tore the kingdom from the ground into the sky, and obscured it with massive wards and shields. As the scourge of Sorcery and the Dusk grew stronger, they worked harder to obscure it in an attempt to protect the rest of the world, but Brindelier could still be found. It wasn't until they enchanted the kingdom to sleep that their security was strongest. Only then, were they able to hide until they were forgotten.

"But we all know the result of that. It has thrown the magic in our world askew. With each Wellspring in our world left to fend for itself, corruption and destruction were left in the wake of the solution. Slowly, as individual Wellsprings weakened, our world grew more open to Sorcery and Darkness. It remained that way for far too long. We have known peace, but it was a false peace, a length of silence which allowed our enemy to grow in strength and numbers. The Dusk is too well-seated now. The only way to ensure its defeat and to reconnect our Wellsprings and our world, is to open the All Source, to bring the disease of darkness and Sorcery to a head."

"Opening it will lure the evil," Keyes says angrily. "It will create a beacon, an invitation for the Dusk to flood our kingdom."

"Then you must warn your people to ready themselves to fight," Queen Margy replies. "As I will mine. We hold the advantage. Only we have control over when the offerings will be set in place. That's why I called all of you here. The time to end this is now. I'm relying on you, all of you, to come together. We must make our plan to stake the Dawn's claim on the All Source, which feeds its strength to all our kingdoms, and we must brace ourselves for the greatest battle the Known Lands have ever faced. It's time to end the threat of Sorcery and Darkness, once and for all, by standing together against it."

"We stand with you, Queen Margary," Pippa says somberly. "Our people have fought before. They will do so again, if it comes to that. Our strength is not in numbers, but in heart. Alex," she says, turning to the fairy, "it is time to end the Festival of Awakening. Our people must be well-rested and prepared for what's to come."

"Will you speak to them, Highness?" Alex asks.

"My brother and I will, together," she says, glancing over her shoulder again.

As if on cue, footsteps approach at a hurried pace. The door at the far end of the room flings open, and Poe rushes in. His eyes are rimmed with red, and as he reaches the mirror, the silver fairy following him unleashes a spell that tidies his hair and neatens his clothing.

Tib steps aside to make room for him, and Poe clears his throat as Pippa takes his arm and looks at his face with concern.

"We need help," he says, his voice strained. "Master Keyes, we need to stop the festivities and prepare. Something is happening."

"We were just discussing that, Your Highness," Master Keyes agrees. "Your sister has proposed a speech. I shall send word to the scribes, and have one written before noontime."

"There isn't time!" Poe shouts. "You don't understand. It's already started. Mother has stopped responding through the

Wellspring. A storm looms over the tower, clouding the sky. It's dark as night out there."

"Oh no," Pippa whispers, clinging to Poe as she looks over her shoulder again. Their two fairies dart away, back through the same door Poe entered from.

"It could just be a thunderstorm, couldn't it?" Tib asks a little dubiously.

The twins shake their heads in unison, their eyes wide. "Not here," they say together. "Not in Brindelier."

The effect is eerie and disconcerting. Even Tib seems to think so. He takes a step back from them and peers up at the ceiling. When he looks back into the mirror, his eyes meet mine.

"They're right," he says. "It's not just a storm. It's them. Dusk. Whatever you're planning to do with those offerings, it has to happen soon."

A slight tremor through the room makes us jump, and a moment later the pale light of sunrise is blotted quickly by a shadow soaring past the tall windows.

"Valor!" Margy cries and starts to run to look out, but Finn and Captain Elmsworth block her way, guarding her. The rest of us make it to the windows just in time to see the dragon glide past, its broad wings gleaming. It snarls as if roaring, though we can't hear anything beyond the silence wards, and releases a powerful stream of fire from its gaping jaws. A figure in the sky bursts into flames and plummets to the ground, landing somewhere near the market square, obscured by rooftops.

Myer, Captain of the Guard, relays the event to Margy from his place at the window. "By your leave, Majesty, I shall go investigate," he says urgently.

Determined to see for herself, Margy nudges in beside me. As a group, we peer out of the window, scanning the sky.

"We need you here, Captain," Margy finally replies to Myer. "We must make a plan, and quickly, to ensure the safety of the kingdom."

"What fool would make such an attempt?" Uncle Gaethon ponders aloud.

"What fool, indeed?" Anod echoes him. "It was a Sorcerer, no doubt."

"Look," Rian says, pointing to the spot where the Sorcerer fell. A pillar of black smoke spirals upward and spreads itself along the rooftops, blanketing them with darkness. He describes it to Tib and Pippa, who can't see from the mirror.

"A sacrifice for a greater purpose," Uncle mutters. "By your leave, Majesty, this is a matter for us to handle."

"Master Gaethon, I need you here as well," Margy refuses.

"Majesssty," Kerr Skalivar, who has remained silent in the background until this moment, steps forward. The orange veins in his scale armor crackle with energy, and he bows low to the queen as the group parts to make room for him. "Allow me to go in their sssssstead. I shall invesssstigate and return promptly."

"Your offer is much appreciated, Kerr Skalivar," Margy says with relief. "Thank you."

When he straightens and turns from the queen, his eyes search the room. To my surprise, they rest on Saesa. He nods to her, thumping his chest with his fist, and whirls to leave.

"My Lady Knight," Saesa whispers, touching my shoulder. "Could I—?"

"Go and be our eyes, Saesa," I whisper, nodding. "Come back safely."

"Hey," Tib calls from the mirror. His lips press into a thin line as the door closes behind them, and he crosses his arms over his chest. "So, what's the plan, then?"

"Where did the prince go, now?" Master Keyes asks, annoyed to see just Pippa and Tib in the mirror again.

"Back to the Wellspring," Pippa says. "He wanted to make sure to be there in case she—" Her eyes go wide, and she interrupts herself. "Mother. In case Mother returns."

"Tib is right," Mya speaks up. Her voice holds a commanding tone that snaps all of us to attention, focusing us on the most important matter at hand. "We need to make a plan to get Her Majesty and the Offerings to Brindelier as soon as possible. We have no way of knowing that storm's intentions. Whatever it is building up to could happen at any time."

"Keyes," Pippa whispers through the mirror.

"Princess, go and gather Alexerin and the High Mages." Master Keyes instructs. "Explain to them what you know. Lift the enchantments and prepare the city, but do not show yourself in person. Make your announcement through the Messenger Line. That would be safest. Tell them to be prepared to receive Her Majesty Queen Margary as quietly as possible."

Pippa nods, steels herself, and rushes off, leaving Tib behind.

"Elliot," Margy says. "Please scout up to Valleyside and the Main Crossroads to Kordelya. I wish to know if there has been any movement since yesterday."

"Majesty," Elliot says. He bows and leaves the room quietly.

"Your Majesty, I offer you our wings," Zevlain says boldly. "By cygnet, we can easily reach Brindelier."

"You'll be too much of a target, flying like that," Tib says. "The Dusk could watch you through that mist."

"They would be a welcome diversion, though," Margy says thoughtfully. "As would our best ships." She nods to Second Admiral Hayse, who salutes her in agreement.

"Could we take her and the offerings?" I ask Flitt and Rian. *"Through the Half-Realm?"*

"I don't think so," Rian replies. *"We weren't able to go that way the last time we went to Brindelier."*

"I thought it might be different, now that the Wellspring is opened," I push, disappointed.

"It's opened, but not claimed," Flitt says. *"You two are a rare case. No other humans can do what you can. Better not risk it."*

"I know a way to get you here safely, Margy," Tib says. "But it's got to be a secret. Azi and Rian, and the fairies, they can know. And the Queen Mother, just in case."

Master Keyes grumbles something under his breath, but doesn't argue.

"Master Keyes, you'll go aboard with Admiral Hayse," Margy says. "We can meet you and the elves at the gate."

The Queen, with the occasional whisper of advice from her council, gives her orders. Bryse and Cort are to go to the main gates of the city. Mya and Mum will go with Captains Myer and Elmsworth to rally Cerion's guard and army, and warn the commoners of the kingdom. Uncle will alert the Academy and start working on wards throughout the city to prepare for battle.

"Before we all part ways, Your Majesty…" With a graceful flourish, Susefen reaches into the folds of her gown to produce King Asio's chalice. A collective gasp whispers through the room as everyone seems to remember the promise of victory Susefen spoke of when Queen Margy had presented the cup to her during the Reception of Allies: "It is said that any who drink from this cup will be assured glory in battle, and victory over even their fiercest, most determined enemy."

"Shall we drink to our impending victory?" Susefen raises the chalice, letting it glint in the light of the rising sun.

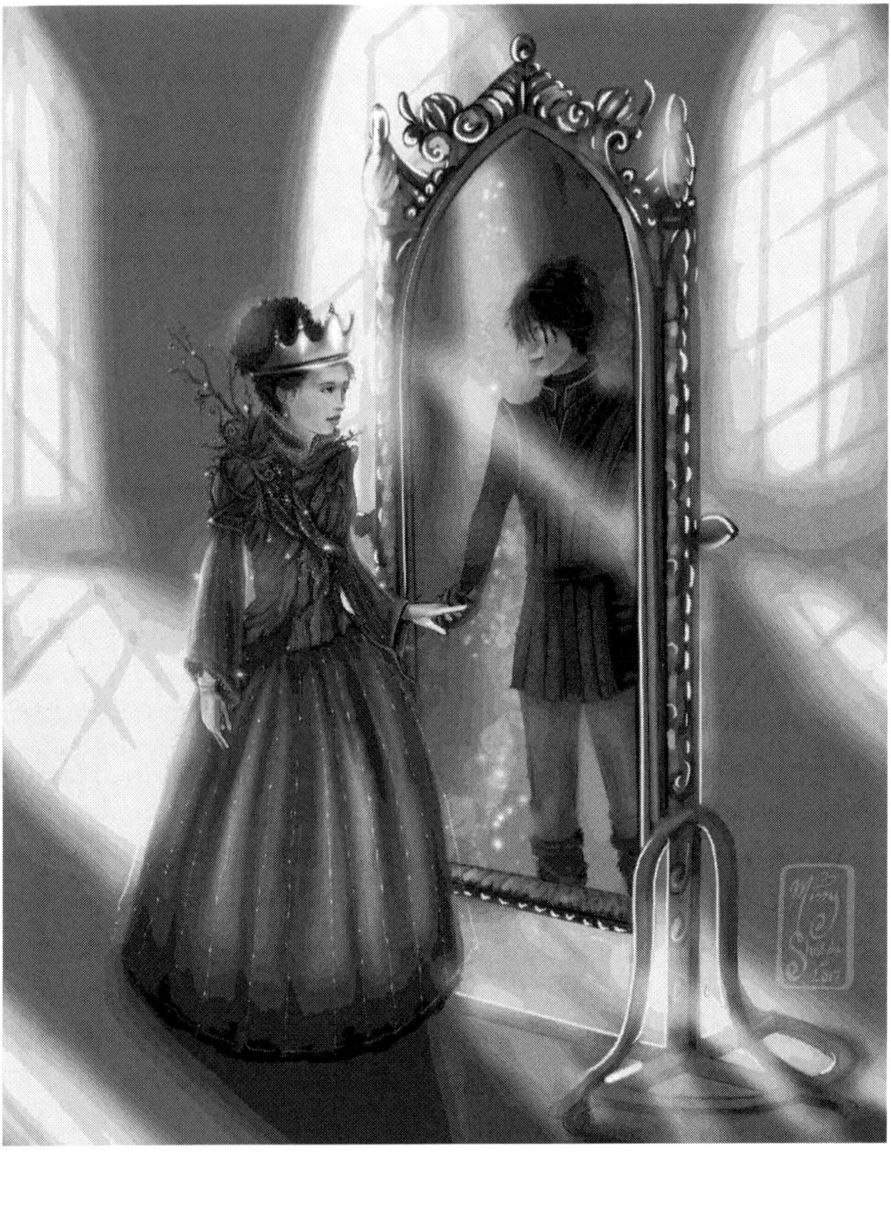

Chapter Forty-One

PREPARATIONS
Tib

Alone in front of the mirror, I watch everyone on the other side drink from Asio's chalice. The magic that surges from it is strong. I can feel it all the way through the mirror. It gives confidence. It assures victory. It's so complex, it's almost overwhelming. While I watch, my thoughts race. I keep thinking about what Keyes said. Marriage or not. What did he mean by that?

I catch Azi's eye again as she, Rian, and Margy gather closer to me. I want to let her do what she does. Let her show me, clearly, what's going on with Margy and Poe and all of that. I remember what Ki said, though. It's not time for that. It's time to do what has to be done, to make sure the Dawn wins. To keep her safe. To keep all of us safe.

I curse under my breath and everyone turns to me with a questioning look.

"I forgot while Saesa was here, but you should know, too. I found the Admiral. I know what happened in Elespen."

Admiral Hayse moves closer to the mirror, his eyes wide. "You've heard from Admiral Ganvent?" he asks.

"I saw him," I explain. "He was in ah…" I look from him to Margy, Azi and Rian. They're all right, but I'm not sure about the others. How much do they know about the Muses and their realms? How much are they allowed to know?

I feel a shift into the space beside me. A presence. Valenor. "Tell them what you will," he says. "There is no longer a point in secrets, especially between allies."

"They've been moved safely to another realm," I explain. "Sort of like the Dreaming, but slightly different. Stellastera, Muse of Magic, created it."

"Is there any way to reach them?" Margy asks. "Can they be returned safely?"

Valenor's form solidifies beside me. He bows to Margy and the others. His cloak settles, draping peacefully from his shoulders to the floor. He's changed his appearance a little. He looks a little narrower. A little more Mage-like. A little less imposing than usual. Still mysterious, though.

On Margy's side, Gaethon and Anod step closer. Both Mages' eyes widen. Gaethon presses his hand to his chest and bows.

"I have seen you in my niece's memories, and heard tell of you from my student," Gaethon says, gesturing to Rian, "but I never would have imagined I would meet you face-to-face, such as we are. Valenor, Dreamwalker, Muse of Dreaming, it is an unfathomable honor to make your acquaintance."

"And you are Gaethon Ethari, Second Magical Advisor to the Crown of Cerion, Master Mage of Her Majesty's Champions," Valenor smiles. "There is no need for further introductions. I know each of you, in my own way. I have seen you in the Dreaming, and I am pleased to speak with you in person, as you say, such as we are." He taps the mirror's surface to make his point.

The small crowd on the other side of the glass stays perfectly still. Everyone's eyes stick to Valenor, like they're afraid if they look away he might disappear. When nobody replies, he goes on.

"It is true that a vast number of Elespen's people have been hidden safely away in the Realm of Magic. At the moment, their lands have been overcome by a darkness which is in the process of being vanquished. I assure you, none of those who chose to flee have come to any harm, and they shall be returned to this realm as soon as it is safe for them to do so. Most of them have no idea they are there, and continue with their lives as though nothing has happened.

"Others of Elespen have been brought to the Realm of Light, where they remain waiting for their homes to be restored. They are the secret, hidden folk who wish to remain unknown by the masses, much like the fae have done until now. When the dark scourge of Elespen has been erased and the All Source is restored, they shall return to their homeland."

He doesn't name them, but I know Valenor's talking about the Savarikta.

"Still others, Your Majesty," Valenor continues, "have chosen another path. They have seen the might the Dusk displays, and they have allowed themselves to be lured into it. Those from Cresten and the reaches of Elespen are not the only ones who have made this choice. There are scores of others, hundreds, even, from all parts of the

Known Lands, who have chosen to join with what they believe will be the winning side."

"A large battalion hails from your own Outlands, Majesty. Your banished lands. Still more have surged southward from Haigh. The force, as your various scouts have informed you, marches on Cerion. They fight in the name of the Dusk, with vengeance and fury heavy in their hearts. When those escaped prisoners fall in battle, the Dusk's Necromancers tear them from the grips of death to fight again. At the forefront of this great army, Diovicus rides on a black steed. Those who knew the Sorcerer King in his prime would fail to recognize him now, Majesty, but you most certainly would. He wears your brother's body like a suit of new armor."

"How do you know this?" Queen Naelle asks. She pulls her daughter to her, and Margy clings to her in fear. I find myself wishing again that I could step through this mirror. Hold her myself. Tell both queens not to be afraid. The Dawn will win. I'll put my dagger through Eron myself. But then I remember when he faced Azi at the king's pyre. How he was still walking around after that with a huge hole through his chest. Still fighting. I shudder and step closer to Valenor as he goes on.

"Even as we speak, my sister, the Muse of Light, stands at the precipice of the darkness. With the aid of a portal, a sort of doorway, she is able to peer into the far reaches of the Void and see its vast workings. We are uniquely linked, you see, when we choose to be, and so I am able to glean these visions from her."

"And you're certain what you are seeing is real?" Naelle asks.

"Indeed," Valenor replies. "I am afraid it is as real as any of this is."

"He's right," Elliot says from the back of the room. The door closes behind him as he rubs his eyes and weaves through the group. "It's as he described. The armies of Dusk have reached Gristen. They're marching for the Main Crossroads at a pace no normal army could keep. They'll reach the gates of Cerion before sunset at the rate they're going. And it's not just men. They've got risen with them, and creatures of darkness like I've never seen before."

"Thank you," Margy says to Elliot. She turns to Elmsworth. "What do you suggest, Captain, now that we know what we're up against?"

"We must alert our troops at Forbend Keep," he says. "They'll intercept them. Other than that, I see no reason to change your previous orders, Majesty. If you must go to Brindelier, we have the ships and cygnets to distract them from your journey. In the meantime, we'll bolster the city, both with men and magic."

"Very well," Margy says, and just like that she's back to Queen again. I see the shift around her. Some of it is magic. How she makes herself seem a little older, a little taller and more imposing. A little more like her father, somehow. The rest of it, though, isn't magic at all. It's pure heart. "You have your orders, everyone. Finn, Azi, and Rian will remain with me. Everyone else is dismissed with my sincere gratitude. I pray that the next time we meet, it will be to celebrate our victory."

"Wait," Gaethon says thoughtfully. "Before we leave, I believe it would be wise, Azaeli, if you were to show all those gathered here the face of the Sorceress, Sybel."

Azi nods. She moves through the small crowd, looking into her palms. Everyone gathers around her, committing the Sorceress's image to memory.

"The Revenant who now contains the essence of our enemy, as Valenor explained, was ultimately created by this woman," Gaethon explains. "Should she be destroyed, there is a fair chance it will negate the magic, thereby weakening or even decimating the creature. Be certain you have your ward charms with you, for she is sure to be traveling with a powerful Mentalist by the name of Xantivus."

"Thank you, Master Gaethon," Margy says. "Admiral Hayse, Lord Zevlain, Twig shall send word to you both when we're prepared to move. Until then…"

She goes to the door and gives each of the subjects a personal farewell and a sincere wish for their victory as they go. Twig taps each of them on one shoulder and the other. The power that comes from him feels old and strong. Roots of trees gripping the earth. Huge trunks, thickened with bark, stretching up to the sky. The magic's like wards, but not really. These will last, I can tell. They'll stick and hold through even the fiercest battle. Between his power and the magic in the chalice, it's hard to imagine how we could possibly lose this fight.

Margy's family is the last to leave. Her mother and sister kiss her forehead, and they whisper to each other to stay safe. While they do, Vorance hands Finn something, and the guard tucks it away. The Prince of Sunteri glances through the mirror at me. Gives me a kind of apologetic salute. I cross my arms and look away as he ushers his wife and Queen Naelle out. With my healed eye, I investigate that scroll case. It's just papers inside. Nothing magical. Nothing unsafe.

Valenor's arm brushes my shoulder. I look up to see a film of white flash over his eyes. Peering closer, I see images playing out there. A swirling mass of black. A streak of green.

"The Keeper has returned to Elespen," he murmurs to me, patting my shoulder. "Well done, dear boy, well done."

"Now that everything is arranged, what was your idea to get me to Brindelier, Tib?" Margy asks, snapping my attention from the Muse.

She's close to the mirror, now. So close, I feel like I could touch her. I press my fingertips to the glass. On her side she does the same. Her eyes meet mine. I never thought one pair of eyes could hold so many emotions. Fear. Determination. Regret. Excitement. Hope. Something else. Something I don't dare to admit to myself. Not now. Not with everything that's going on. My heart races. I reach up and shove the hair out of my face. Scratch my nose. Do anything to try and disguise the hot feeling in my cheeks. To cover it up.

"The Dreaming," I say, tearing my eyes from her to look to Azi. She gives me a smile. The same kind of knowing smile Ki gave me when I talked to her about Margy. I shake my head slightly to clear it. Like the elves taught me, I take a deep breath and center myself. "Valenor can bring Margy to Brindelier though the Dreaming. He's done it before. Can't you?" I ask the Muse.

"Indeed, I can," Valenor says.

"That's a great idea!" Flitt chirps, pushing off from Azi's shoulder.

"Would it be like before?" Rian asks. "Would we have to be granted entry by the gatekeeper, or could you bring Her Majesty straight to the Wellspring?"

"It might be wise, while my sister is away, to arrive at the gates," Valenor replies. "The protections over Brindelier have been shifting ever so slowly, readying the kingdom for the battle to come. Even now, I feel its defenses strengthening."

"I would want them to see me, anyway," Margy says quietly. "We're fighting for them, and they for us. Although the danger would be greater, I want the people of Brindelier to know I'm there. I want to see them, too."

Behind her, Finn's eyes close slowly. I can tell he wants to protest, but a dutiful guard is seen and not heard. Azi puts a hand on Margy's shoulder.

"We'll be beside you, Majesty," she says.

"Margy," the queen grins up at her.

"Margy," Azi says, smiling back.

"When would you like to leave, Your Majesty?" Valenor asks.

"The earlier in the day we leave, the better," Rian advises. "We don't want to arrive too late and invite a battle closer to sunset or even worse, after dark."

"I believe once the offerings are in place, Azaeli and Rian shall be able to return you to Cerion quite quickly, should the need arise," Valenor says.

"Sure, because these things always go smoothly," I mutter. Margy chuckles.

"I agree," she says. "The sooner the better. We'll give Hayse and the elves a little time to get into place, and I would like to know what Saesa and Skalivar find out about that Sorcerer. Perhaps midmorning?"

Everyone agrees. After a quick farewell, the mirror's image fades, leaving me alone with Valenor.

"It seems you have been at this fight for quite a long time. Years, one might say," he says, looking down at me with that smile that always seems to be there. "And now, the conflict is about to reach its peak."

I don't know how to reply, so I just shrug.

"You have some time, and your sister has returned to Kanna's tavern," he tells me.

"Yeah?" I ask, glancing toward the door. It'd be good to see Ki again before things get rolling. "But, what about what's going on right now, between Eljarenae and Vorhadeniel? And what about Stellastera and that girl who pushed me out of the cyclone? And Kaso Viro, where's he been?"

"Tibreseli," he crouches low, fading slightly into the Dreaming. Puts a hand on my shoulder. His eyes change from white to brown when he peers into mine, the flashes of battle vanishing so I know he's not distracted by them. His cloak flaps gently around me. "It is not necessary for you to be everywhere, for everyone, at all times. You're quite a bright fellow. I'm certain you have learned that attempting to carry the world's weight on your shoulders only forces you to drag yourself into darkness. Trust in your friends and allies to do their own part. Go and have some breakfast with your sister. I shall meet you at the gate midmorning, with Margary, Azaeli, and Rian in my charge."

There's no magic in his words, but they have an effect on me almost like a spell could. Like Lisabella's peace. Like Mya's song. I know he's right. Relief spreads over me. Everyone's doing their part. Mine's done, for now. Until she gets here. I smile at him. Let out a long, deep breath.

"Thanks," I say, patting his arm. I step into the Half-Realm and he pulls me into a tight hug that would normally make me want to squirm away. This time, though, I allow it. My feet leave the floor, and he sets me down gently in front of the door of Ki's room in Kanna's before slowly drifting away.

Inside, I hear voices. Ki's. Efran's. I know better than to look through the wood, so I step out of the Half-Realm and knock.

"Don't answer it," Efran's muffled plead comes through the door.

"Stop," Ki laughs. "It might be important."

"This is important," Efran insists.

"Efran!" Ki squcals.

I huff and wrinkle my nose. Slump my shoulder against the door. Pound on it again, three more times.

"Ki!" I shout.

There's a thump, and Ki pulls the door open like she jumped across the room to get to it.

"Tib!" she gasps. With a quick glance over her shoulder, she tells Efran, "I'll be right back," and closes the door to join me in the hallway.

"You'll be right back?" I scowl.

"Won't I?" she asks, grinning, and pulls me into a hug.

"I don't know. They're stopping the festival. Preparing for what's next. It's going to be pretty intense, I think," I tell her under my breath. "Valenor sent me here to have breakfast and get some rest."

I pull free from her hug and look up at her, and she glances at the door again.

"I am pretty hungry," she says. I know what she's thinking. Efran doesn't know me. At least, he doesn't know I'm her brother. The two of them spent a couple days under the ruse of searching for me for the Bordas. Even got a hefty bounty for delivering me to them. From the worried look on her face, it's obvious she never did get around to telling Efran the truth.

"Yeah, he's probably hungry, too," I shrug. Think of what Valenor said. Now's not the time for secrets between allies. I get it, too.

I see how her face glows. How her eyes dance, just because she was with him. If she's anything like me, she can't help being so obvious about it. She was understanding of my feelings. I guess I have to tolerate him. "We should tell him about me, anyway, if he's going to stick around a while. I'll go get a table. Meet you downstairs."

I can feel her eyes on me all the way down the hallway. When I turn around to give her a questioning look, I find her gazing after me with a mix of confusion and pride.

"Hurry up," I say. "I'm half starved."

Chapter Forty-Two

RALLYING BRINDELIER
Tib

"So, you're telling me," Efran whispers, leaning across a heaping plate of sausages, "the kid's your brother? We duped the Bordas? The Bordas!"

He hisses the last of it and slumps against the high booth back. Stabs two sausages with his fork. Chews them, shaking his head. Gulps his ale.

"If they find out—" he says.

"They won't," Ki interrupts.

Efran grunts. Chomps on a biscuit. Declares with his mouth full, "You don't know the Bordas."

"It doesn't matter," I tell them. I check the curtain drawn across the booth. The wards we paid extra for are in place. No one in the crowded tavern can hear us. "Not right now. By noon, the Bordas and everyone else in this kingdom are going to have other things to worry about."

My eyes drift to the window. The streets are completely different today. Quiet. Nearly empty. Almost like it was when we arrived with the first offerings. The Festival is over. The magic forcing everyone to celebrate has been lifted. I wonder where they all went. Home, probably, to get some rest. The streets are still decorated, though. Colorful flags stretched on ribbons across the streets flap in the breeze. Banners of the rich houses of Brindelier wave from lamp posts. Both seem out of place against the sky, darkening with storm clouds.

Efran and Ki follow my gaze. He even stops stuffing his face, shockingly, and says, "Never saw anything like it."

"A storm cloud?" Ki asks.

"Not like that one."

Almost in response to him, thunder rumbles over us. The first drops of rain are plump and heavy. They splat against the window like pebbles. Then it really starts. A downpour so thick I can't even see the row of buildings across the street.

"Definitely not typical weather for Brindelier," Efran says, scooping a heaping spoonful of Kanna's cheesy egg scramble onto his plate.

Lightning flashes, and I narrow my eyes thoughtfully. He must think I'm brooding at him for some reason, so he scoops the rest of the eggs onto my plate.

"If something's coming, like you say, you gotta eat, kid. Seriously. Whatever it is could blow you over like a feather."

I scoff. Look from him to Ki in disbelief. She shrugs, plucks a slice of melon from her plate, and points to mine like she agrees with him.

"Anyway—" I start to say, but I'm interrupted by a shrill chiming sound that floods the tavern, drowning out the noise of the crowd.

"Loyal subjects of Brindelier," two voices boom in unison through the place, and I snap the curtain open expecting to see Pippa and Poe standing on a table or something, shouting at us.

They're not, though. Well, they are, sort of. Their image flashes above the bar, in a mirror hung where everyone can see it. Inside the glass, the twins stand side by side, dressed identically in over-sized silver and gold robes. Their fairies are tucked regally into their crowns.

It's hard to tell them apart, until I remember Poe's red eyes. They have a distracted look to them, like he'd rather be somewhere else. Behind them, three official-looking men in Mage robes dripping with sashes and medals stand rail-straight and serious.

Kanna leaves her cooking and rushes out to look up at the mirror, wiping her hands on her apron. Everyone else in the tavern goes completely silent. The only sound is the downpour of rain and the distant rumble of thunder outside, until the twins speak again in exact unison.

"It is with heartfelt gratitude and great appreciation that we address you on this darkening morning. Do not be alarmed by the storm or its portents, for we are a people of light, strength, and unimaginable power."

"That's creepy," I whisper across to Ki. Ethan's eyes go wide. He shakes his head urgently and points to the mirror while the twins continue.

"For over one hundred years we have slept in anticipation of this moment. Before the day is through, our beloved Wellspring shall once again be whole. Our kingdom will join once more with the world beyond, and our gates shall open.

We know what this means for our kingdom, and for you, our beloved people. We ask you to stand with us in the name of the Light, in the name of the Dawn, in honor of our father who fell and our returned mother, the queen, who now rises.

"We call upon our brethren, the fae, to strengthen us. We beg them to lend us their power and hope in this time, for the greatest challenge we face is not the enchantment of sleep or waking to a new world, but the preservation of the light, hope, and love our great kingdom holds dear.

"Queen Margary Plethore, suitor of the Dawn, arrives this morning to unite our kingdoms and stand with us against any evil which would dare rise against us. Welcome her as only you can. Rally with her, dear subjects, for we do not expect to enter this new era unchallenged. In our streets, from windows and on rooftops, stand together as we stand with you.

"Our long slumber and the celebrations which followed have prepared us for this moment. We are bolstered, we are united. We carry in our hearts the strength and spirit to triumph. We shall restore our fair kingdom to its former glory. We shall be as we once were, the center of power in the Known Lands. Our kingdom shall stand for peace, prosperity, knowledge, and magic. Ready yourselves, one and all, for today is the day of our greatest victory!"

The tavern erupts into cheers. Beyond the window, there's even more celebration. From other taverns across the way, and homes all around us, the rallying cry fills the city.

I turn away from the window and watch. The tavern crackles with energy. Kanna rushes back behind the counter. She clatters around for a bit there. In the meantime, everyone else is abuzz with excitement. Lots of the men who had been lazily enjoying their breakfast are now standing, clapping each other on the shoulders, arming themselves with weapons from packs that had lain dusty and unused for who knows how long.

It's not just them. There are fairies all over the place, diving and ducking and darting around. Bursts of magic flash all over the room. Mages who had been breakfasting together stand up, and several patrons gather around them, pulling out their purses. When they come away, they're decked in full battle gear: Armor, swords, bows, shields.

"Strengthening Squash Pie!" Kanna calls over the excitement, tossing a sliced pie onto one of her magic platters. "Clarifying Crescent rolls! Prowess pastries with cheese, of course! Or also fruit! Everyone eat up!"

She shuffles the food onto each tray like she's dealing a deck of cards. Back behind the counter, a huge pot stirs itself. She takes a handful of something out of the pocket of her apron and it glitters bright red as she tosses it into the pot.

"Accurate Carrot Soup is coming, too! Great for archers!" she calls over her shoulder, winking as she catches Ki's eye. "Don't crowd, you ruffians! There's plenty for everyone! Two silver extra for my boosting recipes! Pay the fae!"

A few more fairies shoot around the room, shouting at the crowd to pay their extra fee. Ki tosses a gold to one of them, and he comes back with a tray loaded down with soup, pie, pastries, and rolls.

"Does it work?" she asks Efran as she sips from a cup of the soup.

"'Course it works," he answers, digging into some pie. "You think my sister's running some kind of scam, here?"

I grab a Prowess Pastry and close my eyes, concentrating. The essence that seeps from it is plain as day. The magic it holds feels nimble. Quick. Precise. I allow the magic, and I take a bite. The light, flaky pastry crunches at first, then melts on my tongue with buttery sweetness. I finish it in two more bites and feel its magic charge through me like the tingle of Mevyn's warnings in my boots, but stronger.

"Wow," I whisper.

"I know," Ki says, her fingers twitching toward her bow. "We'd better go get ready."

We slide from the bench and weave our way through the excited crowd back to their room. While the two of them get their gear together, I start to pace.

"Efran," I ask uneasily as a thought suddenly comes to me, "how many of those mirrors are there? Does everyone in Brindelier have one?"

"Yeah, they're all over the city," Efran explains, hitching up his breastplate as Ki fastens the buckles. "Most taverns have 'em. Lots of—" he gasps and holds his breath. "Looser, Ki!"

"You're getting soft," Ki chuckles, knocks on the armor over his stomach, and shakes her head.

"I just had breakfast!" Efran protests while Ki loosens the buckle a notch. "Anyway, most of the more prominent houses have 'em. They're fairly easy to get."

"So, they probably know," I grumble. "Everyone knows the queen is coming. Everyone."

I clench my jaw hard. My fists curl into tight balls at my sides. I look out toward the city gate, where Margy will be arriving when the time comes. So much for keeping things quiet.

"I know you two've been busy getting rid of Sorcerers," I say, lowering my voice. "How many do you think are left?"

"Efran said he found a little nest yesterday, actually," Ki says, buckling her quiver around her waist.

"Yeah," Efran grins, watching my sister with the sort of appreciation he should probably save for when I'm not around. "It's on the way to the outer gate, actually. They're holed up in there like rabbits in a den. They're probably the last in the city. Just a few of 'em. Three, maybe four."

"We were about to go look into it before you showed up," Ki says. "What do you say, little brother? Are you up for a little Sorcerer hunt to get the blood flowing?"

"Maybe a short one." I grin. "If they're still there. They can leave, can't they? Teleport? Azi said that's how they use those coins. If they have a mirror like Kanna's and they heard the speech, they probably already left to warn the Dusk."

"Mm," Ki agrees. "They use the coins to come and go. Efran and I have done our best to destroy as many of the sigils throughout the city as we could find, but I'm sure there are a few we've missed."

"I know there's one where we're going," Efran says, hitching up his sword belt. "I couldn't get to it without them noticing, though. I'm not very sneaky." He shakes his arm to prove his point, and his chain mail sleeve jingles loudly.

"You have other talents," Ki grins, kissing him on the lips.

"Gross, Ki," I choke and roll my eyes. "Come on. We've got to see if they're still there. If not, we at least need to destroy the sigil to block them from coming back and bringing their friends with them."

On the way out of the tavern, a fairy stops us and offers a drying ward, which we all accept. Good thing, too. Outside, the rain is freezing. Pouring. Drenching. Even though the huge droplets splash on the magical shield set by the fairy, the downpour still makes it hard to hear anything, hard to see anything.

I have to use my healed eye to keep up with Efran, who moves through the streets at an impressive pace. It's obvious he knows his way through around the city. I'd never tell Ki, but I'm actually glad he's here to guide us.

The shift in the kingdom is bold and obvious. Despite the strange storm, Brindelier feels ready. Magic swirls from every single doorway, each spell cast by a different Mage. Wards. Look-aways. Strange battle magic that I can tell would injure any unwelcome visitor with all sorts of different hexes and dangerous energies.

I stretch my awareness to the sky, where the storm rages. It does feel similar to Elespen's fog, but not exactly the same. The clouds seem different. Annoyed, almost. I figure out why almost right away. The city, just above the rooftops, is cloaked with an enormous ward.

The storm stretches along it, searching for an opening, but there isn't any weak point. I crane my neck upward, watching the silent battle rage between clouds and wards, blinking with every raindrop that comes close to splashing my face only to hit my own ward and roll off.

The amount of magic it uses is overwhelming. The magic everywhere, actually, is incredible. I can feel it stretching out from the palace, from the tower that holds the Wellspring, winding through the city, powering every spell, every ward.

I'm so involved in detecting it that I crash right into Efran when he stops in front of me. My nose crunches against the back of his armor. Pain shoots across my face. Stars burst through my vision. Efran whirls to face me, clapping his hand over my mouth before I can yell out in pain. He and Ki duck into an archway where we crouch together.

"Are you all right?" he whispers, shoving his cloak under my aching nose.

"Wasn't watching," I sniffle, tasting blood. "Ugh. I wasn't watching where I was going." I pull a pink vial. Take a sip of it. Feel the bone and cartilage in my nose knit together. The pain fades. I close my eyes. Peer through my closed eyelid, past Ki and Efran who're still watching, concerned.

They don't see the shadow I see approaching. I draw a knife. There's no time to coat it. I remember the battle alongside the *sava*. I hope my hunch is right. I think of white. A white vial, a stripping serum. The magic of Kanna's pastry surges through me I flick my wrist, and my knife whistles between Ki and Efran's heads, landing with a satisfying *thunk* into the robes of the dark figure.

Ki and Efran jump to their feet, weapons drawn. They whirl to face the approaching threat, and I watch with satisfaction when glowing white energy bleeds from the Sorcerer. He screams and drops to his knees, and with two strides and a swing of his sword, Efran finishes him.

Hidden in the archway, I think of my dagger. I imagine it misty green, like I used at Cresten's dock, and draw it. The blade glows softly, the same way it would have if I had coated it myself. I sheath it, and think of it orange instead. My boots tingle softly. I draw it again, and this time, it's orange.

"Huh," I whisper. All I can think of is Stellastera. How I wished for my stuff back. She must have done something to it. My boots tingle again. No, some hunch reminds me. They've told me so many times. It's not the vials. It's me doing it.

"Here," I call to Ki tossing her my last white vial. She catches it and dips a few arrows into it before another Sorcerer emerges. He sees the first one crumpled on the ground. I grab a knife and fling it. Ki's arrow hits him before my knife does. The Sorcerer falls backwards.

Efran, who'd been charging with his sword raised, lets his arm drop. He turns to us in disappointment, and calls, "give a guy a chance, will ya?"

"Shh!" Ki warns, her bow aimed at the door.

Huddled in front of it, I see them. Two more Sorcerers, lurking. Watching. They don't realize I can see through their invisibility. One of them casts a spell. I step in front of Ki as it weaves through the sheets of rain. It licks out toward us, unnoticed by Ki or Efran. It's a searching spell. Looking for something. Not us. Something more important. My boots tingle a warning. Mevyn whispers in my ear. Urgent. Commanding.

"RUN!"

Ki hears it, too. She shoves me away. Screams at me to go. At first, I don't know why. Their magic can't touch me. Can't hurt me.

A sickening feeling pokes at my gut and I clap my hand over the pouch of my bandolier. My stomach lurches as I remember what's inside it. The offering. Why didn't I leave it in the palace? How dumb could I be to bring it out here?

I turn around. Take off down the alley. Behind me, I hear the splintering of wood. The whistle of arrows. Efran grunts. An unfamiliar voice screams. I step into the Half-Realm. Hide myself away. Grip the pouch protectively. Push my legs faster. I have no idea where I am. Where Efran brought us. I just run away. Run until something calls to me. A feeling. A light. A lure. Beauty. Kindness. Love.

"Margy," I whisper, pushing myself faster. It's her. I'm sure it is. I let her energy guide me. I trust my sister and Efran to keep those Sorcerers at bay.

The closer I get to her, the more the rain lets up. Near the gates of the city, in the main square, people mill around. They stand with their hands to the sky, pushing the rain upward and away, warding the storm with arches of light and warm sunshine.

Even though the sight of it is amazing, I don't let it distract me. I don't slow my pace. I speed toward the gate, where a thick crowd is gathered. They're all commoners, I think, but every one of them is dressed in elaborate battle gear. Almost all of it, I can tell, has been created with magic. I wonder if any of it'd hold up against a real sword.

Doesn't matter, I think to myself. Not now. I keep to the outskirts of the crowd, edging my way along it, still hidden in the Half-Realm. Squeeze between the throngs and the statues that line the gateway tunnel. Slide along the reinforced wood doors that open to the space beyond.

Finally, still hidden, I reach the gate. The grassy space between the city wall and the crowd here to greet Margy is empty. I feel the borders, the magic at the end of the kingdom, there not only to keep others out, but to keep the people of Brindelier in.

The scene I'm met with is like a picture from a story book. Queen Margy stands at the edge of the grassy landing. Six floating ships are docked behind her, bobbing gently. Azi and Rian stand at her right side, Finn at her left. The warriors' armor gleams in the prisms of Flitt's light. Twig seems a little larger than usual, perched in the vines that wind across Margy's shoulder. A thick barrier of wards protects the group of them. I can both see them and feel their strength, even from here.

From the nearest ship, Master Keyes scrambles out onto the grass. He rushes to Margy, looking slightly green from his journey. As he reaches her, two cygnets land on the edge of the lawn. All around me, people gasp at the sight of them. In the distance, Opal the dragon, at full size, loops lazily in the sky. I squint to see if Saesa is with him, but the dragon is too far away, and too quick.

"Make way!" someone calls from the crowd behind me. The instruction echoes through them, and the top of an elegant canopy bobs closer.

With my healed eye, I peer through the thick crowd and see Princess Pippa and those same three Mages from the mirror walking beneath it. Another man is with her, dressed in a gaudy bright green tunic and purple hose. Everything else including his cloak and his shoes are gold. I wonder quickly where Poe is, but push the thought aside as the canopy comes to a halt right at the edge of the border.

Before the queen and princess can greet each other, I race to Margy's side, allowing the wards to protect me, too. Undetected by the others, I slip in between her and Finn on Twig's side, and lean close to her.

"I'm here," I whisper. A soft breeze drifts past us, and I breathe in the familiar scent of sea air and green leaves that wafts from her.

Margy takes a slight, secret step closer to me. Her hand reaches quietly in my direction. Her gloved fingers graze mine, leaving a trail of warmth where they touch me. She lets out a sigh so soft I'm sure I'm the only one who hears it.

I want to scoop her into my arms. To pull her away from all this and leave it. Again, what Master Keyes said goes over and over in my head. Marriage or not. Marriage or not.

"Queen Margary Plethore of Cerion," a crier beneath the canopy announces, and the city erupts in cheers.

"Princess Pippaveletti Emhryck of Brindelier," he announces, and the crowd cheers again.

I move closer to Margy until our arms touch. With one hand covering my pouch and the other still grazing hers, I scan the gathered crowd, looking for anything out of place. There's so much magic, it's hard to see anything.

I can feel something off, though. A patch of dark among the light. A sinister force, quiet. Patient. A brighter force pulls at me. Something Azi's holding shines like a beacon. Offerings. Hywilkin. Ceras'lain. I glance over my shoulder at the elves, who have dismounted to join us.

Despite the wards around the group, I can't help but feel uneasy as we make our way closer to the others under the canopy. The guard at the gate post lets us enter without any fuss. Pippa reaches to greet Margy with a hug. I peer around at the watching crowd, positive that any moment, some attack will come. Some threat, waiting to stop us.

"Where is Poe?" Margy asks the princess at a whisper. I try not to let her question disappoint me. I'm actually curious, too.

"Waiting at the Wellspring," Pippa replies quietly. "Something's happened. We must hurry."

"Proceed," Pippa calls to the others, and we move together as a group beneath the canopy. The Mages behind us raise their hands to the sky as we go, pushing up those golden wards, keeping our path dry.

Our pace is way too slow. Even though it's raining, even though the darkness hovers past the wards, people crowd the streets. They surge close, hoping to see. To glimpse Queen Margary. Princess Pippa. The Champions of Light. The great Mages of Brindelier.

When we pass the alley where I left Ki and Efran, I see my sister perched on his shoulders, watching for us. I want to call out to her, to tell her I'm safe. But I don't want to reveal myself.

To my shock, I watch as she draws back her bowstring. She aims it in our direction, closing one eye to get a sure shot. Her white-tipped arrow flies past us. It whistles over the canopy and the dome of wards protecting us and strikes someone on a landing opposite the alley.

The figure plummets from the balcony and hits the ground with a sickening thud. The nearby crowd shrieks and moves away. The procession stops.

Two guards break away from our group to investigate the lifeless figure. One of them swipes his hand to the side, and the attacker levitates limply from the ground. The other guard comes back with a quiver of arrows dripping black. He stands just outside of the wards, unable to enter carrying the wretched things.

"An assassin, Highness," he declares.

Pippa's eyes go wide and dart to the other side, where Ki has climbed down from Efran's shoulders.

"Who shot the heroic arrow?" she calls. "Come forward."

The crowd parts, allowing my sister through. She's got Efran's hand in hers, and he seems a little reluctant to be pulled along behind her.

Before Margy can see her face, Ki ducks her head and drops to her knee in a low bow.

"What is your name, good archer?" Pippa asks.

"Ki, your Highness, and this is my partner, Efran."

I tear my gaze from the two of them to see Azi and Rian exchange glances of disbelief. Neither of them says anything, though.

"Rise, Ki and Efran," Pippa says. "For your honorable actions, you shall take your place with our procession. We ask you to keep your keen archer's eye until we reach the palace."

Ki stands up. She keeps her head low, though. Turns her face away from Margy. Margy looks at her with slight curiosity, but also with gratitude.

Just beyond the canopy, Valenor's cloak swishes in a flash of blue sky. His face emerges beside my sister's, and he winks at me. He's here. Ki's here. I'm not alone. My heart races as we start walking again. I glance behind us, watching my sister and Efran file in at the back edge of the procession.

"Well, that's an interesting turn of events," Rian pushes to Azi.

"Do you think Margy will realize who she is?" Azi asks.

"Maybe not," Flitt replies. *"She's changed an awful lot since she was Viala."*

"I wonder if Tib's with her, too," Azi pushes.

"He is," Twig replies. *"He's been walking next to Margy since we got here. And Margy knows about Ki and Viala. I told her that ages ago."*

"Does she know about Tib and Ki, though?" Azi asks with concern.

"I haven't told her that," Twig pushes. *"That's his secret to tell."*

I glance at Twig, nestled in the leafy shoulder of Margy's gown, and can't decide whether I want to strangle him for keeping that secret, or thank him.

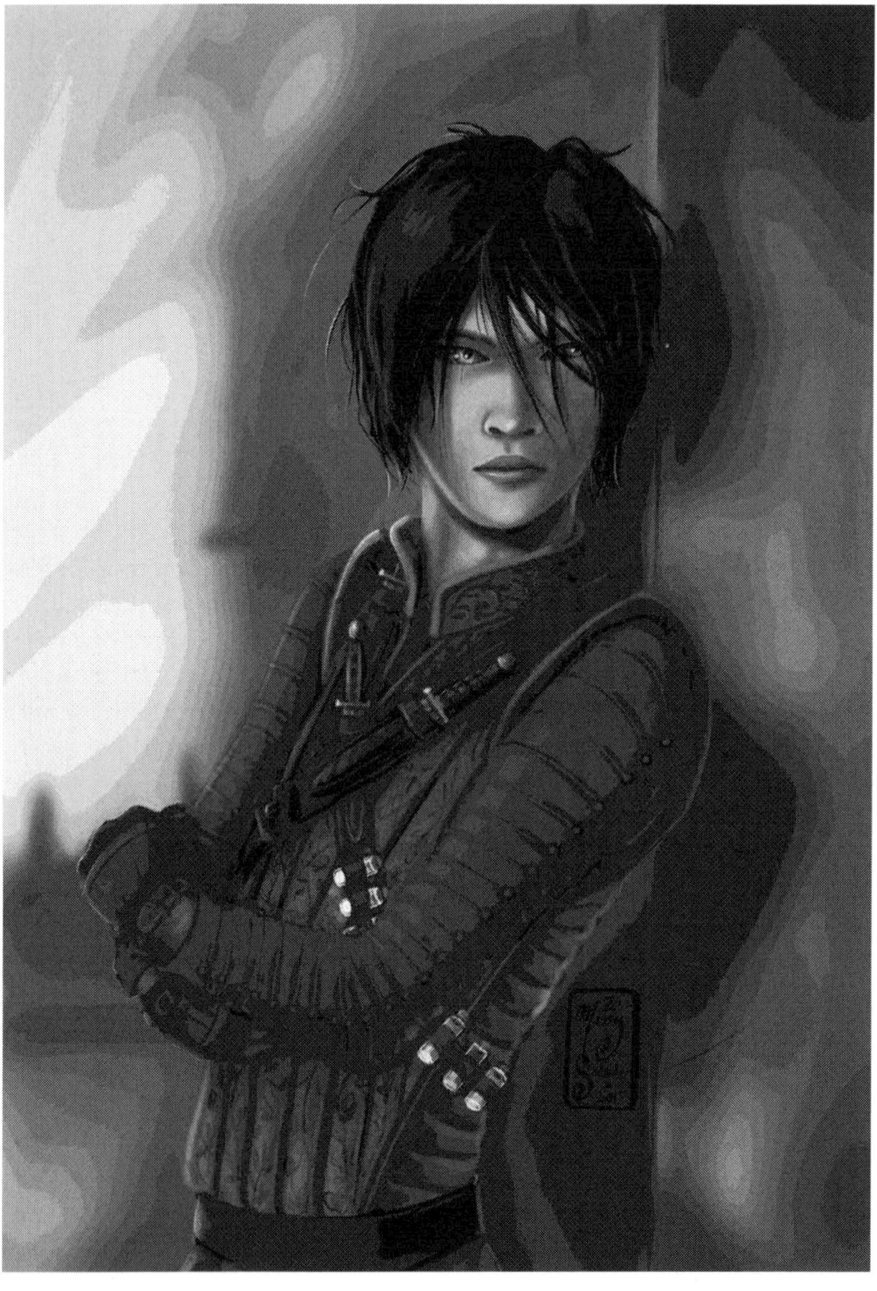

Chapter Forty-Three

ARCANE CHAMPION
Celli

Frozen tendrils of the powerful cyclone slash at my face, whipping my skin. The Muse of Light holds my right wrist firmly, pulling me from the darkness which yanks at my left. I know if Eljarenae were to let go, I'd be lost to shadow. I'd become a tool of the Void forever. I can feel Diovicus's desire for me, spun together with the darkness of the Void. Of the enemy. I force myself to focus on channeling their wicked darkness into light, even though it feels like my body will be torn in half from the force between the two sides.

"Use me," I scream again to Eljarenae as pain spikes through me. If I'm going to die, I want to have done something good with my life. Just one thing.

"Celli, you are not an object to be used," Eljarenae replies, a hint of sadness in her gentle voice, which rises above the torrent with little effort on her part. "You are a person, worthy, as all are, of love and freedom."

She folds her arms around me, tucking me into her light, and I lean into her.

"She was mine, and will be mine," Diovicus's voice roars from the depths of darkness. My left arm twists back, wrenching painfully.

Flashes of a scene unfold around me. Horses thunder through a quiet village. Cerion's crest is trampled into mud. The moon is setting, the fires are embers. A fog of darkness covers the ground, seeping under cracks of doors and into open windows. People cough. Some scream. They can't escape the cloud, though. It overcomes them. The poison it holds snuffs them out. The armies which follow crush everything in their path, burning and pillaging, destroying for no reason but to obliterate and terrify.

This is the army Diovicus showed me through the Void, when he claimed my eyes for his own. At the time, I was inspired by it. I didn't see how anyone could be the victor over such a force. Now I know differently. I look to the flames for light to empower me. My left hand, still wrenched behind my back by my enemy, draws in his powerful darkness, siphoning it. A figure steps out of one of the houses. Behind her, a farmer and his wife, gaunt and wasted, stand blankly in the doorway. I understand what she's done. The poison kills them, and she brings them back as mindless servants to do her bidding. Repulsed, I turn my fury toward the Necromancer. Her face is one I'll never forget.

"Sybel," I hiss. I unleash the light in a blast of white heat that strikes the wretched woman with a force that throws her backward into the house. The energy bursts into flames, and within its walls, Sybel screams in pain. Several Sorcerers rush in after her. Among them are healers, too. This won't have killed her, I know, but Diovicus's bellow of rage diverts me. He twists my arm further, and I snap back into awareness of my body again. His surroundings are closed off to me, his presence smaller now. With a terrible, final crack, I'm released.

"My Champion," Stellastera calls soothingly as the grip of darkness weakens. "Stay with me."

I don't know why she says it. It doesn't make sense. I'm barely aware of anything but light and dark. Dark into my left hand, light out of my right. It spills through me like sand through a sieve. He's gone, but my arm is still heavy. It hangs limply at my side, and yet it keeps doing its work. My head swims with the power that courses through me. There's no room for thought or understanding.

"Take her away from this place, Elja," Stellastera's voice is distant and faint.

I try to protest. My Lady's anguished request makes me more aware. All around me, the nocturnal creatures of the jungle screech and cry. I'm confused by the sounds. How was I just in a village in Cerion, and now I'm in the jungle again?

It barely seems worth wasting a thought on. There's still so much darkness. I have work to do. I try harder, pulling the shadows to me, pushing the light out, cleansing the vast curtain that has fallen on this land.

"Enough, Champion," Eljarenae whispers.

"But I'm not finished," I protest. "You said I'm worthy of freedom. Let me be free to choose. Let me cleanse this darkness."

"There shall be nothing left of you if you choose to remain here. Close your eyes. Come."

Slowly, strangely, my eyes drift to my right hand. Light continues to spill from it, and my fingers move when I will them to, but it doesn't look at all like my hand as I remember it. Now, it's a wisp of a thing, translucent and fading, like the glassy wings of a fairy.

"Nothing left…" I repeat Eljarenae's warning at a whisper. The sight puzzles me and thrills me all at once. I feel a change in me, strange and wonderful. I feel like my heart would be racing, but it's too taken up by the flow of arcane to even exist. I gaze around me, catching glimpses of the broad green leaves of exotic jungle trees and brush. The sky above us is just beginning to brighten, the stars are fading. Morning is near. It doesn't seem as though I've been here so long.

The more I think about these things, the jungle, the sky, time, and my place in it all, the more solid I feel. My mind becomes clearer. The flow of magic fades, and the pain in my arm grows sharper.

"Celli," Eljarenae says with concern.

"Yes," I reply, "Yes, let's go."

The Muse's light surges around me, carrying me off. I drift on white wings, ferried into the purest sunlight. She closes my left hand and rests my fist on my chest. The pain surges, then grows distant and unimportant. I focus instead on the pleasant sensation of magic all around me, inside and out. The delicious buzz of it soothes me. I close my eyes, I don't know for how long.

I'm passed from one embrace to another, and know that My Lady, Stellastera, has taken hold of me. I feel the shift around me from light to true balance. In My Lady's embrace, I'm aware of her reach. I feel battles of magic raging across the lands. When I really focus on her, I can see them as she does, spanning across vast countries to pinpoint our enemies.

Cerion's troops have met with the Dusk, past the village where I encountered Diovicus. In the light of early morning, the Mages of Cerion clash against the forces of darkness with unfathomable power. Though the Dusk's numbers are vastly greater, Cerion's force presses them back. My Lady drifts away from them with a sense that Cerion will likely stand its ground.

In Elespen, the scene is far different. The darkness I had worked to filter has dwindled to a small cloud that lingers weakly in the depths of the jungle. As she carries me through her realm, My Lady opens the way for the people of Elespen who had taken shelter here. They flood into the streets of Cresten, carrying the hope of Eljarenae with them, readying themselves to rally with the Dawn.

Ships sail from docks. Riders of strange creatures thunder through the jungle. A temple rises from ruins, sparkling with gold and green.

Her thoughts flick elsewhere, to Ceras'lain, where the elves of the White Line on their cygnets lift off from a vast wall of white, bows readied, Mages warded. Their formation surges northward, to the Main Crossroads of Cerion.

Far to the north, an enchanted scene unfolds. Hywilkin. I feel the pull toward it as their own magic spills down the great mountain of Kerevorna, charging through battalions of faefolk who charge across snowy tundra toward the sea. Quills rustle, manes blow fiercely in the wind. Scales of dragons sparkle under the light of the rising sun. Waves crash upon the rocky shoreline. Mermaid tails flick and splash in the surf.

An enormous pillar of water shoots toward the sky. Yellow and teal fins flash beneath the surface, and a glorious sea serpent breaches the waves. It rears up and splashes down, and the pillar thickens to ice and plunges to its side like a fallen tree. My Lady's awareness presses nearer. Within the ice, I feel a sense of earth. Of rocks and roots and soil. A statue of a woman.

I feel the pulse of darkness that charges through My Lady. Revenge. Anger.

"What's happening?" I whisper. "Who is that?"

She snaps her attention away from the scene and focuses on me instead.

"The Muse of the Sea," she says, her dark feelings fading, "has captured the Muse of Earth."

"What does that mean?" I ask.

"It means it is now four against one in favor of the Dawn, as far as Muses go. Five, perhaps, if my sister Earth is capable of redemption."

"Muses?" I ask, my thoughts jumbled and confused.

"It is not your concern, my dear Champion," she whispers gently. "Rest now. Be comforted by the knowledge that you have done more than your part. I am proud of you."

Proud of you. The words fill me with such a wonderful contentment that I find myself worrying I'm held under yet another spell. No, I'm sure that isn't it. I'm well aware of what it feels like to be held in thrall. I trust My Lady would never do that to me. What Quenson did was evil. Deceptive. Unforgivable. These feelings are true and real. She is my teacher, and I her student. I've learned well, and her pride makes my heart soar.

We enter Brindelier, which feels very different than it did when we left it. It's no longer jovial and merry. Instead there's a buzz of excitement and preparedness. My Lady floats between storm cloud and rainy streets, watching over the kingdom as it makes itself ready for what's coming.

"What is coming?" I wonder aloud. "Are they coming here? That force? Diovicus? The Void?"

"The darkness has a name, my Champion," My Lady explains. "It is my brother, Vorhadeniel. Muse of Darkness."

I think of moments that seem like ages ago, when I walked in the presence of the Void, when it saw all of me and stole away everything I was. I try to remember his presence there, but they must have been so tangled up together they were indiscernible from one another.

"Rest," My lady insists again as we enter the tower of the Wellspring. Its welcome energy seems to be just what I need. It fills me to the brim, soothing me. "You must rest and allow healing."

She sets me onto soft grass in the courtyard beyond the pool. My head rests on a satiny pillow. Someone speaks, and My Lady answers him in whispers. I don't hear what or know who. My body is too spent and too desperate for the perfect, balanced energy that spills into it from the pool. I try to open my eyes, but the lids are too heavy. My injuries and weakness, once distant and unimportant, surge through me in waves of pain and exhaustion.

Someone strokes my cheek. Poe. My arms and legs shake. Pins and needles prickle me from my toes to the crown of my head. My breath comes in rapid gasps. All of it is strangely separate from me, though. I feel like I'm two beings, the body and the Siphon.

"What's happening to her?" his voice is thick with emotion. Fear, and sorrow.

"She did too much, too quickly," My Lady replies.

"I tried to stop her," he cries. "Mother, please, do something!"

"My child," she says softly, "there is nothing to be done but wait and allow what's to happen to play out."

"Your Highness," a third voice interrupts them. "It is time. The queen has arrived."

"I'm not leaving her," Poe says firmly. "Pippa can go."

"Your Highness, it would be quite—"

"I said I'm staying here, Thalin!" Poe shouts.

"It's all right," Pippa's voice echoes from nearby. Until now, she'd been silent. I didn't even realize she was here. "I can greet Her Majesty."

"Sweet girl," My Lady says. "I shall watch over your procession."

"Come, Alex," Pippa calls.

Her words make it final. I feel her presence move away. The Princess's heels click on the stone walkway. The gate closes quietly.

"Do you want me to stay?" yet another voice asks. Aliandra, Poe's faedin.

"Watch the Wellspring, Ali," Poe whispers.

"All right," Ali says quietly. I feel her leave us, too.

"Celli," Poe whispers. His fingers graze my forehead. I can feel his quick pulse through them, charged with magic and warmth. Pink light tingles behind my eyelids, giving me the strength to open them.

The relief on Poe's face as he gazes down at me is enough to heal me a hundred times over. His deep blue eyes are like Wellsprings of their own, filled with light and hope. He lifts my hand to press it to his cheek, and I'm astonished by what I see. My fingers, white as marble, catch the light of the Wellspring in glittering flecks of gold. With great effort, I raise my other hand to look at it and find it black as coal, with specks of silver. As stony as they look, I can still feel his soft cheek, his gentle hand.

"What's happening to me?" I whisper, peering into his eyes to find my reflection. My face hasn't changed. It's as it was, pale and soft, framed with blond hair.

"Mother said you should rest," he replies. He gathers me into his arms and I close my eyes and drop my head to his shoulder.

My thoughts drift away from here, to places I've been and things I've seen. Oddly, they end up in Hywilkin again. This time, the memory is of me standing before the Guardian of Kerevorna, letting him burn the last of Quenson's blood from me. I think of how he'd drawn in the darkness and let out the light much like I can do now. My palms tingle where the energy had been channeled. My forehead does, too. I think of the spires outside of the palace, the colorful images of fanciful creatures. I think of the people of Brindelier, readying for battle.

The thoughts seem so random and disjointed to me, but somehow, they make sense. My power, my hands. The Wellspring's magic drifts over me, and I don't need to look to know it's blanketing both me and Poe in glittering dust.

I drift to sleep for a short while, and I wake to Poe whispering my name. I feel how close his face is to mine before I even open my eyes. His breath is hot on my cheek. His heart pounds against my shoulder. I turn my head slightly and look up at him, into eyes filled with confused determination.

"They're nearly here," he whispers. "I don't know what will happen when they arrive, but I need to tell you something."

My breath catches. My voice fails me. I can only nod.

"I don't love her," he confesses. "She's so sweet and kind, I really thought I could. I tried to. But I never felt around her the way I do…"

His voice drifts off. He draws me close. I close my eyes. His lips graze mine, soft and sweet. As we kiss, my awareness shifts. The two fractured parts of me become whole again. His kiss unites me with a deeper meaning, a truth that was hidden from me until now.

I see his past, so many years ago, I feel his pain. I share his love for his sister and his closeness to her. I know his fear of the darkness, I understand his responsibilities to Brindelier.

All the magic, all the enchantments of his lifetime filter through me one at a time. I feel the conflict between day and night, between brother and sister, between darkness and light. I watch their Faedins, the Keepers, as they wearily accept their fate, to watch over the Wellspring without the aid of its queen, to keep her children safe from evil. To live torn apart, two halves of something that should be whole.

I feel the twins' pain at the loss of their parents. I see the wedge that was driven by their duties, Alex and Pippa to watch by night and Ali and Poe to watch by day. I feel Poe's suffering when he knew his sister was beginning to fall to darkness. I feel the weight of that, of his need to keep her safe, of his loss of any guidance or true protection from such a force. Of their resignation to enchant the kingdom they loved, to keep it safe and hidden.

I've felt that pain, that helplessness, myself. I know it. I have never known this, though. This love, true and perfect. It makes me ache to keep him safe, to soothe him and protect him and tell him he'll never have to be afraid again. I want to be close to him like this, a part of his heart, forever. His pain flows through me as we kiss, and I draw it in and spill out comfort through my hand at the nape of his neck.

We stay this way until we hear the gate swing open, announcing the arrival of the procession to the Wellspring. My Lady's instruction settles over us: *"Poe, to the throne. Celli, remain where you are."*

My prince leaves me reluctantly, letting my hand slip from his as the distance grows between us. We watch each other until his blue eyes finally disappear behind the lush garden within. When I'm alone, I sink onto a chaise with my hand pressed to my racing heart, straining to hear what's happening inside.

Chapter Forty-Four

Silver and Gold
Azi

"I hope Shush hurries up," Flitt pushes to us as we reach the palace at a painfully slow pace. With Brindelier's strong wards blocking the rain, the whole kingdom seems to have come out to view the procession. *"He said he'd be just behind me, and that was hours ago. I don't want him to miss this!"*

I watch the crowd waiting at the palace gates with great caution, ready to draw Mercy at the sight of anything out of place. That assassin was the only resistance we've met so far, but the prospect of more Blackheart out there somewhere has me on edge, even with the thick wards protecting the canopy.

My gaze comes to rest on Rian, who's also staring out toward the palace, though the corner of his mouth is turned up in a slight smirk.

"What are you grinning at?" I push to him curiously.

"Let's just say I don't envy him right now," he says.

"Who?"

"Shush."

"What's he doing?" I ask.

"It's hard to tell," Rian pushes. *"He's so far away. But whatever it is, it's awkward."*

"Yeah, good job for inspiring him by sticking your face to Azi so much," Flitt pushes, rolling her eyes. *"That fae has always been terrible when it comes to timing. And apologies, obviously."*

"Of all the fairies in Kythshire, though, why her?" Rian pushes.

"Oh, those two have a history," Flitt waves her hand dismissively. *"I told you that a long time ago."*

"Who?" I ask, still lost.

"Ember!" Flitt replies. *"Keep up, Azi, for feathers' sake!"*

"Oh," I groan and fight to keep from rolling my eyes. Ember has never been my favorite fairy. I don't know what she and Shush could possibly have in common, or why he'd bother with her now, when so much else is at stake.

The crowd beside the canopy kneels before the princess and Queen Margy, and Rian chuckles.

"You do realize," I remind him as a few of the subjects glance at my beloved Mage with a puzzled look, *"they don't know you're talking to fairies in your head. They think you're smirking and laughing at them, Rian."*

Rian's expression goes slack, and for the rest of our walk he stays as serious and respectable as any Mage should be. We turn once we're through the palace gates, and Margy and Pippa wave to the throngs who crowd as close as the gate guards will allow.

"You don't think he'll bring her, too?" I ask Flitt, cringing.

"He won't," Rian replies, biting his lips to keep from laughing.

"What's going on?" I ask him.

"Tell you later," he says, going serious again.

We walk along the perfectly manicured lawns, lined by the same row of guards in shining armor that was here the first time we came to Brindelier. Their focus and discipline is uncanny, just as it was then. They could be statues, or suits. I can tell, though, there are men in there. I can feel their minds, bright and alert, within the armor.

The bearers of the canopy step aside once we reach the open doors of the palace, and when Keyes and Thalin usher us inside, the doors close slowly behind Zevlain and Julini, the last two in the procession. Pippa pauses and turns to look over her shoulder at the closed doors.

"You're closing the doors?" she asks the Mages who stand between her and the exit. She seems sincerely shocked at the idea of it. "Are you certain that's necessary?"

"Quite, your Highness," the one in the center says as the other two cast wards of protection over the door. "Once the basins are filled and the All Source restored, we have no way of knowing what manner of resistance we shall be met with."

Pippa sighs and nods uneasily, then turns back toward the great foyer. I follow her gaze and step closer to Rian, in awe of the sight before us. The last time we were here, these polished halls were filled with soft furniture and sleeping courtiers. This time, the walls are lined with soldiers standing shoulder-to-shoulder. Each one has on his shoulder a silver or gold creature, either fairy or imp, perched like a gargoyle.

Margy gasps at the gathered force and takes a step forward. Finn moves with her on her left side, I on her right.

"It's so strange to see the palace this way," Pippa says with a hint of apprehension. "Prepared for battle. Where is everyone else, Alex?"

The golden fairy pushes off from her crown and does a mid-air loop to face her.

"The guests are in the breakfast hall, Princess, preparing for what's to come. Our Mages are at the parapets. The council waits in the planning room. Most courtiers have returned home, but others remain here, barricaded in their chambers."

"And Poe?" Pippa asks.

"Where you left him, Highness," Alex replies.

"Very well," Pippa says, wringing her hands. "I'm not sure what happens next..." she looks to Thalin first, then to Keyes.

"I imagine it is time for the suitor to do what she came to do," Keyes says. He bows, but Rian and I don't miss the bitter tone to his voice.

"Very well," Pippa says, still sounding unsure. "If you're ready, Your Majesty..."

"Princess," Margy says with a smile, "our kingdoms are about to be united. We don't need to be so formal."

"Of course," Pippa says a little awkwardly.

"Have you brought all three offerings, Your Majesty?" one of the Mages asks Margy.

"Yes," she replies. "Sir Hammerfel has them."

She nods toward me, and I press my hand to my chest and bow to the Mage. I don't know why she implies I have all three, but I don't correct her, especially not after I see she and Twig exchange a knowing glance.

"Excellent," Pippa says. "Alex will lead the way."

Alex looks from one of us to the other, pausing only once to wink at Flitt. At my ear, she giggles softly.

"Right," Alex says with a serious tone. "Until the Wellspring is opened to all, it must remain guarded. So, only a few of you are permitted to enter. Her Majesty, Her Highness, Twinkles, Stinky, Sparky, and of course, Twiggish and Flitter, can follow me," he says. "The rest of you will be shown to the breakfast hall where you can remain alert to any attacks."

"Oh!" Flitt laughs flirtatiously with Alex, "I forgot all about that! Twinkles, that's you Azi, remember? Rian is Stinky of course, and Tib is Sparky, though Alex probably shouldn't have mentioned him by name since he's still hiding."

"No point in that anymore, I guess," Tib grumbles, stepping out of the Half-Realm.

"Tib! Have you been there the whole time?" Pippa exclaims, glancing warily at the guards and the Mages. "How clever of you."

A few in the gathering murmur to each other in surprise, and Tib gives the princess a bow.

"I figured it'd be better if I stayed hiding," he says, shrugging.

"Well, then," Thalin clears his throat, looking slightly embarrassed by the fact that no one seemed to have detected the Dreamstalker.

"No worries, Thalin," Valenor's voice echoes beside him, and the Muse of Dreaming emerges from the empty air beside the man. "Tib's ability to hide is quite rare, I assure you. No one else has slipped your Mages' detections."

At his appearance, everyone in the room bends a knee. Even Margy. Even Pippa and every single guard lining the hall.

"My Lord Valenor," Master Keyes breathes, his face red with surprise. "You are most welcome here."

"Uncle!" Pippa grins, and Valenor pats her shoulder.

"Much has happened," the Muse declares. "There is little time to waste. My sister awaits us at the Source."

"Right," Tib says impatiently. "Can we go?"

We split into two groups, with those heading to the Wellspring in one, and those going to breakfast in the other. As we file past the row of gleaming guards and the door to the breakfast hall swings open, a call echoes from inside.

"Azaeli!"

"Kenrick!" I cry and rush toward him.

"I had hoped I'd see you before you went up!" he grins, taking my hand. The group heading to the Wellspring pauses to wait for me.

Kenrick's eyes twinkle with pride as they meet mine, and he offers me a wide smile. "I saw what you did," he says, winking, and Stellastera's face flashes between us.

"I couldn't have, without you," I reply with a grin. "What are you doing in Brindelier?"

"I came along from Cerion with the prince," he explains. When his eyes meet mine again, a quick flash of images leaps between us, showing me exactly what he's been up to. "But we'll have time for all that later. I'll leave you to the matter at hand, then."

The images are faces. Some of them I've seen, others are unfamiliar. One is quite prominent, though: Master Keyes. The faces come with a sense of warning, a foreboding feeling that tells me not to trust.

"Tell me, Your Highness," Rian says randomly to Pippa, interrupting our reunion. "Blood magic is quite illegal in Cerion. Is it the same here in Brindelier?"

"Oh yes, quite," Pippa replies, wide-eyed.

Rian narrows his eyes at Efran, who shifts uncomfortably under his glare. I'm confused, until Councilman Borda Keyes pops up from behind Efran. With a look of shock, Keyes opens his hand and allows the bloodied corner of Efran's cloak to drop.

"Master Borda," Efran says, hiding his bitter tone with a cordial bow to Keyes. He flicks his cloak away from the man and takes a wary step closer to Ki, whose hand rests lightly on her bow.

"That's Councilman Borda *Keyes*," Keyes corrects him. The two glare at each other until Efran looks away, obviously intimidated.

"Been in a fight today, Efran?" Rian asks casually. He strolls to Efran, who nods his head.

"Always work to be done," he says, his brow knit in confusion.

Rian gestures to Efran's cloak, and it flutters into his hand. He traces his finger over the stain of blood on the corner of it, and turns to look at Tib.

"That's mine," Tib says with a scowl. "I busted my nose."

Rian turns to Keyes, who takes a few steps back. With a swish of Rian's hand, the blood is cleared from the cloak and it tumbles down, fresh and clean. Rian flicks his finger at Keyes, and a vial flies from the man's vest into Rian's hand. When he holds it up to the light, red-brown flakes tumble to the bottom of the glass.

"Keyes," Pippa whispers, "what is the meaning of this?"

"I thought perhaps," Keyes stutters. "W-we all thought…" He backs toward the elves, who stand with their arms crossed over their chest, refusing to let him go further. Brindelier's Mages scowl, shaking their heads in denial.

"He thought he could use it," Kenrick explains. "He thought he might change the Queen's heart, or if he could not do that, he had even more sinister thoughts. Did you not, Keyes?"

"The people expect a marriage," Keyes says firmly. "I was doing what must be done for our kingdom. There are those who plot against this joining, Your Majesty. Those in my own family, whom I stand against. They have spoken to the boy who would come between this union. He agreed to put himself between you and the prince." Keyes points to Tib, who glowers darkly at the man.

"Tib would never," Margy says firmly.

"Nor would we," one of the Mages booms. "We had no hand in this, and had we known, we would have ended it immediately."

"You invite darkness, Keyes," Pippa declares quietly. She nods at the Mage, and he thrusts his hand forward, releasing a pink cloud that settles over Keyes. The man slumps to the floor, asleep.

Silence falls over the foyer. Margy looks from Pippa to Tib, to Efran and finally Rian.

"Thank you," Margy says to Rian, who bows. When he straightens, she turns to Alex. "Avoiding any further delay, please show us to the Wellspring."

As if to emphasize her stance in the matter, Margy steps closer to Tib, who offers her his arm. Alex glances between the two of them, then drifts in front of Pippa to guide us to the winding staircase leading to the Allsource.

Kenrick's images play out in my mind as we take to the winding staircase. I see everything that has happened since he arrived in the palace. He shows me Celli: his discovery of her power, her apparent attraction to Poe, and his to her. He shows me her past and the moments of redemption which followed, leading her to Stellastera.

I peer across Margy to Tib, who has shown me memories of the girl more than once, and none of them good ones. He catches my eye, and I smile at him and look away, up to the gilded gateway that leads to the Wellspring. Hopefully, her presence won't complicate things.

"Now," Alex says, bobbing in front of the gate. "There's a certain way this must be done. The prince and princess will take their thrones before the pool. Once they're in place, you can place the offerings. The Champions of Light will place theirs, and Your Majesty, yours should be the last one."

"Does it matter who has which one? We have Elespen, Hywilkin, and Ceras'lain," Margy says.

"Nope!" Alex replies, and darts off into the atrium.

The gate swings open, and I breathe in the rich aromas of earth and leaves as we step into the garden. Rian takes my hand as we walk along the polished stones that wind among huge fronds of fern and gorgeous roses and other fragrant blossoms. The garden seems to have grown much lusher since the last time we visited it, and the air is much thicker with magic than it had been. It feels like a tiny piece of Kythshire, yet the magic here is deeper and more varied.

"Made it!" Shush whispers breathlessly in Rian's ear as the greenery opens up to the glittering pool at the center of the garden.

"Shush!" Flitt and Twig squeak, and the three join together in the usual spinning greeting.

Once they finish twirling and giggling, they settle back into place: Flitt into my pauldron, Shush at Rian's shoulder, and Twig at Margy's. They settle into silence, and a feeling of solemnity comes over the group of us. My heart races as I look to Margy, whose eyes dance with excitement. This is the moment we've all fought for. Glory will go to the Dawn.

Last time we were here, the pool was much lower. There was little sound except for the skittering of creatures and the occasional bird cry from somewhere deep inside the garden canopy. This time, the half-filled pool is lively and bright. Its sparkling light dances on the greenery which hangs over the edges of the pool. The trickle of liquid from the claimed basins makes a pleasing sound like a babbling brook.

The thrones across from the footbridge both sit empty, but between them, Stellastera stands straight and proud, her huge wings stretched out over each seat of the throne, casting prisms of light onto the rich gold and velvet.

"Poe, come to the throne," Stellastera calls, and after a moment the prince emerges from the garden beyond. He glances behind him only once before he steps to his mother's side and offers us a low bow. Pippa crosses the bridge to join the two of them, and beckons for us to follow.

By the time we cross the footbridge and reach the thrones, the twins have taken their places. Poe sits on the right with Aliandra in his crown, and Pippa sits on the left, with Alexerin in hers. Both twins straighten formally, their heads locked forward, their eyes distant as though they're in a trance. Stellastera places a hand on each of their shoulders, and the trio speaks in unison.

"The time has come to unite the Wellsprings of all the Known Lands. Have you the Offerings?"

"Yes," Margy replies.

"In whose name do you unite the Allsource?"

"In the name of the Dawn," Margy says firmly.

"Go then, Margary Plethore, Queen of Cerion, Heir of Asio, and make your Offerings."

I draw the orb containing the offerings from my pouch with a breathless reverence, and Rian whispers the spell over it to separate them from it. The orb fades, and I hold the two in my hand: Hywilkin with its stony, bulbous bottle filled with orange liquid, and Ceras'lain's elegant crystal vessel of swirling purple and blue. With great care, I offer them to Margy, and she directs me to give Hywilkin's to Rian and take Ceras'lain for myself.

"Tib," she whispers, looping her arm through his, "we'll do Elespen together."

Tib tears his gaze from the space beyond the thrones where Poe had emerged moments before. His silvery eye flashes brightly, and it seems to take him a moment to realize what Margy's saying. He looks to the twins and Stellastera, a little unsure.

"Can I?" he asks. "I thought it had to be the suitor putting it in."

"You may stand with her," the twins explain, "but she must be the one to place it."

As we make our way to the basins, the offering begins to vibrate in my hand, pulling me closer to its place. Across from Ceras'lain's empty basin, Kythshire's glows brightly, spilling its never-ending stream of shifting colors into the glittering pool below. I catch Rian's eye as he holds Hywilkin's gently over its matching basin, and he looks across to Margy and Tib, who stand in place before Elespen's.

The queen nods at us, and Flitt darts to my arm to perch on it as I set the crystal bottle into its place. The offering sparks with magic, and the basin begins to fill with liquid from Ceras'lain's Wellspring. It spills over as it reaches the lip of the basin, and cascades into the pool in a breathtaking curtain of glittering blue and lavender.

Rian places his, and the stream of yellow-orange spills over like molten rock. It pours into the pool, mixing with the existing white, gold, blue, purple, and pink like glowing, swirling paint. With all but one offering placed, our attention turns to Margy and Tib at the basin of Elespen.

Chapter Forty-Five

KINGDOMS UNITED
Tib

Everything's distracting, and nobody else notices. They're too involved in what they're doing. The offerings. The Wellspring. They don't see what I saw, the prince hiding behind the ferns, kissing someone. They don't know who she is. They don't even know she's here. It's unmistakable, though. It's Celli. I stare at her, my healed eye pulsing, straining. It's her, but she's different. Different, even, than when I saw her hiding in Hywilkin. Then, she had been drained of magic. Emptied of the darkness that held her. Now, she's filled up with energy. It pulses through her. This time, though, it's neutral. Even light-leaning, just a little.

I tear my attention from her. Whatever reason she's here, whatever she's doing, she doesn't seem to be a threat. The real threat is above us, looming in the clouds. I crane my neck upward. Stare into the churning darkness. See the Void again, the same way I did when I was inside of it. Everything and nothing. Suffocating. Cruel. See him there, too. Vorhadeniel. He's immense. Terrifying. A presence that changes in rapid pulses.

Sparrow. Fox. Boar. Perch. Dragon. Serpent. He's everywhere. In the sky. On the ground. In the water. The darkness. An encroaching shadow. Death. Wherever shadow reaches, he reaches. He can be everywhere at once. Even with his siblings standing against him, the Muse of Darkness is more powerful than we could have fathomed. Even without Sorcerers backing him, he's terrifying.

"Tib?" Margy whispers, tearing my attention from the sky. My eyes meet hers, deep brown and filled with hope, and any doubt that loomed from the shadows above is pushed aside. "The offering?"

I step closer to her. Pull the leaf-shaped vial from my bandolier. Hold it in my palm. Think of what it took to get it here. Elespen. The Dona. Velu. The brave Savarikta. Aleeta, the fallen *sava*. The ruined Keeper.

Its green light casts a strange glow over my palm. My fingers close slowly over the bottle. I think of everyone outside, in Brindelier, ready for battle. I glance up at the sky again. What will happen when this last vial is placed? Will it invite the darkness, like the elves said? Or will the Dawn's victory be enough to keep them at bay? Across the Wellspring, I feel the twins' eyes on me. Pippa's. Poe's.

Margy slides her hand under mine, cradling it gently. A tingle of warmth spreads through me from the place where our fingers touch. My heart speeds up. I glance at Poe, watching eagerly from the edge of his throne. He doesn't seem to mind how close she and I are. He's only interested in the offering. What does that mean? We spent so long getting to this point. We worked so hard. This is it. When it's done, then what?

"Tib," Margy whispers once more, and my eyes meet hers again. "It'll be all right," she whispers so quietly only I can hear. Her fingers graze my arm, and she leans in and kisses me on the cheek.

My breath catches. My fingers go slack around the offering. It slides into her gloved hand. Without it, I feel so much lighter. Valenor's presence moves away, toward the twins. I feel the breeze from his cloak as he goes. I feel the darkness churn above, licking toward us. I feel a pair of eyes on us from beyond the edge of the garden.

Margy takes my hand as she moves toward the basin. Instead of watching her, I fixate on the eyes. Celli's eyes. She sees me. Her own eyes widen. They flick to Poe, then back to us. Some of the energy of the Wellspring drifts in her direction.

"For Cerion, for the Dawn, for peace," Margy says aloud.

"This is it, Majesty," Twig whispers.

I pull my attention away from Celli to see Twig clinging to Margy's arm above the elbow, watching eagerly. Everyone else seems to hold their breath.

Margy leans toward the basin. I grip her hand to keep her steady. The offering slides into place with a satisfying click. Yellow-green liquid floods the basin and spills over. It splashes into the pool, swirling green into the rainbow of colors. Everything goes still. Time seems to stop. For a moment, nobody moves. Nobody makes a sound.

The churning liquid inside the well swirls faster. It swells up the sides and dips low in the center like a whirlpool.

"Our kingdoms shall unite, and none shall divide us," the twins declare eerily.

The floor of the palace pitches, throwing Margy into me. I set her on her feet and steady her by the elbows as we slide away from the basin into the border hedge.

Darkness crashes over us, thick and suffocating. It's like in Elespen. I try to see with my healed eye, but the black is too thick.

"What's happening?" Margy cries, her voice shaken with fear.

"I'm here," I murmur to her. "I've got you."

"I can't see!" she whimpers.

"Me neither," I say, straining into the darkness.

"I'm here, too, Margy," Twig says from somewhere between us. "You're safe."

"Mother!" Pippa cries from across the pool.

"Pippa!" Poe shouts. "Someone help! Mother! Ali! She's gone!"

"A sister for a sister," Vorhadeniel's voice thunders over us deafeningly.

"Alex!" Aliandra cries.

"Deniel, no!" Stellastera screams, and I feel her presence vanish.

Somewhere between us and where I know the thrones to be, Valenor lets out a string of curses. I feel a shift in him. A change. Scales. Talons. Dragon. His wings fan us with a gust of wind, then he's gone, too. A sinking feeling comes over me. Both Muses have left us, and I haven't seen Eljarenae either, since we arrived here.

The floor angles under us again like the deck of one of my air ships. I start to slide into Margy and hold tight to her arm as I cling to a branch of the nearby hedge.

"Majesty!" Azi bellows.

"I'm here!" Margy calls.

"Where?" the knight shouts. "Flitt, your light!"

"I'm trying!" Flitt screeches in reply. Their voices come closer. The floor tilts again. Something heavy crashes into me and I shove it off, away from Margy.

"Found us," I grumble to Azi as I sense the steady energy of Mentalism rolling off her in waves.

"What is that?" Rian whispers from nearby, and my healed eye flicks around, desperate to see what he's talking about.

All around us, the darkness is thick and unending. It's so restricting, it even seems to block out sound. Except for one spot. One space, right near the throne, where a struggle is taking place. Something is drawing it in. The shadow. Changing it. Like a filter. A siphon. It pulls at the darkness, funneling it. I grip Margy's hand as the ground beneath us rumbles, and I inch my way toward it.

Rian and Azi each keep a hand on my shoulders. They follow me. I feel the crackle of magic from Rian's fingertips. He leans forward to peer over my shoulder, just as curious about whatever it is as I am. The closer we get, the easier it is to see. It is a filter, like I thought. It's changing it. Darkness into light. Except the filter isn't an object. It's a person.

"Celli," I whisper. The impulse to attack her is strong, but I fight it. This isn't the enemy I faced before. She's a completely different person now.

Shadow enters her, light leaves. It swirls around her, clearing the evil, banishing the Void, until all the darkness is sifted to light. Beams of it gush up from the Wellspring, blinding us at first. Particles of magic drift through the air, coming to rest on all of us like blown ash. It coats my hair and skin, tingling. It slides off and spills back to the pool when it realizes it has no effect on me.

The others, though, are enthralled. They raise their hands, staring at the glowing dust on them, smiling in wonder. Everyone but Poe, who's on his knees in the dust, his shoulders slumped, and Aliandra, his Faedin, who clings to his neck and whispers comfort to him. The ground slants again, and we all slide a few paces to the side.

Celli rushes to the prince when her work is through. She holds him, stroking his back, whispering words only for him.

A jet of glittering light shoots up from the Wellspring like a fountain. It goes all the way up through the open ceiling and explodes, raining more of the sparkling dust over the palace and the kingdom beyond. It's followed by another one, and another. The clouds above thin out.

I watch them one by one, feeling the power of each eruption surge across us. Dawn. Light. Victory. If that's so, then how did the Muse of Darkness manage to get in here? How could he steal the princess?

I look around. Margy's giggling, waving her hand slowly before her eyes, watching the trail of colorful dust that follows it. Azi and Rian are kissing, oblivious to everyone around them. Their hair and clothes glitter with magic. The fairies are caught up in it, too. They sing and dance in the air, spreading the dust around, laughing.

"Hey!" I shout, snatching Twig in my fist. I shake him, and puffs of magic dust shimmer to the floor. "Cut it out! What's going on?"

He fights free and shakes his head quickly to clear it. "They're aether drunk," he explains, darting to Margy's face. "Margy!" he shouts, slapping her cheeks.

"It's so beautiful," she says vacantly.

"Shush!" I shout, and snatch him as he flies past in a blur. I dust the stuff off him, too, and he blinks rapidly and looks from side to side.

"Oh!" he yelps, and his sudden breath billows over us, clearing the dust toward the pool.

He flies to Azi and Rian and shouts their names, and they break free from each other and look around in confusion as his gusts cleanse them of the aether. He does the same to Margy, who gasps and runs to kneel with Poe. Respectfully, Celli moves away and bows her head to the queen.

"I'm so sorry!" Margy cries, hugging him. "I didn't know."

"Nobody did," Poe shudders. "How could we have known? We had every protection in place. I mean, he got past Mother. He got past Uncle Valenor."

"There was a weak point," Celli's voice echoes meekly around us. "A point of vulnerability within the Princess herself. She knew it was the end of her chance to be with him. Even though she knew it was wrong, she still had a sort of longing for the love that could never be, ended by the Dawn's claim. She was ashamed by her feelings. She tried so hard to resist them."

"No." Poe pushes himself to his feet and Celli does the same. Margy stands, too, and drifts back beside me. Poe stalks two steps to Celli. His hands are balled into fists at his sides. He looks pleadingly at her.

"You fixed that. You took the darkness from her."

"I tried," Celli says with a tenderness that makes me want to look away from the two of them. She steps closer and reaches for him, but he hesitates. "I tried to help her, but I was only just learning. Even your mother's efforts with her were temporary. With the claiming of the Wellspring, those old feelings returned. She welcomed the darkness."

"No!" Poe cries tearfully. "After all we did to prevent it, after everything our kingdom sacrificed, I can't believe it! She wouldn't allow it so easily! How did no one see or try to stop it? How could it be overlooked when it's the very thing we've been fighting this entire time?"

"I don't know," Celli whispers. "The Dusk's power is compelling…"

The ground trembles under our feet, and a thunderous scraping sound rumbles so loudly we all clap our hands over our ears.

"I'll go see what it is," Flitt pushes to Azi, who, along with me, hasn't left Margy's side.

"I just can't believe it," Poe sniffles, clinging to Celli. "How did we not see it?" he repeats.

Margy looks between the two of them, and steps a little closer to me. Her eyes drift to the pool, then up to the sky where the storm clouds have faded, giving way to bright blue. I take a chance. I slide my arm around her. She doesn't move away.

"A sister for a sister," Rian murmurs thoughtfully. "What does it mean?"

"Well," I mutter. "The Muses are all sisters and brothers, right? So which sister is Vorhadeniel after, then?"

"The Muse of Sea," Celli says quietly, "has captured the Muse of Earth."

"What?" Azi asks, wide-eyed. "How do you know that?"

"I saw it, when My Lady Stellastera brought me through her realm," she says. "She showed me many things. Sorcery. War."

"Show me," Azi whispers, stepping closer to Celli.

"Azi," Rian warns, but the knight raises her hand to quiet him.

"She's all right," Azi murmurs. "Kenrick showed me."

We gather around, watching in silence as the golden tendrils stretch between Azi and Celli. The knight holds her hands cupped in front of her, and the scenes spill from Celli's mind into them. We see the rallying of the elves, the wicked battle through Cerion's villages, the return of Elespen's people to Cresten, the gathering of Faefolk in Hywilkin, the moment of triumph when Kaso Viro finally captured Sha'Renell.

"That must be it," Rian says, turning to Poe. "He wants a trade. A sister for a sister. Pippa in exchange for Sha'Renell, his only remaining ally in this fight."

"Everyone!" Flitt's squeaky voice pierces the momentary silence. "Come here! You have to see this!"

Azi's the first to follow the fairy's call, but the rest of us follow quickly into the balcony garden. Margy's hand is still clasped firmly in mine. Her brow is knit. Her thoughts are far away. I wonder, as we skid to a stop, what she thinks of all of this. It should have been a peaceful ceremony. A triumph. Instead, it seems like we just invited more darkness and fear to Brindelier.

"Oh!" the queen gasps, pulling my hand to her chest. Her eyes light with wonder. I tear my gaze from her into the distance, where everyone else is gaping in awe. "That's my palace!"

"But there used to be nothing there," Celli whispers. "Just trees, then sky."

"Our kingdoms will unite," Poe says.

"Well of course, silly!" Aliandra laughs. "What did you think it meant? We're neighbors now! Our kingdoms stand side by side!"

"Is that smoke?" I ask, my healed eye focusing on a pillar of it rising into the sky, where the gates of Cerion would be. A dragon circles over it, its wings stretched, its fiery breath streaming from its mouth. From this distance, I can't tell whether it's Opal or Valor.

"Celli, how long ago would you say it was that you saw that battle in the village?" Rian asks.

"I'm not sure," Celli says, knitting her brow. "Dawn, or a little before it."

"They could have reached the gates by now," Rian says thoughtfully.

"Your Highnesses!" comes an urgent call from inside, and we all run back through the Wellspring garden, where the pool shoots endless streams of magic into the sky. From the other side of the gate, one of the guards from downstairs peers in at us. "The outer gate has been breached. Our guard marches to meet the enemy force, mostly Sorcerers. The kingdom is holding them back. Where is the princess? We must get you both to safety."

"I shall remain here," Poe says firmly. "The Wellspring is whole, and Aliandra and I have a duty to stand with it, along with Pippa and Alex."

"As you wish, Highness. I'll move a thicker guard force to the stairs, then," he says with a bow, and jogs off down the stairs again. As soon as he's gone, a series of explosions thunders outside the palace.

"You didn't tell him about Pippa," Ali says.

"What can they do about it?" Poe asks, scowling.

"The Dusk is coming," Twig says. "They won't give in so easily. Even though you claimed the Wellspring, Margy, they'll fight with everything they have to steal that claim."

My feet buzz with warning inside my boots. At the same time, all four fairies snap their attention to the Wellspring.

"Oh, yes!" Shush whispers excitedly. He, Twig, and Flitt start to cheer. Aliandra gasps. The Wellspring's jets stop abruptly. The pool goes completely still.

"What's happening, Ali?" Poe asks, creeping closer to the edge of the pool.

"They're coming," Ali whispers. "All of them."

I'm about to ask who, when my boots buzz again with warmth. I feel a pull toward the Wellspring. My healed eye focuses on the very center of it. I hold my breath. I know it's him before he even appears. Golden wings. The tip of a gold spear. Waves of golden hair. Strong jaw. Muscled shoulders. Armor of pure gold scale. His toes leave the pool and he drifts toward me. He grows larger and larger, pulling his strength from the infinite pool, until he's the size of a hulking warrior. His wings barely flutter as I back away and he rests lightly on the polished stone in front of me.

"Tib," he says with a curt bow.

"Mevyn," I reply, trying hard to keep my voice from cracking around the lump in my throat. I want to throw my arms around him and hug him. I don't, though. I don't think either of us would actually like it. "Why are you here?"

"I know you," Margy says. "I saw you with Tib a long time ago, when he was sitting on the aqueducts."

"So you did." Instead of bowing to my queen, Mevyn raises his chin and looks down his nose at her. The arrogance, the subtle refusal to give her the honor she deserves makes me want to punch him. To shove him back into the Wellspring. I wish I could figure out why being around him makes me so irrational. So emotional. My joy at seeing him again vanishes. I hate him. I really do. After this, I hope I never see him again.

"Hello," Aliandra chirps, darting to greet him. Her silvery skin shimmers with the colors of the Wellspring, and she grows herself to his size, too. "Mevyn, Keeper of Sunteri's Wellspring, I presume."

"You presume correctly," Mevyn replies, looking her over in his usual haughty way.

"Sapience," Flitt whispers, drifting to hover over the pool as another golden fairy rises from it. This one is muscular like Mevyn, but leaner. His wings are glassy and iridescent like Flitt's instead of golden like Mevyn's. His spear is made of light or glass, and his armor is blue flecked with gold, like Azi's.

He turns to me and Mevyn and, to my surprise, offers me a bow, mostly ignoring the fae.

"I have heard tell of you from many sources, Tibreseli Dreamstalker," he says.

"He and I have long been friends," another voice echoes from the center of the pool.

"Vae!" I shout in surprise, and the imp-like Keeper splashes out of the pool and darts to me, swishing her tail excitedly. "I hope it's all right," she declares. "I brought my own Faedin." She gestures to the pool, and dozens of pointed quills pop up from the liquid. The fae flicks her finger, and the quill-backed figure levitates over to us.

"Tulya!" Azi gasps in disbelief, and the woman beams a smile at her.

"Is good to see you, Warrior," she says, clapping Azi and Rian on the back after she shakes the Wellspring's magic back into the pool. "And you, Magus."

"Ah, a Northwoman," Mevyn says in a tone that drips with sarcasm. "How delightful."

"Is green, here. Warm." Tulya declares, inviting an eye-roll from Mevyn. She cranes her neck, peering around. "Is other Magus here?"

"Kenrick? Yes, he's here in the palace," Azi explains to her as the pool ripples again and more tips of wings emerge.

I recognize the next Keeper right away, even before Aliandra introduces him by name.

"Kiaan, Keeper of the Wellspring of Elespen."

"The Savarikta are restored," Kiaan says to me as he joins the rest of us. "We owe you our gratitude, Tibreseli."

"I owe you my thanks too," I say moving a little closer to Margy, who's gazing up at me with the same amount of wonder that was on her face when she realized Cerion and Brindelier were joined.

"What?" I utter.

"I just, I had no idea..." her voice trails off as the pool ripples again, and this time a slender, silvery-white figure emerges from it. I know who she is, too, even though we've never met. Her greeting as she hovers at the edge of the pool confirms it.

"I am Ienae'luvrie, Keeper of the Wellspring of Ceras'lain," she says with a voice that flows like trickling water. "Well met, friends of Dawn."

"Well met," we reply in awed unison.

Behind her, the pool roars suddenly, rearing up like an angry ocean. Ienae'luvrie speeds away from it, stopping beside Vae at the outskirts of the gathering. A huge, stony, golden fist smashes through the surface of the pool, followed swiftly by a hulk of a creature with deep set eyes and a wide, jutting jaw. He crashes onto the footbridge and heaves a breath like a growl, narrowing his eyes to glare at us. The Keepers make a defensive line between us and the newcomer. Between me and Azi, Tulya's quills shiver in warning.

"Kuvelsk of Haigh," Aliandra announces warily.

Haigh. The offering I stole from the Dusk. Vae glances at me over her shoulder. She was there. She gives me a reassuring nod. Moves closer to Mevyn to conceal me. All the Keepers draw some power from the Wellspring in the uncertain silence. Azi reaches over her shoulder. Her sword leaps to her hands.

"Why do you stand against me?" The Keeper's gruff voice rumbles. "Do you not trust me as one of your own?"

"We were unsure," Aliandra offers gently. "Your offering came from a dark place."

"I did what I had to do to keep our pool safe from outsiders. We struck a deal. Peace from the Dusk in exchange for one vial. We didn't see the harm in it. We knew when we gave it to them, it would end up in the right hands eventually. We in the north are not fools."

The bridge cracks under his weight as he creeps closer to us. "I am with the Dawn," he declares. "I stand with you in this fight."

The line of Keepers seems to relax a little at his declaration. They take a few steps back to make room for the Keeper of Haigh to join us. I can't help but scowl. Anyone who shifts allegiances like that shouldn't be trusted. I decide to hold my tongue, but only because Poe starts to talk before I can say something.

"You have all come here to help us?" he asks. "You've left your own pools unguarded?"

"We are all threatened," Ienae'luvrie explains, "when the All Source is threatened."

"Be assured," Mevyn says, "no agent of Dusk will breach this garden."

"The humans should leave this place," Sapience declares. "Go and defend your own lands. Do not concern yourself with this tower, for even if all of Brindelier falls, the All Source shall remain standing as long as we stand to defend it."

As if to strengthen their point, each Keeper goes to their Wellspring's basin and takes a vigilant stance before it.

"All right, that settles it. Ali, you stay here," Poe says. With a flick of his fingers, his robes transform into a suit of gleaming armor.

"Where are you going?" she asks.

"If the Wellspring is so well guarded, I'm going to find my sister," he says firmly. "And I won't be talked out of it."

"I'll go with you," Celli says. Poe turns to her and rests a hand on her shoulder gratefully.

"Forgive me, your Highness," Rian says, "but, how are you going to do that? Your sister was taken by a Muse. She may not even be in our realm. I have a better idea."

"What is it?" Poe asks.

"Sha'Renell. That's who he's hoping to gain from this. He wants his sister back. If we could heal her, sway her allegiance…" he trails off, looking to Azi.

"She might become our greatest ally in all of this," Azi finishes his thought for him.

"Can you do that?" I ask her.

"I could try," she replies. "I was able to bring Stellastera out of the darkness, to show her her true worth. If nothing else, we will do whatever we can to aid the Muses in retrieving the Princess."

"Could you return us to Cerion first?" Margy asks. "I wish to be with my people."

"Of course, Majes—Margy," Rian says with a bow. "Whenever you're ready."

"Thank you, Margary," Poe says, stepping closer to Margy. He takes her hands in his and bows humbly, and my heart pangs with jealousy even though I know the gesture is just between allies and nothing more. "Our Wellspring is restored, our kingdoms united, just as we both wanted. I only wish our celebration didn't have to be delayed."

"It will be a grand one when this is over, when Pippa is safely returned, and the Dusk is vanquished," Margy says with a confident smile. "I promise you that."

Chapter Forty-Six

CERION'S CONFLICT
Tib

We don't waste much time. We say our farewells to Poe and the others at the Wellspring. I give Mevyn a quick nod. Azi makes promises to Poe. We jog down the spiral staircase to the breakfast room with Tulya trailing behind us, eager to see Kenrick.

"Magus!" she shouts as soon as she sees the Mentalist. Kenrick responds by nearly falling over his chair in shock, then jumping up to hug her, cautious of her quills. They chatter together in Tulya's language, and I pull Ki quickly to the side.

She glances nervously from me to the queen, who's talking to the elves.

"Don't worry," I say. "I don't think it matters anymore. We don't need to be secret."

Ki gives an embarrassed sort of smile. "I feel like I should at least apologize..." she says, trailing off.

"There are bigger things at stake, and she's seen you're on our side," I say. "People change, Ki. Margy knows that."

"Margy," she whispers, laughing softly. "First name basis with the queen..." she waves her hand dismissively, teasing me.

"Anyway," I say, rolling my eyes.

"What happened up there?" she asks.

I fill her in as much as I can. Her eyes widen more and more with each new piece of information, until Efran sidles up beside her.

"What's the plan?" he asks.

"We're going back to Cerion before they breach the gates," I say. I turn to Ki. I know the answer before I even ask the question, but I ask it anyway. "Are you coming?"

"Brindelier's under attack, too," she replies, slipping her hand through Efran's. "It's more of a home to me than Cerion or Sunteri ever were."

"Yeah, I figured," I reply.

"Someone's got to keep those Sorcs out," Efran says, grinning.

"Tib," Margy calls. I turn to her to see the elves filing out, and she and Azi linking arms with Finn and Rian. "Ready?"

"Be safe, little brother," Ki whispers, kissing me on the forehead. "We'll see you when the battle's done."

Margy gives me an excited smile when I join them. Azi knows where to take us. My stomach flips around as our feet leave the polished floor of the palace and we lurch forward through the Half-Realm. The journey is short and disorienting. We nearly crash to the floor in the quiet privacy of Her Majesty's planning chamber.

"Margy!" The Queen Mother cries with a mix of shock and relief. She rushes from the huge round table and falls to her knees, throwing her arms around her daughter. She's alone in here, except for a scribe and her two personal guards, standing at the door.

"Thank the stars and the seas and everything that is good," she whispers into the folds of Margy's gown.

"Mother," Margy whispers, hugging the queen mother around her neck.

"By your leave, Majesty," Azi says the moment we arrive.

"Of course," Margy says, still clinging to her mother. "Hurry. I hope you can get her back safely!"

Azi salutes, and Rian whispers wards over the two queens before they vanish again into the Half-Realm. Behind Margy, Finn sways unsteadily.

"That was something," he mutters to himself. His face is green, his lips thin and white. I shove a chair behind him and he looks like he'll protest, but the queen insists.

"It's all right, Finn," Margy says. "Take a moment. I'm safe here."

"Where is everyone?" I ask, surprised by the empty room.

"Out there," the queen mother explains as the two rise gracefully to their feet. "We're concentrating our defense at the city gates, and a small force has been sent to the new lands to assist. Our navy is nearing at an impossible pace. From what our scouts have described, we have the upper hand so long as our walls are not breached."

Margy goes to the table and studies the magical model of Cerion sprawled across its surface. A sharp glow of dots representing Her Majesty's subjects lines the wall and the gate. A huge force stands behind it, ready. Two lazy orbs loop circles around the city, rising and falling on the wind.

413

"Are those the dragons?" Margy whispers.

"Yes," Naelle replies.

Margy slides her hand along the smooth wood, peering at the clusters of houses where so many dots huddle in hiding. Her lips press together. Her eyes flick to the window. In the distance, there's a muffled roar. A rumble of some attack.

"Thank you, Mother," she says to the queen. "You've served our kingdom well. Will you remain here, in case further council is needed?"

"Of course," the queen mother says, "but, where are you going?"

"To the southwest tower, for a better look," Margy says.

Finn pushes himself to his feet, but Margy places a hand on his arm and shakes her head. "I shall have Twig with me, and Tib. Rest, friend," she commands. "Keep my mother safe."

She gives the queen mother another quick hug, glances again at the table, and rushes out, grabbing my arm on the way. As soon as we leave the room and the door shuts behind us, she starts to run. I assume her hurry is to get to the tower, until I realize she's not going in that direction at all. She's heading for the doors of the palace.

"Margy," I warn.

"I know what you're going to say, Tib," she says, keeping the same quick pace. "Probably the same thing anyone else would say. That I'm too important. That I can't put myself at risk." Her eyes flash fiercely when she looks my way, and she runs faster. She sweeps her hand across her chest, and the bark-like scales of her corset shift to billowing purple Mage robes. Twig flicks his hands at her, too, and the vines that creep to her shoulder transform to gold.

"What is the point of my having gifts if I can't use them to defend my kingdom? What sort of queen would I be if I hid away and let my subjects die? I have powers for a reason. I will stand beside them and inspire them. I will face that creature who was once my brother. I refuse to sit on a throne and wait for victory to be handed to me. I intend to earn it myself."

As she speaks, her image shifts and transforms. Her skin takes on the glow of Light. She grows taller, more elegant, more refined. Beauty spills from her in pulsing waves. The guards lining the great foyer fall to their knees as we rush past. I expect the doors to fling open as we reach them, but, for now, they stay shut.

Margy turns to me. Takes my hands in hers. Even as the guards beside the door go to one knee inspired by the power she gives off, I see her. Even if I couldn't detect all the magic around her, I'd see her. Margy. The youngest Plethore, thrust into a position she never dreamed of. The darling of Cerion. The girl behind the queen. My friend.

Her brown eyes search mine, and I feel the blood drain from my face and spill into the pit of my stomach. A lump forms in my throat and I swallow hard to push it down.

"What is it?" I murmur, stepping closer. My hands, damp with sweat, ache to reach up, to touch her soft curls. To trace her cheek. To hold her close and keep her safe forever.

At her shoulder, Twig sits quietly. Completely still. Like he's trying hard not to exist.

Margy moves closer. She tips her head toward me, so our cheeks almost touch. Her hand rests over my bandolier, on my chest. I freeze. I can't think of what to do. My heart is racing so fast. All it would take is a small turn of my head. That's it. I shuffle my feet nervously. Reach for her arm, but drop my hand awkwardly, losing my nerve.

Outside, there's a huge crash. In the distance people scream. Margy tears her gaze from me. Looks at the carved wood, the only thing between us and the battle outside. She pulls something from the pocket of her robes. A scroll case. The same one she'd taken from Vorance while I watched in the mirror.

"This is for you," she says. "I wanted to thank you for everything you've done."

"Why are you giving this to me now?" I ask, scowling. I don't like it. It feels too much like some kind of goodbye. "Can't it wait until after the battle?"

"Just open it," she says with a sigh. "I want you to have it before."

She stays close to me, watching as I pull the fine leather cover from the end of the tube and fish the parchment out of it. She holds the case while I crack the seal of His Highness Prince Vorance of Sunteri and unroll the page.

Declaration of Property
As Proclaimed by the Royal Throne of Third Sunteri

The words swim on the page, dancing around, taunting me. There are phrases I don't understand. Language beyond what I can read. Feudal Barony. Bequest. Emancipation. Grant. Indentured. One word is mentioned over and over: Everlin.

"What is this, Margy?" I ask when my shaking hands keep me from being able to read any more.

"The throne of Sunteri has agreed to give you the fields, Tib, and everything in them. You can do whatever you want with it. Free the slaves, destroy the Everlin. Build on it, keep it vacant. You could live there, or you could ignore it and never return. Whatever you want. It's a Barony. You own it all."

"What?" I try to whisper, but my voice fails me. My head spins. My heart races. The page flutters from my numb fingers to the ground, and Twig dives to return it to me.

I don't know what to think. Don't know how to react. I can't wrap my head around it. I feel stuck to the spot, unable to breathe, even. Red. Sand. Sun. Heat. The crack of the whip. The sting of the needles. The fear of a basket not full enough.

He listened. I raged and I screamed and I showed him the truth behind that wretched powder, that red, red, red…and…he heard me.

I can't stop the flood of emotions that come over me. I drop the scroll again and pull Margy into my arms. This time, she's braver. Her kiss is sweet and gentle. It charges through me with a force stronger than any magic, any sensation I've ever felt. I burrow into her shoulder, holding tight to her, spilling tears into the golden vines that stretch across her collar.

I'm vaguely aware of the door beside us opening. Of the light that spills across the foyer. I turned my healed eye toward it defensively, then let down my guard as the figure standing there takes off her helm and shakes out her thick red curls.

"Your Majesty," Saesa says, dropping to one knee. She looks up at us, and I try to put some space between myself and the queen for her sake, but I can't. I can barely move. The best I can do is smear away the tears still dripping from my jaw.

Saesa doesn't seem concerned. She's too frantic. Her green eyes flash with warning. Behind her, Opal towers over the courtyard. Her—his tail thrashes urgently.

"What news, Saesa?" Margy asks, peering over her shoulder at the pillars of smoke billowing toward the sky.

"It's him," Saesa says, her voice shaking. "The black rider. He's approaching the gates. Our fire can't touch him. No number of soldiers sways his resolve. Even the spells of Master Mages have done little to slow his approach."

"I shall call for the Royal Guard and my horse," Margy says. "It's time to finish this."

"I have a better idea," Twig grins excitedly. "Valor."

The stony dragon guardian of the palace swoops to land beside Opal before Twig even finishes his suggestion, and Margy gapes from the creature to Twig, who bobs at her eye level.

"I'm about to ride a dragon into battle to defend my kingdom, aren't I?" she asks the fae, her eyes sparkling with excitement.

"I believe so, Majesty. Er, Margy," Twig replies, bowing to the queen in mid-air as he gestures toward the creature.

"Come on, Tib!" Margy shouts, and runs out of the palace toward the dragon.

My eye flicks to every corner of the courtyard, searching for any threat or danger, but the wards on the palace are so powerful and complete that I doubt even an unwelcome fly could breach them.

"Are you all right, Tib?" Saesa asks, as Valor lands lightly in the garden behind her. I feel bad, but even now, I can't take my eyes off Margy as she greets her mount.

"I think so," I answer, my voice shakier than I'd like. "Look." I hand her the scroll, and her eyes get wider and wider as she reads it over.

"Hurry, Tib!" Margy shouts from astride the huge dragon. Valor swings its head in a serpent-like motion. Its eyes flash blue and purple. Urgent. Their excitement is contagious.

"Come on," I say to Saesa, grabbing the parchment and shoving it back into its case. "Let's go burn some Sorcerers."

Climbing onto a dragon's back is easier than I expected it to be. Valor's stony scales make a sort of staircase, and there's a divot between the guardian's wings that's the perfect size for me and Margy to fit in side by side. As he pumps his huge wings and pushes off, I remember the first time I found myself on the back of a dragon: the day we freed Valenor from his prison in the frozen mountains of Hywilkin.

The feeling I have soaring on Valor is about the same. Freedom. Power. Except this time, we're not fleeing from the danger, we're rushing toward it. Margy's excitement is contagious. Valor banks hard to the side and she slides into me, gripping my arm, laughing. The dragon skims along the outer wall of the kingdom, showing us our first glimpse of the war that pounds against the gates.

It's like looking into two separate worlds. On the outside of the gate, everything is black. The ground crawls with darkness, like millions of tiny black beetles. The plague of shadows stretches along the main road, snuffing it out, until it reaches the forest. The forest is in ruin. Diseased trees bend to the ground, rotting and cracking. The ground is littered with bones, covered in black disease.

Dusk's forces hammer relentlessly against the gates with huge rams and strange machines that spew green and purple fire. Cerion's Mages stand sheltered in towers along the wall, casting wards and flinging spells nonstop. The clash of magic between the two sides sizzles in the air, exploding in violent reactions against one another.

Undead creatures scale the walls. Even though some of them are missing arms or legs, it doesn't slow them. They snarl and squeal as a group. The sound is deafening. Horrifying. The stench is even worse.

Valor makes a pass. He heaves a deep breath and blows white-hot fire along the wall. It turns the creatures to ash that spills down the stone like a waterfall. The victory is short, though. More of them surge forward. Skeletons. Risen. Imps. All sorts of other creatures like I haven't seen before. Men with dog-like snouts, long claws, and lashing, pointed tails. Men with mouths full of needle-sharp teeth and the legs of some kind of mountain cat. Stone giants. Golems. Shadow wraiths.

Wyverns circle overhead, mounted by the fierce riders from Hywilkin who I imagine were cast out by the Faedin once their king was overthrown. They're met by the elves on their cygnets, making the battle in the sky just as fierce as the one on the ground.

I look past them into the distance, where the spires of Brindelier poke up over the blackened trees. Smoke rises from their gates, too. They're close enough to Cerion, and the forces of Dusk are large enough, that the battle stretches easily between both cities.

Valor lets out another deafening roar. He dives low, weaving between cygnets and wyverns, and shoots another jet of flames along the battlefield. The action carves a gouge through the attacking force, leaving a wide span of charcoal and smoke between the army and the gates. The siege engines and their operators crumble to charcoal and ash. Twig dives from Margy's shoulder and glides along the ground, leaving a trail of giant brambles behind him, then blinks back to Margy's shoulder.

"They haven't breached the city yet," Margy shouts over the wind, leaning far over to peer at the battle. "Valor, where is he? Diovicus?"

Saesa and Opal speed around us, leading the way. Her dragon dives toward the opening of the blackened forest and arches upward again just as a hulking figure on an enormous draft horse pounds across the ash toward the gates. He wears a cloak of flame-orange splashed with scarlet. The axe he holds over his head bears a banner of red that ripples behind him like a trail of blood. Even this high up, we can hear his battle cry. I look closer at him with my healed eye. His armor ripples with malice. The evil energy surrounding it pulses with fury and death. It's meant to instill fear. To make even the boldest enemies cower. Beyond him, a strange-looking band of attackers starts to emerge from the forest.

Opal loops back. Breathes red-hot molten stone at the rider. It drips off him like jelly, sizzling in globs on the ground.

"Retreat!" Margy screams at Valor, and the dragon obeys.

"No!" I shout, obviously the only one able to see through the fear spell. It isn't even him. Diovicus. It's someone else. A decoy, maybe. A thrall.

I crane my neck, straining with my healed eye as Valor soars behind the city wall. The rider's ax is still raised. He bellows a war cry as he charges the gate. The brambles catch fire. Along the wall, Mages pause in their casting. Some of them lower their hands. The warning magic spewing from him is doing what it's meant to do. Making them pause. Keeping them from casting. I don't know what kind of powerful Sorcerer could have managed a spell like that, but I don't care. Apparently, I'm the only one who can stop it.

"Take me to the wall!" I yell to Valor, and the dragon obeys.

"Tib!" Margy screams. "No!"

"Stay safe!" I shout to her. "I'll come back to you." I trust Valor to keep her out of harm's way. I know if I don't act, that rider will break through the gate. When I'm close enough, I leap from the dragon's back, landing lightly on the parapet. I quickly step into the Half-Realm and race along the upper wall. My legs burn with the effort, but I push them harder. The rider's nearing. A few more hoofbeats, and he'll break through that gate. The enchantments around him seem to strengthen as he whips his horse faster. His cloak catches flame. He'll hit the portcullis. The doors. He'll obliterate them.

Just as he reaches the gate, I leap from the wall, aiming my feet at his shoulder to knock him from the horse. I reach him a heartbeat too late. His ax, charged with impossible power, comes down on the already weakened gate, smashing through it with a horrendous crack. The rider falls to the ground with a crash that shakes the walls. His horse plows through the gate, crashing it open. I draw my dagger and run it through the gap between the rider's helm and his pauldron, thinking of fairy fire and stripping.

He has no chance. His body shakes violently. Blue fire crackles beneath his armor. Dark magic spews from the wound. The fear spell dissolves. He goes still, and I push myself to my feet. I recognize that symbol and those colors. Orange. Red. An old guild of Cerion Saesa once told me about. Redemption. I shove the plate sleeve with my foot, and white ash spills from it.

Through the destroyed gate, I watch Margy and Valor land. A flash of yellow and blue cloaks and tabbards runs to guard her. Her Majesty's Champions.

A row of Cerion's Guard lines up between them and the gate, readying spears and shields.

"Let them come!" Margy shouts. "Let them see the might of Cerion!"

A blinding glow of light surges from the readied force. Beams of that dewdrop Margy shared with her people spear into the sky and crash down in a web of glittering, protective arches. Darkness pulses over my side of the wall, and everything goes silent.

I spin to peer into it. Through the darkness I see three figures riding black, scaly steeds toward me at an unnatural pace. Two of them cross in front of the center rider to guard him. A surge of undead follows the woman on his right. Sybel. She flings her arms forward, and they scurry toward me fiercely. The second rider points, and his own minions charge. These are commoners, raising pitchforks and shovels and ordinary working tools. Women and even children are sprinkled among them. I feel his presence in their minds, like black tar. Mentalism at its darkest form, cruel and merciless. A name is carried on the magic, like a war chant: *Xantivus*.

My healed eye flicks through the mindless crowd as it marches, and my heart leaps into my throat. Brown curls. Silky, ruffled gown. Emmie clinging to her skirts. Ruben beside them.

"Nessa!" I scream. My insides flip. My ears ring with fury. It's worse than when I raged about the Everlin powder. I slip into the

Half-Realm. My mind goes blank. I take off, charging through the crowd, screaming and shoving and kicking and clawing until I reach him. Xantivus. The Mentalist on the horse. I'm still hidden. He can't see me. I draw a dagger. White. I leap, scrambling up the shoulders of peasants. I cling to the Sorcerer, breaking his wards. I stab him through the neck. Watch his eyes go wide in disbelief. Stab him again, this time in the side.

He kicks his horse to speed it. His hands fly up. Fumble over my shoulders. Slide to my neck and clamp around it. The stripping starts to work. White tendrils of magic seep from his wounds. His lips part, baring wet, red teeth. We tumble from the horse, locked together. Into black, stinking mud and ash. My vision closes in as I fight to breathe. I manage to grab two more daggers. Slash them at his wrists. Blue. White. He screams and squeezes harder, slamming my head against the ground. The massive hoof of his horse crushes my shoulder. I try to scream in pain, but he's still squeezing my throat. The fairy fire didn't catch.

The crowd surges over me, grabbing my hair, my arms, my legs. Wrenching me. Pulling me apart. The Mentalist's eyes roll back in his head. His hands loosen and I gasp for breath, fighting to free myself from the grip of his minions. I manage to get a hand free from a boy whose blank eyes stare ahead as he scrambles to grasp me again, and I draw my dagger, white, and ram it through the Sorcerer's middle.

The magic that bleeds from him is black, gold, and white. It spirals into the sky in thick streams. I don't fight off the mind-controlled commoners. I know they had no say in any of this. I know if they had to choose, they never would have come here.

Their hold on my legs and arm loosens. The people restraining me blink, gazing around in confusion. The Mentalist is dead. His spell is broken.

"Xantivus!" Sybel screams.

"Leave him," a dark voice rumbles. Eron's voice. My healed eye flicks to him. Inside blackened armor, I see the face of the fallen prince. Inside him, I see the darkness. The wicked, ancient power, stronger than the other two Sorcerers combined. The Mage King. Diovicus. "He has failed us."

"Run!" I yell at the people around me. My throat and neck ache from the effort, but I keep on yelling. "Run home! Get out of here!"

Some of them listen. They take off, back toward the woods. Others glare around, searching the darkness, looking for someone to fight. Looking to take revenge.

Pain shoots through my shoulder as I push myself to my feet. My arm hangs limply at my side. My collarbone is in more pieces than it should be. It feels like chunks of gravel, scraping around in there. If I breathe too deeply, stabbing pain sears into my chest. I try to ignore it. Pull a pink vial. Gulp it. Search the crowd for Nessa. For Ruben and Emmie.

Relief washes over me when I see them running toward the gates. Into the city. Saesa rushes to greet them. Skalivar towers beside her, shield and spear at the ready. A skeleton ambles toward them, and the warrior takes it out with an effortless bash of his shield. The two of them usher Nessa and the children to safety. Lilen trails behind them, casting layers and layers of wards. Looking over her shoulder into the surge of undead.

I recognize a few of the other faces that rush toward the shelter of the city. Griff and Mikken, the two boys who were stolen way back before we even knew about Brindelier, run past into the gates. I don't have time to wonder how that's possible before the thundering of the remaining two horses is upon me. Spells fly from the parapets into the blinding darkness. Some of them meet their mark, others burst into sparks beside Sybel and Diovicus.

The healing potion has dulled the pain in my shoulder enough for me to at least think straight. It hasn't done much to mend any of my bones, though. I still can't take a deep breath without a twinge. I push what I can't do aside. I've got to get back to Margy. I can fight with one hand. I've done it before.

I pull a knife from my bandolier. Fling it at Sybel as she rides past. It bounces off her wards. The action is like a beacon to her undead. They find me, even though I'm still hidden. Or maybe I'm not, anymore. I'm not sure. Everything's confused. Painful.

A dozen of the wretched things crash into me from all sides, crushing me, hacking at me mindlessly with their swords and hammers, breathing their horrific diseased breath on me.

There are too many to fight off with one hand. One of them stabs its rusty blade through my leg. When he pulls it free, I feel a burn, like acid. Like infection. I stumble backward, slashing the creature with blue, and it catches with fairy fire and crumbles. There's no time to be relieved, through. Two more take its place. Breathless, I fall back until

I'm able to squirm through the city gates. I decide to step out of the Half-Realm, just in case I haven't already, with the hope some healer will see me.

"There!" I hear Bryse bellow over the clash of battle.

"Sybel!" Cort roars from someplace near him. "She's mine!"

The sudden brightness on Cerion's side of the gate stings my eyes. A blur of gold and blue rush past. Her Majesty's Champions charge the riders. Mya's voice rises over the fight, clear and perfect. I allow the magic of it. It bolsters me. Heals me. Works to knit bone back into place. It's slow, though. Painful. The undead are relentless. They push closer, crushing me. I try to stay on my feet, but my leg gives out. It's hot with disease. I feel it swelling inside my leggings, splitting them open. I drop to my knee and slash my blue dagger randomly at my attackers as my stomach churns.

My healed eye flicks around desperately. Gold and blue surge forward. A glowing yellow axe slashes at Sybel. Gaethon blasts her with a spell. Her wards fall. Bryse pulls her from her horse by her hair. Undead flood around them, hissing and screeching. Cort's blades flash. My head spins. There are Margys everywhere. All around me.

"Tib!" Lisabella shouts. A streak of glowing blue whizzes past my ear. Her sword. She stands over me protectively. Strikes two skeletons down with her sword. Sybel gives a gurgled scream. The undead around us crumple lifelessly to the ground. I know what it means. She's dead. Her spells broken. I try to push myself up to look, but my arm is useless. My leg is heavy, like it's encased in stone.

"Healer!" Lisabella bellows.

Past her, the Revenant's horse dances across the cobbles. Eron's lips sneer at the duplicates of the queen. His eyes flash with malice as Diovicus peers through them. My thoughts are jumbled. Confused. Azi said if Sybel fell, the Revenant would fall. I felt her death. Her necromancy died with her. That's why the skeletons and undead crumpled. Why isn't Eron dead too, then? Why isn't Diovicus defeated?

I heave on my knees, emptying my stomach. My heart thumps in my chest. I feel it pumping blood to my throbbing leg. I fight to get to my feet again, my gaze locked on the black rider. On Eron, searching the span of copies of Margy. I know which one she is. I can see it plain as day. I won't look at her, though. Won't give her up.

"Davca," Lisabella calls. "Hurry, he's infected!"

Lisabella catches and cradles me. Her peace pulses over me. The Champions stand between their fallen prince and their crowned queen, weapons readied. I struggle against Lisabella, desperate to get up and fight. To stand between the real Margy and her enemy. I'm too weak, though. I can feel the disease spreading hot through my body. Up from my leg. Into my stomach. Burning my chest. Someone rushes to us, blocking my view. I try to shove him aside so I can see, but I have no strength left. My shoulder throbs with pain. I close my eyes and give in to his healing.

"The Plethore's weak rule has ended," the Revenant's voice thunders over us, rumbling the ground beneath me. "Cerion is mine, and none shall stand against me. I, Diovicus, have come to make my claim."

"You have no claim, and never will!" all the Margys shout defiantly.

I peer through my eyelid and through Dacva into a flash of incredible, pure, and perfect white light. A globe of it, as powerful and pure as the sun itself, bolts toward Eron faster than an arrow. It slams into him, throwing him from his horse. As he flies through the air, his body crackles and sizzles. The light from the web over the city joins with it, driving into him relentlessly. Diovcus and Eron both let out a scream of sheer agony. My heart races. I fight to get up, to see if Margy's safe.

"I'm going to have to put him out," Dacva whispers to Lisabella, and before I can think to deny what I already allowed, he eases me to sleep.

Chapter Forty-Seven

MUSES' MINDS
Azi

Kaso Viro is not where Celli reported him to be. With Rian focusing on his location, we arrive firmly in the center of his tower on the shores of the Stepstone Islands. The circular room with the pool at the center is bursting with light so blinding it makes my eyes water. I almost push to Flitt to tone it down until I become aware of the presence of more than just the Muse of Water in the room.

"Eljarenae?" I ask, taking a step toward her.

"I am here, my Champions," she replies from the center of the strongest point of light. Her voice is tinged with sorrow and exhaustion. She drifts closer to me, and I smile in greeting.

"Azaeli," Kaso Viro says from somewhere near the pool. "You have arrived at precisely the right time. Come."

When I squint in his direction, I can barely make out the Muse of Water bobbing in the pool, flanked by a pair of merfolk: one man, one woman. As my eyes get used to the light and I creep nearer, I can see that they're gathered around a pillar of smooth, crystalline ice. Sha'Renell's stony figure is held captive inside of it, her blackened skin a sharp contrast to Eljarenae's white light.

"You were able to pull our sister, Stellastera, from the grips of darkness and despair," Kaso Viro says, helping me to step into the frigid pool of water. Rian follows, keeping close to me as the fairies dart around us in circles. "Do you think, perhaps, you could accomplish the same results with Sha'Renell?"

"I have tried it myself," Eljarenae tells me, "as has Kaso, to no avail. Her heart is as stone, her spirit swallowed by the Void. She sees only the false power of the Dusk. She cannot see the truth."

"Maybe we should have brought Kenrick along, too," I say, grazing my fingers across the glassy surface of the ice. You can do it, Azi," Flitt chirps. "I believe in you!"

"So do I," Rian says. He kisses my neck softly, sending a flutter of warmth through me, and whispers, "Trust yourself."

"Over twenty years ago," Kaso Viro says to me, "I saw in the stars the figure of a woman. A Knight, bold, determined, graceful. Her heart was open to the light. I saw her lineage, and how that alone would lead her to the fair folk. I saw her acceptance of them, her love of peace, kindness, and charity. I saw the power that nurtured within her."

Beside him in the pool, the mermaid and merman listen, gazing up at Kaso with interest. The man plays lazily with the woman's long turquoise hair, and she floats to lean against him. Both of them smile up at me, and I return the gesture. They remind me of Rian and myself, the way they seem to be drawn together and content to be so close.

Kaso Viro continues, "I did not know her name, but I trusted in the stars and what they showed me. I sent that champion, the golden one, a message. A plea. And wouldn't you know it? My trust in those very stars is what eventually led us to this precise moment. Azaeli Hammerfel, The Temperate, Pure of Heart, Reviver of Iren, The Great Protector, Cerion's Ambassador to Kythshire, Knight of His Majesty's Elite, The Mentalist, The Paladin, Champion of Light, Agent of Light, I ask you, humbly. Help us."

My eyes blur with tears at the Muse's heartfelt plea. I wade to him, and when he steps up out of the water to my level, I take his hand in mine. It's remarkable, I think to myself, how much he looks like Valenor, the first Muse I ever met. I remember how impressed I was by his humility, as well, at the time. These men can command the waters, they can mold dreams. Eljarenae has the power of all light in her hands at any given moment. How could it be possible I'm able to do something none of them can?

Flitt's light dazzles across the man's foamy white beard in lovely shades of teal, yellow, purple, and pink. She settles into my pauldron and pushes to me that she'll be there if I need her. I glance at Rian, who has already closed his eyes in meditation. I feel him gathering the power of Light to him, like he did in Sixledge. I nod to Kaso Viro and wade closer to the ice pillar.

"I'm ready," I whisper, drawing in a deep, calming breath.

I close my eyes, feeling the chill of the water outside my magical armor, aware of the soft warmth of the gambeson and padding against my skin inside of it. I focus on the sound of tiny waves lapping against the sides of the pool. I hear the breath of those around me. My heart speeds up slightly. The pillar of ice drifts closer. I'm aware of warmth. Of the sound of trickling water. I know when I open my eyes, the ice will be melted. I do it slowly, aware of how Kaso Viro has melted the Muse of Earth's prison just enough to reveal her brow, and her eyes just below it.

Sha'Renell's eyes are endless black, like two vacant, empty voids. They don't thrash from side to side when I try to catch their gaze. Instead, looking into them is like falling down a pit into nothing. The infinite darkness spirals around me, pulling me, twisting me, thrashing against me. Firmly inside her mind, I draw Mercy. The light of my sword is a tiny, insignificant needle in the vast space of Sha'Renell's mind.

My own thoughts seem to spiral uncontrollably into chaos and despair. My throat closes. My breath catches. I fight it, remembering a ward Kenrick taught me in Hywilkin. A protection of the mind, meant to keep the darkness out. I build that ward, blocking everything around me. My feet find the end of the pit almost immediately. I squint into the darkness, holding the light of my sword aloft like a torch, trying to see what I'm up against.

The Muse of Earth's mind isn't like Mum's or any other mind I've been in. It's filled with roots, twined together, snaking across the floor, burrowing into the ground. Some memories are giant boulders, stacked up on top of one another as far as I can see up. Everything, though, is coated with black. Like Stellastera's mind had been, it's thick as tar. When I try to move through it, I sink in up to my ankles, to my knees, to my thighs. It drags me down, pulling me deep, holding me fast.

I push the point of my sword into the goo, and it shrinks away from the light in fear. Strangely enough, I notice, it doesn't move away from the center point where my sword is. Instead, it flows away from it in one direction. I center myself again. I focus on the tar-like corruption. It's definitely moving. It flows like a stream away from me. Like a river from its source. I turn away from the direction of the flow and raise Mercy above my head. The light of my sword shines a little brighter. Within myself, I feel Flitt's presence at my shoulder again. I call to her to send me her light, and it pulses through my fingertips in brilliant rainbow colors that shine through roots and boulders into the mouth of an imposing looking cave.

"Stay with me," I whisper, hoping my words carry to Rian and Flitt on the other side of Sha'Renell's mind.

I push against the flow of the muck toward the cave, its source. Mercy's light is dim but helpful. It glints from every surface, giving me courage and strength.

As I near the mouth, whispers skitter from the inky stuff all around me. Warnings to turn back, threats against my life and the lives of my family and allies. Oaths of ruin. Unimaginable fear. I keep pushing, ignoring the voices, aware that I must be making progress since they seem to be growing fiercer against me. I reach the mouth of the cave and recognize the force without even having to step inside. It's the Void. The embodiment of emptiness, the purest force within the Dusk, as Light is the purest force within the Dawn.

"Sha'Renell?" I call into the Void, and my voice echoes back to me in hundreds of thousands of whispers.

The thought is overwhelming. These are the depths of the mind of the Muse of Earth, and it's completely consumed by the Void. I doubt anything remains of the mind she once had. It's remarkable to me, seeing this, that she could even function at all anymore.

There must be something, I tell myself. Some sliver of herself must remain. I take the tip of my sword and push it into the ooze that runs down the wall beside the cave mouth. It plunges until half of the long blade is covered, then it scrapes stone. With both hands, I grasp the hilt of my sword and drag the tip of it down through the muck. To my relief, a beam of green-gold light slices through the black.

"Sha'Renell!" I call.

"I am lost," her voice drifts from the sliver before the muck seeps over it again, snuffing it out.

"I'm here," I shout, scooping frantically at the tar-like stuff with my sword. "Follow my voice! Rian, Flitt, help me!"

My blade meets stone again and scrapes the black free, revealing the earth beneath it. "Now!" I yell, and an unbelievably powerful charge of light surges through me. It beams out of my eyes, my nose, my fingertips, my mouth. With it comes memories of Rian in Sixledge, obliterating Sorcerers with the touch of his hand. This is the power he was meditating for. It's fueled by the Muse, Eljarenae. It carries her own presence with it, the purest, most glorious beaming energy. The Lady of Light bolts past me, spearing into the sliver, bursting with a force that throws me back. I tumble away, into the darkness, into the Void.

My instinct is to panic. To pull myself back out of her, into the light, into reality, away from her mind. I feel something snap to me, though, and realize instead of going one way, I went another, and now my body is with me in this vast, unending darkness, drifting through the Void, one with it. I think of Rian and Flitt, back with Kaso Viro and the others, and my heart races. They don't know what has happened or why I disappeared. I try to reach them, to return to them, but the Void is too thick around me. I hope they don't come after me. This place is too corrupt, too dark and desolate. The fairies would never survive it.

I push away the panic that threatens to consume me with the thought of being alone in this place. I remind myself that I left them, not the other way around. Not on purpose, either. It was a risk I was aware of. Now I'm here, on my own, wherever here is.

I shift my thoughts and focus on what must be done. There has to be a way to defeat this Void, to snuff out this evil once and for all. I just have to find it. Ignoring the hisses and cruel whispers that taunt me, I push myself through the darkness, searching for it. The ward I placed on myself still holds. Their wicked thoughts and cruel doubts can't reach me. I just need to find out where this all came from and how it holds so much power.

I find my answer far more quickly than I expected to. Perhaps it's because my mind is so quiet and my ward keeps me from succumbing to the suggestions of this dark place. I don't know, but I sense him before I see him. The Muse of Darkness, seated on an obsidian throne, seething with fury at the loss of his last ally, his sister, Sha'Renell. I push away the surge of triumph that courses through me at that thought. I aim myself toward him, readying my sword which holds no light in this place.

It's worse than the Dreaming had been under Jacek's rule. Worse than death, this place. It's so desolate, so empty and lonesome, even with my wards to protect me I can't help the tears that spill from my eyes.

"The Champion of Light has found me," he says coolly. "I knew that you would, Azaeli. Of course you would. My perfect sister would never choose a failure, after all. Eljarenae can always be counted on to provide a real challenge. Paladin. Mentalist," he laughs mirthfully. "So perfect. So predictable. I imagine you're the envy of your kingdom. Praised. Worshiped, even."

My feet find solid ground as he speaks, but there is no light in this place. I can't see his shadowy form as it lounges across the throne, I can only sense it.

His words are meant to rile me. To sting me and make me feel small. They're just words, though. I let them roll off me like sand from a cloak. I keep Mercy in a defensive stance, never taking my eyes from the direction of his voice.

"It has been a long, weary little game, hasn't it?" Vorhadeniel sighs. "Ever since I named my own Champion, Diovicus, all those years ago, my siblings took far too long to name their own. But where are the others? Your friends? There are several more, are there not?" He laughs softly. "It doesn't surprise me that it required so many of their champions to stop my only one. He was glorious. He inspired such evil, such cruelty, even long after he died. So inspiring was he, that he was able to cheat death itself in the end. And his following was quite impressive, as well, I might add. I'm sure you agree. There's no record of anything like it in human history books. I checked. Hundreds of Sorcerers have worshiped him since his demise, and aspired to emulate him." He laughs again. "Of course, I played a hand in that, just as much as my sister had her hands in all your pointless little dealings."

"Pointless?" I laugh softly, gripping Mercy, waiting for him to make his move. "I'd hardly call them pointless. By my count, Vorhadeniel, you're on the losing side."

"Perhaps, from your worthless perspective, it seems that way," the dark one answers casually. "One thing the Light always seems to underestimate is their own weakness: love. You see…"

He stands slowly, and I have the sense of a long black cloak spilling out behind him. I imagine a hand, black and spindly, gesturing into the darkness. The figure of a girl appears beside the throne. Her white-blond hair is blotted by the Void, her golden crown dulled by shadow. Black webbing drips from her bare shoulders, pooling onto the floor. Her gaze is fixed on the Muse in a silent, desperate plea.

"…you always have this ridiculous need to *save* each other."

"Pippa!" I cry, and the princess's eyes flick toward me helplessly.

"She is mine," Vorhadeniel roars through clenched teeth. He dives at me, grabbing me by my collar, yanking me to his face. "She is mine. Brindelier is mine. Cerion is MINE. You cannot have it, you cannot save them. You have failed. They belong to me! I'm sick of toying. Sick of scheming. Sick of lying in wait for sunset. I OWN them. I claim them. They are MINE."

I swing Mercy hard to the side, slashing into his cloak and robes. He howls in fury more than pain. Sharp claws rake across my chest, shattering my armor. Shards of it glint reflections of Mercy's light as they skitter across the floor. Flitt's diamond, exposed through the gaping hole in my armor, flashes brightly. It catches the gold of Pippa's crown in colorful prisms that flash across the open Void.

"Azaeli?" a voice echoes toward me from very far away. I recognize it at once.

"Stellastera!" I scream. "We're here!"

"Shut your mouth!" Vorhadeniel bellows. He rips at my armor again, crushing it to pebbles, slicing through my gambeson and grazing the skin beneath.

Pippa screams, "Mother!" and Vorhadeniel snaps his attention back to her. He raises his hand to strike her, and she cowers as much as her cruel bindings will allow. It leaves me an opening. I plunge Mercy into his billowing cloak, stabbing at the chaotic void that swirls around him.

"You made a mistake in underestimating me," I shout at him, desperate to pull his attention from the princess.

My attack works. He whirls to face me again, gouging skin this time with his claws. I feel the sting of it and let the pain of my wounds fuel me. My sword comes down on his wrist, cleaving his hand free.

His reaction is a deep-throated laugh. He thrusts the severed stump forward and a new hand sprouts in its place.

"You are nothing," he hisses. "Barely a flea on the coat of a mammoth." With his attention fully on me, Stellastera easily sneaks behind him. She frees Pippa from the dripping shadows pinning her down, and throws her cloak over her to hide the girl.

Her cloak. The idea rushes over me in a burst of inspiration as Vorhadeniel's billowing mantle flares out behind him. If his cloak is like Valenor's, it holds most of his power. All I have to do is take it from him.

I slash at him again, cutting deep into his neck with Mercy. He rolls his shoulders as though slightly annoyed, and claws at me again, grinning at the sight of blood that soaks the white padding usually hidden by my armor.

As soon as Stellastera and Pippa vanish, I flick my eyes to the empty spot they left behind. I nod slightly, feigning a response to some signal.

The feint works. The Muse of Darkness whirls around to look. He howls in fury to find his prisoner gone, and strides toward the empty space she left behind. While he's distracted, I take my chance. I charge, slipping Mercy up between his mantle and his back. My sword knows my aim. It flicks to one side and the other, slashing at the fastenings at an impossible pace.

The cloak falls free. Before he can react, I yank it away and hold it to my chest. Without any direction from me, the cloak slithers to my shoulders and latches itself there. I feel the vast power in it, the chaos. Night. Shadow. I see the reach of the Muse throughout the Known Lands. Scenes flow around me in layers with myself at the center. Moments at my command. I must only think, and they obey. The darkness seems to retreat a little, giving way to Mercy's light.

"You thieving wretch!" Vorhadeniel screams, scraping his claws over his own face and arms. His body writhes and shudders. He curls into himself, weeping. He has no power to take it back. Without his cloak, the Muse is too weak.

Pushing aside the scenes which play around me, I step closer to him, pointing my sword. The black of my cloak pulses around it, licking at the light. Shadow calls to me, telling me what I must do. He shattered my armor. My chest aches from the wounds he inflicted. He deserves to die. Strike him down. End him. Wear the mantle with pride. Become the darkness. Vorhadeniel watches helplessly as Mercy's bright point spears closer to him.

Within the mantle, I feel other things. Whispers. Secrets. A power that has grown too strong. A corruption apart from night and shadow. The true force behind the dusk. Everything and nothing. The Void. That's the voice that commands me to be merciless. To lose myself to the darkness weighing heavily on my shoulders.

I take a deep breath and close my eyes, searching for the light within myself. The cloak's reach calls to me. It shows me its true nature. Darkness is peace and solace, it is rest and healing. It is a safe place, giving cover to shy creatures who choose not to venture into the light. Darkness can be gentle and comforting. It is a place for togetherness, for quiet comfort. I step closer to Vorhadeniel. There's no need to strike him down. Being so vulnerable to the light and so close to it is enough to keep him at bay for now. The other Muses are coming. The mantle helps me feel their presence.

"Azaeli," Valenor says quietly beside me. I feel his hand on my shoulder and turn to him, keeping my sword aimed at Vorhadeniel's cowering form. Valenor eyes the black cloak warily, and I realize its writhing and wild flapping has settled to calm. The Muse of Dreaming reaches toward me with his free hand. He scoops a handful of the strange, silky material into his hands and closes his eyes.

"Brother," he sighs with a shake of his head. "So long have you allowed yourself to be pulled into taint and corruption."

He crouches to Vorhadeniel's level, meeting his brother's eyes.

"It was the Void," the Muse of Darkness whimpers.

"That, we know," Valenor says. "But you were the one who allowed it."

I watch him warily, pressing my hand to the throbbing wound at my chest. I find it hard to believe that all it took to reduce the powerful Muse to this cowering mess was simply the removal of his cloak.

"Azaeli, sheath your sword, my dear," Valenor says.

I hesitate only for a moment before I do as he says. With Mercy's light extinguished, I can see the details of this place. It's like the Fairy Dark in Hywilkin, like the inside of an ancient tree. The stowing of the light seems to embolden Vorhadeniel, but only slightly. He sits up, his knees drawn to his chest.

"Please," he whispers pathetically, reaching toward me, "give it back."

My fingers flex. I fight the urge, once again, to draw my sword and run him through with it. The cloak ripples wickedly. It whispers suggestions, chiding me, tempting me. It takes a constant effort to keep it from commanding me. Every time I deny it, though, I feel the corruption of the Void unravel just a little more.

"It's true," I whisper to Valenor. "The Void is still present. It's trying to convince me to kill him."

"He cannot die," Valenor explains. He reaches to comfort his brother, but Vorhadeniel sneers and ducks a little deeper into the shadows. "We Muses are infinite. Immortal, your people would say. But we are not without fault, and we do not always choose the righteous path. The Void is an alluring presence. It calls to us constantly with promises of power and recognition. It tells you to kill him only because it knows the quickest way to corrupt you is through your heart."

"What is it, exactly?" I ask him. "Can it be stopped?"

"You have seen it yourself. It is a collection of vengeful, tortured souls. It has been nurtured and allowed to grow by our brother's schemes, and by the desires of Sorcerers and other evil forces. It was emboldened by the division of the Wellsprings.

Vorhadeniel has drawn others into it over the course of decades and therefore, gradually, has become nearly indiscernible from it. We are on the brink of stopping it now that the Wellsprings have been connected and my sisters and brother have been reunited. You see, when the Muses are in alignment, we have the power to suppress chaos and its influences. That is our duty. I imagine the mantle has shown you the true nature of darkness by now."

"Yes," I reply, my thoughts distracted by the scenes still drifting all around me. "When I'm wearing it, am I a Muse?"

"No," Valenor laughs softly. "It allows you the ability to be one with the element, in this case darkness, but no one may take the place of a Muse."

"What will happen now, Valenor?" I ask.

"Now, my sisters and brother shall unite with me, and bring our brother into balance."

As though in answer to his invitation, the others arrive one by one. Eljarenae floats into view as a single, pure white orb of light. Vorhadeniel ducks his head and covers his eyes as she shines over him. Kaso Viro arrives next, his turquoise silks rippling like ocean waves as he settles beside Valenor. He reaches a hand to his side, and Stellastera appears, her wings fluttering softly as they catch her sister's light.

"Lady Stellastera," I say, "Pippa? Is she safe?"

"She is returned to her brother, and to her place at the throne of Brindelier. I did not wish to leave her, but..." she gazes down at Vorhadeniel, her lips pressed into a firm line. "Thanks to you, Azaeli, I was given hope when I was convinced no hope remained within me. Despite what he has done, Vorhadeniel is my brother. I shall not turn my back on him. We all lose our way at times. If he can be brought back into balance, so be it."

The last to arrive is Sha'Renell. The Muse of Earth has changed her appearance completely. Her skin is earthy brown and rich, her hip-length dress alive with beetles, flowering vines and leaves which strategically cover her where they need to, but otherwise reveal her thick curves. Veins of orange like molten stone pulse across her, shining like the surface of the sun. Her hair is an unkempt, bushy nest that bounces slightly as she offers me a nod and a smile, and her green-gold eyes flash brightly as they meet mine.

"Lady Knight," she says, eyeing my cloak. "I owe you my heartfelt gratitude."

"I barely did anything…" my voice trails off. I don't know what to say. The change in her is almost unbelievable. She's like a completely different person.

"Shhh," she says soothingly, coming to stand before me. She sweeps her earthy fingers along the wounds dealt by her brother, and they tingle closed, healing. With another gentle gesture of her earthy fingers, the fibers of my gambeson knit together, and the pebbles of my shattered breastplate sweep up from the floor and mend like new. When she's through, she leans forward and kisses my cheek. The loosened threads of the mantle on my shoulders stretch toward her, licking at her arms and waist, but she simply brushes them away and turns back to her brother.

"Azaeli," Eljarenae beckons. When I go to her, her own cloak sweeps forward like an embrace, and mine seeps toward the light as though they long to touch. I feel the conflict in the fibers of my mantle, the longing of shadow to be restored to its own peace, the cruelty of the Void which taunts it to be something evil and hateful.

"Take the mantle," the Muse of Light instructs me. "Use it to vanquish the workings of the Void. With each act, you will feel the purity of darkness restored to what it should be. You alone have the strength required for this task. When your task is complete, we shall claim it for our brother, whose own balance we come together to restore now."

"Rian and the fae have returned to Cerion," Valenor informs me. "There, you will find the most wicked construct of the Void standing against the queen."

He drifts to me and embraces me. "The hope of the Known Lands rests upon you," he whispers. "The Dawn stands as your ally. Go swiftly."

The mantle flaps around me as I close my eyes and think of Rian and Flitt. Their presence calls to me like a beacon which I pull into my heart. My feet leave the dust of Vorhadeniel's hiding place. I crash hard on cobblestones. Magic explodes all around me. The light is so sudden and blinding that my head throbs with pain.

"Sybel!" Bryse bellows.

"She's mine!" Cort screams.

"Healer!" Mum shouts.

I stumble to my feet, call for Mercy, and blink rapidly into the blur of battle that rages on all sides of me.

Chapter Forty-Eight

DIOVICUS'S STAND
Azi

"Azi!" Flitt squeals with utter delight, sticking her palms to my face and smacking my cheek with a kiss.

"Flitt," I cry with relief.

"Look out!" she shouts. "Kobold!" I swing Mercy hard into the blurry mass that charges us. It yelps in pain and I swing again as my vision comes into focus. A third blow and the creature slumps to the cobbles, swallowed by the surge of attackers who scramble to face me. The chaos, the rage, the hatred all around us is tangible. The sounds of battle ring in my ears, mixed with Mya's strong voice calling a battle chant. A strong, dark presence looms nearby. I can feel the corruption and malice rolling from him in waves. Diovicus. The Revenant. I crane my neck to search for him and see him several paces in front of the gate, a rider in wet black armor atop a steed as dark as midnight.

All around me, the main courtyard teems with his army of creatures. The motley mix of imps, giants, skeletons, huge spiders, undead, and strange beasts I've never encountered spill through the broken gates and push toward the center of the city, skirting around their commander. They fight fiercely against barricades, wards, and magical blockades cast by Cerion's master Mages.

Our soldiers, all in shining chain mail and plate that blindingly reflects the strange bright light above the city, fight with brave determination. Battalions of city guards and the royal army block the entrance to every street, holding their ground firmly against the enemy. A row of twenty decoys of Her Majesty stands before the fountain, safely guarded between two lines of the Royal guard. A quick scan of the rear line finds Brother Donal in his brown robes, his head bowed in prayer, with Elliot beside him firing arrows into the fray.

Valor swoops over us and dives past the wall, raining white fire over the attackers approaching the gate from the outside.

"Rian's over here!" Flitt squeaks. She doesn't settle into her usual spot at my pauldron. Instead, she darts around me, flinging exploding globes of light this way and that while I hack through skeletons and other wretched creatures.

"I'm so glad you're back!" the fairy chatters excitedly in my ear as I run my sword into a strange, hissing black beast. "We were so worried! You left us! How could you do that? We tried to find you, but we couldn't! Not even with the diamond! We waited and waited, then the Muses said you were safe. Valenor told us we should go back to Cerion to meet you, and it took a lot of convincing. Rian trusted him, but I was skeptical. Of course, Shush didn't really argue. He's too easygoing to put up a fight. Honestly, I think he's kind of a pushover. You should see him around—WHOA! Watch where you're swinging that Sorceress, you oaf!"

"'Bout time you got here," Bryse shouts at the two of us. I watch in disbelief as he tosses Sybel, already battered and wounded, roughly to the ground. He and Cort charge her, and she thrusts her hand at us, unleashing a torrent of dark, crackling energy. My cloak swirls toward it, relishing its presence, aching to touch it. I command it with a thought: *"Away!"* and it obeys me. Sybel's bolt fizzles against the cage of light that settles around her, beaming down from the netting of it that stretches over the city. The Necromancer laughs tauntingly and calls out to her minions, who surge through the battle to protect their mistress.

I search through the stinking mass and catch a glimpse of deep blue robes beside a flash of Master Mage's red. Relief surges through me as a gap in the fight reveals Uncle in deep concentration, holding the threads of light that make up the Necromancer's cage. Rian, on the other hand, stands silent. Just like in Sixledge, his head is bowed, his hands clasped before him. Mya's chant weaves over us, strengthening us, giving us courage. Cort and Bryse relish the battle, raking through the crowd of Sybel's minions with barely an effort.

"Rian," Bryse says through clenched teeth as two risen dead scramble up his back. "Any time now!"

I slash the two creatures and they crumple to Bryse's feet. My cloak calls to me in wicked whispers, trying to change my resolve, to show me how I can win it all myself and take the glory. My spirit is too strong, though. Watching this battle unfold with the light of Margy's grace spilling over the city in an enormous web of golden light is breathtaking. This is true power. The power of love, of trust and togetherness, of strength of spirit. Pride of country and the promise of peace is what drives me. I stride purposefully around the outskirts of the fight, toward Rian. Ignoring the pull of the Void causes more threads of it to unravel and drift silently into the wind.

"Dacva," my mother's voice cries from somewhere far across the square. "Hurry, he's infected!"

The cloak shows me Tib, lying in my mother's arms, his body broken and limp. It taunts me with the image of the Dreamstalker, lost. One Champion down. I don't let it needle its hopelessness into me. Dacva is with him. He's held an oath of silence and meditation in the Conclave for many months, concentrating on honing his craft. He's a skilled healer now. One I trust. Tib will come through this even stronger than before.

I see what the cloak is trying to do. It means to distract me. It knows one of its most valued allies is about to meet her end. My awareness weakens the Void's hold. More threads unravel, revealing a velvety midnight blue beneath the black. Darkness. Peace.

I reach Rian with Flitt still buzzing around my ear, chattering excitedly.

"I'm here," I push to him, resting a hand on his arm. *"I'll guide you."*

He doesn't need to answer. I feel the shift in his mood, the light of his mind brightening. Beside him, Uncle grits his teeth. His fingers curl, claw-like, under the effort of holding his spell. Within the cage of light, Sybel has gotten to her feet. A dome of purple mist surges out from her, pressing against the cage, fighting to break it. I hesitate to allow Rian close to it, but Uncle glances sidelong at me and nods his encouragement.

I guide Rian through the fray as he continues gathering light, his eyes closed. With awkward one-handed swings, I slash an opening through her protectors. We reach close enough for Rian to touch her, and Sybel glares through the mist and the cage of light, directly at me.

Ice cold torture spikes down my spine. Undead scrabble at my cloak, tearing at it furiously, trying to steal it.

"Now," I push to Rian, letting go of his arm to snatch the flowing fabric from their grasp.

Rian's eyes fly open. He takes two calm steps and thrusts his arm forward. Sybel tries to dodge him, but the cage grows smaller, forbidding her. His fingertips graze Sybel's cheek. Her eyes go wide as light bursts from them, charging through her with a power that throws all of us back from its center.

Shush catches us with a gust of wind, and we land gently on our feet. Sybel's minions crumple to the ground. No longer under the Necromancer's control, they're reduced to nothing more than heaps of bones and dust. Bryse and Cort stand, swords in hand, scowling at the lack of enemies. Uncle lowers his hand, dismissing the cage of light, revealing the pile of ash that remains of the Necromancer. Shush takes a deep breath and blows a gust of wind at Sybel's ashes, and they swirl away, up over the wall. Rian turns calmly in place and I throw myself into his arms.

"I knew you'd come," he whispers into my hair. "What are you wearing?" The frayed ends of my cloak whip around him and he gathers the fabric into his hand and furrows his brow. The Void's hold on the cloak is far weaker now. The blackened edges of it hang limply from Rian's hand, and the field of midnight blue is beginning to display tiny points of starlight.

"The Plethore's weak rule has ended," Diovicus's voice thunders over us, rumbling the ground, cracking the webbing of light stretched between us and the blue sky. "Cerion is mine, and none shall stand against me. I, Diovicus, have come to make my claim."

"You have no claim, and never will!" Margy's voice is even stronger than his as it echoes from her decoys, scattered around the courtyard.

Rian and I whirl to face him. Despite its weakening hold, the mantle is relentless in its whisperings to my spirit. *This is what you could own. Give in to the power of the Void. Allow chaos into your heart. See the might of it. If you are too weak to do it yourself, surrender me to him. I belong to the Sorcerer King.*

I ignore the cloak's command, recognizing the desperation behind it. Instead, I choose to command it while I can. I pause and feel its reach. Hundreds of creatures still fight to get into the city, just on the other side of this wall. I feel the Void's disbelief as I draw my presence to the scene. With the power of the mantle to aid my Mentalism, I reverse the compelling desires that drew them into this war. I unravel their lust for power, their hatred and thirst for violence. I command them all to stop. To turn away, to flee. Most of them obey.

"The force is retreating!" A guard shouts from the parapet. Within the city walls, everyone goes silent. All eyes turn to our side of the wall, where the decoys of the queen stare Diovicus down from behind her line of defenders.

I push my awareness further along the hold of the Void and find something terrifying. This battle was the smaller one. The main force is concentrated elsewhere: Brindelier. All the Sorcerers of Dusk are there, wreaking havoc over the kingdom, pushing their way closer and closer to the All Source. I try to do the same with them, to order them to flee, but they are not mindless minions. Those Sorcerers believe in their fight. Their resolve is too strong. The Void's presence in the cloak is draining away. I feel it just as Valenor predicted. The essence of night, of darkness, is growing stronger. Slowly, steadily, it pushes the power of the Void out, reclaiming the mantle for the Muse of Darkness.

The Revenant's horse trots heavily from side to side, facing the queen. If he knows he's alone, he doesn't care. He raises his sword, swirling with black energy, and points it from one image of Margy to the next. Black fluid drips from him in streams, like the stuff that ran through the walls of the Sorcerer's keep. Like blood. It streaks down the armored black steed, pooling at its feet and splattering the cobbles with every stomp of its hoof.

He doesn't fool me when he shoves the guard of his helm up to reveal Eron's face, even though a gasp of shock echoes from some of Margy's guard. I know the truth. Eron is gone. All that remains is Diovicus, seething with malevolence and aggression.

The Royal Guard straightens their line. The Master Mages along the wall raise their hands, prepared to cast. I take in the scene, my attention coming to rest on my mother still kneeling, holding Tib, and Dacva working his healing over the boy. A figure I didn't notice before stands over them, his axe held ready to defend anyone who dares approach them. His barrel helm is clamped down over his face, but I'd know him anywhere. Da. What's curious about the scene, though, is the sparking black fae who hovers at his shoulder. She traces her finger along the sharp of his blade, and it drips with molten orange sparks as though it's fresh out of a forge fire.

"*Is that Ember, with my da?*" I ask Flitt in disbelief.

"*Yep! Can you believe that?*" she giggles.

"*But, how?*" I ask. "*When did that happen?*"

"*Well,*" Flitt explains, ignoring my double question, "*when I went back to tell the Ring about the Age of Kinship, lots of fae left Kythshire to come help Cerion prepare. Your da was working hard making weapons and armor. Ember helped him out, keeping his forge nice and hot.*"

"But, Da? Really? Are they Faedin—" I start to ask, but Bryse interrupts my thought.

"I thought killing Sybel would destroy the Revenant," he grumbles as he clomps to my side.

"That thing's not a Revenant anymore," Rian explains. "It's something far more sinister."

"How do we defeat it, then?" Cort asks as one of the Margys raises her hand to tuck a curl behind her ear. I recognize the signal right away from the training I watched her undergo at the palace.

"Together," I shout with a commanding tone, "and NOW!"

Diovicus snaps his attention to the Margy who moved, and as a team, we charge. Before we reach him, Margy unleashes her spell. The orb of light she commands shoots toward him, striking him in the chest, throwing him from his horse. His mount rears up and flees through the gates, and Eron's body, encased in light, crashes against the wall and slides to the street.

Our group changes directions to charge him, weapons raised. The Sorcerer's broken body crackles and shakes violently. Black stuff bubbles from his lips, through the crust of light that surrounds him. It spreads quickly, stretching over his face, head, and neck, down over his shoulders, across his chest. Every place the inky substance touches fizzes and bubbles disgustingly. The stench that rolls off him is nauseating. He pushes himself to his feet, growing until he even towers over Bryse. If ever there was an embodiment of evil and wretchedness, the warrior who stands heaving before us would be it.

We skid to a stop in a tight formation between him and the wards that protect the queen and her line, watching cautiously, waiting for the hulking black figure to make a move.

"Do you remember," Uncle murmurs to Rian, "when I told you to temper your emotions? This is what happens if you do not. All the despair, all the chaos and misery that churns within us, this is what it could become. It builds inside of us, gathering a power all its own, feeding on the Arcane, until it is able to consume a Mage, a Sorcerer, completely. This, my student, is what it becomes at its worst."

The seething warrior stalks closer to us. His eyes snap from Uncle to me, narrowing when he spies the cloak. He knows what it is. I can feel his desire for it.

"You see," I shout at him, advancing with Mercy, "your allies have fallen. The Muses of Darkness and Earth have changed their allegiance. They stand with us, now, and the might of the Dusk is withering. You cannot win here, Diovicus."

He closes the ten paces between us in half of a heartbeat. In a blur of black like a smudge on parchment, he snatches at my cloak. My feet move on their own, dodging his reach, and he catches only the blackened edge of it. The sound of the fabric tearing is like a hundred screams. I feel the Mantle's hold gripping my shoulders through my armor. The force of his pull on it spears through me painfully. I whirl in place, tearing the rest of my cloak from his grip, and swing Mercy with all my might. It catches his forearm, slicing a long gash along it, but Diovicus barely winces.

The others clash into him with their weapons and their spells. Mum and Da charge from across the square. I search for Tib, but don't see him. Dacva slips back to the guard line near Donal, which tells me Tib must be fully healed now. I don't have time to think too much on it.

The Sorcerer King snaps the Void-soaked strip of cloak he managed to tear free from the mantle between his tar-like hands. While Her Majesty's Champions stab and slash at the hulking warrior's legs, he ties the torn strip around his shoulders. With his head thrown back in guttural laughter, he relishes the clever triumph the cloak provides him. The strip of fabric grows long and billowing. Its pointed, frayed edges swirl around him like a storm, lashing out at our small force.

"No," I growl, pressing my attack. Mercy spears through his side, spilling black blood. His cloak of Void and Chaos grabs my sword and tries to fling me back, but I yank away from its grips and stab again. Bryse fights just as furiously on the other side of him, along with Mum and her glowing blue sword, and Da with his yellow-sparked axe. I try not to be distracted by Ember, still floating close to my da, spraying her fiery breath over the Sorcerer relentlessly.

Diovicus brings his hands together before him with a thunderous clap, and the force of the sound sends us sprawling backwards. He begins to walk forward, stalking toward the line of the queen's guard. With one flick of his fingers, he breaks through the wards guarding Margy. We scramble to our feet, preparing to charge him again as he snarls at the Queen. His skin is black as ink. It drips with blood-like liquid. Even his teeth and tongue are black when he opens his mouth to speak.

"Cerion will be mine. The Plethores will fall, and I shall reclaim the throne," he roars.

"Never!" Margy shouts defiantly. "Valor!"

The dragon soars overhead, drawing in a breath. We scramble backward to allow him space, and he sends a jet of liquid fire smashing into Diovicus. With our breath held, we wait for the beam to end. Rian and I cling to each other. Shush and Flitt shield themselves from the heat of the flames by ducking behind us. When the fire dissipates, Diovicus stands at the center of the smoking crater it leaves behind, wrapped in the Void cloak, completely unharmed.

"What now, Plethore?" he asks, grinning wickedly as his cloak slithers back to drape his shoulders.

"I never should have let him rip the cloak," I push to Rian and the others, feeling the neutral presence of my own mantle flapping behind me. The fact that the Void is completely gone from it now is little comfort to me as I watch the seemingly omnipotent Sorcerer creeping ever closer to my queen. It's impossible to know just how much of this power is his own, and how much he's drawing from the Void.

The decoys of the queen stand unmoved by his question, except for one, the third from the end. I see her move slightly and watch the subtle, nearly imperceptible nod of her head.

"We stand together," she and her decoys announce with confidence. "As long as I am its queen, Cerion will thrive in peace. Fight with me, my people. On my command."

The Margys raise their hands to the sky, drawing the light of the web into balls between their hands. Diovicus smirks arrogantly, seemingly barely concerned.

"Charge!" the queen shouts.

The flash of a bright purple blade catches my eye as chaos erupts around us. Diovicus screams under the torrent of Cerion's attack. My guild and I surge forward, weapons raised. A dozen master Mages aim their spells at him. As Mercy spears the Sorcerer through the chest, that purple blade flashes again at the corner of my eye. Diovicus's cloak breaks free. Tib slips out of shadow, gathering it into his hands. With the flick of a silver-white knife, he cuts the Void cloak into ribbons that bleed with dark power.

Diovicus screams in rage, whirling to strike him, and Bryse slams his shield into him, throwing him off balance. A torrent of wind from Shush topples Diovicus completely and sends him sliding across the cobblestones. The light of the webbing over the city strikes the Sorcerer in relentless beams. Each one seems to drain him of his power like a stripping. Add to that the breath of two dragons, and the

Sorcerer King howls. He bellows strange words that pulse with their own power, and scrambles to regain his footing.

We close in on him, slashing and stabbing while he's down. Bryse smashes his chest with his tower shield. Tib slams white-coated daggers into every crevice of his armor. Dark power spills out of those wounds and dissipates into the air. Diovicus turns his head weakly. His chest rattles. Black stuff spills from his mouth. He tries to swipe toward us, but can barely lift his arm. I raise my sword above his neck, prepared to deal the killing blow. When I bring it down hard, Mercy clangs loudly against the cobbles.

"He's gone!" Flitt squeaks.

"No!" someone else shouts.

"Where did he go?" Margy shouts. "What happened?"

"Stay where you are, my queen," Anod directs. "Do not reveal yourself just yet."

"He's still here," Tib screams, pointing at an empty space nearby. He flings a knife and it streaks across the space and disappears in mid-air. "Valor, get her back to the palace NOW!"

"Worthless wretches," Diovicus's rattling voice whispers all around us. "Cerion is barely worth it. Let it burn. I shall rebuild it from the ashes."

Valor swoops from the sky, scooping the queen in its clawed talon, and speeds toward the palace at the same moment the houses and shops lining the square burst into flames.

"No!" half of us shout. Shush speeds toward the flames with Rian close behind him. I sprint to Tib, who's still watching nothing with his eyes narrowed.

"Where is he?" I ask him as he turns slowly toward the city gate. "Where is he going, Tib?"

"Out the gate," he says, glaring. "Toward Brindelier."

Chapter Forty-Nine

FATE OF THE ALL SOURCE
Celli

Hand-in-hand, the prince and I pace from one balcony to the next, watching the battle surge from the edges of the kingdom closer to the palace at the center. Poe doesn't speak. He only stares into the distance, desperate to catch a glimpse of a battle too far away for him to join. Over the course of the morning, we watch the palace doors open to release waves of defenders. Most of them are members of the Royal Guard, but others are sprinkled in with them.

Kenrick and Tulya go out along with a band of commoners. An archer dressed in sleek black leather draws an arrow from her quiver and nocks her bow. The tip of it shines with white light. She aims her shot and lets it loose, and I hear it hit its mark. Moments later, from a space hidden from our viewpoint by rich-looking houses, a spiral of dark energy swirls into the sky and dissipates. A man in plate armor claps her on the shoulder, and they disappear around the corner, into the battle.

In the distance, toward the city gates, a troop of elves on cygnets patrol the skies, volleying their own white-tipped arrows outside the gates. One of the great birds dives to the ground, its rider raising an elegant sword over his head, prepared to strike. When he swoops up again, his blade is tinged with red.

"Thank the stars for the elves," Poe says. He pulls me by the hand, and we jog together through the Wellspring's atrium to the opposite side, where another balcony opens to the east half of the city. Glancing over my shoulder, I watch as the grassy floor of the previous balcony shifts and shrinks, and the glass walls close up to protect it.

"Is that you?" I ask Poe.

"Hm?" he replies absently as he leans far over the balcony railing, craning to see the state of battle on this side of his kingdom.

"The balcony. It changed. It was there, and now it's here," I say.

"Oh," he says, still distracted. "Yes."

I gaze at him as he stares urgently into the depths of his kingdom. His free hand rests on the hilt of his sword, and I wonder whether he even knows how to use. He looks like he could. He desperately wants to. His golden armor glints brightly in the late morning sun, splashing light over the smooth skin of his clenched jaw. He'd be resplendent in battle, I imagine. Seeing his frustration at being stuck up here, I find myself wishing for it. Longing desperately to stand beside him, to protect him in the fight that rages below. We could defend Brindelier together. We'd be a force to reckon with.

A streak of blue erupts from the parapet to our left, cast by a Master Mage in deep crimson robes, startling me. I watch the bolt shoot into the street outside the palace gate, where a huge band of Brindelier's subjects stand against a group of three Sorcerers. Some are soldiers, others merchants and commoners wielding weapons and spells. Fairies dart around them in orbs of every color, lending their unique variety of magic to the fray. The Master Mage's bolt is aimed perfectly at the center of the three enemies. It crashes through their wards, leaving them open to attack.

Another Mage, stationed at a tower beside the first one, unleashes his own attack. His bolt is pure white. It crackles through the air, leaving a wake of steam behind it, and strikes the point Sorcerer right in the center of her chest. Ice spreads over her. Her skin turns blue, her eyes open wide. She starts to scream, but her mouth freezes. The frost creeps up over her face and down to her feet. One of the commoners charges forward with his war-hammer and strikes a heavy blow. The Sorceress shatters. A thousand pieces of her skitter across the square.

Her comrades react with fury, commanding crackling dark energy into the crowd. My left hand aches. I wish I could reach down there and pull that darkness in. I could stop that attack and turn it against them, but I have no power from this far away. Their wicked spell strikes several of the defenders. Fairies tumble backward, screaming. Men surge forward, enraged.

Poe curses under his breath. He draws his sword, aiming its golden blade into the space between the two remaining Sorcerers. With one eye closed to ensure his aim, he whispers a word and a searing globe of golden white light shoots from the tip of his weapon, acting like a sort of wand. The globe of energy explodes between the two Sorcerers, interrupting their desperate attempts to recast their wards. From opposite towers of the palace, more spells shoot into the fray.

The Sorcerers fall. The band of defenders turns to cheer the towers, and Poe waves gallantly to them.

My fingers flex, aching to contribute, somehow. I can feel the conflicts all around the city, if I concentrate hard enough. I can tell, in my heart, how many have flooded through the gates. I'm aware of the balance between dark and light as it tips one way and another throughout the kingdom, even in places I can't see. My heart races. I feel a kinship with Brindelier. Not with the people themselves, but with this land and the magic it holds. Maybe it stems from my feelings for Poe, or my gratitude toward My Lady Stellastera. Toward the both of them, for embracing me despite my flaws. For loving me. It feels like something much deeper than any of that, though. A calling. Like something important is missing here, something I have the power to provide.

I flex the fingers of my left hand in Poe's, and he looks down at them. My skin is still obsidian, like stone, though it doesn't reach as far up my arm as it had before. I place my right hand on the railing, surprised to see how perfectly that one matches the milky white marble.

"Does it feel like stone?" I ask the prince, squeezing his hand as I raise it in mine.

"It feels soft and perfect," he replies, brushing the back of my coal-like hand against his cheek, kissing it tenderly.

As we watch the band of defenders rush into battles raging out of view, I wonder again what's happening to me. I can feel the change, slow and subtle. The rally to defend, the undeniable desire to snuff out the threat.

The intricate carvings decorating the palace towers entice me. While Poe watches the distant war, I find myself caught in the details of dragon scales, elk horns, and gargoyle's glaring eyes. I imagine what it would be like if those creatures were real. If they were able to leap from the towers and fight to protect Brindelier and everyone in it.

"Celli, what are you doing?" Poe asks in a hushed tone. I turn to meet his gaze and find myself head and shoulders taller than he is. The stone, obsidian and white marble, has crept to my chest. Outside of myself, I feel the battle shift slightly, wrongly, to Dusk. Movement in my peripheral vision catches my eye. I turn to look.

"That gargoyle," I whisper. "It moved."

Poe stares up at me from slightly farther below than he'd just been. His head comes to my waist, now. Somehow, it doesn't really seem strange to me. Poe grabs my hand and pulls me inside, toward the Wellspring.

"Ali!" he bellows. "Ali, help!"

I run behind him toward the Source, my large feet booming across the polished stone. His hand is tiny in mine. It barely fits in my palm. I have to bend low in order to keep hold of it. The marble and obsidian have crept across my shoulders. The folds of my acolyte's robes are like skillfully carved marble. Poe seems panicked, but his fear doesn't reach me. Even though I'm not sure what's happening, I feel like whatever it is is meant to be.

"Ali!" Poe shouts again as we reach the pool. The Keepers turn in place to face us. I notice a change in the space since we last paced through here. Each basin now has a mirror behind it. Scenes flash in them, following natives from each Keeper's lands. Vae's is directly across from me. In it, a coppery dragon with white scales along its side like opals, breathes fiery orange breath over some dark form standing before Cerion's gates.

Aliandra steals my attention as she darts from the center of the pool to Poe.

"What's happening to her?" the prince cries.

"How remarkable," Sapience says quietly. The other Keepers look at me in awe.

"Have you chosen this, Celli?" asks Ienae'luvrie.

"Of course she has," Mevyn huffs. "It could not have happened otherwise."

"She wished for it," Kuvelsk of Haigh grunts.

"It was a wise wish," Kiaan from Elespen says. "For it is a great folly for any Wellspring to be without one. Especially a Wellspring such as this one."

"To be without what?" Poe asks as I sink to my knees, carefully avoiding crushing the greenery of the garden behind me with my enormous legs and stone robes.

"A Guardian," Ienae'luvrie replies. "A Protector."

The words unlock something within me. I feel a charge from the All Source as its pure power enters me. I feel the city around me, its dark points, its light points. Poe steps to my marble-white knee and rests a hand on it. He gazes up at me with a mix of wonder and regret.

"But I love her," he whispers, "as she was before."

My heart races, thumping in my chest so hard I fear it'll leap out. My ears ring. My face tingles with warmth. He loves me. He said it.

"And you still do," Sapience says. "I can feel it. What better Protector, after all, than one who is loved?"

"If she concentrates," Aliandra says, floating up to my eye level, "she can change her size. Try it, Celli."

I close my eyes and take a deep breath as my head grazes the high glass ceiling of the atrium. I think of Poe. Sinking into his arms, hearing his heartbeat through his chest as my head rests against it. I imagine myself small again, but nothing happens.

"Try," Ienae'luvrie urges. "You can do it."

"It is a difficult concept for a human," Mevyn scoffs.

"You aren't helping, sun guzzler," Kuvelsk grunts.

I squeeze my eyes shut tighter and try as hard as I can. When I open them, I'm maybe a human hand's-width shorter.

"Perhaps now is not the best time," Sapience says. "She needs to be imposing."

As if to emphasize his point, a flash of blinding light bursts over the Wellspring. I throw my hand down, instinctively shielding Poe. Immediately I'm aware of the new presences in the atrium. My Lady Stellastera, Lady Eljarenae, and—

"Pippa!" Poe cries. He darts around my hand, racing to the place where Stellastera kneels, cradling her daughter. The princess's face is stained with tears, her spirit empty and desolate. Poe slips his arms around her where she lies, and Stellastera works to shift her from darkness into light again, just like I did in my lessons.

"What happened?" the prince asks his mother, and she tells us all about Azaeli's confrontation with Vorhadeniel and how the knight allowed her to steal Pippa from his grasp.

"I tried to help her," a weak voice whispers from the crook of Pippa's arm. "I thought I could shield her."

"Alex!" Aliandra cries, darting to the wasted white fairy who spills out from the golden folds.

"Stand back," Stellastera directs the prince and his Faedin, and Poe draws Ali close to his chest and reluctantly moves away from his sister.

With one hand on her daughter's heart and the other open to the sparkling pool of the Wellspring, Stellastera lifts her chin toward the sky and closes her eyes. Behind her, her sister Eljarenae places her hands on My Lady's shoulders and also looks up. The power of what they're doing is unfathomable. My lady draws perfect, pure energy from the Wellspring through one hand, sending it into the spirit of her daughter. Lady Eljarenae draws the power of Light from all around her and charges My Lady's energy with it.

It doesn't take long. Only a few heartbeats. Pippa blinks and sits up. Poe runs to her, hugging her.

"Sister," says Eljarenae, still holding My Lady's shoulders.

For the first time, Stellastera looks to the rest of us in the Atrium. She peers up at me with a knowing smile, then down to her children again.

"You will be safe here," she says to Poe and Pippa. "Though I hate to leave, I must go and do what I can to ensure your uncle is released from the chaos which has held him and changed him so completely."

"We'll protect each other, Mother," Poe assures her.

The Muse kisses her son and her daughter, and she and Eljarenae vanish. Far below me, the twins fill each other in with everything that has been missed between them since the princess's disappearance. Their tales are filled with such detail, I can see each moment like a play in my mind.

The Keepers listen closely, too. As brother and sister talk and scheme, each mirror around the Wellspring shows flashes of the battles happening across the Known Lands. My eyes are drawn to Sapience's mirror more than the others. There, the war at the gates of Cerion is raging. The scene hops from one perspective to the next, as though shifting through a dozen different fairies.

When Diovicus's voice rings out from his mirror, a hush comes over the atrium. Even the endless jets streaming from the pool's surface seem to quiet. The fight unfolds, and when it seems he'll be defeated, the Sorcerer King vanishes. At first I think he's been defeated, but when the square erupts in flames and Tib declares he's coming toward our kingdom, my blood runs cold.

The twins tip their heads together in whispers. I can't discern what they're saying, but I feel the tone of it. They're conspiring. Neither of them wishes to stay hidden and safe in this tower. Pippa's capture has lit a fire in her spirit. She wants to be a part of the battle. She wants to be the one to face Diovicus. Poe, too.

"Your Highnesses!" Azi's voice rings out, startling us. The knight emerges at the edge of the pool and strides toward Pippa and Poe. "Oh, Pippa! I'm so glad to see you safely returned. I came to warn you. Diovicus has left Cerion. He's charging this way."

"We know," Pippa says. "We're ready."

Azi turns toward the Wellspring and sees me for the first time. Her eyes go wide and her jaw drops in shock.

"What is…" she whispers. "Is that Celli?"

I nod, feeling my head brush against the glass ceiling. Azi starts to say something, but shakes her head slightly as her eyes go distant.

"He's at the gate to your kingdom," she says with an urgent tone.

"How do you know, Azi?" Pippa asks, stepping closer to her.

I can feel it as the knight describes it. The fae, Flitt, clings to Tib in the Half-Realm. The pair follows Diovicus with caution, keeping a close eye on his movements. He's hidden as well, cloaked by a strong invisibility spell. The scene plays out in Sapience's mirror for all to see. The gate of Brindelier was breached when the Sorcerers entered. It's heavily guarded by Brindlians, but none of them see Diovicus slink through. Only Tib can see him.

The Dreamstalker follows him as he weaves through the city streets, skirting around conflicts between Sorcerers and defenders, slipping past guards at their post, ignoring everything but his own determined path.

"He's coming here," Pippa whispers.

I know she's right. I can feel his dark presence, step by step, as he nears.

"Why doesn't Tib attack him?" Poe asks. "He told me of his abilities. He's capable of taking down a Sorcerer with his white blades."

"That creature," Alex explains, peering into Sapience's mirror, "is no mere Sorcerer. He has been championed by Darkness and he has cheated death. His following was the soil that nurtured the seed of Chaos. As weakened as he is, he is the embodiment of the Void with the spirit of a Sorcerer King. His wicked power is unmatched by any Sorcerer or Mage in this land."

"How do we destroy him, Sapience?" Azi asks warily.

"Together," the Keepers reply in unison.

Poe and Pippa exchange a knowing nod. The two clasp hands and lower their heads, and the Wellspring begins to bubble. With a sweeping motion from the two of them, the atrium begins to grow. The ceiling opens completely to the sky, the pool widens, the gardens spill further from the center. A grassy lawn inches over the stone walkway and sweeps forward to the gilded gate. When their spell is through, there's more than enough room for me to stand among them.

Alex and Ali dive into the Wellspring and emerge the size of the other Keepers, as tall as an elf. They take a defensive stance at the base of the footbridge facing the gate. The prince and princess stand on either side of them, and I push myself to my feet and peer down from the open tower ceiling into the kingdom below.

The creatures carved into the towers seem to crane their necks to look at me as I make my appearance. Bears and unicorns, gargoyles and winged steeds, tigers and strange creatures all turn as if waiting for my word. I nod, just once, and they leap from their places and charge into the city, trumpeting and growling and howling battle cries.

In the distance, cygnets circle and dive. Beyond them, I sense ships arriving at docks. A triumphant return. Happy reunions, cut short by the battle already raging. A dragon with coppery wings glides close, circling. On its back, a rider with bright red curls raises her hand in greeting. I know her from Cerion.

"Saesa!" I shout.

"Celli?" she calls in disbelief.

I sense another presence with her, hidden with magic. Two, actually. Fae and queen. The dragon circles again, his sharp orange eyes flashing brightly. When I step aside to give him room, he shrinks to a small enough size that he can fit through the opening still carrying the group, and sets himself lightly beside the prince. As soon as Saesa and the queen dismount, he flicks his wings and they become a cloak, and the dragon transforms into a warrior.

"Thank you, Skalivar," Margy says with a curtsy, and the warrior offers a low bow. His eyes drift across the Wellspring to Vae, and he drops to one knee and bows his head with deep respect for the Keeper. The elves follow their arrival. They let their cygnets roost along the edge of the tower wall, and drop lightly to their feet beside Ienae'luvrie.

Diovicus's nearing presence steals my attention. I peer into the city, watching the empty space he occupies as it urges crowds to part and form again behind him while he progresses. I feel his hatred building, for the followers who fight in his name. He doesn't need or want them anymore. Their purpose is pointless now. This will be a victory all his own. He prowls past them and, Sorcerer by Sorcerer, steals their power, leaving them defenseless and wasted in the face of their enemies.

This kingdom is his, and no mere Sorcerer will remain to stand in his way once he claims it. I stare in disbelief as his shadowed form slinks from one fray to the next, leaving his own allies in crumpled defeat as he grows stronger by their power.

The stronger he becomes, the greedier he gets. His focus changes. He has seen me on the tower. He knows the strong force that waits for him within. He'll leave nothing to chance. Pippa will be his. Brindelier and Cerion will be his. He strays from his straight path toward the kingdom, instead hunting down as many Sorcerers as he can find.

The turn of events is puzzling until I become slowly aware of another presence lurking behind Diovicus beside Tib. Flitt has disappeared. Valenor drifts along in her place. The Muse of Dreaming is both there, and not there. His influence over Diovicus is subtle, but strong. At first, I wonder why he'd encourage our enemy to strengthen himself, but I realize the depth of his plan when the other presences make themselves known to me.

In the Wellspring tower at my feet, a group is gathering. The Muses wait in hushed silence, shoulder to shoulder with each other. All of them are present: My Lady Stellastera of Magic, Eljarenae of Light, and Kaso Viro of Water. Sha'Renell of Earth stands with them. Twig darts around her in joyful loops, chattering about trees and leaves and flowers and dirt. In Sha'Renell's arms, swaddled in a bundle of soft green moss, a baby with deep blue eyes and chestnut skin coos.

The knight Azaeli approaches them, taking a deep blue mantle scattered with stars from her shoulders. She drapes it over her arms, and Sha'Renell passes the child to her.

"A Muse cannot die," Eljarenae explains in a hushed tone as she approaches Azi, "but he can start anew." The Muse of Light tucks her brother's mantle gently around him, and kisses his cheek lovingly.

"See, Rian, we're just in time," Shush whispers as he, Rian, and Flitt emerge beside Azi.

"That baby looks good on you," Rian quips, kissing Azi's cheek. A deep blush blooms from the spot, and the knight passes the child quickly to Eljarenae.

Vorhadeniel's eyes meet mine, and his tiny hands reach toward me.

"What is it?" Eljarenae asks. "Ah." She looks up at me and beckons me closer. I offer them an obsidian fingertip, and the baby grasps it with his tiny hands.

His touch invokes flashes of memories of the Void and the darkness that held me thrall. I feel a slow shift into a deeper understanding. His gift is his apology for all the dark moments he saw me suffer through. It fills me with a deeper understanding of my new role. It charges me with skills and knowledge. I close my eyes and breathe deeply, feeling the change within me as I grow smaller and smaller. When I open my eyes, I'm face-to face with Poe, who sweeps me into a tearful hug.

As much as I want nothing more than to stay here, warm in his embrace, the approaching threat nags at me. I step away from my prince and look from him to his sister and the rest of the gathering.

"He's obliterating his own forces in order to strengthen himself," I say. "He's nearing the palace."

"Let him come," Pippa says, squaring her shoulders and glaring at the gate.

"Rian, what happened with the fires?" Queen Margary asks, wringing her hands nervously as Rian, Azi, Saesa, and her hulking companion move to protective positions around her.

"They're out," Rian replies with a dismissive wave. "They were no match for our Mages. They were extinguished before any real damage was done. It was merely a distraction. Everyone is safe, Majesty. They're working on fortifying the gates and restoring what little damage was done, as you instructed."

"Don't worry," Tib whispers from beside the queen, surprising everyone including myself with his sudden appearance. "Cerion will come through it. I don't know about all of you, but I'm about ready for this to be over."

"As are we all," My Lady Stellastera says, standing between the twins with their hands in hers. The other Muses join her in a line, with Valenor arriving silently at the end.

"He's here," the Muse of Dreaming says, his lips pressed into a thin line.

"Ready yourselves," the Muse of Light advises. Behind her, the Wellspring churns and bubbles. The Keepers come to the center of the pool with Aliandra and Alexerin among them. The light shifts, and another presence emerges, stepping onto the footbridge. Her gown spills into the pool. Her crown of antlers and corals and dew-kissed branches stretches into the sky. Behind her stands an army of fae, poised and prepared for battle.

"Memi!" Flitt cries, darting to greet her.

When even the Keepers bow to her, I know she must be the queen of their realm. The Queen of the Fae.

"Let him come," they all say as they straighten to attention. A few turn to look at me expectantly. I can feel Diovicus just outside, as Valenor said, prowling along the gates of the palace, testing the strong wards. Mages on the parapets shout eerie warnings at each other. Guards at their stations call orders to ready themselves.

Poe leaves his mother's side and takes me in his arms. He gazes into my eyes, and kisses me softly. My heart races with my love for him and my need, as I wished before, to stand beside him, to protect him and his kingdom and everything he holds dear. I feel him let go as I shift again into the role of Guardian, a gargantuan presence large enough to reach all the way down to the wretched creature who paces furiously along the wards.

He pauses when he sees me. Our eyes lock, and I feel the cruelty and malice rolling through him in sickening waves. Scenes of my life as a thrall play back in a distant part of my mind, but I don't let them weaken me. Instead, I'm fueled by them. Empowered. I reach down with my stone black hand and pluck the wretched thing into my palm. He makes his best effort to inflict me with pain. My eyes spike with heat from the hold he had on me before. *Caviena.* My blood burns with the memory of Quenson's mastery over me.

I tighten my fist, feeling his bones crack in my grips, but he doesn't scream out. He seems to relish the pain, to desire it.

"Brindelier will be mine," he screams as I lift him into the atrium. I peer down at the group of Keepers, Muses, Champions, and allies waiting.

My lady nods to me, and without any ceremony, I drop Diovicus to the polished stone like the refuse he is. Chaos swirls around him in ribbons of fraying black. The power he releases is immense and terrifying, and when he pushes himself to his feet, his presence is truly impressive.

He barely has time lift a finger, though, before he's met with the torrent of combined attacks. The Keepers draw from the Wellspring, jolting him with indescribable energy, skewering him with the might of pure magic. The Muses combine their own attacks in a rush of the elements: Light, darkness, water, earth, magic, and dreaming clash together in a beam of sizzling energy that rips at Diovicus's flesh and unravels the Void that swirls around him.

Azi and the others charge, barraging him with their magical weapons, and he falls to his knees, grasping at the floor with claw-like hands. He crawls in stilted movements toward the princess, screaming her name in wretched, agonized howls, pleading for mercy as the relentless attacks continue.

The might of the Dawn is no match for Diovicus. Before long, it becomes clear that his selfish drive to reach us was in vain. He tries desperately to get to Pippa, declaring with every rattled breath that she is his, and he will have her. Poe aims his sword at the unraveling, pathetic creature as it scrabbles closer to them, striking him with bolt after bolt as Pippa stands clinging to him, too horrified to act.

"Save me," Diovicus shrieks, cowering at the princess's feet. "Mercy, my darling, my own. Please. Mercy!"

I step closer, ready to put myself between them and the pathetic creature, but I pause. Silhouetted by the unrelenting surge of magic from the Muses and Keepers, the knight Azaeli steps to the princess's side and offers her sword.

"He begs for Mercy, Highness," she says. "I pray you give it to him."

Her eyes wide with understanding, Pippa takes the offered weapon. Diovicus writhes before her, a blackened shell of his former self, still pleading in chanted whispers. The princess's hands shake, but her lips are pressed together in determination. Alex streaks to her side and wraps his hands around hers, steadying them. Their eyes meet, and he gives her a nod of encouragement. With the might of the Dawn at her back and her Faedin's firm guidance, Pippa raises the sword and plunges it into what's left of Diovocus.

The swift, lethal strike sends a surge of evil pulsing out from it. I throw my left hand out, scooping the energy up, spinning it into me and whirling it out again in a stream of light which streaks into the pool. My lady does the same, ensuring every dark thought and wicked strand is properly cleansed, purified, and returned the All Source.

Pippa lets the sword drop from her hands. She falls to her knees and Alex catches her, holding her close. Aliandra swoops in beside them and burrows herself into Alex and Pippa's arms. Their mother joins their embrace, and rather than join them, Poe turns to me with his arms outspread. In a heartbeat, I return to his size, rush into his arms, and lose myself in his kiss.

The others move in, one by one: Muses, Champions, Her Majesty, Tib, the Keepers, and even the Fairy Queen gather close, joining the embrace. The love and light of Dawn floods over us, melding with the Wellspring, spraying into the sky in golden jets.

In the short-lived silence following Diovicus's defeat, somewhere past the gates of the palace, a single child's voice rises in song. It catches like wildfire, spreading the news of triumph and victory through the streets of Brindelier and beyond, declaring the start of the Age of Kinship throughout the allied kingdoms of the Known Lands.

Chapter Fifty

SKY JOURNEY
Tib
Twenty-Eight Midsummer, Year One of the Age of Kinship

"So, the wind turns the blades outside, and that makes this gear turn, which makes the pole turn, and that connects to the pump arm, which draws the water up," I explain to Margy, who clings to my arm as she cranes her neck to look way down to the first floor of the windmill.

"It must be very deep," she whispers in awe.

"It is, fairly," I say. "We never would have been able to dig it without Sha'Renell's help, and Loren did a great job finding the shallowest places for groundwater."

"It's remarkable, Tib," she whispers in awe. "Truly. What if there isn't any wind, though?"

"In the desert, there's always wind. It's flat and open, like the sea," I explain.

"You can't really call it a desert anymore," she says, grinning. She reaches past me. Unlatches the shutters. Pushes them open. The swift, warm breeze loosens her pinned-back curls. As far away as we are from home, her soft fragrance is the same: green leaves and sea air. I breathe it in as she turns away to lean on the window frame and peer out.

"Did you ever dream it would be like this?" she asks, gazing at the scene.

"No. It used to all be Everlin," I say. I move to her side and look out into fields of green and gold slashed with rivulets of pure, clean water that reflects the deep blue sky, as far as even my healed eye can see. Here and there, the fields are dotted with a dozen sturdy stone farmhouses and barns, each with its own water mill like this one. Tiny dots of brown and white goats and fat cattle drift across every yard, grazing. "It was red, everywhere. Even inside our lean-to, you could smell it. You'd have to walk for a day just to get away from the smell. Not that anyone was ever allowed out."

"That's in the past now," she whispers, sliding her arms around me. She lays her head on my chest and I tip my chin to rest in her sweet-smelling curls.

"Thanks to you, and Prince Vorance," I say.

"No, Tib," she sighs. "No one but you could have turned it into this. Even the Crown of Sunteri is impressed. The king has already declared that Zhilee should be a model to all his other territories."

Zhilee. The name makes my heart race. Margy hears it thumping. She places a hand on my chest beside her cheek. I knew as soon as I saw what our old home was becoming, that I'd name it after her. Little sister. Even so, every time I hear it I'm reminded of Zhilee's terrified face as we were stolen away in that Sorcerer's dark carriage.

"She would have loved it here," I murmur. "She would have been like those kids out there," I say, pointing to the stone house a few hundred paces away. "Running around, chasing pigs."

We stand quietly for a while, listening to the whoosh of the windmill's blades, watching the steady wind shift the color of the wheat from gold to white to brown in waves. Listening to kids laughing and horses neighing and men singing in the fields, making the work go faster. Men who own this land now. Who work for their families, and not the slave master's whip. Free men.

A squawk from below makes us both jump.

"Don't be impatient, Joli!" Margy calls, leaning out of the window. "Eat your lunch!"

"She feels the warmth of the wind, Majesty," Julini shouts over the whoosh of the windmill blade that slices past. "It calls to her."

I slide my arm around Margy's waist and look down at the three cygnets below, pecking at cobs of corn. Joli, Margy's mount, stretches her wings to their full reach and flaps them eagerly, shaking her head and squawking again.

"All right, in a moment!" Margy laughs and turns to look at me. The blue sky catches flecks of gold in her brown eyes, making them look like they're dancing. Slowly, she closes one shutter and then the other, never taking her eyes from mine. "Thank you for bringing me here," she whispers. "I never could have pictured it from words in a letter. Even having seen it in Azi's mind, I couldn't have imagined it to be so perfect until I saw it myself."

"It's perfect because you're here," I whisper. She presses closer. I close my eyes. We lean into each other. Kiss. This one isn't our first, but it feels the same as that first one every time. A spark of warmth as our lips touch. A sweet sigh between us. A secret closeness for only us two.

"Ahem!" Twig yelps, emerging between us. He puts one hand on my chin and the other on her forehead. "Really! I blink way for barely a moment and you two are at it! Your Majesty, I take my role as chaperon very seriously! Remember what the Queen Mother said! Not until you're properly betrothed. You were only allowed on this tour if you promised—"

"I know, I know," Margy says, rolling her eyes. She shakes her head at me, grinning, and starts down the spiral staircase with Twig buzzing around her head. "Honestly, though, I've told you before. Mother isn't stupid. She knows how Tib and I feel. And you said it yourself, kissing is amazing. Fairies don't need to be betrothed. You go around kissing whoever you like, whenever you feel like it."

"That's beside the point! And it's different for fairies! Anyway, I'm just saying that because I'm supposed to. Still, doesn't mean you need to stick yourself to his face every time you two…" his voice drifts off as they reach the lower floor and the door closes behind them. I laugh to myself and look around, making one more quick check that everything's in working order before I follow them out.

Julini leads on her cygnet with Margy and I riding side-by-side on our own. We swoop low along the wheat and soar higher past houses. Mothers come out to porches to wave. Kids laugh and chase us, throwing flowers and calling my name, and we make a show of looping and diving and flying in formation.

Margy's laughter rises on the wind, her hair flying back behind her as she skillfully pulls her cygnet's reins. Flying a cygnet is a lot like riding a horse, Julini had told the two of us earlier this spring, when the two puffballs the elves had gifted us were finally big enough to fly. The only difference, really, is the falling distance.

I had thought it was funny, but Her Majesty the Queen Mother hadn't appreciated the joke. Still, it was obvious nobody was going to talk Margy out of learning to glide. She compromised with the Queen by having Master Anod teach her a Drifting Feather charm, so if she ever fell off, she'd float gently to the ground.

"Beat you to the ship!" Margy shouts from beside me, pushing Joli to her top speed.

"I know you're not going to let a couple of girls beat us, are you, Glyn?" I call, patting the side of my bird's neck and gripping the saddle horn. His answer is a lazy coo. Of the two birds, he's always been more aloof. He picks up speed reluctantly, and the ground beneath us blurs to streaks of green and gold.

As soon as I see the ship's tiny dot in the distance, the shadow of a much larger wingspan crosses over us. Glyn slows in the cool of the shade, and I crane my neck to look up at the glittering belly of the dragon Saesa and I once called Opal.

"Hey Skalivar!" I shout, "We're trying to race, here!"

"She's beating you!" Saesa yells from the dragon's back, laughing, and the two of them bank away.

"Did you hear that?" I yell at my cygnet, but my urgent tone doesn't seem to bother him. "Fine, lazy," I grunt. "Go at your own pace. You're not the one who'll have to hear about it all the way home, though."

I swear if cygnets could shrug, that's what I'd be getting from him right now. He caws indifferently and pumps his wings a little faster.

"Cygnets off the port stern!" Ruben shouts as we near the ship, "and dragon, ho!"

By the time Glyn decides to make his landing on the deck of the ship, Margy and Julini have already dismounted and their cygnets have gone to roost on the lower deck.

"See?" I mumble to Glyn as I hop from the saddle. "If you'd have flown faster, you could already be napping like they are."

"He just needs to grow a little more, don't you, Glyn?" Saesa says, patting the cygnet affectionately. "He's only a little guy."

The ship lists suddenly, throwing me to the side into Skalivar, who has transformed back from dragon to warrior. He scoops up Margy and Saesa, too, and Julini grabs his arm to steady herself as Glyn caws and flaps away to join the other cygnets.

Squeals of laughter and lighthearted screaming echo from the bridge, and the ship levels out again.

"Hey! Easy on the rudder!" I shout. I squirm free of Skalivar's strong arm and run up the stairs to the bridge.

"Great, who let you steer?" I mumble, only half-joking, when I spy Efran at the wheel.

"He had to learn sometime," Ki argues, still giggling. "He's getting the hang of it." She sidles up behind him and rests her hands on his as his brow knits with concentration. "I think he's doing a fine job," she says, resting her head against his back.

"Ugh," I reply, rolling my eyes.

"Sisters," Raefe scoffs, echoing my disgust. He turns away from the railing to concentrate on the navigation instruments, and I glance back to the main deck and see Saesa in her gleaming copper-glazed armor and Skalivar in his matching scale gazing lovingly at each other, hand in hand.

"Think we can be back to Cerion by suppertime?" Ruben shouts down from the crow's nest. "I'm sick of salt fish!"

"You'll never be a real sailor if you can't stomach salt fish for more than a couple days, Rube," Raefe hollers up to him.

"What do we need with boring water sailing when we've got ships like this, anyway?" Ruben yells.

"I take that to mean we're quite ready to return." Valenor's voice drifts to me on the breeze. "Shall I help us along then?"

"Let me take the wheel first," I reply, nudging Efran out of the way.

The others take the hint and file back to the main deck, leaving just me, Margy, and Valenor together on the bridge. The ship shudders slightly, the sails fill out, and with a gentle boost from the Dreamwalker, we speed northward through the Half-Realm.

"Think about it," Margy beams. "From Sunteri to Cerion in an afternoon's journey."

"Yeah," I agree, nudging the wheel slightly. "Thanks, Valenor."

His cloak flutters against us both, and Margy steps closer to me. I take her hand and place it on the wheel, and we steer home to Cerion together.

We arrive at the white cliffs at sunset, with nothing more than a small escort of royal guards to greet us. There's some cheering and fanfare at the sight of the queen, but her people are so used to seeing her around the kingdom, now, that it's barely a spectacle anymore.

"Race you home," Ruben shouts to Raefe as they run down the gangplank. Ki, Efran, and Skalivar wave to us and follow the boys at a slower pace.

The royal guards bows to the queen and files around her, while their captain salutes Saesa.

"I trust you had a safe journey, Lady Knight," the captain says to Saesa, who echoes his salute. He falls into step beside her, two paces behind me and Margy.

"It was mostly uneventful," Saesa replies, filling him in on all the mundane details of the queen's security during our short journey.

As we make our way from the docks to the palace, I keep a sharp eye for any threat. Even though it's been months, I can't help it. Where Margy is concerned, I think I'll always be on alert. Of course, we're met with no hint of any resistance. The queen of Cerion is loved by everyone, especially now that the threat of Sorcery isn't much more than an unpleasant memory.

"Oh, Tib, look," Margy gasps, squeezing my arm. She points at the billowing blue and gold silks and glowing lanterns adorning the outskirts of the forest park as we near the palace. "Twig, did you shape the trees that way? It's like a cathedral!"

"Oh, yes!" Twig chirps. "You know, this is still their favorite spot. Tomorrow, it'll be all lit up with rainbows and fairy orbs. You should see what Flitt's got planned. It'll be a wedding like nothing you've seen!"

"Shh!" Margy whispers urgently. "It's bad luck to share details before the wedding day!"

"Majesty, I think we've all had our run of that!" Twig laughs. "Bad luck! Ha!"

"Your Majesty!" someone calls to us from the gates of the palace. The shock of his orange robes is enough to make me cringe.

"Dumfrey!" Margy calls, laughing. As the bumbling Mage jogs toward her, Sorwa squeaks with excitement and darts around his legs, getting tangled in his robes. He starts to fall, and Sorwa thrusts her hand forward, conjuring a giant spring to bounce him upright again.

"My fault!" she squeaks. The spring, having served its purpose, starts bounding off down the street, careening toward a merchant stall of blown glass. "Ack! Get back here, you!" the fairy yelps, chasing after it, leaving a trail of baubles and gadgets in her wake. Dumfrey chases after her, casting a tidying spell which ends up sweeping dirt from the cobbles instead of retrieving the spring.

With a giggle, Margy flicks her hand. The spring goes still just before it strikes the stall, and Sorwa scolds it furiously, ordering it to return to its pocket. Embarrassed, Dumfrey turns to wave his thanks to the queen.

"Oh, Dumfrey," Margy whispers, still chuckling.

"I'll see you later," I mutter to her, before the Orange Terror can make his way back to us. I kiss her fingertips softly, and she nods and squeezes my hand, then lets it go. She knows how I feel about that mess of a duo. She doesn't make me stay.

I slip into the Half-Realm absently, pushing thoughts of weddings away in favor of new inventions and contraptions. Instead of heading home just yet, I slink toward the former Elite's guild hall and pause right outside the half-door of Mouli's kitchen. The aroma of rich stew and fresh-baked bread rolls drifts into the street, and my stomach growls loudly.

"What comes after the cheese?" a girl shouts frantically. "Oh! It's bubbling over!"

"Stay calm," Kanna's voice drifts distantly from somewhere inside. "That just means you have to stir it. Are you sure you don't want me to come tonight instead of tomorrow? It really isn't any trouble."

"Stirring!" the girl yelps. "It worked! And yes, I'm sure! I want to make Mouli proud."

"She will be!"

I peek into the kitchen through the half-door to watch. Four pots bubble and steam on the cook-top. A small mirror hangs above it, and Kanna's face peers out from it, watching the girl's every move.

Her name is Lia. She's one of about a dozen orphans I picked up from the fields in Sunteri months ago. She's older than me, but came with her little brother. At first, Nessa took them in, but when I showed up with another dozen a few weeks later, she and Mouli had a better idea. That's how, with Nessa and Margy's help, the old Elite guild hall became Cerion's Nest.

I step out of the Half-Realm and rest my hand on the edge of the door.

"Need help?" I ask. Lia jumps and yelps and drops her spoon in the pot.

"Sir Tib!" she squeaks. Frazzled, she starts to reach into the bubbling liquid to retrieve it when Kanna shouts from the mirror.

"NO! That's hot, Lia!"

Lia yelps again and waves her hands near her face, then fishes the spoon out with some tongs. "S-sorry!"

"What did I tell you about apologizing all the time?" I say to her. "It smells amazing, by the way. Where's Mouli, though?"

"Busy with the Champions at the new quarters," she replies, distracted by a newly bubbling pot. "Glad you made it back in time! If you're going into the hall, can you fetch Suri? I need help if supper's ever getting done."

"Sure," I say, ducking past her as she wields a huge pan of steaming rolls.

I slip into the former guild hall, which isn't really any less chaotic than the kitchen. The room is full of kids, old and young, noisily setting the table. A few of the boys toss plates back and forth to each other. Others play a game of chase around the sofas.

Out in the training square, swords clang. A glance through the adjoining door reveals Cort and six or so kids engaged in a lesson of dual-wielding. If Mouli was here, she'd have something to say about that so close to suppertime, I think to myself, chuckling.

Suri's not in there. I didn't expect him to be. I find him just where he always is, tucked quietly in an overstuffed chair at the far end of the hall, his nose buried in one of Rian's old schoolbooks.

"Did you know the most complex spell in known records used to use eighty-six different components?" he asks me without looking up.

"No, I didn't," I say. I like Suri. He reminds me of Ki when she was his age.

"One of the components was so rare, it was worth over sixty platinum! Can you guess what it was?" he asks.

"Dragon scale?" I ask, dropping onto the sofa beside him.

"Nope."

"Uh, snowberry petals?"

Suri rolls his eyes. "You're not even trying. Snowberry petals aren't really rare."

"I know," says the water fairy at his shoulder in a sing-song voice.

"Suri!" Lia yelps from the kitchen.

"Your sister needs help," I tell him.

"She's a mess," he scowls. He flicks his fingers at the page, conjuring a bookmark. Closes the book carefully. Sets it gingerly on the shelf. Rushes to the kitchen.

"Are you staying for supper, Sir Tib?" one of the kids setting the table asks.

"It's just Tib, for the millionth time, and no thanks, I have to get back home."

"Don't listen to him," one of the boys says. "Knights are always called 'Sir,' no matter what they tell you to call them."

A few of the kids groan in disappointment at my reply, but their reaction doesn't last long. They're having too much fun messing around with the table settings, joking together, playing. They barely notice when I slip away, back into the streets, headed home.

Dinner's almost over by the time I get there, but Nessa barely bats an eye at me showing up so late. She's too caught up in the Admiral's story, along with the others, even though it's probably the hundredth time he's told it.

I take a chair beside Ki. She and Efran are staying here as guests until after the wedding. Skalivar's across from me, a guest of Saesa's. He and Raefe are deep in conversation about something else, keeping their voices in a hushed undertone to the roaring reactions of the kids around the table.

I fill my plate with all my favorites, leaning back as Emmie crawls across me to get closer to the Admiral.

"Tell us about the sigil, and how you knew to warn Nessa," Lilen says.

"No, I want to hear about the evil Sorcerer who broke into the ship and stole all those tomes," Ruben yells.

"Gaga! Tell us about when Tib found you!" Emmie shouts over the others, finally reaching the Admiral's lap.

"I couldn't believe it," he says, taking a long puff from his pipe. "There I was, stranded at the inn at Cresten, fully believing I'd lost my mind, and the innkeep comes in and he says, 'someone to see you, sir.'"

"I thought to myself," he puffs his pipe again, "what now? Is it going to be some nonsense dream again? Imagine my surprise," he says, winking at me as Nessa drapes her arms around his shoulder, watching his every move with such an adoring expression it makes my own heart flip, "when the door to our meeting room opened, and in walked this scoundrel." He laughs, pointing at me across the table, and everyone claps and cheers and begs him to go on.

I listen for a while, until my thoughts start to wander to other things. Windmills. Flying ships. Offerings. Weddings. Every thought, no matter how unrelated, leads me to the same place, Margy. Her delight at the first sight of my fields. Her pride at my inventions. Her support of my projects and ideas these past months.

"We should turn in," Ki says, during a lull in the story, interrupting my thoughts. She pats my arm, and the knowing smile she gives me makes me wonder whether she's really tired, or just knows how much I want to be alone. Either way, I'm grateful.

We go upstairs together, while Efran stays behind to talk with the Admiral and Nessa in the sitting room. At my door, my sister gives me a hug and kiss on the cheek. We say goodnight, and I duck into my room.

As soon as I close the door, I feel a rush of relief. I didn't realize how much I needed to be alone until now. It used to irritate me that she knows me better than I know myself. I've let go of my pride, though, since then. Learned to trust her judgment.

I cross to the armoire. Open the door. Take off my boots. New boots. Set them on the shelf. My hands brush the old pair as I do, and the faint magic they hold seems to brighten a little.

I stare at those old boots a while. Since Brindelier, I've stuck with my promise to myself about Mevyn. Never again.

Seeing them every day, though, brings a flood of memories. I think of all the things I've accomplished in those boots. I think of how my life has changed since I took them off and stowed them in here.

Glancing over my shoulder to make sure I'm alone, I reach into the pouch of my bandolier and pull out the small box I've carried for months now. I flick the top open to reveal a ring of gold twined with pearl. The betrothal ring.

I take it out of the box and turn it thoughtfully in my fingers. I meant to do it today, in the windmill, but I lost my nerve. Margy's been wearing hers for months now. She's been ready. Patient. She's told me again and again I could take years if I needed to.

I sink onto my bed and sit cross-legged, thinking about it. How I've been waiting for the right time. A time when I'd finally feel like my life could be peaceful. When I'd feel really, honestly happy.

The weight of the ring, the promise it holds, doesn't scare me like it used to. It's time, I think, for a different kind of adventure.

I slide it onto my finger. Let it sit there. Flex my fingers. I've never worn a ring before. It feels lighter than I'd expected.

A brush of whiskers tickles the back of my hand. She barely appears as Zeze before she pops to Margy.

"Oh, Tib!" she whispers excitedly, throwing her arms around me. "Do you really mean it?"

"Yeah, I do," I say, pulling her closer. "I love you, Margy."

"And I love you," she whispers to me. "Forever."

Chapter Fifty-One

A GRAND AFFAIR
Azi
Twenty-Ninth Midsummer, Year One of the Age of Kinship
(The Next Day)

My fingers drum impatiently against my hips inside the silk wrappings that swaddle me from my shoulders to my toes. Already this morning, I've been subjected to three separate baths with massages in between each one, wrapped each time, and left to rest in my bed and contemplate my future with my husband-to-be. I stare up at the yellow silk canopy and down along the broad, soft blue coverlet of the bed that will be ours, my heart racing.

It's been two days since I've been allowed to see Rian. Two long, agonizing days. This morning I woke up relieved that today we'd finally be together again, but so far, the day has dragged torturously. Having to spend it mostly alone has made it a thousand times worse. I even miss Flitt's constant chatter in my ear.

I tried on more than one occasion to talk Mouli out of these old-fashioned traditions, but she wouldn't begin to listen to me. Mum, Flitt, and even Rian himself have been absolutely dedicated to following them to the letter. Everyone has been so insistent, especially in the Age of Kinship, that we lead by example by keeping Cerion's customs strong.

This period of fasting, meditation, and centering is meant to calm and enlighten me, and I tried, honestly. I've been trying. All I want, though, is to see him. To touch him. To be together.

I huff anxiously and stare at the yellow curtain covering the side of the bed, trying to see through it to the window, trying to hear something, anything. It's no use, though. The silence wards are set, both ways. There's no hint of a noise from the palace beyond our rooms. No comforting ring of Da's hammer on the forge, no scuffle of maids rushing past my door making last minute preparations.

My feet jiggle in the loose bindings, tapping an impatient rhythm. It must be noon by now. It has to at least be past midmorning.

I fidget slightly. The balm they used to soften my skin is getting itchy. I suspect after this, it'll be yet another bath.

As though in answer to my thoughts, the door opens. The footfalls of a dozen feet shuffle in, clunk down what I'm sure is another tub of water, and march out. The yellow curtain is pushed aside, and Mouli stands over me, her eyes wet with tears.

"Last one, dear," she whispers, as though trying not to disturb some deep meditation. She helps me get unwrapped and into the warm, rose-scented water to soak.

Once the final bath is through and I'm wrapped this time in a soft towel, Mum is allowed in, along with my wedding handmaids, Flitt and Saesa. They cover my head with a plain gray veil and drape me in gray robes that cover me all the way to my chin, silent the entire time. It's not until the presentation of gifts that we'll finally be allowed to speak. I glance more than once at the long, wrapped bundle holding my gift to Rian. My heart races as the moment grows nearer.

When I'm finally prepared, Mum goes to the door and opens it. Da steps inside hesitantly, his eyes searching the room until they stop at me. He's dressed all in gray, like the rest of us. The color is meant to represent humility and balance. He looks good in it, with his curly silver hair and his crisp blue eyes. He steps to me as Mum closes the door behind him, and he rests his hands on my shoulders and looks at me.

In his eyes, I see so much more than I had that morning when I'd practiced my lessons with Mum all those months ago. They don't flick away fearfully or seek anything else to look at. Today, they're filled with affection and pride, as they used to be. If anyone had told me back then his change of heart would have been thanks to a fairy, and *Ember*, no less, I would have laughed in their face. Fairies, he'd told me when I asked him about it so many months ago, can be useful sometimes, he supposed.

He cups my cheeks with his rough, calloused hands, and I bow my head respectfully to receive the blessing of his kiss on my forehead. After the exchange, I present him with the long bundle, and he and Mum step into place in front of me, carrying it horizontally before them. In Cerion, each wedding has a theme virtue. For ours, Rian and I have chosen "Generosity."

Saesa opens the door, and she and Flitt, who has grown herself to human size, lead the way down the hallway. This ritual is meant to show respect and restraint toward one another. The bride and groom, escorted by their parents and attendants, are required to keep their eyes cast down during the exchange of gifts.

When I hear Rian's family's group approaching, my heart leaps into my throat. I have to squeeze my eyes shut and press my chin into the thick gray robes to keep from stealing a glance at my groom. Knowing we're so close and yet unable to be together just yet is part of the challenge. Following tradition, the bride's father is the first to break the silence.

"With deepest affection," he says, "our generous daughter Azaeli Hammerfel presents her groom with this, her most prized possession, to keep for her, along with her own heart."

"With deepest affection," Elliot says, his voice much gentler than Da's rough one, "our generous son Rian Dustin Eldinae presents his bride with this, his most prized possession, to keep for him, along with his own heart."

There's a soft rustle of fabric as the gifts are exchanged, and Mouli sniffles quietly. Saesa and Flitt come around my parents and take my arms to lead me back to the room. When the door closes behind us, we breathe a collective sigh of relief and fall, laughing, into each other's arms.

"What is it, what is it?" Mouli asks excitedly, gathering around Mum and Da to get a glimpse at the gift. She tugs my arm as they unfold Rian's guild cloak to reveal his most prized possession. I think of him tucked away with his parents, doing the same, revealing Mercy wrapped in the folds of my cloak. His gift, far smaller, is a blue velvet pouch bearing a note and a single, old button.

"Oh, Azi," Mum whispers tearfully as she reads the note over.

"You gave him your sword and you just got a button?" Flitt scoffs. "I thought your theme was generosity!"

Next to her, Da grunts. It's obvious he's in agreement with the fairy as he turns the button over in his hands, examining it as though hoping there's more to it than its face value.

"Shh, Flitt," I say, taking the note from Mum. I start to read it aloud, but the lump in my throat prevents me. Everyone gathers around me to read over my shoulder.

Dear Azi,

Every single day
Since you were seven
and I was seven-and-a-half,
And we both caught the fury
Of your uncle, my master
For my teaching you a
spell I never regretted
Because that was the moment
I knew, no matter what,
We'd stand together through anything,
I have carried this button.

It's a meager thing, I know
But what it represents
Is the greatest treasure
Any man could ever hope for.

Yours,
Rian

The memory of that moment so long ago plays crisply in my mind as I read the note. The spell had been a simple movement spell Uncle had given him to practice. I was reading my lessons, and Rian was sending the button skidding across the table, this way and that. He held my hands in his and showed me how to move them to perform the spell. It was thrilling, until Uncle discovered us and punished us soundly.

"Oh," Flitt whispers.

"I know," I say hoarsely, wiping away the tears that spill down my cheeks. "I didn't even write him a note."

"Got a good one there," Da says, clearing his throat and clapping my shoulder gruffly as he finishes reading it. "You really did."

"All right," Mouli yelps, blowing her nose loudly with one hand as she waves Da off with the other. "Out with you! We've got work to do! Azi, stop that blubbering, you're going to get yourself all red and blotchy. Benen, I said go!"

Da gives me one last hug and clears his throat before Mouli shoves him out for good.

"Now then," she says, her eyes gleaming with delight as she turns around to look at me. "Let's get to it!"

As she, Mum, Saesa, and Flitt bustle around me, dusting me with powder and guiding me into layers and layers of silk and lace and airy, gauzy fabric with my back to the mirror, I start to regret my decision to give Mouli full reign of the wedding planning. The only thing I wanted to choose, I told her, were the shoes, remembering those awful heels I wore to Sarabel's birthday ball. Thankfully, she let me get away with a pretty pair of woven gold sandals this time.

While Mum and the others laugh and joke and talk, I think about Rian's dream. I see myself in his imagination, walking through the palace of the Fairy Queen in that gown that showed my armor off, and I start to worry that this one is nothing like the one he'd imagined.

Suddenly, the dressing and primping flurry stops, and they all step back, wide eyed.

"Oh, Azi," Mum whispers, and Mouli buries her face in Mum's shoulder and weeps. Saesa takes my shoulders and turns me to face the mirror, and Flitt presses her hands to her mouth like she's hiding some big secret.

The dress stuns me, mainly because it's nothing like what I would have expected from any of them. It's a graceful, simple white gown with short, rolled sleeves that cap my shoulders, showing off the defined muscles of my arms. I see Mouli's influence in the weaving at the bodice, where loops of ribbon hold rows of gleaming pearls, and Flitt's influence in the diamonds sprinkled among those pearls, which cast prisms of rainbows cascading down the skirt and splashing over the loose tails of the ribbons.

I stare at the jewels, watching them flash and glitter while Mum fixes a blue and gold veil to my up-swept hair. Flitt's diamond hangs from a simple gold chain around my neck, and the pearl earrings Mouli clips to my ears finish the look perfectly.

I press my lips together, feeling the sting of tears in my eyes, and Mouli swoops in with a lace handkerchief, scolding me.

"No! No crying! Breathe," she says. "Deep breaths."

Mum's peace pulses over me, calming me as Flitt explains the workings of the dress.

"It's to go with your theme," she says. "Generosity. You pull on a pearl or a diamond, and it will come free. Go on, try it."

I reach for one of the jewels toward the bust line, and everyone yelps to stop me.

"This one first!" Mouli says urgently, pointing to the one on my left hip. "Then work across to the right, then up and across."

"All right," I say curiously, puzzled by her instruction. I pull the pearl off and hold it out, dangling from the ribbon.

"Now don't pull another one out until we get out there," Mouli scolds.

"All right!" I say again, laughing and hugging her. "It's perfect, Mouli, and everyone," I say, my voice cracking with emotion. "Thank you all, so much."

"Oh, you!" Mouli sniffles, squeezing me tightly. "Come now, you can wait in the guild hall until we're sure the coast is clear. I've got to go check on some things, so I'm leaving you in your mum's hands."

They escort me to the new hall, which is much larger than our old one. There are a few desks, one for each of the senior members of the guild, and a wide door that opens into the vast palace library. Like our old hall, it's adjoined to our private armory and training square, and connected to each of our private quarters through a series of corridors. The only difference, and one that still makes me a little sad, is that our meals are served by the royal cooks, now.

Change, Mouli had assured me when the final decisions were made, is often painful, and always inevitable. Still, sometimes when I have a quiet moment, I find myself thinking of her and Luca busy at Cerion's Nest or cozy in their beach cabin, and wondering what they're up to and whether they miss me as much as I miss them.

The others file out and leave me alone with Flitt, who watches my every move but says nothing at all. She's back to fairy size again, and her silence makes me even more nervous than I already feel. When I start to pace and fidget with the diamonds on my gown, she dives and my hand and bats it away.

"Don't touch!" she squeaks.

"What's going on? Are you all right, Flitt? You've been really quiet," I say, drifting toward the desk beside Mya's.

"I'm perfectly fine," she says in a huff. "But I'll have you know it isn't easy for a fairy to keep as many secrets packed into their head as I have right now. My tiny head isn't meant to be stuffed so full of important things I can't talk about. And it doesn't help that you're a Mentalist, either!"

"We could play the question game," I tease her in a sing-song voice.

"We can not, and you know it, so you'd better just drop it." She scowls and crosses her arms, twirling so her back is facing me.

"Sorry," I whisper, moving to my desk. I shuffle through a pile of parchment there, and pick up one of the pages to read it over for the hundredth time.

The Queen's Quest
A TOUR OF THE KNOWN LANDS
IN HONOR OF THE MARRIAGE OF:

MASTER RIAN ELDINAE
KNIGHT ARCANE OF HER MAJESTY'S CHAMPIONS
TO
SIR AZAELI HAMMERFEL
KNIGHT VERITAS OF HER MAJESTY'S CHAMPIONS

It is by the command of Her Royal Majesty Queen Margary Plethore that select members of Her Majesty's Champions shall embark upon a Quest in order to declare Her Majesty's, and therefore the Kingdom of Cerion's alliances and peaceful intentions as friend and ally to each Keeper of the Wellsprings of our Known Lands.

These members shall journey to the Kingdom of Brindelier, where they shall be received as guests in high regard by Her Majesty Queen Stellastera, Muse of Magic, Her Highness Princess Pippavelletti Embryck, His Highness Prince Poelkevrin Embryck and his Princess Celli Embryck, Guardian of Brindelier. Upon reception, Her Majesty's Champions shall embark upon their tour, taking care to ensure peace and light—

"Azaeli Hammerfel!" Flitt squeaks, tugging my veil, "no working! Goodness, I turn my back on you for a half a cricket's chirp and—"

A low whistle from the doorway interrupts her, and I tug my veil from her grip as Cort leans against the frame of it, grinning.

"Will you look at that," he says. Behind him, Bryse breaks into tears.

"What happened to you?" the half-giant groans, clomping across the polished floor to scoop me into his arms. I drop the parchment, letting it drift back to my desk as he swings me from side to side, my toes barely grazing the floor. "Why'd you have to go become a lady, anyway?"

"Put her down, oaf!" Flitt yelps, pelting his arms with her tiny fists. "You'll get her all crumpled up!"

"Sorry," he mutters, setting me down beside Da, who shuffles in beside Mum. Bryse wipes his cheek with his knuckles and then punches my arm hard, leaving a smudge of tears behind.

"Ow," I whisper, feigning pain as I rub my arm to wipe away the tears.

"Lady-girl," he mutters, wrinkling his nose.

"All right, you two," Mum says, laughing. "It's time we're on our way."

Even though the distance is rather short, we know it will take quite a long time to reach the Forest Park due to the crowd, and due to our theme. Our small procession steps out into the street to the cheers of a hundred or more onlookers lined up to see me.

I'm flanked by Mum and Da, with Flitt drifting ahead of me at her usual size, and Saesa just behind her. Bryse and Cort walk behind us, their arms linked together, their sarcastic quips back and forth to each other making me laugh as we creep along.

With every step, as directed by Flitt, I pull a pearl or diamond from the weaving in my bodice, drawing the long tail of white ribbon tied to each jewel through a loop. The first one comes free with no effect, and I toss it into the cheering crowd of well-wishers.

When I pull the second one free, I gasp in shock as a handful of pink powder spills down the white skirt, staining it with rich color and sprinkling it with glittering fairy dust. I look at Flitt, who giggles and urges me on. As we creep closer to the park, I pull jewel after jewel, revealing a rainbow of colors splashed across my skirt. The glittering dust catches the midday sun in brilliant sparkles, casting light dancing in every direction.

By the time I reach the forest park, all the pearls and diamonds have been cast away, revealing a full ball gown of delicate lace and airy silk that billows around me like a cloud. The colors left behind by the fairy dye are bright but subtle. Speckles of pure sunlight catch in the pillows of my skirt like dewdrops in dandelion fluff.

Enormous silk banners of blue and gold billow across trees shaped like the graceful arched open door to a great cathedral. I have to pause and catch my breath as I lift my face to the rich canopy and take it all in.

Leaves of deep emerald green rustle in the breeze far above, revealing the perfect blue sky in shifting patches. From within the archway of trees, Mya lifts her voice in song. There's no accompaniment to her voice, no instrument being played or chorus behind her. There's none needed. The purity of her voice blended with the soft whisper of the breeze carries with it an unmatched, perfect magic.

The sound of a hundred people standing up with quiet reverence overwhelms me before I even reach the archway. My feet seem to plant themselves where they are, unwilling to move forward. Mum offers her left elbow to me and Da his right, and I cling to them both like my life depends on it.

"Go on, traitor," Bryse teases in my ear. I laugh, peering into the sea of faces leaning to glimpse my arrival through the arch. So many have come to see Rian and I wed. I had no idea there'd be such a crowd. It's not just people, either. Hundreds of fairies hover above benches packed with people, their numbers stretching all the way to the tops of the trees.

It's overwhelming. Through the archway, I spot Kenrick and Tulya, and Ki and Efran. In the royal box all the way to the front, Her Majesty the Queen Mother Naelle sits, smiling. Beside her of course is Queen Margy with Twig by her side, and her sisters, Sarabel and Amei, with little Eron on her lap looking all grown up in his velvet and hose. The twins from Brindelier and the newlywed Princess Celli sit with them as honored guests.

In the backdrop of trees beyond the box, shimmering like a mirage from behind the veil, the Fairy Queen watches from her realm. All six Muses are in her company, from Eljarenae to Vorhadeniel, who the Fairy Queen, herself, holds in her arms.

I step through the pointed archway, clinging to my parents' arms, and the moment my feet meet the mossy green carpet, a shimmer of rainbow lights flash through the trees, resting on me. The light splashes over my gown and darts across the gathering in an erratic, spectacular display that makes the entire crowd gasp in awe. As I walk down the aisle, I'm joined by the rest of our guild. Uncle comes to walk with us, joined by Brother Donal, and Tib, who has recently received his official membership by order of the queen.

Mya and Elliot don't join us. They remain at the end of the aisle beside the canopy with their son. With Rian. My heart races. The crowd disappears from my notice as soon as I see him. No one else matters in this moment. No one will ever matter as much as he does.

Dressed in robes of deep blue under a vest of rich, creamy gold velvet, he stands alone under the canopy woven with yellow roses, blue cornflower, and glittering Snowberry blossoms. His auburn hair shines almost a fiery red in the rays of sunlight dancing through the canopy. When his eyes meet mine, even from this distance, they call to me, inviting me.

Scenes of our beautiful lives intertwined play between us as our procession makes its way slowly to him. I know by the nature of them, that Rian must have spent countless hours curating each one. They play in my mind as clearly as if they're happening right now, but at the same time, golden threads of images dance in the space between us for all to see.

We're babies, swaddled in the same crib, being sung to by Mya. We're three, toddling around the Council room while our parents meet with King Tirnon. We're five, crawling around the legs of the table in the guild hall, searching for the source of ants. We're seven, sitting quietly at our studies, practicing our writing. We're ten laughing and chasing each other around the trees of this very forest. We're twelve, and he's meeting me outside the arms guild so we can walk home together. We're fourteen, exchanging Midwinter's Eve gifts with our families. We're sixteen, standing at the center of the Ring at Kythshire, presenting ourselves to Crocus. We're seventeen, battling against Jacek in Ceras'lain. We're nineteen, raging through the tunnels of Kerevorna.

As the memories fade and the applause from the crowd drowns out Mya's song, I realize that while I've been walking entranced by Rian's memories, pieces of my gown have unraveled to trail behind me. By the time I reach the canopy and my parents pass me into Rian's waiting arms, somehow, I'm dressed in my full suit of gleaming blue armor. It's like a dream, more beautiful and glorious than any dream I ever experienced. More perfect than I ever could have imagined. Rian's touch charges me with emotion as he reaches to my face to sweep a tear away, and he pulls me into a deep, passionate kiss.

"We haven't gotten to that part yet," Margy whispers, and everyone laughs as we reluctantly take a step apart to turn our attention to the queen, who has made her way to her place on the dais beside us. She gestures to the crowd, bowing her head gracefully.

"In the deep-seated and honored traditions of our kingdom," the queen says, her voice rising surprisingly clearly over the gathering, "it is the custom for one close to the betrothed to step forward to offer the wedding wishes and present the Promise. Who speaks for our beloved Sir Hammerfel and Sir Eldinae?"

"I do, Your Majesty," Uncle says, his deep voice echoing into the trees.

Blood rushes into my ears. My cheeks go hot, and panic grips me, as it often does when Uncle's attention is turned in my direction.

"Uncle?" I push to Rian, searching his eyes in disbelief.

Rian shakes his head slightly, obviously as shocked as I am. As the Master Mage makes his way to stand beside us beneath the canopy, my heart races. It's against tradition for the bride and groom to know who the Officiant will be. Rian and I speculated for long hours, thinking of everyone from Mouli or Luca to the queen herself, but neither of us ever for a moment thought of him.

"It takes a great deal of wisdom," Uncle begins, and the crowd goes silent. He reaches to scratch his eye, clears his throat, and starts again. "'It takes a great deal of wisdom for a man of learning to admit his mistakes.' This is an adage so old, and found so many times in the writings of Cerion's libraries, that its attribution has been lost to the scholars of Cerion."

"Ugh, why do Mages have to be so overly wordy? So typical!" Flitt pushes.

"Shh!" I push to her, and she scowls at me and drifts closer to Shush, whose presence in the canopy startles me. I wonder whether he's been there all this time, or if I was just too caught up in everything else to notice him. The two of them giggle together, and I snap my attention back to Uncle.

"I have known Azaeli, my dear niece, and Rian, my most esteemed student, since the moment each was born. Through their childhood together, I can honestly say, on more than one occasion, this pair was a direct source of stress to myself and the others of our family and guild. I daresay, at times, the two of them terrified me."

This brings a spatter of laughter from the crowd, though many of them, like myself, seem unsure whether Uncle is serious or joking. Mostly because, as we all know, Mages in general aren't known for their levity.

"As I watched my dear niece work with determination and courage toward her goal of knighthood, and I nurtured my apprentice, Rian, in his own schooling, this terror reared its head more than once. Not in the way that most elders experience fear at the hands of the children they are responsible for, but in another way altogether. You see, as scholars of the Arcane, our first and true love must always be our craft and our studies. Though I saw great promise in my student, perhaps even more so than in any student I've known, I saw something else.

"His love. His attachment to the friend who was always by his side, who stood with him through failures and triumphs, through times of loneliness and times of joy, as he, in turn, stood with her. The emotion, the attachment between the two, I freely admit, caused this Master many sleepless nights.

"I warned my student against it. I had him read, through his schooling, countless accounts of the failures of Mages of varying power. I told him on more than one occasion, once he came of age, how incredibly concerned I was. Each time, he more or less dismissed me."

He laughs softly, shaking his head. Rian and I laugh, too, and he squeezes my hands in his as we gaze into each other's eyes. Uncle pauses until even the breeze in the trees seems to go silent.

"It takes a great deal of wisdom for a man of learning to admit his mistakes. I have seen the folly of my teachings, bearing witness, as all of you have, to the result of the love these two share. Emotions did not impede my student's learning, nor did they entice him into darker leanings. Love strengthened him. The bond shared between these two, between my dear, strong, valiant niece and my determined, diligent, powerful student resulted in the very opposite of what I feared. It strengthened the both of them. It forged within them a power even the fiercest Sorcerer could not hope to overcome. It brought us, with the aid of others, into this Age of Kinship. At its core, that power is love.

"The wish I offer our bride and groom on their wedding day is this: That you continue to live as you always have, with generous hearts and faith in your love for each other, until the end of your days. In the spirit of generosity which is the virtue we celebrate this day, I leave you with this thought: Love lives within us, each and every one. Give it generously to all those around you, and allow it to grow into a power capable of surprising even the most skeptical cynic."

"Oh, Uncle," I whisper through my tears as the crowd cheers his speech, and throw my arms around him. Rian joins us, and the three of us hold each other until Uncle clears his throat softly and we step back to our places again. Beside him, the queen sniffles as she hands him a long, delicate chain of golden links dripping with blue sapphires. Rian and I clasp our right hands, and Uncle winds the chain around our wrists, binding us together.

"Rian Dustin Eldinae," he says loudly, "declare your promise to stand beside Azaeli, taking her as your wife with respect, honor and trust for all the days of your life."

"With my word as my bond, I declare my promise to you," he says, his eyes locked to mine. The gold chain warms slightly, and my skin tingles where it winds around my wrist.

"Azaeli Hammerfel," Uncle says. Somewhere in the crowd, someone blows their nose loudly.

"Sorry," Mouli whispers. "Go on, Gaethon, for stars sake!" Rian and I laugh nervously, but don't break our gaze.

"Azaeli Hammerfel, declare your promise to stand beside Rian, taking him as your husband in mutual respect, honor, and trust, for all the days of your life."

"With my word as my bond, I declare my promise to you," I say, shocked I'm able to manage to make my voice sound so clear in the throes of so much emotion. The chain tingles again, sealing our vow to each other in heart and mind.

"As all of us witness to your promise," Margy says, grinning, "and with a heart full of joy, I declare you, Sir Rian Eldinae and Sir Azaeli Eldinae, now wed. We hope that you'll mark the start of your wedding feast with a show of your affection for one another."

Rian draws our linked hands to his chest, pulls me close, and graces my lips with a kiss to rival every one we've ever shared. The crowd erupts into cheers, and the cracks and flashes of fireworks make a spectacle above us, but we are too lost in each other's embrace to care to look away.

Slowly, our surroundings fade. We tumble through the Half-Realm, our enduring kiss the only thing that matters.

"Don't worry," he pushes, never taking his lips from mine, *"it won't be for long. I just thought it kind of fitting. Disappearing with no trace or explanation is kind of our thing."*

"I'm not worried," I push back, laughing through my nose. Wherever Rian takes me, whatever happens today and in the days and years to come, I'll trust him, always.

Chapter Fifty-Two

ONE LAST THING
Azi

"The feast day that followed was easily as spectacular as the wedding itself had been, with enough fine food and drink to fill every last subject of Cerion and every honored guest to bursting. The bride and groom's reprieve was short-lived, for they only wished a quick, private moment together to gather themselves before joining the feast procession they had looked forward to participating in for so many months."

Curled in a cozy armchair to the side of our bed, I smile to myself at Rian's account of the rest of our wedding day. My stomach growls loudly, surprising me. After yesterday's feast, I swore I'd never eat again. I look over at my husband, who will probably sleep until long after the sun comes up, and rub my stomach as though that'll help. As hungry as I am, I'd hate to leave to find something to eat and have him wake on the morning after we became husband and wife to an empty room.

Empty room. I sigh with pleasure and rest my head back against the chair's soft stuffing, basking in the quiet. My thoughts drift dreamily to the quiet day we have planned. The day after the wedding day, traditionally, is reserved for the bride and groom alone. We don't have to stay in our rooms, but if we choose to, no one would dare disturb us.

"*Azi!*" Flitt yelps in my head. Her colored light beams into my eyes and I scream in utter terror, my heart racing.

"Flitt," I growl under my breath once I'm able to calm down. I glance at Rian, relieved that her sudden appearance hasn't woken him, and glare pointedly at the bright fairy. I want to stay mad at her, I really do, but the tray of Mouli's sweet rolls she's directing to float beneath my nose makes it incredibly difficult. I give in and dive into the platter, devouring two of them, not even too upset that most of the icing has already been licked off.

"*I know the rules, and I promise I'm going to follow them,*" she chatters in my head. "*But you were hungry, and we both know Stinky can sleep for the whole morning, and everyone else was too nice to disturb you.*"

"*If you really know the rules, tell them to me,*" I push.

"*If the silence wards are up, and your diamond is in the dressing room, then you're not to be disturbed,*" she recites like a child going over her lessons.

"*Unless?*" I urge her.

"*Unless it's urgent.*"

"*And what does urgent mean?*"

"*If someone is fatally wounded, otherwise injured, or in danger of death,*" she pushes.

I give her a pointed look as I chew on my sweet roll.

"You could have died from starvation, Azi," she whispers earnestly.

I laugh, nearly choking, and shake my head.

"*Wait,*" I push. "*How did you get in here, if the diamond is in my dressing room?*"

"*I just popped over from there,*" she explains. "*The rules are changing, now that everything's all connected. Things that used to be impossible are getting easier.*"

"*Well,*" I say with a sigh, "*thanks for these. And thanks for yesterday, too. It really meant a lot to me.*"

"*You already said too many thanks for that,*" she rolls her eyes. "*It's getting boring.*"

"*Why don't you go do something with Shush?*"

"*He's too busy with his face stuck to Ember,*" she huffs.

"*You should go find someone to stick your face to, maybe. Like Alex.*"

"*Nah,*" she sighs, scooping some more icing from the roll I'm about to bite. "*He's gotten awfully Keepery lately.*"

"*Twig, then,*" I offer, and she gives me a bashful little smile.

"*Maybe later. You're trying to get rid of me,*" she pushes, pouting. "*Even after I brought you sweet rolls.*"

"*We just want privacy sometimes, Flitt,*" I push. "*I hope you can respect that.*"

As much as she delights me, I don't want her to wake Rian. He needs his rest, and I want to be alone with him when he wakes up. We only have a few days before we leave on our quest, and I have a lot to go over with Mya before we leave. Today is really our only day to relax and spend together, and I mean to make the most of it.

"Speaking of privacy," she blinks excitedly, darting closer, *"tell me about last night."*

"You want me to tell you about my wedding night?" I whisper aloud, too shocked to remember to speak to her mind.

"Yes!" she squeaks excitedly. "I know. Let's play!"

~The End~

Character Glossary

Akkoti *(Ah-KOH-tee)* A Dona of the Savarikta.
Aleetah *(Ah-LEE-tuh)* Meheli's *sava*.
Alexerin *(Ah-lex-AIR-in)* A light and earth fairy, Keeper of Brindelier's Wellspring, Prince Poe's Faedin
Aliandra *(Ah-lee-AN-dra)* A light and earth fairy, Keeper of Brindelier's Wellspring, Princess Pippa's Faedin
Amei Plethore *(Ay-mee)* Prince Eron's wife.
Anod Bental *(Ah-NOD BEN-tul)* High Master of Mages, Advisor to the Throne of Cerion.
Aren *(AIR-ehn)* Guardian of the West, the Golden Coast Embodied, in Kythshire.
Asio Plethore *(Ah-zee-oh)* The first king in the Plethore Dynasty.
Aster *(AS-ter)* An enchanted wand, once in the possession of Kaso Viro, now held by Rian.
Azaeli Hammerfel (Azi) *(A-zee, A-zay-lee) (Not OZZY)* A Knight of His Majesty's Elite, and Ambassador to Kythshire. Daughter of Lisabella and Benen.
Avyn *(a-VIN)* The Guardian within the mountain, Kerevorna.
Benen Hammerfel *(Ben-in)* Knight of His Majesty's Elite, Azi's father, and Lisabella's husband.
Borda *(BOOR-duh)* A well-established, powerful family residing in Brindelier.
Brother Donal Vincend *(DON-ol)* Healer of His Majesty's Elite.
Bryse Daborr *(Brice)* A half Stone-Giant. Shieldmaster of His Majesty's Elite, partner to Cort.
Celli Deshtal *(CHEL-lee)* A street urchin from Cerion, bloodbound to the sorcerer Quenson.
Cort Finzael *(Court)* Member of His Majesty's Elite. Swashbuckler and partner to Bryse.
Crocus *(Crow-cuss)* A plant fairy. Leader of the Ring at Kythshire, partner to Scree.
Dacva Archomyn *(Dock-Vuh)* Apprentice healer to Donal, Azi's former rival in training, former member of Redemption.

Diovicus *(Dye-ah-vik-us)* The Sorcerer King of legend, who nearly overtook Kythshire and was defeated by Asio Plethore over a century ago, ushering in the Age of Peace.
Dub (Wade Cordoven) *(Dub)* A hired assassin who escaped the clutches of Sorcery in *Call of Brindelier* and released many of the prisoners in Cerion's dungeons.
Dumfrey *(DUM-free)* A bumbling, orange-wearing Mage of Cerion.
Efran *(EE-fran)* A mercenary/hired man/freeloader living at Kanna's in Brindelier.
Elliot Eldinae*(El-ee-oht)* Member of His Majesty's Elite. Shapechanger (fox). Husband to Mya, and Rian's Father.
Eljarenae *(ell-JAH-renn-ay)* Muse of Light.
Elmsworth *(EHLMS-wurth)* Davin Elmsworth, Royal Captain of Arms.
Ember *(Ember)* A Fire fairy, and high-ranking member of the Ring in Kythshire.
Emmie Ganvent *(EM-mee)* The only officially adopted child in the Ganvent house.
Eron Plethore (Err-ohn) Son of Tirnon and Naelle. Prince and Heir of Cerion, executed for treason and reanimated to become a Revenant.
Evyn *(Ev-in)* The guardian of the entrance of Kerevorna.
Finn (Isaac Finnvale) *(Fin)* Princess Margary's personal guard.
Flitt (Flitter) *(Flit (like bit))* A Light fairy. Azaeli's Faedin/Illi'luvrie
Gaethon Ethari *(GAY-thon)* Headmaster of the Academy, Member of His Majesty's Elite, Advisor to the throne, Azi's uncle, Rian's mentor.
Glyn *(GLINN)* Tib's Cygnet.
Greshel *(GREH-shul)* A sailor on Ganvent's ship, dealing with cargo.
Hayse *(HAZE)* Temman Hayse -Second Admiral of the Royal Fleet of Cerion. Member of the queen's council.
Hew Deshtal *(Hyoo)* Celli's baby brother.
Ienae'luvrie *(EE-uh-nay LOO vree)* Keeper of Ceras'lain's Wellspring.
Iren *(EYE-ren)* Guardian of the northern border of Kythshire, Spirit of the Shadow Crag. Ki's keeper.
Joli *(JOH-lee)* Margy's Cygnet.
Julini Ensintia *(Joo-LEE-nee)* An elf archer, Deputy Escort of the White Line.

Juvask *(Joo-VOSK)* A past king of Hywilkin who ordered the Wellspring closed.
Kanna *(CAN-na)* Owner of Kanna's tavern and inn in Brindelier. Efran's sister.
Kaso Viro *(KAH-so VEE-roh)* A muse of the Six, the Muse of Water, a Master Mage who aided Rian and Tib in *Call of Brindelier*.
Kenrick Mejliere A vagrant Mentalist from Hywilkin.
Keyes *(Keys)* Adreen Borda Keyes, Master Councilman of Brindelier, Advisor to the throne of Brindelier, sent to Cerion to accompany Prince Poelkevrin and negotiate terms of the wedding contract.
Kiaan *(KEE-on)* Keeper of Elespen's Wellspring.
Ki *(Ki (like eye))* Tib's sister. The redeemed Sorceress Viala, a scout in the service of Iren.
Kit *(KIT)* A fairy trying to earn Mouli's favor.
Kira (KEE-ruh) A page in Cerion's palace.
Krisa *(KREE-suh)* Tulya's daughter.
Kruti *(KROO-Tee)* A Dona of the Savarikta, assigned to Saesa.
Kuvelsk *(KOO-vehl-sk)* Keeper of Haigh's Wellspring.
Leif *(LEEF)* A boy fairy with bright orange hair, trying to earn Mouli's favor.
Lia *(LEE-uh)* A handmaid to Princess Pippa.
Lilen Ganvent *(LILL-in)* A Mage Apprentice, the eldest girl at the Ganvent Manse.
Lisabella Hammerfel *(LIZ-uh-BELL-uh)* Knight of His Majesty's Elite, a Paladin, Azi's mother, married to Benen.
Lowery (LAU-ree) Ansell Lowery. Queen's Council. Royal High Scholar of National Relations.
Luca Salvaneli *(LOO-kah)* Groundskeeper for His Majesty's Elite, married to Mouli, their cook.
Maisie Kreston *(MAY-zee)* A former palace maid who used to live in the Ganvent Manse. Her son, Errie, was kidnapped by Celli and used in a ceremony to raise Eron from the dead.
Margary Plethore (Margy) *(MAR-jee)* The youngest princess of Cerion's Royal Family, the heir to Cerion's throne. Bound to the fairy Twig.
Meheli *(Meh-eh-LEE)* A *sava* rider, warrior of the Savarikta.
Mevyn *(MEV-in)* The Keeper of Sunteri's Wellspring, Tib's Faedin/Illi'luvrie.

Mouli Salvaneli *(MOO-lee)* Housekeeper and cook for His Majesty's Elite. Married to Luca.
Muster *(MUSS-ter)* A half stone giant thug for hire working with Dub.
Mya Eldinae *(MY-uh (not MEE-uh))* A bard. Leader of His Majesty's Elite. Rian's mother, and Elliot's wife.
Myer *(MY-ur)* Lars Myer, Captain of the Royal Guard.
Naelle Plethore *(Ny-ELLE)* Queen Regent of Cerion, widow of King Tirnon, Mother of Queen Margary.
Nan *(Nan (like Ann))* Tib's grandmother. A slave of the dye fields.
Nessa Ganvent *(NESS-uh)* Wife of Admiral Ganvent. Foster mother to Saesa, Raefe, Tib, and whoever else needs her.
On'na *(OH-nuh)* A mermaid captive in the Menagerie.
Osven Chente *(OZZ-ven)* A Sorcerer for the Dusk, killed by Nessa during a confrontation with Rian and Tib in the Ganvent Manse. Bound by magic to Celli after death, by a spell cast by Quenson and Sybel.
Paulin Emhryck *(Paul-in)* King of Brindelier before the Age of Sleep.
Pelu *(PAY-loo)* A native boy of the Savarikta who tended to Tib in their care.
Pippaveletti Emhryck (Pippa) *(Pip-uh-veh-LET-tee)* Princess of Brindelier
Poelkevrin Emhryck (Poe) *(POLE-kev-rin)* Prince of Brindelier.
Quenson Avenaire *(KWEN-sohn)* A Sorcerer for the Dusk, formerly bloodbound to Celli.
Raefe Coltori *(RAFE)* A trainee of the Royal Navy, Saesa's brother, lives in the Ganvent Manse.
Resai *(Ress-EYE)* A *sava* rider, warrior of the Savarikta.
Rian Eldinae *(RI-an)* Mage of His Majesty's Elite, Azi's childhood friend and betrothed. Son of Mya and Elliot. Student of Gaethon.
Richter *(RICK-tur)* King of Hywilkin, owner of the menagerie, defeated by the Faedin of Hywilkin, and stolen away by Sorcerers after death.
Ruben *(ROO-bin)* An orphan living at the Ganvent Manse.
Saesa Coltori *(SAY-suh)* Azi's squire, a friend of Tib, lives in the Ganvent Manse.
Salvia *(SAHL-vee-uh)* A former maid to Princess Pippa.
Sapience *(SAY-pee-ense)* The Keeper of Kythshire's Wellspring.

Sarabel Plethore *(SAY-ra-belle)* Princess of Cerion. Middle child, married to Prince Vorance of Sunteri.
Scree *(SCREE)* Earth fairy. A rock, son of Iren, leader of the Ring beside Crocus.
Sha'Renell *(SHA-ren-ehl)* Muse of Earth.
Shoel Illinviesh *(SHOHL)* An elf. A section leader of the White Line.
Shush *(SHUSH (like rush))* A Wind fairy, and high-ranking member of the Ring in Kythshire. Rian's Ili'luvrie.
Skalivar *(SKAH-liv-ahr)* Royal Consort of the Reformed Kingdom of Hywilkin, Steward of Kerevorna. An imposing warrior from Hywilkin.
Sorwa *(SORE-Wuh)* A bumbling traveler fairy.
Steklin *(STEHK-lin)* A sailor on Ganvent's ship, in charge of navigation.
Stellastera *(Stell-AH-stair-uh)* Muse of Magic.
Stone *(STONE)* Leader of a band of thugs for hire including Dub and Muster.
Stubs *(STUBS)* Just Stubs: an earth and plant elemental who lives in the Dreaming and taught Azi Mentalism.
Susefen Alvierei *(SOO-seh-fehn)* An elf tutor specializing in world conflicts. Grandmaster of Histories.
Sybel *(SIB-bel)* A Sorceress for the Dusk working alongside Quenson, a dabbler in Necromancy who raised Eron from the dead to become the Revenant.
Tanis *(TAN-iss)* A master Mage assigned to accompany the shipment of books to Sunteri on Ganvent's ship.
Thalin *(THAH-lin)* High Advisor and Master of Ceremonies to the Throne of Brindelier.
Tibreseli Nullen (Tib) *(TIB (like bib))* A slave to the dye fields who escaped to Cerion. Faedin and Ili'luvrie to Mevyn, Keeper of Sunteri's Wellspring. Confidant to Princess Margary of Cerion. Dreamstalker (Immune to magic).
Tirnon Plethore *(TEER-non)* His Majesty, King of Cerion.
Tristan Ganvent *(GAN-vent)* Nessa Ganvent's husband, and Admiral of Cerion's Royal Navy.
Tulya *(TULL-yuh)* A faefolk guide living in the mountains of Hywilkin, with porcupine quills.

Twig *(Twig),* Twiggish. An earth fairy. Ili'luvrie/Faedin to Princess Margary. Tufar Woodling Icsanthius Gent Gallant Illustrious Strident Hearken
Vae *(VAY)* An imp in the temporary care of Kaso Viro.
Valenor *(VAH-lehn-or)* Muse of Dreaming.
Valor *(VAH-lohr)* Guardian of Cerion's palace.
Vaecssia (VAY-see-yuh) The Keeper of the Wellspring at Kerevorna.
Velu (VAY-loo) A mystic guardian of the temple of the Savarikta, home of the Wellspring of Elespen.
Viala Nullen *(Vee-AH-lah)* A Sorceress who conspired with Prince Eron. Sister of Tib. Became Ki.
Vorance Evresel *(Vore-ANS)* Prince of Sunteri, married to Princess Sarabel of Cerion.
Vorhadeniel *(Vor-ha-den-YELL)* Muse of Darkness.
Xantivus Ucrin *(Zan-ti-vus)* A Mentalist-Sorcerer working for the Dusk, who was present at the battle in Cerion in Call of Brindelier.
Zevlain Esen *(Zev-LANE)* An Elf Knight and Cygnet Rider of the White Line.
Zeze *(ZEE-zee)* Tib's cat companion.
Zhilee Nullen *(ZI-lee)* Tib's younger sister, who was killed by Sorcerers.

Muses

Eljarenae Muse of Light
Kaso Viro Muse of Water
Sha'Renell Muse of Earth
Stellastera Muse of Magic
Valenor Muse of Dreaming
Vorhadeniel Muse of Darkness

Her Majesty's Council

Anod Bental First Magical Advisor to the Crown
Gaethon Ethari Second Magical Advisor to the Crown
Ansell Lowery Royal High Scholar of National Relations
Lars Myer Captain of the Royal Guard
Davin Elmsworth Royal Captain of Arms
Temman Hayse Second Admiral of the Royal Fleet
Isaac Finnvale Her Majesty's Personal Guard

The Keepers of the Wellsprings

Ceras'lain Ienae'luvrie
Elespen Kiaan
Haigh Kuvelsk
Hywilkin Vaenissa
Kythshire Sapience
Sunteri Mevyn

Acknowledgments

I always have such trouble with acknowledgments, not because I'm ungrateful, but because there really are no words to express how grateful I truly am. My inspiration comes from so many places and people in my life, and without them, the Keepers of the Wellsprings never would have come to be.

More than anyone else, I'm so thankful to my husband, James, and my son, Wesley. Although I try hard to maintain a balance while I'm writing, there are more days than I'd like to admit that find me behind the keyboard of my computer rather than folding laundry and making sure the house is tidy.

To James...I've written five books now, and I still can't think of words to express how much I love and appreciate you. You are the Rian to my Azi. Your support has been endless and constant. You have shown me the meaning of true, unconditional love. I honestly don't know what my life would be like without you in it. I adore you, forever.

Wesley, for all the times I hushed you while I was in the middle of a thought, I want to say thank you for being so patient with Mommy. Even though I always felt bad in the moment, I knew how important it was to show you how hard work can help you achieve your dreams. Never give up on your goals. You can do anything you put your mind to. I love you.

To my mamamama, who read everything I wrote as quickly as I could send it, thank you so much for keeping me going. There were days when I was just completely done with this process, and I knew if I didn't have something to send you, you'd be asking about it. Thank you for urging me on, for being my best cheerleader, and for inspiring Mouli. You are my champion when I'm in the throes of self-doubt. I knew, no matter how awful I thought what I wrote was, you would always tell me it's AMAZING. I am so blessed to have you in my life. Love you, Mama.

To Rebekah: You devoured my first four books and then read this one chapter by chapter (and then a SECOND time when it was finished!) and always had time to chat with me about anything I needed or wanted to chat about, for as long as I wanted to...you are the best. Sorry I made you cry. A lot. Except, not really. Thanks for loving mushrooms and octopuses and weird magical things (like my writing) just as much as I do. You are the best. I know I said that already, but I really mean it.

To Jennifer, five books, and you've stood with me through every one of them! Wow.. You are my eagle eye. You catch things I overlook so well, that sometimes I have to read a passage you highlighted several times before I think aha! That's what I did wrong! Your enthusiasm for my writing and your constant encouragement have been invaluable to me. Thanks for always telling me I'm a good writer when I feel like I am the absolute worst. Your support and input really kept me going, and I'm so grateful to you for that!

To GG Atcheson, gosh, I'm not really even sure how to say what I want to. Things were scary there for a while. I was afraid you'd not be able to read this one. I'm so incredibly relieved you could. Your perspective really helps me see things differently, and your beta reading style never fails to make me chuckle. Thank you so much for every single comment. Honestly, I am so grateful. I'm poised to write a new book soon. I hope you're poised to beta read it. XOXO

Deb! My comrade in writing…to you, I say WRITE YOUR BOOK! Please. I have to read it. Thank you for inspiring me from the beginning, and for being a steady, constant friend even after I slip into the void and disappear for a while. I really hope someday soon, I'll be able to call you fellow indie author. Thanks for always supporting me in my ventures. It's such a comfort to know I have a friend who will always be there.

To Christina McMullen, my marketing and promo guru, thanks for fielding my unending questions about which sites to use, when to use them, and how to do stuff. I don't think this series would have been half as successful without you. It's so great to have someone who has integrity and experience to guide me, especially when she's an incredible author like you! Thank you for all of your help!

To the members of Support for Indie Authors, especially Dan Layfield and Ray Holloway, and to the members of Clean Indie Reads (and Clean Indie Fantasy), it has been a real privilege to call myself a member of your groups, and to stand alongside so many talented, successful, and supportive authors. And to Josh Blum, I'm looking forward to another podcast with you very soon! I wish you all success and happiness, and I hope to be able to support you in the future as all of you have supported me.

To Prospero's Bookstore in Manassas, thank you for showing me how much fun a book signing can be, and for being the first brick-and-mortar store to have my books on your shelves. Thanks especially to McKennah for getting me set up and for encouraging me by keeping my book in your front window! It was always a pick-me-up to drive by and see it there. I hope to have many more volumes on your shelves in the future.

Finally, to my readers, who have followed the journey to the end, thank you from the bottom of my heart. I feel as though these characters are real people who have been given life because of you, the readers. I know it's sad to think their stories have ended, but I assure you this isn't the last you've heard of our heroes. There are still tales dancing in my head, of Benen and Ember, and Saesa and Skalivar, of the origins of His Majesty's Elite, and even of Sorwa and Dumfrey. There's no way I can ignore Tib nagging at me to go on some sneaky, assassin-like adventure, perhaps with a cat at his side. And Azi and Rian will eventually have children, won't they? The possibilities are endless. I hope you stick around a while.

Thanks for being there!

About the Author

Missy Sheldrake lives in Northern Virginia with her amazingly supportive husband, brilliant son, and very energetic dog. Aside from filling the role of mom and wife, Missy is a mural painter, sculptor, and illustrator. She has always had a fascination with fairies and a great love of fairy tales and fantasy stories.

FIND HER ON THE WEB:
Website: missysheldrake.com
Blog: Missyflits.wordpress.com
Goodreads: Missy Sheldrake
Facebook: MissySheldrake
Twitter: @MissySheldrake
Instagram: M_Sheldrake

Printed in Great Britain
by Amazon